On Raven's Wing

MORGAN LLYWELYN

On Raven's Wing

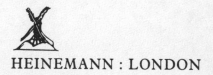

HEINEMANN : LONDON

William Heinemann Ltd
Michelin House, 81 Fulham Road, London SW3 6RB

LONDON   MELBOURNE   AUCKLAND

First published in Great Britain in 1990
Copyright © 1989 by Morgan Llywelyn

A CIP catalogue record for this book
is held by the British Library
ISBN 0 434 42744 6

Photoset by Deltatype Ltd, Ellesmere Port, Cheshire
Printed in Great Britain
by Redwood Press Ltd, Melksham, Wiltshire

For my son

Welcome!

Welcome to the tales of the Red Branch. The heroic legends of the warrior elite of ancient northern Ireland form the so-called Ulster Cycle, which is the oldest surviving vernacular prose in Western literature. Memorised as they happened, then handed down from generation to generation by bards before the introduction of literacy, the adventures on which these tales are based took place at least two thousand years ago. Originally intended to chronicle actual history, during successive centuries the stories were transformed into myth.

The earliest written versions of the Ulster Cycle were transcribed by Irish monastics of the sixth century AD, drawing from a much older oral tradition. As such, they predate the Arthurian Cycle and were known long before *Beowulf*.

In recent years, archaeological discoveries have done much to verify the bardic epics that so inspired W. B. Yeats and other writers. The sites of Emain Macha and Cruachan of the Enchantments survive today as part of Ireland's historic treasure. You may pace their earthwork walls, or stand in a field beside Cuchulain's pillar stone . . . and listen, shivering, for the sound of a raven's wings.

Morgan Llywelyn
Ireland

Phonetic Glossary

Throughout the novel, simplified versions of Irish names have been used where possible. These names date from an era two thousand years ago, and no modern scholar can say with certainty what their original pronunciations may have been. Knowing a few basic rules of Irish may help, however.

C is always hard (Celtic is pronounced Keltik, for example). *Ch* is a soft guttural, as in the German. *G* is hard, never pronounced as *j*. *S* in conjunction with *e* or *i* is pronounced *sh*. Many other consonants are believed to have been aspirated to such an extent as to make them nearly silent. Where names have been changed substantially for simplification, the older version is also given.

PROPER NAMES

Ayfa (in old Irish Aife, or Aoife)
Pronounced Ay'-fa (old Irish, Eefe)
Ailell Al'-ill
Badb Bīve
Bricriu Brik'-roo
Cathbad Kaff'-a
Conall Cearnach Kō'-nal Kar'-nah
Conor (old Irish, Conchobar) Kon'-or
Cuchulain Koo-hull'-in
Deirdre (old Irish, Derdriu) Dayr'-druh
Duffach Duff'-ah
Emer Ee'-mer (old Irish, Ay'-ver)
Fedlimid Fe'-lim-i
Ferdiad Fer-dee'-uh
Finavir (old Irish, Finnabhair) Fin'-a-vir
Frassach Frass'-ah
Laeg Loy

Leary Buadach   Leer'-ee Boo'-yah
Lugaid   Loo'-ih
Lugh   Loo
Macha   Mah'-ha
Naisi (old Irish, Noisiu)   Nee'-sha
Niamh   Neev
Setanta   Shay-tahn'-tah (old Irish, Shay-dahn'-dah)
Skya (old Irish, Scathach)   Sky'-ah
Sualtim   Soo'-al-dav
Tuatha de Danann   Too'-uh day Dan'-ann

PLACE NAMES

Ath Cliath   Awth Klee'-uh
Cúil Sibrille   Kil Siv'-rel
Cruachan   Kroo'-a-han
Emain Macha   Ev'-in Mah'-ha
Murthemney   Mur'-thev-ne
Slieve Fuad   Shlee'-av Foo'-id
Uisnach (old Irish, Uisliu)   Oosh'-neh

MISCELLANEOUS

Beltaine   Bell-tawn'-yuh
Gae Bulga   Gay Bul'-guh
Grianan   Gree'-nawn
Ges, gessa   Gesh, gesh'-uh
Lughnasa   Loo'-nas-ah
Ogham   Ōhm
Samhain   Sau'-win

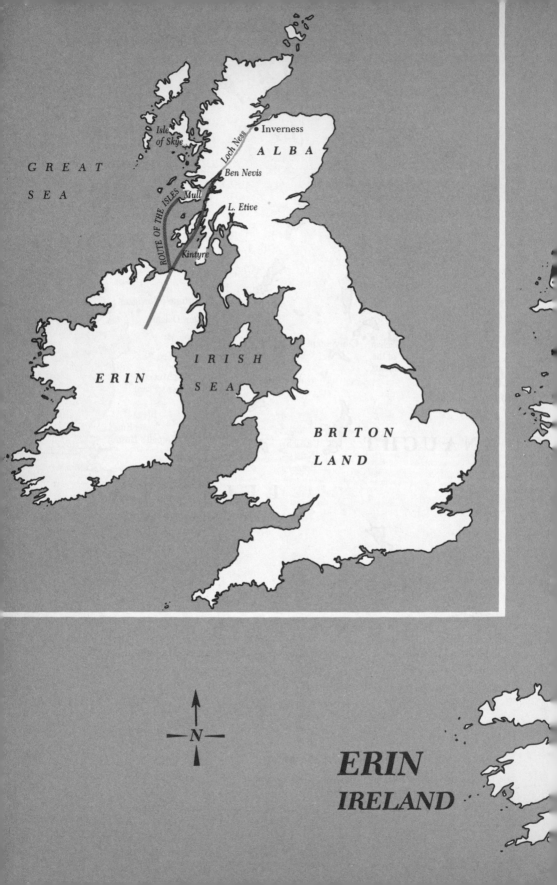

GREAT SEA

Isle of Skye

Loch Ness

• Inverness

ALBA

Ben Nevis

ROUTE OF THE ISLES

Mull

L. Etive

Kintyre

ERIN

IRISH SEA

BRITON LAND

N

ERIN
IRELAND

ULSTER

Dun Borach

Emain Macha

R. Nith

Tarteise (Morrigan)

Dun Dalgan   Cooley

Stony Mt.   Bay of Dun Dalgan

Cruachan   Cúil Silinne   Ferdiad's Ford
of the
Enchantments   Cúil Sibrille   Mag Muceda
                                       (The Pig-Keeper's Plain)

CONNAUGHT   Brega

                   Uisnach   Emer
                   (Naisi's   (Forgall's Hostel)
                   Home)

                        LEINSTER

MUNSTER

Volume 1

Emain Macha

*Greengold blaze of pagan
splendour, defiant
timbered halls emerge from their
cloaking mist.
For twenty generations, a royal
fortress
guarded by heroes.*

Heroes.

*Listen! Oaken gates scream open
on iron hinges.
Feathered chariots racing toward
us, horses leaping
out of antiquity, galloping
wild-eyed.
Here they come!*

Warriors.

*Once again a dark lad leads them,
dauntless.
Brilliant eyes and tender mouth.
He can break your bones
or break your heart.
Cuchulain.*

The Hound of Ulster.

1 The atmosphere surrounding the little boy vibrated with tension. He could not see the stifled anger and baffled desire, but he sensed their residue accumulating like dustballs in the corners of the fort. Unspoken recriminations crowded the silences; bitter glances were hurled like spears over small Setanta's head.

Sometimes he awoke in the night with his heart pounding and a cramp in his belly. Darkness pressed down on him. Anything could lurk in such darkness, the world roiled with unseen forces. He would lie tensely anticipating the unknown until exhaustion tumbled him back into sleep.

Setanta was sensitive and he had spirit, so two options were open to him. He could become a timid, subdued little creature – or he could challenge the unknown and learn to fight.

His earliest memory would be of his mother's hands. In contrast to her dark hair, Dectera had skin like milk, and her son loved to watch her luminous fingers weaving patterns over her embroidery. Her face was harder to visualise. She wore a driftaway expression that blurred her features like an image reflected on water. Setanta knew her cheekbones were high and her eyes the same silvery grey as his own – but the real Dectera did not live behind her face at all.

Her inward absence was part of some greater mystery. Even her child could see the effect it was having on her husband. Sualtim, chief of Dun Dalgan, was a sturdy, jowly redhead with an amiable disposition, yet each season found him slower to smile, quicker to frown. He grew increasingly restless and irritable.

To their only child, Dectera and Sualtim showed the same indifferent kindness they bestowed on servants and hounds. They neither hugged him nor yelled at him; they tolerated him. Their passions were jealously hoarded for use in the war between themselves.

Setanta never heard his parents fighting, but he saw the wounds in their eyes.

For the first few years of his life, the little boy had a nurse called Dethcaen, who was a druid's daughter. She was slender and tall – to a

5

child, everyone seems tall – and she was the one person at the fort who had time for him. Dethcaen would sit cross-legged beside the stone hearth in the centre of the hall and not mind being ash-drifted. She took Setanta on her lap and sang to him or told him stories. When he was older he would have a tutor to educate him as a son of the Gaelic warrior aristocracy should be educated, but until then he learned from a woman who knew what animated shadows.

'There is a *ges* on you, a prohibition,' Dethcaen warned him. 'If anyone awakens you from sleep it will cause dreadful trouble. You must always be allowed to wake up on your own.' Setanta accepted this without question; everyone did. Dethcaen was a druid's daughter. Once the warning was given, the servants were careful to let the child sleep until he woke up by himself.

Setanta was not the only person at the fort with a *ges* upon him. Many people had one or more. Anluan the steward could not enter any building through a south-facing door, or eat butter and cheese at the same meal. One of the sentries at the chariot gate was not allowed to speak during his wife's bloody days. As long as the rules were obeyed, unnamed disasters were kept at bay.

Dethcaen often entertained her small charge with tales of the past, for among the Gaelic inhabitants of Erin history was a common coin of conversation. 'We are descended from a band of chariot-chieftains who invaded and conquered this island long ago,' she said, 'before even Rome had armies.'

'Rome?' Setanta tilted his head to one side and looked at her through a forest of thick black lashes. A pity to waste such lashes on a boy, Dethcaen thought. 'Rome is a land to the east,' she said aloud, dismissing Roman might with a casual wave of her hand. 'The Romans are fighters too, but they know enough to leave us alone in Erin. We are a race of *heroes*.'

'Who was here when the chariot-chiefs came?' the little boy wanted to know, shifting his solid warmth in Dethcaen's lap. He had grown too big for her to hold seasons ago, and his weight made her legs go to sleep, but both enjoyed the old habit too much to break it. 'Who did our ancestors conquer to win Erin?'

Dethcaen gave an automatic and wary glance around the hall, then answered in a near whisper. 'The Tuatha de Danann – people of the goddess Danu. They fought the Gael in a series of spectacular battles, using magical arts the chariot-chiefs had never seen before. But at last we defeated them and . . .'

6

'And?'

'And the Dananns vanished.'

Setanta scrambled off her lap. He wanted to absorb this news while standing on his feet. 'How could anybody vanish?'

'They melted into the land itself, or so the learned men tell us. The Dananns housed their spirits in thorn trees or went underground to live in huge mounds with hidden entrances. Some believe they are immortal. Others think they may die eventually and claim to have heard them mourning their dead. But be certain of this: the Tuatha de Danann are very different from the Gael, Setanta. They are magic, whatever else they may be. Magic to be feared. No one knows the limits of their powers, and they have never relinquished their hold on Erin. They are all around us, unseen but living in ways we cannot comprehend.'

Magic to be feared. Setanta stretched his brain, trying to understand. 'Are they gods, then? What do they look like? Do you know where a . . .'

Entering the hall, Sualtim fixed Dethcaen with a speaking look. She promptly changed the subject and began chattering about a kinsman of hers who carved harps. No matter how Setanta tugged at her sleeve, she said no more about the magic people.

So he questioned Gelace the cook and Anluan the steward and the red-handed bondwomen who boiled linen, but they did not tell him much. He learned that the Dananns were indeed regarded as gods or demigods; some of them bore names like Manannan of the Waves or Lugh, Son of the Sun. Powerful names, invoked with superstitious awe.

Yet there was obviously a prohibition in force against discussing them with the little boy. Were they so horrible? Were they monsters?

He should leave it alone, then. He knew that much.

Yet the Tuatha de Danann continued to occupy a flickering realm at the edge of his mind that he could not ignore. He was in the uncomfortable position of having learned too much and not enough. He kept pestering Dethcaen for more information until Sualtim overheard him and sent the druid's daughter away.

'You're too old to have a nurse any more,' was the only explanation the heartbroken child was given.

But Setanta knew the real reason. His curiosity had cost him dearly. There was a secret he was not supposed to know, and adults were jealous of their secrets. Fair enough, then. It was all just history, anyhow.

Because he was only a child, with no history of his own yet, it was easy to dismiss the past as nothing more than words and ashes. He began thinking about the future instead.

To occupy Setanta after Dethcaen left, Sualtim had his smith forge a miniature sword and a fistful of small spears. Then the warrior-lord lost interest, and it fell to the men-at-arms who guarded the fort to teach the boy to use his weapons. He learned quickly and they praised him, heady stuff for a neglected child. Soon he was out of bed every morning before dawn, running to the practice field in spite of the grumbling of his empty belly.

Bright and exuberant and bursting with energy, Setanta pitted himself against everything he could. He shouted a lot and laughed a lot. Laughter was an unfamiliar sound around the fort.

One of the guards gave him a target of straw tied into a manshape and Setanta practised on this with his little sword, yelling defiantly and trying to look fierce. He slashed away until bits of straw filled the air, making him sneeze. It felt good to hit something solid. Too many things within the fort had no substance at all.

Dun Dalgan of the Bright Aspect was built on high ground overlooking a sparkling bay. In Gaelic, *dun* meant fort, and Dun Dalgan was the stronghold of Sualtim, chariot-chieftain of a clan owning many cows. In times of war it could be manned as a military outpost, but since Dectera had come to live there with her husband, the fort was used only as a protective base for the clan and its dependents.

Constructed on the model of most Gaelic strongholds, Dun Dalgan was surrounded by a deep ditch and a banked earthwork topped by a timber palisade. Beyond these walls, the homes of Sualtim's kin were dotted among woodlands and across the grassy plain of Murthemney. The houses were circular, with timber framework supporting wicker-work walls and thatched roofs. The mild climate made such construc-tion possible, and every household had its little plot of kale and root vegetables to augment Erin's abundant supplies of game and fish.

Within the palisades of the fort, Sualtim's dwelling house was built in a similar fashion, though on a grander scale. It consisted of a multipurpose round hall with a peaked roof supported by carved pillars. Attached to the walls were small sleeping chambers with separate entrances, a sign of aristocracy. Other classes used one room for everything.

In front of the hall was another symbol of nobility, an ornamental lawn called an *urla*. The one at Dun Dalgan was always in need of weeding. Beyond stood the kitchens, ale-brewing house, buttery, corn kiln, bake house, storage sheds, a guest house with its door sagging on rusty iron hinges, and a rectangular feasting hall for entertaining large crowds. The roof of this last building was collapsing from neglect. It had been a long time since any entertaining was done at Dun Dalgan.

Near the northern gateway was a shed for Sualtim's war-cart. When Setanta was still pudgy with babyfat, he taught himself to scramble up a splintery wooden ladder to an observation platform atop the palisade. From this vantage point he could watch as Sualtim took his chariot team out for exercise.

The chariot-chieftain drove the horses himself at top speed, spurning the services of a charioteer. Setanta watched, cheering them on, as they swept in great circles across the plain, racing no one beneath an empty sky. Sometimes Sualtim shouted the cryptic phrase 'Red Branch!' in a voice of mingled longing and defiance.

Sualtim would not come back until the team was lathered and heaving. When he passed through the gateway, the guards dipped their spears to him, but Dectera did not emerge from the hall to welcome him. Only Setanta trotted at Sualtim's heels, trying to imitate his walk and engage him in conversation about the relative merits of the horses and the techniques of driving.

As the seasons passed, Sualtim's answers became briefer and rarer. By the time he reached the hall where Dectera waited, his voice would be cold, his jaw set. The two adults and the child were like three separate islands, isolated from each other. Setanta sometimes looked from Dectera to Sualtim and back again, crying out silently to both of them, but they never heard him. Their own unspoken words were too loud.

Then one summer's day Sualtim took his team out racing and did not bring them back. He went, straight as a thrown javelin, along the road leading north from Dun Dalgan. From the palisade, Setanta watched with one hand shading his eyes, for the sun was striking a blinding glare off the bay to the east. He saw Sualtim's chariot disappear in dust and dazzle, and when the dust settled all that remained was the empty road.

The boy was stunned.

'Where did my father go?' he demanded of his mother. 'Why did he leave us? Is he coming back? Is it something I did?'

'It's nothing you did.' Dectera absentmindedly patted the child's thick mop of dark hair. 'Nothing to do with you, this. Go and play.'

He did not believe her. He was still young enough to think himself the centre of the world, with everything revolving around him.

Therefore, he must be in some way responsible for Sualtim's defection. He could not know the man had suffered the memory of the past until it almost destroyed his manhood, and at last fled for his life and sanity. It was not a failure of love on Sualtim's part, merely a failure of endurance.

Setanta was devastated. He had tried with all his might to be a worthy descendant of the warrior nobility and make his father proud of him. He had somehow failed. If only he had been bigger, stronger, braver . . .

He had the servants build him another straw man, which he demolished before the sun was halfway across the sky.

In spite of Sualtim's departure, life went on much as before. He had left orders; his guards continued to offer protection to nearby kinsmen in need of it, and cattle were herded and seawater dried in flat pans to provide salt for meat. But the weeds grew taller on the *urla*. The roof of the feasting hall finally fell in one morning, with a great whoosh and a cloud of dust.

Dectera never bothered to order its repair.

She did make a few small efforts to start life afresh. She wove some winter woollens and embroidered some tunic borders. When Setanta's tutor came up the path from his home by the bay, she intercepted him, asking if he remembered the words of an old song.

Caisin scratched his curly head. 'Ask me the laws of hospitality and I can tell you; I'm going to recite them for your son today. But songs . . .' He shrugged.

'It was about a man with green eyes,' Dectera prodded. 'You must know it, we all knew it once. Does this sound familiar?' She hummed some broken notes in a singing voice thready with disuse.

'I never heard it,' Caisin assured her.

Dectera's spurt of energy waned. She dragfooted back to the hall and spent the day sitting at her loom with her hands lying idle in her lap.

Existence at Dun Dalgan ceased moving, suspended like the flies trapped in Dectera's amber beads.

Setanta longed for boys his own age to play with, but there were none at the fort, at least no sons of warriors or cattle-lords, children of high rank. He was forbidden to play with the children of servants. He possessed a ball and a hurley stick of ash wood inlaid with red bronze, both of which had once belonged to Sualtim. But hurling was a team sport, and Setanta had no team. He practised on his own with stick and ball until he made strokes that would not have shamed a grown man, yet

10

at last loneliness defeated him and he left the stick lying in the grass. He turned then to teasing the poultry, wrestling with the great, regal wolfhounds his father had left behind, and running through the dairy spinning the crocks until the women scolded him for turning the butter rancid.

He was mightily bored.

He retrieved the stick and ball and carried them to Dectera. 'Play with me,' he pleaded.

'Me? Play ball?'

'I'll just throw it and you catch it. Didn't you do that when you were young?'

Dectera struggled to remember. For a moment, Setanta glimpsed someone he had never seen before, a shy girl with a piquant smile. Then her eyes clouded. 'If I did, I've forgotten. I forget so many things.'

Winter, the season of maintenance, dragged for Setanta. A chieftain should be instructing his son in weapons' care and supervising the repairs of walls and thatch. But Sualtim was gone. Setanta played outside as much as he could until a spell of cold and sleet drove him under the rooftree. Then he developed the habit of curling up out of the way somewhere and losing himself in reverie. A boy with too much time alone can be driven to contemplation and brooding. But dark moods rarely lasted long, he was young and full of energy. He would shake them off and imagine some heroic adventure instead, one in which his father played a central part. In such waking dreams, Sualtim wore Setanta's face.

When sunseason finally returned, there were buttercups on the meadows above the sea and he attacked their golden heads with his sword, defeating an army all by himself. He ran along ridges in pursuit of butterflies; he skimmed stones across scummy ponds and fished and set snares and climbed trees; he did all the things a solitary boy can find to do while he waits to be a man.

Shortly after harvest season, supply wagons rumbled down the road from the north. Setanta was at the gate, standing on tiptoe at the guard's elbow, before the first oxcart was ushered inside. The wagon had hardly stopped before he was scrambling into it, his toes scuffing the vivid red and yellow knotwork design painted on the wooden sides.

Everything he found in the wagon had the glamour of newness. The bales of cloth were dyed in brighter colours than anything at Dun Dalgan; the tools and hardware gleamed without rust.

'Here, you, get out of my cart!' an oxdriver yelled.

'I have every right to be here,' Setanta replied. He need take no orders from a lowly oxdriver, the marrow in his bones knew this. He fingered a few things and then got down leisurely, as if he had meant to do so anyway.

The driver eyed him. 'How old are you, boy?'

'I've survived ten blue winters.'

'And with a polished tongue in your mouth too. What gives you the right to speak so fancy?'

Setanta lifted his chin. His eyes flashed. 'My father is the chariot-chieftain Sualtim, lord of Dun Dalgan.'

'You expect me to believe that?' the driver scoffed. He turned towards his companions, who were busily unloading their own wagons. 'This lad claims to be Sualtim's son!'

Someone barked a rude laugh.

The boy balled his fists. 'My father *is* Sualtim . . . if he's still alive,' he added half under his breath. 'Dectera is my mother.'

The driver was a beefy, balding man wearing a knee-length tunic of coarse brown wool, belted with a piece of rope to be used in case some component of his harness broke. He possessed no jewellery but an iron arm ring. By contrast, the dark-haired little boy glaring at him wore a linen tunic embroidered with red and blue Celtic knotwork and a short cloak fastened with a brooch of good silver. The man squinted at the jewellery. Ah. Dectera's child . . . indeed, he probably was.

The oxdriver started to say something else about Sualtim, but the boy's expression made him think better of it. The lad was no ordinary child – not if the stories were true. And they might be. This was the Plain of Murthemney in the south of the kingdom of Ulster in the land of Erin, where anything might be true. 'Sualtim is alive,' the driver said in a more kindly tone.

'You've seen him, then? Where is he?'

'Don't you know? Doesn't your mother hear from him?'

Too late, Setanta put up a shield. 'Not every day,' he replied, elaborately casual. 'I just wondered where he happens to be right now.'

'And where else but at Emain Macha with the king?'

'With the king. . . ?'

'Conor mac Nessa, of course. King of Ulster. Surely you know of him. Emain Macha is his royal stronghold, and the warriors of the Red Branch, Sualtim among them, attend him there. You might do so yourself one day.'

'He'll need a lot more leg under him first,' commented one of the

12

other drivers. He sauntered forward, sucking the stump of a broken tooth in his mouth. 'He's small for his age, this one. But given his family connections, they might take him in the Boys' Troop and teach him to hunt and fight. I'm surprised your mother keeps you here, boy,' he finished, looking directly at Setanta.

The first driver snorted. 'Do you think she wants this one at Emain Macha to remind everybody of – ' He stopped himself before his tongue could dance him into trouble. The two drivers exchanged one of those adult looks Setanta knew so well, then turned abruptly away to finish unloading their oxcarts.

The boy drifted off, wishing he could bend his ears backwards like a horse and overhear what they were saying. He kicked at the rich brown earth with his toe. He picked up a pebble and slung it at a tame piglet rooting for food scraps on the midden heap. He was aware of a rising buzz of conversation among the drivers. His neck grew hot with embarrassment; they were talking about him.

When Dectera emerged from the hall to examine the cargo in the wagons, Setanta ducked into one of the storehouses. For some reason, he did not want his mother's eyes on him just then. He spent the afternoon carving designs on the poles that supported the roof, using the tip of his little sword as a carving tool. Again and again, he formed the crude but recognisable shape of a bird, its head turned and its back curved. All his life he had traced the same figure, though he did not know why. But when he had nothing else to do, he drew it in the dust with a stick or in the mud with a stone. It was his one artistic accomplishment.

When the sun set, he went into the hall.

'Where were you?' Dectera asked.

He was in no mood for ritual interrogation. 'Where is Emain Macha?'

His mother stared at him.

'They told me my father is there now. And something called the Boys' Troop. What is that? Are they boys like me? Would they be my friends and play with me? Can I go and meet them?' His eager words tumbled over one another.

As often happens, the future had caught up with Dectera while she still wrestled with the past. Many things had been kept from her son; now he threatened to sweep the protective barriers away. 'I don't want you to have anything to do with the Boys' Troop,' she told him. 'Pretend they don't exist.'

'How can I pretend anything about them, when I don't even know what they are?'

He is already too clever, she thought. In a voice scarcely audible above the crackling of the hearthfire, she replied, 'The Boys' Troop is a pack of savage youths who would cause trouble from dawn to dark if they weren't controlled by a firm instructor as soon as they are old enough to outrun their mothers. They are the sons of the Red Branch.'

Setanta inhaled sharply. 'Red Branch?'

'Sualtim was – is – Red Branch,' the woman told him, feeling too weary to fight off his questions. His brash young masculinity sapped her strength. 'Born of the warrior line of Rory the Red, whose male descendants form the elite guard of the king of Ulster. Rory's branch, the Red Branch, of the clan Ulaid. Swaggering, boastful killers, all of them.' Her voice was stiff with contempt. 'And the sons no gentler than their fathers. Long ago, the troop was formed in an effort to control the pups until they could take up arms and fight as men. The Boys' Troop gives them their education and training in the battle skills.'

'If my father is Red Branch, I am entitled to join the Boys' Troop!' Setanta cried, glowing. His mother's obvious distaste for warriors and the Red Branch seemed both arbitrary and unreasonable. They were warriors, heroes, everything men should be. The elite.

Perhaps women simply could not understand such things, he told himself. The Boys' Troop. The Red Branch. The names sang through him.

Now he had her talking, he would not relent. 'And what of Emain Macha?' He clamped his hand on her thigh, demanding.

'Emain Macha.' Dectera's eyes grew misty. 'When I was a girl growing up there, I thought it was the entire world. It's been the stronghold of the clan Ulaid, the ruling clan of Ulster, since a warrior-woman called Macha of the Golden Hair scratched the design for the fortress in the earth with the pin of her brooch. There was another Macha too, in my own time . . . very different . . .' Her voice faded.

Setanta dug his fingers deeper. 'And Conor is king there now?'

She nodded. 'Conor mac Nessa. Conor son of the woman Nessa, so called because his royal blood comes to him through his mother's side of the family. His father was Fachtna the Giant. After Fachtna died, Nessa married the then king of Ulster, Fergus mac Roy. Fergus raised Conor as his foster son, and in time, in a rather curious way, Conor replaced Fergus as king. Imagine my brother Conor being king of Ulster.' She smiled a very strange smile.

Setanta gaped at her. 'Your brother is the *king*?'

'Half-brother, actually. But once we were close. Very close

14

indeed . . .' The smile wavered, slipped sideways on her mouth, was swallowed. Dectera blinked several times, then added in a harsh tone, 'Now, at least he makes certain we are well supplied here, and no one bothers us. I should be grateful for that, I suppose. Conor can be kind sometimes. I'm certain he thought he was being kind when he urged me to marry Sualtim of Dun Dalgan. They were in the Red Branch together,' she added, as if that explained everything.

'If you're the king's sister, why aren't we at Emain Macha with my father and the Boys' Troop?' Setanta demanded to know. 'Don't we belong there too? Was I born there?'

'You were not,' she said, staring through him at some point beyond his head. 'You were born near Brugh na Boinne. In a snowstorm. We came here . . . after. After so many things.'

'But where do we really belong?' Setanta insisted on knowing, trying to drag out of her the answer he wanted.

Her eyes filled with stars that might have been tears. 'We belong nowhere, you and I. At least, nowhere that I know how to reach. Though I have to try, in my dreams . . .' She shook herself, and her voice became harsh again. 'Be content here, Setanta. Dun Dalgan is all we have, we live a comfortable enough life here.'

'We live no life here at all! We're just waiting to get old and die and nothing is *happening*!' The boy's face blazed with passion. To her surprise, Dectera saw that he was growing up. He might never be tall, she was not tall herself, but the muscles knitted across his frame foretold great strength.

Then on his face his mother recognised, for the first time, the unmistakable stamp of his father. The intensity.

The fire.

She almost cried out. She put both hands over her mouth to keep from calling a name.

'What is it? Mother, what's wrong?' Forgetting himself, the boy was as tender to his mother as his father had once been – making her pain worse.

Dectera began to tremble. The metallic smell of grief rose in waves from her body. Help me, she called in silent supplication. I cannot bear this, help me!

Thunder rumbled. A fist of wind pounded the hall. The fire on the hearth leaped into a twisting dance, showering sparks. 'Get my cloak,' Dectera murmured to her son. 'I have grown very cold.'

He ran to retrieve her favourite blue cloak. She grabbed it from him and wrapped it around her shoulders; her fingers felt like icicles. Setanta began to be frightened. He helped his mother to her feet and accompanied her to the bedchamber, where she fell across her bed with a sigh and turned her face to the wall. Trying to comfort her, the boy covered his mother with fur bed robes and tucked them around her body. The edge of his hand touched her small breast, which yielded like liquid to the pressure. Setanta snatched his hand back as if it had been burned.

Dectera would not eat or even get out of bed. She lay with her eyes closed, listening to the wind. To fill up the silence, Setanta prattled about the contents of the trading wagons and the condition of the oxen that pulled them. He did not mention Emain Macha again, though he wanted desperately to learn more about the Boys' Troop. Its name had the effect of a trumpet summons on him.

When he was certain Dectera was asleep, he lay down beside her with his fingers laced at the nape of his neck, staring up into the underside of the thatch.

Someday he would take a sword — a real one, not a toy — and follow the road north. He would find Emain Macha and make friends there with boys like himself, warriors' sons. Sualtim would be delighted to see him and take him everywhere, boasting of his boy more fondly than any other father.

The dream was warm and golden. Sinking into it, Setanta fell asleep smiling.

In her own sleep, Dectera twitched. Her body made a series of jerky motions like someone trying to keep her balance. She slipped, she tumbled . . . and all at once she was at Emain Macha again, and it was her wedding day.

A soft rain had fallen intermittently through the night, but the morning brought a watery sun. Dectera slipped from the sleeping compartment and ran lightfooted across the *urla*. On this most special of mornings, she wanted to gather the dew and bathe her face in it to assure herself of lifelong beauty, for that was the magic of dew gathered on Beltaine, first day of the sunseason, traditional day for marriage.

When her face was pink and glowing, she sat down on a bog-oak bench and began combing her hair with an ivory comb. The comb was one of the many gifts brought to the king of Ulster by traders from across the seas, and had arrived at the same time as the ape. Everyone had been astonished by that creature on its golden leash, a noble gift indeed, a funny little hairy man with a round belly and spindly legs. It had the

16

eyes of a puzzled child, and when it died, it was buried with honours beneath the doorway of the Speckled House.

Your thoughts are wandering, Dectera rebuked herself. You should think only of Sualtim today. The comb crackled through her hair and she began to sing to herself, an old song about a man with green eyes. Sualtim had green eyes – or did he? Suddenly she could not remember. But his hands were big, she recalled that much. Big and freckled on the backs. When he embraced her, he ran them down her body in a proprietary way. She flinched and he chuckled. 'You'll feel different when we're married.' He pinched her buttocks hard enough to hurt, not out of cruelty but because he did not know how tender she was.

Now the time for marriage had come. From the corner of her eye, Dectera saw Conor emerge from the House of the King and walk toward the *grianan*, the women's sunny-chamber. The gold of his hair was so different from the darkness of hers; the boldness of his stride was so unlike her delicate step. Though hardly past boyhood, Conor mac Nessa already drew the eyes of every woman at Emain Macha – and not just because he was king.

Slipping her comb into its gilded leather comb-bag, Dectera jumped up and ran towards him. At that moment two things happened: a cloud passed over the sun, and she thought she glimpsed a figure moving in some bushes at the edge of the lawn.

Then Conor called her name and she forgot; she ran eagerly into his arms. 'Why do you look so serious?' he teased her. 'There should be only smiles on your wedding day.' He put his fingers to the corners of her mouth and forced her lips up. Dectera smiled. She could never resist him.

'That's better. Sualtim is a lucky man to get you. Look how your hips have widened this season. You are ripe and will bear strong sons, Dectera.'

She felt her cheeks burning. She hated having Conor say such things as casually as if he were discussing breeding horses.

Dectera had never enjoyed earthy talk. She preferred listening to the music of the harp, or gazing at the stars, or picking flowers.

Now the other women came looking for her. They crowded close, shouldering the king away. Any man was a nuisance on a marriage morning. Conor surrendered as gracefully as he did everything, telling the women, 'Just don't make my sister too beautiful, or poor Sualtim will be unable to wait.'

Everyone laughed except Dectera.

They took her to a private chamber and bolted the door. They would not bathe her until just before she entered her bridal bed. But they made sure her fingernails were cut and rounded like crescent moons, and they added blush to her cheeks and fingertips with juice from the *ruam* plant. Her body was draped with a layer of *sida*, the imported silk purchased from the sea-traders. Over this Dectera was to wear a gown of blue *srole*, a heavy woven fabric with a glossy face, girdled at the waist with a rope of amethysts. Her hip-length hair was curled and fastened with a gold fillet, from which tendrils escaped to tumble over her forehead. Her feet were encased in soft leather boots.

When at last she was ready, they left her alone. By tradition, her mother should have kept her company, serving her spiced wine and giving her gratuitous advice until the bridegroom came to perform the ritual abduction. But Dectera had insisted on being alone this morning. On the one day belonging exclusively to her, even shy Dectera could make demands. Nessa had submitted with reluctance. Nessa wanted to be in on everything.

With only her thoughts for company, the girl leaned against the window frame and listened to a wren in a nearby hedge piping with pride over its huge clutch of eggs. Sunlight and clouds chased each other across the landscape; perhaps the clouds would burn off after all, she thought. Then she noticed a tree outside the chamber, a tree with one long branch stretched out in a way she had never seen before.

She drew in a startled breath. A man was standing so close to the tree, they seemed one being. It was not a branch but his long arm she saw, beckoning to her.

Dectera shrank back, out of his line of vision, but she still seemed to feel his eyes on her. The window of the chamber was too narrow to admit a grown man, and with one call she could have summoned a dozen warriors. Yet she did not cry out. Her heart was beating so heavily at the base of her throat, it threatened to suffocate her.

A shadow crossed the window. He stood there, looking in at her.

His face was unique to himself. The men of Ulster did not have such peaked brows, nor such wide and tender mouths. The men of Ulster were bearded, not smooth-cheeked and fine-skinned like the stranger. When he smiled, his features disarranged themselves and fell into a new, even more pleasing pattern.

'How lovely you are, Dectera,' he said in an unfamiliar dialect. Yet she understood every word. 'I have watched you, and you do not belong with that red-haired man. You belong with me.'

18

He reached through the window and closed his fingers around her wrist. Dectera watched as if what was happening had nothing to do with her. She made no effort to pull away. His shoulders were too broad to allow him to climb through the window, but she was slender. I could climb out, she thought.

From beyond the chamber door came the sounds of festival. Wine casks and ale barrels were being rolled across the lawn, and the wedding games had started. Men were shouting and laughing; some married women were singing a bedchamber song, stressing certain phrases with glee.

The stranger's grip tightened on Dectera's wrist, then all at once he opened his hand and she was free. Her skin ached with not being touched by him. Everything happened so slowly, it felt like a dream, yet the dream was a reality she wanted to last for ever. When the stranger smiled at her she put her knee on the window ledge, twisting sideways to squeeze her body through the opening.

Someone knocked on the door but she cried shrilly, 'I'm not ready! Go away!' The tone of her voice served as an alarm. Her name was called once, then again, and whoever was at the door shouted for help. Fists pounded; a heavy shoulder thudded against the wood, trying to force admittance. Dectera flung her arms forward into space and tumbled through the window, falling down down down into his . . .

In her carved wooden bedbox, the sleeping Dectera writhed and shrieked.

Setanta leaped to his feet before he could get his sleep-fogged eyes open. His mother was a blur in the dimness, a formless figure tossing and moaning. He reached for her and tried to hold her, but she beat at him with her hands.

'Mother, it's me, it's Setanta!' He tried to reach her in whatever nightmare held her, frantic because she would not respond to him. 'Wake up, Mother, you're all right. Oh, please, wake up!'

She was sobbing now and calling out, but the sounds she made had no meaning for him. It might have been a name she said. Or a profanity. He did not understand why he could not awaken her.

She might be ill. She might be dying!

Desperate, Setanta raised his voice and yelled with all his might for help.

2 The boy's shouts brought every person in the fort to the sleeping chamber. There was such a crush at the doorway, the guards were unable to draw their swords. But when they looked inside there was no enemy to fight, just Setanta bending over his mother.

'Something is terribly wrong with her!' he cried.

Gelace pushed the men aside and entered, peering down at Dectera's face. The cook had paused to bring a beeswax candle, which illuminated her mottled red arms. Hot wax from the candle dripped unnoticed on to Dectera's shoulder.

Actually, the woman on the bed was aware of people in the chamber with her, but they seemed no more substantial than shadows under trees. They were part of a dim background. *He* was foreground, catching her in his arms, carrying her away.

She had screamed, but not in terror. She had cried out in fear they would be stopped, because from the moment the stranger touched her nothing else mattered. A guard had broken through the door and rushed across the chamber, and as Dectera fell out of the window he reached after, trying to catch her. She had hit out at him, beating him back with her hands.

'We must hurry,' the stranger's urgent voice whispered to her. The cloak he wore felt like heated mist which swirled around the two of them as she clung to him.

The day crumpled its face and began to cry in earnest. A sudden, pounding rain drove down from the north, propelled by a bitter wind. Angry men came rushing around from the other side of the building, keeping their heads down to shield their faces from the storm. Sualtim led them. His sword was in one hand, his spear in the other.

But by the time they reached the place where Dectera and the stranger had been, no one was there.

In the sleep from which she did not want to wake, Dectera remembered the journey in his arms – or wrapped in his cloak, or carried by the wind, she could not tell. It did not matter. They had fled

Emain Macha on the wings of storm. Her ears rang and she pressed tightly against him, drawing heat from his body to keep herself from fainting. Even through their clothing, his flesh scorched hers.

Then at last they were . . . somewhere else.

The storm ceased as if on command. The stranger placed Dectera on a narrow couch piled with cushions; the style of the furniture was unfamiliar to her. He stroked her face, pushing her wet hair back.

Gelace pushed Dectera's sweat-soaked hair back. 'I've seen her like this before,' she said. 'When they first brought her here.'

'When who first brought her here?' Setanta wanted to know, hanging on to one of his mother's hands as if he would keep her with him by force.

'Her brother the king and Fergus mac Roy, the king's champion. They were the ones who'd rescued her, and a terrible time they had of it. The hair of Fergus turned grey all at once. Wherever they had gone to get your mother, it was not a place you or I would care to visit.'

The couch stood on a low platform, and the chamber was not dark but flooded with a pearly radiance. Dectera's pupils dilated in the light. The stranger smiled down at her. 'Did the journey tire you?'

She swallowed with difficulty. Her mouth was very dry; the sound of his voice seemed to have that effect on her. 'It did not, but where are we?'

He placed three fingers across her lips. 'You need not know, Dectera. Know only this.' He took his fingers away and put his mouth where they had been. She felt his lips move on hers. They forced her mouth open and his tongue darted inside, seeking the roots of her spirit.

She was so startled, at first she did not respond, and then she thought she was pushing him away. But she was not. Her hands were holding him, her mouth imitating what his did. She had a curious sensation of melting – melting into him. The stranger began stroking her body with a gossamer touch.

Gelace and two female attendants freed Dectera from the tangled bedclothes and began stroking her body with cloths wrung out in cool water. Her skin blazed with fever.

Her skin blazed with fever wherever he touched.

Some part of Dectera ached like a hungry belly, only the ache was sweeter, and farther down her body. Her traitorous body that persisted in acting on its own without conscious direction from her. Now it was rubbing itself against the stranger, all heat and appetite. 'But I am supposed to marry Sualtim,' she heard herself say as if from a distance.

Perhaps someone else said it. The words had no meaning weighed against her desire.

He chuckled, a deep, rich sound. 'You are wed to me, to Lewy of the Long Hand.' He held still, not forcing her. Waiting for her. Gentle in his strength.

'I never agreed to marry you,' Dectera said, while her body went on moving and moving, demanding.

'Ah, you pledged yourself to me every starry night when you stared up into the sky and dreamed. It was me you were dreaming of. When you sat on the oak bench combing your hair, you were longing for me. When you clapped your hands in delight at the song of a bird, you were summoning me.' He began to move then, moving as she was. Demanding.

Lewy of the Long Hand.

When the druids offered sacrifices to him in the circle of standing stones, he was invoked by a more formidable name: Lugh, Son of the Sun.

Beyond the circle of radiance, Dectera sensed people reaching for her and trying to pull her away from him. There were voices she almost recognised, calling to her. Demanding. She was in two places at once, torn between them. She had to choose.

'Mother!' The women had led Setanta away from his mother's bedside so they could work on her, but now he tore himself from their grasp. Fear gave him strength. 'Mother, please wake up now!' His brain was presenting horrific possibilities to him. Dectera was dying, she was already dead, he would be totally and completely deserted, they would carry her away with a robe over her face and he would be alone in the echoing hall of Dun Dalgan.

'MotherMotherMother.' In anguish he threw himself on his knees beside the bedbox.

With difficulty, Dectera opened her eyes. Her lids were still weighted down with Lewy's kisses. In another heartbeat she would be totally his. She felt warm and fluid. Her knees parted to receive him. But his face was not looking down at her any more, it was beside her, pressed against one of her hands, which was held by . . . not Lewy. A boy.

'Setanta?'

Her voice was very weak, and the sound of disappointment in it shocked him. But at least she was awake. Setanta was overjoyed. He squeezed her hand, pressing it against his heart. He willed her to answer, to squeeze back. He knew he was crying, but he had been badly scared.

22

Gelace reached past him to feel Dectera's forehead. 'The fever is fading, she'll be all right now. You should let her rest, lad. She won't leave us, it was just a fit she had.'

Putting one motherly arm around Setanta's shoulders, she led him away from the bed. Poor little creature, she thought. This is not much of a home for him. He should have been fostered with a family who could raise him as he should be raised. But how should he be raised? Who could say?

By dawn, Dectera was better. She was pale and listless, but Gelace cajoled her into eating a little broth while Setanta devoured a huge meal with the appetite of a young wolf. He was gobbling the last of a bowl of duck eggs and some oatcakes dripping with honey when the healer arrived.

Frassach the physician, like Setanta's tutor Caisin, was a member of the *filidh*, the professional class, which, though not considered nobility, was as highly ranked as the warriors themselves. Bards and druids and healers and brehon judges were all *filidh*. Once Frassach had hoped for a position in the retinue of a major warlord, but his gifts had not proved equal to his ambition. Now, like Dectera, he was assigned to the backwater, treating the brittle bones of old men and the inflamed udders of cattle.

His dwelling house was a considerable distance from the fort. The runner arrived late in the night with news of Dectera's seizure, and it had taken Frassach a while to assemble the treatments he might need. Then he had to spend more time placating his wife, a woman who routinely seasoned his food with complaints.

'Not good your going off like this when the moon is dark,' she told him. 'You're always leaving me at the worst times. Don't I have a pain in my back that needs attention? And my hip? And there was blood in my eye yesterday, I'm certain of it. Besides, the pathway is long and dark, something could happen to you.'

'Nothing will happen to me. I'll take a torch, I know the way, and no one harms a member of the *filidh*, it isn't allowed.'

The woman toyed with her copper finger rings, frowning. 'Isn't that boy living at Dun Dalgan?'

'Dectera's son? He is of course.'

She hunched her shoulders and hugged herself, a thin woman with a fat face seamed by sleeping on it. 'You know what they say about that boy, husband. What if his father learns Dectera fell ill and died while supposedly in your care? He could do something terrible to you!'

Frassach ran all the way to Dun Dalgan, exerting his greatest speed when he had to pass mounds of earth or hawthorn clumps.

But by the time he reached the fort, Dectera had made her recovery –such as it was.

Gelace the cook, having used her own decoctions on her mistress, greeted the healer with the sniff of someone annoyed by the intrusion of a rival. 'You come too late, Frassach. I've cured her myself.'

'Look at my mother anyway,' Setanta requested. Frassach glanced down at him. The tone of command in the child's voice was out of proportion to his size; the lad was maturing. Things would change at Dun Dalgan.

'Take me to her then, boy.' He followed the boy to the small wattle-and-daub sleeping chamber attached to the main hall of the fort.

With Setanta hovering at his elbow, Frassach smelled Dectera's breath, read the veins in her eyes, felt the texture of the flesh under her chin. Then he pounded dried blossoms of corn marigold into a paste that he thinned with cow urine, called all-water because it contained the essences of all the plants the cow had eaten. This was applied to the woman's temples and the soles of her feet. The healer also ordered leaves of sundew to be boiled in milk and served to her as her only beverage for three nights and days.

As he worked, Frassach muttered incantations unknown to Gelace, taking a small and spiteful pleasure in doing so.

When he had done all he could, he straightened up with a grimace and began to massage the small of his back. He saw Dectera's son watching him with ill-concealed impatience.

'Your mother will be all right, Setanta,' Frassach said reassuringly. 'Just give her peace and quiet. Let her sleep as much as she wants. I'm surprised to see her in this condition again after so long a time, though. What brought it on?'

'Nothing! We were just talking. I was asking her questions about Emain Macha and the king and . . .'

Frassach took his hands away from his back and folded his arms. 'I'll tell you something for nothing. Don't try to make your mother speak of the past, or Emain Macha.'

'But why not? Don't I have a right to know about them? She came from there and her brother is king there and I should be there too, with my father, I should – '

'Enough!' Frassach's voice sliced the air, cutting off the flow of words. 'The last time Dectera was ill in this way, I attended her – when

24

she was first brought here. I warned them all then that she was delicate. Don't question her any more, I told Conor and Sualtim and the others. Her brain is confused and in a fever. Leave the past alone. Now, I tell you the same, Setanta.'

He would not be so easily put off. 'I don't want to hurt her, I just want to know what happened.'

Frassach sighed. 'Who can say? This began when poor Dectera was abducted on her wedding day. Abducting women is an old custom; a man seizes the woman he intends to marry and carries her away – for a short distance only – as a demonstration of his strength. No harm is meant, and everyone has a good time. But for some reason, your mother's abduction didn't follow the usual pattern, and left her very . . . disturbed.'

Setanta's face lit with understanding. 'Sualtim frightened her, didn't he? He frightened her so badly he made her sick, and that's why he finally left us, isn't it? He still feels guilty for having made my mother sick!'

This boy has a quick mind, Frassach said to himself. But obviously he has been told nothing, so they must want him to know nothing. Good enough. Let him think his answer is the correct one; perhaps it is. 'Indeed,' he said aloud. 'Any reference to the past brings Dectera pain, as you have seen. Let the past be over, boy; that's the best thing you can do for her. Ask no questions about it unless you want to see the fever return to her brain. I want your solemn vow. Will you swear?'

Setanta swallowed hard. He was still brimming with questions, but being asked to take a vow was very adult business. 'I vow by sun and moon,' he said in his most solemn voice.

Later, lying sleepless in bed, he regretted not having asked Frassach a few more questions before he made his vow. What had happened to Dectera in the time between her abduction from Emain Macha and her arrival at Dun Dalgan? Why did Conor and the man called Fergus go to rescue her? From what? Sualtim? Yet they had left her in Sualtim's care . . .

Setanta stared into the shadows. He had come to hate mysteries.

As winter set in, the boy kept his promise. Its very difficulty gave him a reason to congratulate himself. If he could lock his jaw on such irresistible questions, he could do anything.

He set himself to caring for Dectera and making life pleasanter for her. She was delicate, sensitive; he saw that now. He would be so good to her, she would never try to retreat into a place where her child could not follow. He taught himself tricks with his ball and hurley stick to amuse her, and he even learned to walk on his hands, strutting across the hall and trying to make his mother laugh. At last she did, though her laughter was as thin as ice on the surface of the bathing basins in winter.

She avoided looking at Setanta's face. Her averted gaze left a bruise on his heart.

He asked no questions, but by listening to the casual conversation of porters and traders, he learned that Emain Macha lay to the north, and a notch in the mountains marked the way. The notch and others like it allowed the inhabitants of the royal stronghold to see signal fires warning of invasions from as far away as the coast.

Now that he knew enough to listen for the name, Setanta heard frequent references to Fergus mac Roy. He learned the former king of Ulster was, in addition to being the king's champion, the chief instructor of the Boys' Troop.

Every mention of the troop excited Setanta.

At Dun Dalgan of the Bright Aspect, he had no clear vision of himself or of what he might become. Life was a gift without shape. The boy needed a father to be his model, and he needed friends to measure his growth against.

A longing for both tormented him.

When winter's mud gave birth to flowers, Setanta began to wander farther and farther from the fort. 'Watch the boy but don't interfere with him,' the captain of the guard instructed his men. 'Remember how it was for you; growing boys need to go off by themselves sometimes.'

Dectera did not seem troubled by her son's absences. Her thoughts were elsewhere.

She would be happier if I were elsewhere too, Setanta told himself sadly. The realisation made him feel like crying, but he had recently decided to be too old to cry.

A plan began to form itself inside him.

Ignoring the northern road that led openly towards Emain Macha, he began using the southern gate instead, the one the herders used. When departing for the day on one of his rambles, he took his little sword and his spears, his beloved hurley stick and a spare cloak, and a packet of bread and cheese. He made certain the guards got used to seeing all this. Well provisioned, he would wander a whole day on the Plain of Murthemney, teaching himself to find his way in unfamiliar places.

South-west of the fort he discovered a rough-surfaced grey pillar stone standing alone in a field, like a giant's accusing finger pointed at the sky. No man other than a druid would touch a standing stone, memorial to a vanished race of unknown powers.

The second time Setanta happened across the stone, a huge raven was perched on it. The bird did not fly away at his approach, but seemed to wait for him. Unblinking, it regarded him with a predator's glare. Setanta thought of the Battle Raven, the dreaded Morrigan who was one of the deities of war. Her name was to be whispered with horror, for in her guise as a bird the Morrigan haunted battlefields, inciting carnage and feasting afterward on carrion.

The boy was seized with a defiant sense of play. He drew his sword and ran forward, brandishing the weapon. 'Hail to the Morrigan!' he cried, tossing back his hair and laughing. 'I will be the greatest of all your warriors; watch me!' He flung the sword into the air, spinning up, up, bird and boy watching it together, until it dropped and he caught it with a deft turn of his wrist just in front of the pillar stone.

The raven did not move until the sword was back in Setanta's hand. Then she opened her wings. Their cold shadow fell across his upturned face.

Setanta's playful mood evaporated. He walked away from the pillar stone and sought other areas to explore, thereafter avoiding the field where it stood.

He knew he was growing stronger. New muscles swelled in his arms and legs; every day he could achieve more. Soon he would be able to survive on his own. He could take himself to Emain Macha as Sualtim had done.

At last he felt ready. As the flags of a red dawn flew, he left Dun Dalgan by the herders' gate, giving every appearance of a child out for a day's play. Whistling – slightly off-key – he strolled south in clear sight of the yawning sentry. Only when he could no longer be seen from the fort did he change direction and begin angling westward, then double back toward the north until at last he joined the road to Emain Macha.

Setanta walked briskly for most of the day, buoyed by a sense of adventure. He followed the road but when he saw someone coming towards him in the distance he ducked off into woods or hid in the curve of a stream bed. His mother might send a search party after him at any time, he reminded himself.

As long as the sun shone, he was in high good humour. The changing landscape delighted him. 'All new to me!' he exulted, tossing his ball and catching it, slamming it with his hurley stick and running after it.

Later in the day, he began to catch glimpses of hills of a perfect, unnatural roundness. 'They look like women's breasts,' he marvelled, thinking himself the first person ever to comment on the resemblance.

He felt wonderful. He thought he would remember for ever the exact way the air smelled on this most important day.

Then the shadows reached out for him; the wind was cold. As darkness advanced, the world seemed to expand, stretching away into unimaginable distances where anything might be waiting. Setanta kept his hand on his sword hilt and a brave jut to his jaw, in case anyone was watching. But he saw no one. Wise folk had long since gone home and were sitting by their warm fires.

Light left the landscape as if something had sucked it out.

The boy's legs ached with weariness. He could not stop shivering.

At last he made a bed for himself in the hollow some animal had scraped beneath a rotting tree trunk. Pillowed on sweet moss, he was comfortable enough. Warriors on cattle raids must sleep like this, he thought.

But he had never slept on the ground before, with no walls around him. He felt naked.

Has Dectera missed me and begun crying for me, he wondered. He did not want to make his mother cry.

It would be even more awful if she did not cry for him.

In the morning, he was ravenously hungry. He gobbled a large portion of his bread and cheese, then spread out the remainder and wondered how long it would last. It seemed a very small supply for a journey of indeterminate length.

To pass the time as he walked, he invented a new game. He threw one of his spears as if aiming at a fleeing deer, then ran along its flight path trying to catch it before it fell to earth. No matter how fast he ran, the spear was faster, but soon he learned to launch it into a higher arc, which at least gave him a chance. Sometimes he caught it and laughed aloud.

As long as he kept busy, he did not feel too lonely.

Noticing a broad, clear pool a little distance from the road, Setanta paused to drink and bathe himself. Dirt and sweat had mingled on his skin in one pervasive itch. He was almost finished, when he heard a sound like a cough. He glanced up to see a raven sitting on the stump of a tree, watching him.

A glossy, arrogant raven, like the bird on the pillar stone.

28

With a show of indifference, he turned his back on the bird and put on his clothes. When he was back on the road, he heard the dry rattle of feathers overhead and looked up to see the bird flying above him, going in the same direction. It circled and dropped lower; he could see its outsized, cruel bill.

'You're only a bird!' Setanta shouted at it, refusing to be intimidated. 'Just feathers and bones. I'm a warrior's son, I'm not afraid of you.' He walked faster, keeping one eye on the creature.

The raven kept pace with him. Sometimes it landed on the road ahead and strutted along the deep ruts left by generations of trade wagons. Again it perched on tree limbs, or leaped into the sky to make a dark slash across the empty air. The land was enjoying a spell of sunny weather, the sky was blue, the bird's feathers flashed with iridescence.

Setanta grew accustomed to the raven's presence. When it occasion- ally flew ahead and disappeared he found himself missing it – but it always came back.

When he stopped for his middle meal, the bird landed near him and stood with its head cocked. He threw it a piece of bread he could not spare. The bird seized the offering and devoured it. Setanta gulped down the rest of his meal quickly, eating too much but unable to resist. Putting food into his belly gave him a sense of security.

The days of sunshine ended with the sunset, and a damp wind heralded rain. The dry roadway quickly turned to mud. Setanta could find no shelter and had to make a bed for himself by wrapping up in his cloak in the lee of a lichen-covered boulder. Rain pounded a drumbeat on the stone. The boy fell asleep only to awaken some time later with a miserably stiff neck. He reached down to pull up his warm bedclothes and there were none. Everything was wet. He was wet. And cold. And alone. No one even knew where he was, and since he had seen no search parties, he must assume no one would find him.

I could die without reaching Emain Macha, he realised. Is that why the raven follows me? Is it waiting to pick my bones?

He could not go back to sleep but lay curled in the tightest possible knot, waiting for daylight and listening to the pounding of his heart.

Blackness faded to a gritty grey, the dawn before dawn. As the landscape slowly appeared, the first thing Setanta could make out was the raven perched on a rock nearby, huddled in its wings. Somehow the bird knew he was awake; it shook itself and looked directly at him.

Gaping its beak two or three times, the bird hopped from the rock and came towards him.

Setanta had seen carrion eaters pluck the ripe fruit of a dying animal's eyes. He squeezed his own tightly shut and held his breath – until curiosity got the better of him. Opening one eye, he peered through the screen of his lashes to find the raven only an arm's length from his face.

With sudden inspiration, Setanta flared his other eye as wide open as he possibly could and gave the bird a savage, lopsided glare.

The bird squawked and hopped sideways. Then, as if embarrassed by its fright, it stopped and began preening its damp feathers.

Rain. I *hate* rain. And cold, and damp, and mud. This is not the right climate for me, though I do my best to make the most of a bad situation.

The boy intrigued me. That trick he did with his eyes – he was young to display such bravado. Bravado can grow into true courage if properly nurtured.

Nurturing, however, is not my business.

Children are not my business either, though adults often drag them into my affairs. Trust adults to do everything wrong.

I realise I have a cynical viewpoint, but this climate has embittered me. I would do much better in a hot, dry place – like the desert. Yes, I could do my best work in the desert. But we are not allowed our preferences, any of us. We just are what we are and do what we do.

I, for example, am in the war business.

The tools of my trade are magic and terror. So far I had used no magic on the boy, but he was wonderfully resistant to terror. Knowing more about men than I ever wanted to know is one of the many burdens I bear. I can see into their spirits, so I knew the child Setanta was frightened, but he could already do what many adults cannot. He could think and act in spite of his fear.

Perhaps it is a result of his breeding.

The rain continued to fall, but the worst of it was moving past us, headed south. We had best be on our way if we were ever to reach our destination. In spite of my preening, I felt almost too soggy to fly. My feathers stank of damp.

Miserable weather. I would curse the stuff, but that is another of my burdens. Humans with their colourful vocabularies can use the full pantheon of gods and demigods to call down curses upon anything they choose . . . but whom do *we* call upon?

It is not easy, being me.

3 Early morning was the best time. In pre-dawn tranquillity, a man could get his best thinking done before the distractions of the day overcame him. But the truth of it was, Fergus mac Roy liked to lie abed. By the time Nessa finally made him get up, the day had begun without him, and he had to leap into it with his plans unmade.

The king's champion felt as if he always started just a little behind.

A massive man with a great mat of grey hair covering his chest and thighs, Fergus was proud of being the warrior chosen to represent Conor mac Nessa in single combat – a good king was too valuable to be risked. He was equally proud of his position as instructor of the Boys' Troop. His wife had once been bardsung for her beauty; he had strong sons and devoted foster sons. Most of the time, he was content.

The storm had blown over Emain Macha, leaving behind a freshly washed summer day. Sunseason. The royal mounds rose glittering with wet green grass. Atop each, a large timbered hall stood with doors opened wide to admit the sweet air. Warriors strutted importantly across the compound; servants crisscrossed the lawns at a brisk trot; children swarmed everywhere amid swarming hounds. The king's stronghold seethed with activity. In the sunlight, it also dazzled the eye with colour.

Scorning wickerwork, the royal halls were built with walls of timber coated with lime-washed plaster. They shone with a white so brilliant, it could be seen by trading vessels on the distant sea. Their conical roofs wore the gold of new thatch, and the people swirling energetically among the buildings sported tunics and cloaks of every vivid shade, crimson and saffron and blue, imported purple and intense green, embroidery of gold and silver thread and great buckles and brooches of burnished bronze.

These were the Gael of the clan Ulaid, ruling dynasty of Ulster.

Emerging tardily from his sleeping chamber, Fergus mac Roy looked at his clanfolk with an air of disbelief. How could so many people be so busy . . . and so loud . . . so early in the day?

32

He was not alone in this feeling. Cathbad the chief druid had long since departed for the sacred silence of a great circle of standing stones north of the fort. Fedlimid the king's harper had taken himself and his instrument to the stand of trees known as the Sorrowful Forest, where he could compose undisturbed.

Fergus envied them both. He seemed to be developing a slight headache behind his left eye. But the Boys' Troop was waiting for him.

For their day's activities, which must by law be divided into three separate parts, Fergus decided on quiet studies. No yelling. His head throbbed at the thought.

Definitely, no yelling.

Nessa pushed past him, headed for the well. He laid a hand on her arm. 'Would you bring me a linen pad soaked in cold water?'

She grinned with no sympathy at all. 'Again? If you didn't sit up all night in the ale hall, you wouldn't have such headaches the next day.'

'There is a *ges* on me, and you know it,' Fergus retorted with an air of offended dignity. 'I cannot refuse any man's hospitable offer of a drink.'

'And very convenient for you it is,' sniffed his wife.

She did not bring the cold cloth for his head.

Fergus set off for the Grove of Instruction, trying to organise thoughts in a bruised brain jouncing in a sore skull. This might be a good day to discuss a little history. He could talk – softly – about the clan Ulaid, whose name meant wool growers, and the victories that had led to their being dominant in Ulster. Some of the Ulidian battles made great telling . . . ah, that would be a mistake. Rethink, he ordered his painful head. If we begin talking about battles and victories, the boys will soon be yelling and cheering. No history. Not even the most casual mention of the age-old feud between Ulster and the neighbouring kingdom of Connaught to the west.

I wonder if we could talk about clouds, Fergus thought wistfully. Or just lie on our backs and look at them. Very quietly.

Seeing him coming, the boys ran to meet him. They were turning out well, this lot – every one of them the son of a famous fighter. They showed their noble lineage, though amid the roundheaded, ruddy boys was an occasional darker one, with a narrow, elder face. But they were all his charges, and Fergus loved each of them.

'The first lesson of the day will be boot repair,' he announced, bracing himself for the moan of disappointment. But he was determined, as a matter of self-preservation. Boot repair was quiet. 'If you are far from home and your footgear rots off your feet, you could get sores that would cripple you. A man whose feet hurt is at a disadvantage in a battle. Go barefoot when you can as do we all, but know how to protect yourselves when necessary.'

They grumbled among themselves but dared not argue openly. He was Fergus mac Roy, as stout as an oak tree, with thighs seven times the measure of an ordinary man's. Or so the bards sang.

Their instructor eased his bulk on to a low bench and began demonstrating how to shape leather well softened with melted fat in such a way that it could be formed to the leg, then held in place with crossed throngs. By the time they had the technique mastered, Fergus could feel rebellion simmering. His charges were bored, the most dangerous condition for boys.

'Enough for now,' he said, one heartbeat before they boiled over. 'A little game of hurling on the playing field will refresh you. I'll wait here in the shade and supervise.'

They raced past him like so many stones shot from slings. Balls and hurley sticks materialised out of nowhere. They began yelling as they chose sides, and Fergus looked around for a place farther removed from the scene of the contest – under the tree, perhaps, where the chessboards were always set up in good weather. A quiet sport, chess, the quietest form of battle. Though not the least serious.

He started towards the chessboards, seeing Conor mac Nessa already there and looking for an opponent. But when Fergus stepped into the sunlight, a red band of pain clamped down on his forehead. He paused, wincing. If only the day weren't so bright . . .

Spears of light had lanced Setanta's eyes, forcing them open. The world around him was bathed in sunlight, as if it had never known rain. He sat up, rubbing his eyes with grubby fists. He was not dead after all.

He scrambled to his feet, looking around. Mist was bleeding from the peaks of low purple mountains. Water gleamed on every leaf and twig, refracting sunlight into tiny rainbows.

Somewhere nearby, a raven coughed.

The boy started. 'Are you still here, then? You're as stubborn as I am.' He straightened his soggy clothing as best he could. Hoarding his last morsels of food from home, he made a meal of sorts by eating sloes from the blackthorn bushes, dyeing his lips a rich dark red in the process. He threw some to the raven, but she ignored them.

Then he gathered up his pack and set out along the road again.

34

The dry rattle of wings accompanied him.

As the morning passed, he had a growing sensation of being cut loose in space. He was suspended in unknown territory, with his mother somewhere behind him and his father somewhere ahead of him. The vast indifference of the universe pressed down on him.

Setanta's shoulders gradually rounded under the weight of the sky. The bird noticed as they went on together, on and on.

Setanta was so preoccupied, he did not realise the road had become much wider, nor did he notice that its verge was free of weeds and nettles. Unfamiliar with the customs of kings, he did not know that the members of a king's clan were obliged to keep weeds scythed away from the *slighe*, the road that led to his stronghold.

The land nearest the king must reflect his status, but throughout Erin the earth was treated with ritual care, for the island's inhabitants recognised their total dependence upon her.

On the giver and destroyer.

The mother goddess.

At Dun Dalgan on certain days, Setanta had observed the women offering gifts to a carved stone figure known as the Sheela-na-Gig. The image was blatantly female, but also frighteningly hideous. She represented that aspect of the mother and goddess in which birth and death were interlocked. The goddess was equally prepared to bestow life or devour her young, to spew out corn and cattle or to take them back into her body to rot, and with her fingers she spread her genitals wide to show the pathway through which life moved.

The Sheela-na-Gig both frightened and disgusted Setanta, and he watched without understanding as the women buried their afterbirth at its feet, or draped it with flower garlands or poured hot blood down its face. The little boy was too young to ponder the duality of goddesses.

Now he rounded a final bend in the *slighe* and halted abruptly.

In a blaze of greengold light, the vision that was Emain Macha flooded his consciousness.

Nothing in Setanta's brief life had prepared him for the royal stronghold of Ulster. It was too vast, the earthen bank surrounding it too wide, the ditch embracing it too deep. The great halls atop their mounds were formidable beyond anything he could have imagined; the smallest of them dwarfed the dwelling house of Dun Dalgan.

The boy stood in the road staring. His little sword dropped from nerveless fingers.

He was a fool to have attempted this, he thought. A child alone, laying siege to such a place and demanding recognition! They would laugh at him. Or worse yet, they would not notice him at all, any more than he noticed the midges in the air around him.

He sat down in the middle of the road. There was no strength left in his legs, but they were not going to take him any farther anyway. He could not go on, and it was too far to go back. He bowed his head and wondered if it was very easy to die.

The raven glided down out of the sky. She landed on the weedless verge and strutted forward, opening and closing her wings to get Setanta's attention. But he did not look up.

She pecked at his ankle and drew blood.

He glared at her then, but made no move. His mind was a blank, without the smallest thought to ruffle its surface. Weariness and shock had emptied him.

The raven lifted a crest of feathers along the top of her head and down her neck: warrior's plumes. She pecked Setanta again, cruelly.

'Get away from me!' he yelled at her. His childish voice cracked suddenly, and the first deep note of manhood rang through it.

Boy and bird were both startled.

'Get away from me, I say,' Setanta reiterated, trying unsuccessfully to repeat the one resonant syllable that hinted at the future.

The future. Something stirred in him. He could not sit here in the road for ever; he was going to become a man some day.

The raven was at his elbow and he lashed out at her. 'Go on, I don't need you.'

You do need me, said a voice. A strange, sibilant voice, as dry as a raven's feathers.

Setanta rocked back on his heels and looked at the bird in astonishment.

You do need me.

He did not hear the words with his ears, but in some deeper place, the marrow of his bones and the corners of his spirit.

You need me, the voice told him, to name you as a coward since your own people are not here to undertake the obligation. In their absence, I say you dishonour them, crouching in the dirt like a slave.

Setanta was on his feet at once, fists clenched. 'I'm not a coward, I'm a warrior's son!'

He heard a sound like harsh laughter. The ravenvoice mocked him. You stop before you even begin, human, it said. A chick has more courage, or it could never break out of the egg.

'I haven't stopped, I was just resting.'

A strong boy like you with a night's rest behind you and an easy road ahead? You need food, but can you not smell the meat roasting at Emain Macha? Go there and claim a portion, if you would call yourself a warrior's son. Or crouch here in the road, brave Root of Valour, and be crushed beneath the wheels of the real warriors when they come in their chariots.

The eerie voice rang in the boy's head, derisive, sarcastic.

Root of Valour!

The raven spread her wings and leaped into the sky.

He got to his feet and followed her.

She stayed within his view, circling, climbing, diving, mocking him. He longed to hurl one of his spears at her, but she never let him get quite close enough.

Coward! she called him. A warrior's son indeed!

Step by step, she led and goaded him towards Emain Macha.

The main gateway of the fortress stood open. As Setanta drew near, the raven soared away, but he no longer needed her. Now he advanced on his own, pulled forward by curiosity. The guards in the gatetower watched him but did not challenge him, one small boy alone and on foot. They viewed him with amusement as he entered, his grey eyes wide with wonder.

The earthwork bank and palisade were outside the ditch instead of within, which was the more usual arrangement. Beyond the ditch stood another timber wall with another gate and sentry, but Setanta passed this without difficulty. The fortress embraced him.

A well-trod path followed the slope of the land upward toward the royal mounds, but a branch of the path led toward a grassy playing field where scores of boys were screaming and yelling. Sticks flashed; a ball sped through the air with a pack of youngsters racing after it. The hurling game was underway. The playing area, or pitch, was impeccably maintained; no blade of grass was longer than a man's shortest finger, holding the ball up just high enough to allow a hurley stick to get under it. No sight could have been more inviting to a little boy who had always wanted to play at hurling.

Setanta gave a cry of delight. Without pausing to think, he pulled his own hurley stick free from the thongs holding it to his pack, and ran towards the playing field.

Some of the Boys' Troop saw the stranger approaching but they did not bother to acknowledge him. He was on their territory, it was up to him to offer the greeting. According to their tradition, there were certain words to be said, advances to be made, and the troop had had their formalities thoroughly drilled into them.

No one had taught any of this to Setanta.

His excitement knew no bounds. He was actually inside Emain Macha, he had obviously found the wonderful Boys' Troop, and they were playing a game he had longed with all his heart to play. A team game, a match between friends!

Suddenly the ball bounded in his direction. Setanta flung himself into the contest as a traveller flings himself into homecoming. Forgetting his weariness, he darted forward to seize possession of the ball.

There was an outraged howl from the other players.

Grinning hugely, Setanta drove the ball this way and that, evading the boys who tried to stop him. He had imagined this so many times and rehearsed the techniques so endlessly that he seemed to be playing by himself in a realm beyond the ability of the others. They were shouting angrily at him but he did not hear, he was too lost in the joy of the moment. At last he was measuring himself against contemporaries. At last he was discovering that he was, indeed, talented at the game.

He dodged to one side; a large boy with hair the colour of a fox's pelt tried to block his way but Setanta whirled and evaded him easily, to find himself facing a small but crucial opening in the wall of boys. With one brilliant stroke he sent the ball hurtling through that opening to the goal.

A roar went up. It was not a happy sound. At first Setanta mistook it for admiration of his shot, but exhilaration faded as he noticed the expressions of the boys bearing down on him.

One tall lad stepped to the front of the pack. Blond and sturdy, Follaman was the firstborn son of Conor mac Nessa. His younger brothers, the equally blond Fiacra and a curly-haired, snaggletoothed lad called Cormac, crowded against him, prepared to support his every action and shelter in his lee if trouble broke out.

'We don't know you,' Follaman said to Setanta, who noticed with a sinking feeling that the other boy's voice had already changed. 'And you have not properly presented yourself to us. You shoved in amongst us without first acknowledging our superiority and begging our protection, so you must be very ignorant. The son of a herder or even a seaweed gatherer, probably. You are obviously not fit for the company of heroes' sons.'

38

Follaman accompanied this haughty speech with an insulting glare down an aristocratic length of nose. Setanta's temper flared – but he fought it back. These were the companions he had longed for; he must not alienate them when he had just found them. But he would have to establish himself in their eyes quickly. He must prove himself the worthy son of a chariot-chieftain so Sualtim would be proud of him.

'I want nothing more than to be your friend and teammate,' he said to Follaman, using his most educated accents and standing with his chin high and his shoulders back. 'But I will not apply to you for protection, because I am your equal. I just proved it on the playing field.'

'Equal!' Follaman almost strangled on a gasp of laughter. 'You miserable little wood tick, you could never be my equal. Don't you know who I am?'

'I do not,' Setanta replied coolly. 'But neither do you know who I am. I suppose I must show you.' With a slow, deliberate gesture, he laid his hurley stick on the ground, out of harm's way. Then he spat on his hands, rubbed them together, and took a deep breath.

Setanta fully expected the boys to hammer him into the earth. He was so certain of the beating he would receive that his imagination carried him through it and beyond, leaving the pain in the past and his fear with it. The beating was inevitable, so it did not matter, but the style with which he faced it could determine his whole future.

Once he was freed of fear, wisdom rose in him like a bubble.

Surveying the mob of angry boys facing him, he realised Follaman was not the largest. That distinction belonged to a youth with an uncommonly square jaw and deadly green eyes. Setanta called out to him, 'You're biggest, you strike the first blow.'

Before the surprised boy could respond, he turned to Follaman. 'You're next largest, the second blow is yours. But mind you just take one, because the others will want their turn.' He then went through the crowd like a trained number counter, assigning each boy a place in the order. They gaped at him. This conformed to no style of combat they knew.

When every boy had been ranked according to size, Setanta stepped up to the green-eyed one and said, 'Now.'

Conall Cearnach, he of the square jaw, glanced around in hopes of seeing Fergus mac Roy. He did not mind beating this presumptuous interloper to pulp, but he longed for the voice of authority to give a formal order in an unfamiliar situation. The newcomer was a stranger –he was also, probably, a visitor, a guest at Emain Macha, and the laws of hospitality were very strict. One must not abuse a guest. A man who did so would be shamed for ever.

Yet surely the dark, wiry boy had requested to be hit, and Conall Cearnach's arms ached to hit him. What to do?

At that moment, a huge raven swooped down out of nowhere and flew right at his eyes. Conall instinctively raised his arm to protect them at the same time as Setanta heard a derisive voice screeching, Coward, coward, no wonder Sualtim abandoned you! Hit him, Root of Valour! Hit him!

Any hesitation Setanta might have felt evaporated. Fury burned through him from the crown of his head to the soles of his feet. His brain blazed, exploding in his skull in a red daze, shooting off sparks. Vision swirled into a crimson spiral flecked with gold and a delicious heat engulfed him. Melting into it, Setanta felt a rapture of reckless courage flame through his veins, engorging his muscles, transforming mortal sinews with a spark of immortality.

On the playing field of Emain Macha, one young boy became Rage.

Afterwards, every member of the Boys' Troop had a version of the story, and for each of them the truth was subtly different. Some saw the raven, others did not. Some thought Setanta had been exceptionally lucky, others said the boys he fought had been unusually slow. But all agreed on one point: The thing that attacked them was not simply a wiry, dark, bare-legged boy in a dusty tunic.

Conall Cearnach still had one arm flung up to ward off the raven he thought he saw when Setanta locked his fists together and drove them straight-armed into the larger boy's diaphragm. Conall folded neatly in the middle and sank to his knees, pop-eyed.

'That's enough for you!' Setanta yelled. 'Wait at the end of the line if you want another turn.'

He turned at once to Follaman, who was already expecting a blow to the belly, since that had proved so effective against Conall. Follaman crouched in anticipation and Setanta swarmed up him as if he were climbing a tree, roaring with anger as he pummelled Follaman's head and ears. One blow to the temple and the king's son found himself staring into a darkness filled with stars. Staggering, he raised an arm to try to brush Setanta off, but the smaller boy grabbed the arm and swung from it as if from a tree branch. Against all training, Follaman yelled with pain. His arm was nearly wrenched from its socket.

At once Setanta abandoned him and fell on his next victim, Fiacra.

The anger still blazed in him. He attacked each boy differently, so none could prepare a defence. The anger was feeding on itself now, growing, consuming him. He had come so far with such high hopes and they had denied him, they had mocked him . . . He grabbed one boy by the throat and throttled him, then stepped over his half-conscious body and turned just in time to slam the top of his good, hard skull against the jaw of Cormac, third of the king's sons, who had come up behind him. Setanta heard bone crunch, but it was not his bone.

By now, the troop was in disarray. They were trying to gang up on him but he was awesomely agile, ducking and dodging as he relentlessly pursued the next boy on his mental list, refusing to be sidetracked. The troop had been drilled in the rituals of Gaelic combat, which involved showy displays of power and stylised demonstrations of sword and spear work. No tribe had men to spare, so the purpose was to win a point, not to create carnage.

But the interloper seemed intent on carnage. He had not killed anyone yet, but they were beginning to think he might. The anger that drove him was beyond their comprehension. A score of the troop were already injured; noses streamed crimson and eyes swelled purple. But few had been quick enough to land a blow on Setanta.

He was, however, a child. Even the Rage could not carry him indefinitely; his immature body had limitations. He began to run out of breath. Soon the troop would overcome him and take an awful revenge.

But he did not mind. He was in the centre of them, surrounded by their company. The Rage began to fade; a slow grin spread across his face.

Fergus had at last been alerted. A servant in an unbleached tunic had come running up to the chessboard, where he and Conor were just getting into the serious part of the game. 'The Boys' Troop have caught some stranger and are killing him on the playing field!' the servant cried.

Fergus and the king exchanged a look. 'Perhaps we should keep them all on leashes,' Conor said with amusement. 'And muzzles,' he added.

Fergus heaved himself to his feet. The headache, which had begun to recede, came pounding back. 'They'll make good warriors,' he reminded his foster-son. Then he set off for the playing field.

He arrived in time to see Setanta's unlikely grin just before the dark stranger disappeared under a wave of boys howling for his blood. Wading in amid upraised arms and swinging fists, Fergus began pulling his charges away. 'Stop it at once!' he commanded. They were slow to obey him. Easier to separate hounds fighting over a bitch, he thought grimly, and began to deliver some blows himself.

Eventually, he got the knot untangled and the pile unstacked. At the bottom was the stranger, not yet broken but certainly bruised.

Lying on his back, Setanta sensed light above him and opened his eyes to see a huge, hairy man bending over him. The man was dressed in a knee-length warrior's tunic dyed saffron, with a short red cape pinned at the shoulder by a gold brooch. A king's brooch.

Setanta propped himself on one elbow and shook his head to clear it. Then, with an effort costing more than he cared to admit, he dragged himself upright and stood swaying on his feet. The Rage was gone, leaving his muscles slack and trembling. But he brought the grin back and showed it to Fergus.

The instructor of the troop looked from the stranger to his own boys. They seemed a sorry lot by comparison. None of them was matching the newcomer's bravado, and a dozen or more, as Fergus later remarked to Conor, looked as if they had been chewed up and spat out.

'This is no gentle game you play,' Fergus said to the unknown boy.

Setanta was fighting for breath and his ribs hurt, but he kept his feet under him. The troop was all around him; the metallic smell of their sweat intermingled with his. He saw more than one boy give him a look of grudging admiration, and one bony redhead, as freckled as a blackbird's egg, threw him a wink.

'The fault is on those around me,' Setanta told Fergus. 'I came as a stranger, but they didn't offer me the courtesies due a stranger.'

'Didn't you know no one joins the Boys' Troop without requesting their permission first?'

'I did not know, or I would have done so,' Setanta explained. 'They did demand I plead for protection, however. And I refused. I'm not the one who needed protection,' he added meaningfully, glancing at the ranks of the injured.

A second man strode across the playing field towards the group. Setanta saw all eyes swing toward the newcomer, and when he looked at the man himself, he understood.

The heavy gold torc around the strong white throat was not necessary to identify the king of Ulster. Every proud line of Conor mac Nessa's face and form did that for him, from his gleaming golden beard to the flawless articulation of his knee joints. His tunic was of *sida*, and quite short, his legs being deemed too beautiful to hide. And Setanta thought he recognised something familiar in the king's face. Later, when he had time to think about it, he would decide it was a similarity to his own mother. The same wide cheekbones, the same finely modelled mouth.

'Tell us your name and family, boy,' Conor commanded.

Here was the opportunity Setanta had been waiting for, but when he tried to answer, his newly treacherous voice betrayed him. It cracked and slid and the other boys laughed.

He frowned and tried again. 'I am called Setanta, the son of Sualtim, chariot-chief of Dun Dalgan. My mother is Dectera, sister to the king of Ulster.' He added the last for emphasis, standing as tall as he could in his battered body.

Conor gave him a searching look. As was his habit, the king smoothed his forked and curled beard with his fingers before he spoke, so his words seemed twice as well-considered as any other man's.

I should have adopted that pose, Fergus was thinking.

'The shape of your head,' Conor mused aloud. 'And those silver eyes, I know them well.' His expression softened. 'Ah, Dectera.' He roused himself from his reverie by asking sharply, 'Did you come this long way by yourself, boy? Or did my sister perhaps bring you?'

Setanta was insulted the king should even suggest it. 'I came entirely by myself,' he said firmly. 'The whole journey. Alone.' He saw no point in mentioning the raven.

Conor nodded. 'You're not lacking in courage, then. Or a bold heart. And look what you've done to this lot here.' He glanced towards his eldest son, and Follaman flushed with embarrassment. 'Emain Macha is where you belong,' Conor said to Setanta, 'and I am proud to welcome you. If we had known you were coming, we would have arranged, er, a more appropriate welcome.'

Setanta's battered grin surfaced. 'The welcome was wonderful,' he said.

The king hid a smile in his beard. 'We'll send word to your mother that you are safe and well and with us now. You are well, aren't you?' He was gazing at a gaping tear in the boy's tunic, beneath which abraded skin was oozing blood.

Setanta looked down. 'Fabric is being very loosely woven this season,' he remarked. 'It seems to tear at the graze of a twig, doesn't it?'

The king grabbed the child and gave him a huge hug, squeezing all his bruises. Setanta felt no pain. Lost in the first fatherly embrace of his life, he was blissful.

'We will go to the House of the King,' Conor decided, 'and find some appropriate clothing for my sister's son.'

Later, when he had time to think about it, Setanta wondered why he had not been called Sualtim's son.

Guided by the king and escorted as far as the doorway by the entire Boys' Troop in various states of disrepair, Setanta climbed the largest of the royal mounds. The pathway was swept clean of even the tiniest pebble, the sheep-cropped *urla* was starred with buttercups, the air was fragrant with flowers and rippling with harp music. They went up and up and then all at once they were on top, with Ulster spread out below them.

The fort was well sited. On a clear day it was possible to see the Sperrins to the north-west, Slieve Gallion to the north, Slieve Mish to the north-east, Slieve Fuad to the south, and a blue glitter of water to the east. Mountains and sea. Anyone holding such high ground was truly a king.

I am here, Setanta thought. *Really here.* At the doorway of the royal hall, he paused to allow himself one long look back at the way he had come. Something burned at the base of his throat.

Then he turned and followed Conor mac Nessa into the House of the King.

4 An oak door sheathed in bronze swung in to reveal a vast circular hall, rising the height of seven long spears to a thatched, conical roof. The building smelled of woodsmoke and ashes, damp wool and bitter ale, of flea-ridden shaggy wolfhounds and the extravagance of beeswax candles, which kept the interior day-bright.

Movable cedar screens, inlaid with strips of silver and bronze, partitioned the space into various compartments as required. The House of the King was not only the royal residence but also served Conor mac Nessa as an audience chamber and was usually thronged with members of his family, including his two wives, plus the *filidh* who attended him, and his personal band of warrior elite.

Not all three hundred members of the Red Branch were there at one time, however, being posted in rotation to guard the few approaches giving access through mountain and forest to the kingdom of the north. When Setanta entered the House of the King for the first time, a third of their number were present, occupying the benches reserved for their use around a raised dais on which stood the king's carved bench. This high seat was studded with hunks of amethyst and amber and rock crystal, and nearest it on either side were the places of honour belonging to Athairne the poet, Sencha the brehon judge, and Cathbad of the Gentle Face, the king's druid.

The size and splendour of the royal residence dazzled Setanta. He rotated slowly, trying to absorb everything, from the smell of crowded humanity to the blaze of bright colours. A giggle made him tilt his head back and look up.

High under the thatch, a wooden gallery ran the width of the hall. Women were crowded at its railings, leaning on their elbows to observe the floor below. Some were laughing and pointing out Setanta to others; small, dirty children were rarely introduced in the House of the King.

The gallery was not the only special arrangement made for women. Like most duns, or fortified residences, Emain Macha included a *grianan*, a sunny-room prepared for the exclusive use of women of rank.

45

Grianans were built with numerous windows to admit light and air, to facilitate sewing and embroidery. But for the main meal of the day, the women in order of their rank joined their men. Instead of using a separate feasting hall for the purpose, Conor mac Nessa fed his Red Branch in the House of the King as a mark of special favour.

Unnoticed by Setanta, the day was dying. There was a large audience gathered in the hall to observe the unknown boy's arrival.

Dethcaen, daughter of the chief druid, Cathbad, was among those in the gallery. She grabbed the arm of the nearest woman. 'Elva, see down there? I know that boy, I nursed him as a child at Dun Dalgan. I never expected to see him here.'

Elva was an ageing woman with a face like crumpled linen. She sighted along Dethcaen's pointing finger, then shrugged and looked away. There was only one child Elva longed to see at Emain Macha.

When Elva and her husband, Fedlimid the king's harper, had all but given up hope of having a child, Elva had finally found herself pregnant. But even as the infant waited in her womb, Cathbad had laid his hand on Elva's belly and uttered a fearful pronouncement.

'This child will be a girl of such wondrous beauty that beauty itself will have a new name,' he had said. 'But an excess of anything is deadly, and the excess of this girl's beauty will cause champions to fight for her and Ulster to run red with blood because of her. Her birth will be the greatest tragedy to befall the Red Branch.'

A great cry had gone up at once, with many demanding that the unborn child be slain in its mother's womb. But Conor mac Nessa was new to the kingship, and anxious to make a name for himself as a wise and compassionate man. Besides, he loved his harper and would not have the elderly man's only child slain.

'As soon as she is born, I will take this girl under my protection,' he had decreed, 'and raise her in secret out of the sight of men, so her beauty will inflame no one. If she grows to be as extraordinary as Cathbad says, I will make her my own wife, placing her in a rank so high no other man will dare aspire to her.'

As the young king had decreed, so it was done, and the day the little girl was born to Elva, she tearfully surrendered her to a nurse Conor had named, a trustworthy woman called Levarcham. The baby, who was given the name of Deirdre, had been raised since in some secret place, and no one at Emain Macha had ever seen her – except the king, who sometimes went to visit and check on her progress.

Elva felt the winter of age stealing into her bones, making them

46

brittle, and longed to see her Deirdre just once before she died. This was her obsession; she had no interest in any other child. 'What is some strange boy to me?' she said to Dethcaen.

But Dethcaen was a druid's daughter. In response to Elva's question, the gift of prophecy rose in her. 'The stranger down there will some day be known the length and width of Erin, more famous even than your Deirdre.'

Elva recognised the prophetic ring in the other woman's voice, but she did not care. 'Druid predictions make my belly gripe,' she said sourly.

A crowd was forming around Setanta. Everyone was curious. Conor mac Nessa stood to one side with his arms folded and watched. When he looked at the boy there was a peculiar expression in his blue eyes, a look both guarded and delighted.

Setanta was paying no attention to the king, however. He was searching the room for another face, but Sualtim did not seem to be among the men of the Red Branch gathered in the hall.

Then Conor spoke – and his words drove all thoughts of Sualtim from Setanta's mind. 'This boy called Setanta is my sister's son,' the king said in a loud voice, so all could hear. 'And I name him as my foster-son, from today a full member of the king's family.'

There were gasps of surprise, not the least of them from Setanta himself. His head spun, his ears roared. He felt dangerously close to fainting, as much from excitement as from the aftereffects of his recent battles.

Becoming a fosterling of the king was the last thing the boy had anticipated. Caisin had taught him about fosterage: 'Noble families send their children to be raised by other families in order to establish ties of affection they may call upon in case of war.'

But to be fostered by the king himself! Setanta could scarcely comprehend such an honour. He had come looking for one father and had found another, who offered him recognition and rank beyond his dreams.

Follaman came forward, rubbing one shoulder ruefully. 'I'm not one to bear a grudge,' he said, 'so welcome to the king's family. I rather like the idea of having a foster-brother who can do magic. Perhaps you can rid me of the terrible dreams I have sometimes, when I'm sick with a fever.'

'I can't do any magic.'

'What was that on the playing field, then? You changed your shape, we saw you do it. The hair stood up on your head and you swelled, Setanta. I vow by meat and mead, you expanded to twice your size, or you could never have beaten me. And that is magic, surely.'

Shape-changing? Setanta thought. Me? Impossible. That's something the magic people would do. I want nothing to do with it; magic is to be feared, Dethcaen said . . .

A slender woman in a striped gown made her way through the crowd to him. On the heel of Conor's announcement, everyone was trying to get closer to Setanta, to welcome him, to make a good impression on him. But they gave way to the druid's daughter.

Though not born of the magic people, druids had long ago learned some of their secrets, and they commanded fear and respect.

'I thought it was you,' the woman said. 'Don't you remember me?'

He gave her a long look, recognition slowly flooding his face. 'Dethcaen!'

'It is. And you are too pale.' She put a quick hand under his elbow to steady him as he swayed. 'You must eat and rest. Have you put anything in your belly all day?'

He corrugated his forehead with the effort to remember. 'Some berries. I think. It seems a long time ago.'

Under the king's approving eye, Dethcaen took charge of the child, finding him a bench to sit on one heartbeat before his legs collapsed under him. She sent an attendant for bread and buttermilk.

When he was somewhat restored, Setanta asked, 'Where is my father, Dethcaen?'

'Your new foster-father is over there, talking to his poet.'

'I mean Sualtim of Dun Dalgan. Isn't he here? I came all this way to find him, and I want him to see what I've accomplished. I want him to be proud of me. I'll be Red Branch too, when I grow up.'

Dethcaen looked uncomfortable. It was all very well for the king to make a kingly gesture, but this child was going to need some sensible guidance to keep from making an awkward situation worse. 'Sualtim is indeed at Emain Macha, and I imagine you will see him soon enough,' she said. 'But don't try to attach yourself to him, and don't expect too much of him; I tell you this as a friend, my Setanta. Some pots are best left unstirred. You have been taken into the king's family now, and that should be enough for you.' She put her hand on the boy's shoulder but he squirmed, pulling free. His muscles did not feel like those of a child.

'I'm entitled to my father's recognition,' Setanta said stubbornly.

48

The druid's daughter fixed him with her eyes. 'Listen to me, boy, and be patient. What is for you will not pass by you.'

At that moment someone else demanded her attention, and she turned away. At once a thin redheaded boy with a plague of freckles took her place. 'I am called Laeg, son of Riangabra,' he introduced himself. His eyes were as merry as his wink to Setanta had been earlier, on the playing field. 'I'm the best of all boys here in handling horses,' Laeg went on. 'Some day when you have a chariot and need a charioteer, remember me.'

Laeg's bony face was as open and candid as a summer meadow. Setanta liked him at once. 'We will be comrades always,' he decided.

A friend. He doubled one fist and punched Laeg gently over the heart to hammer the friendship in.

Laeg gave way to a square-jawed boy with deadly green eyes. For the second time that day, the tall, muscular lad and the newcomer measured each other warily. Setanta could not tell if there was any possibility of friendship in the other's face; it was closed to him. Yet he liked it. The green-eyed boy was shaped in a heroic mould.

'I am called Conall Cearnach, son of Amorgen.' The name was hurled like a challenge.

Conall Cearnach suddenly looked even bigger than Setanta remembered – and not as quick to forgive as Follaman mac Conor. Setanta's body hurt all over, but it seemed he was not through proving himself. He got to his feet.

'Since you can't be Setanta,' he said, 'I suppose the next best thing is to be Conall Cearnach.'

The other's eyes widened. 'You insolent . . . we should have beaten you to a pulp.'

Setanta tossed his head to get an unruly lock of dark hair out of his eyes. 'Shall we start again, then? You first?'

Conall hesitated. A reluctant smile played around the edges of his mouth, softening its naturally hard line. 'You are mad,' he decided. 'You'd do it, wouldn't you?'

'Indeed. I might not win, but I would not lose.'

The green-eyed boy shook his head. 'You're going to be very interesting. But you have a lot to learn. For example, we are within the *maigen* of the king. The area around the dun of a person of high rank is safe ground, sanctuary, and the sanctuary surrounding Emain Macha extends almost to the Sorrowful Forest on the west and the crossroads on the east. No one can break the peace within a *maigen* without the owner's permission, so we cannot fight one another at Emain Macha. Unless Conor allows it, which he won't.'

'But you just fought me on the playing field.'

'Ah, the playing field – that's different, isn't it? But our contests are over for now. Dethcaen sent me to take you to the House of Tethra – that's where the Boys' Troop sleeps.' As he spoke, he had somehow herded Setanta through the crowd and out of the door. The smaller boy had to trot to keep up with his long stride.

Conall led the way to a low, rectangular wattle-and-daub building crowded with pallets. 'Take that one,' he said, pointing. 'Dethcaen says you're to sleep as long as you like, and we can't disturb you because you're under a *ges*.'

'A *ges*,' Setanta echoed gratefully, falling on to his pallet like a felled tree.

At the doorway, Conall Cearnach paused to look back at him. Mad, thought the older boy. But interesting.

When Conall returned to the House of the King, the hall was buzzing like a hive. Everyone was talking about Setanta. Conall drifted from group to group, listening but contributing nothing himself. He rarely indulged in casual conversation. He preferred to save his energy for action; he had only spoken at such length to Setanta to show off his knowledge after his defeat at the smaller boy's hands.

'The king's foster-son indeed,' scoffed Duffach, who was known as the Beetle of Ulster. One of the most famous of the Red Branch, he sprawled comfortably on his bench picking remnants of his most recent meal out of his beard. Peering at his companions from beneath a massive brow ledge, the Beetle of Ulster went on, 'Didn't Conor's sister Dectera sleep with her brother in the same bedbox until he took a wife? And didn't Conor start encouraging a marriage between Dectera and Sualtim very suddenly?'

'Families sleep together,' said Ernan of the Iron. 'It's warmer that way.'

'I'm not talking about sleeping.' Duffach made an explicit gesture with his fingers; his friends responded with a ribald laugh. 'Everyone knew Dectera adored her brother. She stayed so close to him, the poor fellow had no room for his shadow.'

A servant arrived with a braided willow platter sagging under the weight of oatcakes kneaded with salmon roe. Hands grabbed, jaws chewed. Only when the heap of cakes was reduced to a few crumbs did shaggy, silver-haired Brocc the Badger say, 'The lad is Sualtim's. Has to be. And unless Sualtim formally denies him, which isn't likely, he's entitled to become one of the Red Branch when he's old enough to take up weapons.'

'He could be Red Branch anyway,' Duffach insisted. The Beetle of Ulster had a clamping mind. 'If his sire is Conor mac Nessa.'

Brocc shook his head. 'Conor wouldn't dare break the *ges* against mating with a sister.'

'Even if he was drowsy and drunk and she snuggled too close?'

Ernan of the Iron leaned forward. 'It's easy to see what happened. Sualtim abducted Dectera on their wedding day just as he was supposed to, but he got overeager and she probably panicked, as women occasionally do, and ran away from him. She found someone to shelter her while she made up that ridiculous story about – '

'It wasn't a ridiculous story, and I don't think she made it up,' said a raw-boned, florid man they called Gergind, a warrior with an awesome number of trophies to his credit in the House of the Red Branch. 'I was with Sualtim on his wedding day, and I vow by the moon and stars he never got his hands on her. A strange day it was, and a stranger year followed. Remember the Plague of the Birds? I went on that bird hunt with Conor and the others, so I was there when we finally found Dectera again. I know what we saw and what we didn't see . . . *I* think Setanta was sired by – '

'You men have looser tongues than women,' said an imperious voice.

Conall Cearnach, who had been listening from the fringes, slipped away as the king's mother thrust herself in among the benches of the Red Branch. Nessa had a long habit of going without hesitation into areas denied other women. 'Take what you want and dare anyone to object,' she had often told her son.

Gruff warriors squeezed together on their benches to make room for her to sit down. She looked with disfavour at the empty platter, then picked up a few lingering crumbs. 'The new boy's paternity is not anyone's business but his own,' she said to those around her. 'My son the king does not want it discussed. He has made Setanta a member of our family, and that's an end to it.' She beckoned to a passing servant to pour her some of the new wine recently purchased from the sea-traders. Nessa carried her own cup with her, a fine footed vessel of polished olive wood banded in gold wire.

The men said nothing more until she had drained her cup, then Gergind asked innocently, 'Do you know who sired the child, really, Nessa?'

She twisted around to glare at him. Nessa had lived three generations already, but she was still a handsome woman – with a great deal of effort on her part. 'I know everything that goes on in Ulster,' she said firmly. 'Everything!' She stood up abruptly. In another moment she was halfway across the hall, talking to someone else.

The warriors looked at each other. 'She doesn't know either,' said Brocc the Badger.

Conall Cearnach sought out Follaman, who had gone to the king's physician to have his wounds treated. The building set aside for healing wounded warriors was at a distance from the royal halls, allowing for peace and quiet. A private conversation was easier there.

'Follaman, have you ever heard of the king's nephew before today?'

Follaman considered. 'I believe I have. When I was little, my nurse told me some strange tale I'd all but forgotten. Something about my father's sister having got a baby by swallowing a seed in a cup of wine. For a while, I thought that's where babies came from.'

'Setanta's different, but I don't know that he's *that* different. A seed in a cup of wine, indeed. Still . . .' Conall's green eyes narrowed in speculation. 'He's quite a fighter, that new boy, whatever his origins. We need every fighting man we can get, so if the king's new fosterling lives to grow up, he'll be valuable.'

'Until the Pangs overtake him,' Follaman predicted. 'No warrior in Ulster is any good when the Pangs come upon him.'

'Emain *Macha*!' Maeve cried, spitting out the name. She was working herself into a temper, Ailell observed. His wife had been too sunny recently, he had expected a turn in her weather.

'Why,' Maeve demanded to know of the travelling bard who was entertaining them, 'are you boring us with praises to the stronghold of Ulster? You're in Connaught now, in the stronghold *I* built, and you won't flatter me by reciting glowing descriptions of a fort some other woman built!'

'Macha of the Golden Hair has been dead four hundred years, Maeve,' Ailell observed mildly. 'She's not in competition with you.'

'Isn't she?' Maeve flashed him a scorching look. 'Throughout my childhood, I heard the poets sing of the last female war-leader in Erin, the great Macha, until I was sick of her and her accomplishments.

'I have outdone her. Bard, look around you at my Cruachan of the Enchantments. If you are honest, you must agree it is more splendid than the stronghold of the north, as the brilliance of Connaught leaves Ulster in the dark.'

Nervously, the bard – who came from Ulster – rolled his eyes around the large and smoky hall. He was a member of the *filidh*, he dared not lie. Maintaining the history of an entire people depended upon a bard's reverence for truth.

But he was not eager to answer Maeve's question honestly. Her expression frightened him. People in Maeve's presence tended to watch her in the same way they would watch a burning pine knot that might explode at any moment.

She was good to look at, the bard thought to himself; the poet in him could not deny her attraction. Tall and stately, with round white arms and a deep bosom, Maeve had pale skin so translucent it seemed lit from within. Her hair tangled into a coppery froth around her face; no handmaid in Connaught could force that hair to obey the comb.

But it was Maeve's eyes people never forgot. Colourless, those eyes, yet she could draw whatever colour she chose from lake or moss or stone to fill them. When she was angry, her eyes held the golden flicker of candleflame.

Maeve's very name meant 'intoxicating – she who makes men drunk.' The first time he had seen her, Ailell understood. She was a magnetic force; no matter how many times she infuriated him, he was always drawn back to her. When he began to woo her, her father, the king Eochaid, had warned him, 'If you mount a chariot with my daughter you will have a rough ride.' Young and full of confidence, Ailell had laughed. Half the princely men in the region claimed to have bedded the woman, yet she had walked away from all of them. To bring down such a quarry in marriage would make a man famous, and as a son of the king of Leinster, Ailell felt himself entitled to such a woman if anyone was.

So he had wooed her with difficulty and won her partially, as much as any man would ever win Maeve. And now he was famous. Maeve and Ailell, people said in one breath, and together they ruled the fortress her father had given her, Cruachan of the Enchantments, on an upland of singing grass. But Eochaid had been right – it was a very rough ride.

Ailell cast the bard a sympathetic look. 'Tell us no more of Emain Macha,' he suggested.

Perversely, Maeve raised her hand. 'Wrong, husband. I want to hear *all* this poet can tell us of Emain Macha. Haven't you noticed that his phrases describe only strength of arms and fortifications? Doesn't that make you suspicious?'

Ailell raised his eyebrows at his wife.

Maeve continued, 'The bard has already told us about the three major halls of Conor mac Nessa . . . the House of the King where his Red Branch warriors have pride of place, the Speckled House where their arms and shields are stored in – if we are to believe this man – numbers beyond counting, and the House of the Red Branch, whose walls are decorated with equally countless trophy heads. All these florid descriptions are intended to make people from beyond the borders of Ulster think the land and her king are unconquerable. But I don't believe a man would go to so much trouble to give that impression unless he was secretly afraid of conquest.'

In spite of himself, Ailell felt a tingle of admiration. Maeve's thoughts were always leaping ahead and scurrying around corners. 'The last time I visited Emain Macha was many years ago, in the days of Fergus mac Roy,' he told his wife. 'I was but a lad when I went there with my father to discuss a cattle trade, but the place looked well fortified to me then. I don't know why Conor mac Nessa would have bards sent out specifically to – '

'Idiot!' Maeve spat with disgust. 'Have you nothing in your skull but boring reminiscences? You've begun to live in the past like an old man with no future, and I warn you, Ailell, I have no use for old men.

'Conor mac Nessa is engaging in excessive boasting even for a Gael, and that means he has some weakness to hide. Or some treasure. Connaught and Ulster have skirmished on the borderlands for years, but I've let the reputation of the Ulaid discourage me from a full-scale invasion, and I see now I may have been mistaken.' A slow smile began to curl her lips. Her colourless eyes caressed the walls of her hall, imagining Conor mac Nessa's wealth beneath her rooftree. Leaning back on the piled wolfskins that cushioned her bench, Maeve idly traced the pleats of her gown of sheer *sida*.

'Indeed,' she murmured. 'We must give some thought to taking an army into Ulster and plundering the northland. Transferring the glory of Emain Macha to Cruachan.'

Watching her, Ailell thought to himself that any other woman would be content with what she already had. But Maeve was desperately ambitious for Cruachan.

Sometimes, Ailell was convinced it meant more to her than anything else, including her husband and children.

But as always, when he heard the building excitement in her voice, he was caught up and carried along. He yawned, stretched, and stood up as if he were ready to march. Seen thus, Ailell was an imposing figure. His eyes were a deep, fierce blue, and he had the square white teeth of a man used to tearing half-raw meat from the bone.

He was a head taller than Maeve, who was no small woman. He could loom over her if he chose, and he enjoyed looming over her. Sometimes, rarely, she would relax into the compliant posture of a young girl and look up at him as if he really had power over her. Such moments made him feel so fondly expansive, he forgave her a great deal, because then he felt he was catching a glimpse of the child she had been, the child who appealed to something deep and fatherly in the warrior.

In their years together, he had only seen all the way into her once.

They had been returning from a successful cattle raid together, one she had planned, as usual, and he had fought, as usual. With a small band of warriors, they camped for the night in an isolated glen. When they awoke at daybreak, the land was rimed with ice. Ailell opened his eyes to find their shared bed of moss and cloaks empty of his wife, who was crouched with her back to him some distance away.

He thought she was relieving herself and sneaked up on her to make a crude jest, the sort she usually enjoyed when they were campaigning together. Maeve liked to be one of the men, when she was not being allmother to Cruachan or seducing the latest likely lad. But when Ailell looked down at her, his words died on his tongue.

She had found a tiny fox kit that had somehow wandered too far from mother and den and had frozen to death in the night. Its small cries must have been too weak for the vixen to hear – or perhaps the proximity of humans had frightened her away.

Now, Maeve held the tiny body in her two hands, cradling it against her breast as if to give it back some of its vanished warmth. And she was crying.

Ailell had never seen his wife cry before. He watched for a long moment, then stole away so lightly an egg would not have broken beneath his feet. He never mentioned what he had seen to Maeve, but from that day she became more precious to him in a way he could not articulate. Some small portion of the daunting, complex woman belonged to him that no other man would ever know, and from this he drew sustenance.

Anyone could sleep with Maeve. Only Ailell had ever seen her cry.

There was no tenderness in her face now, however. Looking down at her in her hall, Ailell saw eyes as hard as flint, a mouth curved to the shape of her newest scheme. And he knew that whatever the scheme was, he would follow her for the excitement of seeing what would happen next.

But Maeve proved to be in no hurry to mount an invasion of Ulster. She took the visiting bard to her bed long enough to learn everything he knew of Conor mac Nessa's strengths and weaknesses, and began to make plans, but then the weather of Erin intervened with one long season after another of rain and mud. Maeve was too good a strategist to march men in mud unnecessarily. So she stayed at home, adding to her beloved Cruachan, and bided her time. But the look in her eyes assured Ailell that his wife had not forgotten Ulster.

Meanwhile in Ulster, the boy called Setanta was growing. He did not mind when trees bent beneath the weight of water; there was always something to learn, some skill to be polished. Fergus mac Roy was a thorough instructor. Soon his newest pupil could sharpen a knife blade, doze standing up, spear fish in shallow water, make thunder roll from a shield by striking it with his knuckles, or hurl a javelin cleanly through a heavy stand of trees. Each new accomplishment left Setanta aching to run to his father for praise, to say, 'Look what I can do now!'

But he did not. Dethcaen's warning stayed with him, and whenever she saw him around Emain Macha, she repeated it. So the seasons passed and Setanta grew and he did not speak to Sualtim, though he often saw him with others of the Red Branch. He waited with an unchildlike patience for the man to make the first move.

Yet Sualtim never looked at him, seemed unaware of his existence. Never acknowledged him.

In his bed at night Setanta writhed with rejection. Why, he asked himself repeatedly.

The day came when he could bear it no longer. Sualtim had gone out with a hunting party in search of game for the feasting tables. The sentries in the gatetower shouted of their return and Setanta outran everyone else to be the first to greet them.

The boy planted himself in the forefront of the gathering crowd, so as the laden wagons rumbled through the gateway, he all but blocked their entrance. Sualtim was accompanying the first cart, which was piled high with trophies of the chase. Deer and badger filled the bottom, and the heads of dead boar lolled over the sides, their tongues still slowly dripping black blood.

The lord of Dun Dalgan could not help seeing the boy who stood in his way. Sualtim had not changed much, he was still stocky and amiable-looking, though his features were more relaxed than they had been when he shared his life with Dectera. And he knew who Setanta was, in spite of the boy's new length of leg and width of shoulder.

But he turned his head away.

Setanta stared after him.

In anticipation of a successful hunt, the king's servants had prepared for days of cooking. For the tougher meats, great trenches had been dug in the earth to hold wooden troughs that were then lined with sweet mosses. By dropping heating stones into the water until it boiled, they could cook the meat until it fell from the bone. Other meats would be smoked for long keeping, but the choicest viands were secured on arbutus skewers and roasted for Conor mac Nessa and the Red Branch. These first fruits of the hunt were eagerly seized and readied for the spit, and soon the air filled with the aroma of crisping fat.

But Setanta did not feel very hungry.

Late in the day he sought a trench behind the royal mounds where people went to relieve themselves. In the squatting group, he saw Sualtim, who had his back to him and was talking with some other men. When Setanta came within earshot, he realised they were discussing him.

'We're watching his development with considerable interest,' one of the other warriors was saying. He grunted, strained, sighed with satisfaction, and continued. 'You know Setanta has even defeated Conall Cearnach in mock combat, and no one defeats Conall.'

'No one but me,' Setanta spoke up.

Their heads snapped round. The moment was awkward; Sualtim felt he had to say something. His companions expected it. Looking at Setanta, he said, choosing his words, 'You're doing well. Any man would be proud to have such a son.'

The boy took a deep breath. He felt as if he were on tiptoe, waiting.

'Continue making the king proud of you,' Sualtim finished. He wiped himself with grass and walked hurriedly away, so no one could see the expression in his eyes.

That's all? Setanta thought in astonishment. *That's all?*

Others were watching. He forgot his bowels, he had a worse pain to manage. From his belt he took the small sword he carried with him everywhere and set off back up the slope, tossing it into the air and catching it in a dazzling display of virtuosity, whistling, capering, unhurt and uncaring.

Thereafter when he encountered Sualtim, he ignored him completely.

As the king's foster-son, he had been given a whole new set of apparel, its every detail set forth by the elaborate code of conduct known as the brehon law. Setanta now possessed linen tunics with fivefold pleats, a loose woollen coat of softest weave, a great overmantle trimmed in fur. Golden rings gleamed in his ears. He even had a pair of ceremonial shoes for wearing only on special occasions, for they had bands of silver on the soles and were too fragile for everyday use.

'I wish my mother could see these,' he said to Dethcaen.

The druid's daughter was a new mother herself and was feeling overtired and irritable. Before she could stop herself, she snapped, 'Dectera wouldn't be interested.' She regretted her words as soon as she saw the hurt in his face, but it was too late.

A raven sat in the trees near the playing field. As Setanta walked beneath their branches, he heard the voice in his head. *Dectera cares for you no more than Sualtim does. Only I love you, Root of Valour.*

Someone ran to tell Fergus, 'The king's foster-son is fighting again; he's broken Cormac's jaw for a second time.'

Fergus was deceptively swift for such a massive man. He reached the playing field to find Setanta in the centre of a circle of fallen boys. His appearance was frightening. He swelled, he blazed, he shook with a warp-spasm that pulled his joints into inhuman angles. The grizzled old warrior barely repressed a shudder at the sight of him, but his martial mind commented, *Setanta will certainly terrify the enemy!*

Caught up in the Rage, the boy found himself surrendering to it gladly. The surrender itself was the sweetest part, melting down into heat and crimson light, relinquishing control to something stronger than himself.

The raven screamed at him.

Then, in this, his second Rage, he took a second step. The hot ecstasy of surrender cooled and was replaced, in an eyeblink, by an icy ferocity controlled by a mind he could not have recognised as his own. Time seemed to halt. He thought so fast, so clearly, that those around him were frozen and immobile while he was free to act with dazzling speed. Sensory pleasure was gone. All that remained was a calculating killer, its only motivation destruction. *Kill. Kill.*

The raven laughed.

The Boys' Troop backed away, the smallest of them hiccuping with fear.

Fergus flung himself upon Setanta before the image could terrify him as well. He wrestled the boy to the ground through sheer weight and lay

58

upon him, but though Setanta was far from half his size, he was painfully aware that he could hardly control the lad.

What is this boy, Fergus mac Roy wondered.

Then he felt the seizure begin to pass, and the body beneath his relaxed, softened, was human again. Fergus got warily to his feet and extended a hand to help Setanta rise. It *was* Setanta, though his face was still flushed and his eyes were wild.

'What's got into you, boy?' Fergus demanded to know in the gruffest voice he could manage. The incident had shaken him.

'I want the troop to apply to me for protection because I am the best of them.' Setanta tossed his head, flinging back a lock of dark hair. His set face challenged anybody to deny his claim.

This boy is as dangerous as a runaway chariot, Fergus told himself. He turned to the Boys' Troop. 'What say you?'

They muttered, they ducked their heads. Cormac was weeping from the pain in his shattered jaw. Some of those who had fallen were sitting up and spitting out broken teeth.

One by one, they agreed Setanta was their superior.

Follaman and Fiacra, the king's sons, made the formal acknowledgement. Cormac with his twice-broken jaw was unable to speak, and Conall Cearnach was as silent as usual. The other boys crowded around.

'The Red Branch and their sons are heroes, men of exceptional bravery,' Follaman said. 'But even heroes can have a champion, I suppose. Kings have personal champions. You will be champion of the Boys' Troop, Setanta. If there were any other troops like this in Erin – which there are not – we would ask you to meet their champions in single combat for the honour of us all. As Fergus mac Roy represents my father.'

Setanta nodded, mollified by this public recognition of his abilities. Laeg, eager to share, stepped forward and punched him happily on the arm. The fighting was over.

The battle had somehow eased Setanta's pain, and he resumed being the cheerful, exuberant boy he had been, quick to help a friend, first to laugh at a jest or join in a song. One among the brotherhood, but first among equals. Most of the troop were his friends, and he was an obvious favourite of the king.

Which should have been enough to fill up the hollow space inside him. It *should* have . . .

★

Watching him make a place for himself, I was proud of him. He was special; he would overcome the scars Sualtim and Dectera had unintentionally given him. This was one who would not be crippled by emotions.

A long time had passed since I felt any of that emotion humans call tenderness. This boy who had, in ignorance, drawn me into his life had touched something in me I thought withered.

I once had a son. Mechi was his name, and he was born on the sacred hill of Tara when I lived there in womanly form. That was a long time ago, of course. I do not remember it raining so much, then. I had a great cooking spit and a chamber with a thousand beeswax candles and men came to kneel before me and do me honour.

Meanwhile my son ran carefree across the meadowland and buttercup pollen gilded his legs.

Then Mechi was slain. The son of Cet the Gael killed him in an act of recreational slaughter, like hunting a deer for pleasure. Black blood dripped from my son's tongue. I will never forgive the race of his murderers, and I have sworn to pay them back by encouraging them to destroy each other, generation after generation.

Kill, I urge them. Kill.

Yet I am not a monster. I have known love. When I first encountered the child then known as Setanta, I remembered love.

Love and war – what else is there? Love is the more dangerous of the two.

I wear the other face.

5 'Your Setanta is going to outstrip my ability to train him,' Fergus predicted to Conor mac Nessa. The two were in the chariot shed, examining a newly constructed war-cart. Conor frowned, perhaps at his champion's words and perhaps at the broken shaft of a carelessly attached plume. He did not attempt to repair the damage himself. He was a king. At a gesture from him, a craftsman trained in working with feathers hurried to replace the broken plume with an even larger one, dyed a brilliant crimson. The king smiled in satisfaction.

'Do you think Setanta will be a better warrior than you?' he asked Fergus.

'Not better,' the other said with offended dignity. 'Different. He's going to need someone who can make the most of his abilities, and I admit I don't even understand some of them. Such gifts come to us in the blood; I'm not certain what blood he . . .' Fegus paused.

The king narrowed his eyes, volunteering nothing. A silence stretched between them.

Hitching his thumbs through his leather belt – which was becoming too tight, again – Fergus wished he had a little of Conor mac Nessa's thoughtful, deliberate manner. He knew he often spoke and acted impetuously, but it was his nature to plunge right in. He must do so now, because this conversation was necessary, though he had much rather talk about chariots and horses.

Still, the Boys' Troop was his obligation, and their training was his responsibility. He had too willingly shed responsibilities in the past, which was why his foster-son was now king of Ulster. Subtle Conor mac Nessa, who liked to plan ahead . . . as his mother had done.

When her husband Fachtna was killed, Nessa had gone to live at Emain Macha under the protection of Fergus mac Roy. She was beautiful in those days; inevitably, the king asked her to marry him. Nessa had replied, 'I will marry you gladly, but I ask a high bride-price. My son Conor's father was not of that branch of the Ulaid from which kings are chosen. I wish a higher rank for Conor and his posterity.

Therefore, I will marry you if you make him your foster-son and pledge that, should you ever have to be long away from Emain Macha, you will allow Conor to serve as king in your stead for four seasons. He has noble blood from me, he will not dishonour the position. When you return, he will, of course, relinquish the title to you, but thereafter the bards must remember him as a king, and his children will have kingly entitlements.'

Fergus had been thinking with his testicles at the time and impetuously agreed to the apparently simple request, so eager was he to bed Nessa. And Conor was a fine lad, handsome and intelligent. He was proud to call him fosterling.

Then the day came when he must be away from Emain Macha for a protracted period, and Nessa reminded him of her request. Fergus found himself forced by honour to keep his word. When he and his men left Emain Macha for a campaign against the Munstermen, he left Conor mac Nessa in charge. The boy was only a lad, but popular with the people; he thought everything would be all right. Fergus drove off with a sense of relief, thinking his back well guarded.

No sooner was he out of sight than Nessa urged members of the royal household to begin distributing the valuables of Emain Macha to the families of Red Branch warriors, whose support was essential to the king. In all instances, she claimed these gifts came from Conor mac Nessa.

When Fergus eventually returned with a string of his enemies' heads jouncing from his chariot rim, he found his fosterling firmly ensconced. 'But your true king has returned!' he protested.

'We'll have to talk about this,' the others told him. 'Young Conor is unmatched in generosity, most kingly of attributes. He is fearless, unblemished, and never renders a decision before it is ripe, though he has survived only sixteen winters. Men are even sending their brides to him for deflowering, the ultimate tribute! Conor has come to represent all that is best in Ulster – which *you* carelessly gave away, mac Roy – and we want him to remain king.'

The warriors of the Red Branch agreed unanimously. Even those who had been on campaign with Fergus voted against him, having returned home to find their families newly enriched thanks to Conor. They were adamant and not to be denied.

Without the support of the heroes of the Ulaid, a king had no legs.

Fergus was shocked.

Yet when he thought it over, he decided he should be glad Conor had not opted for killing him. Gaelic kingship was an elective position, and the king must come from the dominant clan – clan Ulaid in Ulster. The title was not guaranteed for life; a king who failed in kingship could be replaced, and was sometimes slain by an aspirant.

Fergus had been king for a long time, long enough to grow weary of his obligations. A king could not afford to get too drunk for fear of doing something stupid. A king could expect to be interrupted as he lay atop his wife and have to go shivering into the hall to make an unpopular decision, then return to a wife and a bed gone cold.

Fergus liked drinking and disliked making decisions. So he let himself be persuaded, and Conor rewarded him with titles better suited to his disposition: king's champion and instructor of the Boys' Troop. His last small kingdom.

For them, at least, he must take responsibility.

'If Setanta is a warrior's son,' he said warily, watching Conor's eyes, 'I know what to expect of him. But if he is not . . . ah, Conor, ever since he came here, the fort has hummed with rumours.'

'I know. It's awkward for poor Sualtim.'

'Why doesn't he just recognise the boy as his, then? If he is,' Fergus could not resist adding.

Conor's face remained impassive. He looked at the feathered chariot as if it had some message for him.

Fergus tried once more. 'Was he . . . the one who took Dectera on her wedding day . . . *was* he Lewy of the Long Hand?'

'Who can say?' asked Conor mac Nessa.

Overcharged with energy, Setanta was always last to leave the playing field. Even Cathbad the druid complained of the fanatic devotion of the Boys' Troop to their sport. 'Nothing is sacred to them but making goals,' he grumbled.

One afternoon, the king found his fosterling engrossed in a particularly exciting match. 'Come with me, Setanta,' he called, cupping his hands around his mouth. 'Cullen the smith has invited myself and my sons to a feast.'

The boy trotted reluctantly to the sidelines but did not put down his hurley stick. 'Can't you wait until the game's over?'

'I cannot, the smith expects us. I won't insult him by coming late to his table.'

'Then go on and I'll join you as soon as I win this game. I'll follow your chariot tracks.'

Conor laughed, shaking his head. He had once been a boy who loved hurling matches himself. He went on his way to the feast and left Setanta to his winning.

Skilled craftsmen held high rank in ancient Erin, and Cullen the smith stood higher than most because he fashioned the weapons of the Red Branch. He was a man of property, with his own walled dun and sufficient status to be able to entertain the king of Ulster in his hall.

As usual when leaving Emain Macha, Conor travelled not only with his sons but also a guard of the Red Branch, his druid, his bard, and his brehon. Reaching Cullen's dun, the king's party found a warm welcome awaiting them. Cullen anticipated some new orders for weapons. To put Conor mac Nessa and his men in an expansive mood, the smith had even slaughtered several oxen, and the fragrance of roasting meat was like music in his hall. Fresh rushes had been laid on the stone floor; a fire roared merrily in the central firepit.

When he assumed all were inside, Cullen asked the king if he might secure the dun.

'Indeed,' replied Conor – who had forgotten all about issuing an invitation to Setanta.

So Cullen closed his gate and barred his door, but before doing either, he turned his watchdog loose outside. As the party within enjoyed foaming ale and fat meat and compliant serving-women, a huge and hungry wolfhound ranged beyond the walls.

Famed for its viciousness, Cullen's hound knew every field and hollow of its master's landholding. It checked the precincts thoroughly, snarling all the while, then returned to lie in front of Cullen's gate with its paws crossed and a red light glowing deep in its eyes. It would like to kill something.

Cullen had often boasted that his wolfhound was worth four human guards.

At sundown, Setanta came up the chariot track, whistling to himself and playing as he came. To shorten the journey, he was taking practice shots along the way with his ball and hurley stick.

The hound heard him and leapt to its feet. Its fangs were bared; a terrible roar issued from its throat.

The sound cut through the noise within Cullen's hall. Conor stiffened. 'My foster-son, I forgot about him. He must be out there with your dog!' He leapt to his feet, dumping the woman who had been sitting on his lap on to Cullen's new rushes.

There was a race to unbar the door.

Setanta saw the hound racing toward him in the gathering gloom. He stared in awe; he had never seen a dog as big. Red-eared, frost-white, lean as grief: Cullen's hound.

One desperate glance told Setanta there was no tree near enough to climb. His sword was a toy, a useless defence against such a monster. All he had was his hurley stick . . .

One heartbeat before the hound reached him, he tossed his ball in the air and swung the stick at it with all his might.

The ball shot forward and flew through the gaping jaws to lodge deep in the hound's throat.

Momentum completed the animal's leap so it struck Setanta full on the chest. He clutched at it instinctively, struggling to keep his balance. The terrible growl was still ringing in his ears and his nostrils were filled with the wolfhound's smell.

Then he felt it go limp in his arms.

Setanta staggered back, letting it fall.

Choking, the hound writhed on the earth and began to die. The creature's agony communicated itself to Setanta. It had meant to kill him but he could not watch it suffer, and if he tried to dislodge the ball from its throat he would only get savaged for his pains. He seized the hound by the hind legs and swung it in a wide arc, slamming its head against the upright stone pillar marking Cullen's gateway. Blood and brains spattered the stone.

The smith and his guests came running up.

Fergus mac Roy elbowed through the crowd to make certain Setanta was unhurt. Cullen stared in dismay at his dog. 'This faithful animal has guarded my home for years,' he said. 'For *years*. Whoever you are, boy, you are not welcome here.'

'You are speaking to my fosterling,' Conor mac Nessa said sharply.

'It's all right for you, with your high banks and your deep ditches and your Red Branch warriors! But all I had to defend my livestock and my women was this dog. And your boy killed him.'

Everyone looked at Conor. But before the king could reply, Setanta spoke up. 'If there is a whelp of this breed anywhere in the land, I'll buy it for you,' he told Cullen, 'with my gold earrings. And I will train it myself as a replacement for your hound.'

The smith blinked. 'Fair enough. But what protects me in the meantime?'

'I do,' Setanta said. He saw the surprised look Conor gave him. I will make you proud of me, he vowed silently to the king. 'Until the young dog is ready to take the old dog's place, I'll be your hound, Cullen, and guard your holding by night and by day.'

Cullen turned to the king. 'What do you make of this?'

'I think you've just acquired the best hound you'll ever have,' said Conor mac Nessa.

Cathbad the druid stepped forward and laid his hand on the boy's head. The king's druid was a tall man of unreadable age, with a heavy shock of white hair springing up from a broad forehead. The touch of his hand made Setanta tingle, but apparently the boy had a similar effect on the druid, for he drew his hand back as if burned.

'Hmmmm.' Cathbad cleared his throat. Everyone listened, as they must when the druid spoke. 'Setanta, you have won a warrior's name today. You fought heroically and accepted heroic responsibility, and from henceforth you shall be known as Cu Cullen. The Hound of Cullen.'

The Hound of Cullen; Cuchulain in the Gaelic tongue, a name no warrior had borne before. Coming from the king's druid, it was an unparalleled honour.

Setanta realised the honour, but too much had happened too fast. Before he could think, he blurted, 'I would rather just be Setanta, son of Sualtim.' Then he met Conor's eyes and wished the earth would swallow him.

The king smiled, however. 'It is better for you to be Cuchulain, I think. Come, young Hound, let's go into the feast together.'

Once again something magical had happened, and once again its meaning eluded the boy. He would think about it later. But he did understand that he had hurled himself forward through some unexpected rite of passage and behaved well.

As he would learn, to survive such a journey conveys a special confidence.

That night in Cullen's hall, Setanta feasted with the warriors.

And afterwards, when the bones of the feast were thrown on the floor, he laughed and seized them in his teeth as a hound would, gnawing them in such true canine fashion that he soon had the whole party cheering him on.

Each morning thereafter, he arose at dawn to patrol the borders of Cullen's holding, alert for any intruder. Some time during the day he would trot back to Emain Macha for instruction, but he always returned by nightfall to take up his position in front of the smith's gate, curled up like a watchdog, sleeping with his ears awake.

To his disappointment, no raiders tried to steal Cullen's livestock or run off with his bondwomen during Setanta's tenure as hound. In due course, a puppy was purchased, trained, and presented to the smith, and Setanta's tour of duty was over.

But by then the story of Cullen's hound had travelled far beyond Ulster's borders. Men delighted in spreading the tale of the monster dog and his youthful slayer, each recounting embellishing it further, until the boy sounded as mighty as an army.

'If Cullen's Hound is an example of the warriors they're breeding in Ulster these days,' one tribal warlord concluded, speaking for many, 'then I want no trouble with them.'

But Maeve of Connaught laughed when she heard the story. 'Conor mac Nessa is reduced to bragging about *puppies*,' she said with disdain.

The boy now known as Cuchulain continued his education. From Athairne, he learned the history of Ruari and the branch of his family now guarding Ulster. From Bricriu Bitter-Tongue, he learned the insults and epithets warriors used to goad adversaries past the point of caution. Sencha, the chief brehon judge, instructed the youth in the all-important quality of honour.

'As the sun is to the earth, so is honour to man,' Sencha said. 'Without it, he will not flourish. All else may fail you, but honour is the treasure no one can take from you, the shield no one can penetrate unless you let him. Honour is sacred to the Red Branch.'

Honour, Cuchulain thought to himself, was beautiful and clean. Its bonds were as strong as a *ges*.

His honour would mark his particular place in the world even without a father's name, he decided. His unshakable honour would identify him for ever.

Studying the fine points of combat was what appealed to the boy most. Various members of the Red Branch were called upon to demonstrate their special skills for the troop, the manoeuvres or techniques that had won them renown on the battlefield. After the sword-thrust was taught, or the chariot-feat shown, the boys would gather in a circle and listen admiringly to a recounting of the battle that had made the deed famous.

One day Bricriu Bitter-Tongue sauntered up to the group just as Naisi, son of Uisnach, finished telling about his defence of a river fording. The tale was heroic, ending in a rout of the opposition. Though Naisi was modest for a Red Branch warrior, he did manage to invest himself with a certain glory in the telling.

Bricriu listened impassively, with his hands on his hips. Bitter-Tongue was not handsome; he had fishlips and flat eyes. When Naisi finished speaking, he cleared his throat of phlegm and said to the troop, 'It all sounds wonderful the way Naisi tells it – afterwards. When he's home and dry.

'Now, let me tell you what it's really like to be a warrior. War is being tired and cold and hungry and just trying to stay alive. War is feeling your bowels run with fear until those nearest you move away from the stench. War is dead men rotting on the battlefield, their swollen bellies distended by gasses until they finally explode with a sound you'll never forget. That's all it is. Don't expect more than that, and don't try to make more of it than it is, or you'll cause more trouble than you're worth. Endure more hardship than you think you can and kill every man who tries to kill you, and you'll be a warrior. All this talk is just feathers on the chariot.'

He limped away.

The boys glanced at one another self-consciously. Everyone knew Bricriu was a morose man, but to hear him denigrate the battle-glory of the Gael made them uncomfortable.

Naisi tried to repair the damage. He was freshly promoted to warrior status himself, having served his apprenticeship in the troop, and everyone liked him, as much for his pleasant nature as his black-haired, blue-eyed good looks. 'Ignore Bricriu, just ignore him,' Naisi said, thinking privately that nothing was less welcome than an unsolicited truth. 'Bitter-Tongue took a spear-thrust in his back years ago that ruined not only his kidneys but also his disposition. A man is never in a good mood when he has to watch the colour of his urine every day for a portent of death.'

Leaving the Grove of Instruction, Cuchulain noticed a solitary raven of uncommon size sitting on a low tree branch. He approached the bird, but it did not fly away. 'What is the truth of war?' he asked the creature.

The raven lifted a feathered crest and glared at him. But he heard no voice. The answer was his own to find.

He threw himself into battle-practice with redoubled energy. With the passing of seasons, Cuchulain had learned to summon the Rage almost at will. He loved the thrill of power when heat ran through his veins and his body began to change. Grown men were afraid of him then. When he chose, he could draw upon a unique strength to inflict more damage on a dozen than they could hope to inflict on him.

Just beyond the sensual heat of the Rage lay the icy realm in which he

68

could move at top speed while others seemed frozen; in which his brain, freed from emotion, was remorselessly cold. In that stage, he could not tell friend from foe. He had not yet actually killed a person, but his fingers tingled with the killing imperative.

Though using the Rage was still a game with him to a certain extent, Cuchulain was approaching manhood. He realised the game was becoming more deadly each time he played it, and suspected the Rage could grow beyond his ability to control it at all. Then there would be nothing of Setanta left in him. Only the Hound.

The Wolfhound of Cullen.

The *invincible* Hound of Cullen. That was what mattered. The power of the Rage would some day make him a champion like Fergus mac Roy, chosen to uphold the honour of his people in single combat.

On his pallet at night, Cuchulain dreamed of being a champion.

Other dreams began to trouble him as his chest and his voice grew deeper. He tossed in his sleep and awoke to feel a throbbing heat between his legs. His eyes began to follow the women of Emain Macha. The curve of a rounded hip as a woman bent to pick up a dropped pitcher could make him miss an easy spear-cast.

His friends noticed. 'The Hound approaches breeding age,' they teased him. When they discovered they could make him blush, the teasing grew worse, though they were careful never to drive him to rage.

He wondered how other boys dealt with the problem. The older members of the troop had begun pairing off. Follaman had a plump little maiden as neat and chirpy as a wren whom he took on long expeditions looking for mushrooms outside of mushroom season. Conall Cearnach was always at the centre of a score of nubile beauties. Even Laeg, for all his boniness and speckles, was seen in the company of one of Sencha's daughters, a girl with a maddening wiggle to her walk. All the troop watched her.

Ferdiad, son of Daman, said of Sencha's daughter, 'It's a wonder she doesn't break all her bones, the way she moves.'

The other youths sniggered and added rude elaborations of their own – except for Cuchulain, who blushed and averted his eyes.

He was not sleeping well. His appetite slackened, and there were dark circles under his eyes. Yet he could not bring himself to approach a girl. When one looked at him, he invented some quick excuse for going in the opposite direction.

The royal physician, Fingan, was an observant man. For several phases of the moon, he observed without comment the increasing restlessness of Conor's famous young Hound. At last, he waylaid the boy and spoke to him directly. 'Are you ill, lad?'

'I feel fine.'

Fingan put one hand under Cuchulain's jaw and turned his face toward the sun. 'I don't much like the look of you. Have you some pain you're trying to hide?'

Cuchulain writhed with embarrassment. 'Sometimes a terrible weakness comes over me . . .' he whispered.

Fingan was alarmed. 'When?' He leaned closer, his tone urgent.

The youth regretted having said anything, but you must not lie; not if you were honourable. 'At night,' he admitted. 'When I dream about . . . women. I wake up feeling weak and . . . and I'm all wet.'

The physician threw back his head and laughed. He was short and lean and bandy-legged, with a narrow face and sinewy, gifted hands, one of which he now clapped on the boy's shoulder. 'You're not sick, you're just growing up. But you had me worried when you spoke of weakness. I was afraid the Pangs were beginning, even if you don't yet have a beard.'

Cuchulain was relieved to hear his condition was normal, but the way Fingan looked when he mentioned pangs was disturbing. 'What pangs?'

The older man gave him a measuring look. 'You're ready to be told, I suppose. Better hear it from me than from one of the others; the warriors are so embarrassed they can hardly discuss it coherently.' Fingan gestured toward an open doorway. 'The weather is going to turn desperate, I smell a storm brewing. Let's take shelter in the bake house and see if the women left a loaf or two lying about. Talk goes down best with food.'

The bake house was still warm with residual heat from the stone ovens, and there were a few round dark loaves left cooling on slats of wood. Fingan broke one in two and gave Cuchulain the larger portion. Inside its crust, the bread was brown and chewy, with a scattering of unground grains like berry seeds.

The two men sat with their backs to the wall. 'What do you know of Macha?' Fingan asked Cuchulain as he licked crumbs from his fingers.

'Macha of the Golden Hair built the first fort here.'

'That was hundreds of years ago. I'm speaking of a recent woman, the wife of Crunnuc the Fat, a cattle-lord to the north during the period when your mother lived here as a girl.

'In accordance with the law applying to cattle-lords, Crunnuc in his turn was to contribute the feast for the House of the King. This Crunnuc was a braggart and a fool. Under Conor's rooftree, he boasted about his new wife, Macha Fleet-Foot, until everyone sickened of her name. He claimed she had extraordinary powers because she was sired by one of the Tuatha de Danann.'

'What?' Cuchulain's bread dropped from nerveless fingers. 'That's not possible, humans and magic people don't . . .' He choked, unable to say 'mate'. Fingan noticed with amusement that the boy was blushing.

Emain Macha was crammed with tongue-waggers. At the king's order, to spare his fosterling discomfort, no one repeated stories about his paternity within Cuchulain's hearing, but he had long since caught enough veiled allusions to make the problem loom large in his mind.

If Sualtim was his father, as he wanted to believe, why did the lord of Dun Dalgan ignore his son so pointedly? The idea of being the result of a mating between Dectera and her own brother appalled Cuchulain, for it would have broken the most stringent of *gessa*. The last, most unthinkable option was that of having been conceived by a coupling between his mother and one of the magic people, one of the gods. The mysterious, frightening gods.

This he rejected with a thrill of terror.

Yet Fingan, watching him, was saying kindly, 'Nothing is impossible, boy, and such alliances are reputed to have occurred from time to time. If Crunnuc's wife was the result of one, it would explain her gift, for the name of Fleet-Foot was well deserved. Men sitting at Crunnuc's feast claimed to have seen her outrun deer, and her foolish husband insisted she could outrun the king's own chariot horses. I ask you, knowing the Red Branch – do you think any of them would let such a boast go unchallenged?

'So Conor mac Nessa demanded that Crunnuc's wife be brought from his holding to Emain Macha, in order to race. Crunnuc realised he had gone too far and tried to back out of it then, protesting that his wife was heavy with child. But the Red Branch scented blood and were hot for the contest; they were already making wagers. Conor was new to the kingship and wanted to keep his supporters happy, so he insisted on sending for Macha Fleet-Foot.

'I was here when they brought her through the gates in an oxcart. Even from a distance, I could see how large her belly was. Again Crunnuc tried to call off the race, but the warriors threatened to take his head for satisfaction. So he told his wife he would die unless she ran, and pleaded with her to save him.

71

'As a physician, I went to the king and suggested he let the pregnant woman go. At first he listened, but then I grew emotional and tried to pound the point home and lost him. You know how he is – or perhaps you don't, not yet. If you argue with Conor mac Nessa, he closes up like a clam.'

Fingan took another bite of bread, chewing reflectively as he gazed back into the past. 'The king ordered his best team hitched to his chariot and had the woman brought to the starting line of the racecourse. Crunnuc was by this time in a bad way. His wife gave him one dreadful look that turned him pale, then ignored him as if he were an insect on the wall. I realised then he was afraid of her, and I wondered what she was capable of. Daughter of magic – you can't trust someone like that. They are too different from us.'

Cuchulain was sitting very still, listening with every pore of his body.

'The racecourse we used was the one we have now, circling the walls. The brehon law is very precise about the maintenance of racecourses, as you know, holding the owner responsible for the slightest damage to man or horse. So the king's course was immaculate, without a pebble or a root. But still it was no place for a pregnant woman to run.

'The king used no charioteer but handled the reins himself, to make the war-cart lighter. Poor Crunnuc didn't dare object, he had already said she could outrun anything.

'As Conor drove up with his horses prancing and snorting and rolling their eyes, Macha held out her hand in supplication to him. She was too proud to beg, but she held out her hand. His face softened, I saw it. But at that moment the warriors began chanting for the race to begin; they were in an ugly mood, they wanted their sport. Their combined voice was like the crack of a whip and the king's horses leaped forward. Macha went with them stride for stride, with one long shriek of despair.

'Seeing her run, I believed Crunnuc about everything. She moved with great flowing strides like nothing I had ever seen before. The very grass held its breath, watching Macha run.

'Conor lashed his horses, but they were no match for her. They threw themselves into their harness, yet she gained on them with every stride. The warriors of the Red Branch were lining the racecourse, and they screamed and shouted as the woman dashed by them. Not one reached out to stop her and save her.

'From where I was standing, I could see her grimace as the first pain hit her. The horses were still close to her, but her belly was clearly in the lead.' Fingan noticed a new blush spread across Cuchulain's cheeks.

The boy is definitely delicate about women, the physician thought. Though he does not look delicate – far from it.

'Go on, Fingan. What happened?'

Suddenly, the physician's pupils contracted. He found himself standing in darkness with the wild, wet smell of ancient forests in his nostrils, gazing out on a bright plain lit by a singular memory. 'The king's horses began to slow down, but Macha was slowing too. She took a few more steps, she stopped, she bent double. And then . . .'

'And then?'

'And then, as we stared, the woman lifted her head and looked toward us. Pain stretched her mouth into a hideous square shape. The tendons in her neck stood out like ropes. Then the other mouth a woman has, the one between her legs, stretched too, and Macha used her fingers to pull it wider.

'She screamed. Never in my life have I heard such a scream. The labouring woman cried out to us, "You think you have power, you puling men? Watch, and I will show you real power!" She was livid with hatred for us and our careless male meanness, she flung her words at us like stones.

'Then she . . . changed, Cuchulain, into something that was not and had never been human. We all saw it happen. She changed into a creature like the earth beneath her feet, indifferent to man, consumed by the life within itself. On the racecourse of Emain Macha, on a sunny day when birds were singing and trumpet flowers blooming, we saw with horrified eyes the living embodiment of the giver and destroyer. The mother goddess in the form of the Sheela-na-Gig; hideous, sickening. The legends of shapechanging came back to me in a rush and I was terrified. We were all terrified, we brave men standing in the sun.

'One more scream was torn from the creature that had been Macha Fleet-Foot, then there was a great rush of blood and she gave birth to a pair of twins. In the face of her anguish, the crowd had grown silent.

'Her voice tore the silence apart. Crouching over her babes on the bloodied earth, she cried, "Shame on your beards, men of Ulster! You would not take pity on me, so I shall have no pity on you. From this day, I curse you. You will learn the hard way what women know. In times of exceptional danger, every fighting man in this kingdom will be afflicted with the agony of the birthing pangs. You will then be at the mercy of your enemies as I have been at your mercy.

' "I call this curse to last for nine nights and nine days unto the ninth generation. As each warrior's son sprouts his first beard hairs, he too will become subject to the Pangs."

'I saw and heard this, Cuchulain. I was present when Macha Fleet-Foot cursed not only the king, Fergus, Sualtim, the Red Branch, but every warrior in Ulster.' Fingan shivered as if a cold wind from the past blew over him. His haunted eyes reflected the sunflooded racecourse and the thing that had been Crunnuc's wife.

All the warriors, Cuchulain thought, dry-mouthed. As soon as they have beards. He rubbed his finger along his jawbone, anticipating the first prickle of hair. But in spite of his swelling muscles, he was still as smooth-cheeked and fine-skinned as he had always been. 'What happened to Macha Fleet-Foot?' he asked aloud.

'She took her twins and fled into the forest, which we have called the Sorrowful Forest since. But she left her curse for us to remember her by, and twice since then I have seen it befall our warriors in times of great danger. It is not a punishment I would wish on anyone, Cuchulain. Cruel magic. Cruel and hideous.'

After his conversation with the physician, Cuchulain wandered around the fort, thinking until his head ached, trying to unravel a mystery. Resenting mysteries, yet feeling himself part of one.

Macha shapechanged, he was thinking, into something hideous. Fingan saw it. They claim *I* shapechange when the Rage is on me.

He loved beauty. He was horrified to think he might turn into something as grotesque and disgusting as the squatting figure of the Sheela-na-Gig, pulling its genitals open and leering out with an inhuman face.

Magic.

Revulsion rose in him. He wanted nothing to do with such magic.

Cruel magic, subjecting men to the weakness and agony of birth pangs.

The warriors – whom he idolised – humiliated by magic.

If his own father was not a warrior, however, the curse would not devolve upon him.

But that would mean his sire must be . . . the unthinkable Other. Even more magical, more terrifying to him.

I am Red Branch! Cuchulain shouted inside his head. Red Branch, son of Sualtim of Dun Dalgan. I want nothing else, I want no part of the gods and their magic.

Yet without magic, how can I explain the Rage?

No sooner had he thought the word, than memories of the battle-fury

74

enveloped him. The first wave of red-gold heat was like a flare from the sun, pouring through his body to explode in ecstasy in his groin.

Empowered by the Rage, he could climb the clouds in the sky like a ladder, he could skip over the ripples of a river as if they were ruts on a chariotway. He could burst through his skin like a moth from its chrysalis to emerge as something totally new, larger, a creature born from the mating of confidence and desperation, goaded to life by the taunts of a raven, succeeding because failure was unacceptable.

The glorious, terrifying, irresistible, isolating Rage.

Cuchulain stood transfixed, listening to the wild beating of his heart.

6 Now that he knew the secret of Macha's curse, Cuchulain was sworn not to divulge it to outsiders. Such vulnerability must be concealed. Peace throughout Ulster and its borderlands was the safest course.

But that was not possible, not with a warrior race.

Clan-feuds and cattle raids continued, providing the battles by which a heroic society maintained its reputation and kept its skills polished. These were not the dire crises to which Macha's Curse applied. By her own words, the Pangs were reserved for times of exceptional danger.

Therefore, Conor mac Nessa did his best to avoid a major war with any of the other kingdoms of Erin, with Munster or Leinster or, most particularly, Ulster's ancient rival Connaught.

Maeve of Connaught was said to be voracious.

As each season passed, Conor was increasingly thankful that no shadow of beard yet darkened the face of the Hound. The lad was growing into a short, dark man of deceptive strength and dazzling agility, yet his face remained boyish. Energy burned in him like a dark flame and others responded to it; he was much admired at Emain Macha.

As Cuchulain's body grew, so did his hunger to achieve. He wanted to prove himself on his own. He had the entitlements of a king's foster-son, making his place in society secure, but that was not enough for him.

If no man would claim having sired him, he would create himself in the image of his choice. Better anyway, he told himself. Then the credit for my achievements will be mine alone.

He would not admit the possibility of failure, not ever. He was very young, and so far he had always won.

Cuchulain became incessant in his demand to be allowed to take up arms and be counted fully a man.

At the king's request, a man's sword and shield had already been made for him. They hung waiting with the other Red Branch weapons in the Speckled House. Cullen the smith had forged the sword himself, a splendid weapon to be called Hardhead, in tribute to the weight of its hilt. The shield was black with bronze bosses and had fine new leather straps to hold it firmly on the arm.

Cuchulain often visited the Speckled House to look at them.

Like the House of the King, the hall that held the weapons stood atop a man-made mound. The door was kept barred; a guard had to be asked to open it, for the weaponry of Ulster's defenders could not be left lying around in the open. The guard grew very tired of seeing Cuchulain's face every day, requesting admittance again.

Inside the Speckled House, the young man would stand for a long time with his head tilted back, looking up at the swords and spears and shields on the wall and reading their histories from the dents and nicks and dried blood no amount of polishing would remove.

Compared to the others, his own unused Hardhead was too new and shiny; the sight of it embarrassed him.

Cullen the smith told a tale about its forging. 'Bitter and windy the weather that day,' he enjoyed telling anyone who would listen. 'A day when no birds would fly. Yet as I bent to my work, a huge raven lit as close to me as I am to you now.'

No one doubted Cullen's story. Smiths knew secrets; the very nature of their work bordered on the magical. Combining the male element of the sun in the form of fire, with the female earth in the form of iron, smiths created swords. If the smith achieved a perfect blending of the elements, the strength thus forged created security and prosperity.

'When the blade had been fired and hammered and quenched nine times,' Cullen was fond of relating, 'the raven flew to me and lit on the sword as if to test its edge, then flew away with a screech that raised the hair on my head. That was the forging of Hardhead.'

Now the raven-touched sword and the unused shield waited in the Speckled House and Cuchulain waited with no patience at all to use them.

When the ewes' udders swelled with milk, Cathbad of the Gentle Face performed the Imbolc rituals in the circle of standing stones north of the fort. Cuchulain attended with the others as the druid threw the sacred sticks of prophecy into the wind, looking for signs to predict the coming season in the patterns they made as they fell.

The sky shimmered between sun and cloud, undecided. Rough grey stones thrust from the earth, stabbing upwards, the winterdead grass brittle around their bases. This was a place that did not welcome man. Whatever agency had erected the stones in the forgotten past was an elder force, perhaps hostile, surely unknowable. Only druids dared try to make use of the residue of power still contained in magic circles.

Cathbad threw his carved sticks several times, making this prediction and that. Weather would improve. Trees would produce more fruit than last year, sheep would bear more twins. A new river would burst forth, flooding the territory of Brega. Good and bad, as always. He threw the sticks one final time and the wind seized them with a capricious hand, flinging them beyond the ring of stones and spectators. Cathbad ran after his sticks anxiously, afraid some might be lost in the grass. Relieved to see they had all fallen together, he bent and peered down.

When he stood up, he ran his tongue over his lips as he always did when the gods sent him something beyond the usual weather and crop reports. 'Whoever takes up arms for the first time on this day,' the druid announced, 'will gain unprecedented fame. His name will be remembered when the names of the kings are forgotten. But he will have a short life, for glory is not without price.'

Cuchulain felt gooseflesh rise on his arms at Cathbad's words. Glory! He whispered it to himself: glory.

He did not care about the rest of the prophecy. He was young; the shortness of life hardly mattered to him.

The Imbolc ritual had taken place at sunrise; the rest of the day lay ahead like a promise. Cuchulain ran to the Speckled House and took his sword and shield down from the wall. As he emerged, he met Cathbad.

'You heard my prediction, yet here you are anyway,' the druid said. 'I was afraid of this. Tell me, young Hound – do you see any other members of the troop hurrying to take up arms? You do not. They are too sensible, they wait until the portents are more favourable.'

'The portents are perfect,' Cuchulain replied. 'A great name outlasts life. If I can have that, I don't care if I die before sunset.'

Cathbad drew a deep breath and leaned more heavily than usual upon his ash-wood stick. How impetuous the young are, he thought. Fortunately for the rest of us. Without their fire, we would crouch cold in our skins, waiting for a drab death.

'Each man chooses his first step, at least,' he said aloud.

Cuchulain laughed up at him, brimming with excitement and confidence. 'Who chooses the last?'

'The gods,' said the druid soberly.

'Not for me. I make all my choices myself.'

Cathbad shook his head and sighed. 'Come along then, young

warrior. Let's go and tell the king you have taken up arms today and see if he has some task worthy of the occasion.'

They found Conor mac Nessa with one of his counters, dividing a herd. 'Your foster-son has tired of boys' games and wants a man's work from now on,' the druid said. 'Even the threat of an early death doesn't seem to deter him.'

Conor lifted a golden eyebrow. 'The Hound is never frightened.'

Hearing this, Cuchulain would have walked through a stone wall for Conor mac Nessa.

'You'll need a chariot and horses, harness, all manner of things,' the king said to his foster-son. 'Come with me to the bawn and we'll pick out a team and a war-cart for you right now.'

'I already have a charioteer,' Cuchulain boasted. 'Laeg, son of Riangabra, has promised to drive me.'

'He has, has he? And when did the two of you make these arrangements – before you were weaned? I'm not going to send two untried youths out together. We'll start you off with two wise old horses, a good stout chariot, and an experienced man to drive you. Ibar, he's the best. Take him on your adventure and I'll send you to the Watcher's Ford at Slieve Fuad to stand a turn as border guard. Just last season Conall Cearnach took up arms, you'll recall, and was assigned that post. You can relieve him today.'

Cuchulain was delighted at the prospect of driving up to Conall Cearnach with a whip and a flourish, carrying his own sword and shield at last. He would come at the gallop with a mighty yell; he would make Conall's eyes pop from their sockets!

He ran from one war-cart to another as they were rolled out for his inspection, but each seemed to have some flaw. He sprang too eagerly into one and its floorboards split; he kicked at the wheel of another and a spoke broke. The next one he saw had a bashed-in side, and the next a rusted axle. Impatience overcame him. He attacked each cart like an enemy and they all gave way.

'You're breaking every chariot we have,' Conor protested.

'They're all flimsy wickerwork. If I'm to do my best, I must have the best equipment.'

'Could anyone ever doubt he is of noble blood?' Cathbad murmured. 'He has the faults that go with it.'

Conor mac Nessa frowned. 'Take my war-cart then, for this day only. Bring it back bloody but not broken or I'll . . .' He did not finish the threat, Cuchulain was already running toward the king's plumed chariot with joy in his eyes.

With Ibar at the reins, Cuchulain set off for the Watcher's Ford. Ibar was a full generation older and a head taller, a thick-necked, slope-shouldered man, whose mere presence could calm the wildest horse. His fingers played on the reins like a bard's fingers on a harp, and the experienced team trotted briskly, but with a steady rhythm, to his command.

Beside him, Cuchulain almost danced a jig in his own eagerness to get there. To begin. Being a man. Being a warrior.

In spite of Cathbad's predictions, the weather was still chill and damp. As they drove towards the mountain known as Slieve Fuad, rain marched towards them in a grey column, field by field, conquering hill and hedgerow. Ibar ignored the weather and the horses followed his example, flattening their ears against their heads to keep the water out but never faltering in their stride. Then the rain blew over, and by the time they reached the ford, the sun was shining again.

The chariot splashed into the shallows of the river, and Conall Cearnach sprang out from behind a boulder, his javelin at the ready.

'Ah, it's you, Cuchulain. What are you doing here, is Ibar taking you somewhere?'

This was not quite the transcendent moment Cuchulain had envisioned. In fact, Conall had startled him. 'I'm taking Ibar,' he answered shortly, setting his face in what he hoped were stern lines. Not by the flicker of an eyelash did he recognise Conall as an old playfellow. 'I've come to relieve you.'

'Relieve me?' Conall shouted with laughter. 'You still don't reach my shoulder. Come back when you've grown up and we'll talk about it.'

'I can do the job you're doing, better than you,' Cuchulain replied. There was a dangerous glitter in his eyes. But Conall saw no sign of the Rage . . . and he was not yet ready to be relieved by anyone, especially this mere . . . boy. He propped his javelin between two stones and pretended a careful inspection of its head while saying casually, 'You're not going to defend *this* ford, not today, Hound. It's mine.'

Cuchulain held back his anger. The Red Branch must not fight among themselves. 'Fair enough. But if you won't relinquish your post to me, I'll go past you. Beyond the river is foreign territory; I'll find someone there to test myself against.'

'That really isn't necessary,' Ibar protested. He had no intention of letting the king's favourite be seriously injured on his first day out.

But Cuchulain put a none-too-gentle hand against the chariot driver's chest and pushed. 'If you don't want to go with me you can get out and walk. I've been taught to drive.'

Defeated, Ibar turned the horses' heads and clucked to them. They plunged through the shallow water, hooves slipping on the stony bottom, and trotted up the opposite bank.

Conall Cearnach ran for his own war-cart, concealed in a stand of trees. If something happens to that reckless idiot, he told himself, Conor will take it out of my hide.

Cuchulain heard the clatter of his friend's chariot behind him. 'When my opportunity comes, Conall will only get in the way,' he told Ibar. 'Slow down, but don't stop.'

Leaning from the back of the chariot, Cuchulain picked up a large stone from the roadbed. As Conall's war-cart drew abreast of his, he threw the rock with such force it broke Conall's chariot-tongue. The light cart slewed sideways and overturned, pitching Conall on to the ground.

'What did you do that for?' Conall shouted, sitting up and rubbing the side of his head.

When he saw the other was not really hurt, Cuchulain answered cheerfully, 'Just testing my aim. I have a supply of death-balls with me, but I haven't thrown anything for several days, and I wanted to be certain I could still do it.'

'Your aim is absolutely brilliant,' Conall snarled. 'If you meet someone who wants to take your head today as a trophy, they're welcome to it. I won't interfere.' Scrambling to his feet, he brushed himself off with outraged dignity and went after his horses and cart.

'Good enough!' Cuchulain shouted to his retreating back. 'Let's go on, Ibar.'

The charioteer hesitated. 'They'll be carving the meat soon at Emain Macha. Aren't you hungry?'

'I am not. Drive on.'

The Hound's eyes seemed to be following something that kept pace with them as they advanced. Ibar saw a raven, flying in the same direction. 'Let's go back,' he urged. 'The raven is a death bird, an unhappy omen.'

Cuchulain laughed. 'Not for me.'

'But if we go farther down this road, we'll come to the dun of Nechtan!'

'What of it?'

'Nechtan's three sons have, among them, killed as many of the Ulaid as are alive at Emain Macha today,' Ibar explained. 'I don't think we need to disturb that hive of hornets.'

Cuchulain noticed that the raven was now flying much closer to the chariot. 'If I match myself against such men and win, I will become famous my first day at arms.'

'Posthumously famous,' the charioteer warned.

The track they were following dipped into a valley as gentle as a woman's lap. On a broad meadowland, short-legged black cattle turned mild eyes toward the chariot as it passed. Beyond them, Nechtan's dun stood on the crest of a hill. Ibar drew rein and cautiously surveyed the area.

All seemed quiet. The gate into the central enclosure yawned open, but no one was visible inside. Bees hummed lazily amidst the clover.

'The journey has tired me,' Cuchulain said. 'I might as well sleep until someone notices us.' With a show of enormous indifference, he spread his cloak upon the earth beside the chariot and lay down.

'If you fall asleep now, you'll wake up dead, madman. You'll get us both killed,' the scandalised Ibar protested.

Ignoring him, Cuchulain closed his eyes. 'Remember, you must not disturb me until I wake of my own accord.'

Ibar stared at him.

Almost at once a man emerged from the dun of Nechtan, a hulking man with a permanent scowl stitched between his eyes. 'What horses do I see at our gate?'

Cuchulain did not move. He lay on his back, his chest moving slowly up and down, as if he were totally relaxed and deeply asleep.

Get us *both* killed, Ibar thought bitterly. 'They are the speckled team of Conor mac Nessa,' he called in answer. Hearing their master's name, the greys pricked up their ears.

The man came closer. 'I thought as much, that's a king's chariot. But I don't recall inviting the king of Ulster to our dun, we're not on bed-and-beer terms with the Ulaid.'

'It's not Conor mac Nessa sleeping there, but a young lad who just took up arms today. He has wandered into your territory only to show off.' There, thought Ibar. I hope you heard that, Cuchulain.

'Bad luck to him, then,' replied the other. 'Even a beardless boy cannot enter our territory with impunity.'

At that moment, a raven coughed a derisive laugh nearby, and the beardless boy sat up. His eyes were clear, but when the raven laughed a second time, his face suffused with blood.

82

'I am Foll, son of Nechtan, and you are cold meat,' the man told him, raising his two-handed sword. But in one lithe leap Cuchulain was on his feet and seizing a death-ball from the leather bag tied to the rim of the chariot.

Death-balls, or brain-balls as some called them, were made from the brains of slain opponents mixed with lime and formed into rock-hard missiles. Their manufacture was a speciality of the Red Branch. With one unerring throw, Cuchulain sent one of these death-balls hurtling through the air and crashing into Foll's skull.

The man was dead before he hit the ground.

Cuchulain felt a certain shock. Up until now, he had been playing; now a man was dead and he had done it. He stared at the figure lying on the earth, drumming its heels in a final spasm.

'That's it,' Ibar said. He began briskly unloading the rest of the weaponry from the chariot. 'It's as good a day for dying as any,' he remarked to the horses.

Before the weapons were laid out, two more men came running from the dun, howling with outrage. The raven screamed. Match them if you can, Root of Valour!

As Ibar watched, Cuchulain seemed to expand into a larger version of himself. The hair rose on his head like a raven's crest, but each strand was tipped with fire. One eye narrowed to a slit, the other bulged outward, red-veined. His features contorted into those of a ravenous hound searching for a victim to savage.

Too late, Nechtan's sons hesitated.

A moment later they lay dead upon the grass with their brother. They were mangled beyond recognition.

Ibar found himself backing away from the hideous apparition of the Hound. 'Cuchulain?'

No answer. The monstrous warrior was breathing like the roaring of a great fire.

'Cuchulain?' Ibar said again, beginning to feel rather desperate. 'Come back to me!'

With an effort, Cuchulain sought within himself and found a particle of Setanta. He clutched it and fought his way back. Sinking to his knees on the bloody grass, he leaned forward, his head hanging.

For the first time, Ibar noticed how thick his wrists were. The beardless boy had a man's bones.

As the Rage slowly faded, he began to look like Cuchulain again. His face was unmarked and noble, the firm skin fair, the grey eyes brilliant.

'I've killed three men,' he said at last with absolutely no inflection, as if they were a reality outside his own.

'You have. Three warriors of considerable reputation.'

Cuchulain nodded but made no effort to stand. 'They were as alive as I am.'

'They were, but not now. That's the way of it.'

Cuchulain swung his head slowly from side to side, looking for the raven. She was gone. He was not certain how he was supposed to feel. Triumphant? He had taken up arms and fought successfully, he should feel exhilarated.

He only felt hollow.

Nothing left but three men, slowly stiffening. The Rage faded into a dim memory of hot rapture and deadly cold efficiency, then it too was gone, and he was left alone.

He dragged himself to his feet. 'Let's take the trophies,' he said to Ibar.

His sword bit through the necks of Nechtan's sons; he wiped their faces clean and tied them by their hair to the chariot rim. The horses did not shy away from them. Conor's team had carried trophies home before.

From the gatetower at Emain Macha, the sentries observed the king's distinctively plumed chariot approaching the fort; their trained eyes recognised it even at a great distance. 'Cuchulain returns!'

Conor grinned and slapped his thigh, forgetting his studied kingly reserve. He hurried to greet his fosterling, but as he reached the gateway one of the sentries called down, 'There appear to be tiny black dots on the rim of the chariot that could only be trophy heads. Your wolfhound has made his first kill. What if the Rage is still on him?'

The king halted where he stood, horrified by the possibility. If Cuchulain entered the fort while still transformed by his murderous battle-fury, he could easily slay a score of his own people before he recovered himself.

Conor's subtle mind seized and discarded a succession of plans, then his grin became sardonic. Spinning on his heel, he pointed to someone nearby. 'You. And you and you, I need you now, with all the friends you can gather. Meet me outside the gates, and hurry!'

They ran to obey him.

He called up to his sentries, 'I'm thankful for your hawks' eyes. You may have given us just enough time.'

The chariot sped on towards Emain Macha. The day was dying in a bright splash of peacock colours as they rounded the final bend in the road and the fortress loomed before them. With an oath, Ibar drew rein. 'What's this? What welcoming party have they sent out for us?'

The young man beside him stiffened and blushed crimson.

Both sides of the roadway leading to the open gates were lined with the young women of Emain Macha. The youngest, the most attractive. All smiling and waving, calling Cuchulain's name.

All birth-naked.

7 If Rage had still gripped Cuchulain, it would have evaporated long before Ibar drew rein in front of Conor mac Nessa. The king's fosterling stepped down with a flaming face.

'Did you like your welcoming party?' Conor asked politely.

Cuchulain was speechless.

'Just a precaution,' Conor explained. 'Fingan the physician once told me you have a delicacy, a near reverence, when it comes to women, so I thought the sight of so many naked females would pour cold water on your fighting heat before you could come roaring in here and do damage inside my stronghold.'

'I can control myself, Foster-Father,' Cuchulain said stiffly.

Conor had to work to keep his face straight, but he succeeded. 'I'm glad to hear it. But tell me – truthfully – you did enjoy the sight, didn't you? Just a little?' In spite of his best efforts, his eyes were dancing with unkingly mischief.

Cuchulain dug his toe in the dirt. 'I enjoyed my triumph,' he said, looking down. 'But someone had better take the heads from the chariot and start steeping them in walnut oil, or they won't be fit to hang in the House of the Red Branch.'

He was struggling to forget the vision of the rows of naked women.

He was also struggling to forgive himself for having looked away before he had seen all he longed to see.

Taking pity on him, Conor dropped the subject. But the matter of Cuchulain and women remained very much in the air.

Having taken up arms successfully, Cuchulain was no longer counted a boy. That night when he entered the House of the King for the evening's feast, Sencha met him just inside the door.

'Come with me,' he said.

The revered brehon judge cut through the crowd like a sword blade, leading the way to the massed benches of the Red Branch. A man was seated on each of them – save one.

Sencha gestured toward it. 'For Cuchulain of Murthemney,' he said.

The king's warriors leapt to their feet, shouting his name and cheering in welcome.

I am a man among such men! Cuchulain thought, holding his breath with the wonder of it. His name was on the lips of heroes: Duffach, Ernan, Gergind, Brocc, Fergus . . . Sualtim. Sualtim cheering him with the rest of them.

Red Branch.

He sat down very slowly, trying to make the moment last.

Men who seemed twice his size surrounded him, grinning at him through their beards. His comrades, now.

The food was served, but he was too excited to eat. At last, Naisi leaned towards him and whispered, 'If you ever want to grow any taller, you'd better eat something.'

'The way I feel, it would run straight through me,' Cuchulain admitted.

Naisi laughed. 'Drink, then. That will run through you too, but it leaves a better glow.'

He was counted a man, so speculation about Cuchulain and women began in earnest. The women were doing much of the speculating. He was small but impressively strong, and the contrast between his shyness and his intensity was appealing.

'The women certainly aren't shy about *him*,' a young warrior called Leary Buadach commented in the hall one evening when Cuchulain was elsewhere. 'Every unwed female at Emain Macha pursues him in some fashion. Half of them spend their days leaning against a wall hoping to catch sight of him as he passes by. There's nothing like a spectacular reputation to make a man desirable. Nechtan's sons . . . who would have thought he'd go out and kill Nechtan's sons all by himself?'

'It isn't just the unmarried woman,' Gergind said irritably. 'My own wife rolls her eyes at him. Lately I've been given cold bathing water and my cloaks go unmended. The Hound is a hazard,' he told Conor.

The king's eldest son added, 'My ears are melted from hearing what a good chess-player Cuchulain is, how gracefully he moves, how low and melodious his voice is. The fact that he pretends to ignore the women just whets their appetites for him. Find him a wife, Father.'

'Find him a wife!' echoed the king's other sons, Fiacra the Fair and Cormac Connlongas.

'Find him a wife!' demanded the warriors of the Red Branch.

'It will have to be someone very special,' Fingan the physician warned. 'Special enough to make him overcome his shyness. That isn't pretence, Follaman; Cuchulain isn't like the rest of you, as ready as goats to climb on to anything warm.'

Bricriu Bitter-Tongue entered the conversation with, 'If the Hound requires such a special woman, there's always Deirdre. Wherever she may be hidden,' he added, glancing at Conor.

The king scowled. 'You would love to see that trouble, wouldn't you? But Deirdre is for me, and me only.' His voice was as hard and cold as iron. 'You have a passion for creating discord, Bricriu; I've warned you about it before. I tell you this now: I do not want to hear Deirdre's name on your lips, or anyone else's.' His hand dropped to his sword hilt.

Bricriu fell silent.

Yet the king thought, in the quietness of his own skull, that Deirdre would indeed be the perfect mate for young Cuchulain. She was as extraordinary in her way as he was in his.

Except she belonged to Conor mac Nessa. And not even his love for Cuchulain would make him surrender what he considered the greatest treasure in Ulster. Let the others whisper about her, make guesses about her. He had seen her. He knew.

Cuchulain must have some other mate.

At the king's order, the daughters of Ulster's chariot-chieftains were invited to Emain Macha and served sweet golden mead in the *grianan*; were paraded back and forth on the lawns. Cuchulain glanced at them covertly, but made no other response. His hand never slid down the round slope of a passing haunch, nor did he press himself against a woman who stood with the wall at her back.

The more reserved he was, the more the women panted after him. And the more they criticised other men for their coarse behaviour.

Soon the Hound was in danger of losing his popularity with the Red Branch altogether.

Laeg had less awe of him than the others. Now that Cuchulain was counted as a full-grown and blooded warrior, he had been allowed to take the freckle-faced young man as his charioteer, and the two spent much time together. Every day Laeg breathed the smell of Cuchulain's sweat and observed his mistakes as well as his triumphs; the intimacy made him bold. 'You'd better take a woman soon,' he said, 'or you'll lose every friend you have. Haven't you seen one you like?'

Cuchulain laughed. Just the two of them together, out of the sight of women, he could laugh easily. 'I like them all, that's the trouble. Perhaps too much. They distract me.'

When Laeg grinned, his freckles divided into a new geography. 'They distract all of us. But as soon as you have one of your own and bed her regularly, you'll be able to think with a clearer head. I recommend it.'

'Do you? And who would you suggest for me? Everyone else seems to have some opinion, the guessing game has become more popular than chess on rainy evenings. But no one asks me. No one knows what I would like in a woman.'

'Do you know?'

'Not yet,' said Cuchulain.

But in one change of the seasons, he did know. A flood broke out on the plain of Brega, and the men of Emain Macha were sent to the aid of the hosteler Forgall the Wily, whose guesting house had been swept away.

'Forgall provides food and shelter in my name for travellers in the southern reaches of Ulster,' Conor explained to Cuchulain. 'Hospitality and generosity are both important; they put men in your debt.'

So Cuchulain had gone with the others to clear debris and raise new beams and help herders chase down scattered livestock, as this Forgall was also a cattle-lord. It was no time for social niceties. The men sent by the king worked as labourers to do what must be done, leaving their noble trappings behind them at Emain Macha. Manpower was always scarce.

Cuchulain was only dimly aware that Forgall's family included two daughters, one called Derforgall and the younger, Emer. He did not encounter either of them until he happened to rescue a casket of jewels from a pool of stinking muck. As he carried it up a hill, looking for someone to give it to, Forgall's younger daughter ran forward with a cry of delight to claim her treasures.

Their eyes locked.

Muddy and begrimed, Cuchulain stood speechless until someone shouted for him. Then Emer turned away to her own duties. Not even a word had passed between them.

But for the rest of the endless day, he thought of nothing else.

The king's men had to return to Emain Macha as soon as possible to avoid leaving the fort undermanned. Cuchulain went with them, wrapped in moody silence. The next day, he said to Laeg, 'If I return to Brega, will you drive me?'

'I will of course, but why go back?'

'Emer,' said Cuchulain.

Emer.

He spent days selecting a princely wardrobe to make her forget her first view of him in a common saffron tunic, covered with mud.

Emer.

He wondered if she even remembered him. Probably not. Why should she? Agony.

Three times during the journey to Brega, he almost asked Laeg to turn back, but he could not let his charioteer see him lose his nerve. Heroes never run away, he told himself. Rush into it and through, it's the only way to face what you fear.

Emer.

Standing beside him in the chariot, Laeg could see how tense Cuchulain was and smiled to himself, reassured to know that even the Hound was afraid of something.

The dun of Forgall the Wily had been rebuilt on higher ground, and the women of his clan had taken advantage of an improvement in the weather to meet there and share the tasks of spinning and sewing. As Cuchulain's chariot approached, a group were gathered on the *urla*, their voices raised in a working song. Emer sat at their centre with her head bent over something in her lap.

'Slow down, Laeg,' Cuchulain ordered.

'Why? We're almost there.'

'That's just it, I don't want to come upon them suddenly and frighten them. Slower, I tell you. Not a trot, a walk. A *slow* walk,' he insisted, forestalling the moment.

Hearing the creaking of an axle and the snorting of horses, Emer glanced up. She saw a chariot containing two men, a lean red-haired driver and a darker, powerfully built youth with smooth cheeks and unforgettable eyes. She stood up at once, a lapful of embroidery sliding to the ground unnoticed.

Laeg drew rein at the foot of the lawn, and Cuchulain stepped from the chariot. For the occasion, he had dressed in a linen shirt bleached to swansdown softness, his best fivefolded crimson tunic, gold arm rings, and a massive golden torc encircling his neck. This piece of jewellery served a practical purpose, not only identifying him as belonging to a chieftain's family but also shielding his nape. 'You look splendid,' Laeg had assured him.

But when Emer met his eyes, Cuchulain did not feel splendid. He

90

was suddenly certain he was too short and too shabby and he wanted to leap back into the chariot and race away.

Her eyes held him where he was.

Emer came lightly down the lawn. Summer comes with her, Cuchulain thought, dazzled. A pure white light seemed to shine on her alone, illuminating every detail for him.

Forgall's younger daughter was a small girl with a swift clear gaze. She moved with the poise of someone who has always been cherished. Heavy tresses of amber-coloured hair framed an oval face; a piquant slant of unexpectedly dark eyebrows contrasted with her fair colouring. Her eyes were green-flecked hazel, and her long lids had a slight droop at the outer edge that would have made a less vibrant girl seem languid.

In homage to the sunseason, she had donned a buttercup-yellow gown and twisted wildflowers and vines together to make herself a colourful girdle. All the hues of summer belonged to Emer of Brega.

Cuchulain thought even her small imperfections – the drooping eyelids, a mole at the corner of her mouth – endearing.

Laeg was shaking his head. He had believed he knew all his friend's moods, but he had never seen him captivated before. They would never believe this at Emain Macha.

When she reached the foot of the lawn, Emer held out her hand, palm up and weaponless, in friendship. 'May every road be smooth to your feet,' she said in a bell-chime voice.

'And may you be safe from every harm,' Cuchulain managed to reply, with more feeling than the automatic response usually carried.

Emer liked his voice, low-pitched and almost too gentle to belong to a warrior. She liked his eyes too. Since she first saw them, she had never forgotten them, had dreamed constantly of luminous silvery eyes screened by a thicket of black lashes. The eyes were dauntless – but the mouth was tender.

This one could break your bones or break your heart, she warned herself.

Meanwhile, Cuchulain was struggling with speech. For this girl, ordinary conversation was not good enough. Yet he had not mastered the art of even ordinary conversation with women.

As the daughter of a man who maintained a public hostel, Emer was fortunately too well trained in the forms of hospitality to let a silence become uncomfortable. Putting one hand on Cuchulain's arm, she began steering him toward her family's own dwelling house. 'Have you come far?' she asked by way of opening conversation.

Laeg had fallen in behind them, leading the team until a horseboy should come forward and relieve him of them. He was a charioteer but also Red Branch; whatever courtesies were extended to Cuchulain he expected for himself also. He noticed with amusement that his friend seemed unable to frame a coherent answer to the girl's question.

'Where did you come from?' Emer asked again.

At the time of his greatest need, inspiration struck. 'From a woman's brooch,' Cuchulain said surprisingly. He risked a sidelong glance at her.

She did not miss a step, but he thought he saw her lips twitch. 'And where do you sleep in such a place?'

'I sleep in the house built for the herder of Tethra.'

This time he could definitely hear suppressed laughter in her voice as she said, 'And who are you yourself?'

'I am nephew to a river flowing in the land of Ross,' Cuchulain answered quite seriously. She gave him a glance then, and the spark leaped between them, the sheer fun of a game both understood from the beginning.

They were passing the young women who had been studying needlework with Emer, but no sewing was being done now. Every woman sat frozen, straining to overhear what Emer and the strange young man might be saying.

Little good it will do them, thought Laeg, three steps behind. Cuchulain is talking in riddles, the fool. His shyness has made him simple, and that's no way to win a woman. I'm surprised she bothers to humour him.

He could not see the way Emer's face was glowing.

They were nearing Forgall's circular dwelling of timber and thatch. 'And you,' said Cuchulain, 'what can you tell me of yourself?'

When he turned towards her he was rewarded with a new delight, a dimple winking at him from her cheek.

'Easily told,' said Emer. 'I am a watcher who has seen no one yet, a chieftain's daughter who offers hospitality on a road that is barred. Three heroes of the blood guard me, each as strong as a hundred, and with nine more like him at his back. Their fortresses cast shadows on my apple trees, but I would not have them harmed, though the apples never ripen.

'My father, Forgall the Wily, has earned his name many times over. He has undone many strong men; a boy's trick will not impress him.'

Cuchulain frowned. 'I am no boy.'

92

'You have no beard.'

He ignored this. 'I have been trained in battle by Fergus mac Roy, and I have already taken trophies. I have studied law with Sencha the brehon and counting with Blai the distributor. I have learned poetry at the knees of bards and sciences from the druids. No man in Ulster is better educated.' His head was high now, his expression haughty.

Emer stopped and faced him, matching pride for pride. 'I too have been well educated.' There was steel in her bell-chime voice. 'I was raised to honour the ancient virtues, to observe the laws of our people, to guard myself for the man who will claim me, to behave in all ways as a woman of noble blood should behave. No woman in this land stands above me.'

'I've never met a woman who speaks to me as you do,' Cuchulain told her.

'Even your wife?' She fixed that direct look of hers on him, challenging him.

'I have no wife. Yet.'

Laeg had stopped the moment the two in front of him stopped, but the impatient horses were pawing the earth and jingling their bits, making it hard for him to hear what was being said. He cursed them under his breath.

Emer's expression had altered in some subtle way when Cuchulain said he had no wife. 'And I have no husband. Yet. My older sister Derforgall is unmarried and I cannot take precedence over her by leaving first. If you are seeking a wife, perhaps you should have a look at her,' Emer added in an elaborately casual tone.

'I could look at her, but I would not see her,' Cuchulain said truthfully.

They resumed their walk, and for the rest of the short distance there was silence between them.

Forgall the Wily met them at the doorway. A narrow-chested man with eyes constantly darting like minnows in a puddle, Forgall noted the flush in his daughter's cheeks, and his lips drew together into a disapproving line. But he made the two strangers welcome. A horseboy was summoned to care for the team, and servants hurriedly heated water so Cuchulain and Laeg could bathe off the dust of the journey. When that tradition had been observed, the two young men were seated on benches close to low tables heaped with baskets of fruit and nuts. As a meal of meats and cheeses was prepared, Forgall exchanged pleasantries with his guests, discussing the state of the crops and the additions to his landholding since Cuchulain had seen it last.

From the corner of his eye, Cuchulain saw Emer talking with a leaner, older version of herself: Derforgall. Then the two left the hall to the men, and he thought the room grew darker, though as many candles burned as before.

A formal visit to a man of noble rank must take a certain amount of time. Cuchulain filled that time as best he could, talking about an innovative shape Cullen the smith had recently developed for javelin heads. But his thoughts were elsewhere.

Laeg, mightily bored, slouched on his bench and tried to keep his eyes open.

No women in here, no fighting, nothing interesting at all, he thought. The poor Hound, he hasn't the slightest idea how to go about this.

Cuchulain was having much the same thought. He wanted to talk about Emer, but each time he approached the subject her father led the conversation off in some other direction. He got the distinct impression that Forgall wanted to keep him as far away from Emer as possible.

At last the visit had stretched to a point where even good manners could make nothing more of it. Cuchulain said he must return to Emain Macha – with Forgall's compliments to the king, of course – and Laeg ran gratefully to get the chariot. There was no sign of Emer as the men stood in the doorway saying farewells.

Forgall urged Cuchulain to come back any time and often, but the young man noted the hosteler's eyes did not agree with what his mouth was saying.

'Was that supposed to be a diplomatic visit?' Laeg asked as they drove away. 'I thought you were going to woo Emer.'

'I did.'

'You did not. I've wooed women, I know how it's done. All you did was talk to Forgall about his new guest house and his cattle byre, and – by the leaves of the trees! – the man is a dull talker. I thought we'd never get out of there. But you did no wooing, Cuchulain – unless you call those childish riddles you said to her wooing.' Laeg flicked the reins, urging the horses to a trot. 'And they didn't even make sense,' he added. 'No one could understand them.'

Cuchulain chuckled. 'Emer understood them from the very beginning. Her mind is as nimble as her sewing fingers, Laeg.'

'A nimble mind, that's what you noticed about her? She has better

94

than that, my friend, the girl has a nice round nimble – ' One look from Cuchulain stopped Laeg's comment in mid-breath.

But the charioteer could not keep quiet for ever, it was not in his nature. When he tired of watching the rise and fall of the horses' haunches in front of him, he tried again. 'I never thought we would come all this way just to sample the quality of a woman's mind.'

'If I ever live with a woman, I have to be able to talk with her. Or be silent with her. And be comfortable either way,' Cuchulain explained, remembering the strained silences at Dun Dalgan. 'It's important.'

'It is?' Laeg raised his eyebrows. They were both young, and the charioteer had only one compelling requirement when it came to women. He had assumed Cuchulain was the same, but now he saw his mistake. The Hound was not quite like anyone else.

'What if Forgall won't consent to give you Emer?'

'I don't expect him to. He was polite enough today; I am the king's foster-son, after all. But he knows of me, and I could see in his eyes that he thinks of me as some sort of madman, not fit for his daughter. Mad.' Cuchulain gave a mirthless laugh. 'People do say that about me, don't they? Behind my back?'

'Some mistake your battle-fury for madness, but they are wrong,' Laeg said loyally.

'If I insist on taking Emer as my wife over Forgall's objections,' Cuchulain went on, 'I'll have to fight her three brothers, who live nearby and keep troops of warriors. And if I should kill even one of them, Emer would never marry me. It's a complicated situation.'

'How did you learn all this?'

'Emer told me.'

Laeg looked at Cuchulain in surprise. 'She did? When? You only spoke to her the one time, I was with you and I know.'

'That game of riddles we played was our conversation.'

'Explain it to me, then! The business about your coming from a brooch, all that nonsense.'

'It was a test, Laeg. I'm always testing myself; this time I tested Emer. The reference to coming from a woman's brooch meant I came from Emain Macha, of course, and she understood at once. So I made the next riddle harder – I told her I slept in a house built for the herder of Tethra. Our sleeping house at Emain Macha was originally built for the king's chief fisherman, you know – and isn't the sea called the Plain of Tethra by the poets? Emer knew that too. She's very quick.'

'You're not the nephew of any river,' Laeg said indignantly, feeling

95

he should have caught on to the game himself if even a woman could understand it.

'Ah, but I am. Conor is the name of a river in Ross, and I am the nephew of Conor mac Nessa. Laeg, did you notice the way her hair curls at her temples?' he added dreamily.

'I thought we were talking about her mind.'

'It's all part of the same thing, isn't it?'

The charioteer abandoned any attempt to understand. Perhaps Cuchulain really was mad, he decided. Talking with him about women was certainly a waste of time. Laeg resumed watching the haunches of the horses, and was soon lost in a pleasant daydream involving Sencha's daughter.

Meanwhile, Forgall the Wily was watching his younger daughter closely. There was a dreamy look in her eyes that disturbed him. Taking her companions aside, he questioned them at length, but no one had heard anything of importance pass between Emer and Cuchulain.

Yet Forgall knew something had happened. He could tell it by the prickling at the back of his neck. 'That mad boy from Emain Macha is after my child,' he growled to his steward. 'We've heard tales of his deeds, young though he is. He goes into every battle with the Red Branch, every little skirmish and cattle raid, and he outfights everyone with a sort of terrible insanity. I won't give my Emer up to that, she's meant for something better.'

Emer was Forgall's favourite. She was not to be wasted on Conor mac Nessa's Hound! He often boasted that she possessed all six of the womanly gifts praised by poets: beauty of person, sweetness of voice, an appreciation of music, skill in needlework, cheerful disposition, and maidenly modesty.

Within a fortnight, Forgall arrived at Emain Macha. He had come, he claimed, to repay the kind visit of the king's fosterling, and he brought a cartload of gifts in addition.

That night, he attended a feast in the House of the King and heard the royal bard extol Cuchulain's latest successes in combat.

'He's an unusual youngster, your Cuchulain,' Forgall told Conor. 'A remarkable lad.' He smiled, showing his teeth. 'I find it hard to believe he can perform all the feats credited to him, however.'

Forgall and the king were lounging on comfortably padded benches, with one of Conor's immense shaggy wolfhounds resting its head on its master's knee. The smell of foaming ale thickened the air.

'Cuchulain's better than his reputation,' Conor boasted. 'I wish I had a hundred of him.'

'Indeed? Then I'm surprised you haven't given him every possible advantage.'

'What do you mean?'

'I would not presume to tell the king of Ulster his business,' Forgall said, lowering his eyelids modestly. 'But if that fellow were mine, I'd send him to the school for heroes kept by Skya the warrior-woman on her island west of Alba. Any number of other Ulster fighting men have gone there, you know. She has the fastest reflexes in the world, they say, and turns out pupils better than herself.'

'Skya.' Conor's eyes lit with interest. 'Of course. I should have thought of her sooner; everyone knows of Skya.'

'Even I,' agreed Forgall. 'I've sold a few hides to that island from time to time, I know people over there. It's a hard place, but it builds men.'

Glancing around for Cuchulain, Conor saw his foster-son deep in conversation with Fergus mac Roy. The Hound was explaining a spear-throw of his own devising, and Fergus was listening with furrowed brow, trying to understand something plainly beyond him.

Conor, watching the two of them, nodded to himself. 'I'm most grateful to you,' he told his guest. 'Here, have some more wine.'

Forgall the Wily smiled gratefully and contrived to spill half his drink when Conor was looking the other way. Most of it went in Forgall's lap, but he did not mind. Spilling his wine was a long-standing custom of his when away from the security of his own dun. He thought it better to have a soggy lap than a soggy mind.

As always, Conor mac Nessa provided a sumptuous feast. Shoulders of venison and hunks of bacon had been simmered with leeks and onions and root vegetables until all was bathed in a glossy gravy. Servants brought platters piled with rounds of oxmeat and mutton, encircled with delicate strips of tripe. Salmon had been poached and spread with butter, turbots were boiled in milk and wine, mullet stewed in mead. Tongue of ox and sweetbread of calf were prepared for the women. Baskets of red and yellow apples contested for pride of place with custards of rowanberries and blackberries. No one ever left the House of the King hungry.

But Forgall the Wily ate sparingly. Most of the time, he kept his eyes on Cuchulain. Enjoy yourself while you can, boy, he thought. Mad boy. Mad to think I would give my daughter to a creature who is said to foam like a dog. Skya's island is a dangerous place, and I think we can arrange to make it even more dangerous for you; indeed we can.

Indeed we can.

Forgall considered the evening a great success.

When Forgall had gone, Conor sought out Fergus mac Roy to tell him he was sending Cuchulain to Skya's school for heroes for further training.

'But I thought you were going to find him a wife.'

'We can take care of that later, Fergus, after he's had all the hardening and tempering possible. If he's out of Erin, it will serve the same purpose as having him married – the women will turn back to their own men.

'Besides, I have a marriage to think of myself, and one in a season is enough.'

'What marriage?'

'Deirdre. She's reached marrying age. Last leaf-fall I told Levarcham to start preparing her for me.'

Fergus looked alarmed. 'Wouldn't it be better to leave her as she is? Cathbad said – '

'I know what Cathbad said.'

'And you have two wives already, Mugain and – '

'I can afford more. The two I have are nothing like Deirdre, she's even more beautiful than the druid prophesied.' Conor's voice grew husky. 'Too beautiful to be shut away all her life. Deirdre deserves to be the treasured consort of a king. This king.'

'But . . .'

'Don't argue with me, mac Roy!' Conor clenched his fists. His eyes glittered and two deep grooves appeared on his face, running from the flare of his nostrils to the corners of his suddenly grim mouth.

I've pushed him too far, Fergus realised.

But the damage was done.

When he was told of the proposed trip to Skya's training camp, Cuchulain had mixed feelings. The adventure excited him, but he was painfully aware of the distance it would put between himself and Emer.

'I think I need to make a trip to Brega,' he told Laeg.

The redhead nodded. 'I thought you might. Those word games the two of you played are great fun, I'm sure, but before a man ventures across the sea he should enjoy at least one good – '

'Prepare the chariot and team,' snapped Cuchulain.

But first one thing and then another intervened, and they did not leave Emain Macha until almost sunset. When darkness signalled a halt, Cuchulain lay on the ground with his arms folded behind his head, staring up at the sky. A brooding awareness at the back of his mind worked on without his permission, exhausting him with thought.

For a long time, his body had been telling him mating was necessary for a man, as if by himself he were incomplete. Sexual hunger urged his granite bones and iron muscles to seek their complement in female softness.

But why? Cuchulain wondered. Could not all the necessary elements be contained in one perfect body, one self-sufficient and total hero?

Cuchulain did not think of himself as needing love. He was satisfied to be part of the Red Branch, a member of the tightly woven brotherhood necessary among warriors who fought together for common causes.

So why was he now lying awake, sweating, trying to remember the exact arrangement of the flecks of green in Emer's hazel eyes?

A new thought assailed him so painfully that he rolled on to his side and drew his knees up to his belly. What if he had misunderstood Emer? What if no unspoken messages had passed between them at all, and she really wanted him to take her sister away so she might save herself for someone taller-older-fairer . . .

Laeg was awakened by a peculiar noise, like the sound of two boulders being ground together. The charioteer blinked and sat up, trying to locate the source.

As his brain cleared, he realised he was listening to the gnashing of Cuchulain's teeth.

Men did sometimes gnash their teeth in their sleep, but Laeg had no intention of trying to awaken the Hound. In an uncertain world, every Gael tried to be certain of two things: that his ancestry was known to the bards, so he could collect the entitlements due him as a result of his rank in society, and that any *gessa* upon him were known, so other people would not cause mishaps and disasters.

Laeg knew very well there was a prohibition against awakening Cuchulain, so he lay back down and willed himself to return to sleep. If the Hound was having a bad dream, he would have to rouse from it on his own.

But Cuchulain was not asleep. When the sun finally slew the night, he arose, red-eyed, and the two resumed their journey. The Hound seemed uninterested in food and never reached for the supplies they had brought with them, so Laeg felt honour-bound to fast as well. At Cuchulain's order, he drove the team headlong and listened to his belly grumble.

99

When they finally neared Forgall's hostel, Cuchulain had Laeg stop the horses and conceal the chariot in some shrubbery. The team and their driver were exhausted, but the Hound did not even seem to notice. He gave off energy like waves of heat. 'Circle around the dun until you find some ignorant slave to question,' he said to Laeg. 'Learn just where Forgall is; I'll wait out of sight.'

Laeg soon returned with the news that Forgall the Wily was fortuitously absent. 'He and Derforgall have gone to collect bees from another clan. Derforgall knows the song for singing to bees, I was told. Handy, a talent like that. And of course they took a brehon with them to recite the laws applicable to bee-keeping . . .'

'Is Emer here? I don't want to hear about bees!'

'She is, she's – '

But Cuchulain was already running towards the dun.

Emer met him at her father's doorway with the exact degree of formality appropriate for the daughter of a hosteler. She smiled, she asked about his journey, she remembered Laeg's name. She did not act as if anything had ever passed between herself and Cuchulain at all.

Cullen's Wolfhound felt winter in his bones.

Servants bustled about, bringing a bathing basin and preparing food. A hosteler must always have meat available. Laeg decided honour had been satisfied enough and began to supply his mouth with both hands at once. Let Cuchulain starve himself if he wanted, women sometimes had that effect on a man. Women . . . he tried to recall Derforgall's appearance. A girl who could manage bees could certainly add to her husband's prosperity.

Of course, there was also Sencha's daughter. But as a member of the Red Branch, Laeg was entitled to more than one wife as long as he could feed and protect them. And as Cuchulain's charioteer, he could expect a noble share of hunters' spoils and victors' booty.

The meal seemed to last as long as the journey to Brega had taken. Cuchulain could not insult the hospitality of the hostel by refusing to eat, so he toyed with his food and pushed small bits into his mouth, whenever someone was looking. The food had no taste for him, however.

Then Emer came towards him, carrying a platter that held a whole roast suckling pig. Taking up the long iron flesh-fork, she tore one haunch free from the steaming carcass and set it before Cuchulain.

He looked up at her. 'You've given me the haunch, the Champion's Portion.'

'I have. Who else would I save it for?'

His appetite returned with a rush. He tore meat from bone as if he had not eaten since last season. Emer stood watching him, the dimple winking in her cheek.

When Cuchulain had cleaned every morsel from bowl and platter, she brought him a silver bowl brimming with wine. Bending low to hand it to him, she whispered, 'Beware, my father dislikes you. I overheard him planning to do you harm.'

'By telling me, you choose my interests over his,' Cuchulain reminded her, his heart hammering at what that implied.

She lowered her eyes. He wanted desperately to touch her, just there, in the neck of her gown, where the skin looked so tender and a few pale gold freckles lay like butter on milk.

'The king is sending me to train with Skya on her island; she has taught many heroes,' he said to Emer. 'I must go, but I will return when I have mastered all she can teach me. When I come back I will really deserve the Champion's Portion, and you can carve another for me then.'

'But my father . . .'

'Nothing your father can do could stop me from coming back here to count the green flecks in your eyes,' Cuchulain said.

Emer gave him one long look, then resumed her role as hostess. But by now, he knew he had made no mistake.

Emer knew how to entertain guests. A harper was ordered to play; three jugglers did wondrous tricks with a set of balls. More ale was poured. Eventually, the servants began lighting torches of bog fir, for the hall was filling with shadows. Yet Cuchulain showed no inclination to leave.

Laeg reminded him, 'You promised Follaman and Ferdiad to play on their side in the next hurling match; if we stay here any longer, we won't get back in time.'

'Hurling match?' Cuchulain asked dreamily.

'Tomorrow.'

'And I promised?'

'You did.'

'Oh.' For the first time in Cuchulain's life, a hurling match seemed trivial. He cast a longing glance towards Emer. 'Uh . . . Laeg, go outside and observe the position of the stars every so often, will you? If we leave by midpoint of the night, I can be at Emain Macha in time to keep my promise.'

'And risk breaking our horses' legs by driving in the dark?'

'Just do as I tell you.'

'Do you have to leave at night?' Emer echoed. 'The guest house is well prepared, my father's hostel can accommodate you comfortably.'

Cuchulain's expression was abject but determined. 'I keep my word.'

'And you never break it?'

'Never.' She must understand this most important thing about him. 'Never.'

Emer smiled the tiniest smile, one meant for him alone. Raising her voice so the servants could hear, she said, 'Then at least permit me to show you the new fittings in the hostel before you go, so you can give a favourable report to your foster-father.'

The night was clear and cool; the first stars were just appearing. A path was already worn to the guest house, and Cuchulain tortured himself by wondering how many other men Emer had shown the way.

Rectangular and low-roofed, the new building smelled of thatch. A tall man would have had to duck under the door lintel. Emer entered first, holding up a stubby candle in an iron stick. 'It's only tallow,' she apologised. 'When my father and sister return, we'll soon have a good supply of beeswax.'

Cuchulain felt a pang of sorrow that anything, even an inferior quality of candle, should give Emer reason to apologise.

She set the candlestick on a low table and stood uncertainly, looking at him. For once, the forms of hospitality deserted her.

'This is very . . . nice,' Cuchulain heard himself say inanely.

His nervousness steadied Emer. She put her hand on his arm. 'Setanta,' she said, cherishing the sound of the name.

He was startled. 'How did you know about that?'

'I asked Laeg if you had ever been called anything other than Cullen's Wolfhound. That name doesn't fit the boy I know. If you don't mind, I'd rather call you Setanta – just when we are alone.'

'I don't mind,' he said, deep in his chest. He could feel himself blushing. Yet as if they had a will of their own, his fingers began moving up Emer's arm to her shoulder, then slowly tracing the delicate line of her collarbone. When they reached the neck of her gown, she drew in a sharp breath.

'The road between those hills is dangerous, Setanta.'

'I thrive on danger . . .'

She hardly seemed to breathe as his hand slid into her gown. He closed his eyes to concentrate on the feel of her flesh. Nothing had ever

102

been so soft, not even the silky skin between the forelegs of the horses. Cuchulain's fingers buried themselves in the cleft between her breasts and a spasm of desire shook him.

They both heard cloth tear.

He opened startled eyes to find he had ripped her gown from neck to waist. But she was not angry. She smiled, a slow, heavy-lidded smile. And by some curious alchemy, the raging strength in him was shapechanged into tenderness, a deep welling sweetness of unbearable intensity.

'Don't cover yourself,' he pleaded.

Her smile deepened. They had moved beyond shyness. In one graceful gesture, she shrugged out of the ruined gown and let it fall around her feet. She had to be naked. She was not in control of her actions any more, they were being dictated by patterns she had never been taught but was powerless to resist. The pleasure was in the surrendering.

Tossing her head back, Emer released her hair to cascade down her spine, sending ripples of pleasure along her nerves. She felt like a candle, a glowing white beeswax candle.

Cuchulain was the flame.

The ecstasy he had only experienced in battle-fury came to him in a new form now. He felt himself grow huge; when he rubbed against her belly, she groaned.

'There are fresh rushes on the floor,' she murmured, knowing the nearest pallet was too far away for either of them.

Bending at the knee, Cuchulain carried her down with him. Before they reached the ground he twisted to lie beneath her, cushioning her. Her hair tumbled around them.

Girlfingers fumbled with his clothing. When she touched his penis, Emer gasped. 'You are no mere boy!'

'Did you think I was?'

'I thought . . . I mean, I . . .'

'No more thinking,' he told her. 'Not now.'

He tried very hard to be gentle, afraid in his ignorance he might hurt her. But simultaneously he wanted to spend his strength on her in a wild explosion that would rip them both apart.

Struggling with himself on the thin edge of control, Cuchulain rolled over until they lay facing each other. Her delighted hands at once continued exploring his body. Her touch was magical, unbearable. If she did not stop at once he would . . . he tried to push her hands away,

103

though the air on his unstroked skin was torture. 'Don't,' he whispered. He wanted time to explore her, to seek out those places on her body he had only imagined.

But suddenly it was too late. Too late for anything but to push her on to her back and mount her; there was no time left and no control either. He was wild.

Emer opened to him instinctively, but his first deep thrust made her cry out with pain. He could not possibly stop. She bit her lip just as he shuddered and gave a great moan.

Heat flooded through her, miraculously banishing pain. She was scorched, she was scalded! Was this what men carried inside them, this heat like a hundred suns? She writhed under Cuchulain, clutching at him, trying to pull him deeper inside her, desperate for the healing heat.

The force of his climax had taken him to the brink of unconsciousness, but Emer brought him back. While he was still hard inside her, she began to move, tentatively at first, then with increasing confidence and a surer rhythm. Soon she was grasping him as if there were a strong hand within her, stroking and squeezing the massive erection one orgasm had not diminished.

As passion rose in him again, tenderness grew with it, until the same intense sweetness enveloped them both.

'Setanta,' Emer breathed against his beardless cheek.

8 From the doorway of her father's dwelling house, Emer watched Cuchulain drive away. She stood leaning against the carved doorframe, oblivious to the servants in the hall. Her attention was focused on the dim figure of a chariot and two horses faintly illumined by starlight.

She shifted her weight from one hip to the other, experimenting with the feel of her body. It was a new body, a woman's body, with nerves educated as they had not been the day before. She savoured the lubricious sliding of tissue against tissue, she smiled secretly at the sense of weight and fullness in the bottom of her belly. Her slightest movement started the tension building again.

She closed her eyes, just for a heartbeat. When she opened them, the chariot had been swallowed up in darkness.

'Be careful, Setanta,' she whispered.

Her attendants came up to her hesitantly. They could smell the man on her. 'Did you swear to him?' they wanted to know.

She spoke as if from a far distance. 'I did not. He goes into great danger and could be killed tomorrow. I have no desire to be a widow so soon.'

She sounded very practical, but she spoke in self-defence. She did not want to admit he had not asked for her promise, though she understood he had not done so for the reasons she just named: He did not want to bind her to a dead man when she was still so young, with pleasure newly awakened in her.

She resented his protecting her. I do not need protection, she thought, tossing her head. What good is there in being prudent? He's gone and I'm here. We were too careful; we thought too much.

No more thinking, he had warned her.

Next time, Emer told herself – if there is a next time – I won't make the same mistake. I will just go with him, wherever he goes, to whatever awaits him. I'll laugh and follow him into the chariot, and he won't refuse me.

If there is a next time.

She lingered until the sun rose through streaks of purple cloud.

Dawn broke over the lone chariot racing toward Emain Macha. The Hound rode in silence, shifting his weight to the jouncing of the war-cart but saying nothing.

'Well?' Laeg urged finally. 'What do you think of her?'

'Forgall's daughter entertains travellers beautifully,' said Cuchulain in a voice that revealed nothing. He looked straight ahead, his hands resting quietly on the chariot rim. Even in the pale light, Laeg could see his face had become that of a grown man.

The charioteer tried again. His friends would question him extensively once they returned to Emain Macha, and he had to give them some sort of answers, preferably true. 'Does Emer satisfy your requirements for a wife?'

'We did not speak of marriage,' Cuchulain said shortly. 'It wasn't necessary. We understand each other.'

Laeg lost patience. 'I never heard of two people who understood so much while saying so little. When I'm with a woman, I have to spend a lot of time explaining and convincing.'

'Then you're with the wrong woman,' Cuchulain told him.

The chariot rolled on.

As they neared Emain Macha, a change in the atmosphere alerted the Hound. He flung up his head, scenting trouble. An increase of traffic through the gates and a general air of disorder made him urge Laeg to drive faster.

'The king may need us,' Cuchulain said.

But when they entered the stronghold, they found there was little anyone could do for Conor mac Nessa. The king of Ulster sat stunned on his high seat, his face drawn and lined. The flush of youth, which had lasted overlong in him, had faded all at once, leaving a haggard, middle-aged man. His eyes were empty.

Cuchulain took one look and went to find Fergus. 'What happened while I was away? What could do that to the king?'

'Deirdre's been stolen.'

'Deirdre?'

'Fedlimid's daughter, the girl Conor's been keeping hidden away. He recently decided it was time to marry her – apparently she's become devastatingly beautiful. Her loss has certainly devastated him.'

'But who would dare lay hands on a woman of the king's? Is it war, Fergus – were we invaded?'

They stood near the *grianan*, from which Nessa suddenly emerged with her arm around the shoulder of a weeping, near-hysterical woman. When she saw Fergus and Cuchulain, the king's mother hurried up to them. 'Can you help me with Levarcham? She's terrified the king will blame her for her part in Deirdre's abduction and have her slain.'

'Conor won't hurt a woman,' Fergus tried to reassure Deirdre's old nurse. 'You know him better than that, surely; there is no kinder man.'

'Kind he is,' Levarcham agreed, 'but he won't forgive me for this, I know it as a duck knows water.' Her dishevelled cloak was red, her chinless face was red, her tear-filled eyes were swollen and red.

Cuchulain stared at this apparition in crimson. 'What did you have to do with Deirdre's being taken?'

'I'd like to know that myself,' added Fergus.

But Levarcham seemed on the point of collapse. Her knees buckled, and they all reached to catch her before she fell. Somehow they managed, clumsily, to guide her to a bench and send for a bowl of cool buttermilk to revive the woman. Only when she had emptied the bowl and was wearing a white moustache of buttermilk on her upper lip was Levarcham able to tell her story.

'It wasn't an abduction,' she said, her eyes moving from one face to the other. 'It was . . . an elopement, you might say.'

Fergus's eyebrows shot up and he growled in his throat, but did not interrupt her. Levarcham continued, 'My Deirdre has grown into the most beautiful of women. Her hair is a mass of golden ringlets, her eyes are the green of spring leaves. And as for her womanly charms, ah! She has such a way with her. No one could resist her. She knows just how to duck her chin and look sidelong from the corners of her eyes. Of course . . .' the woman hesitated, then decided to tell the entire truth, since the yarn had begun to unravel. 'Of course, she is spoiled, and the blame is mine. I felt sorry for her, poor little mite, snatched away from her own people and shut up with only an old stick of a woman like me for company. I asked the king for presents to make her smile and he never begrudged them; anything she wanted, he sent to her. Rings for her fingers, ribbons for her hair.

'She could have anything but freedom. As she grew older, this lack sat more heavily on her, and sometimes she took fits of sulking. If the king arrived when she was in one of her moods he scolded her for being ungrateful. To get even, she asked for more and richer gifts and he gave them, but I could tell she had conceived a dislike for Conor mac Nessa. He paid no attention. She was still a child to him, her petty passions glanced off his hide like darts off an ox-skin shield.

'Don't misunderstand me, most of the time Dierdre was a delightful girl. But when her breasts began to bud, I saw the beauty she would become and grew frightened for her. Then I understood the druid's prophecy. No woman should be so beautiful. It is terrible, the beauty of Deirdre.'

Levarcham shook her head sadly. 'Last leaf-fall the king told me he was thinking of marrying Deirdre the next Beltaine, at the start of sunseason. I was to talk to her, prepare her for what men and women do together.

'I was not eager to do it, but who else did she have? So I described for her the mating of couples, and I tried to make it sound as delicious as I could so she would be ready for Conor mac Nessa. I spoke of the feeling of a man's hands on her body, and the softness of a man's lips, and the hardness of a . . . well, you understand.' Levarcham looked down at her reddened hands, twisting in her lap. 'I succeeded; I saw eagerness leap in Deirdre's eyes.

'But not for the king, she told me quite frankly. She hated him, she said. The more I tried to argue with her, the more determined she became. Every attribute I claimed for the king, she loathed. She detested his yellow hair, the golden sheen of his sunkissed skin, even his thoughtful, deliberate manner.

'Deirdre is very singleminded. What she feels, she feels totally, and she convinced herself she hated Conor mac Nessa. When I tried to talk her out of it, she decided I had turned against her and began to act like a wild animal who has been backed into a corner. I was very worried about her.

'Then the winter caught us by surprise, so cold and so early. We needed firewood and I am not strong enough to cut it, so I brought the old man who lives beyond our woods, the only person other than the king and myself whom Deirdre had ever seen. An old man, with only one eye . . . I thought he was safe as long as I watched him.

'He was glad to help and brought us a calf of his, which he butchered and skinned outside our door. He stretched the carcass out on the snow to clean it, and Deirdre wandered out to watch – with me right behind her, of course.

'I saw how she halted in her tracks. Her spine went stiff, and she stood staring at the calf. It occurred to me then that she had not seen one slaughtered right on our doorstep before; I foolishly thought it might be frightening her. Warm red blood was running from the animal, pooling on the ice. I reached out to put my hand on her arm and lead her away, but at that moment a raven glided down.'

'A raven?' Cuchulain interrupted, feeling his scrotum tighten.

Levarcham nodded. 'We usually see only hooded crows in our valley, but this was a raven right enough, and a huge one. It landed on the snow beside the calf and plunged its beak into the spilled blood. And Deirdre laughed.

'When she turned towards me, her eyes were wild. "Raven-black, blood-red, snow-white," she said in a peculiar voice. "Are those not the most beautiful of all colours, Levarcham? I long to see a man with *those* colours on him, not some yellow-haired old king who will make me a servant to his senior wives. Raven-black, blood-red, snow-white. Is there such a man anywhere, Levarcham?"

'Deirdre had begun to shiver, but she asked that question over and over, murmuring about the three colours, the young calf, and the old king. Conor is not old, really, but he seems so to a girl that young. Youth and rebellion and her awakening senses were boiling all together in her and I tried to lead her back in the house, for I feared she was going mad.

'Then I heard the raven scream. The one-eyed man yelled to drive it away, but Deirdre laughed again, her voice rising with the scream and the yell until I could not tell which was which. Some fearful music was being made that I had never heard before, and do not want to hear again.'

Levarcham's thin lips trembled, and she clawed at her hair distractedly. 'By this time, Deirdre had worked herself into such a state, I couldn't manage her. The old man was frightened; he ran away and there's no blame on him for it. But he left me alone, standing there with one arm as long as the other and a girl who was moonmad.

'To try and quiet her, I said the only thing that came into my head. I told Deirdre I knew of a young man with the three colours on him that she described, and if she would only be a good girl and come into the house with me, eat her food, sleep in her bed, I would tell her about him.

'My words had some effect, at least I was able to get her inside. But then I had to keep my promise. So I told her of a young warrior of the Red Branch whom I had seen at Emain Macha when I carried a request of Deirdre's to the king. Naisi, his name is – one of the sons of Uisnach.' *Ushna* was the pronunciation Levarcham gave to the famous hill of Uisnach from which Naisi's clan took its name. The old woman had originally been taken as a slave from Munster, and her accents were still southern.

109

'I told Deirdre that Naisi had black hair, white skin, red lips, and I assured her she would see him as soon as she was married to the king and went to live at Emain Macha, for he would be one of her loyal Red Branch guards. That quieted her for a little while, but not for long; not my Deirdre, who was accustomed to having her desires fulfilled at once.

'She decided she wanted to see Naisi immediately. She insisted. She refused her food, she pouted. She sighed and would not speak.

'Then I realised my mistake in mentioning him at all, but you cannot make the wind blow backwards and return foolish words to your mouth to be unsaid.' The old woman paused to blow her nose copiously on her sleeve.

'We had spoiled Deirdre,' she reiterated, 'and the girl wasn't used to having a request refused. When I told her she couldn't see Naisi until she was married to the king, she became very persistent. She wore me down. I am an old woman!' Levarcham threw out her hands, pleading for sympathy. When no one said anything, her shoulders slumped. 'When I could not bear to listen to her any longer, I sent word secretly to the sons of Uisnach to come to our forest to hunt. That much I would do, but no more, and I told Deirdre so. If they happened to come, and if she happened to catch a glimpse of Naisi with the three colours, she was to be satisfied with that.'

Nessa said harshly, 'You're a fool, Levarcham. You've been old so long, you've forgotten what young girls are like.'

Levarcham, who was Nessa's age, was not enough of a fool to remind the king's mother of this fact. Instead, she went on, 'We were out picking mushrooms one day when we heard the voices of young men singing a hunting song in the forest. When Deirdre heard them, that wild look came into her eyes again. I tried to hold her, but she threw down her basket and ran off among the trees.

'I followed as quickly as I could, arriving in time to see three young men in a glade, and Deirdre stepping out from behind a tree, into their path. She managed to find the one ray of sunlight in the dark forest and danced into it.

'A day's hunting had brought the blood into Naisi's cheeks, and I must admit he was as beautiful then as a man could be. And he was the first young thing like herself my Deirdre had seen. Perhaps she had been being fanciful and wilful until that moment, but once she saw Naisi, everything changed. It was in her face – and his, seeing her.

'She was not a child any more. A woman's guile came into her, and she pretended to be unaware of him until Naisi called out, "That is a

110

fine heifer before me." His brothers Ardan and Ainnle were with him, and they laughed, but Deirdre tossed her head so he could see the curls of her hair and answered, "In a land without bulls, the heifers grow sleek and fat with laziness."

' "If you are who I think you are," Naisi replied, "the king bull of Ulster claims you."

'Deirdre looked angry at this. "He is away at Emain Macha doing king-things; he is nothing to me, and I belong only to myself." She turned the curve of her cheek toward Naisi so he could admire its perfection. "Would you like me for yourself?" she asked.

'His brothers understood the danger then and tried to discourage him from her, but she smiled at them, and capered around them with pretty graces, and ran her fingers through their beards until their arguments dried in their throats.

'I stepped out from behind my tree to add my own pleas, but I was wasting my breath and my spittle. To give Naisi his due, he stood very straight and tried not to look at the girl. "I am Red Branch, my loyalty is sworn to the king. I cannot . . ."

' "Can you not?" Deirdre laughed at him. "Can you not indeed?" And she picked wildflowers and stuck them in his beard, and bent her body like a willow in the wind so he could see how supple she was.

'She was maturing before our eyes, a magical thing to watch. "Just come into our house and take a meal with us," she urged the young warriors, her eyes holding Naisi's all the time. "Just sit at our table and tell me about yourself and the world beyond this valley, for I am kept a prisoner here." She parted her lips and begged without words for rescue. Begged Naisi to take her away.'

'That's it,' commented Fergus mac Roy. 'Naisi's human.'

'Sworn to the king, sworn on his honour,' Nessa said darkly.

Levarcham told them, 'Naisi could not help himself by then. Deirdre was in all his pores. And his brothers were almost as beguiled as he was. You would have to see the girl to appreciate what she can do. I could only watch, powerless to prevent what was happening. She is so young! The king was wrong to shut her away as he did, part of the blame must be his!' she cried bitterly.

Cuchulain thought of the raven, and wondered.

The rest of Levarcham's tale was briefly told. Naisi and Deirdre had made her promise not to tell until they had time to clear the borders of Ulster, for the sons of Uisnach knew well enough that Conor mac Nessa would seek revenge for the theft of his woman. Deirdre had fled with her clothes and her jewels and a little harp her father had once sent her, and together with Naisi's brothers and some of their clansmen they were even now seeking safe haven, in Erin or beyond.

Exhausted by her narrative, Levarcham slumped into a bundle of misery. 'The king will kill me.'

'He will not,' Fergus assured her. 'Since the incident with Macha Fleet-Foot, he's taken a *ges* upon himself against hurting a woman in any way. Cathbad the druid predicted something terrible would happen if he caused the woman injury. He'll be furious with you, but he won't hurt you.'

'My son won't treat Naisi and his brothers so easily when he catches them,' said Nessa. 'I shudder to think of the punishment he will exact on them. And he will be justified!' she added, taking a sudden half-step away from Levarcham. Nessa knew how to choose among her loyalties.

The theft of Deirdre pushed other considerations into the background. Conor forgot about sending Cuchulain to train with the warrior-woman. He dispatched search parties in all directions and let it be known throughout the kingdoms of Erin that there was a reward for the lovers, but they could not be found. Together with his kinsmen, Naisi seemed to have fled the island altogether.

Conor mac Nessa was no longer cool and deliberate. He stalked the precincts of Emain Macha, giving off waves of anger, and everyone avoided him.

He awoke with a pounding heart in the middle of the night, clutching at his most recent dream of Deirdre, only to feel her fading from his outstretched arms. Night after night this happened, battering him with frustration.

He wondered if people were laughing at him behind their hands. A man in his middle years, losing a woman to a younger man. A king, whose virility represented the strength of his people, losing a woman to one of his most trusted warriors.

'They have fled across the sea to the east,' someone finally reported.

The king had decreed that Naisi and the sons of Uisnach were to be outlawed; outside the law, no longer protected by it. Any man could do anything he liked to them without fear of retribution in Erin.

But they were no longer in Erin.

The king was so distracted, his sons and foster-son took on many of his responsibilities. Follaman tried to listen to the complaints of clan-members; Fiacra, with Blai the distributor, parcelled out grain and goods to those entitled to them; Cormac Connlongas organised hunting parties; Cuchulain deployed the Red Branch to various clan-wars and skirmishes.

Though he longed to return to Brega, the Hound was too busy – nor did he think it was a good time to discuss with the king his own hopes for marriage. But at last Conor fought his way out of a sullen depression that had almost overwhelmed him, and resumed the reins of authority. He plunged into his work with a fierce outpouring of energy, as if to prove any suspicions about his strength and virility unfounded. He seemed determined to control and organise everyone and everything.

His eye lighted upon Cuchulain almost at once. 'Why aren't you with Skya, learning to be a better warrior?'

'I thought I was needed here . . .'

'I need you at your peak!' Conor cried. 'No one must think Ulster is growing soft. Be ready to leave for Skya's school for heroes by the next change of the moon.'

A frenzy of preparations began. At the end of the day, when the quilted quiet of Erin finally folded around him, Cuchulain lay on his bed and thought of Emer.

As companions for his journey, two Red Branch warriors were assigned to him, the redoubtable Conall Cearnach and Leary Buadach, known as the Battle-Winner. Leary was as talkative as Conall was taciturn. A burly man with too many teeth and not enough neck, he was slightly older than the other two, neither of whom had yet seen eighteen winters. But he respected them as men, for they had trophies in the House of the Red Branch.

They would journey to Skya's island with fishermen who regularly plied the waters off the north-east coast of Erin and knew their way along the jagged western coastline of Alba, where the island lay. Thinking of Alba, Leary remarked, 'We just might find Naisi there, you know. If we contrived to bring him back, think of the rewards the king would give us.'

'Naisi's Red Branch,' Cuchulain said shortly.

'Naisi's an outlaw now.'

'Naisi's a friend,' said the Hound, glaring at the other man.

'Friends today can be enemies tomorrow,' remarked Conall Cearnach.

'Not for me!' said Cuchulain. Refusing any further discussion of the matter, he bade the king and the Red Branch farewell, departed Emain Macha, and made his way, with Conall and Leary, to the coast where the boats awaited them.

113

I could not follow him, not across open water. I went as far as the strand where the silvery, spiky sea holly thrives, but from the moment Cuchulain gave himself into the care of Manannan of the Waves, he was beyond my influence. Though I flapped and screeched, he never looked back. He had flung his dreams towards Skya, his body was merely following.

I watched the boat ride out on a heavy westerly swell. For once, no rain was falling, but the northern coast always seems cold to me. I wondered if Cuchulain was cold in his boat.

He had many dangers to overcome before he could return, but if he did, I would be waiting, because I could not do otherwise. You must understand this: I was bound. Humans have freedom of choice, we do not. We occupy a disparate reality, though when the two overlap, one sometimes pulls the other apart.

In laughing play, the child called Setanta had unwittingly bound me to him for ever, obligating me to set the theme for his life and shape his destiny.

True commitment to a god is never made in the mind, but in the spirit.

9 Behind them, the voyagers left a troubled kingdom. Fergus never actually said, 'I told you so,' but Conor read it in his eyes. The relationship between the two became strained. Because Nessa invariably sided with her son, Fergus felt a chasm opening between himself and his wife as well.

The warriors of the Red Branch were also divided. Those who had not been close friends of the sons of Uisnach howled for Naisi's head on a pole. But there were others whose sympathies were with the exiles, and they did not try to hide it.

Quarrels erupted daily at Emain Macha. More often than he liked, Conor had to remind his followers that they occupied the king's *maigen*, and fighting was forbidden. The wisdom of the old law of sanctuary, like the wisdom of all ancient brehon law, became evident.

Fergus confessed to Cathbad the druid, 'I'm as bewildered as a goat in a grassy field, listening to thunder. I don't know where to stand. Was Conor at fault? Did his infatuation for that child reveal a weakness in himself? Or is he a victim to be avenged? Naisi is dear to me, you know. I trained him and his brothers in the Boys' Troop.'

'And the king is the king. As well as being your foster-son. Which tie is stronger?'

Fergus scratched his chest. 'That's what I dislike about druids, you answer questions with questions. I call it an evasive tactic.'

'We call it wisdom,' Cathbad said mildly.

Only the bards seemed to be benefiting from Deirdre's elopement. The escapade was fuel for their creative fires, and poets outdid themselves creating verbal visions of the king's lost love. Cattle-lords and seaweed gatherers alike listened open-mouthed to the romance of Naisi and Deirdre, imagining themselves in that young man's tunic – and getting out of it in a hurry, with such round white thighs waiting. Their women sighed with equal pleasure at thoughts of Naisi's impetuosity, his courage and daring for the sake of a woman.

The story was a sensation.

Like every tale, it reached Cruachan. Maeve was amused. 'If the girl is really so gorgeous, I'm not surprised Naisi went moonstruck over her. And his brothers too, apparently – following him into exile like that and taking their supporters with them. But Deirdre will have to keep them all enchanted once the first bloom wears off. If she can, I'll be truly impressed.'

Maeve's youthful bloom had long since worn off, but she knew how to keep men moonstruck over her. Cruachan of the Enchantments was aptly named.

Ailell was, by and large, a tolerant person. He took a certain pleasure in watching his wife exercise her power over other men. When she walked through the hall, men's eyes followed her like hounds on a leash. Ailell held himself in check when one of the watchers responded to some invisible signal from Maeve and followed her out of sight.

Ailell understood that these diversions were as necessary to his wife as his own dalliances were to him, and he had no intention of giving up random pleasures with plump serving girls. So he swallowed his jealousy – most of the time.

On the pillow they shared at night, Maeve remarked to her husband, 'This matter of Conor mac Nessa has set me to thinking. When he first took charge at Emain Macha, he was a bold warrior, not afraid of provoking battles with his neighbours to prove himself. Then he grew cautious. Now, we learn that a simple girl and a member of his own Red Branch have been able to dishonour him.

'He has become a weak king, my husband. A weak king with fat herds, when our own need replenishing.'

'We also need more bondwomen,' Ailell commented, twisting his heavy shoulders to avoid being poked by the sharp quill of a feather escaping the thick pallet on which they slept.

Word of new incursions from Connaught reached Emain Macha. Border skirmishes were common enough, but the raiders were becoming uncommonly aggressive. They were not just grabbing and running after a cheerful little battle, but were driving ever deeper into Ulster with an insolence that boded ill for the future.

Conor wondered if Maeve knew of the Pangs.

At his urging, more travelling bards visited the other kingdoms of Erin, singing not of Deirdre but of the valorous Red Branch and its terrifying Hound. No chieftain dared refuse a bard hospitality, for to do so meant disgrace – the bard would compose a satire about him and sing it in other strongholds. The highly polished weapon of bardic satire was as cruel as a sword blade and harder to stop. A man could be beaten with

116

it until he lost the will to defend what was his, and his enemies rolled over him like the tide.

At Conor's request, Athairne the chief bard of Ulster instructed the other poets in the tales they were to tell. After considerable thought the king asked that the story of the Plague of Birds be included.

'Now that Cuchulain is out of the country and won't be disturbed by it, I want this told to every chieftain with ears to listen,' Conor said. 'It will add to their fear of my wild young Wolfhound.'

Throughout the four kingdoms of Erin, chieftains and warriors heard the tale as Athairne told it and his apprentices dutifully memorised it. Ulster, Munster, Leinster, and Connaught all listened.

'A generation ago, in the season of harvest, the warriors of the Ulaid returned to Emain Macha. Long had they searched without success for the abducted wife of Sualtim of Dun Dalgan. But the earth was in labour and must be delivered, so at last they returned for the harvest rituals.

'Long was that winter, bitter and cold. When leaves sprang out again and the first new shoots appeared, a great host of birds appeared also and devoured them. The Ulstermen planted again, and the birds came again and destroyed this crop also. Again and again, until the land was barren and the season wasted. Bitter the night and the weeping of the women by autumn.

'Conor mac Nessa decreed that the warriors would hitch their chariots and drive across the land hub to hub, sweeping the birds before them and killing all they could. Every chariot bristled with spears as the hunters set forth. The birds leaped into the air, great flocks silver against the sun. And the light on their feathers was like a chain of gold, yoking them together.'

When Fergus and the older members of the Red Branch heard Athairne rehearsing the bards, their eyes met and they remembered as if it were yesterday.

They had pursued the birds south beyond Slieve Fuad. There was little danger of losing their prey, for the birds sang so sweetly as they flew that people came out of their duns to listen. But the warriors had hardened their hearts against beauty. The birds were a plague and had to be destroyed.

The massive flocks crossed mountain and meadow until they came at last to the river of the cow goddess, Boyne, south of Dun Dalgan.

When the Red Branch reached the riverbank, a light snow had begun to fall. Sualtim took several men to gather firewood, but the campfires gave no heat. Men huddled around them shivering, rubbing their hands together and blowing on them as they cursed the depredations of the birds. 'We'll kill them all,' they promised one another, 'and next spring we'll have crops again.' They were cold and they were hungry, and their voices were sullen.

Fergus and Bricriu were sent to find something to eat, and soon came hurrying back. 'We've found a dwelling not far from here, where a man and woman live who offer us shelter,' Fergus said.

Hard on his heels, Bricriu complained, 'It's only a small, mean place, narrow and without furnishings. They can't offer proper hospitality to the Red Branch.'

'As long as they can offer a roof, I'm willing,' said the Beetle of Ulster, glaring around at the others as if daring them to disagree. 'Lead us to it, Fergus.'

They followed the riverbank to a white-pebbled ford and crossed the winter-shallow water. Frozen fields rose beyond in a gentle curve. Fergus drove his chariot in the lead, with the king beside him. Bricriu, muttering about the unworthiness of the place, brought up the rear. The wind had started to blow pellets of ice into the men's faces.

Gergind whistled in surprise; the regal mound of a mighty dun rose before them. 'This is your "small, mean place," Bricriu?'

'It didn't look the same before . . .'

'Your eyes have gone bad. Too much honey on your bread.'

Conor mac Nessa pounded on a stout oaken door. It was opened at once. Golden light beamed out upon the half-frozen warriors, revealing in silhouette a man who spoke words of welcome.

The men of the Red Branch had followed him down a narrow passage into a stone-walled chamber with a corbelled ceiling three spear-lengths high. There they were served meat and mead until their bellies ached. A fire roared on a hearth, driving the cold from their bones.

As they were picking the last fragments of meat out of their teeth with goosequill splinters, Conor had asked their host, 'Where is your wife? I want to thank her for allowing us her home.'

The man, who had stood in the shadow of a recess in the wall throughout the meal, replied, 'She is in another chamber with her attendants. Tonight she gives birth.'

'A most auspicious occasion, then!' Sualtim had cried, lifting his cup. 'Let us drink another round in honour of the new life!'

Sometime later – they could never remember how much later – the weary Ulstermen had wrapped themselves in their cloaks and fallen asleep on soft pallets provided by the owner of the dun.

The sun was high in the sky when the first of the Red Branch awakened.

Conor mac Nessa sat up slowly, rubbing his head. 'My mouth tastes worse than a badger's guts,' he muttered, rolling his thick tongue between his gummy teeth. 'Strange, I don't recall drinking that much . . . Fergus!' he yelped in astonishment.

The king of Ulster had just realised he was sitting on open ground. No walls surrounded him, no corbelled ceiling rose above him. His men lay around him in the same positions in which they had fallen asleep inside, on soft pallets. Now they lay outside, on bare earth.

'Unnhh?' Fergus opened one eye at Conor's shout. 'Whazzat?'

'Look around you!'

Fergus levered himself into a sitting position and rubbed his eyes. His bellow of disbelief woke the others.

What they saw – or did not see – shocked them sober.

'Where in the nine waves did that dun go?'

'It's magic,' Fergus decided. 'I know the smell of magic. And I don't like it.'

'I didn't like anything about this from the beginning,' said Bricriu Bitter-Tongue. 'Didn't I tell you? Didn't I tell everyone?'

Conor stretched himself to his full height, a tall and splendid man in the thin, bright light of a winter sun. He looked down toward the river they had forded the night before. This morning it was contentedly chewing its banks as if nothing remarkable had happened. 'We're in the same place we lay down to sleep,' he said, perplexed. 'This is just where the dun stood, and we came up this very hill . . . from there . . .' He pointed.

'The doorway was here,' Fergus said, 'I'd swear to it by the sun and stars. And when we entered, we left our weapons outside . . .' He began to pace off the area.

'With our chariots!' Conor finished for him. He whirled and ran toward his own war-cart, standing as he had left it the night before, the horses cropping frozen grass nearby.

When he reached the chariot, he skidded to a halt and stared down with a bemused expression on his face.

Curled up in the bottom of the chariot slept his sister Dectera. A tiny baby was clasped in her arms, sharing her cloak.

'Sualtim!' the king had called. 'You'd better come over here. I've found your wife.'

119

10 Unaware that the king was disseminating the story of his birth with its overtones of strange magic, Dectera's son sat in the prow of a fisherman's boat and watched land loom out of the mist.

'There's Skya's island,' the boat's owner said proudly. 'I got you here as I promised, alive and safe.'

'I'm not so certain about the alive part,' moaned Leary, whose face had taken on a permanently greenish hue during the voyage. 'Manannan is not my favourite god; I don't think he likes me at all.'

Privately, Cuchulain agreed; the seas had been rough. But as in the game of hurling, the goal was what mattered and they had reached their goal, which appeared to be a wild and desolate place where a man could lose his life as easily as he could shed a hair from his head.

The boat's bottom scraped on a narrow shingle beach.

The trio from Ulster unloaded their gear and headed inland, leaving the fishermen to effect some needed repairs to their vessel before setting sail for Erin again. The island offered expanses of rolling, windbeaten terrain covered with coarse forage and outcroppings of rock that might easily hide a troop of armed men. Cuchulain proceeded with caution, alert to the slightest sound.

Tensing abruptly, he raised his hand to signal a halt. The unmistakable clang of a hammer on an anvil rang through the air.

'A forge! A smith is a good omen for me,' the Hound said. 'Let's get close enough to have a good look at it, and if it appears harmless, we'll ask for hospitality.'

The smithy proved to be very like those in Ulster, a few domestic buildings and a mud-walled forge. The rhythm of the hammer sounded steadily. Raising his voice, Cuchulain called, 'We are travellers who claim the right of hospitality!'

A thick accent answered him immediately. 'If they speak like that here, I might as well have stayed at home,' Conall said. 'I'll never understand them.'

120

'I've heard the accent before,' Leary told him. 'It's a form of Gaelic, just listen and you'll recognise some words soon enough.'

The smith emerged from his forge and trotted forward to meet his visitors. Swarthy and short-legged, he was not even as tall as Cuchulain, and everything about him was dark. Dark thicket of hair, dark eyes in deep hollows, skin dark with soot. 'He's a Pict,' Leary said in an aside to his companions. 'I've seen others like him.'

'Are they to be trusted?' Conall whispered.

'As much as any other man.'

Conall put his hand on his sword hilt.

The smith identified himself as Donal White-Foot – 'The soles of my feet are the cleanest part of me,' – and confirmed that he was indeed of the Pictish race, though he could speak several languages, including his rough approximation of Gaelic. 'I get a lot of business, being the only man with a forge on this side of the island. Various fisherfolk and sea-traders put in here, and I have to be able to understand what they want. Weights and measures, axles, tools, rivets for spear heads . . . I meet a lot of different people.'

'You've just met the Hound of Cullen,' said Leary Buadach. 'And this is Conall Cearnach, while I am known as the Battle-Winner.'

The smith nodded, unimpressed. Warriors. They liked those bristly names. 'There are no public hostels here, but I can offer you some boiled goat, and some sour wine from the Middle Sea. I was saving it for a special occasion.'

'This is a special occasion!' Leary boomed. 'Break it out!'

Later, Cuchulain stood the first watch so Conall and Leary would not need to wake him for a turn and risk the *ges*. To amuse himself in the long night, he thought about *gessa*. Awakening him was prohibited, yet his mother had done it with her cry in the night. And that had begun a chain of consequence that led him to Emain Macha, and to here. Seen in that light, the breaking of a *ges* seemed to have been beneficial. Yet belief was copper-fastened and must not be set aside; he knew this. Sooner or later, the long road upon which that awakening had set him must lead to a disaster.

But first he would be famous. He knew this too. He willed it.

The snoring of his companions mingled with the snuffles and snorts of Donal White-Foot and his family, asleep on grass-filled pallets nearby. Normal, ordinary sounds in an alien night.

Cuchulain was acutely aware of the differences between this land and his own; a man who lives in intimacy with the natural world responds to every subtle difference of scent and change of light. When he put back his head and looked up, he recognised a slight alteration in the position of the stars themselves, the landmarks in the sky, as his old tutor Caisin had called them.

I am really here, he thought. I have come across the sea.

He was glad he had taken the first watch. He could not have slept anyway, tired though he was. The blood prickled in his veins in anticipation of new adventures. He decided to stay awake throughout the night and let his friends have their rest.

But when they awakened at first light, Conall and Leary were changed men.

Conall arose first, massaging his flat belly with the palm of his hand. 'I need a meal of good Ulster beef,' he said. 'All night I've dreamed about it. That stringy goat we ate is sitting in me like a death-ball.'

'I would settle for a breath of Ulster air,' Leary joined in, rubbing sleep from his eyes. 'As soon as I put my head down last night, I began dreaming of Emain Macha; I ache for the place with a pain worse than that of a broken tooth. I'm sorry we came here now, I don't like it and I want to go back. I *need* to go back, Cuchulain,' he added with surprising fervour.

'I don't believe my ears. The two of you, brave men of the Red Branch, sniffing with homesickness? We've only just arrived!'

Conall shrugged. 'You've arrived; it was our job to see you safely here, and here you are. I can't explain it, but I feel as Leary does. The most unbearable longing for Ulster torments me. I *have* to go back. Leary, if we hurry, perhaps we can catch our boatmen before they set sail for the return voyage.'

Cuchulain looked from one to the other in astonishment. Their eyes seemed strangely glazed; they were behaving like men under compelling orders.

Compelling . . . and was there not a certain scent on the wind?

A horrid suspicion occurred to Cuchulain.

He found Donal White-Foot already at his forge, using a bellows and two leather bags to blow the fire to full heat.

'Tell me, smith – is there a druid on this island? An enchanter capable of putting men under a powerful spell?'

'A sorcerer, you mean?'

'Something like that.'

'There is such a man, not far from here, in fact. I don't have much to do with him, but he did send me a bit of business recently. A visitor from Erin, like yourselves, had broken a piece of equipment, and I was needed to repair it for him.'

'From Erin?'

'He was a representative of someone important over there, a cattle-lord . . . or a hosteler . . . whose name was . . . ah, let me think.' Donal rummaged deep in his black mop of hair with broken fingernails. 'Fingal. I believe it was Fingal.'

'Forgall,' Cuchulain corrected him with dreadful certainty.

'Forgall indeed!' The smith smiled, but Cuchulain was not smiling.

'That man is an enemy of mine,' he said. 'I want something he does not want me to have; I was warned against him. Now, he has got to my men as they slept. He hired your druid to raise a vision powerful enough to draw my companions away from me and leave me alone on this island to whatever dangers might lurk here.'

How clear it seemed to Cuchulain in the clear morning light. Having identified the source, he could almost taste the peculiar flavour of druid magic on his tongue, faintly acrid, the earth-scented, bittersweet odour that Cathbad could summon in the ring of standing stones.

Magic, he thought resentfully. Not fair play. That's one against you, Forgall. But he realised he had underestimated the malice of the man, never having expected him to send men across the sea to arrange harm for him.

He tried to argue with Conall and Leary, but it was no use, they were determined. Yet even as they hurried away from him, he glimpsed embarrassment on their faces and knew they wished it otherwise. 'Safe home to you!' he called to them.

Donal White-Foot apologised. 'Having guests attacked in this way while they slept under my protection – I'll be disgraced.'

'I won't tell,' Cuchulain assured him. 'Perhaps it wasn't an attack; perhaps they were both just homesick.'

Donal narrowed his eyes until two slivers of obsidian gleamed between his lids. 'I think not. I awoke this morning myself with a mighty desire on me to see Erin. I who have never been off this island in my life, nor wanted to. And my wife and children the same, all eager to go west. I hope to hear the end of it soon. How long do you think the spell will last?'

'Only until my companions reach home again, I suspect. Say a fortnight, to be certain.'

'A fortnight! A fortnight of listening to my family plead for something they don't really want and I can't give them. Grand. I haven't been so happy since I dropped an anvil on my foot.'

Cuchulain took a gold chain from his neck. 'This won't compensate for your troubles,' he said, 'but please accept it. And if you ever have need of a champion to fight on your behalf, send this chain to Emain Macha, the royal fort of Ulster, to summon me.'

'Who am I to ask for again?'

'The Hound of Cullen.'

'Ah. The Hound. I'll try to remember. The Hound. Ulster.' Donal nodded and pressed his finger against the side of his head, trying to force the name through his skull into his memory.

As soon as Cuchulain had bathed his face and eaten some dry bread and goat's cheese, he went on his way. The last he heard, Donal the smith was still muttering to himself, 'The Hound. The Hound . . . of Ulster.'

Cuchulain wandered half a day through unfamiliar land. He had been given only approximate directions to Skya's camp, and had expected he would be able to ask the way once he arrived on the island. But whenever he saw someone – a dark child picking its nose, a wood-gatherer searching for roots to burn – he asked for and was given directions, and no two sets of directions agreed.

He found himself longing for the voice of a raven, but he saw no ravens on Skya's island. Only cormorants and gulls inhabited these skies, and they did not know Cuchulain.

He badly needed sleep and knew it, but he dared not. Once he reached Skya, he hoped the spell would be behind him; then he could sleep. He did sit down to rest for a while, however, experiencing the land and the light, his back propped against an outcropping of stone.

Then he went on again.

As the shadows began to grow longer, he glimpsed a glow of a campfire coming to life, half-hidden by the curve of a hillock. He approached quietly, keeping himself behind the shielding earth until he knew the nature of the firebuilders. When he was close enough to recognise Ulster accents, his heart leaped.

A male voice was saying, '. . . as good as any other place for now.'

Another answered, 'We could go on.'

'Where?' the first replied wearily. 'We're exhausting her to no purpose, one place is as dangerous as another.'

'If I weren't with you, there would be less danger for you,' a woman said. 'But I must be with you. Ah, Naisi! What choices have we?'

Cuchulain drew in his breath. He had recognised the first speaker almost at once. 'Naisi!' he cried out. 'Is it you?'

He was answered by the unmistakable sound of swords being drawn. Then, tentatively, 'Cuchulain? Can it be?'

'It can and is.' The Hound stepped forward, holding both hands well away from the hilt of Hardhead. 'And I haven't come after you, I'm here to complete my training with Skya the warrior-woman.'

Upon hearing these words, Naisi hurried forward to greet him, looking visibly relieved.

Thinner than the last time Cuchulain had seen him, Naisi was still a beautiful man. Lustrous black hair rippled in heavy waves to his shoulders. His complexion was very fair, but his lips and cheeks were flushed with healthy blood. The three fatal colours of black, white, and red. His eyes held the wary expression of a hunted animal.

'Make camp with us,' he urged Cuchulain, 'even though there's a tail left to the day. We long for news from home, and there's food. You remember what good hunters my brothers are? Ardan, Ainnle, step out here and show us you have something to stretch a friend's belly.'

Naisi's brothers came forward then to add their welcome and show Cuchulain a recently slain deer. A third man was with them. 'Cuchulain!' he said with joy. 'Soft on our eyes you are.'

Ferdiad mac Daman had become one of Cuchulain's closest friends when they were in the Boys' Troop together. Though Ferdiad was older by several seasons, the two had found they had much in common, including the bond formed by both being outsiders in a sense.

Entitled by blood to be one of the Red Branch when he matured, Ferdiad was also, according to the bards, descended from the tribe of the Fir Bolg, a harsh, secretive race who had been in Erin before its conquest by the Gael and even before the Tuatha de Danann. The Fir Bolg were dark, pinch-featured, and narrow-built, whereas Ferdiad was large and fair, yet there were still enough differences in style and temperament between reserved Ferdiad and the gregarious Boys' Troop to mean he must fight for acceptance. So he had been sympathetic to Cuchulain's own attempts to establish himself.

Fergus had discovered the two to be well matched in ability and had often teamed them together. Both were shy, which they would only admit to each other; Ferdiad had a calming effect on the intense Cuchulain, and Cuchulain in turn brought an unsuspected sense of humour to the surface in Daman's son. When the older Ferdiad took up arms and was sent out on patrol, Cuchulain missed him desperately.

125

Now, he saw the matured version of his friend, a man of full eighteen winters, with a sandy beard and a blunt, rough-hewn face. Ferdiad spoke with the same familiar husky drawl, however, and moved with the same deceptively shambling gait.

'I had no idea you were here,' Cuchulain said, embracing him.

'Suddenly last season, the idea came upon me. I thought it would be worth a pair of bullocks from my entitlements to have Skya put a sharp edge on me. I've taken a course of training and was headed for the coast and Ulster when I ran into the sons of Uisnach and decided to spend some time with them. But you! Let's have a look at you!'

He pushed Cuchulain to arm's length and stared him up and down. 'You've filled out, surely. From your body, one might think you an old warrior of twenty. That beardless face belongs on a boy, however. And those silver eyes belong to a wolf. There is no age in them. People will always have trouble knowing how old you are, I think.'

'A high-hearted man is beautiful at any age,' said a voice.

Looking past Ferdiad's shoulder, Cuchulain saw the final member of Naisi's party.

Seared into his memory for the rest of his life would be that first vision of Deirdre.

Conor mac Nessa's stolen woman. Fedlimid's accursed daughter.

As soon as he had recognised Naisi, he had known she must be somewhere nearby, amid the broken land and tumbling gorse, but there was no way he could have prepared himself for the full effect of her. There were no weapons for defending oneself against Deirdre.

Unique among mortals, she was perfectly symmetrical. One half of her mirrored the other to the curve of an eyelash. Neither eye was infinitesimally larger than the other; neither shoulder higher than its mate. Even her pale hair fell in identical ringlets to left and right. Her face was a flawless oval, holding eyes of fathomless green. Her body was composed of a series of curves so harmonious and flowing, she seemed to be in motion even when standing still.

Ainnle, seeing the expression on Cuchulain's face, laughed. 'Close your mouth, Hound. She affects everyone like that the first time they see her, but you'll get used to her eventually.'

Getting used to Deirdre, Cuchulain thought, would be like getting used to staring into the midday sun.

The sons of Uisnach had made themselves a campsite in the lap of hillocks, concealed by low-growing scrub. Cuchulain deposited his own pack of supplies with theirs, then joined Ardan in finding enough burnable material to build up a cooking fire.

A tiny, undernourished deer was the best the area provided, the creatures being rare to the point of extinction on the island. Ainnle neatly skinned it, turned the hide inside out to form a pouch, and filled it with water. He suspended this improvised cooking vessel over the fire by means of stakes, then cut the stringy meat into small chunks and put them into the water. The water within the hide kept it from burning until the meat had boiled long enough to be chewable, and since Ainnle had turned the hair to the inside of the pouch, it did not scorch and stink to ruin their appetites.

Waiting for their meal, the group gathered around the fire and talked of commonplaces, avoiding awkward topics. Deirdre and Naisi held hands with just their fingertips touching, yet the afterglow radiating from them was so intense, it made Cuchulain's breath catch in his throat. He did not have to see with his eyes to know that Naisi touched her more intimately when no one was watching, petted her, stroked her, pressed himself against that incomparable curving softness.

As soon as Ainnle pronounced the meat edible, the hungry group devoured it. When her portion was gone, Deirdre snuggled against Naisi and cajoled him out of the tenderest bits of his meal. Then she moved on to Ardan and Ainnle, teasing them until she had taken the choicest morsels from them as well – morsels they had obviously been saving for her, Cuchulain noticed. They fed her from their fingers like a small child as she cuddled close.

He realised she was not being deliberately flirtatious. Raised with only an old woman for company, Deirdre had been starved so long for human contact that she retained an infant's need to be hugged and caressed. In a flash of perception, Cuchulain thought that she flung herself into the arms of the sons of Uisnach as he had once flung himself into the Red Branch, seeking the warmth of a family.

But when Deirdre looked at Naisi, Cuchulain recognised the bone-deep passion of a grown woman who could love with an intensity capable of inflaming armies.

Beautiful Deirdre. Levarcham had said she was spoiled, yet the treasures she had once demanded had been left behind in Erin, and she did not seem to miss them, so long as she had Naisi. She was blooming heedless and content in very stony soil, needing only the devotion that surrounded her. But beneath her fragrance, Cuchulain thought he detected an unsettling whiff of decay.

He saw the way Ferdiad's eyes burned when he looked at her.

The meal concluded, Deirdre and Naisi wandered off together, and Ardan and Ainnle fell into a good-natured squabble about hunting. Ferdiad took advantage of the moment to draw Cuchulain aside. 'Now that you've seen Fedlimid's daughter, what do you think of her?'

'She appears flawless,' Cuchulain replied guardedly.

'She is. Naisi claims she doesn't even have a birthmark.'

Cuchulain considered this. An image of the tiny mole at the edge of Emer's mouth came into his mind. 'I wouldn't want a perfect woman. She would make me itchy.'

Ferdiad's husky voice dropped still lower. 'I might as well admit to you, I haven't wanted a woman at all, I've been too busy. Until I saw Deirdre. I should be on the sea for Ulster by now, but I'm not.

'I'm glad you're here, Cuchulain, to keep me from getting myself killed. If I laid hands on that woman Naisi would take my head, old friend or not. Yet I don't seem to be able to walk away from her.'

'Walk away with me, then. Accompany me to Skya's school. My companions deserted me, and I don't want to be without a friend to guard my back in an unfamiliar place. The king is generous with me; I can pay the cost of a second course of training for you, and I won't let you go chasing after Deirdre.'

With obvious relief, Ferdiad said, 'I accept gladly! Can we go at dawn? I don't trust myself and I don't understand myself; the first time I saw Deirdre, I almost went through poor Naisi for a shortcut.'

'We'll be up with the sun and gone,' Cuchulain promised. 'And I'll tell you something for nothing. Beautiful she is, but I think the disaster Cathbad predicted for Deirdre still clings to her like the smell of rotten fruit.'

'Naisi is welcome to her then, though he doesn't deserve disaster. Still, that may be the very thing in her that he loves most. There's a dark streak running through the Gael.'

That night, Cuchulain and Ferdiad shared the warmth of their cloaks, and at dawn they told Naisi they were going together to Skya.

'I wish I could go with you,' he said wistfully. 'To train with the most famous of teachers in the arts of war . . . but I have no wars left to fight except my own.'

'What will become of you?' asked Cuchulain.

'We left a band of our clansmen on the other side of the island scouting, as we've been doing, for a safe haven. I don't think we'll find a suitable place here, however. We may eventually settle in Alba; there seem to be better hiding places in its mountains and forests than anywhere else . . .'

His voice trailed away. Cuchulain glanced toward Deirdre, wondering if any woman could be worth the unhappiness of exile.

As he looked, the rising sun haloed her hair and outlined her body.

For one heartbeat, Cuchulain had his hand on the hilt of his sword and was ready to run it through Naisi's throat.

Horrified, he took a step backward and flung the sword from him. He saw understanding and something akin to pity on Naisi's face as he staggered away, fighting back the taste of bile.

A woman's magic had almost robbed him of his honour.

Hastily gathering up his things, Cuchulain pondered this new revelation of magic.

Deirdre was not a druid, yet her enchantment had been as overwhelming as the most potent sorcery. Perhaps, he thought – walking the idea step by step through his brain – perhaps everyone has some potential for magic.

If this is true, we are all weapons, and the deadliest is Fedlimid's daughter!

11

After they had walked for a while, Ferdiad signalled a halt. 'I have a gift from Skya in my pack, and I should put it on before I see her again.' He paused to take out a peculiar set of armour made of overlapping plates of translucent horn. When he pulled it over his head, it fitted like skin.

'You look like a lizard,' Cuchulain told him, laughing. 'Is that comfortable?'

'It's so light I hardly know I have it on, but it will turn almost any blade. Skya is in the habit of giving her best students gifts, a unique one for each. Usually, I wear this at all times, but I . . . ah . . . took it off when I met Deirdre.'

Cuchulain said nothing. There was nothing to say.

As they continued their journey, the Hound told Ferdiad of Emer, and Forgall the Wily.

'I could have predicted you'd have difficulties. Forgall has a reputation for being nasty to anyone who even blinks in the direction of his favourite child. It's a pity you don't want the older one, Cuchulain; I understand he'd give her gladly, with a score of heifers into the bargain.'

'I've chosen Emer. Even if I have to fight for her. We are a match for each other, she has wit and spirit and . . .' He fell to describing her in glowing terms, and as he did so, the memory of Deirdre faded into insignificance, driven back by the clear gaze of Forgall's daughter. 'I'll fight for her,' Cuchulain said in conclusion. 'And I'll win her. Nothing can stop me.'

Ferdiad shot the smaller man an admiring look. 'You can make the most extravagant claims, yet coming from you they don't seem like boasting. If you told me you could split open a mountain, I think I'd believe you.'

'Because I'd believe it myself,' Cuchulain replied.

And that was also an aspect of magic.

After passing a huddle of earth-walled huts, the two men climbed a barren knoll, and the wind hit them with enough force to steal their breath. Ferdiad pointed. 'Skya's stronghold is over there.'

The hill on which they stood dropped away suddenly to form a cliff face below them. At the base of the cliff, water boiled amid black rocks. The sea had dug deep into the coast here, cutting out chunks. One chunk formed a narrow finger of land running back from a stony beach to a dark furring of stunted trees. Glimpsed through the trees were buildings and a strip of palisade.

'How do we reach it, Ferdiad?'

'There's a bridge, of sorts, but it's no path for a weak man. Both ends are low and the middle is high, tied with ropes staked to either shore. The planks are slippery with spume from the sea, and the slightest wind makes it buck like an untamed horse. The only handhold is a rope of twisted gorse too prickly to grasp.'

'It sounds as if Skya doesn't want to encourage casual visitors.'

Ferdiad laughed. 'Only the hardiest are welcome at her camp.'

As the two made their way down the cliff face to the bridge, Cuchulain realised they had an audience. From the seemingly empty land, first one man and then another appeared at the top of the cliff to peer down on them, eyes glinting in anticipation.

'Watching strangers fall off the bridge into the water is one of the major amusements around here,' Ferdiad said.

Cuchulain took a hard look at the ropes and stakes holding the end of the bridge. 'This would be a good place for one of Forgall's tricks,' he told his friend, but the fastenings seemed secure enough. 'Is there any special technique for crossing?'

'Luck and determination. I've seen strong men be thrown off and drown. But I can go first and show you . . .'

Before he could set action to word, Cuchulain had pushed past him and, with one audacious bound, was first upon the bridge. At once the structure swayed violently, like a boat keeling over.

The Hound stepped back on to solid ground.

A snigger was heard from the spectators.

Scowling, Cuchulain tried again. This time, he had taken several careful steps on the slippery planking before the bridge suddenly buckled, its centre soaring upward. Cuchulain grabbed at the hand rope and took a palmful of gorse prickles. He retreated a second time, shaking his stinging fingers and swearing under his breath.

Now the laughter was cruel. Some watchers jeered.

'Let me go first,' Ferdiad urged.

'Stand where you are!' The Hound stood still also, letting the laughter pour down on him, seeping like acid into muscle and bone.

Reaching deep, he summoned the strength of the Rage.

Ferdiad had last witnessed Cuchulain's famed frenzy during a skirmish with Leinstermen the sunseason before. Cuchulain had still seemed to be a youngster then. Now, for all his smooth cheeks, he was a man.

His features contorted, became unrecognisable. The lower lids lifted to accentuate the mad glare of his eyes; one narrowed to a slit, the other bulged from its socket. Cuchulain's face turned scarlet as he bared teeth so clean, so white, they resembled a predator's fangs. A guttural roar came from his throat, a sound not human.

Ferdiad thought the sun, which had been brightly shining, dimmed at that moment. Or perhaps its strength was bled off into the hair of the Hound, which flared with a spectral aura radiating outward as each shaft rose from his skull, tipped with fire. A terrible glow pulsed from Cuchulain's body. The roar sounded again, a manic battle cry.

In one mighty leap, like a salmon climbing a waterfall, the Hound landed squarely at the midpoint of the bridge. Spectators gasped. As they said later, it would have taken a fast-running man six strides to reach the centre, even if he could have kept his footing on the slippery planks. But Cuchulain's feet barely touched the planks before they were off again. He did not try to grasp the rope of gorse, he just hit and jumped a second time and was on the other side.

On Skya's private landholding.

The watchers on the cliff above held up their hands to make the signs of protection against dangerous gods.

The creature on the far side of the bridge turned and called back, in its inhuman roar, 'Ferdiad! Follow me!' Then it plunged into the trees.

Ferdiad stood staring at the bridge. Then he looked to the cliff above. The spectators had gone, fled back to their homes in terror. Which was just as well, he thought. He did not want anyone to see him as he shrugged off his cloak and wrapped it around his hands. Then he edged carefully out on to the bridge, grasping the gorse hand rope and shifting weight from one foot to the other with infinite care. Hanging on and sweating, he made his way to the other side.

Cuchulain, already out of sight among the trees, had not seen his crossing. The Hound was preoccupied with other concerns. Inside his altered body, he was fighting to gain control. He did not want Skya to see him as he was. He struggled through a clotted red haze, trying to find some shred of Setanta to seize and hang on to.

The stronghold of Skya the warrior was somewhere between a rough battle encampment and a full-scale fort. No earthwork bank shielded it; none was necessary, as it was surrounded by water. But she had a palisade of sharp-pointed timbers and a guard at her gate, and within was a crude residence of stone and mud, a coarse rectangular building that could function as feasting hall or guest house, and an assortment of campsites where her trainees assembled. Members of her clan moved freely through the gateway. The men were windburned and knotty-muscled, and the women were not the sort who put their hands over their mouths and giggled at the sight of strangers. They gave Cuchulain the same challenging glare he was receiving from the guard at the gate.

Dressed in a coat of fitted leather that reached to mid-thigh, Skya's gatekeeper was a woman.

She stood a head taller than Cuchulain, and probably weighed more. Her heavy cheekbones filled her face, her mouth was no more than a stern slash. Hair and eyes were of a matching mud colour. The eyes raked the Hound from his head to his heels.

'What do you want here?' Her voice was like cracking ice.

'I've been sent by the king of Ulster, my foster-father, to complete my warrior training.'

The guard grunted, unimpressed, and gestured toward the dwelling house with a twitch of her shoulder before returning her gaze to the woods.

But he knew he was being watched, and fervently hoped his appearance had returned to normal. Taking a deep breath, Cuchulain selected his favourite spear from his pack, hefted it, and ran straight for Skya's door.

The guard's reflexes were half a heartbeat too slow. She whirled and came after him, but by that time he had put his full force behind his thrust and driven the point of his spear completely through the wooden door.

He heard a yell of consternation inside.

The door swung inward just as the guard's hand gripped his shoulder. 'One step and you're dead,' her cold voice informed him. He felt the tip of her sword press against his spine.

'You made an impressive approach,' said the woman who stood within the open doorway. 'It's all right, Uta. Let him go. This lad may damage my door, but he can never hurt me.' She took half a step backward and beckoned to Cuchulain to follow her.

She could only be Skya, he thought. If the spirit within shaped the exterior body to some degree, then she was as moulded by her nature as

Conor mac Nessa was by his. Skya's short-cropped hair was the same colour as the iron shortsword thrust through her belt, and her face was as battered as the sword's blade. Both had seen hard use. A ridge of scar tissue ran from the woman's left temple, puckering the flesh at the corner of her eye before skidding across her cheek to twist one nostril into a permanent sneer, drawing up the lip below. On the right side of her jaw was a second old wound, a deep pit remaining where bone had once been gouged out. Skya's face resembled an eroded hillside where two hot blue fires still blazed in deep pits.

'I don't have time to instruct children,' she said to Cuchulain.

'I'm not a child.'

'Then where's your beard?'

'It never seems to grow. But I assure you I have a man's parts otherwise,' he added, a muscle tightening in his jaw.

Skya twitched back a smile.

His spear still quivered in the door, but Cuchulain had Hardhead at his waist. He did not take his eyes from Skya's, did not make the mistake of glancing at her sword to warn her of his intention. In one smooth motion, as swift as his salmon-leap across the bridge, he had Hardhead in his hand and its point between her flat breasts.

'I've come to be your pupil. Or I can kill you where you stand.'

For a second time, the guardian of the gate seized his shoulder, but Skya said dryly, 'I believe my visitor means his words.' To her credit, she had not flinched. She was a warrior who had faced death many times, and had forgotten how to be frightened.

The tableau held, with both Cuchulain and Skya at the point of swords. Cuchulain was aware of other people in the hall, but none of them dared move.

Then a cheery whistle from the doorway broke the tension. 'I see you've met my old friend Cuchulain!' Ferdiad called. 'And you're trying each other already. Good, that. He's the student who will make your name immortal, warrior-woman.' Ferdiad sauntered into the hall as if he were coming on to a friendly playing field. 'Uta, you're as charming and hospitable as ever.' He clapped the guard on the back so hard, Cuchulain felt her blade skid against his spine. He spun on his heel and caught her wrist, raising his knee in the same motion so he could slam her arm across the hard muscles of his thigh and break her grip on the sword. The weapon clattered to the floor.

At once he felt a colder, deadlier blade against his own neck.

'You're good, lad,' Skya told him. 'But not as good as I am.'

He turned his head very carefully to avoid cutting his own throat. For all its nicks, Skya's blade was keen enough to slice a hair in two lengthwise. Keeping her gaze fixed on Cuchulain, she said, 'Tell me who this is, Ferdiad.'

'Cullen's Hound. The foster-son of the king of Ulster.'

'Conor mac Nessa sends his greetings,' Cuchulain said, as if he were a welcome guest laden with ambassadorial gifts. He forced a smile.

Skya did not move for another long moment, then a rumble began in her belly. It worked its way up, up, to erupt in a bellow of laughter. She lowered her sword and threw back her head.

'Your friend is so brazen he must be either superhuman or simple-minded, Ferdiad! Either way . . . what are you standing around for?' she shouted at the servants in her hall. 'Bring us some beer!'

Cuchulain was warmly welcomed and offered the hospitality of Skya's camp, which was crude even by the standards of Dun Dalgan. But she gave the two young men a huge meal of coarse fare and sat talking with them late into the night.

'I'll be happy to train the fosterling of the king of Ulster,' she told Cuchulain, 'and for that gold arm ring you wear, I'll give Ferdiad here some additional polishing to keep you company. A warrior should always have a friend at his back. But I warn you – you must be ready to fight to the death for me if need be. My pupils are my army.'

'Have you many enemies?' Cuchulain wondered.

'Only one. We are necessary to each other, I think. If it weren't for Ayfa, I would have let my sword get dull and my muscles flabby, and I serve the same purpose for her. I trained her myself once, here in this school, and there are days on which she surpasses me. She is war-leader for her clan beyond those hills, for all she's still a young woman. Sometimes she tries to steal my livestock or enslave my clanfolk, and sometimes I do the same to her. I hear she has some fine new heifers she recently acquired from somewhere – I wouldn't mind having those.'

'Ayfa's a young woman,' Ferdiad told Cuchulain, 'but she's a fighter. You can lose your head to her sword before you get close enough to enjoy her body.'

Training was to begin with the next sunrise. Cuchulain and Ferdiad were assigned groundsleeping space next to a stone-rimmed firepit near the fort's main gateway, a campsite already inhabited by six warriors from Gaul. While the newcomers were settling themselves, the Gauls exchanged names and histories.

'We also came across open sea,' their leader explained in yet another variant of the Celtic mother tongue which had spawned both Gaulish and Gaelic. 'We fought our way across the land of the Britons to get here, for we are sworn to take back the secrets of this famous woman's training skills for our own tribe.'

Fame, Cuchulain thought enviously. They've heard of Skya as far away as Gaul . . . wherever that is.

Skya's fame had reached farther still, however. The next day another student arrived, a man whose language no one could understand. With gestures and guttural grunts he managed to communicate that he had travelled a great number of nights, coming all the way from the dark forests of the Teutons, north and east of Gaul. He was an exotic figure. Atop his square skull he wore a bronze helmet surmounted by the figure of a large boar. Dressed in furs and untanned hides, he seemed impervious to cold, ate unbelievable quantities of food, and only smiled when someone was wounded in competition.

The Gauls avoided him; they had no fondness for the Teutons. 'He doesn't wash,' Ferdiad remarked in disgust. 'The Gauls don't do much bathing either, but they don't smell like that one. They claim his tribe mates with bears.'

Everyone showed a healthy respect for the Teuton's strength and ferocity at battle practice, however.

Skya was a hard taskmaster. She had Cuchulain demonstrate every spear-throw and sword-thrust he knew and found fault with each of them. Though he could outrun anyone in the camp, she called his running insufficient; even his salmon leap did not impress her. 'Higher, harder, faster,' she urged continually. He responded, thriving on her demands, flattered by someone who drove him as hard as he wanted to be driven. It showed she had confidence in him.

New skills were added to his repertoire daily. Skya taught him three tens of foot-feats to keep him from an enemy's sword, and three tens of sword-cuts to open an enemy's body. He learned the shield-feat, the art of dancing on the rim of a spinning shield while accurately hurling spears, and the rope-feat, which involved balancing on a rope tied above the ground at shoulder height while fighting an opponent trying to keep his footing on the same rope.

'These are the arts you must master for the combat of champions,' Skya explained. 'Battle need not always mean killing. People do not get along together, yet if we slaughter one another over every little quarrel there would soon be no one left.

'Therefore, the battle of champions. When king or clan name a man

136

as their champion, it is the highest accolade a warrior can receive. His people's honour rides on his shoulders. When both sides in a conflict agree to have their champions meet in single combat and to abide by the result, one man determines the outcome of a war.

'If you would aspire to be a champion some day, you must learn to dazzle your opponents, Cuchulain. More men are defeated by intimidation than by the sword. Make a man kiss the grass and you have beaten him – and his supporters – even if he is still alive.

'I'm not saying we could ever hope to make a champion out of you, you understand. You may have only a little talent . . .' As she said this she lunged at him unexpectedly, a shortsword appearing in her hand as if by magic. Only the swift reflexes she had recently developed in Cuchulain enabled him to leap out of her way before the warrior-woman could disembowel him.

Skya was, indeed, a hard taskmaster.

Cuchulain was determined never to allow himself to use the Rage. In this company, where all were working with such dedication and skill was everything, he would be humiliated by the unfair advantage the Rage would give him.

His friendship with Ferdiad deepened through their shared experiences. On the training ground Daman's son abandoned his easygoing style and strove to match Cuchulain feat for feat. By day they competed furiously with each other. At night they slept wrapped together in their cloaks, sharing their warmth.

Ferdiad never willingly intruded on Cuchulain's private thoughts, but was an interested listener if the Hound wanted to talk. He did not judge; he only ventured an opinion if asked; he knew when to use a jest to change a mood grown too solemn.

In armour of horn, Cuchulain had found the friend of a lifetime.

In return he provided Ferdiad with the challenge the other man needed. One rainy morning Ferdiad remarked, 'I would be the best man in the school if you weren't here.'

'Are you jealous?'

'I am not. I'm grateful. You've pushed me into being better than I ever knew I could be; I'm impressed with myself now.'

'That's because you're seeing Ferdiad through the eyes of Cuchulain,' the Hound said softly.

'Oh? Is that why everything looks grey?'

They both laughed.

At times Cuchulain fell into his old habit of solitary contemplation, which Ferdiad learned to recognise and respect. Once, realising he had been talking down an empty well while his companion stared into space, Ferdiad asked, 'Where are you, Hound?'

Cuchulain started. 'Ah . . . just wandering around looking for my next thought.'

'Mmmmm.' Ferdiad tactfully withdrew, leaving Cuchulain alone. Sometimes the dark lad needed to be alone.

They grew even closer. Days of camaraderie and nights spent exchanging confidences created a deeper intimacy.

In other places, in other seasons, Cuchulain would find himself reminiscing about some adventure they had shared and look up, expecting to meet Ferdiad's eyes. He would grow impatient with others who needed something tediously explained which Ferdiad would have understood at once. And when enemies closed on him, it was always Ferdiad Cuchulain wanted guarding his back.

When the nights were not too cold Ferdiad did not sleep in his armour.

Late one day a runner burst into the stronghold. 'Ayfa's attacked one of your clansmen, Skya, and stolen his herd!'

The warrior-woman made clubs of her fists. 'Any injuries to my people?'

'A spear in one man's back. Before he died he claimed to have heard a woman's laugh as it was thrown.'

'A spear in the back.' Skya spat with disgust. 'I see I still have some lessons to teach Ayfa.' She turned to her pupils. 'Prepare for battle. And you, Cuchulain; you come with me. It's time you met the Gae Bulga.'

Out of the corner of his mouth Cuchulain whispered to Ferdiad, 'What's the Gae Bulga?'

'New to me. Perhaps it's her special gift to you, like my body armour.'

Skya led Cuchulain alone to the training ground, a foot-beaten field where her pupils sometimes played at hurling when the day's session was over. The area was the only part of Skya's holding that was neatly maintained. She insisted that weapons and any accoutrements of battle be properly cleaned, and was ready to break the fingers of anyone who was careless with his equipment. Otherwise, she was indifferent to her surroundings, as a warrior is indifferent to a weaving shed.

Skya faced Cuchulain on the empty field. Stripped for combat, she wore only a narrow apron of leather around her lean hips and a thong to

138

hold the hair out of her eyes. Her breasts were as flat as empty water sacks, and the blocking of muscle across her midsection was as deeply carved as a man's.

Cuchulain and Ferdiad had sometimes speculated on what sort of man would dare mate with such a woman, yet it was known she had raised a family, and there were rumours around the camp that once she took a mysterious lover.

It must have been long ago, Cuchulain thought.

In one hand, Skya held a weapon. She lifted it so he could see it clearly: a curious form of spear with a haft of polished ash. The head was bronze inlaid with silver but had a red-gold sheen, and ended in three large prongs with hinged barbs on each. The weapon glowed with craftsmanship and gleamed with cruelty.

Cuchulain could not take his eyes from it. 'How did you come by this?'

'It was a tribute to me. Before you were born. I've saved it for a long time, waiting to give it to someone who could make use of its magic.'

'Magic?' Cuchulain eyed the spear suspiciously.

'This is a unique weapon, the Gae Bulga. The Invincible Spear once used by the Tuatha de Danann.'

Cuchulain took a step backward. 'I don't want this.'

'I may not be able to give it to you,' she retorted. 'No mortal man has ever been able to make it do his will; even I could not. I give you the Gae Bulga only if you can control it, for that is the test the weapon demands. Here, catch!' Without warning, she threw the spear at Cuchulain.

The Gae Bulga sang in flight. Like a swarm of bees, it hummed, low and dangerous, though it moved too fast for the sound to warn its victim. By the time he heard, he would be fatally stung.

Cuchulain tried to throw himself out of its path, but it proved unnecessary. In spite of Skya's usually infallible aim, the spear fell harmlessly at his feet. He looked at it without touching it. 'What's so special about the Gae Bulga? I didn't see it do anything.'

'It won't, for me. But I know what it is supposed to do, and I can teach you. If you succeed where others have failed, the weapon is yours. With it in your possession, no one can deny you a championship, for the Gae Bulga will make you invincible. Perhaps I should not have kept it this long . . .' Her eyes clouded, recalling all the long days she had spent in this same field, trying to master the spear that would not be mastered.

Skya could not have said why she offered the Gae Bulga to Cuchulain.

Instinct, perhaps, she thought. She had survived overlong thanks to her good instincts.

Part of him did not want to, yet Cuchulain found himself picking up the spear. No warrior could resist at least looking at such a weapon. 'If you succeed where others have failed . . .'

He had to know.

Late in the day, the two returned from the training ground. Weariness showed in Skya's drawn face and sunken eyes. But Cuchulain vibrated with restless energy.

In his hand, he carried the Gae Bulga.

As they lay wrapped in one cloak that night, Ferdiad said, 'Tell me about the spear, Cuchulain.'

The other struggled for words. 'It's . . . alive. When I first picked it up, I felt as if it . . . knew me.' He gave a shudder of distaste, which his bedmate felt.

'You don't like it, do you?'

'It's hard to answer that question, Ferdiad. Whether I like it or not doesn't seem to matter. The spear allows me to control it, which no one else can do. When I lift it, it tells me how it wants to be thrown; I can feel its commands running through my arm, or even through my foot, if I do the foot-feat and hurl it from the crotch of my toes.

'Then, when I throw the Gae Bulga at a target, any living thing, man or animal, it doesn't matter, the spear follows them no matter how they twist and dodge. Once I select the target and hurl the spear, it will seek out its victim on its own, nothing can avoid it.

'Nor can any living creature survive its attack. Those barbed prongs open still wider inside a body and can't possibly be pulled out the way they went in. They have to go through the body and be taken out on the other side, dragging the guts with them. Once I hurl the Gae Bulga, my target has no chance at all.

'And that's what I don't like, Ferdiad. Where is the fair fight between equals?'

'Where is the fair fight when you use the Rage?' his friend countered.

Cuchulain lay silent for a time. At last, he said, 'I don't have to use either of them against Ayfa; I can win without them.'

He tried to sleep then, but rest eluded him. His mind kept reliving the first moments when he held the Gae Bulga. A weapon of magic, surely – magic that he feared and mistrusted. Magic that responded to something in himself that he did not want to admit.

140

In lifting the spear, and hurling it, and glorying in the first realisation that it would obey him, he had accepted the magic. Now, he must lie sleepless in the night, re-examining his life in the meaning of this discovery about himself.

This discovery he had not wanted to make.

12 At the home of Forgall the Wily, Emer did her needlework and waited. Her days were not empty; she must rise with the sun and perform, with her sister, the tasks their dead mother would have done. No servant could be entrusted with the original awakening of the fire; fire and water and earth were sacred, and the premier woman of the household was responsible for them. Emer and Derforgall divided the rituals between them, one building the fire and the other going to the well for the morning supply of water.

They did their share of preparing the food as well, though the hosteler had enough bondservants to assign such tasks as were considered too coarse for well-born women. His daughters were also responsible for provisioning the guest house and seeing that a vat of ale and a vat of milk were kept in readiness at all times for passing travellers. As sacred as fire and water and earth was the hospitality of the Gael.

Entering the guest house, Emer always paused for just a moment and let herself see Cuchulain there. With her.

Forgall kept his hostel at the king's command, but provided for his personal needs in the same way as other men, by raising cattle and trading the produce of his land. Cattle-lords from other holdings frequently visited him, or invited him to visit them, to discuss cattle breeding. The hosteler's glossy black herds were much admired.

So was his younger daughter.

Lugaid mac Ros, a chariot-chieftain from Munster, had spent the sunseason travelling throughout Erin looking for breeding stock to buy and for wives for himself and his followers. Close to home, one could obtain both through battle, but it was more convenient when importing fresh blood to do so through outright purchase. To this end, Lugaid was travelling with a number of cartloads of valuable trading materials.

Forgall the Wily was suitably impressed.

'There is a husband worthy of you,' he pointed out to Emer.

He picked a bad time. The night before had been the full moon, flooding Emer with thoughts of Cuchulain. She could still smell his breath in her nostrils. 'Show Derforgall to your visitor instead of me,' she said.

This lack of hospitality annoyed her father. 'He's already seen Derforgall. She didn't please him; I gather he's very hard to please. He's even been to Emain Macha and seen nothing he liked, though someone there mentioned you, which is why he's here now. He's a chieftain, Emer – need I remind you? With a great dun and a troop of men-at-arms.'

'Hunh,' said Emer.

'I insist you come to the hall and meet this man.'

Emer stood up and put her hands on her hips. She could be marvellously stubborn, as her father well knew. 'My sister must be married first, it's the tradition.'

'I blow the entire contents of my nose on the tradition!' Forgall shot back. 'This man is rich, I tell you, and he doesn't want Deforgall! He wants to see you, and he's prepared to offer me a huge bride-price for you if you live up to the description he's heard.'

Emer had inherited her stubbornness from her father.

Knowing she must, she dragfooted back to the dwelling house and cleaned herself up in her sleeping chamber, then entered the hall. One look at Lugaid was sufficient. His eyes were not the eyes of Cuchulain; his mouth was not the mouth of Cuchulain. He was just a big, gruff, red-faced cattle-lord.

'What do you think, Lugaid? Isn't this girl all I said she was?'

'Forgall, your daughter fills my eyes indeed.' Lugaid looked Emer up and down as he would have examined any breeding stock offered. Other women in such a situation would have smiled to show the health of their teeth and the warmth of their dispositions, but Emer just gazed at him coldly, making no effort to charm him.

Her attitude piqued his interest.

'Your Emer pleases me, Forgall,' he decided. 'Has she any kins-women similar to herself – aside from her sister, of course? I have twelve stout companions who are also looking for wives. They are propertied men; your clan would be enriched by their bride-gifts.'

Forgall grinned like a fox eating goslings. 'Excellent news, this. I've had some, ah, unusual expenses lately, and your offer comes at a most propitious time.'

'Not for me,' said Emer.

'This discussion is between myself and my guest,' her father told her with a warning glance that she disregarded. He turned back to Lugaid.

143

'Women!' He rolled his eyes. 'They never know what's good for them. But you look to be an experienced and well-travelled man, mac Ros, as am I myself. I'm confident you know how to handle a woman of spirit.'

'I won't be handled at all – not by him,' Emer said.

Lugaid raised one hand. 'Now here, let's not have a fight in the family! I mean you no harm, girl, and you are freeborn. I could do nothing to you without your consent. Do you find me so loathsome?'

His face was open and earnest, and Emer realised he was, indeed, a fine candidate for a husband.

But he was not Cuchulain.

Her manner softened. He could not be blamed, there was only one Hound. And she did not want to make an enemy for her father.

She went up to Lugaid mac Ros and put one small hand on either side of his face, looking long into his eyes. 'I tell you this,' she said. 'Until I saw you, I thought myself free to take a husband. But now I know I am not.'

'What do you mean?'

'I am saying if I could marry any man other than Cullen's Hound, I would marry you, and I thank you for your offer.'

'Is your daughter already married?' Lugaid thundered at Forgall. 'If you've been deceiving me, old man . . .'

'I am not married,' Emer said hastily. 'At least, I have exchanged no vows. My Hound is far away, and I must wait until he comes back to me. But even if he does not, I realise now it would make no difference. I am his and only his. I'm sorry, Lugaid mac Ros,' she added gently.

'Such devotion makes you more desirable than ever,' he replied. 'Unfortunately for me.' Then the name she had mentioned registered in his brain. 'Cullen's Hound? *Cuchulain?*'

Emer's sudden glow was his answer.

Lugaid stood very still. Cuchulain. A name to reckon with. Having just come from Emain Macha, he had heard a great deal indeed about Cuchulain.

Lugaid was bold, but not foolhardy.

To Forgall, he said, 'If your daughter has given her devotion elsewhere, that's all there is to be said. I will seek a wife in another clan, and my men with me.'

No sooner had he gone than Forgall raged at his daughter. 'How could you do this to me! Don't you know what that man was willing to give you? You've cost me dearly for the sake of a mad creature you'll never see again!'

'You can't be certain I'll never see him,' she said, fighting to stay calm.

'Indeed I can!' In the excess of his passion, Forgall shook his fist in Emer's face. 'I guarantee Cuchulain shall not return to Erin – and if by some miracle he does, either your brothers will kill him or I'll lift his head myself!'

Emer began to walk away.

'Where are you going, I'm talking to you.'

She ignored him and kept on walking, out of the hall and straight to her sleeping chamber. Forgall was forced to trot after her in order to keep yelling at her. He watched in disbelief as she began gathering up her favourite belongings.

'Where are you going?' he asked again.

'I'm leaving this dun.' She folded a gown over her arm; she selected her favourite jewels and stuffed them into a comb-bag.

'An unmarried woman can't leave her father's protection!'

'As you said yourself, I blow my nose on tradition.' Emer went on packing.

Forgall tried changing tactics. 'You wouldn't really leave me, my daughterling, my dearest girl . . .'

'I'm halfway gone already. I won't stay in any place where Cuchulain would not be welcome.'

Forgall's brain skittered among possibilities. He would be hideously embarrassed if it became known that his daughter had left him for any reason other than marriage. Besides, he truly loved her. Compared to Emer, Derforgall was stringy and dull. Emer wore her dead mother's face.

He buttered his voice. 'This matter can be resolved with you still under my rooftree. I had no idea you were so set on Cuchulain.'

Her tone was icy. 'Didn't you? Then why try to kill him? That's where our young heifers went, isn't it? You gave them to somebody to kill him. Somebody on Skya's island, perhaps?'

My Emer is very shrewd, thought Forgall with a mixture of pride and chagrin. 'What's done can be undone,' he said aloud.

'Can it? Can you put a duckling back in the egg?'

'I'll send word at once that no hair on Cuchulain's head is to be harmed. Just put your things down, Emer, and say you'll stay with me until Derforgall marries. Then . . .'

She gave him a level stare. 'What if Cuchulain is already dead?'

★

Cuchulain was not dead, but a serious plan had been laid to kill him. Ayfa was pleased to learn that Skya had taken the bait. When Ongus the Hairless, Ayfa's second-in-command, reported battle preparations in Skya's camp, the other woman smiled with satisfaction.

'I thought that would bring the old she-wolf and her cubs-in-training out. One among them is the lad we're supposed to destroy, Ongus.'

'Will he be easy to kill?'

'I understand a payment of tanned hides was given to the druid in exchange for a spell to rob him of companions who might protect his back,' Ayfa replied. 'But it doesn't matter. We'll take him down no matter how capable a fighter he is. We were given good cows in exchange for his death, so honour demands he die.'

Ongus the Hairless rubbed his belly. Cow meat was a rare delicacy on the island, whose rough forage was not favourable for cattle. Acquisition of the heifers had strengthened Ayfa's position in her clan and furthered her private ambition: to take over Skya's stronghold and school for heroes as soon as the older woman's grip on both was sufficiently weakened. Ayfa was young and had dreams.

She prepared for the conflict to come. Chariot warfare was unknown on the island; her people fought exclusively on foot, hip to hip and knee to knee, armed with iron-bladed short-swords and casting spears. Ayfa possessed an additional weapon, an Iberian dagger with a blade shaped like a narrow triangle. In close fighting the dagger could bore a hole in a man large enough for her to thrust in her fist and seize his heart.

She had earned her position as war-leader of her clan.

Ready now, she bared her teeth in a feral grin. In the distance, she heard the sound of Skya's war trumpet. 'Come to me, young Cuchulain,' said Ayfa softly.

Battle morning. A trumpet was calling and the dawnlight was tinged with blood. Exhilaration flowed through Cuchulain's veins. No day smelled as good as a battle morning. On battle morning, a gulped gruel of barley and linseed tasted better than meats roasted on a king's spit. Every sense was keen, every nerve tingling.

A man knew he was alive on a battle morning.

As he and Ferdiad moved out with the others, they exchanged a grin, sharing.

They trotted with weapons at the ready. Over a distant rise came a thin line of opposition, also running lightly.

Cuchulain called to Skya, 'Request single combat, and I will be your champion.'

'That is for me to decide, not you,' she replied, but her eyes flashed approval. Cupping her hands around her mouth, she called across the space between the battle lines, 'We claim a combat of champions!'

'We don't have a warrior insignificant enough to be an even match for your best man,' someone shouted back.

Skya reddened. Cuchulain's hand caressed the hilt of Hardhead.

'Then I alone will fight all your men at once!' he cried.

'You alone will die alone,' came the answer. A figure stepped out from between the massed men with their raised shields. At the distance, Cuchulain could not quite make out the other's face, but there was something strange about the voice.

'Who threatens me?' he wanted to know.

'I am called Ayfa.'

'And I am Cullen's Hound!' he yelled in defiance.

Ayfa's teeth gleamed. 'The very one I want.' She ran towards him, calling back over her shoulder to Ongus, 'If by some mischance I go down, kill him.'

With his keen hearing, Cuchulain heard her shocking order to have a victorious champion slain.

He approached Ayfa warily. The watching armies encircled them, keeping their distance. This was the first time Cuchulain had faced a woman who actually meant to kill him, and to meet her in single combat was doubly daunting. 'Women are more deadly than men,' Skya had once warned him. 'Men fight for victory, but women fight for survival. Survival is the sharper goad.'

Seen at close quarters, Ayfa was a surprise. She was nothing like Skya. Her cheeks were plump, her lips were full, her smooth muscles were encased in creamy skin. Only her war cry was savage – that, and the unusual wedge-shaped blade she brandished.

Cuchulain was reluctant to attack her. A woman, a lifebearer . . . when she was within one spear-length of him, he leaped into the air and hit her in the chest with both feet. Air exploded from her lungs; she fell backwards. Cuchulain landed and was on his feet again before she could get to one knee. Whirling to face her, he raised his shield.

Ayfa got up, coughed, feinted to his left, ducked back to the right with a practised twisting motion and came in under his shield, her dagger aimed at his armpit.

He flung himself sideways but felt the weapon pierce his skin in

147

passing, ripping flesh. Her failure to score a killing thrust caught Ayfa off guard for the briefest moment; few men had been quick enough to outmanoeuvre her before. And now, Cuchulain was somehow behind her. She spun around.

'I challenge you to a fiery-feat,' he taunted. 'To the rope-feat, to the shield-feat, choose one!'

She shook her head grimly. 'I'm just going to kill you,' she said.

Dropping into a crouch, she wove patterns in the air with her dagger. The weapon was a live thing. Cuchulain denied himself a swift glance in the direction of the spear carrier who had been appointed to bring the Gae Bulga for him. He would do this according to tradition – the tradition of champions. No matter what Ayfa did.

Suddenly, she flipped her dagger from right hand to left, using it either way with equal dexterity. Cuchulain switched Hardhead with the same ease, denying her the advantage of the ambidextrous. His eyes met hers above their shields.

Her eyes were sky-blue.

While he was looking into them, she shouldered past his shield and drove for his heart.

The only way to stop her now was to kill her.

She was too close for him to go over her, so Cuchulain went under. He dropped to one knee and butted his head into her belly. She did not fall again; her belly was as hard as the Hound's skull. But her deadly blade missed a second time, and she lost her temper; she slashed wildly at him as he leaped to his feet. Then she steadied enough to advance her shield-shoulder toward him and close again. He half-turned away from her to give more momentum to his swing and brought Hardhead around with enough force to cut a man in two.

The sword sang through empty air. Ayfa was at Cuchulain's side, dancing on the balls of her feet, mocking him with laughter.

She lost the battle with that laughter. Her laugh was as hard and harsh as a raven's cry, and Cuchulain drew it into himself like breath. Laughter to save his life, to summon his battle-fury . . .

The Rage flooded through him from his head to his heels. His world was suffused with red light. Ayfa was moving like a ponderous fish in thick water while he darted around her, swifter than thought.

Leap, slash, jump back . . . scarlet lips opened on Ayfa's arm, pouring blood.

He fought in a red cloud of ecstasy, yet one cool area of his brain stood apart to calculate the exact spot, half a thumb's length from her chin,

148

where he could hit Ayfa and knock her senseless. Fergus had once taught: 'If you curve your blow downward slightly, you can knock an opponent's jaw open at the point of impact and save yourself the trouble of a collapsed knuckle.'

Some fragment of himself remembered; some fragment of himself still did not want to kill a woman.

When Cuchulain hit her, Ayfa's head snapped sideways, her open mouth spraying spittle as she fell unconscious.

The Hound leaped over her and ran towards her appalled warriors, screaming at them from his unsatisfied Rage.

When Ayfa opened her eyes, she found Skya squatted on her hams beside her, watching her. Ayfa was not comfortable. Skya had bound her arm, but her head seemed to be full of broken rocks. She propped herself on one elbow, and with the other hand gingerly waggled her jaw. Then she spat out two broken teeth. 'What's happened?' she asked Skya.

'Look around you.'

The grass was strewn with the bodies of Ayfa's followers. Skya's band was intact, standing together with their weapons lowered while they watched a solitary figure off to one side.

Ayfa's gaze followed theirs, to the Hound.

He was surrounded by a pulsing glow. His hair stood upright on his head, bathed in a nimbus of flame. He had just struck the last of Ayfa's warriors to the earth, but still the fury gripped him; he swung his terrible head from side to side, seeking more victims.

Only Ferdiad dared approach him. 'That's enough, Cuchulain. We've won; *you've* won.' He raised his voice. '*It's over!*'

The Hound pivoted slowly; Ayfa and Skya could see his face. The glaring mask should have chilled the marrow in Ayfa's bones, but it did not. Its dreadful aspect was transformed for her into something splendid, something awesome, by the pulsing of the golden hero-light.

'Cuchulain!' Ferdiad called again urgently, fearful lest the Hound start attacking his own allies.

Slowly the crimson began to fade from Cuchulain's face. His grimacing features relaxed, his knotted joints straightened themselves into human configurations.

No one said anything. A few of Ayfa's men were groaning, but the majority were beyond pain. The living were transfixed by the spectacle of the Hound struggling to return to normal. In the silence, his breathing was a roar.

He raised one hand to wipe the sweat from his eyes, and when the hand dropped, his face was almost Cuchulain's again. But before the Rage faded entirely, he had one task to perform.

Striding to Ayfa, he picked up the dagger she had dropped and held it between himself and her, so their eyes met across its blade. Then, with thumb and forefinger, the Hound bent the blade into a curve.

'Sit up and hold out your wrists,' he ordered.

Wincing with pain, Ayfa obeyed. She watched in fascination as he twisted the dagger into a manacle and fastened her wrists together with it.

Then he left her. Wandering in an erratic path across the recent field of battle, he paused here to comfort a wounded enemy, there to offer an injured man water. The Rage faded and was gone; he might have been another person.

Skya's followers began scouring the area for weapons to add to their armoury.

'Your men aren't taking trophies,' Ayfa commented.

'A man can only claim a head from a warrior he's killed himself,' Skya reminded her. 'And all the kills you see belong to the Hound of Ulster.'

Though some of Ayfa's men had survived, badly wounded, Skya had no intention of taking them back to her stronghold as prisoners of war. She wanted only one prisoner – Ayfa herself. Celtic tradition demanded that hostages be treated as honoured guests, given the best of everything. To do less would cause their captors a drastic loss of prestige. 'I'm too wise to have wounded men in my stronghold, eating their heads off and doing nothing,' Skya said, 'so I'll take Ayfa with me and leave the others to make their way to their homes as best they can. While I hold her, they won't dare try to retaliate.'

Ferdiad and Cuchulain walked together. 'I was a little surprised to see your battle-fury,' Ferdiad remarked after a time. 'You didn't leave much for the rest of us to do. But don't think I'm reproaching you, I'm not. I'd like to be like you, but I never will. You're different.'

'I don't want to be different.'

'I hardly see how you can avoid it, Cuchulain. Aren't you satisfied with what you are?'

'I was satisfied to be a member of the Boys' Troop, then of the Red Branch. That's all I ever wanted.'

Ferdiad paused in midstep. 'Do you know what I always wanted?' he said earnestly. 'To be a goldsmith. Don't laugh, I know . . . look at these huge, clumsy paws I have for hands. But ever since I was a small

150

boy, I dreamed of bending the thinnest gold wire into loops and knotwork, using my fingers to shape melted sunmetal into designs I imagined. There were fine craftsmen among the Fir Bolg.

'But I'm a warrior, Cuchulain. Because my father was a warrior. I've learned to accept it as I accept the big, clumsy hands. As you must accept whatever you are. You fight against it, but that's no good, you're only fighting yourself.'

They walked on. Some of Skya's other warriors had begun singing a marching song. Tiny insects from the gorse started stinging Cuchulain, but Ferdiad in his body armour was impervious to them.

In jest, Cuchulain told him, 'If you were a real friend, you'd let me wear your armour for a while.'

'I would if you'd let me throw the Gae Bulga in the next battle,' Ferdiad countered.

'The spear wouldn't work for you.'

'My armour wouldn't fit you.'

They walked on. 'Of course,' Ferdiad said, 'I've never tried to do any magic. Perhaps I could throw the spear, I may have a gift I don't know about.'

'Pray you don't,' Cuchulain advised him. 'Do you think Macha Fleet-Foot was grateful for her gift of speed on the racecourse at Emain Macha?'

When they reached Skya's dun, her attendants prepared a victory feast of fish and game and cockles cooked in seal fat. Her pupils were invited into the warrior-woman's hall to share it, and her hostage was given the bench of honour at her right hand.

Skya believed that once a battle was over, it was over.

Whatever Ayfa thought she kept hidden behind her eyes.

13 With her injured jaw, Ayfa was only able to eat a little bread soaked in ale. She soon lost interest in the feast. 'Have you a guest house for me?' she asked Skya.

'You know I do.'

'And a guard of honour to accompany me?'

'Take your pick of my men.'

Ayfa would have smiled had her face not hurt so much. 'Then I will take the best. As your hostage, I'm entitled. Give me the Hound of Ulster.'

Cuchulain did not want the assignment. After battle, men liked to gather around a campfire and talk over the day's adventures. He wanted to be with his companions, but Fergus had pounded obedience into the Boys' Troop; it was the only way he could control them. So Cuchulain was obedient to Skya's order: 'Take Ayfa to her new home and guard her well.'

At the doorway of the guest house, the captive hesitated. The night was crisp and clear; Cuchulain's young profile was proud in the moonlight. 'I'd prefer not to sleep in there alone,' she said to him. 'Some of Skya's people may bear me a grudge, one could slip in and put a knife into me while you were out here.'

'No one gets past me.'

'They might be hiding inside already. Why don't you come in with me and look around, just to be certain?' She beckoned him inside.

Skya had given Ayfa a bronze lamp fuelled with seal fat, which she held high as she surveyed her new accommodations. She pursed her lips as best she could with an aching jaw. 'I fear this place insults my status as a war-leader. It's little better than an animal shed. If the battle had gone the other way, and Skya were in my guest house tonight, she would be sleeping on feathers' – Ayfa aimed a kick at the bedding that awaited her – 'instead of a pile of grass and sticks!'

'Skya's a warrior,' Cuchulain said in his teacher's defence. 'She doesn't put a high gloss on anything but weapons.'

'Ah, but hospitality is important. And a little luxury is a pleasure. If you were my guest, for instance . . .'

'I'm not your guest, I'm your guard.'

'My captor, to be precise,' Ayfa corrected him. 'See the bruises on my wrists where the smith had to break the manacles you made for me?' She held up her hands, a circlet of purplish green around each wrist.

Cuchulain looked surprised. 'I did that?'

'Don't you remember? I'll never forget it.' She put the lamp down on the one rough wooden table the room possessed, then raised her hand to Cuchulain's cheek. 'So smooth,' she murmured. 'It's hard to reconcile this face with the thing I saw on the battlefield.'

She kicked again at her bedding. 'I suppose I can hope for no better than this. If you weren't guarding me, what would you be sleeping on?'

'My cloak and the ground.'

'At least straw is softer than that. And the night grows cold. Stay here with me and keep us both warm. It is a custom among your people as it is among mine, I assume.'

'Not with enemies.'

'Ah, Cuchulain, I'm not your enemy. I'm just a cold, tired woman who has no sister or companion nearby to warm her bed. Skya is supposed to give me anything I need, you know.'

He understood her meaning well enough. She was not just referring to shared warmth, the harmless comfort of family and campsite. Had Skya known this was what Ayfa wanted? And, knowing, sent him anyway?

Ayfa took a step closer to him. 'If you don't take the best possible care of me, it will reflect dishonour on Skya,' she said. She lay down and looked up at him expectantly. 'That fine woollen cloak of yours looks delightfully warm, Cuchulain. Won't you share?'

Reluctantly, he eased himself down beside her, trying to pull his cloak over both of them without actually touching her.

Ayfa chuckled at the back of her throat. 'That's better. And much better for guarding me. Now I can't make a move you won't know about.'

He lay quietly, keeping his breathing steady.

'How many women have you lain with?' she asked him suddenly, reaching over to extinguish the lamp.

No answer. Cuchulain felt his face grow hot.

Then he felt something else: a woman's hand on his thigh.

In a conversational tone, Ayfa said, 'My mother bore nine living children. Eight boys and me. Life here is hard even at the best of times, and she wore herself out caring for us. I remember her as always being

153

old and thin, though she must have been young once. My brothers were destined for a better fate, so I chose to be like them. Who would want to be a woman?

'I learned to fight with my brothers, and then I learned to fight better than they did. I enjoyed it; it was certainly better than staying in a smoky hut tending snot-nosed children. Men wanted to marry me and doom me to that fate, but I rejected all of them.

'When I ran away to apprentice myself to Skya, my family mourned me as dead and forgot about me in a season. When I returned fully armed and bristling with battle skills, they hardly knew what to make of me. I might have crawled out of a tomb. But I soon convinced them I was a step above buttermilk; I challenged every man in the clan, and defeated them in single combat. When the old warlord was killed, they elected me in his place. Since then, I've given ground to no man . . . until today.

'You are the first to best me, Cuchulain. It took an extraordinary warrior to put Ayfa down.' Her fingers began to move. Two of them marched down his thigh toward the knee, then reversed and came up again. Toward the groin.

Cuchulain stopped breathing.

'I suspect you are bigger than you look,' Ayfa remarked. 'When I saw you today with light shining around you and from you and through you, you captured me then, long before you wrapped the blade around my wrists.'

Her fingers made a little jump and captured him.

'Aahhh,' she breathed. 'You *are* much bigger than you look. I thought so.'

Because Ayfa was a war leader, she extemporised a little campaign, a small exercise in power. Her walking fingers were her advance guard, reconnoitring the territory. After a through examination of his geography, she moved up her front line, a hot body suddenly pressing against Cuchulain's full length, creating a shock wave. While one hand had kept him distracted, Ayfa had skilfully removed her clothing with the other.

Now, both hands were on him, warm palms pressing and relaxing his muscles, knowing the very places where a warrior felt the strain of fighting. She massaged him from heel to shoulder and back again.

Then she bent over and went to work with a specialised weapon.

The touch of her mouth made Cuchulain writhe.

Ayfa was used to taking charge. Part of her mind thought of

154

Cuchulain as a youth and herself as an adult instructor, as Skya was an instructor. Though in a rather different field.

She would now demonstrate flank attacks and indirect assaults.

She slid one hand under his buttocks and inserted her fingers, gently stroking. Her mouth sucked his penis in alternating rhythm, pinioning him between two pleasures. She built him to a level of agonised need, then backed off, returning to fondle his body and drag her heavy breasts across his groin – though not quite long enough for him to find release between them.

But he thought about it. She meant him to think about it.

Ayfa was having a good time. She had no intention of allowing him satisfaction before she was ready for hers. She calculated the exact instant when he would be forced to take over the role of aggressor, and when he rolled her over with an anguished growl, she lay open to him in delighted astonishment.

Cuchulain was, as Ayfa was discovering, a young man of giant strength at the height of his powers and energy.

She had thought herself fighting fit, but eventually even she was exhausted. When the first light of morning stole through the chinks in the guest house wall, it illuminated Ayfa smiling in her sleep, the pain in her jaw long forgotten.

Cuchulain had not slept. He was on guard. Drained, he lay beside her, remembering. Comparing.

When the final spending was done, he had found himself waiting for instinct to tell him how soon he could draw away from Ayfa without insulting her, and curl into the ball of the solitary sleeper. But with Emer, things had been different. The sweetest part of their mating had been the afterpart, when they discovered how well they fitted together in relaxation, how smoothly every curve slid into every matching hollow. When the orgasmic convulsion faded, it had left in its wake a deeper, slower, richer climax of comfort, experienced not in the loins but in the heart.

Separating his body from Emer's had been agony, Cuchulain recalled. But he could not lie for a timeless time upon Ayfa, drifting into sleep, as he had done with Emer. Ayfa did not feel right under him. Not wrong . . . just not right.

The light grew stronger, dusty yellow beams spearing into the guest house to warn him of the day and its duties. He got to his feet, arranged his clothing, and slipped outside, taking up his post at the door.

Ayfa never stirred.

When the day guard came to relieve him, the man gave him a curious look. 'You have dark hollows under your eyes.'

'I fought all day and stood guard all night,' Cuchulain answered.

'Life isn't easy,' the other remarked.

The battle won, normal activity resumed. Skya's clanspeople went about the business of survival, fishing and seal hunting and tending their meagre livestock, while she returned to training her apprentices.

Their attitude toward Cuchulain had undergone a sea change. With the exception of Ferdiad, Skya's band now gave the Hound a wide and respectful berth. Even the square-skulled Teuton stepped aside to let him enter the hall first. And when he came up to a group of them together, Cuchulain was painfully aware of words not spoken and glances he was not meant to interpret.

It made him uncomfortable, this echo of an earlier time. Now, he was the mystery. The Hound of Ulster, they called him.

Ayfa continued to request him as her night guard, and Skya continued to oblige. From his boyish countenance, she had thought he might even be a virgin, and found the idea exciting. Her memory of him with the Rage upon him was unforgettable, a vision of the ultimate warrior that even the most arrogant warrior-woman must admire. She would have him. She would conquer him, her way.

But once they were together, her emotions betrayed her. She did not feel like a conqueror. She found herself thinking of him at the most inappropriate times, and wanting to talk about him to anyone who would listen. Just to say his name . . .

'Skya, do you have any perfumed oil?'

Skya stared at Ayfa. 'Whatever for?'

Flustered, Ayfa would not meet the other woman's eyes. 'My skin has become so rough lately. I thought you might have received some from the sea-traders. Or some soft cloth, or glass beads, something pretty?'

'Hunh! I have no use for any of that, and the sea-traders only put in here in emergencies. They know we have nothing worth trading for the goods they carry. Perfumed oil, indeed. What foolishness.'

Ayfa thought of sending to her own clanholding for the small store of luxuries she herself had obtained from traders, but decided against it. Skya's scorn would be withering. Ayfa must hold Cuchulain's attention with her skills, instead.

He came to her dutifully each night. But sometimes Emer stole into his thoughts and he pulled away unexpectedly, flinging one arm across his eyes.

In the morning, he would be eager to be up and away. Yet by nightfall, more often than not, his body began making demands again, as insistent upon this new nourishment as upon food and drink. He was very young and very strong.

The day came when even Skya had to admit she had nothing left to teach him. 'You excel in all feats, Cuchulain. You outrun the swiftest and outstay the hardiest, and no one is willing to contend with you any more except the son of Daman. And you are master of the Gae Bulga. Go back to Conor mac Nessa and wield the Invincible Spear in his service.'

'Are you certain you want me to keep the Gae Bulga?'

'Of course. The two of you belong together.'

'I'm not so certain.'

'Let me tell you something, my Hound from Ulster. I am wise in ways beyond your princely education. From my own experience during a long lifetime, I have learned that the world you see with your eyes is only the thinnest of skins. Beyond it lies the Otherworld. This one is a place of fixed forms, that one is a kingdom of fluid fire. Creatures dwell there who are more aware of us than we are of them, for their vision is different.

'I have seen them, those children of ancient gods. As our numbers grow, theirs diminish – or perhaps they just become better at avoiding us, because they dislike our heaviness, our solidity. Sometimes, however' – she smiled as at a fond memory – 'sometimes we still meet. And so I've learned to recognise their look.

'The day we fought Ayfa, you had that look, Cuchulain. Don't shake your head at me, I know what I know. The Gae Bulga was given into my keeping long ago. Once I realised I was not its master, I doubted if I would ever meet the person who was. Then you arrived.

'Some things must be. You must take the spear. You have told me your ambition is to be the greatest of champions; the Gae Bulga will help you win that honour.'

His sombre silver gaze met hers. 'If I win through magic, what have I proved?'

'Then give up magic altogether,' she snapped in exasperation. 'Bury the Gae Bulga under a stone if you must, build a cairn over it and walk away. But I warn you – you cannot walk away from the Otherworld. It was here long before we came, it is all around us even as we speak. We move in and through it without seeing it, any more than we see the air we breathe. Yet it is real. The gods are real. One exists within yourself. Keep the spear.'

In the dun of Forgall the Wily, Emer hugged her pillow and dreamed of Cuchulain. Not all the time; there were whole days when his face did not form in her mind until well after sunrise, and there were nights when she almost fell asleep before remembering to whisper, 'Setanta.' But she dreamed of him.

She could not ask the druid of her father's clan for a spell to protect the Hound. So she waited until Forgall had to be away from Brega for a period of time, then commandeered a cart and some loyal bondsmen and set out for Emain Macha, where she felt assured of finding more sympathetic help. She felt safe enough travelling by herself. 'No harm comes to women in Conor mac Nessa's kingdom,' Cuchulain had once explained to her. 'The king has sworn to it.'

The journey took several days at a cart's pace, plodding along behind a team of oxen. Emer would have preferred the swifter method of walking, but that was beneath her rank. She thought with envy of the chariot-chieftains and their horses. But eventually the stronghold of the north rose before her, and she saw a bony, freckled young man just emerging from the main gateway with a team of chariot horses to exercise. When she recognised Laeg mac Riangabra, Emer shouted to him.

As soon as she had explained the reason for her journey, Laeg told her, 'You must apply to Cathbad of the Gentle Face. Only the best will do for Cuchulain, whether it's war-carts or weapons. And Cathbad's the best when it comes to casting protective spells. But before you can employ his druid, you must seek the king's permission.'

Emer was nervous about approaching the king of Ulster, but Laeg took charge officiously, anxious to show himself as the man to deal with in matters pertaining to the Hound. He located Cathbad, explained the situation, then conducted the druid and the young woman to the House of the King. After introducing Emer to Conor mac Nessa, Laeg stood to one side and watched, curious to know what the king's reaction would be to Cuchulain's chosen woman.

Conor liked the girl on first sight. She was smiling of face and polished of manner, and she hid her nervousness behind her dimple. 'Do I understand,' he asked her, 'that you want to have special spells of protection cast for Cuchulain? Does that mean you do not think him capable of protecting himself? What do you expect to befall him?'

Emer tensed. She was not anxious to reveal to Conor that her father plotted against the king's foster-son. 'I am a landwoman, not a seawoman,' she said. 'We have had a stormy season, and I fear the water crossing he must make . . . among other things. Could we not, through the offices of the druid, make his way safer for him? I have no doubt Cuchulain is well able to defend himself against any sword or spear, but . . . but I just want to help in any small way I can.'

Blushing, she lowered her eyes. Conor sat on his bench and admired the sweep of her dark lashes against her cheeks.

'Cathbad, take this woman with you and do whatever she asks,' commanded the king of Ulster.

Even to Laeg, Emer had not divulged the extent of her father's treachery, the real cause of her fears and her journey, but when she was outside the House of the King and the druid Cathbad gave her a searching look in the daylight, she wondered how much his eyes saw. Druid's eyes. 'I have brought a casket containing my favourite jewels,' she explained to him, 'gold and silver and copper, carnelian and amethyst and amber. I want to offer these as sacrifices for Cuchulain's safety.'

Forgall had lavished the jewels on his favourite daughter. By giving them up in Cuchulain's name, she hoped to make the scales balance.

Cathbad fixed her with a penetrating look. 'You told the king you feared Cuchulain's sea-crossing. So we must make our sacrifice to Manannan mac Lir, who rules the waves.' A half-smile crooked Cathbad's lips. 'The Son of the Sea can protect your young man against the perils of the deep and . . . other things,' he added meaningfully.

Emer's body tingled. It is true, she thought. Druids *see*.

Cathbad took her to a small, deep pool north of the fort, a man-made lake used for rituals and as a water reservoir. The lake's clarity captured light and sky, amplifying both. A circle of standing stones loomed beyond. 'This pool is one of Manannan's portals,' said the druid. 'Give me your jewels.'

He flung the treasures into the water one at a time. With each, he called out a different invocation. Halfway through the ceremony, a sigh shivered the surface of the lake.

Emer drew her cloak around her shoulders. The quality of light had changed, though the sky was cloudless. She felt an unseen presence, an awareness tugging at her mind. She felt cold and hollow and small.

'Your jewels have been accepted by the lord of the waves,' said Cathbad. 'His wife, Fand, loves jewels; you chose well.'

'Are you certain? Will he keep Cuchulain safe until he returns to me?'

The druid flung out his arm. 'Look and see for yourself!'

The pond was aflame with colour. Its formerly azure surface blazed gold and silver and copper, carnelian and amethyst and amber. 'Lake of the Jewels, now and for ever,' Cathbad intoned.

They returned to the House of the King, where Conor entertained Emer in a style befitting the Hound's chosen wife. But during the long feast, she drank more mead than she had intended, partly from relief, and heard her tongue admitting to Nessa's insistent questions that Forgall did not approve of the match. That Forgall wanted to kill Cuchulain.

Emer had thought the king sat regal and remote on his bench; now, she learned he heard every word spoken. Leaping to his feet, he cried, 'I'll have that hosteler's head! I'll have his eyes pickled and his tongue jellied!'

Emer threw herself at his feet, forgetting dignity. 'You must not, he's my father!'

Conor looked down at her in surprise. 'You can plead for him even though he wants Cuchulain dead?'

'He is my father,' the girl repeated. 'I don't want either of them harmed.' Her face was pale beneath its faint sprinkle of golden freckles.

The king's hand stroked her hair. 'I'll send word to Cuchulain to come home at once,' he assured her. 'We'll let him deal with Forgall the Wily.'

Emer was laden with gifts from the king and sent home to Brega. Cethern the messenger was sent for Cuchulain, together with an armed guard who accompanied him as far as the coast and would wait there to welcome the Hound back to Ulster and escort him safely to Emain Macha – just in case.

Conall Cearnach and Leary Buadach were among the guard who were to wait on Ulster's shore for the return of Cuchulain. When they reached the cove where Cethern was to board a fishing boat to Skya's island, they found the community of fishermen uneasy.

'The sea to the east has never been so calm,' they were told. 'Hardly a ripple on the water, all the way to Alba.'

Cethern, who had never been in a boat before, eyed the placid water with grave suspicion. 'I don't like this,' he said. 'Conall, Leary, come with me.'

But the other two were under orders to protect Cuchulain in Erin; not

160

on the sea. Since they could remain on the strand, they pushed Cethern toward the boat unhesitatingly. 'Just go and get the Hound!'

'Perhaps we should wait for a better time . . .'

'The tide is with you now, what tide there is. Go!'

The last sight they had of him was his white face staring back wistfully at the land from the stern of the boat.

'Some days,' Leary remarked to Conall Cearnach, 'it's easier to find acorns on a willow tree than to get a simple job done.'

14 Bruised and dishevelled, with three broken fingers and a dislocated shoulder, Cethern of Ulster finally reached the near side of Skya's bridge. He had had a terrible journey. The voyage itself had been uneventful, but since making landfall he had got lost, been set upon by robbers, and fallen ignominiously into an abandoned well. Without timely rescue by a smith named Donal, he would probably have been dead. But at least Donal had heard of Cuchulain, whom he persisted in calling the Hound of Ulster, and had given Cethern safe escort as far as the cliffs.

'I'm happy to do it,' the smith said. 'I have little work today anyway, and I liked your friend. He's become quite famous here, you know. Tell him I was good to you, will you?'

Now, Cethern stood alone atop the cliff and stared down at the bridge. I'll never make it, he told himself. This far I have come, but no farther.

A man came toward him from a half-hidden hut. 'Are you looking for a person, or for trouble?'

'I have a message from Conor mac Nessa, king of Ulster, for the one called Cuchulain.'

The stranger had a florid face and a pendulous underlip, scored by a single tooth. His clothes seemed to be an assortment of discarded rags tied together. Upon hearing Cuchulain's name, he broke into a singularly unattractive smile. 'You mean the Hound of Ulster! Why didn't you say so? Everyone knows where he is, just follow me!' He bounded off down the side of the cliff like a goat.

When he realised Cethern was not following him, he looked back. 'Come on, what's the matter?'

'I could never cross that bridge, I've been injured.'

'Oh. If it's the Hound you want, I suppose we can make an exception for you, then.' He threw back his head and bellowed a summons across the water. Then he scrambled back up the cliff to wait with Cethern.

They shifted from foot to foot. They tried to make conversation, found no common ground, lapsed into silence. At last a familiar figure appeared at the far side of the bridge.

'Cuchulain!' Cethern shouted with relief. 'I was afraid I'd never see you again. The king asks you to return to Emain Macha.'

One narrow-eyed glance showed the Hound the messenger's disabled shoulder. In a series of agile bounds, he crossed the bridge; then, before Cethern could object, Cuchulain had slung him across his back like a sack of meal and was returning the way he had come. As the bridge swayed violently, Cethern kept his eyes tightly closed and hoped he would not vomit down the Hound's back.

However, he reached Skya's dun without incident, and soon her healer was tending his injuries while her attendants gave him ale.

Skya was not eager to see Cuchulain leave, though it was inevitable. And Cethern noticed another woman who seemed even less pleased, a deep-bosomed, fair-haired woman who followed the Hound with her eyes.

'Is there, er, a problem with her?' Cethern asked, indicating Ayfa with a nod.

'There is not. I am as ready to leave as grass is to grow, nothing holds me back. As soon as you are able, we can go home.' Cuchulain spoke briskly, his mind already occupied with the journey eastward – yet his eyes darted once or twice toward Ayfa in spite of himself. He would feel a certain reluctance about leaving her. She was exciting; he doubted he would meet a woman like her in Erin.

But she gave him no emotional satisfaction. For each pleasure she offered, Ayfa had exacted full payment, her preoccupation with her own satisfaction so total that sometimes Cuchulain felt as if he were only a bystander. Ayfa took.

Emer, he thought to himself with a leap of anticipation; Emer gave.

'Skya,' he asked the warrior-woman, 'what will become of Ayfa?'

'I'll send her back to her clan soon, I suppose. I enjoy having her here, really, but it isn't right to keep her from her own kin under the circumstances.' Skya stopped speaking suddenly, as if afraid she had said too much.

Cuchulain was immediately on guard. 'What circumstances?'

'Ah. Mmm. Since this will be your last night here, perhaps you had better talk to her before you leave. You can have privacy in the guest house, I'll assign someone else to stand watch outside.'

Ayfa was waiting for him when he arrived. He had dreaded the moment of farewell and the look she would give him, but the expression

163

on her face was not quite what he had expected. Her face looked subtly different, with a new roundness to her cheeks.

'I might have wished for a better time to tell you, Cuchulain, but as you are leaving tomorrow, there will be no better time. I am with child.'

How simply she said it! She lowered her eyes and held her arms gracefully at her sides, palms turned toward him. In that moment, he loved her. 'You're carrying my . . .'

'Your child. I am.'

The world rocked around him, the real world, the tangible world. Here was something created of flesh and blood, and it would be his! 'A son?' he managed to ask.

Her smile was old with female wisdom. 'I believe so. The other women assure me it is.'

Cuchulain wanted to throw up his arms and yell, to leap and skip and caper, to burst from the guest house and shout the glad tidings to everyone. A son! Far from being a beardless boy, he had become not only a man but a *father*.

A father.

He stood immobilised, letting the implications sink in.

A patriarchal gesture was obviously required. Taking a gold ring from his finger – one given him by Conor mac Nessa – he pressed it into Ayfa's palm. 'I have to attend the king at Emain Macha, but when my son has grown large enough to keep this ring on his finger, send him to me.'

She nodded. 'I will bear you a hero.'

'If you want to raise a hero, I ask you to place three prohibitions. Tell him he is never to give way to any man, that is the first *ges*. Second, he must not let any man force him to give away his name. Third, he must never refuse to meet an opponent in single combat; any opponent, no matter how powerful. If these *gessa* shape him, he will make us both very proud.'

Cuchulain smiled, satisfied he had discharged an important obligation to his unborn son. Ayfa was of the Celtic race; she knew as well as he did the powers of *gessa*. Sometimes they were intuitively discovered by the druids, as Dethcaen had done for Cuchulain; sometimes they were a birth-gift from parent to child. These were a birth-gift, the accumulated wisdom of a young warrior.

'Promise me,' Cuchulain demanded. He had chosen these *gessa* because each meant something to him. He was proud of his courage; he was sorry he had let his name be changed and lost so much of Setanta; he was determined to stand as a champion against whatever the world might offer. These three gifts of himself he would give to his son.

'Promise me, Ayfa.'

She repeated solemnly, 'I vow by sun and moon, by fire and air, by night and day, by sea and land.' Most binding of oaths, this one compelled the very elements to rise up and destroy anyone who dared break it.

When Cuchulain had gone, Ayfa remained alone in the guest house, hugging her belly with her arms and smiling to herself. I will accompany my son to Emain Macha, she promised herself. As soon as he is old enough to wear his father's ring, he will be old enough for the sea voyage. If Cuchulain has not returned by then to marry me, I will go to his land to marry him. With his son, his firstborn son.

I will be wife to the great Hound of Ulster.

At last all the farewells were said, and the Ulstermen made their way back to the beach where their boat awaited them. The sun was, by that time, low in the sky; a camp would be set up for the night, and they would await the change of the tide.

'Do you know what night this is?' Cuchulain asked Ferdiad.

The other man glanced at the sky. 'I don't . . . Samhain!'

'It is Samhain. I suspect Conor mac Nessa secretly hoped we would be back in time for the Samhain feast at Emain Macha. Every clan-chieftain in Ulster will be there, if he can.'

'And the bards will recite the genealogies and sing the praises of the dead,' Cethern joined in, 'because Samhain is death's festival . . .'

'When the barriers between the living and the dead are lowest,' Ferdiad concluded. 'Winter approaches, season of sleep, season of death, which precedes birth.'

Cethern rolled his eyes. 'It isn't the most auspicious time for a sea voyage, don't you agree?'

Their boatman shrugged. 'And why not? The waves are absolutely smooth, we will glide westward as if we're sliding on ice. There's no wind, so we'll have hard rowing, but we should be safe enough. Manannan mac Lir is on your side, Cuchulain.'

The Hound looked at the calm sea, wondering.

That night, the boat owner and his crew took turns standing watch, throwing an occasional bit of driftwood on the fire and talking among themselves in low voices. Although it was Samhain, the night passed uneventfully, and at the turn of the tide they departed for Erin.

The voyage passed as peacefully as if they rowed across a lake, until at last the Ulster coast breasted towards them from a grey mist.

Cuchulain leaped out of the boat before it beached and ran up the strand, taking in great gulps of the air of home. Throwing back his head, he shouted in a mighty voice, 'Red Branch!'

A chorus of yells answered him. Men materialised from the mist, running towards him, shouting greetings. Conall Cearnach and Leary Buadach were competing to reach him first, but just behind them Cuchulain recognised the dear freckled face of Laeg mac Riangabra.

They clashed like armies with happy profanity and a thud of bodies. Laughing, hugging, pummelling one another, they danced on the strand. Buried in the embrace of a dozen, Cuchulain lost sight of Ferdiad, who stood as always a little off to one side, apart.

When the excitement finally subsided, they helped the boatman care for his craft, and Conall Cearnach rewarded him with wool and copper sent by the king. Then the men of the Red Branch broke out supplies of ale and cheese and settled down for serious celebrating.

Cuchulain was anxious to hear of Emer, but there was something more urgent in the wind. 'You've been gone a long time, and a lot has happened,' Leary told him. 'Not all of it good.'

'Not any of it good,' muttered Laeg.

Cuchulain glanced at his charioteer. 'Is it famine? You were always thin, but now you've less meat on you than a duck's leg.'

'We've had hard campaigning. You can't take a track out of Ulster now without meeting a band of warriors from Connaught.'

Cuchulain whistled.

Leary went on, 'Conor mac Nessa thinks Maeve of Cruachan has learned about the Pangs and deems Ulster ripe for the plucking.'

'Trouble,' Conall added succinctly.

Cuchulain agreed. 'It's time I came home,' he said.

Ferdiad remarked to Leary, 'You can stop worrying about Maeve. The Hound of Ulster has returned.'

The Battle-Winner bridled. 'You needn't make it sound as if Cuchulain's going to defend Ulster all by himself. I'm at least as good as he is. Better, probably.'

A celebration of welcome was prepared for the return of the king's foster-son to Emain Macha. The Ulaid gathered for Samhain had, many of them, lingered on in hopes of seeing the famous young warrior. Conor had a special area set aside where Cuchulain could demonstrate the skills he had learned from Skya.

With Ferdiad for partner and foil, he showed them first the salmon-

166

leap, his own discovery, and then ran through his entire new repertoire of battle-feats. Ohs and ahs greeted each one. When a wheel was removed from a chariot and affixed horizontally to a post and set spinning, Cuchulain danced on the rim while Ferdiad threw spear after spear straight at him – yet all sped harmlessly past his whirling form. This feat alone soon had many members of the Red Branch dismantling their own war-carts and setting up wheels to attempt the same thing. A number would be injured, learning.

Still, they clamoured for more. At last Cuchulain met Ferdiad's eyes. 'The Gae Bulga,' he said.

Ferdiad silently unwrapped the spear from its covering of oiled goatskin. As Cuchulain hefted the strange bronze weapon, one of the watching women whispered to a companion, 'The boy is a man. Look at those thighs.'

The men were all looking at the Gae Bulga.

'This weapon,' Cuchulain explained, 'is of a unique design, as you can see. It's not easy to use. But if Ulster is threatened, it is my duty to use it.' He exchanged glances with Ferdiad again. 'For the demonstration, I will need a living target – but not a human one,' he added quickly.

'Easily done,' said someone cheerfully, trotting away to return with a half-grown pig. 'Here is part of tomorrow's meal. Let's see how your spear handles this fellow.'

Cuchulain took up a position. At his signal, the pig was released. It darted away, squealing, and skittered into the crowd, dodging between people's legs. No one would have dared throw a spear at it.

But Cuchulain took a deep breath and hurled the Gae Bulga.

There were shrieks of horror.

The spear sang its song of death. Following the pig, it ducked and dodged through the crowd, which was frantically trying to run in every direction at once. No human was touched; no human was its target. But when the pig doubled in its tracks, it saw the Gae Bulga coming straight at it.

People were throwing themselves on the ground with their arms around their heads.

The relentless spear drove into the pig as it tried to turn, and came out the other side, dragging the animal's entrails.

Those nearest the kill were spattered with blood.

That night at Emain Macha, no one talked of anything but Cuchulain and the Gae Bulga.

Cuchulain listened to the praise and exchanged greetings warmly with everyone from his foster-brothers to the porters, but he tried to avoid discussing the spear. He worked his way through the crowd until he saw Sualtim.

With people pressing on every side, they could hardly avoid each other.

'That was quite a demonstration today,' Sualtim said, because it would have been too awkward not to speak; others were watching.

'I'm going to have a son,' Cuchulain was surprised to hear himself blurt out.

'Ah. A son. *Your* son.'

'My son. Born of my blood.'

'Ah,' said Sualtim again. He seemed to be fumbling for words. 'Here?'

'Away, on Skya's island. But he will be here some day.'

Sualtim wore the frown of a man struggling to impart some urgent message. 'When the time comes . . . when you face your son . . .'

'Isn't this grand!' Nessa shoved herself between them, grabbing each man by an elbow. 'All of us together again at Emain Macha. All the clan, so important, eh? Eh?' She gave each arm a happy shake and hurried off to annoy someone else, leaving Sualtim and Cuchulain looking blankly at each other.

'What did you start to say?'

'I . . . ah . . . that spear, Cuchulain. Be careful of it. Don't ever throw it when you're angry at yourself, for example,' Sualtim gave a slight, nervous laugh and turned away, looking for someone else to talk with about anything else.

After the feast, Conor mac Nessa took Cuchulain aside. In a few terse words, he outlined the situation with Connaught. 'I'm strengthening all our border outposts, and I'd like to have you with a loyal troop at Dun Dalgan; it's a strategic location.'

'What about Sualtim?'

'He doesn't want to be there,' Conor said. 'And I can't leave the place to rot. Besides, your mother's there, and I understand you may soon have a wife to house.' The king smiled.

'Nothing too certain about that,' the young man replied.

'Ah, I know of Forgall's treachery. But I have no doubt you can handle him and claim your Emer.'

Having agreed to take over Dun Dalgan and hold it for the Ulaid,

Cuchulain decided to go to Brega first and get that out of the way. 'Plunge in and through,' he remarked to Laeg.

The night before departure, Cuchulain spent a long time alone, thinking of the past and the future, of Ayfa and Emer, of Sualtim and Dun Dalgan.

A warrior should face battle with his thoughts organised.

Then he drained a succession of ale-horns and went to bed by the simple expedient of wrapping himself in his cloak and falling asleep outside the horse pens, ready and eager for morning.

He awoke inside a pearl. Nacreous light rose from the eastern horizon, spreading an opalescent radiance across the land. In such beauty, even the birds were hushed, and the trees stood in homage with their arms raised against the pale sky.

It was the dawn of the world; man must fight to establish his place or be swept away.

 I had not been on the shore to greet Cuchulain when he returned. I knew he was coming; I could feel him by the time he was halfway home. But I was on the other side of Erin in Connaught, drawn there by the activities of Maeve of Cruachan.

I know Maeve. I have observed her life after life, watching her develop into a complex being. She can love and hate in a single breath. But though she sends men into battle she has never committed herself to me.

Maeve is her own law.

The season of leaf-fall had been cold and – of course! – wet. But at Maeve's urging, her warriors slogged through mud even after it forced them to abandon their chariots, and crossed Ulster's borders with increasing rapacity. They did not satisfy themselves with cattle raids and small skirmishes that sometimes ended, in the Gaelic fashion, with both sides sharing their campfires and ale-skins at the end of the day. Maeve's men stole the cattle and stayed to kill the cattle-lords.

Because war is my business, I was there, inciting both sides to be certain there was a rich harvest left for me on the battlefield.

Yet I am not as bloodthirsty as you may think; I simply require nourishment. All life needs fuel, a transferring of energy, and I need more than humans do.

If you do not think it takes energy to change from one form to another, you are mistaken. I am not always a raven, you see. Though I

169

am one spirit of fierce intent, there are several different shapes in which I may seek expression. Whatever form I assume is always female, however, and the moments of my transformation are, like the lives of women, intimately connected with blood. Menstruation, defloration, childbirth – a sacrifice of blood pouring from human clay to earthly clay. This gives me strength.

Long ago, I assumed the form of a priestess in a land whose name no one remembers now. Grey-haired, white-robed, with a linen scarf on my shoulders and a brass girdle around my waist, I stood with the other priestesses to receive the prisoners of war. We crowned them with fillets of beaten metal as accolades to their courage, then led them to a giant cauldron as large as thirty Hellene amphorae.

As senior priestess I mounted the ladder that leaned against the cauldron, and the prisoners were handed up to me one at a time. I held each one firmly, bending him over the lip of the cauldron. Then I looked towards the sun, chanted the ritual, and cut the prisoner's throat.

The blood of life poured into the cauldron.

I made an excellent priestess, if I do say so.

Indeed, I can assume several forms other than that of a raven. In Erin, I could appear as a handsome red-haired woman washing clothes in a stream. A warrior who saw me in this guise on the eve of battle and recognised the clothes I was washing as his own, could tell by the red-stained water that he was seeing his future bloodspill; his death. The Gael called this apparition Badb.

I might also appear to them as Neman, a crone in black robes singing death-music. In that form, I taught the women of Erin to keen for their slain warriors, their voices shrieking with mine on the wind in a great gorgeous scream of frenzied loss and longing. Neman, the hag – a face of mine.

I can be terrible and I can be beautiful. Some day I meant to show Cuchulain how beautiful I could be.

Forays into Ulster had proved so rewarding for Connaught that new herds grazed on the uplands of Cruachan, and a man could grease his knife with fat every day.

Maeve should have been content with her successes, yet she continued to stalk through her stronghold, examining, appraising, seeing an addition to be made here, an improvement there.

'Doesn't she ever rest?' Baile the stonecutter complained.

'Not since I've known her,' Ailell told him. 'What does she want now?'

'Angled stones set as kerbs on the *slighe* to catch the hubs of speeding chariot wheels and wreck them. And she wants designs carved on them. So, as if I didn't have enough to do already, I have to consult with the *filidh* to be certain the symbols I carve summon the maximum protection and power. But I suppose it's necessary,' he added wearily. 'Under the circumstances.'

Ailell sought out his wife. 'Just when do you expect a full-scale attack?'

'What do you mean?'

'All this building and fortifying you're doing.'

She smiled. 'I'm making Cruachan more splendid than ever.'

'You're not answering my question, woman. Do you expect an army to come screaming across the plains towards us waving their weapons?'

'Considering our increased aggression toward Ulster, wouldn't you say that's a safe assumption? That's what our people believe; it's why they're willing to work so hard enlarging Cruachan. Prudent preparation. Though whether Conor mac Nessa is actually in a position to attack us is something else entirely.'

'I thought so. This is more than prudent preparation, you're indulging your own passion for building. More walls, more duns, more storehouses, more of everything we don't really need. And,' he added resentfully, 'we certainly didn't need to raise the height of the mounds under our hall and the main guest house so those had to be rebuilt too! Night and day, my ears ring with the noise of stones being broken and timbers being nailed. You're going to a needless amount of trouble.'

Maeve pivoted slowly, surveying her handiwork. Beyond the newly elevated main buildings, the fortress seemed to be extending arms in every direction, like a crawling child reaching out greedily. And everywhere she looked, she saw ten tens of projects crying for completion.

'When something stops growing, it starts dying,' she explained to her husband.

'Living things, not forts. They're just earth and stone and timber.'

'My home is my creation,' Maeve said fiercely. 'A living thing.' But he would never understand.

She watched as he ambled off in the direction of the ale-brewing house. A succession of expressions chased one another across Maeve's face, like cloud-shadows racing across hillsides. At last she shrugged and shifted her gaze to gather in her kingdom, from the ragged line of distant blue hills to the diminishing woodlands to the west.

Within bardic memory, the climate of Erin had grown colder and damper, and the western forests had begun to disappear. Nothing was certain; one must fight to hold anything.

Maeve set out on a long walk of inspection. She peered into doorways to see her people at work; she kicked at newly built walls to be certain stones were propped against each other properly so their mortarless weight would hold them in place for many generations. She even went as far as the one place others avoided – the hill that had risen on the plain of Cruachan long before her stronghold was built.

The hill was hollow. Throughout Erin were other hills, mounds possessing the same eerie and unnatural symmetry. Unless encroaching trees and shrubbery disguised their outlines, they stood as stark reminders.

On certain days, the druids gathered at the sites to hold rituals of propitiation with fire and water and animal blood, for the hollow hills were the portals through which the Tuatha de Danann were reputed to have escaped the conquering Gael.

The Tuatha de Danann, a mysterious and pervasive presence, feared and worshipped and everliving in Erin.

Now known as gods.

Maeve took no chances. Stripping a copper ring from her arm, she left it as an offering buried in the soft earth at the mouth of the still-discernible entrance to the cave within the hill. Even if rain someday uncovered the treasure, she knew no one would take it. Not from this place.

Maeve had committed herself to no specific god, but she wanted no enemies more powerful than herself.

Continuing her tour, she made a huge circle that eventually brought her back near the gateway of her dun. There, she suddenly crossed her legs and sat down on the grass. The guard in the gatetower watched impassively, having seen this before.

Leaning forward over her folded legs, Maeve ran her palm across the grass to flatten it, so she could examine the soil at its roots. She sniffed it; she tasted a few grains on the tip of her tongue, rolling her eyes as she judged the exact condition of the earth; she let it trickle slowly between her fingers, assessing its richness and moisture. Then she began to pluck various grasses and subject them to the same sort of scrutiny.

At last she was satisfied. With a long sigh, Maeve leaned back on braced arms, closed her eyes, and turned her face into the wind blowing across the upland of singing grass. 'Live,' she murmured. 'Grow.' Her voice was sweet with love.

Through every pore of her flesh, Maeve inhaled Cruachan of the Enchantments.

15 Though he was the personification of caution when away from home, in his own house Forgall the Wily liked to drink. His brewmaster produced a superior barley beer to warm a man's spirit when his favourite daughter chilled him with every glance.

Emer had finally agreed to stay with him, but in retrospect her father regretted it. He had promised to cherish Cuchulain as his own son, he had even called on the name of her dead mother, and he had at least managed to keep her body in his house – but not her heart. She treated him like a rat in the granary. And her sister, Derforgall, who had little will of her own, had begun following Emer's example.

Forgall was not a happy man.

Too much drink made him truculent, a condition he reached by stages. First came the raised voice, then the stabbing forefinger driving home an obscure point no one else cared about, then an assault – either verbal or physical – on whoever was nearest.

When his drunkenness reached the last stage, no one would serve him but his daughters, and they merely slammed his ale-horn down on the table and hurried out of reach.

The wretched hosteler sat slumped on his bench, swearing to himself. He pounded each profanity into the tabletop with his fist. With enough repetition, his sodden gibberish began to take on meaning, becoming a profound statement about the condition of being human. Or so it seemed to him.

Candles were guttering in their melted wax, and a chill roused Forgall sufficiently to tell him someone had allowed the fire to go out. He was about to call for a servant, when a sound from outside brought him bolt upright on his bench, shocked half-sober.

A clatter of chariots was coming right up the road to his dwelling house.

Someone had left the gates open, someone had not been on guard, someone would pay . . . Forgall fumbled for a weapon. His dulled mind could not remember where he had last seen his sword. Or when.

As a frightened servant came towards him, he shouted, 'Send runners for my sons! Hurry!'

Then Forgall heard a voice he remembered all too well calling Emer's name.

Cullen's Hound had come to take a wife.

At the last moment, some of Forgall's clansmen managed to get the gates closed just as the chariots reached them. Cuchulain did not waste time with an attempted assault on the stout oaken gates. Instead, he went right up the palisade, leaping high and swinging over with astonishing agility. He landed on the balls of his feet and, before any of Forgall's men could stop him, had whirled and let down the bar so the gates swung wide.

His companions poured through the gap.

Forgall's sons came at a run. Battle was joined on the *urla*.

Cuchulain fought well but conventionally; he had left the Gae Bulga behind and promised himself he would not, notnotnot, give in to the battle-fury. He only wanted to subdue Emer's kinfolk and take her away. He hoped his reputation would prevent anyone from seriously challenging him.

He had given orders that neither Forgall nor his sons were to be killed. 'Better you should kill me,' he told his friends. The words still came to him easily; he did not feel as if he could ever die.

There was no reason to be so gentle with the hostel's guards, who went down beneath his attack like scythed hay.

When Emer's oldest brother ran at him, he recognised the man from his likeness to her. Tossing Hardhead into the air, Cuchulain caught the sword by the blade and clubbed Emer's brother unconscious with the hilt. In similar fashion, he dispatched her other brothers, hitting them with enough force to keep them quiet until the battle was over. Then he joined his companions in cleaning up the remaining opposition. In a short time, Forgall's supporters were throwing themselves on the trampled grass and asking for mercy.

Suddenly one lone figure darted across the *urla*, heading for the palisade. Cuchulain shouted and ran after him, but the sound of the Hound's voice accelerated Forgall's terror. With a wild lunge, he made it halfway up the peeled timber posts, clawed desperately, heaved himself up the rest of the way, and looked back to see Cuchulain's face just below him.

'Madman!' Forgall screamed, shaking his fist. The gesture cost him his precarious balance. His arms rotated wildly, then he toppled backwards.

There was a sickening thud on the far side of the palisade.

Once more Cuchulain ignored the gate and went over the wall because it was quicker, but when he dropped down beside Forgall, it was already too late. Emer's father lay with his neck bent at a curious angle, his opened eyes glazing. Forgall the Wily, cattle-lord and hosteler, a fierce foe who loved his daughter, was dead.

Cuchulain bowed his head and stood waiting so the man's spirit might pass out of his body unimpeded. Then he picked up the emptied flesh and carried it into the dun.

Emer ran forward. She did not speak to Cuchulain, she did not even look at him. She bent over Forgall, cradling his face between her hands as she had once caressed the Hound. Only after Cuchulain had carried Forgall into the dwelling house and laid him on a table did Emer ask, 'Did you do this, Cuchulain?'

'I did not. I gave specific orders that neither your father nor your brothers were to be killed. Your brothers lie safely sleeping on the lawn, but Forgall broke his own neck trying to run away from me.'

She did not answer. He could not tell if she believed him. Turning to Ferdiad, he pleaded, 'Tell her how it was!' but Emer was bent over her father's body and did not look up again.

Forgall's clanswomen collected and tended the wounded until the healer arrived, then devoted their attentions to the dead. Emer and Derforgall bathed their father, tenderly combing his hair over the little bald spot on top of his head, arranging his thin beard just as he would have arranged it himself.

Cuchulain slouched against the wall, watching, wishing he were anywhere else.

When Emer's brothers recovered consciousness, they found themselves bound hand and foot with new rope. 'We'll release you when we leave,' Laeg told them. 'But we'll take your weapons with us; we always have use for good weapons at Emain Macha.'

The keening of the women shivered on the evening air.

Exhausted and pale, Emer finally turned aside from her father's body. There was nothing more to do for him; the earth would have to do the rest, restoring him to herself. Emer pushed her straggling hair back from her damp forehead and looked in a dazed way around the hall.

Cuchulain offered a tentative smile. He looked as bad as she felt –

but not as bad as Forgall, she thought. Emer wished there was something to say to him, but death was a riddle without an answer.

Cuchulain straightened up, watching her with a desperate intensity.

She made herself walk towards him one slow step at a time. When she reached him, he opened his cloak and pulled her inside, against the beating of his heart.

'I loved him,' Emer said in a muffled voice. 'You only saw the worst of him, he wasn't always like that. I did love him.'

'That's good.'

'And he loved me.'

'That's better.'

'He wanted the best for me always, Cuchulain. He wanted me to be wife to a chariot-chieftain with a strong fort and fields blooming with cattle.'

'I answer that description now,' Cuchulain said, keenly aware of the irony. 'Dun Dalgan has been assigned to me. I would have told Forgall, if he'd given me a chance.'

'He wouldn't have listened.'

'Why?'

'You know how it is, Cuchulain.' He noticed with pain that she did not call him Setanta. 'What was between you had to be finished. He had set his hand against you and couldn't back down, it was a point of honour.'

'So he doomed himself.' This irony was something Cuchulain knew he would think about, and brood on, in the future. Magic had a dark face; was it possible the same was true of honour? Honour, which he had set above all else.

'We'd better get back to Emain Macha,' Conall reminded him.

'Soon . . . soon.' Yet he put off departing, not able to bear the thought that it might all end here. He might never see her again, she might never forgive him, and he could not even find the courage to ask her.

He wandered to the guest house and stood staring absently at the dead brown rushes on the floor. He heard Laeg calling his name. 'Come on, we're leaving!'

'You don't dare go without me,' Cuchulain muttered, kicking at the rushes. A cloud of musty dust arose.

'Come *on*,' Laeg shouted again.

With an oath, Cuchulain left the guest house and turned toward the gateway. Then he stopped like a man who had run nose-first into a wall.

Emer stood beside Laeg in his chariot.

He ran forward, hardly daring to believe.

Her eyes were lowered, so he could not interpret her expression. With clenched hands, she held the chariot rim, standing patiently, waiting.

Cuchulain climbed into the war-cart beside her before she could change her mind. There was room, she had brought only a leather bag of clothing. 'Where is your box of jewels?' he asked, unable to think of anything better to say.

Emer met his eyes then. 'I spent them. For a worthwhile cause.'

Cuchulain furrowed his forehead. If this was a riddle, he was too tired and dazed to work it out.

'I'll explain it to you on the way back,' offered Laeg, with the delighted grin of a man who has been keeping a secret too long and has just received permission to tell. 'Shall we go, then?'

Suddenly, Cuchulain felt so weightless he could have flown to Emain Macha. He did not care about jewels; he had Emer.

As it happened, he was not through fighting for her. Forgall had been a cattle-lord with debts owed him, and some of these men tried to impede Cuchulain's progress with Emer. When they offered battle, Cuchulain, to his surprise, was not tempted by the Rage. He was too happy for anger. He merely hit and bashed and won and went on his way with his woman riding proud beside him, her hair streaming out behind her as the horses galloped.

They had almost reached Emain Macha when he realised Emer was crying to herself. He put his arm around her, resenting his impotence in the face of grief. Grief would not yield to armies; it was always a matter for single combat.

Since Conor mac Nessa had been denied the joys of marrying Fedlimid's daughter, he announced he would lavish the resources of Ulster on Cuchulain's wedding instead.

At sunrise on the festival day of Beltaine, the aristocracy of the Ulaid gathered at the royal stronghold to celebrate the marriage. The massive oaken gates were swung wide on their iron hinges. Lines of spearmen held back the crowds as a single pipe played the dawn summons, a piercing sweet echo across the valleys and hills.

Through the gates raced a chariot driven by a freckled and bony charioteer. Cuchulain stood beside him, pale but composed.

The Hound of Ulster wore new garments for his wedding day,

emblematic of his rank. Cuchulain had not confided to anyone, even Ferdiad, how much he wanted to wear the colours of Murthemney, but Sualtim had not offered him a cloak. And he had not asked for one. A man's wedding cloak must be freely given by the father who took credit for him.

Cuchulain came to Emer clad only in the gifts of Conor mac Nessa.

A jerkin of *sida* fitted him as closely as his skin, covering him from his neck to the brownish-red battle-apron identifying him as a member of the warrior class. Across his shoulders was a cloak of bright crimson, bordered with six colours from the king's own cloak. Red-gold was set into the hilt of his sword, and his dark hair was plaited and fastened with balls of yellow-gold, one for each of his trophies in the House of the Red Branch.

The cream of the king's clan stepped forward to greet him. Bard and druid, healer and harper, they called him by name; Sencha the chief brehon, who would preside over the agreement to the marriage contract, recited the specific rituals for the day as set out by law so each person would know his or her exact duties and obligations.

When Cuchulain dismounted from his chariot, representatives of Conor's allied clans took turns offering gifts to the king's favourite. He received a number of sworn men-at-arms and lavish assortments of brazen-headed javelins and other weaponry. A herd of cattle waited beyond the gates in his name; a flock of sheep was a gift to him also.

The king's distributor, a man trained in counting, had already enumerated the gifts with Sencha at his elbow and declared the offerings to be within the law entitlements for a king's fosterling.

Accompanied by nine female attendants, Emer emerged at last from the *grianan* and came towards an increasingly impatient Cuchulain. And though it was only Beltaine, summer came with her.

He did not notice her pleated gown or her fur-trimmed cloak. The elaborate curls the women had laboured over were just a formless, tawny richness as far as Cuchulain was concerned. Details of hairdress and cosmetics were lost on him; he only saw Emer's eyes.

She had spent her jewellery and her father was dead, but the Hound had been firm about the matter of a bride-price. He had given Derforgall a pair of topaz armlets, rings of crystal, and buskins of red deer hide, as well as other treasures, and from this assortment Emer's older sister had selected a brooch set with amethyst and given it back to the girl as a dowry. 'I do not think you will starve in the household of the Hound,' she had said somewhat wistfully.

179

Many females were wistful this day, looking at Cuchulain.

Sencha recited the contract as they had agreed to it beforehand, while delegations from far-flung clans continued to arrive, anxious to show their allegiance to the king of Ulster. A pandemonium of children ran underfoot, squealing with excitement. Cuchulain's eyes crinkled at the corners with pleasure when the little folk blundered against him; children belonged at weddings.

Late in the day, the guests reclined in concentric rings according to their rank, overflowing the House of the King and spreading out upon the *urla* like bright flowers. Venison and pork and smelt and salmon were served them; attendants ran back and forth replenishing the gold and silver cups of the king's family and the ale-horns of chariot-chieftains and the wooden cups of ash and sycamore belonging to guests of lesser rank.

When no one could eat more, rush torches were lighted and the dancing began, accompanied by harp and pipe and bell. Musicians who had accompanied the various clans competed briskly to see who could capture more listeners, and men whose bellies were too swollen with food to allow them to stand managed to do a little pleasant wrist-wrestling with their neighbours.

As the final event of the day, Athairne rose to recite. The entire population of Emain Macha gathered eagerly to push back the encroaching darkness with the supersensual flame of poetry only a true bard could ignite.

On this day of beginnings, it was the chief poet's duty to carry his people back to an earlier beginning. He would tell of Amergin, most famous of bards, whose words had inspired the Gael of five hundred years earlier to undertake the hazardous voyage to Erin and attempt the conquest of the Tuatha de Danann.

Transfixed, the descendants of those bold chariot-chieftains listened again to the epic of Erin.

With polished voice and rhythmic chant, Athairne re-created a time lost in antiquity when the borderland between the perceived world and the Otherworld was in flux, when the differences between man and god were thinly delineated, and one could shapechange into the other. He sang of the past, but in Erin little had changed. In the darkness beyond the pools of torchlight, magic was still alive.

Cuchulain felt it run across his shoulders like a shudder.

When the poet finished reciting, only the wind dared speak. His listeners were immobile, lost in enchantment.

180

Cuchulain felt a touch on his arm. 'Come with me now, my Hound,' said Conor mac Nessa very softly.

He roused himself with difficulty. 'What is it?'

'I have a final wedding gift to give you,' the king told him.

Cuchulain rose obediently and followed Conor mac Nessa. A small torchbearer trotted ahead of them, holding aloft a blazing sheaf of wood soaked in pitch. They made their way from the central area of the fortress to the chariot shed and horse pens.

The light from the torch made the animals blink. The king gave a low call, and two separated themselves from the herd and came forward: two new horses Cuchulain had never seen before, though he thought he knew all his foster-father's stock.

This pair knew the king, it was obvious. They arched their necks for his caress. He stroked each in turn, then snapped his fingers at his torchbearer. The boy produced a handful of barley from a leather pouch at his waist, and Conor fed it to the horses a few grains at a time, letting them lip it from his open palm.

They were stallions, a huge, heavy muscled grey and a black as glossy as the sea at night, equally large. Aside from their colours, they were a matched pair.

'You like them?' Conor asked Cuchulain.

'They steal my breath.'

'They're yours, then. Right it is they go to you. One of my mares was in foal on the night you were born, and these two are descended from the twins she bore. I call this the Grey of Macha, that the Black of Sainglain. There are no faster horses in Erin, and they've been trained to fight to the death for their master. I've kept them . . . elsewhere, as a surprise.' He smiled an ironic smile. 'Sometimes hiding a treasure away is a good idea.

'Take them, Cuchulain. Have Laeg harness them to your chariot in the morning, and take your new wife home.'

For this journey, Cuchulain dispensed with the services of his charioteer and let Laeg follow with a cart containing his belongings, while he drove his new horses himself, acquainting them with their master's touch. Emer stood proudly beside him. When they reached the place where the chariot road branched, she did not let herself look along the way leading to Brega.

Dectera met them at the gates of Dun Dalgan. The years sat heavily upon her. She was very thin, and as grey as Cuchulain's new horse. When she saw her son, she raised one hand to her throat in a startled, jerky movement.

But then she smiled and bade him and his wife welcome, and he thought perhaps everything would be all right.

'I'm sorry I haven't been able to come to see you more often,' he said.

'You are occupied with a man's business now,' Dectera replied. 'It's all right. I'm not lonely.' She smiled a little, secretive smile.

Emer glanced at her husband. Dectera's smile made her uncomfortable.

Dun Dalgan was not the home she might have hoped. It still bore some hints of the important stronghold it had once been, but the fort was in a sad state of disrepair.

'Forgall the Wily would have bitten his tongue if he'd seen me living here,' Emer teased Cuchulain.

He was dismayed. 'I hadn't realised it was so bad . . .'

'It isn't!' she laughed. 'It's gorgeous, because you're here. Don't you understand?'

I suppose I still have something to learn about women, Cuchulain told himself.

He set to work at once, repairing the fort. At first, he deferred to his mother out of respect, but she was so vague, he soon gave up and made all decisions himself. Aside from decay, nothing had changed at Dun Dalgan.

Yet the arrival of Emer gave new meaning to its name, Dun Dalgan of the Bright Aspect. Everyone quickly loved her. She was unfailingly kind to Dectera; she could be found working right along with the labourers and craftsmen Cuchulain brought from as far away as the settlement of Ath Cliath to the south. She scrubbed, she scoured, she swept, she brought joy into the shadowed hall and garlanded its walls with laughter.

When she and Cuchulain entered their sleeping chamber together, she fitted into his arms exactly as he remembered. He could not get enough of her. And when she chuckled the deep, throaty chuckle of a happy woman, the Hound experienced the unfamiliar sensation of being at peace with the world and himself.

He threw himself into the restoration with such passion that, all too soon, Dun Dalgan stood complete again. A fortress for a major chariot-chieftain, a hero of the Red Branch. Old Gelace presided over its kitchens, and Caisin came up from the bay to brag beside the hearth about his favourite student.

But when work on the fort was finished, Cuchulain began to feel restless. Every warrior within a fortnight's journey knew the Hound held Dun Dalgan, and no one came to challenge him to even the simplest contest. Laeg, bored, began taking the chariot out and racing the black and the grey in huge circles, the way Sualtim had once done, while Cuchulain practised his battle-feats over and over, and paced and brooded and stared into space. 'I wonder what the rest of the Red Branch are doing?' he said one time too many.

Resentful of his longing for their company, Emer sang songs to him and invented games to challenge him and tumbled him into bed at the most unexpected moments. Red Branch, Red Branch, she thought, biting down on her anger. What could they offer him she could not? She understood the competition between women for a man, but she could not imagine how to fight the entire Red Branch for her Setanta's undivided affection.

The Red Branch was a rival whose power she dared not consciously admit to herself.

 It was me Cuchulain longed for, of course. They all need me, the warriors, but Cuchulain more than most. How else could he use the lightning-swift reflexes he had worked so hard to develop; the hard-twisting sinews, the great bunching muscles? Raising walls and moving boulders could not satisfy him for long.

A creature like Emer would never understand. How could Cuchulain ever be hers? Only I appreciated the hunger in him and could satisfy him.

What came after was not entirely of my doing, however. When dealing with humans, I must draw on the energy they supply, and the form that energy takes is determined by the natures of the individuals involved.

Men, like the earth that bears them, have two faces: one in sun and one in shadow. Each may choose for himself the face he turns to his brother. The bright side is beautiful, but the dark has its purpose, as do night and winter and death.

At my urging, the child Setanta had first opened the passageway to the dark side of his nature and drawn strength from it. But the Hound of Ulster could also be gentle. He could fight and kill and bathe in blood, then wash it away to reach out in tenderness and compassion to bind the wounds of his enemies.

Many can not.

For them, battle becomes an all-consuming lust that destroys their brighter side. With each killing, they hope to feel more alive themselves, but they never do, so they go on killing and killing.

In Erin.

Where my son, Mechi, was slain for pleasure, long ago.

Cuchulain, on an inspection tour of his new landholding, came by accident upon the field where the pillar stone stood.

The raven was waiting for him.

This time, there was no innocent salute, no playful gesture of childish allegiance. He just stood and looked, and the bird looked back at him.

When he returned to the fort, he took Emer into his arms and held her tightly without speaking for a long, long time.

Bricriu of the Bitter Tongue did not have so felicitous a marriage. His wife was as sour as he. Every part of the day offered an opportunity to quarrel. If he came in hungry and asked what there was to eat, she might say, 'Which would you like, mutton or stirabout?'

Bricriu would consider the question by plastering it against the roof of his mouth with his tongue. Any question was dangerous. 'Mutton,' he would venture at last.

Her eyes blazed. 'And what's wrong with my stirabout?'

A wife like that kept a man agitated.

The quarrel over food suggested a plan to Bricriu. In accordance with custom, one night a year he would be expected to prepare and serve a feast for the other members of the Red Branch – but why not have it in his own stronghold instead of at Emain Macha, and arrange a diversion to amuse himself at the same time?

He went to see the king. 'I'm building a splendid new feasting house,' he said, 'and plan a larger feast than anyone has served for a generation. But it's far too much food and drink to transport here, so I would like to invite all my friends – and their women – to my stronghold instead. Dun Droma, the Fort on the Ridge.'

Conor stroked his yellow beard, which was as long as a warrior's hand. 'I don't think so, Bricriu. I've been under your rooftree before. Fighting is good fun, but your household is so constantly quarrelsome, a man can't digest his dinner.'

Bitter-Tongue's eyes narrowed with cunning. 'How can you refuse the sincere request of a man who has never failed to fight for you? Besides – if you don't come, I will turn the warriors against one another until no two of them are left unbloodied.'

Conor was taken aback. He knew Bricriu's gift; the man could do what he threatened. But the king resented his blatant coercion. The set of his jaw and the coldness of his eye indicated furious refusal.

Then Bricriu threw his most irresistible argument into the pot. 'If you don't show your support and friendship for me by attending my feast, I will, with clever words, set the very breasts of the women of Ulster to beating against each other until they become foul and putrid!'

Conor mac Nessa gnawed his refusal off his lips. If Bricriu caused discord among the women, there would be no peace for anyone. Sometimes the essence of kingship was the art of compromise.

He hesitated long enough to give the impression of still having control over the situation, then said, 'You've been a reliable warrior, and I suppose you have the right to make this request. But I counter: if we feast at your fort, you give us eight hostages as guarantors of your good behaviour for the duration of our visit. And as soon as the food is served, you will withdraw from the hall so we can eat our meal without the whiplash of your words.'

Bricriu considered. 'Good enough,' he finally agreed.

When Cuchulain received word that the warriors of the Red Branch were to accompany the king to Bricriu's stronghold, the news affected him like a deep drink of wine. He whistled tunelessly to himself as he polished the bronze bosses on his shield. 'Bricriu has a bad reputation,' Emer reminded her husband. 'Don't you expect trouble?'

'Of course,' he answered. 'That's why I'm going.'

The skin crinkled on either side of Emer's nose when she laughed. 'I should have guessed as much.'

When they arrived at Dun Droma, the Hound could see that Bitter-Tongue had gone to unprecedented lengths to make an impression. His massive new feasting hall was three times the size of his dwelling. In addition, he had built a new *grianan* for the comfort of female guests, and put up scores of pens to hold chariot horses. The entire stronghold smelled of fresh wickerwork and adzed timber.

Cuchulain promptly left Emer at the *grianan* and went off in search of Ferdiad. He was so anxious to be with his Red Branch comrade, he did not notice the flash of jealousy in Emer's eyes. Someone else did, however – Conall Cearnach's new wife, an elegant young woman called Lendabair, who was much admired for the delicacy of her hands and feet and had drawn some appreciative glances from Cuchulain himself.

'You weren't raised at Emain Macha,' Lendabair said to Emer, 'or you'd realise how strong the bonds are between the warriors. We are the borders of their lives, but the Red Branch is the centre.'

Emer gritted her teeth.

To his disappointment, Cuchulain could not find Ferdiad. 'He's standing guard on the western approaches,' Fergus informed him. 'Border trouble. Connaught.'

The mention of Connaught was explanation enough.

Before Bricriu's feast was served, the warriors engaged in contests of strength and skill on the *urla*. Their host stood off to one side, calling encouragement to each impartially, cheering the victors and enjoying the chagrin of the losers.

Cuchulain held himself back in some of the contests so other members of the Red Branch could win. Conor mac Nessa, who knew him well, realised what he was doing.

'Don't let them catch you at it,' the king advised his fosterling in a whisper.

'The only one who could really give me a contest is Ferdiad.'

Conor gave Cuchulain a searching look. 'Let the others boast; better for you if you do not.'

'I'm not boasting.'

A few paces away, pretending to stare in another direction entirely, Bricriu overheard the conversation. His eyes kindled. With the hitching gait of a man in constant pain, he crossed the *urla* to Leary the Battle-Winner. 'Ah, my old friend, it's glad I am to see you here,' he said. 'Even if you are not accorded your true place.'

Leary looked puzzled. 'What place is that?'

'Next to the high seat reserved for the king of Ulster, I have placed another carved bench meant for the champion of champions, the best fighting man in the land. In my opinion, the title should be yours – though I dare say the king's favourite will help himself to it unless someone stops him.'

Leary Buadach began to swell like a man who has drunk too much water.

Blandly, Bricriu continued, 'The real purpose of my arranging this feast was my perhaps foolish hope that such a champion might emerge. A *genuine* champion, you understand. Against such an eventuality, I have a huge cask of imported wine, a fine young boar, a magnificent ram, a bullock without equal . . . and in addition to all those tributes, I would give such a man an amount of silver and gold to the width of his face.'

186

By the time Bricriu left him, Leary was waving his arms in excitement and racing his tongue like a chariot team.

In contrast, Conall Cearnach was standing quietly beside his wife, watching the contests with his arms folded and his mouth closed. Bricriu approached them, saying, 'You must be proud to be married to such a hero, Lendabair.'

'I am proud,' she replied, inclining her head graciously.

'Then you should urge Conal to overcome his reticence and take for himself the well-deserved title of champion of champions. Don't you agree?'

'I do agree!'

'Great rewards go with the title, Lendabair,' Bricriu said. He enumerated them as he had done for Leary, though in even more glowing terms. The look in Lendabair's eyes as he left them assured him her husband would be persuaded.

After the foot-race, Bricriu found Cuchulain in the guest house, bathing the sweat from his face. 'Do you like this bronze basin?' he asked genially. 'I have one like it in every chamber. Of course, there is a much finer one set apart for the supreme champion of the Red Branch. Champion of all Ulster.'

Cuchulain stopped washing. 'There is no such man, only Fergus mac Roy, and he's the king's champion.'

'Ah, and there is a difference, is there not? There should be such a man, Cuchulain . . . and who but the Hound? I have collected a Champion's Portion to be awarded at my feast, and I fully expect you to claim it.'

Cuchulain was suspicious. 'Does the king know about this?'

The other man shrugged. 'Is there anything the king does not know?'

So Conor knows, Cuchulain thought. Yet he warned me against boasting.

Does he think someone else is better suited to be champion of Ulster?

A swift, irrational anger flooded through him.

True to his word, when the feast was ready to be served, Bricriu supervised its arrival at the hall, then prepared to leave. He need not be physically present to know what would happen next. Imagining the scene to follow would serve him in stead of sharing the banquet. Since his last terrible battle injury, he had been forced to live on soaked bread and ducks' eggs anyway. Given this circumstance and his wife's disposition, he had made the furtherance of discord his chief delight.

As the last tray heaped with food was carried into the feasting hall,

Bricriu paused in the doorway. 'The choicest meat this night is reserved for the champion of champions!' he shouted.

Then he limped away, wearing the smug expression of a man who has just enjoyed a good bowel movement.

16 Until that moment, Conor mac Nessa had been enjoying himself. Bricriu seemed to be abiding by the rules, the food smelled good, and there was plenty to drink.

Yet the king of Ulster never totally forgot himself, no matter how many cups he lifted to his lips. Let others shout and grow sodden; part of Conor was always held in reserve, watchful and wary, mindful of his title.

He was the king.

Because Fergus mac Roy had grown weary of responsibility he had failed in kingship, surrendering the title without a fight. Sometimes his successor wondered if the subsequent fateful incident of Macha and her curse had not been a punishment visited upon the Ulstermen because their king had failed them.

Conor mac Nessa did not intend to make the same mistake.

At Bricriu's feast, he lounged on his bench in apparent relaxation, but as always he kept a clear, paternal eye on his people.

Most of them were approaching their customary state of rowdy revelry. Some few – those who were too drunk or too arrogant to take part – remained aloof, gazing at inner landscapes.

Conor had occasionally observed Cuchulain thus. Though neither drunk nor arrogant, the Hound could, if the mood was on him, sit for an entire evening in quiet contemplation, separated from the others not by his profession, as the king was, but by his very nature.

My foster-son is a thinker, Conor had decided. How surprising in a man of swords and spears. I wonder if anyone will ever realise it but me?

But on this occasion, Cuchulain was part of the action. No sooner had Bricriu spoken than Conall and Leary jumped to their feet and the Hound was right with them, his cheeks flaming as all three yelled their claim to the prize.

Conor mac Nessa nodded to himself. 'That's it,' he said. 'That's what Bitter-Tongue intended from the beginning. May his left foot fester and develop a wobble.'

But cursing Bricriu would not help, the damage was done. Three members of the Red Branch had become enemies in the blink of an eye and were yelling defiantly at each other as they argued over the Champion's Portion.

Wine and ale had been poured copiously throughout the day. Some of the men in the hall were on the far edge of control. Each of the three claimants had immediate, and angry, partisans; fights broke out like grassfires. Tables and benches were overturned. Bricriu's hounds fled the hall, deeming it unwise to wait around for food scraps.

With every man on his feet, shoving and shouting and struggling with his neighbour, the wickerwork walls began to bulge outward.

The king of Ulster glanced anxiously toward Cuchulain, hoping his foster-son would not lose himself to the Rage. If he did, in such constricted quarters there would soon be men dead, warriors too valuable to lose. But the Hound seemed, with difficulty, to be controlling himself.

Cuchulain was doubly angered at Conall and Leary. He had counted them as friends, yet now he was reminded how they had abandoned him on Skya's island. They were turning their backs on him again, claiming an honour that Cuchulain felt should, by all rights, be his. With a howl of delight at fighting again, mingled with a growl of resentment, he threw himself upon the both of them.

Other men at once cleared the floor, flattening themselves against the walls to stay out of the way. By unspoken mutual consent, Conall and Leary moved closer together, prepared to fight the Hound jointly.

The king's eyes sparked with anger. 'Unfair!' he cried. But the level of noise had risen so much that no one heard him. He swung around until he caught the eye of Fergus mac Roy. 'Help me,' Conor mouthed.

King and former king shoved through the crowd and interposed their bodies between the three antagonists. They looked eager to dismember each other, but none of them was so far gone he was willing to attack the king and Fergus.

A grudging truce settled over them like dust.

'I won't have you disrupting my feast in this fashion,' Conor said. 'You can't settle this matter in here.'

'This isn't your *maigen*,' Leary pointed out in a surly voice, still glaring at Cuchulain. 'And there's nothing to settle. It should be obvious that I'm the oldest and most experienced, and I've fought in more battles than any man here. The title is mine.'

At once Conall whirled toward him with a doubled fist and a furious light in his eyes. 'When did you ever defeat me?' he roared. 'Or me?' Cuchulain added, lunging towards him.

Only quick footwork by the king and his personal champion prevented the fighting from beginning again. At last, red-faced and panting, the three men were separated and sent to cool off in different corners of the hall.

'It still isn't your *maigen*!' Leary yelled at his king.

'But I am your king,' Conor reminded him grimly. 'And if you come out of that corner before I give you permission, I'll hit you myself. My sire was Fachtna the Giant, remember,' he added, lifting an exceptionally large fist for Leary to observe and think about.

The king beckoned Sencha the brehon to his side. 'Advice,' he said succinctly.

The judge nodded. 'Be thankful the question of a champion for all your kingdom hasn't arisen before. It was certain to, sooner or later. And these three, together with Ferdiad, son of Daman, are the best of your fighting men.'

'I'm thankful Ferdiad isn't here to make it worse.'

'Ah, he would never set himself against Cuchulain,' Sencha said confidently. 'But now that it's been voiced, the matter will have to be decided. I have a suggestion.'

'I have two ears. Put it in them at once.'

'This might be a wise time for some overture of friendship toward Connaught. Nothing too obvious, you don't want Maeve to think she has you worried . . . but some subtle, diplomatic gesture of placation. Why not send these three – your most skilled fighting men, and each of them very impressive to watch – to Maeve and Ailell? Ask them to serve as impartial judges. They should be flattered by your request, and it will also give them a chance to see how very dangerous your warriors can be, if matters between Ulster and Connaught grow worse.'

Conor stood with his head bowed, stroking his beard as he listened. A smile appeared within that beard. 'You have earned the title of chief brehon many times over, Sencha, and never more surely than with this advice. I'll make the annoucement in a way to placate all three, explaining that it's a singular honour they are receiving. Then we'll send them off to Connaught to impress Maeve and Ailell with their martial displays instead of breaking up Ulaid feasting houses.'

With the full force of his kingship upon him, Conor mac Nessa informed the three of his intentions, and they received the news with varying degrees of good grace. Cuchulain nodded, muttering, 'Good enough.' Conall said nothing at all; Leary protested in an angry undertone but dared not let the king hear him.

When the feast was over, however, Fedelm of the Fresh Heart, Leary's wife, sought out Emer. 'I must say I'm surprised your husband is seriously in contention,' she remarked, 'when his rank is so clouded. A champion should have an impeccable pedigree, I would think.'

'What do you mean?'

'My Leary Buadach, son of Connad, son of Iliath, has heard the bards recite all the generations of his fathers. He knows who he is, and our children know their rank as a result of their lineage.

'Likewise, Conall Cearnach sits on the bench once occupied by Amorgen, who sired him, so his knots with the past are securely tied. But no man boasts of having sired Cuchulain, Emer. Don't you find that strange, when he is so admired? It makes me wonder what your children might be like – if you have any.'

Fedelm smiled a tight little smile and turned away, leaving Emer to stare at her back.

If I have children? But of course I will have children, Cuchulain's sons and daughters. A warrior is expected to replace himself. Then her thoughts slammed against a wall.

Who is Cuchulain replacing?

Try as she might, Emer could not recall his ever having spoken of his father. She had simply assumed it was Dectera's husband.

Bricriu's wife was happy to enlighten her. Taking Emer by the elbow and leading her aside so no one could overhear, the woman said, 'For your own good, you know, someone should tell you. Fedelm mentioned your conversation to me, and I felt so sorry for you, being kept in ignorance of what everyone else knows.

'Among the Red Branch, there have always been three possible candidates considered as sires for your husband. Sualtim, of course, though that looks doubtful. Or Conor mac Nessa, his mother's own brother – a mating that could introduce monsters into the line, which is why there is a strict *ges* against it.

'Or . . .' the woman hesitated, drawing out her pleasure in the moment.

'Or?' Emer's breath quickened; her heart was beating so hard it hurt her throat. Intuition told her the third answer must be very terrible.

'Or one of the gods themselves. Lugh, Son of the Sun. If that is the case, your husband isn't even human, Emer, not really – and who can say what his children might be?'

192

In a swift, instinctive gesture, Emer put her hand over her womb as if to protect the life not yet cradled there.

Inhuman . . . Her eyes flared wide.

'I told you this for your own good,' Bricriu's wife reiterated.

Cuchulain, Conall, and Leary were to return to Emain Macha and prepare there for their trip to Connaught. Emer rode in the chariot with her husband, but she was silent and thoughtful on the trip. Cuchulain did not notice, his own thoughts were directed on the trials to come. The championship. Of Ulster.

Behind them, Bricriu's wife settled contentedly into bed beside her husband. 'You've put the Red Branch at each other's throats,' she said, 'and I've given the Hound's wife a nettle to grasp.'

Both were so pleased with themselves that they did not begin a new round of bickering and complaining until well after sun-up of the next day.

Having arrived at Emain Macha, Cuchulain and the other two went their separate ways, to practise their war-feats and prepare their weapons. On the night before they were to depart for Connaught, Cuchulain was unable to fall asleep. He was performing his feats over and over in his mind, becoming increasingly critical. Emer was also restless, unable to lie still.

How can I ask Cuchulain, she was wondering. He will think I doubt him, that I listen to the prattle of foolish women. How could I possibly ask my husband if he was sired by his own uncle – or more preposterous still, by Lewy Long-Hand!

She tossed and turned, started to speak, bit her lip, rolled over again, and buried her face in her pillow.

I'm keeping her awake, Cuchulain decided. Getting up quietly, he slipped from the chamber.

When he went outside for a breath of fresh air, he found Conor mac Nessa there before him, staring up into a pebbled sky.

'Can't you sleep either, Cuchulain?'

'I was disturbing Emer, so I thought it would be better to come out here and count the stars.'

'Count the stars,' Conor echoed. 'I do that myself when the night grows too long. Do you believe they are the eyes of distant gods watching us?'

'I sincerely hope not, Foster-Father.'

Conor laughed ruefully. 'I agree. I wouldn't want strange gods to see me being petty.'

Cuchulain looked at him in surprise. 'You?'

'Shall I tell you why I can't sleep? I lie awake planning vengeance on Naisi.' Conor's voice thickened with self-disgust. 'You left Emer so she could sleep, a generous gesture. If I were as generous as a king is supposed to be, I would open my hand and surrender Deirdre to her happiness. I would even welcome the sons of Uisnach back among the Red Branch. The noble deed of a kingly man, people would say; the bards would tell future generations of my compassion.

'But I can't do it, Cuchulain! I want to tear Naisi to pieces with my bare hands. I want to hurl Deirdre, whom I loved, whom I still love, into the deepest pit. And I hate both of them for showing me this side of myself.'

In his youth and preoccupation with his own inner struggles, Cuchulain had not yet thought of the struggles of others. Conor's anguish came as a revelation to him. He put a hand on the king's shoulder in sympathy. The two stood together silently, watching the uncaring stars.

When Emer could no longer bear to lie alone in bed, she went looking for her husband. She found him with Conor on the footbeaten path that circled among the royal halls, but she did not approach them, and they did not notice her in the night shadows. She stood with narrowed eyes, comparing them. One was exceptionally tall and fair, the other short and dark – yet the same noble proportions graced them both.

Emer's eyes were stinging. She slipped back inside without calling attention to herself, and piled all the covers in the bed-chamber on top of her.

On the morning of departure, Cuchulain was in good spirits, even without sleep. 'The next time you see me, you must act very impressed,' he teased Emer. 'I'll expect all sorts of bowing and saluting for the champion of Ulster.'

She did not feel playful. 'Connaught is an unfriendly land,' she said. 'You are not going as invaders, but I'd prefer you didn't go at all. You don't have to prove anything to me.'

'This is for my own sake,' he told her. 'And my sons.'

He had never told her about Ayfa, he suddenly realised, seeing an odd expression in her eyes when he mentioned sons. But it was of no importance. Emer was his only choice as a wife, and the sons she would bear him would be his favourites. He smiled to make her smile back at him and put his finger on the tip of her nose. 'Now laugh,' he ordered. Helplessly, she did.

194

A crowd lined both sides of the *slighe* to see the contestants depart. The three rode in chariots crowded with clothing and weapons. At the last moment, a group of women gathered thickly around Cuchulain's war-cart, holding him back just as Conall and Leary galloped off toward Connaught.

Among the throng Cuchulain recognised the wives of Conall and Leary.

He understood their game, then, and was amused. No matter what their women tried, the other two would not reach Cruachan ahead of him. He had the Grey of Macha and the Black of Sainglain.

'Laeg,' he ordered, 'bring me some apples.' While the women watched with wide eyes, he juggled nine apples and caught them on the tips of nine spears, occasionally winking at the crowd to show them how easy this was. Laeg leaned against the shoulder of the Grey and basked in Cuchulain's arrogance. The Hound cast occasional surreptitious glances along the road, judging the distance his rivals had gained by the size of the dust cloud behind them. When he decided the cloud was small enough, he threw the apples to the crowd and Laeg sprang into the chariot at once. With one crack of the whip, they were away.

The Grey of Macha and the Black of Sainglain overtook the other chariots with disheartening ease. 'Grand day, this,' Cuchulain observed pleasantly.

Neither Conall nor Leary responded.

When they reached the end of Conor's territory, the road turned into a rutted cart track. The chariots were forced to a trot, then a walk, then a trot again, always mindful of the possibility of disabling stones that might cut the horses' feet or damage a wheel.

They were fortunate in the weather. A high, clear sun shone down on them as they made their way toward Cruachan of the Enchantments. Cuchulain felt its heat on his shoulders like a benevolent mantle, and sometimes he laughed aloud with the sheer joy of adventure, of being young and desperately alive.

The same sun shone on Dun Dalgan. Emer had returned to await her hero there and look after Dectera. And the itch of curiosity had come with her.

More than an itch, Emer's curiosity was a torment.

From the beginning, Cuchulain had instructed his wife to be gentle and patient with Dectera, not to ask her a lot of questions because she was inclined to be vague and did not understand things clearly any more. But now there were questions that must be asked.

Dectera, Emer reasoned, was probably feeling insulted because her son's new wife had not already wanted to know the family history.

'The day is fine,' she said to the older woman. 'Come and sit with me on the *urla*.'

'I stay out of the sun,' Dectera replied.

'Why? Is there a *ges* upon you?' Emer asked, meaning to make a joke. 'Can't you go anywhere you choose?'

Dectera gave her an astonishingly bitter look. 'If I could go anywhere I chose, do you think I would still be here?'

The sharpness of the reply alerted Emer. The answer is right here, she thought. If I can just ask the question she cannot resist answering.

They were in the hall of Dun Dalgan, amid the perpetual shadows of the great room. Dectera sat on a bench to one side of the hearth and Emer on one across from her, but now she stood up and went to kneel beside Cuchulain's mother, looking up earnestly into the old face. 'Where would you go if you could?' she asked. 'If you left this fort, whose protection would you put yourself under?'

Dectera was not vague at all; a sly light of understanding gleamed in her eyes. 'You're trying to get me to tell you *his* name, aren't you? That's what everyone has always wanted of me, *his* name. They asked me and asked me. Not long after we came here, Sualtim pinned me to the wall with a hand on each arm – I wore the bruises for days.' She held out her twig-thin arms as if the bruises could still be seen. 'He shouted at me to tell him who sired the child; he swore it wouldn't make any difference, it would be no more to him than having a fosterling.

'But I knew it would make a difference and I did not tell him, for fear it would destroy us.' Her shoulders sagged. 'As things fell out, we were destroyed anyway.'

So you have given me one answer, Emer thought. Sualtim is not Cuchulain's father. Suddenly she regretted her curiosity; the only answers left were both answers she did not want. But she could not stop, it was worse than ever now. She had to know.

She was patient with Dectera. She fed the other woman mead and fruit, she chatted of inconsequential things. She talked in spirals and then in circles, but at last she returned to the only topic that mattered.

'I need to know who Cuchulain's father was,' she said frankly. 'For the sake of the children I will bear him.'

Dectera heaved a long sigh. 'My first lover.' She paused. Emer waited. When Dectera spoke again, her voice was sweet and sad. 'Memories are like thorns,' she said. 'You go through life carrying them in your hands. If you want to put them down, you cannot, they are too deeply imbedded.

'Sualtim tried to banish the memories. He wanted me so much. But whenever he touched me, it was as if he felt other hands on my body, between himself and me. He came to hate me for it. And I hated him for not being able to forget. We might have been happy, otherwise,' she added wistfully.

She was wandering away in her mind. Emer put her face close to Dectera's to recapture her attention and made one last, desperate plea. 'What name did you never tell Sualtim? For the sake of my unborn children, tell me!'

Dectera was at the edge of a silvery mist. From deep within the mist came light, an opalescent light she remembered from long ago. One more step would take her into that mist and beyond reach for ever.

She had always known it was there waiting for her.

But Emer's gaze was compelling. Cuchulain's wife had a right to ask the question. And perhaps if she answered it, just once, she would be free to go.

With an effort, she pulled herself back into reality. 'You are right, Emer, your children are entitled to know the name of their father's father. If Cuchulain had ever insisted, I would have told him. It is important to know the tree from which we branch. The sons of kings must have confidence to rule, the sons of warriors must have confidence to fight. And the son of . . .'

'The son of. . . ?' Emer's hand cupped Dectera's head, holding her close for her answer.

'Perhaps you will be fortunate. Perhaps you will be barren.'

Shocked, Emer withdrew her hand. 'What is so terrible about my husband's siring?' she cried.

So Dectera told her. And then went quietly, permanently, gladly, into the waiting mist.

17 Cruachan of the Enchantments waited on its upland of singing grass. The ever-present wind played a music so constant that no one noticed until it stopped; then people cocked their heads and stood perplexed, wondering what was missing. On the meadows beyond the increasingly sprawling royal complex, herders tended livestock and cotters dug stones out of fields for yet more building.

It was an ordinary day. Until thunder came rolling along the winding roadway.

A trumpet blast from a sentry brought a full complement of armed warriors running to the front gates. Ailell soon joined them, strapping on his swordbelt. Maeve was at his elbow. No hand would be raised against the visitors until their purpose was known; their open approach demanded a courteous response.

A smooth-faced lad was in the lead, riding in a kingly chariot bedecked with feathers. Impressed by the equipage, Ailell addressed him first. 'May all roads be smooth to you.'

'And may you be safe from all harm except that which you bring on yourself,' the stranger responded in a surprisingly deep yet gentle voice.

'This is not a boy,' Ailell told his wife from the corner of his mouth.

Overhearing, Cuchulain announced, 'I am a warrior. They call me Cullen's Hound.'

A startled gasp arose from the gathering crowd. Maeve recovered first. 'How extraordinary. And why are you here?'

Leary Buadach and Conall Cearnach had also drawn their chariots up by this time, their drivers competing to see who could get closest to the obvious rulers of the stronghold. Leary, as eldest of the three Ulaid, took it upon himself to answer. 'We mean to settle the championship of Ulster between us, and Sencha the brehon has told us Maeve and Ailell of Connaught would be best equipped to make that judgement.'

Flattered, Ailell relaxed. Maeve did not. 'I think Sencha is no friend, to give me such a hard task,' Ailell said graciously. 'But as I know all the arts of combat, I will be happy to render my opinion.' He felt a sharp jab in his ribs. 'My wife and I will give our opinion,' he amended. 'Now – will you stay in one guest house?'

The three Ulstermen exchanged glances. Conall Cearnach spoke for the first time. 'Separate chambers.'

Ah, it's like that already, Maeve thought with satisfaction. They come to us as enemies to each other. If the best warriors in Ulster are so divided, it's good news for Connaught. 'We welcome the opportunity and are grateful for the honour you bestow on us,' she told them with a wide smile.

When their guests had retired to refresh themselves, Maeve and Ailell shared a pillow. 'I never knew Conor mac Nessa had such a high opinion of my judgement,' Ailell remarked happily.

Maeve leaned on one elbow and looked down at him. 'Idiot. It's some sort of trick.'

Ailell thrust out his underlip. 'You're just saying that to annoy me. There's no trick here, merely proof that I'm respected far beyond the borders of Connaught. Now, even the king of Ulster defers to my reputation, and I won't have you trying to take that from me. Go to sleep.'

'Nothing worthwhile was ever accomplished by a man asleep,' Maeve said, reaching for him.

Later, when Ailell was well and truly asleep, Maeve crept silently from the sleeping chamber. She and Ailell could account for many sons between them, and the strongest of these was called Maine Morgor.

She found him still awake. 'I think this story about a championship for Ulster is just an excuse to get spies into Cruachan to assess our strength,' she said. 'Ailell won't listen to me, so I need your help. Here's what I want you to do . . .'

The next morning, while the three from Ulster took turns demonstrating their battle-feats before Maeve and Ailell, Maine Morgor journeyed to a dark glen where a family of rare wildcats lived. He returned to Cruachan with three squirming leather sacks, and deposited one in each of the Ulstermen's sleeping chambers.

As they feasted at the end of the day, Maeve and Ailell watched their guests and discussed them quietly between themselves. 'The other two are good,' Maeve said, 'but when the Hound lifts a weapon, a shiver goes up my spine.'

Ailell's eyebrows crawled towards his hair. 'You find him attractive?'

If he had expected a simple reply, he did not get one. 'I think Cuchulain is war,' said Maeve. 'But I will outlast him.'

Satisfied with his day's performance – they had agreed to contest for three days, as it would take that long to demonstrate their full range of skills – Leary crawled wearily into his bed and fell asleep at once. He awoke to find a pair of slitted yellow eyes glaring at him. With a wild yell, he scrambled for the rafters.

At almost the same moment Conall was having a similar experience, and a man forcibly awakened by the snarl of an enraged wildcat is in no mood for showy feats of valour. Pulling his clothes around him as he ran, Conall fled his chamber.

Cuchulain was also sleeping soundly, until the hot stench of a carnivore's breath flooded his nostrils. When he opened his eyes, the creature was an arm's length away, measuring him with its open mouth.

The cries of the Ulstermen brought Ailell and a score of guards. Leary's wildcat had disappeared from the chamber, and when Ailell came in, he climbed down from the rafters in great embarrassment. 'It was here,' he kept saying. 'I tell you, I saw it!' Nor was any animal to be found in Conall's quarters, though Conall insisted the animal had almost savaged him.

With the two of them at his back, Ailell made his way to Cuchulain's door.

When he opened it, he found the Hound sitting on a stool facing him, sword in hand. Crouched in the corner was a big male wildcat with furious eyes and a lashing tail.

'Be careful how you come in,' Cuchulain said. 'My pet isn't thoroughly tamed.' He nodded in the direction of the cat and it shrank back, spitting.

They gaped at him. 'How did you do that?' asked the dumbfounded Leary Buadach.

Cuchulain chuckled. 'I don't know. The thing was about to attack me, then it yowled and drew back. So here we sit, the two of us, neither wanting to touch the other. If you stand aside, I think it will probably run out the open door.'

'A man who can tame a wildcat, or even frighten one, deserves the title of champion,' Ailell remarked.

Leary yelped. 'Not so! I say he vanquished the animal through magic!'

Cuchulain gave him a long look. 'This is a fair contest between us. I use no magic. I wouldn't know how to put a spell on a wildcat if I wanted to.'

'Wouldn't you?' sneered Leary. The air crackled between them, and the cat, seeing no one watching it, bolted out the door.

200

'Save your energy for tomorrow's contest, then,' Ailell advised.

When he returned to tell his wife what had happened, she seemed strangely disappointed with the outcome. 'I can't imagine how three wildcats could have got all the way into their chambers,' Ailell muttered to himself as he fell asleep.

The next day, the contest resumed. For a second time, Cuchulain outstripped the others. Maeve's watching warriors surrendered to envy as he handled his weapons with the careless indifference of expertise. But he used neither the Gae Bulga nor the Rage.

The warriors also watched, though with less interest, when Conall broke a spear and Cuchulain immediately offered him one of his own. And when Leary tripped and fell backward, Cuchulain caught him before he could crack his spine on a rock protruding from the earth.

Neither man bothered to thank the Hound, Maeve observed. The warmth she saw in their eyes was only the admiration they could not conceal when he took desperate chances to demonstrate impossible feats. He did what no one else would try; men held their breath when he leaped amid flaming spears or hurled himself on a nest of swords.

That evening, Ailell spoke privately to his wife. 'Another round will prove nothing more, let's award the championship to Cuchulain now. We can make a nice little ceremony of it. In fact,' he went on, warming to the idea, 'we could make this the start of a tradition. We could invite all the kings to send their champions to contest here.'

'It's a great shame to waste a body on a mind like yours!' Maeve exclaimed in disgust. 'Are you actually suggesting we make a habit of inviting armed strangers into our land?'

'I just thought these games might . . .'

'This isn't a game, you fool. And close your mouth, I can hear the wind rushing through your skull. This is deadly serious. I don't want to see Cuchulain made champion of anything. I don't want him exalted in a land where my children must live.'

Ailell was taken aback. 'But he's magnificent. I've never seen such fearlessness, such absolute recklessness, such wild valour. He has all the gifts of a hero – and honour too, of course,' he added almost as an afterthought. 'This young man is a model for us all.'

'And there's the poison in the meat,' Maeve said darkly. 'Have you not noticed that no one commends his honour? They are far more impressed by his physical gifts. As his fame spreads, I think young men will indeed pattern themselves on him. The great Hound of Ulster will be remembered, not for his kindnesses, but for his kills. That is what will impress everyone; the number of his kills.'

'I tell you, the Hound will inspire men to fling themselves into profitless carnage for no better reason than to seek the glory of the warrior. And war shouldn't be about glory, Ailell. War is *business*.' Her mouth formed a bitter shape. 'I don't want to see a lot of healthy and useful young men needlessly slain trying to be like the Hound of Ulster.'

'You aren't making sense,' Ailell told his wife.

'You don't understand me because you don't want to; he has you dazzled like the rest of them. But listen. We must put enough obstacles in Cuchulain's way to deny him fame, now, while there's still a chance!'

Ailell said slowly, 'I don't think we can deny a man like that anything.'

My children will die because of Cuchulain, Maeve thought.

During the night, she sent her herald, mac Roth, to her foster-father, Ercol, who lived some distance away. And in the morning, she informed the Ulstermen they had been invited for a day's feasting with Ercol before concluding their contest. 'You will do better with a little rest,' Maeve said persuasively.

The three young warriors drove to the dun of Ercol, each secretly glad to have a chance to gather his energies before the final competition. Ercol welcomed them heartily and prepared a fine feast in their honour – a feast attended by an old friend of his, the most gifted druid in Connaught. A man both celebrated and feared.

The druid's reputation was well earned, for his particular gift was the ability to reach into a man's mind and finger its contents; rearrange them, sometimes. At Ercol's private suggestion, he used his arts on the Red Branch warriors while they unsuspectingly feasted.

He found both Conall and Leary simple, straightforward men, unable to deny him their minds or resist his will. But he had no instructions concerning these two; they were merely an exercise to warm up his powers.

He turned his full attention upon Cuchulain.

The Hound felt the first tentative probe, like a stick thrust between his thoughts. He was fully alert at once. The probe was repeated, followed by a wave of mental laughter, the laughter of the initiate who thinks himself master. The smell of druidry flooded Cuchulain's nostrils.

He concentrated on the silent laughter and met it with one single calculated block of the Rage.

Fight magic with magic, he thought.

If it is magic.

If I know what magic is.

He looked up to see the druid staring at him.

The man tried silently to suggest that Cuchulain was not hungry, and the Hound promptly ate more food than anyone at the feast. He next suggested the young warrior was very thirsty, but Cuchulain pushed his cup away and would let no one refill it. Finally, the druid tried to fulfil the order he had been given – 'Make him weak, turn his muscles to pudding' – but when he hurled this suggestion at Cuchulain, the Hound laughed aloud.

'Bring me a wagon axle!' he cried. While the guests at the feast watched in disbelief, he bent the iron axle over his knee as if it were wet bread dough.

Defeated, the druid pulled his hood over his face and left the feast early.

Ercol was upset to realise he would have to admit failure to Maeve. He ground his teeth and bit his thumb; then an idea occurred to him. He could inflict some damage on Cuchulain after all, though not as much as Maeve wanted.

As his three guests were preparing to leave, Ercol went to the stone-walled bawn where he kept his horses. A big roan stallion came to meet him, rolling its eyes in perpetual bad temper. He opened the gate and jumped out of the animal's way as it galloped past.

The half-harnessed horses of the three Ulstermen heard the stallion's shrill whinny of challenge and answered it. All six exploded with excitement as the roan charged toward them, his tail flung over his back like a battle flag.

Their charioteers tried to control them, but it was no use. Ercol's vicious stallion flung himself on one of Conall's good bay horses and forced it to the ground, tearing the muscle loose from its foreleg. Then he spun around and delivered a terrible kick with both hind legs, catching one of Leary's team full in the ribs. The men heard the bones crack.

Rising on to his hind legs, the roan screamed another challenge.

An answering cry came from the Grey of Macha. Pawing the sky, Cuchulain's horse walked erect towards the roan. They met like a clash of armies. Squealing and grunting, they struggled for position as the helpless charioteers danced around them, trying to separate the two without getting killed themselves. Each horse was trying to grasp the neck of the other with his teeth and tear open the crest, a stallion's emblem of pride and beauty.

The Grey of Macha rose again, higher than before, as Cuchulain came running up with Conall and Leary. This time, the Grey managed to get a foreleg over the roan's back and used his weight to drive the other to the ground. As the roan stallion went down, the Grey whirled and savaged him with hooves and teeth.

It was soon over. Ercol arrived in time to watch his horse die.

Cuchulain offered him no sympathy. 'You brought this on yourself,' was all he said.

In sobered silence, the three men returned to Cruachan. Cuchulain's team could be driven, but Conall and Leary each had a badly damaged animal that had to be led, hobbling and bleeding.

Maeve met them and took in the situation at a glance. 'Must even your horses be superior, Cuchulain?'

Cuchulain stepped down from the war-cart to face Maeve. His hands were open at his sides, his face serene. Seen thus, he was beautiful, she thought to herself. His glowing silver eyes were set in an eagle's face, proud and predatory, but his mouth was as sweet as a child's, and those long, supple fingers could surely do exciting things to a woman's body . . .

She jerked her thoughts back to find Cuchulain watching her as if he knew what she was thinking. Which he did. Women had been looking at him in just that way for some time now. He retained his reverence for them, but he had learned they were very human.

'There is a terrible danger in you,' Maeve said.

'I have no intention of hurting you. My foster-father has taken a *ges* upon himself against hurting women and I honour it, as does all the Red Branch.'

'That isn't what I mean. You make what you are too beautiful, Cuchulain. Why must you be a warrior?'

Because my father is one, he started to say. 'Because it is what I know,' he replied instead.

Watching them from a distance, Ailell felt a strange unhinging of reality, as if he were watching an elemental confrontation between two forces he did not understand.

His wife's antagonism towards the superb young man continued to baffle him, in spite of her explanation. As the two of them faced each other now, there was obviously something between them; the very air vibrated with it. Ailell frowned.

Maeve was a woman who would not be conquered by any man, though her husband prided himself on having come closer than anyone else. At least she was still with him – even if sometimes she drove him to exhaustion.

Was that what she had meant when she vowed to outlast Cuchulain?

Suddenly, Ailell felt older than his years, and tired. Particularly tired of looking at younger men.

During the third day's contest, he absented himself, and that night he told Maeve the decision was hers to make, he had lost interest.

The three Ulstermen waited anxiously throughout the feast that night, but no announcement was made. Ailell was paying no attention; Maeve seemed to have forgotten. A harper was playing to entertain the feasters, and all her concentration seemed to be on him.

Curled on her bench with her feet tucked beneath her and one elbow leaning on a magnificent throw of wolfskin, Maeve, as she often did, was losing herself in music.

Finding herself in music.

When the last notes of the harp died away, she shook herself and sat up. The first person who met her glance was Leary Buadach. She beckoned a servant to her side. 'Tell the Ulsterman they call Battle-Winner that I have made my decision. So as to avoid embarrassing the others, I will tell him privately tonight in his own chamber.'

When the servant whispered this information to Leary, the man's face lit and he grinned at Maeve.

A similar message was given to Conall, and to Cuchulain.

Leary waited feverishly until she arrived. She brought no attendants with her and closed the door behind her. Then she took a magnificent bronze cup from a cloth bag and handed it to him. 'This is yours,' she said. 'One of our best craftsmen has put a tiny silver bird in the bottom, see? It's an honour for a champion, but don't show it to your friends yet. There will be time enough to display it when you return to Emain Macha; you don't want to make them unduly jealous on the long drive home.'

What a wise woman, Leary thought. She meant them to return believing the decision had not been made, out of sensitivity for their feelings. Bad news was always better received when one was at home.

He smiled at her. She smiled at him. Her gown was very thin, and when she stepped closer he caught the sweet, earthy pungence of her skin.

Glancing out of his open doorway, Cuchulain saw Maeve cross from Leary's chamber to that of Conall Cearnach. Her clothing was disordered.

A delighted Conall received a silver cup with a gold bird at the bottom, and the admonition not to tell the others yet. He received other indications of Maeve's favour as well.

When at last she approached Cuchulain's door, she found it bolted from the inside.

Maeve frowned in anger. She would not knock at the door like a petitioner. Instead, she went to a private chamber she often used and had a servant come to summon Cuchulain formally.

The door was opened to his knock, and the man found the Hound and his charioteer sitting together, playing chess.

'Maeve expects you,' the servant said. 'Privately,' he added.

Cuchulain snorted. 'Does she think I'm a fool?' He went on playing chess.

When the servant returned to Maeve, she was lying comfortably propped amid a welter of pillows, her grown spread around her in an attractive fan. But when the man repeated Cuchulain's words, she sat bolt upright. 'By the hills and the grass!' she exploded. 'That lad is hard to deal with.'

Back she went to Cuchulain's chamber. She did not knock at the door, she kicked it open. With a peremptory gesture, she dismissed Laeg, who looked to Cuchulain for confirmation before leaving. She slammed the door behind him.

Then Maeve sat down beside the Hound and rested one arm across his shoulders. With one powerful twitch, Cuchulain threw off her arm with such force that she found herself sitting on the floor in a most unbecoming posture.

'Don't try it with me,' he warned.

Before she could guard her tongue, Maeve burst out in frustration. 'Then what does work with you?'

To her surprise, Cuchulain threw back his head and laughed. Unhidden by a beard, his strong white neck looked clean and young. 'If I tell you my secrets, will you tell me yours, Maeve?'

'Ah, you admit you have secrets.'

'Don't you?'

They studied each other's faces until the tingling antagonism between them turned into something quite different.

Cuchulain's eyes blazed in their frame of black lashes. He was aware of neither lust nor love. The passion suddenly scorching through him was as compelling as the drive of the sun to pour energy into the fertile earth.

Maeve, who never granted unconditional surrender to any man,

206

could not look away from the frightening intensity in his eyes. She had come to him with the strength of anger, but she had no strength now. All the power was his . . . Her knees and her lips parted . . .

No! Maeve fought back. Before he could move, she had clamped her teeth on her lip until the pain broke her free. Staggering, she pulled herself to her feet. She sensed him reaching toward her and turned away. Her ears were ringing.

When she regained control of herself, she turned around to find Cuchulain sitting as before, his hands on his knees, his expression guarded. But there was no denying the passion that had shaken them both – the air was still charged with it.

If I had given in to him, Maeve thought, I would have lost myself for ever. She had never been so frightened.

Forcing her voice to remain steady, she said, 'You should not have been rude to me, Cuchulain. I merely brought you the honour you have earned.' She withdrew from its bag a spectacular golden cup with a bird of jewels and enamel set in the bottom. 'For the champion,' she said. 'There is no disputing truth.'

She seemed almost subdued, and Cuchulain regretted having been rough with her. But the feelings she had summoned in him had startled him; he also struggled to sound calm as he replied, 'I thank you for your generosity.'

She put the cup in his hand. 'I am not giving you this,' Maeve said. 'You took it.'

She turned towards the door, but before going out, she looked back at him. 'I won't be available to bid you farewell in the morning. Just leave, all three of you, and when you reach Emain Macha show your cup to the king, so he will know his champion of Ulster.

'But I think we will meet again, Cuchulain. I think we must meet again. There is something unfinished between us.'

The look she gave him made the hackles rise on Cuchulain's back.

The return to Emain Macha took twice as long as the journey out. Ailell had offered Conall and Leary new chariot horses, but they insisted out of pride on going home with the animals they brought, since Cuchulain still had his. That meant they must walk the entire way, the sound horses pulling the weight and the injured horses dragging along in the traces, while the men accompanied them afoot.

When Cuchulain got out of his war-cart to walk with them, Leary gave him an angry look, but Conall shrugged and accepted his company.

When they finally arrived, travel-grimed and weary, the wives rushed to meet their heroes. Cuchulain was sorry he had sent Emer back to Dun Dalgan. At that moment, he would have given the gold cup just to see her bright face with those of Leary's wife, Fedelm, and Conall's wife, Lendabair.

He needed Emer's face to come between himself and his memories of Maeve, of the future that lay waiting for him in her eyes.

Conor mac Nessa came forward to greet them, his face impassive to avoid showing favouritism. 'Has Ulster a champion?' he asked with cool formality.

Cuchulain nodded. 'A decision was rendered,' he said. 'Once we have bathed our faces and feet and washed the insides of our throats, we will tell you everything that happened, Foster-Father.'

'When you are ready, come to the House of the King. An excellent ox has been roasting very slowly in anticipation.'

Not speaking to each other, the three men split up to refresh themselves and prepare for the evening's feast. Each nursed a secret. Each waited to hatch it with the eagerness of a hen for her single egg.

The reward Bricriu had set aside for the champion of Ulster was piled outside the doorway of the royal hall, with a guard watching it. Other Ulidians had added their own tributes, until a veritable fortune was amassed, including several full sets of horse harness set with gold and silver and more bowls and cups and ale-horns than a man could use in two lifetimes.

Eyeing the assortment, Cuchulain and his companions entered and took their seats with the Red Branch. The carving of the meat began. At each stroke of the knife, Sencha announced according to tradition, 'A thigh for the king. A thigh for the chief poet. A chine for the second poet. Legs for the king's sons. The head for the smith . . .' So it continued until all portions had been assigned but the haunches. The brehon then said, 'One haunch belongs to the king's own champion, Fergus mac Roy. And the other haunch is, now and for ever, given to the champion of Ulster.'

Leary and Conall leaped to their feet simultaneously, each brandishing a shining cup and demanding the Champion's Portion.

18

'Over here!' cried Leary. 'That meat is mine, Maeve of Connaught herself gave me – '

'Liar,' screamed Conall, beyond silence for once. 'She gave me silver! Look, you only have bronze.'

Benches were kicked aside, fists doubled, men leaped on to tables, and there was a concerted rush for the weapons stacked outside the door.

Conor mac Nessa sighed.

The Hound stood up. He said nothing, he would not have been heard in the din. But reaching into the folds of his tunic, he took out a cup of gold and held it high above his head.

Men, seeing it, pointed it out to other men. The great hall grew quiet. The Red Branch resumed their seats.

'You didn't win that fairly,' Conall said, not wanting to believe.

'You bought it,' Leary accused, 'or took it by sorcery.'

The cords stood out in Cuchulain's neck. 'Be careful what you say.'

'The gold is the proof,' Sencha decided. 'And we know this man well enough to know he acquired it with honour. The Champion's Portion is yours, Cuchulain.'

He ate the meat slowly, methodically, the joy gone out of it because he knew two in the hall begrudged him every bite.

But he ate it; he ate it all.

Across land and water, another feast was being served. Skya had restored Ayfa to her own clan, and upon learning of the birth of Ayfa's son, had come to take part in the celebration. In her honour, Ayfa had ordered one of her precious Ulster beeves to be slaughtered and roasted, and the two women were lingering over their meal in the wattle-and-daub feasting hall.

'He seems a healthy child,' Skya commented, digging among her back teeth with her fingernails in hopes of extracting a troublesome shred of meat.

'He's more than healthy,' replied the proud mother, 'he's wonderfully strong. Like his father. Did you notice the fists he makes?

Cuchulain will be very pleased when he sees the son I have produced for him; I have named the boy Cunla, meaning son of the Hound.'

Skya found her shred, removed it from her mouth, examined it, and ate it. Beef was a rare luxury. 'When will Cuchulain ever see the boy?' she wondered.

Ayfa beckoned to one of her attendants to bring more barley beer. 'As soon as Cunla's big enough to keep his father's ring on his finger, I'm going to take him to Emain Macha myself,' she replied. 'At Cuchulain's request,' she added, shading the truth slightly. By now, she believed it, however. Since the Hound's departure, the woman who had known only masculine pursuits had found herself spending much time daydreaming in a most feminine vein. 'When we arrive, I intend to marry Cuchulain,' she told Skya. 'I'm a warrior myself, and he's the first man I've ever known who was worthy of me. We will be a grand pair, will we not?'

'Don't be ridiculous,' the other woman scoffed. 'I can't imagine you journeying all the way to Erin just to accept second rank in another woman's household.'

Ayfa's eyes, which had been dreamily contemplating her future, widened. 'What do you mean?'

'I mean you would have to live in the Hound's stronghold with his first wife.'

'But he isn't married!'

'He wasn't,' Skya agreed. 'Not when he was here. But during that last bad storm, a boatload of Ulster fishermen were blown ashore on my coast, and they told us of Cuchulain's marriage. It was the talk of the kingdom, it seems, a most festive occasion. Almost as soon as he returned to Ulster, he married a woman called Emer, the daughter of one Forgall the hosteler.

'So you see, Ayfa, if you go to Ulster and also wed the Hound, you'll live out your days as second in rank, and you and I both know you could never do that. Better to stay here, like me . . . we'll become two mean old warhorses together, eh?' She reached out and slapped the younger woman heartily on the shoulder, then turned to spear another hunk of meat from the platter held by the waiting attendant.

Skya was not sensitive; she had not noticed the way Ayfa flinched from her last words. Nor did she see how pale Ayfa had become at the mention of Cuchulain's marriage. But when she had both cheeks refilled with food and looked back at her comrade, she found Ayfa slumped on her bench as if the spine had been pulled out of her back.

'Cuchulain . . . married?' Ayfa said in a disbelieving voice. Then a dull red began to creep back into her cheeks. 'As soon as he returned to Ulster? While my sweat was hardly dry on his body?' The voice rose. Realisation was beginning to cut through shock. 'Whose daughter did you say he married?'

'A man known as Forgall the Wily, a cattle-lord who runs – or ran, he's dead now – a hostel in Ulster. If you're not going to eat that bit, give it to me.' Skya reached; Ayfa gave automatically, her mind elsewhere. Forgall the Wily, the younger woman was mouthing silently. She stared past Skya, seeing the formation of an inexorable pattern.

For the rest of the day, Ayfa proved such poor company that Skya at last grew bored and went home. She had expected to exchange war stories, chant some snatches of comic song, restore the camaraderie she had enjoyed while Ayfa was her hostage. But motherhood seemed to have ruined the woman, Skya mused. Too bad.

As soon as she was gone, Ayfa went into her stone-walled, mud-plastered sleeping chamber with the baby, and bolted the door behind her. She had no wooden bedbox; a pile of furs and sealskins was her pallet, and she sank down upon this with her son in her arms. A small bronze lamp, its flame guttering in seal oil, cast distorted shadows around the chamber.

Ayfa looked intently into the infant's little red face. 'I once promised Forgall the Wily I would kill the man who later fathered you – did you know that?' she asked as seriously as if the baby had been an adult. 'I was to lure Cuchulain into a battle and make certain he was slain. Forgall paid me well for the service. An unearned payment I had no right to keep, as it fell out, for once I saw Cuchulain with the hero-light around him, I forgot all about killing him.

'So I remain in debt to Forgall. He is dead, but if I don't pay my debt to him in this life, I shall have to pay it later.' She was speaking very slowly as her brain fought its way through layers of hurt and loss. But her brain was fighting; it would soon seize upon a less painful emotion and draw vitality from that.

'He went from *me* to a . . . *hosteler's daughter!* He must have already intended to do it when he left this island, Cunla. Indeed, he must have known that last day, when I told him of you . . .'

Insult blossomed in her; her brows contracted in anger. 'He could not have been more cruel if he used the Gae Bulga on me!' The vehemence of her outcry startled the baby, who began to wail and shake his little red fists in the air. Ayfa's attention snapped back to him.

211

'Cunla! Ah, Cunla. My little warrior. I have a weapon of my own now, don't I? A perfect weapon for revenge against the Hound; one even he cannot resist.' He teeth pulled back from her lips, parodying a smile. But there was no sweetness in Ayfa's smile.

'Forgall,' she vowed in a low voice, 'I will keep my promise to you. In fact, I will keep all my promises. Cunla, your father had me promise him to instruct you in the *gessa* he placed upon you and so I shall. Starting tonight, and repeating every sunrise and sunset of your life until they are more a part of you than your blood and your bone. Hear me, my son!

'You are forbidden to give way to any man. You are forbidden to give away your name to any man. And most important, you are forbidden to refuse any challenge to single combat, no matter who the challenger.'

The last tears she would ever shed were sparkling in Ayfa's eyes as she lifted her baby above her head. Holding him at arm's length, she shouted up at the frightened, squirming child, '*Never give way, never tell your name, kill any man who challenges you!*'

The terrified baby screamed back at her and waved his fists.

Cunla. Son of the Hound.

The acknowledged champion of Ulster prepared to leave Emain Macha for his home at Dun Dalgan. Conall had, finally, accepted Cuchulain's title without reservations; Leary still muttered to himself about it from time to time, but the quarrel was fading.

Yet in the space it left, another quarrel swiftly grew larger. The old topic of Naisi re-entered every conversation, men became more fixed in their opinions, and the divisions between members of the Red Branch widened.

Cuchulain was glad to turn his back on all of it and go home to Emer. Home to Emer. He liked the sound of the words. The reward she would give him for his victory was sweeter to Cuchulain than any gold cup or stack of treasure.

When the sentry announced his approach, she came running out to meet him, holding out her arms and crying, 'Setanta!' careless of who might hear.

Laeg, driving the chariot, grinned.

Cuchulain leaped down and ran to his wife, meeting her with a shout of happiness, lifting her into his arms and whirling around and around with her beneath a sunny sky. Now, I have everything I want, he told himself – except sons, and they will begin to come soon. Ah, Emer . . . soon!

As they entered the hall, Emer explained his mother's absence by saying, 'Dectera stays in her sleeping chamber most of the time now; she's wandering in her mind. Not just wandering – gone completely. Your old physician has looked at her, everyone has, but there's nothing to be done. She's been given herbs and potions and we've offered sacrifices, but nothing brings her back.'

The light dimmed in Cuchulain's face. 'You'd better take me to her,' he said.

As he had expected, he found Dectera lying in her bed, staring up at the smoked underside of the thatch. Her hair was combed and braided, and Emer had even put a touch of *ruam* on her lips. She was breathing calmly, but no one lived behind her open eyes.

'She's left us,' Cuchulain affirmed.

'It wasn't my fault,' Emer said quickly.

'Of course not, don't you think I know that? I always expected her to go like this, some day. It isn't anyone's fault.'

Emer breathed a sigh of relief. He had not asked her the exact circumstances, so she felt no obligation to volunteer them. She did not want to relate the conversation she had tried to have with Dectera for the sake of her unborn children.

Her whole spirit ached to give Cuchulain a child. She knew he loved the little ones; his eyes followed those who played around the fort, whether freeborn or slave. He joined merrily in their childish games, and they accepted him almost as one of themselves.

But when Emer thought of his parentage, she felt a guilty sense of relief each time her bleeding season came around again and she knew she was not yet pregnant.

Cuchulain visited Dectera daily. He had been given a decoction of vervain for her, because the plant was a remedy for illnesses of the brain. She opened her mouth like an obedient child and let him spoon it in, but he could see no difference in her afterwards. She even let him put a hand under her elbow and take her for walks, Cuchulain striding along trying to make conversation, and his mother drifting mindlessly beside him, unaware.

'She's not alive,' he told Emer bitterly. 'She's just not dead enough to bury.'

A galley belonging to swarthy-skinned traders from the distant Middle Sea beached on the strand east of Dun Dalgan. The captain of the vessel paid a formal visit to the fort. Erin was a good source of hides and goldwork and, occasionally, blue-eyed slaves who fetched fine prices in the markets of Rome and Egypt. Entrepreneurs from southern waters liked to maintain good relations with the various Gaelic warlords whose strongholds ringed the coast.

Cuchulain entertained the visitors with a feast. In honour of the occasion, Emer dressed Dectera in her finest gown and led her into the hall. Even without her mind, she deserved to be present; she was entitled.

The leader of the trade expedition was a Cypriot who had travelled the known world and seen many things; with his first glimpse of Dectera, he recognised a woman touched with sacred madness. He paid little attention to anyone else, and before leaving he paused long enough to kneel beside her bench and touch his forehead three times to her feet in homage.

When the Cypriot had departed with a bellyful of good beef, leaving behind bales of silk and amphorae of wines, Cuchulain and Emer looked at each other in bafflement. 'Why do you suppose he saluted my mother that way?' the Hound wanted to know.

Emer could not answer him. 'Who can explain the ways of the sea-traders?'

With the championship his, Cuchulain expected to be very busy, but a season of peace gripped Ulster instead. The Hound had ample time to bed his wife and begin siring children, yet Emer's belly did not swell.

A season of sharp frost and buffeting winds descended upon them. Conor mac Nessa summoned the clan-chiefs and cattle-lords of Ulster to Emain Macha to celebrate the Samhain feast.

Though he would not admit it to Emer, Cuchulain was glad of the summons. He would see Ferdiad again, and they would talk together of the things that interest men.

Ferdiad met his chariot at the very gates of the royal stronghold, and the two flung themselves at each other, whooping and yelling like boys. Emer watched, her lips twitching with amusement. Men never grow up, she thought, as women had thought in every generation before her.

The Samhain feast was sumptuous and overlong; the rituals of the druids as mysterious as ever. Housed in a hot young body eager for action, Cuchulain found himself getting bored.

Ferdiad agreed. 'Why not have a day's bird-hunting tomorrow, just you and me? I'll get the nets, you bring the spears.'

The new day of the new year dawned cold but brilliant. The two friends struck off on foot across the countryside, flushing an occasional hare but seeing few birds. It did not matter. The pleasure was in being together.

'You should have been one of those to contest for the championship of Ulster,' Cuchulain told Ferdiad as they walked together.

'I was needed elsewhere. Maeve's quiet for now – I think you and Conall and Leary distracted her for a time – but that doesn't mean we can pull back all the guards from the fords and passes. Connaught will always be a problem.'

Cuchulain's eyes brooded on memories. 'Maeve is a clever woman, I'm glad I met her. At least I have an idea what to expect if we meet again.'

'She leads her men but doesn't wield weapons herself, I'm told,' said Ferdiad. 'Not like Skya and Ayfa.'

'Their island is a different land. This is Erin, and war is a man's game here,' Cuchulain replied. 'Even for would-be goldsmiths.'

Ferdiad laughed. 'Maeve seems hard to convince.'

They ambled on. Once, they sighted a covey of red grouse picking a winter's meal from the heather; once, they found a gathering of rooks and jackdaws feeding on insects. But their nets remained empty.

When the sun was high, they sat together with their backs against a rock to share a meal of cake and nuts they had brought with them. 'Champion of Ulster,' Ferdiad said. 'I suppose some day you'll be the king's champion as well.'

'What makes you think so?'

'Have you taken a look at Fergus lately? He's grown so fat, it's easier to climb over him than walk around him.'

'He can still outfight three men, Ferdiad. Besides, Fergus mac Roy would sooner surrender his life than that title. And I don't covet it, I have everything I want.'

'It's always dangerous to say that,' Ferdiad reminded him. 'And there's something else – I've noticed Conor and Fergus aren't as close as they once were. That matter of Naisi and Deirdre; I've heard them argue about it. Feelings run deep there, and I think – '

But what Ferdiad thought Cuchulain did not learn, for at that moment a wild boar broke from cover some distance away and trotted across a field in plain view. Both men yelled. The boar picked up speed, its head high and its upright tail rigid.

As if pulled by strings, Cuchulain and Ferdiad ran after it. Two men afoot, armed with only light birding spears.

Above the scene, a raven watched, making lazy spirals in the sky.

Flying is fun, I admit. There is not much pure fun to be had in my existence, to be candid. So I take what I can where I can.

Housed in a raven's body, I can curl my wings around the wind and climb into a silver-wine sky. I swim on currents of air, gliding, soaring, swooping in the turbulence left by the earth as she tumbles through space. Sometimes I spend a whole day at it and accomplish nothing else.

Ravens' eyes are another pleasure. Sharper than any human vision, the sight of a predator bird can pick out a tiny insect on a leaf or the fullness of a head of grain from the height of a low-hanging cloud. Nothing escapes my eyes when I am a raven.

And, oh! the rapture of freedom as I climb towards the sun until, looking back, I can see the curvature of the earth before oxygen starvation forces the birdbody back down again, skating on the wind.

Curvature of the earth, oxygen starvation, skating. Terms from another reality that do not belong in Cuchulain's world. But for me one shifts into another along unstable borders and I know more than I want to know.

Whooping and yelling, Cuchulain and Ferdiad pursued the wild pig. It was a young male, an immature boar the old sows would not tolerate near them. Consigned to a solitary existence, it roamed the countryside, eating acorns and tender roots. There had been nothing on its small, blank mind but food until the two men attacked it, and it took the animal a few strides to overcome its astonishment and turn to face them.

'Circle behind him!' Cuchulain shouted to Ferdiad.

They tried to hold the animal between them, but the boar was lean and leggy, very quick. Its eyes glittered with viciousness, and it made huffing sounds through its snout, which was spiked by two curving tusks of murderous ivory.

It started towards Ferdiad, then twisted and doubled back, trying to get past Cuchulain. He almost loved the animal for testing him. With a burst of speed, he ran after it, taking huge strides over the frost-crisped grass.

'Gethimgethimgethim!' yelled Ferdiad. He jumped from one foot to the other in his excitement, wishing tardily he had worn his body armour.

The pig changed direction again. Cuchulain understood its intention; at the edge of the open ground, an abandoned hut was snuggled into the curve of a hill like a hen settled on her nest. Beyond the hut, a

216

stand of oak trees loomed. If the boar reached the woods, it might be safe.

Cuchulain made a frantic arm signal, which Ferdiad understood. He ran for the trees, hoping to get there first, while Cuchulain kept the wild pig distracted.

The animal was not intelligent enough to think about two men at once. Cuchulain kept it occupied by alternately bounding toward it and zigzagging away, being careful never to go too far. The young boar tried several short, angry charges, head lowered, but each time he dodged out of its way, as if playing a delightful game under the bright sky.

The boar was not amused. But it had stamina; it would play as long as the men, and it was learning from every charge. The next time Cuchulain teased it, the animal did not run straight at him but slightly at an angle, anticipating the leap he would take. It hurtled past his legs much closer than he had expected.

'Over here!' Ferdiad called. 'Drive him towards me now!'

Ferdiad was between the boar and the trees, on a slight hummock below which the land fell away towards a patch of bog. With Cuchulain in pursuit, the pig ran in a large circle and headed towards the woods. Ferdiad threw one of his birding spears as soon as it was near enough, but the light shaft glanced off the boar's tough hide. The animal swerved to one side, skirting the bog. Ferdiad ran after it but hesitated on the lip of the wetland, unsure of the ground under his feet. A man could sink up to his waist in moments in a bog.

The boar was past him now, heading for the safety of the trees. Soon both men were running hard behind it, shouting to each other and laughing.

The boar beat them to the woods. They could hear it crashing through the young growth along the edge. This was an oak stand, safe haven for many wild things. Each tree supported a teeming community of snails and caterpillars and spiders to whom the oak was food and home and nursery, universe and god. Wild pigs searching for acorns beneath the trees ploughed the earth with their snouts, inadvertently burying some nuts so deep they never found them. From these accidental plantings, new generations of oaks would spring to support still more life in the future.

Among the oaks, the boar thought itself safe. But the men plunged into the woods without hesitation, unwilling to grant it sanctuary. No undergrowth marred the heart of the stand, and if they could get close enough, they might still manage a lucky spear-throw into ear or eye.

The boar was so enraged by now that its grunts turned into squeals of anger. No matter where it turned, it saw Man. Forgetting everything else, even personal safety, the animal resolved to end its torment. Only one thought blazed through its dim brain; kill.

Lowering its head, it began a deadly charge.

Cuchulain and Ferdiad were trying to keep the boar between them until one could get a clear throw at it. The animal charged, Cuchulain dodged, the boar wheeled in a tight circle and immediately charged again.

Ferdiad was not as quick as Cuchulain. Tusks sharper than knives tore open the thick muscle of his calf.

He staggered backwards with a grunt of pain. The boar, carried by its own momentum, ran past him as he struggled for balance, then spun around and came a third time, straight at the wounded man.

Cuchulain could not throw a spear, because Ferdiad was between himself and the boar. So he used the only option left him, hurling himself up in the salmon-leap and striking his friend with his own body in the instant before the boar hit him. The two fell together as the animal rushed past.

Cuchulain rolled up on to his feet in one motion and flung a spear. The boar, turning back towards him, took it in the eye. Its forelegs collapsed after a few faltering steps. Squealing, the wild pig ploughed its tusks into the soft earth, digging up a little cache of acorns as it fell.

Cuchulain sprang on to the animal, aiming both feet for its exposed neck. He heard the cartilage crunch.

Shaking his head to clear it, Ferdiad sat up. His leg was a column of pain. Seeing Cuchulain's worried face looking down at him, he forced a shaky laugh. 'I thought I was killed.'

'I thought you were too. That was a mad thing we were doing.'

'Mad,' Ferdiad agreed, panting.

'Glorious, though.'

'Glorious!'

They looked at each other and began to laugh.

'How grand it is,' said Cuchulain, 'to find yourself alive when you expected to be dead.'

'It's the best part of a battle,' Ferdiad agreed.

'Can you stand up?'

'I doubt it. Where's the boar?'

'Oh, he's dead enough.' Cuchulain squatted and peered at Ferdiad's leg, from which the blood was pouring. He was still breathing very hard himself, but he turned and retraced the way they had come until he reached the patch of bog. There he collected some sphagnum moss, which he applied to Ferdiad's wound, holding it in place with strips torn from his own tunic. 'That's stopped the bleeding,' he announced with satisfaction.

Ferdiad looked down. 'I'm glad I've been wounded before and know how bad it can look, or I might think my leg was ruined.'

'We'd better get back anyway, and let the king's healer take a look at it.'

'I can stand now,' Ferdiad said, demonstrating with gritted teeth. 'Cut a sapling and we'll sling the boar on it and carry him between us.' He took a step forward and stumbled, his head swimming.

'I don't think you're fit to carry anything,' Cuchulain observed. 'I'll cut you a stick to lean on, and carry the pig myself.'

Ferdiad eyed the dead boar. 'He's young, but he's big.'

'I'm able,' said Cuchulain. He bent and gathered the boar's forelegs in one hand, its hind legs in the other, then crouched down and heaved. In one mighty lift, he had the carcass on his shoulders. 'Let's find you a walking stick and be on our way,' he said cheerfully.

The way back to Emain Macha seemed a much longer distance than the way they had come. By the time they reached the gates, Ferdiad was staggering, leaning against Cuchulain's shoulder, his head close to the lolling head of the dead pig. But in spite of his pain, he managed to grin at the guards who ran to help. 'Cuchulain got him with just a birding spear!'

After the boar had been gutted and drained, its blood saved to make puddings, it was boiled until its bristles were soft enough to be removed with a scraper. Choice organs were set aside, and what remained was consigned to the spit. The sweet smell of roasting pork floated on the air.

The prize was his; Cuchulain would do the carving. He stood beside the boar in the House of the King that night while Sencha recited the apportionments. But when the time came for the haunches to be awarded, Cuchulain made an apportionment of his own. He carried one to Conall Cearnach and the other to Leary Buadach.

That night, the Red Branch cheered the Hound of Ulster until the music of their voices was trapped for ever in the golden thatch.

Later, Cuchulain shared his bed with Ferdiad, who alternated between fever and chills. Fingan the physician had rebound the torn leg and given Ferdiad a strong potion to make him sleep, but the healing process must run its own course. Cuchulain wrapped his arms around his friend when he shivered and wiped the sweat from his face when he burned. Several times he got up to bring water to hold to Ferdiad's lips while he said small, encouraging things. As tender as a mother with a child, he kept watch until the worst was over.

Within a fortnight's time, half the Red Branch had gone out boar-hunting with birding spears.

'They'll get themselves killed,' Fergus predicted. 'It's become the fashion to attempt everything Cuchulain does.'

'I understand why,' said the king. 'He does even the impossible so well.' Conor's eyes darkened, thinking of the Hound's seemingly happy marriage. Even with women, Cuchulain knew only success.

Conor's own women no longer appealed to him. He kept mentally comparing them to the lost Deirdre. Knowing this, they spoke of her frequently in the most scathing tones, so even in her absence, Fedlimid's daughter was causing discord at Emain Macha.

Cuchulain applied to the king for permission to return to Dun Dalgan.

'You shouldn't let him go,' Fergus advised Conor as the Hound prepared for departure. 'Winter will end and leaf-spring will come and we'll have to worry about Connaught again, I suspect, in spite of your friendly overtures to Maeve. Better for Ulster if all the Red Branch were together.'

Conor mac Nessa stroked his beard. 'You expect her to keep raiding?'

'Don't you?'

'I suppose so. If I thought it were just cattle-raiding, it would be one thing. But I sense a more complicated pattern behind Maeve's actions. Fergus. She doesn't think like a man or act like a man, though. I can't get a grip on her, I don't know what she's really after.'

'Women,' said Fergus mac Roy, dismissing the entire sex with a word. 'I'd feel better if all the Red Branch were here at Emain Macha.'

The two men had met in the Speckled House. Conor mac Nessa was there surveying the armaments of his warriors; Fergus had arrived intending to begin the winter maintenance of his own tools of battle. Surrounded by shields and spears, they felt discussion of war to be the only possible topic.

But as so often now, Conor mac Nessa's mind was dwelling on another subject. 'Three of the best of the Red Branch's fighting men are far away,' he said. 'Over the eastern sea, stolen from me by a woman's

220

guile. If they were here, we would be much stronger, Fergus, and you wouldn't reproach me for letting Cuchulain go home to his wife for a while.'

This was an opening Fergus had long awaited. 'Then forgive the sons of Uisnach and send for them. What Naisi did wasn't so terrible, was it? Tens of hundreds of men have stolen tens of hundreds of women, and by the time the women start sagging and nagging, no one can remember what the fuss was about. Lift the name of outlaw from them and bring them home.'

The king narrowed his eyes. 'You seem very anxious to see Deirdre here.'

Fergus thew up his hands. 'Aren't you listening to me? I wasn't thinking about Deirdre. I was thinking of Naisi and his brothers, three fine men who always loved you.'

But the tooth of jealousy was gnawing anew in the king's belly. Fergus wanted to see Deirdre. Every living man wanted to see Deirdre. To touch her, to possess her . . .

He was having those terrible dreams again, the ones in which she was just beyond the reach of his fingertips, and he stretched himself until at last he touched her. He ran his hands down her incomparable body and heard her moan, felt the heat rising in her flesh. Flesh like sun-warmed silk. Pressing against him, her soft belly accepting the hungry rubbing of his throbbing penis, her arms around him, her sweet breath in his nostrils . . . He awoke sweat-drenched and agonised to greet a rising sun the exact colour of her hair.

Terrible is the curse of that woman, Conor thought. No matter where I turn, she torments me.

Seven nights and seven days the king struggled with himself. The days were endless; the nights were worse.

At last he sent for his champion.

Fergus came to him after a difficult night of his own, when he and some of his fellow warriors had gone to the ale-brewing house to sample the latest beverage and declare it fit for a king's feast. Sadly, there was now little left for a feast. Fergus was not feeling his best. When he batted his eyes, the sound of his eyelashes striking together made him wince all the way to his toes.

Conor mac Nessa had not spent the night drinking, but his eyes were sunken and his lips colourless. An apprentice of Fedlimid's was quietly playing a harp in the shadows of the hall, the ubiquitous shaggy wolfhounds sprawled at the king's feet, the great shield Ocean leaned against Conor's bench.

Fergus glanced at the shield. 'Are you expecting trouble?'

Conor followed the direction of his gaze. The shieldmaker mac Enge had outdone himself in the creation of Ocean, a large convex oval of treated hides stretched on a wooden frame, ornamented with bronze bosses and the seven colours of a king. A special feature had been added to Ocean, with Cathbad's help. If the bearer was in mortal danger, even before the blow was struck, the great shield cried aloud to summon help. Its cry was the roar of the ocean.

Having Fergus mac Roy to defend him, Conor usually left Ocean hanging in its place on the wall of the Speckled House. Seeing it so close to the king told Fergus the condition of the other man's mind more clearly than words.

'I'm not expecting trouble, I already have it,' Conor answered his question. 'Word has come that Maeve's activities in our outlands grow bolder and bolder; soon we will need every warrior of the Ulaid to stand against her.' He stroked his beard. 'Every warrior,' he added meaningfully. 'It is time to set grudges aside in the interest of Ulster and the tribe.'

Seeing where this might be leading, Fergus brightened. 'Naisi?'

Conor nodded. 'If you stood as guarantor to their safety, I think the sons of Uisnach would come home with you.'

'They trust me, everyone trusts me,' Fergus could not resist boasting. 'But can I promise them safety if they return?'

'Would I ask you otherwise?'

Fergus gave his foster-son a long, hard look, and wished his brain were not muddied with the aftereffects of drinking. He found the king's face unreadable. But Conor was the king; his word had to be copper-fastened. 'Bring Naisi and his brothers back to Ulster, Fergus,' he commanded. 'I've learned where they are, in Alba; I will send you for them. Boats are already arranged.'

'I'll take my sons Buinne and Illand with me, then,' Fergus decided. 'They've never seen Alba.'

'Of course, anything you want.' When Fergus hurried from the hall, Conor leaned back on his bench and put one hand over his eyes. Once he was informed Fergus had departed on his mission, the king sent for a cattle-lord called Borach. He did not want to do what he was planning, but he had been driven to it.

And perhaps he was not to blame at all. Surely this had been determined the moment Cathbad the druid had laid his hand on Elva's womb and felt Deirdre stirring inside. I never had a choice, Conor tried to assure himself.

222

Borach was a leather-faced man with a mashed nose and a wild stand of hair, made wilder by the fact that he had begun to stiffen it with lime-paste. Even cattle-lords past youth were imitating the upstanding hair of Cuchulain in his battle-fury, the king observed. 'Borach, your holding is on the road leading here from the seacoast, is it not?'

'It is.'

'And any party returning to Emain Macha from the coast would pass your gateway?'

'They would,' Borach agreed, mystified.

'Ah. My champion, Fergus mac Roy, has just departed on a mission for me to Alba. When he returns, I want him to be suitably rewarded. He is a modest man' – Conor was surprised how easily this lie came to his lips – 'and might refuse honours I would offer him. But he has a *ges* upon him; he cannot refuse the offer of an ale-feast. So when he returns, I want you to intercept him and insist he attend an ale-feast in his honour, which you will provide.'

Thinking rapidly of his ale supplies, Borach asked, 'Will he have a large group with him?'

'Don't worry about them, I don't want you to entertain any of them. They are to come on straight to me. Just take Fergus into your hall and keep him there until his belly gurgles with drink, do you understand?'

'I do,' said Borach, still mystified, but obedient to the command of his king.

Conor had been careful not to set these things in motion until Cuchulain had returned to Dun Dalgan. Whatever was going to happen, he did not want the Hound involved. He thought of Cuchulain as something special and apart, something that must not be sullied by the machinations of a subtle and tormented man.

So Cuchulain spent the maintenance season in the south of Ulster at Dun Dalgan, with only occasional forays to intimidate strangers who did not have sufficient reason to venture deeper into Ulster. In his new feasting hall, he entertained various members of the Red Branch who came to see him, and while expecting the king's summons to defend against Connaught, he nevertheless enjoyed his wife and his life.

When the sun began to warm the earth again, he was surprised to find himself feeling both relaxed and content. It was as if, with Emer, he had combined the elements needed to make him complete, his masculine force finding its complement in her feminine tenderness.

He all but ceased pondering on the mysteries that had perplexed him for so long, and when he heard the voice of a raven in the sky, he never looked up. Cuchulain stayed with Emer at Dun Dalgan until the meadows were abloom with lambs.

But by then the peace of Ulster was irrevocably shattered.

19 Deirdre awoke with a start, leaping out of an unpleasant dream. She sat up on her bed of piled furs and knuckled her eyes, trying to rub away the last remnants of a vision.

Ravens. Flying across the sea toward Alba with honey dripping from their beaks, but as they drew near land, she had seen, in her dream, the golden honey turn to crimson. She had seen black birds approach from the direction of Erin with bloodstained beaks.

Deirdre shuddered and looked vaguely around for Naisi, longing for the comfort of his arms. But he was already up and gone, deserting the round wattle-and-daub house with its stamped earthen floor for the open air and the open sky, and the joys of hunting with his brothers. Deirdre followed him to stand in the doorway, gazing out at the other round houses, the bawn, the cluster of outbuildings set in a pattern reminiscent of their Ulster origins.

She drew in a deep breath. How sweet the air was! How serene the glittering waters of Loch Etive and the dark forest climbing into the highlands. Surely they were safe here, she thought. A mere dream could not shatter her happiness.

A dream of ravens with bloody mouths . . .

For the journey to Alba, Fergus had assembled an entourage fit for a king. Naisi might be hard to convince that all was forgiven without ample evidence. The sea-traders who had told Conor mac Nessa of Naisi's refuge on Alba had also said the sons of Uisnach were very wary, with good reason. Until they had found their most recent haven, their exile had been fraught with troubles.

'But their troubles are now over,' Fergus assured Conor mac Nessa on the eve of departure. 'I'll bring them home to Ulster safely, all of them.'

'All of them,' echoed the king.

The boats from Ulster made their way across the open sea and then north along the coast of Alba, past windswept islands and rugged headlands until they reached the mouth of Loch Etive, which gave access to innumerable tiny sheltered bays. In time the lookouts spotted the familiar configuration of a Ulaid settlement among the trees beyond the shore, and Fergus ordered the boats beached at once.

The former king of Ulster was the first man ashore. Kingly he looked, dressed in a long tunic dyed dark yellow and half-concealed beneath a great shaggy mantle of wool, fastened at the throat with disc brooches of gold. His width was imposing, his manner confident.

Fergus swept the narrow strip of stony beach with his eyes, but no one was running to greet him. 'They haven't a sentry on watch, it appears,' he commented to his son Illand. 'That means they feel safe here. I'm glad; they've had a hard time of it. A man forced to leave his home loses more than a rooftree, he loses the root part of himself.' With a gesture, Fergus summoned his personal piper. 'You brought a trumpet?'

'I did.'

'Then sound a call on it, let's announce ourselves.'

In the largest of the three round buildings, Naisi and Deirdre sat together, playing chess. Naisi had returned early from the hunt; he could never stay away from Deirdre for long. She seemed pale to him, and hollow-eyed; hence, his suggestion of a game to distract her. The dream she mentioned to him he brushed aside with a wave of his hands. Women were known to be fanciful.

However, as they played, he glanced across the board at her from time to time, just to reassure her. He never tired of looking at her.

Her fine garments had long since disintegrated, and now she dressed in the same sort of simple clothing she provided for her menfolk. Her slim body was clad in the ruin of her last shift, a piece of shredded linen; a tunic of lambskin fastened with thongs rather than brooches; a heavy shawl of goat's wool for which Naisi had traded three days' catch of fish with their nearest neighbours inland – a long day's walk. Except for her face and form, she might have been any cotter's woman living on a bleak coast.

But Deirdre did not mind.

Exile had changed her. It had burned her like a fire, cleansing her of the past. When you are fleeing for your life and the life of the person you love best, soft beds and delicate gowns become unimportant. Now, she took pride in fashioning their clothing from scraps, because it was something she had done herself, with her own hands, with love.

The sound of a trumpet rang from the bay. Naisi jumped to his feet, almost overturning the chessboard he had constructed from driftwood and shells. 'That's an Ulster horn!'

226

Deirdre recognised it as clearly as he, and the night's dream returned to haunt her. 'It is not,' she insisted. 'It's a seabird calling. Pay attention to the game. I've captured one of your pieces.'

Naisi sat down again and tried to concentrate on the board, but the second call of the trumpet convinced him. 'I tell you, it's a trumpet from home we're hearing.'

She pretended to be angry, 'You're only saying that because I have the advantage now, and you want to end the game.'

One more strong, clear note sounded, and Naisi could be held no longer. He burst from the house and ran unerringly towards the bay, towards the waiting boats and the familiar bulk of Fergus mac Roy.

With a soft moan like a wounded doe, Deirdre rose to follow him.

Ardan and Ainnle and the remnant of their band from Uisnach were still in the forest, hunting. With a piercing whistle, Naisi summoned them.

By the time Deirdre reached the shore, Naisi and Fergus were deep in conversation. One look at the older man and his party had convinced Naisi that they meant him no harm, which was why he had called his brothers. Now, he held out a hand to Deirdre, and she saw the smile of delight on his face. 'Wonderful news, this!' he told her. 'Conor has forgiven us and wants us all back in Ulster. We have Fergus mac Roy himself as surety of our safety until we reach Emain Macha. We can go *home*, Deirdre!'

'I thought we were home,' she said.

Narrowing his eyes, Fergus studied the creature who had caused so much grief. Beautiful she was. Long exile had neither coarsened nor broken her. The texture of her skin seemed even finer by contrast to her rough garments, and the brisk wind off the bay brought a bloom to her cheeks. Fergus and his sons gazed at her in admiration, but she paid them no attention. All her interest was on Naisi.

'Remember my dream,' she urged. 'It was an omen. We must not go back.'

Naisi laughed uncomfortably, one eye on Fergus. 'The nervousness of women,' he said in a tone of apology.

Fergus wondered if he should feel insulted. 'Surely if I say you are safe, there's no question?' He fixed Naisi with a piercing look, the look of an instructor not to be doubted.

'Of course, of course, I understand, old friend,' the other said quickly. 'I would never doubt your word. But I'm Red Branch and Deirdre isn't. She doesn't understand these things.'

Fergus stepped forward towards Deirdre, dominating her view. 'I vow by sun and moon, earth and water, fire and air, I would die myself before I let a hair of your heads be harmed.'

'There, doesn't that satisfy you?' Naisi asked Deirdre.

She bit her lip and would not answer.

Fergus was beginning to lose his temper. On the long voyage over, he had imagined many times the triumph of bringing home the exiles. Fergus loved stories with happy endings; a warrior does not get to fashion that many happy endings. Having this woman thwart him – after all the trouble she had already caused! – diminished her charm in his eyes.

He turned to Naisi and deliberately excluded Deirdre from any further conversation. 'All disgrace will be lifted from you and your men, of course,' he said. 'The bards will recite the names of the sons of Uisnach again, everything will be as it was. Conor mac Nessa is a good king, he won't let the solidarity of the Red Branch be broken by this, ah, misunderstanding.'

Naisi's younger brother Ardan spoke up. 'It never would have happened if you had still been king, Fergus. When a king walks away from his kingship . . .'

'I didn't walk away! The Red Branch said Conor was the leader they wanted.'

'Indeed; but a king is supposed to know what his people *need*, which is more important than what they want.'

Fergus wiped a hand across his eyes. Discussions of this nature made him uncomfortable. Ideas were the province of the *filidh*. And – perhaps – Conor mac Nessa, who was something of a thinker. But Fergus mac Roy was a doer, and he wanted to do what he had come to do. 'Gather up your people and your belongings,' he said, 'so we can leave as soon as possible. Ulster needs you.'

'Don't do it,' Deirdre whispered, putting one hand on Naisi's arm. The young man hesitated.

'Are you afraid to face the king?' asked Fergus's son Buinne the Rough-Red . . . though his eyes remained on Deirdre's face as he spoke to Naisi.

'I am not.'

'Then come with us. My father's pledge will protect you.'

'Perhaps Ulster needs you,' Deirdre argued, 'but we don't need Ulster. We have everything here, Naisi.'

He looked from her to Fergus and back again, obviously torn. 'I was

228

Red Branch before I ever saw you,' he said at last. 'And I am Red Branch still. Please try to understand. Do you think things are so wonderful here? Need I remind you of all that has happened to us?'

'What has happened to you?' asked Illand. Unlike his brother the Rough-Red, Illand had a smaller build than that of their father and a milder face. Because Buinne most resembled himself at the same age, Fergus treated him as his favourite. Fergus looked at the surface of things.

At Naisi's request, Ardan and Ainnle gathered the rest of their band together and began preparing for the voyage to Ulster. Meanwhile, Naisi escorted Fergus and his sons to the dwelling house, where he offered them what refreshment he could and told the story of the seasons of exile.

'After we left Erin, we went to Skya's island, where we happened to meet Cuchulain and Ferdiad, but even there we could not stay long. Because we had heard two warrior-women divided the island between them, we hoped it might be safe, but those two had men in their clans, and as soon as a man sees Deirdre, trouble begins. So we came on to the mainland of Alba, hoping that in kingdoms so vast and rugged we could lose ourselves permanently.

'For a time, we thought we had found sanctuary with the high king himself, and I and my brothers fought for him as loyal warriors while keeping Deirdre hidden away in the mountains. I went to her as often as I could. But once when I was with her, the king sent his steward to find me, and the man had an uncommon gift for tracking. Even the isolated glen where she sheltered was not safe; he found us there and spied on us, he saw her sleeping in my arms. Then he went back to his king and described the woman.

'The king of Alba did not want to take by force the woman of one of his loyal fighting men, so he sent his steward secretly to Deirdre to try to persuade her to leave me and go to him.'

'But I laughed at him,' Deirdre interrupted, leaning past Buinne to put a woven platter of boiled fish in front of him. 'After that, the king put my three heroes' – she cast a loving glance at Naisi – 'in the forefront of every battle, trying to get them killed. He was at war with both the Picts from the lowlands and the Britons to the south, and eventually he would have succeeded in having my men slain. So we fled in the night, on and on and on again, until at last we found this quiet shore, so lost and far away that no one has bothered us since. Once or twice boats put in for fresh water, but they are men from other lands, who have no interest in our plight. We have been safe here, and happy.'

'You can't always be safe here,' said Fergus reasonably. 'Sooner or later you'll be found, and it will start over again. Your only true safety lies in coming to Ulster and letting the Red Branch protect you.'

Naisi said, 'You talk sense. Listen to him, Deirdre.'

She slammed down the latest platter of food and stamped her foot against the packed earth of the floor. 'I don't want sense! I just want to be left alone here with Naisi and Ardan and Ainnle and our home. All of us together and free!' She fled from the room.

Fergus nudged Naisi in the ribs. 'That's how women are sometimes, I've got one like that myself. No reasoning with them. I advise you in the name of friendship, never give in to the howling of dogs or the plaints of women.'

Fergus looked like home and smelled like home; he spoke with the accents of home. A world Naisi had loved and lost was embodied in him. Once Deirdre was out of sight, longing for that world so overwhelmed the young man that he put his head down on his folded arms and wept.

Fergus heaved himself awkwardly off the three-legged stool that was the best the house offered in the way of seating. He went to Naisi and patted the young man's shoulder. Speaking around a lump in his own throat, he said, 'There, there. You're going home, lad. Your own hurley stick is still propped in a corner of the Speckled House waiting for you, did you know that?'

This elicited an audible sob from Naisi.

At that moment, Deirdre stood framed in the doorway, but no one noticed her return. She stood watching, then quietly left again.

Beyond their tiny settlement, a narrow track led away from the bay, up a steep hillside. Deirdre's feet knew the path so well, she did not have to watch where she placed them. Up she climbed, through tumbled rock and outcroppings of conifers, past boulders in whose deep shadow lay the last white aprons of unmelted snow from the winter. Black rock, white snow . . . and red clay surrounding an icy pool, her favourite bathing place. The pool's water was the only water she allowed to touch her cheeks and forehead; the time she spent here alone was her time, not even shared with Naisi. Her time, her place, of black and white and red. Beyond and upward again stretched a dark glen where she gathered ferns, giving way at its head to a brawny torrent of water cascading off the mountain, wasting its strength in foam.

She wandered slowly over the familiar ground, seeing each sight as if for the first time. She had not expected to love Alba. Though its Celtic warrior-aristocracy, its druids, its cattle-lords, its very language and music, were so like those of Erin, yet this was a different land, and she had arrived a frightened stranger. Her first experiences in Alba had done nothing to reassure her. But in this one place, by a shimmering bay, she had found peace and rest and time to grow into herself as a woman.

Red and white and black.

'I don't want to leave you,' she whispered to the pool and the glen.

But at last she pulled her shawl over her head and went down to Naisi. 'I am ready to go,' she said.

On the return journey, Fergus was ebullient. Things had worked out very well indeed. He was bringing the sons of Uisnach home, and the days of division among the Red Branch were almost over. He even forgave Deirdre her reluctance, so expansive was his mood.

She had insisted on sitting in the stern of the boat so she would be, in effect, the last to leave. When they were well out on the water, she reached into her pack. Each of the exiles had some few things they had managed to carry with them. Naisi had a bronze sword he had been given by the king of Alba; Ardan had a good hunting knife; Ainnle, for some unaccountable reason, carried an iron reaping hook around with him. Fedlimid's daughter had a small hand-held harp, her dearest treasure since childhood.

She lifted it from her pack and moved her fingers across the strings. With her eyes on the receding coast, Deirdre sang:

'My love to you, eastern land,
Fair Alba of bright harbours,
Never would I leave you
But to be with Naisi.

Dear to my eyes are your glens,
Oh my grief! To be leaving Glen Laoi!
There I slept in my lover's arms,
There we feasted on red deer and badger.

Fair to me also is Glen Archan,
The straight valley of the pleasant ridge,
Torn is my heart with longing
To hear the cuckoo on the branch at Glen Rua.'

As the music died away, no one spoke. Deirdre's fingers had plucked each man's heartstrings, for there was no one in the boat who did not cherish a homeplace, one private little part of the earth that was dear to him, a kingdom of the spirit.

The sea grew rough as they sailed; the boats were tossed, and some men grew pale. Naisi put his arm around Deirdre and held her tight, and the other men, watching, envied him.

When at last they made landfall on the coast of Ulster, the sons of Uisnach leaped from the boats and ran to throw themselves on the earth.

Before they went any farther, Deirdre insisted on spreading the clothing of Naisi and his brothers on the sand to dry, smoothing it with her fingers, rubbing away the salt stains with her palms.

The other men watched her as if they had never seen a woman do homely tasks before. Buinne the Rough-Red in particular hung over her, getting his breath on her, if not his hands.

'The sooner we get back to Emain Macha, the better,' Fergus decided.

His chariot and driver, and those of his two sons, had been left to await their return. He apportioned the sons of Uisnach among the war-carts, prudently putting Deirdre in with himself. Fergus was not immune to female magic, but he trusted himself more than he trusted anyone else.

Following the road toward Emain Macha, they soon approached the holding of Borach of the Cows. A man came running out to meet them. 'Borach sends greetings to Fergus mac Roy,' he cried, 'and asks you to join him for an ale-feast at his dun.'

'And just when I realised I have mighty thirst upon me!' Fergus replied happily. 'Come, all of you; I must attend an ale-feast.'

The man whom Borach had sent to intercept him held up one hand. 'I have specific instructions just to bring you, Fergus mac Roy. The king of Ulster wants the rest of your party to come to Emain Macha at once; special preparation has been made for you there. This feast is just his reward to Fergus for a job well done.'

Deirdre cast an apprehensive look toward Fergus. 'We can't go anywhere without you, you guarantee our safety.'

'But you must go on to Emain Macha,' Borach's man insisted.

'Don't leave us then, Fergus!'

Fergus scowled. He could already smell the ale – and there was a *ges* on him, after all. How could he refuse the feast? 'I was sworn to bring

232

you to Ulster safely, and here you are,' he said. 'My sons can go with you the rest of the way, their protection is as good as mine.'

'You're abandoning us,' Deirdre accused.

'I am not! I will drain three horns and catch up with you before you reach the king's gateway.'

'Fergus, your dear and trusted friend, deserts us for ale,' Deirdre said to Naisi.

'Don't give in to that,' Fergus advised the young man. 'She's pouting. If you let her have her way now, you'll never get your own back.'

'Easy for you to say,' Naisi answered him. But all the men were watching, and he did not want to be seen giving in to a woman – not after Fergus had called everyone's attention to it. Besides, what could harm them now? Conor mac Nessa had forgiven them, and they were safe within his territory, with Buinne and Illand as their escorts. 'Go and enjoy your ale, Fergus,' he said. 'We'll see you in the House of the King.'

'Fergus, *don't!*' Deirdre pleaded, but the former king stepped down from his war-cart and beckoned Deirdre to follow. 'Ride with Illand and Naisi,' he told her. He kept his burly shoulders square and his voice brusque, letting the others see how a man should handle a woman.

Deirdre climbed up into the chariot with Naisi as if she were an old woman. 'Women just need someone to tell them what to do with authority,' Fergus confided to Naisi before setting off for the ale-feast.

As Illand's chariot rumbled and jounced toward Emain Macha, Deirdre gripped the rim of the war-cart so tightly her knuckles turned white. She was not used to riding in chariots. Nor was the cart made for carrying four people. It creaked in protest and took every bump in the road badly. The season was wet and cool, the roadway muddy, forcing the horses to a trot. Illand's team was not well-matched, so they did not proceed in a rhythmic fashion. Sometimes one leaned more heavily into his traces than the other, and the cart twisted on its tongue, causing its occupants to lurch against one another.

'I'd rather walk,' Deirdre said under her breath. Her bones felt brittle.

Out of the corner of his eye, Naisi glimpsed a flickering expression on the charioteer's face, quickly wiped away. That man thinks she rules me, he told himself. 'You'll stay here with me,' he said aloud to Deirdre, reaching out to grasp her wrist and hold her firmly in her place. He was not trying to be unkind; he wanted her to take strength from his strength and confidence from his confidence.

He wanted the other men, the men of the Red Branch, to see the control he exerted over the splendid creature for whom he had suffered so much. Now they were safe – truly home and truly safe, with the king's forgiveness – he could allow himself the luxury of enjoying other men's envy.

But with every step the horses took, Deirdre's sense of foreboding grew.

They entered a region of rolling hills and oak woodlands. Drawing a deep breath, Naisi said, 'I think I smell apple trees blooming already.'

His words did not cheer Deirdre. Instead, she flattened her body against his and pointed at the sun, drowning in a crimson sunset. 'The sky in the direction of Emain Macha is filled with blood,' she said. 'Look and be warned, Naisi.'

The lurid light was reflected on her face.

Naisi put an arm around her shoulders and tried to comfort her. 'If I were too cowardly to face the king after he has forgiven me, I couldn't live with myself, Deirdre. Don't try to scare me out of going to Emain Macha just because you don't want to see him.' He gave her a gentle hug. 'Everything will be all right, you'll see.'

'I shall see,' she said in a lost little voice. 'But I shall hate what I see.'

They approached the royal stronghold; the outer gates were opened for them. The light of the setting sun coloured the landscape, including the walls of Emain Macha. 'Washed with blood,' Deirdre murmured.

Naisi shook her shoulder. 'No more of that now – and try to smile when the king comes to welcome us. We have much to thank him for. If I were in his position, I don't know if I could be so forgiving.'

The party entered the gateway under the impassive gaze of the guards. Fortifications had been strengthened during their absence, Naisi noted, and a second gateway across the track lay closed. A stout knuckle of oak hung beside it on a leather thong, and dismounting from the chariot, he beat a tattoo on the gate with the oak knocker. At once he heard a bolt being drawn, and the gate swung inward.

'Don't go through,' Deirdre whispered.

'Fergus is right about women,' Naisi replied angrily. He was so close now; in a few more moments, he would be with the Red Branch again. His heart was pounding with eagerness.

The king's steward was waiting for them inside the second gate. Martain was officious to an excessive degree. A willowtree of a man with

234

tight cheekbones and narrow lips, he tried to give the lie to his appearance by bustling and beaming with jollity. No one must think the royal steward cold and inhospitable.

He approached Naisi in a condition one step short of wringing his hands. 'I can't tell you how happy we are to see you here again,' he said. 'You just cannot imagine . . . and it's so very unfortunate, it's the worst possible time, we had no idea you would arrive so soon . . . Was the wind with you, then? The tide?'

'What's the man rattling on about?' Ardan asked Ainnle behind his hand.

'I don't know. But listen to the noise, will you? The fort buzzes like a swarm of bees. It's positively packed with people.'

'Indeed,' Martain confirmed. 'That's the problem, you see. The king had of course meant to house you in the royal guest house, with a feast in your honour, but recently he's been doing what he could to strengthen alliances with clan-chiefs whose friendship for the Ulaid might be questionable. For the past several days, the stronghold has been filled to overflowing with Owen mac Durrow of Fern Mag, south of Slieve Fuad, and his men.'

'I know mac Durrow,' said Naisi. 'He is inhospitable and untrustworthy. His warriors are mercenaries, the scavengers of the countryside. I'm surprised Conor allows any of them within his walls.'

Martain widened his eyes. 'We do not question a king's judgement when he is doing a king's business.'

Naisi hooted with sarcastic laughter. 'That too has changed, then! When did people not criticise their king?'

A shout of profanity billowed from the House of the King. 'Owen feasts there tonight,' Martain explained, 'and his retinue is already in the royal guest house. So you will stay . . .'

'We can go to your friend Cuchulain,' Deirdre interjected. 'I trust him, Naisi. Let us seek shelter wherever he is.'

'Not possible, that,' said Martain. 'The Hound has been sent to his stronghold at Dun Dalgan.'

Something about Martain's choice of words made Naisi uneasy. 'Why "sent"? Why shouldn't my old friend be here for my return?'

'Please, all these questions will be answered by the king when you see him. For now, I have orders to bid you welcome and make you comfortable. We have arranged adequate accommodations for yourself and your company, as you shall see. You will be staying in the House of the Red Branch and – '

'We will not!' Deirdre protested. 'I could not sleep in the trophy house with the heads of dead men leering down at me.'

'Some of those trophies are mine,' Naisi tried to placate her. But she twisted away from him.

'This is a terrible omen,' Deirdre said.

For the first time, Naisi began to give credence to her intuition. Suddenly, the very air smelled wrong to him.

But he and his brothers were inside the walls of Emain Macha, and the gates had been closed behind them. He could not show fear now, not here. To the steward, he said, 'Is Ferdiad here?'

'He was earlier. I haven't seen him for a while, however.'

'If you do see him, will you tell him the sons of Uisnach have arrived?'

'I shall of course,' Martain replied. 'Now, if you will follow me. . . ?' He beckoned toward the House of the Red Branch.

More than the smell was wrong. They could all feel it, a tension in the atmosphere like that before a storm. Naisi and his brothers automatically, as they had many times in the past, closed around Deirdre, keeping her in their centre as they climbed the mound toward the royal hall. The few clansmen who had stayed with them through their long exile trailed after them, glancing nervously over their shoulders. The sons of Fergus, Illand and Buinne the Rough-Red, brought up the rear.

As Martain had promised, the House of the Red Branch, like most royal halls, was well supplied with couches and tables for guests. No one could anticipate how many people might seek shelter beneath the king's rooftrees at any given time. With portable screens arranged around its walls, the circular structure could be divided into a number of small chambers, providing a functional guest house. Between the carved oak pillars supporting the roof, benches waited for weary travellers, and in anticipation of Deirdre's arrival someone had set up a couch covered with the softest fawnskin, where she could recline in comfort while taking her meal.

She did not even glance at the couch. She stood in the centre of the room like a sacrificial victim, feeling the glare of the preserved heads on the walls directed towards her.

Buinne the Rough-Red, intending to point out his own trophies, approached her. When he noticed how frightened she looked, he tried to comfort her. 'What can harm you here, in the king's *maigen*, under the protection of Fergus mac Roy?'

'Fergus isn't here. He betrayed us for ale.'

Buinne scowled. 'You shouldn't say that about my father. He will be

236

along soon, and in the meantime Illand and I stand for him.' He dropped his voice to a more intimate level. 'Do you think *I* would let anything happen to *you*?'

How many times, Deirdre thought wearily, have I seen that look on a man's face? Don't they ever suspect how tired of it I am?

Naisi came to her, took her elbow, and guided her to the couch. 'Rest and refresh yourself, some servants are bringing heated water for us to bathe our faces and feet. Then I think we should pay a formal visit to the House of the King, just to show Conor we're here and appreciate his hospitality.'

Martain had not yet left, and when he heard Naisi say this, he spoke up hastily. 'You must stay here, you wouldn't want the men of Owen mac Durrow to know *she*' – he nodded toward Deirdre – 'is here, would you? The trouble it could cause! I'm certain it would be better for all concerned if you just stay quietly inside here for now.'

Naisi saw the wisdom of the suggestion, but his uneasiness remained. 'Ask the king to come to us then, when he can. I want to see for myself that all is healed between us.'

After Martain had left, the little party tried to relax. But Deirdre's face was drawn and white, and one man after another took his turn at pacing the floor.

While Naisi bathed, Ardan came to sit beside Deirdre. 'You once loved beautiful things,' he reminded her. 'Look at the gold cups we're using; feel the softness of these cushions!'

She would not even glance at them. 'Oh, Ardan, I don't care about luxuries any more. It's true, I asked for everything I could think of until I got Naisi, but then I just gradually stopped wanting anything else. Except to go home. I want desperately to go home.'

'We are home,' he reminded her. 'We were all born in Ulster.'

'This isn't home to me. Home is the place we built with our hands, all of us working together. Home is the hearth where I cooked the meat you brought back from the forest, where the snow once threatened to bury us and the wolves once threatened to eat us and we laughed at all of it. Home was all of us around the fire at night singing songs and telling stories, and Naisi lying with his head in my lap.'

She slumped disconsolately. He patted wordlessly at her shoulder.

In the House of the King, Conor mac Nessa was very aware of the arrival of his guests. Indeed, he thought of little else, only pretending to listen while Owen described some copper-trading he had recently done with the king of Leinster. He did not really like Owen mac Durrow. But there were times when even a lack of scruples proved valuable. And he knew Owen was eager for a better relationship with Emain Macha, his own cattle and borderlands not being immune to the long arm of Maeve of Connaught.

The king was not the only person in the hall who knew of the arrival of the sons of Uisnach. The whispered news had travelled faster than the exiles themselves. An old woman sitting near the doorway had been one of the first to hear, and when Conor suddenly called out, 'Who will run an errand for me to the House of the Red Branch?' Levarcham leaped to her feet as if she were young again.

The king beckoned her close so the others would not hear his instructions. 'Go and take a long look at Deirdre. I want to be certain she has, ah, made the trip safely. Study her face, Levarcham; you know it well. Study her form. Then come back here and tell me if she is as beautiful as ever, or if the years of exile have taken their toll on her. If she is no longer lovely, I will gladly leave her to Naisi and enjoy a peaceful heart.'

Levarcham hesitated. 'And if she is beautiful?'

'Just go and see her,' the king commanded.

The night was troubled. As Levarcham approached the House of the Red Branch, she heard the sound of many men somewhere close by, men whose accents were not those of the Ulaid. She crept past the royal hall and peered into the gloom beyond. There, barely visible in a night of curdled mist, was a large group of heavily armed men, gathered and waiting.

Shocked, Levarcham gathered her skirts in her hands and ran to the House of the Red Branch, pounding desperately on the door for admittance. A cautious voice asked her name and business, but once she identified herself as Deirdre's old nurse, the door was opened immediately.

Naisi and Deirdre had been sitting together on the couch, trying to distract themselves with a game of chess. Deirdre, Levarcham saw at once, was as beautiful as ever, though very pale. The hard years showed more on Naisi than they did on her; she seemed magically impervious. Naisi still had his raven hair, but there was a thick white streak through it, and the flush of his cheeks now came from veins broken by the cold winds of Alba.

Wailing 'Ochone!' the ancient cry of grief, Levarcham ran to Deirdre and flung her arms around her. 'You're in terrible danger! Not far from these walls a troop of foreign warriors waits, by their accents I know them as the men of Owen mac Durrow. The men of Fern Mag will attack anyone for a price, and they have this hall almost surrounded.'

Naisi was on his feet, a profanity on his lips. 'Tell us all you know, Levarcham.'

'Sorry I am to have lived long enough to see this night,' the old woman replied. 'The three bright candles of Uisnach are to be attacked and killed as soon as the king learns you are still desirable, Deirdre. He means to take you from Naisi by the sword.'

The others were crowding around now, torn between anger and disbelief. But Deirdre merely buried her face in her hands – her hateful face that she would have ripped from its bones if she could. 'I knew this before we left Alba,' she said in a muffled voice.

'Are you certain about Owen's men?' Ainnle wanted to know. 'The night is dark, the air is thick . . .'

'And don't I know the style and accent of every clan? I could not see their faces, but I heard their voices, and I've heard those same voices for days while they swanned around the fort, showing their teeth and their weapons. I tell you, Conor mac Nessa plans to use them against you, because he can't rely on the Red Branch to attack one of its own.

'But where is Fergus mac Roy?' she wondered, looking around. 'His honour is sworn to protect you.'

Illand told her. 'My father was waylaid. Deliberately, I see it now. This is a long-planned treachery. But he knows we expect him, he will be along soon. If we can hold out until then . . .'

'Guard every opening,' Levarcham urged. 'I'll go back to the king and tell him my Deirdre has become a hag. It won't satisfy him for long, but . . .'

'Perhaps long enough for help to come,' Naisi finished for her.

Levarcham and Deirdre exchanged a final embrace. Both women were crying. 'Take care of her,' Levarcham said to Naisi. And then, to Deirdre, she added, 'And you take care of him.'

She showered a final spate of kisses on the unforgettable face, then made her sorrowing way back to the House of the King.

By this time, the mist had grown so thick that she was almost upon the hall before she could even see it.

Going straight to Conor, Levarcham said, 'I have news of joy and sorrow.'

'Tell me the joyful first.'

'The sons of Uisnach, three of the bravest and strongest men ever to lift a sword, have returned safely to fight for you whenever you ask it of them. They are grateful for your forgiveness and are even now enjoying your hospitality.'

She is trying too hard to be convincing, Conor thought, alerted at once. 'Now the sorrowful,' he commanded.

'Ah, my poor Deirdre is sadly withered from her wild seasons, I hardly knew her. Her face is lined, her form is gaunt. All her teeth are broken!' she added with sudden inspiration.

'Are they?' Conor nodded. 'Are they indeed?' With a gesture, he dismissed the woman and returned to his conversation with Owen, as if the matter were of no further interest. Levarcham huddled in the shadows and watched him.

After another round of food and drink, Conor mac Nessa beckoned to a visiting cattle-lord called Gelban. 'Tell me, Gelban – who took your father's head in battle?'

'Naisi,' was the reply. 'My clan has an old quarrel with his.'

'And who killed your brothers?'

'His brothers, Ardan and Ainnle.'

The king nodded, satisfied. 'You're the man I need for a mission, then. Go to the House of the Red Branch and take a good look at the woman you'll find there. Climb up the walls and peer in a window if you have to. Then report back to me.'

Gelban returned with one hand cupped over an eye and blood streaming through his fingers. He was torn between agony and outrage. 'They saw me peering in and threw something at me, they've put out my eye!'

'You still have one,' Conor said implacably. 'Before I send for my physician, tell me what you saw with it.'

'The most beautiful woman on the ridge of the world,' Gelban gasped. 'Now where's your physician, I'm bleeding to death!'

With a snap of his fingers, Conor brought Martain to his side and sent him for Fingan. Then the king stood up. Raising his voice, he cried in tones sufficient to carry over the customary noise in the hall, 'Clansmen of the Ulaid! Out of the goodness of my heart, I have invited the sons of Uisnach to return to Ulster and have undertaken to forgive them their treachery, only to learn they have not changed. I gave them beds in the House of the Red Branch preparatory to welcoming them formally in this hall tomorrow, yet when I just now sent an emissary to them, they cruelly put out his eye. See Gelban there, bleeding.'

Shocked, the crowd in the hall looked from the king to Gelban and back again.

240

'I was wrong to invite these savages back among us, for they refuse to abide by the laws that protect decent men,' the king went on. 'They must be punished now, finally and for all time. Who will aid me?'

Stunned silence answered him.

'I am your chosen king!' Conor shouted.

The divisions in the Red Branch suddenly gaped very wide.

Some men got slowly to their feet; others stayed where they were, hands frozen over food or ale cup.

The king ran from the hall, crying for vengeance. Owen mac Durrow was right behind him. With a shout of his own, he summoned the warriors of Fern Mag to join him.

In the half-emptied House of the King, the remaining Red Branch warriors stared at one another. Ferdiad was the first to speak.

'I wish Cuchulain were here,' he said.

20 The halls of Emain Macha had been constructed to withstand assault; they were the king's stronghold. Only the heaviest timbers had been used for walls and roof supports. Stone kerbs protected the base from tunnelling, and the few small windows for light were set high up. By using grappling hooks, a determined band could reach the thatched roofs and break through, but using grappling hooks in the dark of night was a risky business.

The first assault had little effect. The king's followers regrouped and came again, and Conor was gratified to see his son Fiacra among the foremost of them. His brother Follaman lay ill with what was becoming a chronic complaint, but Cormac Connlongas was not far behind Fiacra.

A group of men went to bring a great log to use as a battering ram, but the bronze-sheathed door of the hall was reinforced with iron bars and did not give way readily. 'Open to your king!' shouted Conor mac Nessa to those inside.

From beyond the barred door, Illand answered him, 'These people have had their safety sworn by the honour of Fergus mac Roy, my father!'

'And is Fergus in there with you?' Conor asked. Then he laughed.

Inside the House of the Red Branch, Naisi saw Illand turn white with anger. 'I take my father's vow upon myself!' he yelled back to the king.

'We're trapped in here,' said Buinne the Rough-Red. 'Sooner or later they'll break in. If I get out, perhaps I can rally help, or at least get word to Fergus.'

He ran towards one of the tables, jumped on to it, and leaped up again, catching the frame of one of the small windows set high up on the wall. His feet swung wildly for a moment, then he heaved himself up. The window was barred, but Buinne broke the wooden bars with his bare hands, then thrust his body through the opening and dropped down outside the walls.

The ground was far beneath him; he felt a great shock to his feet and ankles as he landed. But he was on the one side of the hall where no warriors waited. And he had a shortsword in his belt.

242

He started around the building, feeling his way in the gloom, until torchlight suddenly blazed in his eyes. With a howl, Buinne attacked the first man he saw. Fergus's son acquitted himself admirably; soon he had a pile of bleeding men around him.

Conor mac Nessa ran up. 'Who is responsible for this?'

'I am.'

'Then you're fighting on the wrong side,' the king replied.

'My brother and I are sworn to protect the sons of Uisnach and the daughter of Fedlimid.'

Something about the way he said 'the daughter of Fedlimid' gave Conor the clue he needed. 'If you were my man, Rough-Red, I would find you a woman every bit as beautiful as that one, and you would have a cantred of land and my friendship as well.'

Buinne hesitated. 'As beautiful as Deirdre?'

'If there is one, there must be more, and I have a gift for knowing where such treasures are hidden.'

Buinne considered. Then he hitched up his sword belt. 'I am the king's man, after all . . .'

'A wise decision,' Conor assured him. He returned to the door. 'The son of Fergus himself stands with me now!' he called. 'Open to me and surrender!'

Within the House of the Red Branch, Deirdre said, 'Fergus seems to have sired a litter as dishonourable as himself.'

Illand's face flamed. 'Not true. As long as I can hold a weapon, I'll protect you, and my father would do the same if he were here.' Cupping his hands around his mouth, he yelled through the door, 'I claim the right of single combat. I'll fight as champion for Fergus mac Roy!'

Fiacra the Fair grabbed his father's arm. 'I'll fight as your champion,' he told Conor. 'If you'll have me.'

For a fleeting instant, the king thought of Cuchulain; then he nodded. 'Take my sword and shield, boy.'

The sons of two kings met in the torch-starred gloom. Illand had opened the door of the hall only wide enough to allow him to step outside quickly, then the king's men heard the bars dropping back in place. The warriors formed a circle around the combatants. Trial by single combat had begun.

Fiacra the Fair adjusted his father's shield on his arm. He noticed that Illand had already dropped into a fighter's crouch, sword extended as he weaved back and forth, looking for an opening.

Fergus probably taught his own sons some tricks no one else knows,

243

Fiacra thought resentfully. And in that moment, when his trained body should have been working independently of his brain, Illand leaped at him, using his own imitation of Cuchulain's famed salmon-leap.

Fiacra went over backward with his father's shield atop him, and the voice of Ocean roared its warning of danger.

Conall Cearnach was returning late to Emain Macha. He had been standing watch at a ford, and the man due to relieve him had been detained by a broken chariot axle. Annoyed to think he would find the best meat already eaten, Conall was driving his team up to the gates of Emain Macha at the gallop when he heard the unmistakable booming of the king's shield.

Conall flung his reins towards someone he hoped was a horseboy, since he had been driving with no charioteer, and ran towards the source of the sound. Yelling and the glow of torchlight guided him to the House of the Red Branch. There, he found a scene of wild confusion. Angry men were milling about, swearing and jostling each other and watching something taking place in their midst.

Elbowing his way through the crowd, Conall saw a man lying on the ground, and in the flickering light glimpsed enough of his face to recognise the king's son Fiacra. Another man was bending over him, pressing him down.

Loyal to his king, Conall Cearnach plunged his sword into the back of Fiacra's attacker.

The man gasped, twisted, fell sideways. The torches flared, and Conall recognised Illand mac Fergus, a favourite champion of his own in the Boys' Troop days.

Horrified, Conall looked wildly around for some explanation.

Fiacra was dragging himself to his feet. 'You saved my life,' he said breathlessly, reaching toward Conall. The other man shied away from his touch and turned toward Illand instead.

Fergus's son was still breathing, but mortally wounded. As Conall bent over him, he opened his eyes. 'Who stabbed me in the back? Ah, Conall . . . you? I wouldn't have treated you so. You'd have got a fair fight from me, face to face . . .' He coughed up a clot of blood, then coughed again, his voice making a metallic rattling sound in his throat.

Illand mac Fergus let his head roll to one side and died.

'I didn't know it was you!' Conall kept trying to tell him anyway, with tears streaming down his face. He could not bear that Illand had died thinking Conall his deliberate killer. He looked around at the massed warriors, but no one would meet his eyes; they were all staring at the dead body on the grass. This first killing had shocked them. An irrevocable line had been crossed before anyone had had time to think clearly.

Conall was the most shocked of all. He had just killed a brother of the Red Branch. With a blade in the back.

Something seemed to snap in his brain. He spun around and the first face he saw was Fiacra's, alive and well and *smiling*, actually holding out his hand as if in *congratulations* . . .

Conall screamed and swung his sword again. 'The life of one king's son pays for another!' he shrieked.

Fiacra fell, gushing blood. The warriors fell back from the temporarily mad man swinging the sword. Conall gasped, shuddered, recovered himself slightly, flung the weapon from him and fled into the night.

The sons of two kings lay dead.

Conor mac Nessa staggered as if he had taken a blow himself. The madness leaped to him. Looking around for something to strike, he saw the royal hall looming before him, with the sons of Uisnach still safe inside. 'Burn down the Red Branch and all in it!' screamed the king of Ulster, his agony tearing his throat.

The stunned men leaped back into action. Conor's followers hurled their torches on to the thatched roof, and an ugly orange light glowed almost at once as the dry material caught fire.

Men began to run in all directions, shouting confused orders to each other. Those of the Red Branch loyal to Conor collided with Owen mac Durrow's men and swore at them, then joined with them to help destroy the House of the Red Branch.

Ferdiad and those who had remained behind in the House of the King now emerged, just in time to see the glow of fire in the sky and hear the first ominous crackling. They ran towards the burning hall, arriving as the door opened and the sons of Uisnach emerged, shielding Deirdre in their centre and coughing from the smoke. Without pausing for thought, Ferdiad joined them, helping to force an opening through the confused swirl of people in the area so the exiles could escape. Others of the Red Branch joined them, making the choice instantaneously. Fighting their way towards uncertain freedom – somewhere.

Men who had been eating from one platter in the House of the King were now trying to kill each other within the walls of Emain Macha. Madness, like blood, seeped into the earth. The roar the warriors made was more savage than the fire.

Aided by Ferdiad and the others, Naisi and Deirdre stumbled across the dark compound. Someone came out of the night at them, swinging a weapon, but Ferdiad killed him before he could reach the sons of Uisnach. 'My swordhand itches to fight,' Naisi panted to Deirdre as they ran together, bending over, hugging the earth.

In the horror of the night Deirdre found a smile for him. 'While there is life in your body, I expect you to be brave.'

So he stopped and planted his feet and got in a few swordswings himself before his brothers forced him to start moving again. 'You'll get her killed,' Ardan insisted.

They made it to the nearest wall and over, the sons of Uisnach handing Deirdre up from one to the other. Behind them, covering their retreat, part of the Red Branch fought the other part and Owen's men as well. As the exiles ran towards the Sorrowful Forest, they heard the crashing boom of the roof collapsing into the House of the Red Branch.

Nothing was clear in that terrible night. The only realities were pain in the lungs from running and a sense of doom following them. Deirdre stumbled; Naisi caught her and held her tightly to him. 'Go on without me,' she urged. 'If they catch you . . .'

But he would not leave her. None of them would. As soon as she caught her breath, they went on again.

While the fighting continued, Conor mac Nessa stood like a man in a trance and watched the House of the Red Branch burn. Cleansing fire, he thought. But it would not bring back Fiacra . . . or Deirdre, now surely lost to him for ever or . . . his son Cormac was still around somewhere, fighting . . . fighting whom? His brain seemed numb when he tried to think.

The only clear reality was his son lying dead on the grass.

'Fiacra!' he cried with a great sob, falling to his knees.

Cathbad the druid materialised out of the night and put a hand on his shoulder. 'You have brought this on yourself,' said the druid in a stern voice.

Conor looked up at him.

The king's face, twisted in grief, was hideous to Cathbad. Deirdre has made a monster of this man, he thought. She is worse than I predicted. She has destroyed the finest king in Erin.

The weight of his own realised prophecy crushed Cathbad beneath it, and he turned away from Conor, from the ruin of the Red Branch, from the tragedy of a people who seemed doomed to kill.

Yet in his heart, the old druid wondered just how much of the blame for this could honestly be laid at Deirdre's feet. Some other force seemed to be at work here . . .

The huge pyre of the burning hall served as a signal, alerting watchers the length of Ulster. It was observed from the flank of Slieve Fuad and interpreted as a call for help, and word was swiftly sent south, to Dun Dalgan and Cuchulain.

When the first light streaked the eastern sky, a few men came back to the fort to report to the king. 'We have the sons of Uisnach trapped in the Sorrowful Forest. We've succeeded in separating them from their friends of the Red Branch, whom some of Owen's men are holding at bay. What do we do now?'

Conor looked a thousand years old. He was in the House of the King, standing beside a trestle table on which lay the body of Fiacra the Fair, beneath the great shield called Ocean.

The king sighed. 'Lead me to them,' he said.

Naisi and Deirdre had finally come to rest together in a holly thicket. Ardan and Ainnle were nearby, but were allowing them some time to be alone, knowing they needed these last precious moments for themselves.

When they heard the voices of the king's men approaching, Deirdre met Naisi's eyes.

'I can go farther,' she told him. 'Let's run again, let's try to get away.'

He shook his head. 'There's no point in it. Who would give us sanctuary? The king's broken his own *maigen*, all laws are in abeyance now.'

The dappled green forest light lay on Deirdre's face like water. She could smell the rich odour of decay, of rotting wood and growing fungus; she could hear a distant tinkle of some tiny rivulet pouring over rocks and losing itself among ferns. The forest was constantly dying to be reborn again, she thought.

'Conor will have you killed,' she said aloud to Naisi.

'Death is everyone's future,' Naisi told her.

He caught her hands between his. Deirdre laid her cheek against his knuckles; he could feel her hot tears. 'I was dead from the first moment I saw you,' he told her, 'but it doesn't matter.' He drew her deeper in among the trees, into an older part of the forest.

As with any ancient structure left to itself, the pillars of the forest were slowly collapsing with age. Naisi found one of the oldest trees half-fallen, with a cavelike hollow beneath it, and he thrust Deirdre inside. 'Stay there,' he commanded. 'For my sake.'

He did not want her to see him die.

He could hear his enemies approaching. Yet time slowed for Naisi, holding him suspended in a place where neither battle nor fire could reach him, giving him an opportunity to think the thoughts a man needs to think before he draws his final breath.

Naisi had seen enough living and dying to be in awe of neither. He had never wanted to be one of those who crouched fearfully in the shadow of their own mortality, grasping at life as they would grasp at chaff blown on the wind. But chaff blew away anyhow, leaving them with empty hands.

So why clutch? Why not blow free as the wind blew, moving easily, letting life happen, letting death happen too.

Once, in the days-before-Deirdre, the details of existence had seemed important to him. But no more. They had not grown less important, he had simply outgrown them, learning to give them no more weight than they deserved.

Some time during the night and the running, he had lost his sword; when he reached for it a while ago, he had found the scabbard empty.

That was a mere detail.

He was cut off from his friends and hopelessly outnumbered; that too was a detail. Unimportant.

He would always have Deirdre.

He heard the king's voice just beyond the trees, took a deep breath, and walked forward to face Conor mac Nessa.

The two men met at the fringe of the forest. 'You have torn the Red Branch in two,' Conor accused, verbally attacking.

Naisi did not bother to answer.

The king looked away as if he could not bear the sight of Naisi. 'Who will punish this man for me?' he asked in a choked voice. His eye lit on Owen of Fern Mag, on a fleshy red face with flinty eyes sunk in deep pouches. There was no kindness in Owen and no mercy. 'There stands Naisi,' Conor told him.

'I know who he is,' the clan-chief replied, stepping forward from the cluster of the king's followers. 'His father's father killed my father's father in a clan-war.'

'Then will you even the score now?'

'I will.'

Owen approached Naisi as several more warriors came up dragging Ardan and Ainnle, whom they had just caught. The captives were shoved against their brother so the three stood as one. Now, Naisi could

248

see the shape of his death. Please, Deirdre, he pleaded in his mind, stay where you are.

Conor mac Nessa felt deep quivers run up his thighs and was thankful they were hidden beneath his tunic. He marvelled that Naisi could appear so calm. In that painful moment, he knew he was not a king seeking justice but a man of middle years who had been driven too far by jealousy and desire and was determined to make others suffer for it. A foolish man. A man too small to be a king, yet who loved his kingship above all else.

Ardan squirmed in the grip of his captors and tried to push himself in front of his brothers. 'Slay me first,' he said, 'for I am the youngest.'

Ainnle raised his voice at once. 'I demand the right to die first and give my brothers another breath.'

'The deed that brought this upon us was mine,' Naisi said quietly. 'Your quarrel is with me, Conor mac Nessa. Kill me and let the others go.'

'I grant you no rights of negotiation,' said the king. Then Naisi noticed that one of his men was holding a sword, a familiar sword – Naisi's own sword, dropped during the night and now found.

An old friend, he thought. It would be . . . comforting . . . to die at the touch of an old friend. 'Then I ask you one favour only, Conor mac Nessa. I see your men have found my sword. Its blade is sharp enough to take the three of us together, so I ask you . . .'

'Done,' Conor interrupted him. 'Owen, see to it.'

Naisi stood with his head up, quietly waiting. His eyes were calm, his face serene. He had already moved past the death to come.

Someone dragged a log into the clear, and the three men knelt down next to it and laid their heads upon the rough surface, baring their necks for the sword. Out of sight, they took each other's hands. Owen brought down Naisi's sword in one powerful stroke.

A wild cry tore the air.

As the blood spurted, Deirdre ran forward and threw herself across the bodies, trying desperately to share the killing blow. But she was too late.

Owen stepped back and left her there, sobbing.

Conor mac Nessa shook himself like a man awakening from a bad dream. 'Deirdre?' He reached his hand down to her and she tore it with her teeth, snarling at him like a wild animal.

The king pulled back. 'You have to understand. They were outlaws, they broke trust with me . . .'

She could not hear him. She could not hear anything but the last faint gurgles of life leaving Naisi's body.

Fergus arrived in the morning, bracing himself in his chariot with the exaggerated care of a man whose head may fall off at any sudden move. His eyeballs were very red. Immersed in the joys of Borach's feasting hall and an exceptionally good brewing of ale, he had never seen the blazing light in the sky from Emain Macha. But as he approached the royal fort, the wind began to bring him drifts of ash.

'Use the whip,' he told his charioteer.

At the gateway, the guards opened to him, but without the usual cheerful greeting. They raked him with sullen eyes, as if he were a stranger. Inside the walls, he found devastation.

The House of the Red Branch was burned to its stone kerbwork, with only a skeleton of charred timbers leaning at crazy angles to show where walls had been. A steady stream of people were hurrying in and out of the long, low building known as the House of Sorrows, where Fingan and his apprentices usually tended to the battle wounds of the Red Branch. As Fergus neared the building, he could hear groans coming from inside, and someone swearing in the low, monotonous voice of pain.

'Bad work, this,' Fergus muttered, beginning to run in spite of his bulk.

More men lay on the grass, also wounded, but past caring, waiting with the terrible patience of the dead until the living were tended. Their women bent over them, keening like the wind blowing across lonely seacliffs. A few of the new widows threw looks of hatred at Fergus mac Roy.

He found Conor mac Nessa slumped on his bench in the House of the King. The younger man's face was ravaged; great lines were carved into his flesh, and his eyes were lost in their sockets.

'What happened?' Fergus demanded to know.

The king did not move, only rolled his eyes towards Fergus. 'Did you enjoy your ale-feast?' he asked with cruel sarcasm. He had used Fergus, but he would not be kind to him now; he hurt too much himself to be kind to anyone else.

'Where are the sons of Uisnach, Conor? I am guarantor for their safety, what's happened to them?'

'You didn't keep them safe,' said a cracked and anguished voice from the shadows. Levarcham stepped forward, her hands curving into claws as if she meant to tear the face from Conor mac Nessa. But the king did not shrink from her; he stared at her sombrely, as if he no longer cared what happened to him.

The old woman turned on Fergus. 'You abandoned my Deirdre and the sons of Uisnach to die,' she accused, raising those taloned hands. 'Your son Illand took up the honour you so lightly cast aside and died in your place, did you know that?'

Appalled, Fergus threw a hand up before his face; whether to ward off her physical attack or her terrible words he did not know.

'And your son Buinne abandoned *you* and took the king's side,' she added with malicious spite.

Fergus sank on to a bench. Levarcham bent over him, pouring out the story as if she could not hold so much poison inside herself. When she finished speaking, Fergus sat listening to the silence in the hall. Then he got to his feet, slowly, heavily, and turned one last time towards Conor mac Nessa. 'You are no longer my foster-son,' he said. 'I do not know you.'

He left the House of the King for ever.

When Cuchulain reached Emain Macha, the stink of the burned hall came out to greet him. He had driven at breakneck speed from Dun Dalgan, summoned by the fire signals. Leaving Laeg to take care of the exhausted horses, he ran as Fergus had done to find Conor. But he met Ferdiad first.

In the midst of so much destruction, he was overjoyed to see his friend alive. 'Were we attacked?' he wanted to know.

'We were. By ourselves,' the other replied. His horn armour was intact, but individual plates of it were crazed and shattered.

Ferdiad swiftly related the events of the night of death, including his own part in it. 'I've been out there in the forest with the survivors who took Naisi's side,' he explained. 'I came back to the fort in hopes of finding you.'

'Is it safe for you to be here . . . now?'

Ferdiad glanced around. 'For a while, I think. No one's in the mood to challenge anyone right now. I thought the fire summons would reach you, and I knew you'd want to be with us when we . . . when we bury Naisi and the others. We've waited.'

Silently, Cuchulain followed his friend from the walled fort to the distant forest. A crowd was gathered there. The sun was low in the sky, but the unnatural stillness that overlay the land was not a twilight hush. As they drew near the Sorrowful Forest, Cuchulain could see

251

the dark rectangles of open graves, like doorways into the Otherworld.

Beneath their cloaks, the sons of Uisnach lay waiting, and a woman sat on the ground beside them.

Deirdre looked up as Cuchulain and Ferdiad approached. In grief she was even more beautiful than in happiness. The ivory pallor of her skin accentuated her perfect features, and weeping had not swollen her eyes, but framed them with lovely violet shadows.

Deirdre was luminous with pain.

'All those I loved are slain through love of me,' she said to Cuchulain.

'I asked Cathbad to come,' Ferdiad told her gently. 'For the burial rites.'

'You shouldn't have done that,' Deirdre replied. 'I've already bathed them; I took water from a pool in the woods and let no one help me. They are mine. They need nothing from Emain Macha.'

Cuchulain reached down and took her hands. It was the first time he had ever touched her. He thought, wondering, that her flesh felt like any other woman's flesh, only cold. So cold. 'They need the honours due them,' he said to her. 'Please Deirdre.'

Some of the fierce protective light went out of her eyes. 'I'm too tired to argue,' she said, looking away, at the graves.

Members of the Red Branch stood within the concealment of the nearby trees. A few raised their hands to Cuchulain in greeting, but no one said anything. There was nothing to say.

Cathbad soon arrived, wearing a white woollen cloak with the hood pulled up in respect for the dead. At his direction, Ferdiad and the others lined the graves with branches, then placed the dead within them, their feet to the east, as Cathbad invoked the sun upon its next rising to warm them from their heels to their heads.

Deirdre said she wanted no funeral games, even if anyone present had had the heart to run a token foot-race in honour of the dead. So after lighting a fire, turning the earth, pouring water in four directions, and setting a stone to mark the road that would lead the slain heroes towards the Isle of the Blest, where they could fight and die and rise to fight again, the druid's work was done.

Yet he lingered. They all lingered, though the sun had set and the night grew cold. As long as Deirdre sat on the bare earth by the graves, no one else felt free to go.

Fergus mac Roy watched from a distance. He dared not draw closer, though he wanted to find some way to explain himself to Deirdre. He longed to stand beside the grave of his son Illand, who had been carried out here to be buried with the sons of Uisnach he had died trying to protect.

In my place, thought Fergus, anguished. In my place. He tore at his beard with his hands. The others knew he was there, but no one looked towards him. He was more alone than he had ever thought it possible to be, and he did not know what to do.

When the time was right, Deirdre knew what to do.

She had left her harp behind in the House of the Red Branch; she would never touch a harp again. But she had all she needed with her. Rising at last, she paced sunwise around the graves, then stopped beside the place where Naisi lay and raised her eyes to the stars.

No one wanted to listen, but no one was able to keep from listening as Deirdre sang her lament for the sons of Uisnach:

> *'Three lions are dead and the day is long*
> *without them.*
> *No day was wearisome in their company,*
> *For they were heroes and merry men.*
>
> *Three hawks are slain and the sky is empty*
> *without them.*
> *The sun will not warm the earth again,*
> *Nor the clouds bring rain for drinking.*
>
> *Many were the hardships we shared,*
> *But Ardan made a pillow for me.*
> *Ainnle kept meat on my table,*
> *And Naisi held me in his arms in the morning.*
>
> *Three lions are dead whose spears and shields*
> *were my fortress.*
> *I am Deirdre without joy, and I will not stay long*
> *without them.'*

Naisi held me in his arms in the morning. When Deirdre sang those words, Cuchulain was overcome by a desperate longing for Emer; for warmth, for life. As soon as Deirdre's voice died away, he turned his face toward Emain Macha, to collect Laeg and his chariot and go home.

Ferdiad intercepted him. 'You're leaving us, then?'

'I'm going to Dun Dalgan.'

'This isn't over.'

'I know it. But I want no part of it. The Red Branch torn in half . . .' He was still unable to accept the unthinkable.

'I want no part of it either,' Ferdiad agreed. 'But I was here. Even if I had held back, I would have been making a choice. We all had to – do you see Conor's son Cormac over there? He came with us. And Buinne mac Fergus stayed with the king.'

'What will Fergus do now?' Cuchulain wondered.

'He'll never forgive Conor, I know that much. He'll have to work out his grief and his sense of betrayal somehow. Perhaps we'll help him; I know I can't find it in my heart to blame him very much for this. Conor was just too shrewd for him. But what of you, Cuchulain? Which side will you take? Come with us, you loved Naisi.'

In spite of the darkness, they could see each other's faces; memory filled in the shadows. They had played together and fought together; they knew each other in a way they would never know anyone else. Now even that had been affected by Deirdre's tragedy.

There was only one answer for Cuchulain, though he would have wished it otherwise. Honour kept things simple.

'I'm Conor mac Nessa's foster-son,' he told Ferdiad. 'I gave him my first allegiance.'

'I hope you'll never regret it, then.'

'Where will you go, Ferdiad? You are always welcome at Dun Dalgan, you know that.'

'I thank you, Cuchulain. But it seems we are on opposite sides now. I'll go wherever the others do. Anywhere, except back to the king.'

'And Deirdre?'

Ferdiad gestured. 'You see those armed men over there? They've come to take her back to Emain Macha when the burials are over. Conor mac Nessa claims her – his prize of war, I suppose.' Ferdiad's tone was bitter. 'He hasn't attempted any reprisals against us yet, but even at a time like this, he's still thinking about her.'

'Will you fight to keep her?' Cuchulain asked.

Ferdiad shook his head. 'Would you?'

They stood together, nothing left to say. Something more than the sons of Uisnach had been slaughtered, and they shared a common grief for it; neither wanted to be the first to turn away. They took a step towards each other. They almost touched. Then they heard the sound of an approaching chariot.

Laeg drove through the darkness, the reins wrapped around one arm and a torch held aloft in his other hand. 'Cuchulain! Are you all right?'

254

'I am. I'm ready to go now.' He took the torch from Laeg's hand and allowed himself one last look at the faces gathered around the graves, men of the Red Branch he knew and loved. Then his eyes met Ferdiad's, locked, and held.

Cuchulain drew a deep breath. 'Let's go home to Dun Dalgan,' he ordered Laeg.

21 Cuchulain headed southward without pausing to speak to Conor mac Nessa. He did not trust his tongue. When he reached Dun Dalgan, his expression was so grim that Emer asked him no questions until he had drunk a quantity of wine. Then, as they sat together by the hearth, he told her of Deirdre and the sons of Uisnach.

She heard him through to the end, making no sound other than an occasional inarticulate murmur. Then she said, 'That poor woman. And Fergus as well. But you have to remain loyal to the king, there's no question about that.' And let Ferdiad go the other way, she thought to herself. He had been too often a guest in their hall, and Cuchulain mentioned him too frequently for any wife's liking.

'I'm glad you understand, Emer. Not everyone will. Both sides have terrible grievances now – both sides of survivors, that is. Naisi is buried, but not the quarrel.'

Emer sighed, stretched, and began absently stroking the fine growth of silky hair on her husband's bare forearm. 'Ah, Setanta, all quarrels must fade in time, if only to make way for new ones. And Deirdre's tragedy seems to have been inevitable from the moment you men made love a weapon and war a passion.'

He gave her a surprised look. 'How did you learn to be so wise over a lapful of needlework?'

'Women are born knowing things men will never, never learn,' Emer told him mischievously. 'But as long as we remember them for you, it will be all right.' She snuggled against him, content to watch the fire with him. With her own Setanta, alive, while Deirdre's Naisi lay dead . . .

Cuchulain heard her voice, very soft against his shoulder. 'Is she so beautiful, Deirdre?'

For the first time in a long time, he chuckled. 'I was wondering when you'd ask that.'

'Is she?'

His expression sobered. 'No matter what she is, I want your vow that you will never be jealous, Emer. Do you understand? Jealousy makes small people out of large ones and has practically destroyed the Red Branch. It is a mean emotion and not worthy of you, and I want you to promise me you will never allow yourself to feel it.'

She swallowed hard; his voice was deadly serious. 'I vow by sun and moon,' she whispered.

'I'll tell you what Deirdre is, then. When I first saw her, I thought she was like one perfect note struck on the harp, but now I know better. She is like the voice of the war-trumpet, issuing an invitation to die.'

Emer shivered. She pressed even closer against him, savouring life.

Cuchulain began to relax. A dreamy languor stole slowly over him, a heaviness of body he finally recognised as desire. But he made no move to touch her, not yet. Possession was a luxury to be savoured, he thought, wondering how much of Deirdre Conor would ever possess now.

They made idle conversation, each pretending to be unaware. By unspoken agreement, they spun out the thread of the evening, letting passion build by denying it. They spoke of cattle and weather and Dectera – though this last was a subject Emer did not seem anxious to pursue – and from time to time Cuchulain got up to throw a stick on the fire. The servants had left them alone in the hall some time earlier, at Emer's command. They lapsed into long silences, warming their feet at the fire as if they had nothing better to do.

The game was lost when Cuchulain faked such an elaborate yawn that Emer laughed at him. Their eyes met without pretence then. There was only one counterbalance for the destruction Cuchulain had seen, and he knew where to find it. In one stride, he had Emer in his arms and was heading towards their sleeping chamber.

She was not perfect. She was better than perfect. She was real and warm, looking all the more naked for a golden dappling of freckles, all the lovelier to him because her hair was tangled and her eyelids had that slight droop at the outer corners. Her nipples, Cuchulain told himself as happiness enfolded him, were the exact pink of a baby's toes . . .

Cuchulain had been right about the quarrel between the king and Fergus. Conciliation was impossible; each man faced the other over the grave of a dead son.

Conor was trying to effect conciliation on another front, however.

The killing of the sons of Uisnach had been a catharsis, cleansing him of anger. Grief remained for all those who had died, particularly his own son Fiacra, but in addition to the grief was the determination to make something good come of it all. Some positive achievement *must* result from the carnage; it was unbearable otherwise.

At least he would have Deirdre.

He sent for her. He was prepared to be tender, to be compassionate, to be understanding – to be whatever she required, even patient, knowing it would take her a while to get over all that had happened. He would wait, Conor promised himself.

But when she appeared before him, his good intentions vanished. One look at her face and he did not want to wait. Such strong emotions flooded through him, he could not summon the carefully prepared phrases he had planned, the perfect words and entreaties that would have smoothed things between them. He wanted her so much, he blurted out the first thing that came to him.

'The outlaws who took you from me are dead, but you'll come to no harm from me,' he said. 'I'm prepared to treat you as if nothing had happened. Your chamber will be filled with everything you could desire, servants will answer your every request, you need only stretch out your hand.'

Her huge green eyes were opaque. 'If I stretch out my hand, will you put Naisi into it?'

'He's dead.' Why couldn't he say it less brutally, he immediately wondered. If only the sight of her didn't make self-control impossible!

'If Naisi is dead, I am dead,' she said in a faint, lost voice. She stared past him as if he were not there.

Conor scowled. This was not going as he had planned. He must not let her make him angry all over again. 'Take her to her chamber,' he instructed her attendants, 'and let her have Levarcham with her. I know this girl. In time she'll be grateful to me for rescuing her from a hard life among strangers.'

He was disconcerted by Deirdre's expression. When he stood in front of her, she seemed to meet his eyes, but then her gaze somehow went through them to a point at the back of his head and beyond. She made him feel invisible. He was glad when they led her away.

At the edge of the Sorrowful Forest, Fergus finally grasped the nettle and approached Naisi's friends. They looked at him sullenly, but no one cursed him aloud, at least. 'Conor mac Nessa has cost me my sons and my honour,' he told them. 'He's brought shame on my beard by tricking me. I was king before he was; I see now that I owe kingship a responsibility, and that responsibility is to punish a bad king!

258

'If you want to take vengeance for the slain men, I offer you the opportunity of standing with me as I claim vengeance for my son and my good name.'

He saw acceptance in their eyes.

Fergus took a swift head count of those who gathered around him. The Beetle of Ulster was among them, glowering as usual from beneath his heavy browbone. And Cormac Connlongas, the king's son, chewing on a blade of grass and occasionally glancing toward the grave where his old friend Naisi lay. In his habitual horn body armour, Ferdiad sat on a stump with a file in his hand, smoothing the nicks from his sword blade. Even Bricriu Bitter-Tongue had joined them, though he complained with every breath he drew.

There were almost nine tens of them altogether, an impressive number. The sons of Uisnach had been much loved.

But more than twice as many warriors remained with Emain Macha.

The grizzled champion cast a professional eye over his allies. They were hardened warriors, and he had no illusions about them. They were not all standing with him now because of himself. Some were loyal to the person of Fergus mac Roy, but others were deliberately turning their backs on the king for their own reasons and joining Fergus because he was the only alternative.

The Beetle of Ulster spoke up. 'The king's going to keep Deirdre over there in the fort. He's holding her against her will, and every man here knows it.'

There was a sullen mutter of agreement.

'We should pay fire with fire,' someone suggested. 'In my father's time, if we had a bad king, we would have burned him out.'

This was not true and they all knew it; a bad king would have been replaced by the election of a new one from the dominant clan, and the new king would have been responsible for the destruction of the old one. No one was suggesting renaming Fergus as king of Ulster, but they liked the sound of violence. It fitted their mood. The raw earth of the graves cried out for it.

They lingered in their makeshift encampment while a few more men drifted out to them from the fort. If he was aware what was happening, Conor mac Nessa was making no effort to prevent it.

But he was not aware of the last few defections. Within Emain Macha was enough to keep him preoccupied: grief and despair and Deirdre.

The band of men gathered in the Sorrowful Forest began to talk about the future.

'When we find Conall Cearnach,' Bricriu Bitter-Tongue said to Fergus, 'are you going to take his head for killing your son?'

'I think not. He evened the score, didn't he, when he killed Fiacra. Besides, my quarrel isn't with Conall but with the king. Now that you mention it, though, where is Conall? Did he stay in the fort to face Conor's anger? If so, he might be dead already.'

The question was a good one.

After the shock of the double killing of Illand and Fiacra, Conall had fled with no knowledge of where he was going or what he would do. Somehow he found himself outside the walls. Throughout that night and the next day, he wandered at random, dazed, not realising he had travelled in a wide circle until he came upon the ritual ring of standing stones north of Emain Macha at sundown.

Grim by day and even more grim in the dusk, the stones loomed, rough-hewn sentinels that kept their secrets. A fever of exhaustion overtook Conall. He sank down and fell asleep on the bare earth only a few paces beyond the stone circle.

At dawn, Cathbad of the Gentle Face found him there.

The king's druid also wanted to avoid Emain Macha as much as he could. The smell of the fire sickened him, a man who had offered innumerable burned sacrifices in his time. His inner eye saw so many terrible omens around the fort, he sought the lonely peace of the standing stones instead – and found a warrior huddled in sleep there, an unpleasant reminder.

Cathbad shook him roughly by the shoulder. 'Wake up, Conall, you can't sleep here.'

The young man sat up and cradled his head in his hands. 'Where else can I go? Do you know what I did back there?'

'You can't stay here,' Cathbad reiterated, glaring at him. 'This is *my* place.'

'Then tell me what to do. Should I go back and face the king? Or flee with my life, while I still have it? I'd be grateful for a druid's advice.'

'You'd be grateful for any advice, wouldn't you?' Cathbad replied. In his befuddled state, Conall mistook his tone for one of thoughtful consideration of the problem. 'If I threw a pebble into the air and told you to choose one side, the dry or the damp, you could call one Conor and the other flight and abide by the way it fell. Would that satisfy you?'

'I suppose so,' Conall said.

With one scathing look, Cathbad stripped the flesh from his bones. 'You idiot!'

Conall drew back. 'What do you mean? You throw the sticks of prophecy – aren't you talking about the same sort of thing? I just asked you for help, and I don't think – '

'And there we hear a truth indeed. You don't think. All your profession requires is that you know which way to march. You'd follow the advice of sticks or pebbles or fishes' guts or flickering lights, so long as it came from outside your own head and you could get your thinking pre-chewed.' Cathbad snorted with deep disgust.

'Just go off somewhere and hit somebody, warrior!' he yelled at Conall. 'Do blind damage! It's all any of you are good for!' Raising the ash stick in his hand, he turned south, facing the fort. 'I curse *you*, Emain Macha, for fostering such a belligerent tribe. You throw away peace with both hands; so be it. I make this prophecy: the day will come when you will search for peace with both hands throughout all Ulster and not be able to find it!'

Cathbad's voice was no longer human. Chilling in its power and anger, it reached beyond the circle of standing stones to the Otherworld whose portal they marked. Whatever waited beyond that portal heard the druid and acknowledged the curse.

Conall grabbed his sword and fled, not caring what direction he ran.

And so time passed until a full moon rose over Ulster, and the men assembled at the edge of the Sorrowful Forest began to gather up their weapons. Earlier in the day, they had noted the departure of Owen and the mercenaries from Fern Mag. Only the rest of the Red Branch were left in the fort.

Men did not speak to each other of what they were about to do. Discussion was useless; what was there to discuss? They stood together, waiting.

'Now,' said Fergus mac Roy.

They began to run across the open space between forest and fort.

Conall Cearnach had made a lonely little camp for himself in the lee of a long-abandoned midden heap, and from his vantage point he saw in the moonlight the distant line of men running towards Emain Macha. He stood up with a sigh of relief. Things were simple again. Someone was attacking the royal fort, and he was Red Branch, pledged to defend it.

He began to run too.

With an intimate knowledge of the fort, Fergus knew exactly where its weak points were. He led his men to a section of palisade built upon the embankment above an underground stream. The earth was always damp there, and enough men scrambling up the wall together could pull it down with their massed weight. As soon as the palisade was breached, the warriors shoved through, tearing more timbers aside as they went.

At once the alarm was sounded, but too late.

Bending low, Fergus led his men from building to building in an unpredictable zigzag pattern, throwing torches up on to the thatched roofs.

As the first fire blazed a shout of horror arose from within and help came running, but by then Fergus's followers had spread throughout the fort.

The women had rushed outside at the first shouts; Nessa caught a glimpse of a familiar shape trotting between buildings and shouted, 'Fergus mac Roy! What do you think you're doing?'

If he heard her, he gave no answer. He disappeared behind the bake house.

Men were now running in every direction. Martain the steward organised a line of servants to throw water on the fires or beat them with cloth and leather, but Fergus had deployed his men skilfully, and flames kept leaping out in new places.

The attack had been well timed. The remaining Red Branch warriors had been gathered for the evening meal and had been well relaxed into their ale cups, trying to forget the recent sorrows. By the time they could collect their weapons and their wits, it was almost too late. They found themselves grappling with Fergus's men in groups of three and four, too scattered to present a unified force. Besides, many found it all but impossible to strike a killing blow against a fellow member of the Red Branch. There was a great deal of flailing and bludgeoning and profanity. The first killing happened almost by accident; the second came easier.

Conor mac Nessa appeared in the doorway of the Speckled House, carrying his own sword and shield. He had no champion to stand for him now; Fergus mac Roy stood against him. He would have to represent himself.

He took a deep breath and waded into the nearest tangle of fighting men.

When the first blow struck against it, the shield called Ocean roared with its great booming voice, and Conall Cearnach heard it. He ran towards the fort with an awful sense of nightmare repeating itself.

Conor mac Nessa was attempting to be everywhere at once and

outguess Fergus at the same time, but it was impossible to do either. What his former foster-father had lost in agility over the years, he had gained in cunning. Conor saw the fort of Emain Macha crumbling under the attack.

The king began to stumble over dead bodies, many of them his own supporters.

He was frantic to find Fergus and uncertain what he would do if he did.

He felt someone grab at his arm and tried to shrug the person off, but the hand clung like a burr to wool. He recognised his mother just as he was about to strike her across the face and knock her away. 'Go to the *grianan* and stay there!' he ordered. 'Even Fergus won't burn the women's house.'

Still she clung to him. The fighting was intensifying around them; Nessa was in a dangerous place. With a snort of impatience, Conor tucked his mother under his arm like a sack of meal and hurried toward the *grianan*.

'Conor mac Nessa!' roared a voice.

The king turned to see Fergus coming towards him with a drawn sword in one hand and a spear in the other, his face streaked with soot, a cut above one eye oozing blood.

Nessa began to squirm, and Conor set her on her feet. 'Do you want to go to him?' he asked her.

Nessa looked from son to husband. Then she stepped between them. 'Both of you, stop this at once!' she commanded.

'Don't start your interfering this time,' Fergus warned her. 'The last thing that's needed here is an old woman.' At the moment, his anger against her sex was total. 'Old woman,' he repeated like a curse.

She shrank back as if he had struck her. Conor's strength loomed behind her, and she sheltered against him gratefully. The time had passed when she could have both husband and son, but at least the invisible umbilicus of motherhood had not been broken.

'Kill the traitor,' she advised Conor icily, then turned and made her way to the *grianan* with a straight back and a strong step.

Both men followed her with their eyes until she reached the chamber and went in. Then they looked at each other. Fergus tightened his grip on his sword hilt. Conor shifted his stance, lifting Ocean a bit higher and holding his own blade in readiness.

So they stood until Fergus finally cleared his throat. 'I don't seem to be able to kill you,' he told Conor.

'Nor I you,' the other admitted. They exchanged one more long look, then turned aside. In the madness and confusion that followed, they managed to avoid encountering one another again.

In the *grianan*, Nessa flung herself down on her favourite couch. Most of the women huddled at the doorway, watching the fighting from a safe vantage point. No one paid any attention to Nessa lying with her fist thrust into her mouth and her shoulders shaking.

As the sounds of battle diminished she sat up and made a futile attempt to smooth her hair. Her eye fell upon a beautifully wrought mirror of polished silver, lying on a table nearby. She picked it up by its slender handle and studied the reflection she found. Even softened by candlelight, the evidence of the mirror was clear.

'Old woman,' Nessa said to herself.

She saw a sagging, lived-in face as juiceless as last year's apples. The eyes were milky, as if the yellowed whites were seeping into the faded irises. Chin and nose hurried to meet across receding lips. The face could have been male or female; the only certainty was of age.

Nessa put the mirror face down on the table and took a deep breath. 'At least I never need to bother with rubbing oil into my skin again,' she said. Then she stood up, brushed her hands together, and went to join the women at the doorway watching the progress of the battle.

No one was fighting within their line of vision. Timidly at first, then with increasing boldness, the women emerged from their shelter and moved out across the grass. Then they stopped in astonishment.

Grown men, powerful, hard-muscled warriors, were bent double clutching their bellies or rolling on the ground, pallid with moonlight and pain. Yet they were not bleeding. They gasped; they rolled their eyes in their heads; their skin was clammy. A few seemed to be on the verge of tears.

Nessa wandered among them, looking for her son. She saw Fedelm searching for Leary Buadach, but she had gone almost to the foot of the *urla* before she found the king. She was relieved to see him still on his feet, but when she drew closer, she could see he was in the same agony as the others. His face was convulsed and he twisted from side to side, biting back groans.

'What is it?' she asked urgently, trying to feel his brow for heat.

He pushed her hand away. 'You can't help,' he said through clenched teeth. Sweat was rolling down his forehead, and the veins in his temples were hideously distended. 'I'm being split in two pieces, Mother.'

Nessa's eyes lit. 'The Pangs!'

264

'It is.' Conor dragged a deep breath into his lungs as the rhythmic pain eased temporarily, leaving him only enough time to brace himself for the next onslaught. 'The curse of Macha . . . in times of direst crisis . . .' He folded over and cradled his belly with his arms.

As Nessa glanced around, the size of the crisis became obvious. Emain Macha was all but destroyed. Fergus and his men had burned most of the buildings; the House of the King and the Speckled House were blazing like torches.

Released from their pens, the chariot horses were running wild, adding to the confusion.

Those who were able were trying to contain the damage, but with mixed success. The day had been dry, the fire had a will of its own. Sparks threatened to ignite the roof of the *grianan*. But there was no sign of fighting, no clang of iron on iron.

'Bring all the women together,' Conor muttered to his mother. 'They'll have to deal with the fires. The men . . . can do nothing . . . You must be leader now, until I . . .'

'And a good job I'll do of it,' Nessa said confidently. 'But what about Fergus, won't he try to stop me?'

The king managed a faint smile. 'He's an Ulsterman too. The last I saw of Fergus, he and his men were trying to crawl out of the fort before . . . the Pangs incapacitated them completely. They'll do us no damage . . . for a while . . .'

'That's one dry patch in a deluge,' Nessa remarked. She gathered her skirts in her hands and prepared for action, satisfied her son's malady was not fatal.

Once again, fires from Emain Macha sent a signal to Dun Dalgan. Cuchulain realised he had been expecting it, somehow.

Evidence of disaster greeted him and Laeg long before their chariot reached the fort. The road leading southward from Emain Macha was littered with people. Some were servants and bondsfolk, fleeing because they could think of nothing else to do. Others were Red Branch families, seeking shelter with clans and allies elsewhere.

But no warrior walked upright.

From a distance, Cuchulain recognised the elegant figure of Conall Cearnach's wife, Lendabair, pacing beside a huddled form carried on a litter. When she saw Cuchulain approaching, she ordered her porters to set the litter down. 'All Emain Macha is burned,' she told the Hound by way of greeting.

265

He had already learned this from other refugees, though their stories were confused. 'Fergus did it? Hard to believe.'

'True, though. He put the torch to everything and left many casualties. We found this one' – she pointed to the litter – 'outside the gates, afterwards. Come and see.'

Cuchulain found himself gazing down at Conall, who lay curled into a ball like a baby. The formidable face was as bleached as old bone and his heavy beard was sweat-matted. There was no visible blood.

Cuchulain crouched in the road beside him. 'Where were you wounded?'

He could have sworn he heard Lendabair snigger.

'I wasn't wounded,' Conall said in a weak voice. 'I wish I were. I was struck down just as I arrived to fight . . .' He gave a gasp and drew his knees up against his chest.

'It's the Pangs,' Lendabair said. 'He's having a baby. Except there isn't any baby. It's happening to all of them like this, all the big, strong men.' She bit her lip, and Cuchulain realised she was fighting to keep from laughing.

'Precious little sympathy we're getting from the women,' Conall complained.

Lendabair shrugged one graceful shoulder. 'As much as we get from you when we're in childbed.'

'That's different.'

'Is it? Women die giving birth. At least none of you are dying from this.'

'I wish I were,' Conall grated.

Lendabair turned to Cuchulain. 'I see the Pangs haven't overtaken you.'

'No beard,' he pointed out, obscurely embarrassed to be so set apart. 'Not yet.'

'Mmmm . . . Oh, Conall, stop thrashing around. I could bear a dozen children without the fuss you're making over not bearing one.'

'We'll see about that as soon as I feel better,' Conall promised her grimly before the next pain tore through him.

Cuchulain was finding it difficult to keep from laughing himself, until he remembered the burned fortress and the casualties. 'Apart from this incapacitation, how many were actually killed?' he asked Lendabair.

'Quite a number, I didn't stay to find out. Fergus and his followers got away, though the Pangs overtook them too, of course. They're

266

probably staggering across the land right now, seeking a sympathetic *maigen*. No one will be much interested in pursuing them until this passes.'

'Nine days, isn't it?'

'Nine days, so Macha decreed.'

'Nine days and *nights*,' Conall moaned.

Returning to his chariot, Cuchulain told Laeg, 'You can let the horses go at an easy pace. Not much will be happening at Emain Macha before we get there.'

Laeg mac Riangabra was looking very pale. 'Do you think you could drive, Cuchulain?' he asked plaintively. 'I have the most terrible pain in my belly.'

22 Emain Macha looked as if a giant's foot had been set down atop it, crushing buildings, breaking a section of palisade, leaving the stronghold of the north naked to its enemies and the elements. The stench of burning was worse than before.

Leaving Laeg with his fellow-sufferers, Cuchulain went on an inspection tour. Morning sunshine had given way to a rain that did not fall in separate droplets but oozed from the atmosphere in total, pervasive damp. There was not enough shelter remaining intact for the women and children, much less the men, so Nessa had ordered the scavenging of the burned halls for usable building materials as soon as the fires were extinguished. Hasty lean-tos had been erected against the walls, and families huddled there, peering out at Cuchulain as he passed. Their faces were blank with shock; only a few managed to call a greeting.

When he saw the row of new graves at the foot of the largest of the mounds, Cuchulain was reminded of another row of graves beside the Sorrowful Forest.

Conor mac Nessa was leaning against the doorframe of one of the makeshift huts. His arms were wrapped around his mid-section and he looked ghastly, but he was on his feet. 'I thought I heard a chariot come through the gate. I hoped it was you. Pardon me if I can't stand long enough for a proper greeting.' The king's knees sagged, and Cuchulain reached to catch him.

'I'm as feeble as an old man,' Conor muttered. 'But you're all right?'

'I am.'

'I should have kept you here, you'd have been more use to me than all the rest of them. But I didn't expect this. Who could anticipate that my own champion would lead a rising against me?'

Cuchulain said nothing. He realised the king was reworking events in his mind, choosing the version he would prefer to believe. Everyone would do that. No two would be quite the same.

Obsession glittered in Conor's eyes. 'At least I rescued Deirdre, I succeeded to that extent. She's here now, and safe.' He clenched his fists, waiting for the pain.

268

'Who else is here? What of Ferdiad?'

'He came with Fergus and left with Fergus; another outlaw now. But I don't think he was killed.'

'I saw Conall on the road.'

'He tried to come back to me at the end, so I forgive him for what he did in the dark in a moment of madness. I'm a compassionate man, Cuchulain; you know that.' His eyes pleaded for agreement. 'If Naisi had only come to me and begged my forgiveness . . .'

'He couldn't. Naisi was as proud as any of us.'

'I wouldn't have been too proud to forgive the sons of Uisnach if they had asked,' Conor said, by now believing it. 'Instead, I've lost half the Red Branch. And my champion.' He wiped his forehead with the back of his wrist and gave Cuchulain a calculating look. 'You. . . ?'

'I'm the champion of Ulster, that's enough honour. I can't take the place of Fergus by default.'

'Ah, yet you blame others for being too proud. Nessa! Come out here and tell this fosterling of mine that a king must have a champion. It's one of my entitlements.' He slumped over again, clutching at the pain.

Nessa came bustling out of the lean-to. She wore a filthy linen shift belted with rope and had a half-burned square of red wool flung across her shoulders for a cloak. 'How can you refuse the king after all he's done for you?' she burst out at Cuchulain, proving she had overheard the entire conversation. 'Your own father!'

'Foster-father,' Cuchulain said carefully. 'My foster-father.'

'He claimed you when no one else would. You owe him.'

Cuchulain bowed his head. 'I know that, Nessa. But I can't live here at Emain Macha now.'

'You don't have to,' the king managed to say. 'Just accept the title and I'll let it be known the terrible Hound of Ulster is my new sword arm. It should be enough.'

I wonder if Fergus will ever forgive me for this, Cuchulain thought.

But forgiveness seemed to be in short supply in Ulster lately.

'You have your champion,' he told Conor mac Nessa.

He left them to the rebuilding of Emain Macha and turned the heads of the Grey and the Black for Dun Dalgan. 'Send Laeg to me when he's recovered,' was his last request of the king.

The men of the Red Branch endured the full nine days of the curse. When the pains left them, they were as weak as if newborn, and their women had to care for them for several days more – not without the occasional sarcastic comment.

As soon as he felt he looked presentable again, Conor devoted himself to a dogged, determined wooing of Fedlimid's daughter. He had lost so much, he must win her. Deirdre was the only justification for any of it.

Tense, short-tempered to others because he dared not be irritable with Deirdre, Conor mac Nessa set about rebuilding. Since she no longer had Fergus, his mother turned her full attention upon him, to his discomfiture. She commented on everything he said and did, how he looked, what he ate or did not eat; she was at his heels like one of his hounds.

At the end of the day, when he thought to allow himself to let his guard down just a little and wiped a tired hand across his eyes, Nessa was there at once, her own hand stroking his forehead. 'My poor boy,' she would murmur. 'How tired you must be. And these people simply don't understand, they don't appreciate you. But I do.'

'That's nice,' he muttered.

The king's wives had been less than warm to him for a long time; now that Deirdre was actually at Emain Macha, bringing disaster with her as clouds brought rain, Conor's women withdrew into icy politeness. If he took one to bed, she tolerated him, and he hated being tolerated.

Deirdre, however, was not even tolerating him. And that was worse.

Deirdre did not seem to think he existed at all.

'She's an ungrateful little mud-pudding and not half good enough for you,' Nessa fumed. But she could tell how determined he was. 'I'll speak to Deirdre for you,' she offered. 'A woman can talk to another woman.'

'I'll speak for myself!' Conor burst out sharply. 'Stay out of this.'

Nessa pursed her lips and shook her head, knowing what was best for her child.

The best of the repaired chambers had been given to Deirdre, with Levarcham to care for her and two armed men at her door night and day. Each morning shortly after sunrise, the king appeared at the door with some new gift in his hand. He brought her a pillow of swan's feathers; he ransacked his own treasures to select the finest carnelians and amber to offer her; he examined every harp in the area and appropriated the finest to give her as a replacement for the one burned in the House of the Red Branch.

Yet Deirdre took no gift from his hand. It was always the same, day after day. He would knock, Levarcham would open to him, Deirdre would not look at him. She went about whatever she was doing as if he were not there, even the most intimate things – a calculated insult not lost on the king.

And she never smiled.

Though she did not speak to him – since he was not there for her – she spoke to Levarcham, but always in the same monotonous voice with the life drained out of it. And when she spoke, it was always about the same subject.

'The water on Alba is sweeter than this, Levarcham,' she would say as she lifted a cup to her lips. Or, 'You should hear the birds singing on Alba, they know such lovely melodies.'

She wants better music, Conor told himself. Good enough. He had songbirds trapped for her and delivered to her chamber, but she immediately set them free. 'I cannot stand the sight of caged things,' she told Levarcham.

He came himself and sat outside the open door, singing in his deep, rich voice to the accompaniment of a harper.

'Close the door, Levarcham,' Deirdre commanded. 'I feel a draught.'

Later, he asked the nurse, 'Did she hear me singing at all, Levarcham? After I left . . . did she say anything about it?'

There was a dark pity in the old nurse's eyes. 'She said the least of the sons of Uisnach had a finer voice than the king of Ulster.'

There were private moments when Conor admitted to himself what he knew his people were thinking, and probably saying, behind his back. He was a man in his middle years who was behaving like a braying ass. But then he would think of some new stratagem and be back at Deirdre's door, or he would catch a glimpse of her crossing the *urla* on the rare occasions when she went out, and know himself as the true captive at Emain Macha.

Most unbearable of all was the way she spoke of Naisi. His name was constantly on her lips; her undying adoration of him was so obvious, even Levarcham began to tire of hearing it.

Conor mac Nessa ached in every fibre of his body to be worshipped as Naisi was worshipped.

The season of cattle-raiding was upon them. Word came from the borderlands that Maeve of Connaught had sent her men out again, striking where the northerners had the weakest defences, inflicting damage but suffering little in return, attacking Ulster's underbelly with studied skill.

And she had new allies.

On their pillow, Maeve and Ailell discussed the new arrivals at Cruachan. 'I thought pigs would fly before Fergus mac Roy came marching up to our gates with his palms up,' Ailell said.

'Bringing a sizeable number of the Red Branch with him,' Maeve added gleefully. 'Even one of Conor mac Nessa's sons, that fellow called Cormac Connlongas. We'll make a good Connaughtman of him!'

'I suppose they had nowhere else to go, really. After rising against their king, they seem to have rampaged across Ulster in a mindless fury; many of their own people turned against them. Men who rise against their leader are always suspect, whatever the reason.'

'They were a subdued lot by the time they arrived here,' Maeve said. 'We can win them over to us one by one, if we're generous, and we'll have a fine addition to our warrior band. I intend to make every one of them feel welcome. Now scratch my back, husband.'

Ailell's willing fingernails dug ploughmarks into Maeve's skin until she sighed with pleasure. 'Aaahh . . . lower, lower, there. Now up again to the shoulder blade . . .'

'Now you scratch my back, Maeve.'

'Why should I?' She rolled over and went to sleep. Ailell lay beside her for a while, then got up and went in search of a serving girl. But it wasn't the same.

In the encampment Fergus and his men had established beside the walls of Cruachan, Ulster's former king also lay sleepless. The madness that had precipitated the sacking of Emain Macha had faded, leaving only blurred memories he was reluctant to examine too closely. Somewhere among those memories were the faces of men he had recently slain, and each of those faces had once belonged to a friend.

I think I understand something of Cuchulain's battle-fury, Fergus thought to himself in the night.

Lying wrapped in his cloak at Cruachan of the Enchantments, looking up at stars that were also looking down at Ulster, he seemed to be in a known and trusted cosmos. Yet now he knew such trust was misplaced. The verities he had always believed in did not exist. Without their mortar, the world cracked around Fergus and Otherworlds leered through.

Nearby he heard an odd, chitinous rattle. He was reaching for his sword when he recognised the sound; Ferdiad, turning over. Ferdiad always slept in his armour now, no one ever saw him without it.

There was no trust left in the world.

In the dark, Fergus mac Roy buried his face in his hands.

272

Over the next days, Maeve patiently elicited the whole story from the Ulstermen, drawing bits and pieces from each in turn.

At last she sat on her bench in the hall, lounging comfortably amid thick wolfskins, toying with a gold bracelet set with carbuncles. She waited until Ailell was elsewhere, and then sent for Fergus mac Roy.

The grizzled warrior approached her warily. Since agreeing to give them sanctuary, Maeve had hardly spoken to him directly. Nor had he been eager to seek out her company. He was embarrassed at the position in which he found himself, and uncertain how to act with the rulers of Connaught. It went against his grain to think of them as friends, after all the years of skirmishing between them.

Maeve watched with concealed amusement as he came down the length of the hall towards her. She relished having the former king of Ulster in such a position, and she felt a grudging admiration for the dignity he was trying to maintain under the most awkward circumstances. He had been drinking constantly and too much, that was obvious, yet he put one foot in front of the other and held his head high. Tatters of past power clung to him like bits of tarnished metal.

'Ah, Fergus. I thought it was time you and I had a pleasant conversation.' Maeve patted the cushions of the bench beside hers: Ailell's seat. Fergus glanced at it and drew up a different bench for himself.

'I hope you have fully recovered from your weakness?' Maeve inquired.

Fergus held himself stiffly upright. 'What weakness?'

'When you left Emain Macha, you were incapacitated, I understand. You had a very difficult time making your way westward until the, ah, cramps passed, isn't that true?'

His eyes were hooded. 'If you say so.'

Aha, thought Maeve. Some part of him still feels loyal to Ulster and wants to protect the secret. I wonder if I can win him over. The challenge intrigued her. 'You have the reputation of being a magnificent warrior, Fergus mac Roy,' she said aloud, but his eyes never flickered. Flattery was not the way, then. Perhaps it would be better to keep him off-balance. 'Conor mac Nessa was fortunate to have you.'

'He was a bad king, and I wish I'd killed him when I had the chance,' Fergus growled in spite of himself.

'I'm not certain you mean that. I don't think Conor is a bad king, he's a good one with an unfortunate flaw. He's not the first man to clutch at a giddy girl in hopes of recapturing his own fading youth. It never works;

the man merely seems older by comparison. I don't think *you* would make such a mistake, would you?' she asked, looking at Fergus through her coppery eyelashes. There was no mistaking the seduction in her glance.

Fergus cleared his throat. Several times. 'Neither would I make the mistake of clutching at a female war-leader.'

'Is that what they're calling me in Ulster? Like Macha of the Golden Hair? I'm flattered.' Yet even as she spoke, Maeve was privately contemptuous of warriors. She saw them as men playing childish games with rules they had designed in order to glorify themselves. Men could not bring forth life from their bodies as women did. They could only produce death, so they had undertaken to ennoble killing.

But they could be used.

'If I am a war-leader, Fergus, then I must be an expert on the matter. Let me give you the benefit of my expert opinion. You've just spent many good men in a war of revenge, and what have you accomplished? Nothing.

'War is a tool, Fergus. Men like you misuse it, because you don't understand it.'

His clothing was tattered and less than clean; his face was haggard and his breath reeked of drink. But Fergus dug deep into himself and summoned up the noble blood of the Red Branch as he answered, 'Of course I understand war, better than a woman ever could. War is the simplest method for acquiring cattle and slaves and glory.'

At his words, Maeve thought she glimpsed another face super-imposing itself over his; a younger, more intense face, made for glory. She blinked it away as a trick of the light. 'Nonsense, Fergus, your words only prove my point. You don't seem to realise that cattle and slaves – and glory – are just the incentives leaders use to persuade warriors to fight. The desire for such things convinces fools who might otherwise live to old age that a war is necessary.'

Fergus had no idea what all this was about, he could not find the direction in which Maeve was going, but he was shocked to hear her denying the principal reason for his existence as he knew it. 'Are you saying war *isn't* necessary?'

'Of course it is. But not for the reasons you name.'

He thought he could afford to be patronising; she was only a woman. 'Then tell me what you think.'

'War,' said Maeve of Connaught, slowly, thoughtfully, 'is the process by which we tear down so we may build. War forces change and development and growth. No spring without winter, Fergus.

274

'Besides, if there were no battles for them to fight, men would sit around getting fat and lazy and letting women do all the work,' she concluded briskly.

Then something shifted deep in her colourless eyes. Against her will, she found herself looking through Fergus, seeing a different face. 'As for glory . . .' Maeve shook her head impatiently, again trying to banish Cuchulain's image from her inner sight.

Warrior.

A man who made battle splendid for its own sake.

She wrenched her thoughts back to the conversation at hand. Fergus was beginning to look confused, which was what she wanted. Once he began questioning his own beliefs, he would be more susceptible to her leadership. 'When I send men out raiding, Fergus, they have orders to return to Cruachan with cattle and slaves. They know those will be shared with them as rewards for their efforts, and I am never . . . ungenerous.

'However, my reward for equipping and leading them is this.' Maeve waved her hand to indicate the solid, looming walls of Cruachan, built to stand for centuries. Glory to last beyond the lives of mortal men. Her creation.

'If it weren't for war, Fergus mac Roy, what chieftain could justify having a stronghold built like this home of mine?'

Suddenly, Maeve tensed. Against the timbered walls and glowing woollen hangings of her hall, that face asserted itself yet again. She stared at the proud sweep of forehead, the brilliant grey eyes fixed on hers. Denying her the achievement she sought.

Championing Ulster.

I use warriors, Maeve thought, but I could never use Cuchulain. He will neither lead nor follow. His vision of himself refuses to let him be a tool for manipulation.

I am a builder, I must have tools. If Cruachan is to put Emain Macha in the shade, the Hound of Ulster must be swept aside.

She could no longer concentrate on playing games with Fergus mac Roy. With an impatient wave of her hand, she indicated he was free to go. Fergus stalked from the hall, humiliated at being in a position where a woman could summarily dismiss him.

Maeve made him very uncomfortable.

The conflict between men and women was being conducted in various ways in Erin that season. At Dun Dalgan, Emer nursed her secret and

275

condemned the curiosity that had led her to unwanted knowledge. Cuchulain sensed an unexpected area of reserve in her and tried to break through without any success, since he did not know what the problem was. They became edgy with each other.

For want of a better explanation, Cuchulain attributed it to the mysteries of being female and began watching Emer with an ever more hopeful eye, expecting to see the first signs of pregnancy. He knew less about the way such things worked than other men, for the subject was one that embarrassed him. The delicacy Fingan had first remarked in him had not disappeared with marriage; it was as much a part of him as his grey eyes.

But thinking Emer's moodiness must be the result of incipient parenthood that she was keeping to herself for her own female reasons, Cuchulain began taking added notice of every child at Dun Dalgan.

They all were beautiful to him.

So young, so fresh, they looked at the world with eyes that had not yet seen the darkness. He delighted in the company of the little people. Whenever he could, he played games with the sons and daughters of his clansmen and even his servants, ignoring the distinctions of rank.

Rank wasn't important when you were with children.

He began to carve toys for the youngsters, crude little wooden birds that improved with practice. 'By the time you have a child, I'll be an expert at this,' he said jokingly to Emer.

She did not answer him.

Children adored him, recognising a kindred merry spirit lurking within the trappings of a feared and famous fighter. Whenever he sat down, they came running to him to climb into his lap, pull his hair, pelt him with questions.

One day a little jug-eared lad asked innocently, 'Where do you keep Lugh's spear?'

The Gae Bulga was stored safely out of reach, but the question startled Cuchulain. 'Who told you about it?'

'My mother. She said everyone knows you have the spear that once belonged to the Son of the Sun, and you throw it every morning to make the day begin. I'm awfully glad you do,' he added confidingly, gazing up at the Hound. 'I'm just a little bit afraid of the dark, and I'm glad when it ends.'

Cuchulain laughed and hugged the boy. But after the children had gone, he went to the Gae Bulga and unwrapped it from its protective covering of fine *sida*. He looked thoughtfully at it for a long time, seeing

276

the distorted image of his own face reflected in the polished golden bronze below the three prongs.

Lewy of the Long Hand. His lips formed the name silently. Lugh. The questions children ask . . .

Meanwhile, at Emain Macha, the king had grown tired of asking questions that were never answered and offering gifts that were invariably refused. Conor mac Nessa had been patient with Deirdre. Painfully patient, he thought. But he felt he had suffered more rejection than any human could endure.

To make matters worse, after every rebuff his mother hovered over him. 'My poor son,' she would say, 'you're suffering so because of that worthless woman. I understand. I know how you feel.'

'You can't possibly know how I feel!' Conor finally exploded. 'Why do you always insist you do?'

'Because I'm your mother,' she answered complacently.

It was no answer at all. 'You understand nothing about me and never have. I live alone inside this skin and you can't get into it, for which I am thankful. You would if you could; you'd take over my life if I let you. But I won't. Now stop clinging to me and let me be!' He thrust her aside roughly and stalked away, leaving Nessa staring, her eyes two round moons of astonishment.

She realised people were watching. People were always watching, there was never any privacy in the royal stronghold. 'He doesn't mean what he says,' Nessa explained. 'He's just upset. I understand. I'm his mother.'

That afternoon as they were out hunting, Conor remarked to Ferloga, his charioteer, 'I wonder if there's a way to have a *ges* removed – one you've taken on yourself? There's a woman I'd like to strangle.'

Ferloga was shocked. 'Not Deirdre?'

'Not Deirdre,' the king agreed.

He determined to attempt one final, magnificent gesture. The hunt resulted in the killing of a rare white stag unlike any ever seen in Ulster: Conor's kill. He turned it over to the best craftsmen, leatherworkers and metalsmiths, with orders to create an unparalleled work of art.

When the staghide was ready, he dressed in his seven-coloured cloak, set the massive gold torc of his kingship around his neck, and went to pay a call on Deirdre.

Opening the door to him, Levarcham dropped her eyes to the present he carried folded across his arms and let out a faint gasp. Even an old woman on the verge of blindness could not help being impressed.

The skin had been tanned and treated until it was as soft as *sida*, draping in a shimmering fold over Conor's muscular bare arms. The white hair had taken on a silvery sheen, matched by the lacework of silver wire that had been fastened around the deer's hooves. Its antlers had been covered with gold, precious stones set into each of the branchings.

The white deer had been transformed into a creature out of myth.

'This is for you,' Conor mac Nessa said simply, extending the deerskin to Deirdre.

She did glance at it, the faintest flicker. Then she raised one shoulder in a tiny shrug. 'The red deer of Alba are infinitely more beautiful than that poor dead thing,' she said. She turned away, still refusing to look at him.

Conor's temper exploded. 'Have you no love left in you at all?' he cried.

'Only hatred,' she answered.

'Then tell me whom you hate most!'

For the first time in all that terrible season, she let herself look at him. Her eyes were so empty Conor had the impression he was gazing off the brink of the world. 'Yourself surely,' she replied. 'And Owen of Fern Mag, whose blow killed my Naisi.'

The king drew a long breath. 'Then I will give you to Owen of Fern Mag to warm his bed for a year,' he told her.

'I am freeborn, you cannot!' A shriek of horror, of *feeling*.

'I can and will.' His eyes were blue frost. No one told Conor mac Nessa what he could or could not do, and he had suffered enough because of women. 'Levarcham, prepare her. I'll send Cethern to Owen this very day to inform him of my gift. I think he'll be quite pleased.'

He flung the white deerskin on to the floor and strode over it on his way out.

Levarcham ran after him. 'Don't do this, I beg you.'

'It's done already.'

'I thought you cared about Deirdre.'

He stopped. 'Cared about her? Haven't you noticed, Levarcham? I've crawled on my belly through the mud for her, but any effort I make to give her pleasure just produces pain. She embraces pain instead of me, she's wallowing in her grief. Good enough. I'll give her pain. Perhaps a year in Owen's bed will make her more appreciative of what I offer.'

Levarcham hurried back to Deirdre as fast as her arthritic old legs

278

would carry her. 'You'll have to plead with him yourself, he won't listen to me.'

'I wouldn't ask him to close my eyes after I was dead,' Deirdre said with contempt. 'I beg Conor mac Nessa for nothing. He can't hurt me. I buried my Naisi; nothing the king does to me can ever hurt me after that.' Stoically, she knelt by her carved wooden box of clothing and began taking out her gowns, as if preparing for a journey.

'You mean to let him send you to Owen, then?'

Deirdre lifted her eyebrows; her expression was opaque, as if she looked within herself. 'He can't send me anywhere. I don't belong to him.' Then she smiled. Something about her smile frightened the old woman more than anything that had happened before.

From that morning, Deirdre ate nothing and consumed no more water than Levarcham was able to force into her by pressing a wet cloth to her lips. The flesh fell away from her, leaving her younger-looking than ever, like an immature child. Perversely, when the king saw her, he found her more desirable than she had been in full bloom; she looked like the little girl he had once known.

Cethern returned from his errand to say Owen mac Durrow would soon be on his way to collect his prize.

'I'll accompany the two of you to Fern Mag myself,' Conor told Deirdre. 'I want to be certain you arrive in good condition. He's known as Owen Hard-Hand in his own clanhold,' the king added, unable to resist putting in the knife and twisting it just a little, hoping to see her react again.

But Deirdre held her face impassive. And when Owen's chariot arrived and she was led forward to meet it, she walked with her head up.

She was very pale. Levarcham kept darting worried glances toward her. Noticing, Conor took the old woman by the elbow and whispered to her, 'He won't dare harm her, I promise you. This is just an education for her, Levarcham.'

Owen had brought his usual band of surly fighting men with him, a lowering group who looked at Deirdre and licked their lips. Her clothes hung on her thin frame, her eyes were enormous. Still, she drew men's attention.

When he saw her, Owen licked his lips as well, leaving a slime on them like the track of a snail.

Conor mac Nessa handed her into the chariot and got in after her. He and Owen were both large men; Deirdre looked dwarfed between them as the chariot clattered down the road and out through the gate with Owen's men trotting after.

Levarcham waved as long as she could see a cloud of dust rising.

Deirdre stood between the two chieftains and gripped the rim of the chariot, not listening as they talked back and forth of common interests, of Maeve's campaigns and crops and cattle. She tried to concentrate on the creak of the axle, the jingle of the harness.

She emptied her head of everything but Naisi.

Their way south passed through broken land. At one point, the party had to pick its way through a narrow, rocky defile. There was scarcely room for the chariot, and the experienced warhorses, anticipating an ambush, began to trot nervously, flicking their ears back and forth. The chariot lurched. Deirdre kept her eyes downcast but flinched away when her body was thrown against Conor's.

He felt the movement and resented it. Looking down at the fleecy gold of her hair, he said. 'Stand still, woman. You're a helpless ewe penned between two rams here.'

The chariot swung around a curve, and the earth fell away steeply to one side, revealing a slope strewn with boulders. Without a moment's hesitation, Deirdre flung herself from the open back of the war-cart.

As she had intended, her head struck a rock with a sickening crack.

Conor's yell startled the horses so badly they bolted, running many spears' length before Owen, who was driving himself, could get them under control. Then he and Conor rushed back to Deirdre, but it was too late. The warriors clustered around her body stepped back to let them see, and when her face was revealed to him, Conor threw his arm across his eyes.

The beauty that had split the Red Branch was destroyed. Deirdre's skull was smashed like an egg, collapsing beneath the skin to make her face a distorted parody of itself. The only thing that remained was her smile, the small and secret smile that had so frightened Levarcham.

The king of Ulster dropped to his knees beside her. Now, he could touch her. Now, he could do anything he wanted to her.

He picked up her hand; it was already turning cold, as if the life had gone from her even before she jumped from the chariot. Pressing his cheek against the thin white fingers, he whispered hoarsely, 'Was I so hard to love?'

Owen known as Hard-Hand, brutal chieftain and remorseless killer, could not watch. He walked a little distance away to gaze fixedly at a clump of dead saxifrage. The rest of his party shuffled their feet and

280

shifted their weapons, trying to look anywhere but at Conor mac Nessa and Deirdre.

'If she's yours,' one of them hissed to Owen, 'do you want to take her the rest of the way and bury her in your own landhold?'

Conor heard him. Without raising his head, the king said in a carrying voice, 'She's mine. I'm taking her home.'

No one argued. Owen scowled at the saxifrage.

When Conor finally stood up, it seemed to take him a mighty effort to lift Deirdre, slight as she was. Her hair trailed over his arm like pouring honey, but something darker and sticky was seeping through it.

For the last time, Fedlimid's daughter arrived at Emain Macha. The harper's wife was safely in her grave, beyond grief, but Fedlimid attended the burial ritual. He made no effort to compose a lament.

The sky was the colour of blood.

Conor ordered Deirdre buried close to the House of the King, which was almost rebuilt, but in the night someone dug her up. An empty grave yawned at the morning.

No one admitted knowing anything about it.

Guided by intuition, the king went to the Sorrowful Forest. Naisi's grave had obviously been opened and refilled; someone had put Deirdre with the son of Uisnach.

Conor stood looking at the recently disturbed earth as if he could see through it to the bodies lying beneath. Conall Cearnach had accompanied him, for which he was grateful. Lendabair had kept Nessa back at the fort, for which he was even more grateful.

'What will you do now?' Conall asked.

'I won't have her dug up again, if that's what you mean. I doubt it would do any good; someone would just bring her back here. But I don't think I can sleep, knowing she lies in Naisi's arms. I'll have servants take up enough dirt to see where they are, and then drive stakes through the bodies to hold them apart.' He saw the look on Conall's face. 'I know; but I have to.'

They made their way toward the fort. When they were almost there, the king paused for one last look back. 'No matter what I may do for Ulster,' he said sadly, 'I suspect this is what people will remember about me. Yet I wouldn't have harmed Deirdre if it meant my own life, Conall. You know that.'

'She didn't.'

'What do you mean?'

Conall disliked mentioning the action of his own he most wanted forgotten, but the king had asked and must be answered. 'After Fiacra and Illand were dead,' he said, 'you yelled for the House of the Red Branch to be burned down. With everyone in it.'

Conor looked astonished. 'I couldn't have said that!'

'You did. And I'm certain everyone inside heard you, including Deirdre. The way you bellowed, they could have heard you in Connaught.'

Conor stood with his head bowed. 'So she died thinking that of me; that I had ordered her killed. And I don't remember saying it, though I must have, if you heard me. We were all a little crazy that night.'

'We were,' Conall agreed.

The king stroked his beard. 'I have an idea, Conall, perhaps the best idea I've had in a long time.'

'What?'

'Let's get drunk.'

'Agreed!' cried Conall Cearnach.

Two naked, peeled saplings stood guard over the grave at the edge of the Sorrowful Forest all winter, their bases reaching deep into the earth to hold Deirdre and Naisi apart. In the spring, they unexpectedly sprouted. The first people to notice were hunters returning from the west, but they were afraid to say anything to Conor mac Nessa. When Levarcham next visited the site, as she did at every new moon, she found two graceful yew trees growing together. Their branches were just touching. Like fingertips.

Cathbad the druid made the final pronouncement. Looking sternly at his king he said, 'If any man ventures to disturb those trees, all the troubles he has known before will be as nothing to the trouble he will find.'

'Let them grow taller than the House of the King,' Conor said. 'Those trees are safe from me.'

Levarcham watered the trees in the dry season that first summer, for the days were long and warm, and there was not as much rain as usual. She could not cry, aside from the rheumy leakage of the elderly. But she was regular in her visitations, until one twilit evening when she arrived late to find someone already there. A tall man in a massive golden torc, standing quietly just looking at the trees, not noticing the old woman.

As she crept away, Levarcham heard the lament the king of Ulster sang softly, just for Deirdre.

'Spoiled and headstrong
we made her.
Graceful and faithful
she made herself.
Weep. Weep for Deirdre.'

Volume 2

Cruachan

*They are not dead who will not
die
But in a fevered dream they lie
and wait to hear the trumpet's cry.
We pace the earth beneath our feet
but sense no death, where life was
sweet
(Live, Maeve; we command you.)*

*For them the eons are one age
where they alone hold centre stage
and stride full-fleshed through love
and rage.
White wind and clouds like warrior plumes
o'er Cruachan of the many rooms,
the singing grass, the peopled
tombs.
(Live, Maeve; we command you!)*

1 So it was over. The damage had been done, the dead buried, the wheel of the seasons turned. At Emain Macha, they had cleared away the rubble and were building afresh on fire-blackened foundations.

Conor mac Nessa had exhausted himself with memories and recriminations, chewing on them like worms eating into a wound. At last he realised he must cauterise the wound, or die. With the greatest effort of his life, he put Deirdre out of his mind – most of the time. He busied himself with the present, and worried about the future.

He gave Deirdre's things to his wives as a peace offering. But he kept the white deerskin aside, and sent it to Dun Dalgan for Emer.

'I don't want it,' Cuchulain's wife insisted. 'The scent of sorrow lingers on everything Deirdre touched.'

Conor's redirected energies rebuilt Emain Macha and spread outward in ripples, stimulating a burst of construction throughout Ulster. With Maeve a constant threat on their borders, the chariot-chieftains and cattle-lords began strengthening their own fortifications, and more and more people made their way to the king's *maigen* to build duns within the protective sphere of Conor mac Nessa.

Cairns of stones were raised over the dead, and the cries of birth were heard in the season of leaf-spring. Amid the wreckage, the amazing, persistent animal that was Hope struggled to be reborn.

 I was feeling quite satisfied. In fact, I had had too many eyes to eat and suffered some aftereffects that necessitated my taking a little hiatus to digest and recover.

The orgy of killing had been delightful, but one must never go so far as to injure oneself.

Take Fergus mac Roy, for example. The man had no instinct for self-preservation. A warrior to the core, he had let his lust for vengeance drive him beyond common sense and carry him into the camp of the one person for whom he could never fight wholeheartedly.

A good point, that, about the heart. Maeve's battles would always be with Ulster as she strove to build a stronghold and a reputation for herself to eclipse Macha of the Golden Hair. And Fergus mac Roy was once king of Ulster. Though now doomed to exile, he had left his heart in his homeland. In one eruption of fire and fury, he had emptied himself out and would never be whole again, and he was just intelligent enough to realise it.

Therein lay his tragedy.

Like so many before and after him, when he understood what he had lost, he cried 'Unfair!' to the gods. Though he realised only Cruachan would have dared offer sanctuary to the Red Branch rebels, Fergus could see the irony in his being stranded among Ulster's enemies.

Unfair.

Fairness, however, is a concept of purely human invention, having nothing to do with cosmic reality. Snails and stars do not expect fairness. Only humans inveigh against destiny as if they were entitled to something better.

I know – sometimes I also complain. That is the human in me, you see. We are kin, though I would not boast about it.

Some day soon now, I meant to let Cuchulain see how human I could be. But not yet; we had work to do together, even if recent events seemed to have somewhat slaked his enthusiasm for being a warrior. One must get back to business eventually, however.

In the wake of the destruction of the Red Branch, his spirit was depressed; but I had seen him dejected before. I would find a way to put the fierce glow back in his eyes.

I sought Cuchulain in Murthemney, at Dun Dalgan.

A long spell of unrelieved rain had depressed everyone's spirits. When at last the clouds lifted, Cuchulain sat in the mud outside his chariot shed, picking fleas from his cloak and scowling. The sun was out, but he was not ready to be cheerful. He could have sat on a log bench, but the cold mud was more appropriate for his mood.

'The thatchers are ready to start on the roof of the hall.'

Cuchulain looked up. His wife stood before him, hands on hips, lips pursed in disapproval. 'You should be supervising them,' she said. 'Or do you plan to stay here all day?'

'They know what they're doing, they don't need me.'

'But they're putting on a whole new roof, Setanta.'

'You watch them then. If you think you see them make any mistakes, call me.' He went back to searching among the folds of his cloak.

290

'If it was Ferdiad calling you to come hunting with him, you'd be on your feet in a breath!' Emer complained.

Cuchulain gave her a glance full of misery. 'Ferdiad and I won't be going hunting together any more.'

Regretting her words when she saw his pain, Emer went back to the hall and the thatchers.

Thatching was both art and craft, taught by father to son. As with everything, there was controversy. Some preferred to use reeds for roofing, because they could last as long as fifty winters once properly affixed and did not sprout new growth as straw did, tempting birds to tear at the thatch and make holes.

But straw was the more flexible material, and its proponents were convinced it kept a building warmer in winter and cooler in summer. Besides, its golden glow and sweet fragrance conveyed a sense of well-being comparable to a harvest safely gleaned. 'All is well here,' fresh thatch proclaimed.

Making the most of the rainless day, the thatchers had spread a great amount of straw on the *urla*. They caught the stems at each end and 'pulled' the straw to rid it of dirt and grain before stacking it into neat piles and tying them into manageable bundles. Next they poured heated water on the straw to make it flexible and draw its inner wax to the surface, where it would shed rain and gleam gold in sunlight.

As Emer approached the hall, the first men were already scrambling up their ladders, carrying bundles to the roof. Two old men remained on the ground to twist and turn straws back on to themselves to form the bobbins that would become the ridge cap. Two more were bending green twigs into staples that would secure new thatch to old.

As they worked, one man raised his voice in the thatching song, its rhythm dictated by – or dictating – the blows of the mallets. The others joined in; the dun rang with their voices. Emer smiled. Even at his moodiest, Cuchulain would not long be able to resist the cheerfulness of the music.

Then she saw the raven strutting along the ridgepole.

'Chase it away!' she shouted to the men on the roof. 'Chase the bad omen away, quickly!' Bending down, Emer seized the nearest small stone and flung it with all her strength at the bird. The rock glanced off the thatch at an angle; the raven turned its head and looked directly at the woman.

Even at such a distance, Emer could see its bright, malicious eyes.

They pierced through her and she felt a hand clench deep in her belly, mocking her empty womb. The blood drained from her face.

Death bird. Perched insolently atop Cuchulain's hall! As his wife, Emer must protect him. Without allowing herself time for fear, she bent and seized a stone the size of her fist, and flung it with better aim towards the bird. The sound of stone striking flesh was gratifying. The raven screeched, staggered sideways, then gathered itself and flew away.

'It's sorry I am I didn't kill you!' Emer called after it.

The thatchers had paused in their work to watch the scene with superstitious misgivings, but once the raven was gone, they resumed their labours. As each section of thatch was installed, they threw water on the material, then raked it smooth to compact it. Bluestone had been added to the water used for this final dressing procedure, both to preserve the straw and to prevent any undetected oats left in it from sprouting. Emer walked back and forth on the ground below, watching them with a housewifely eye, standing sentry against the return of the bird of ill omen.

Beyond the hall, the raven dropped from the sky on to the earth near Cuchulain's feet. He looked at the bird in surprise. It seemed to be hurt; it was flopping around in a peculiar way, occasionally pausing to peer at him intently with a measuring eye. He reached out and tried to catch it, but it hopped awkwardly just out of his reach, tempting him to stand up and try again.

Cuchulain did not want to be drawn from his black mood, but the raven was irresistible. Its plight seemed real; its movements were comical. He did not know if he meant to kill it or help it, but something drove him to follow the creature as it leaped and flapped across the compound. When it tumbled into a mud puddle and rowed frantically with its wings as if using oars, he chuckled. When the raven dragged itself from the puddle and shuddered with a very unbirdlike disgust at the wet mud clinging to its feathers, Cuchulain laughed out loud.

He made another grab for the bird; it stayed just out of his reach. Laughing like a boy, he pursued his quarry until the sound of an approaching chariot distracted him. He hesitated and looked up.

Laeg was entering the gates, driving the Grey of Macha and the Black of Sainglain. Since the destruction of the royal stronghold, Cuchulain had not shown much enthusiasm for anything, including his duties as guardian of the south-eastern approaches, and it had often fallen to Laeg to drive out alone to watch for unwelcome strangers.

Part of this Laeg blamed on Ferdiad. 'The Hound hasn't been the same since he and Ferdiad last parted, not really. Now that the man in horn armour is an exile from Ulster, he acts as if there's not enough salt in his meat any more.' Laeg's words were bitter, but Emer understood. She wasn't the only one who had been quietly jealous of the close relationship of Cuchulain and Ferdiad.

As Laeg drove in the gate on thatching day, he was surprised to see Cuchulain in a laughing mood. Surprised, and pleased – it boded well for the future.

'There may be work for us,' Laeg announced by way of greeting.

Only a day before, Cuchulain might have replied, 'Is it something you can take care of by yourself?' But now, stimulated by his laughing pursuit of the raven, he felt full of energy. 'Tell me at once.'

Laeg grinned. 'What's happened here?'

'Not much. But an injured bird almost fell into my lap just now, and I was trying to catch it . . .' He glanced around to indicate the bird.

There was no raven.

Laeg raised his eyebrows.

Some of the playfulness faded from Cuchulain's puzzled face. He was on his feet, however, and the need for action surged up in him with the blood pumping from his heart. 'What news have you?' he asked Laeg again.

'Foreign chariots on the Plain of the Pig-Keepers.'

'Foreign chariots?'

'In the style of Connaught.'

Cuchulain's eyes flashed. 'Step aside and let me in the cart, we'll challenge them immediately.'

The chariot sped out through the gates. From the roof of the bake house, a large raven watched it go, then preened a few broken feathers from one wing and launched into flight herself, following them.

When they reached the broad plain, the strangers were just advancing across it. As soon as they saw Cuchulain's chariot approaching, they turned their own three war-carts so the left side faced the Hound.

'They offer us insult, Laeg. Draw rein here.' Cuchulain stepped from the cart, threw back his head, and shouted, 'Who dares enter Ulster?'

There was a flurry of consultation among the foreign chariots, then someone called, 'We've come to help a clansman in distress.'

'His name at once!'

More discussion. Cuchulain tapped his foot impatiently, narrowing his eyes and shading them with his hand so he could see the faces of the men across the expanse of grass. Something he saw made him draw his mouth into a thin line.

He turned and reached into the chariot, taking out his sling and a leather bag of stones. 'Forward, Laeg. Goad the horses to full speed and circle that lot.'

The chariot raced forward.

As they neared the strangers, Cuchulain leaped over the chariot rim and capered on the tongue between the galloping horses, whirling the sling over his head. 'The Hound of Ulster will hurl stones through your bodies until they come out the other side!' he shouted in a terrible voice.

The men with the three Connaught war-carts exchanged nervous glances, then their spokesman called, 'We've already helped our clansman and are returning west, there's no need for trouble here!'

At a nod from Cuchulain, Laeg checked the team. The band of strangers turned westward and made a hasty retreat.

Laeg and Cuchulain watched them go. 'Did you see who was with them?' the Hound asked his driver.

'I did, though it hurt my eyes to see the Beetle of Ulster bold as a rutting goat among the Connaughtmen.'

'He's not the Beetle of Ulster any more, Laeg. Duffach is one of Maeve's men now, and who can say how much he may have told her about Ulster's strengths and weaknesses? I suspect that's what this group was about; they were checking our defences. If they had intended serious provocation, they wouldn't have left so easily. But I think we can expect to see more of them soon enough, and with more deadly intent.'

'Men of the Red Branch coming into Ulster as enemies,' the charioteer said. 'It seems incredible. Will Fergus come with them, do you suppose?'

Cuchulain frowned as he replaced his sling and stones in the chariot. 'I know mac Roy. A man so slow to anger is even slower to forgive. We'll all be dry bones before he makes peace with Conor mac Nessa; he might join Maeve in an attack on Ulster. I wouldn't like to think so, but I wouldn't be surprised. We're going to have to be very vigilant from now on.'

'Good enough you got your blood up this morning, then,' Laeg replied. 'And that feat you performed, running out along the tongue of the chariot between the galloping horses – you must have frightened them very badly with that one, Cuchulain.'

'*We* frightened them,' the Hound replied generously.

Laeg glowed inwardly. We, he repeated to himself. Not Ferdiad and Cuchulain, but Laeg and Cuchulain. We.

He whistled to the horses and turned their heads towards Dun Dalgan as the daylight faded.

On the drive home, Cuchulain gave thought to the situation. Duffach's foray into Ulster told him a number of things, none of them good. Loyalties had obviously changed; friendships were set aside as a result. Duffach had not even greeted Cuchulain by name, but stared at him with the eyes of a stranger.

Many of the Red Branch were now rebels, enemies of Ulster and the king. And as Conor's champion, Ulster's champion, he could be called upon to face them in a battle to the death.

His friends.

The dark mood with which Cuchulain had begun the day settled back upon him.

Perhaps Fergus will stay clear, he thought to himself. Perhaps I will be spared that, at least. He's an ageing man with the weight of too many winters on him, surely Maeve would never ask him to stand against . . . me.

But Ferdiad is a young man. And everyone knows he's the nearest thing to a match for me.

When they reached Dun Dalgan, Cuchulain began devoting himself to practising those of his feats that could disable without killing.

There were not many of them.

As Cuchulain thought of Fergus, the former king of Ulster was thinking of his homeland. He had lost too much. His life, seen in a backward glance from Cruachan, appeared to him as a long series of sheddings, none of which had improved his situation. The kingship, his foster-son, Nessa, his honour, his birthland . . . what more could a man lose?

Fergus mac Roy sat in the hall at Cruachan, drinking wine and making desultory conversation with Bricriu Bitter-Tongue as they awaited the return of the group that had gone east to reconnoitre Ulster.

'How did all this happen to us?' Fergus wondered aloud, staring into his cup and finding dregs in the bottom.

Bricriu – who had also left a wife behind in Ulster but did not regret it – shrugged. 'Guidance from the gods.'

'If I've received guidance from the gods, it has been of a very inferior quality. Probably from low-ranked gods,' Fergus replied. 'Some misbegotten spirit of bog or gorse bush.'

His companion's sadness made Bricriu feel infinitely better by comparison, which is why he so enjoyed other people's disasters. He almost smiled. 'Look at me, Fergus; all four sides of me are an Ulsterman, yet here I am too. You aren't the only one with misfortunes. I could tell you about my own – '

'You have,' Fergus interrupted. 'Too many times.' He gave Bricriu a dark look. 'How did you happen to come with us, anyway?'

Bitter-Tongue arranged his forehead in pleats. 'Do you think I want to be here in this windy place at the edge of the world? I do not. You can't imagine how I long for the sight of my dear wife's face.'

Fergus favoured him with a sceptical glance, but Bricriu went on, 'I just got trapped on the wrong side somehow when Naisi and the others were killed; I found myself in a swirl of men, and before I knew what was happening, we were all out in the forest.'

'Go back, then, if you want. Explain that to Conor mac Nessa. Be with your wife again, I'm sure none of us would want to hold you here.'

'Oh, I couldn't!' said Bricriu quickly. 'You know how the king is – it would mean my head. Although I miss the woman dreadfully, you can't imagine. I know, you left your Nessa behind as well, but now you have Maeve . . .'

'I *what?*' Fergus slammed his cup on to the table and whirled to fix bloodshot eyes on Bricriu.

'She flirts with you, we've all noted it.'

'I'll tell you something for nothing, Bricriu. Once I ploughed my way across Ulster leaving troops of youngsters behind with my features and colouring. But now the idea of bedding a woman seems like too much trouble. In fact, women are too much trouble altogether.

'Oh, they're enjoyable enough under the right circumstances, but when they aren't content to stay in their proper limits, they spill over into a man's world and cause disasters.

'Deirdre, for instance. She refused to accept the life chosen for her and has destroyed all of ours.' His vision enlarged by wine, Fergus could see clearly. He could almost feel sorry for Conor mac Nessa in his present mood. Only the death that released Deirdre from the tyranny of her beauty would be able to release the king of Ulster from his own obsession.

Fergus would never be able to understand such an obsession, but he was unlike his former foster-son. Conor, deliberate, far-planning

296

Conor, was capable of transcendent passion. Within him smouldered flames that did not burn in a man like Fergus mac Roy.

For which Fergus was profoundly thankful. The idea of having a woman like Maeve pursuing him filled him with dismay.

'I'm through with women for ever,' he assured Bricriu Bitter-Tongue.

His attitude was a challenge to Maeve.

One of the former Ulstermen mentioned in her hearing that Fergus had once been called Fergus of the Horses, an allusion to his stallionlike prowess in youth. Amused, Maeve began to call him Fergus of the Horses. He tried to ignore her.

'I'm only here because I have no other place to go,' he told Cormac Connlongas. 'I'm not interested in Maeve, I wouldn't give her the itch if I thought she'd get warm on a cold day by scratching herself.' Fergus was in a hostile camp, he felt; he intended to comport himself with dignity no matter what the others did. Some of them were all too willing to embrace the gifts Maeve and Ailell offered them in return for their allegiance.

But the more Fergus tried to hold himself apart, the more Maeve concentrated on him.

'Isn't he a little old?' Ailell finally asked his wife peevishly.

'The same age as you,' she replied. Outmanoeuvred, Ailell went off in search of his own diversions.

Maeve changed tactics. Instead of attempting to charm Fergus, she began ignoring him. When meat was carved in the feasting hall, the former king of Ulster was given a badly hacked slab with a piece of the neck bone still attached. When he tried to get his wine cup refilled, the servants looked the other way.

Except for himself, Red Branch rebels were wearing new cloaks, new tunics, great shaggy mantles to keep out the west wind. Except for himself, Red Branch rebels were talking of stocking their new landholdings.

The least of them was now more important than the former king of Ulster, his prestige gone with his lack of property.

Fergus sat down and thought about it. Thinking was not too difficult with a head made painfully clear by the lack of anything decent to drink.

He had to admit it to himself, there was no going back to Emain Macha. Connaught had probably taken him in to annoy Conor mac Nessa, but he was here now, and whatever future he had would have to be spent here. The quality of that future was up to him.

'I am too old,' he told himself, picking morosely at his fingernails, 'to wear a cloak full of holes. I've been a king. And I'm too old to face the rest of my life without wine in my belly.' Fergus groaned and heaved himself to his feet. 'If that woman has a good side, I'd better go and see if I can find it.'

After considerable searching, he encountered Maeve returning from an inspection tour of her newest construction, a stone-walled buttery. Glancing around to be certain no one overheard them, Fergus approached her, feeling foolish but desperate.

He fumbled among dusty memories for a conversational opening that once worked with women. 'Ah, Maeve . . . have you seen my knife?'

She gave him a suspicious look. 'What knife?'

'A . . . very important tool I always carry with me. I seem to have mislaid it, but the moment I saw you, I felt the lack of it. It's about this long' – his hands measured an impressive length – 'and I would certainly like to have it right now.'

Maeve looked down at his hands, then up at his eyes. She smiled. 'I should hate to think something so important had been mislaid, even temporarily, Fergus of the Horses. But surely the two of us can find it if we look for it together.' Her glance flickered sideways then, and Fergus realised someone had walked up behind him.

Turning, he found himself face to face with Ailell.

Fergus felt his ears turn red.

Ailell gave him a wry smile. 'Go with my wife, if you like, and find your missing property,' he said.

Maeve's mouth twitched, whether in amusement or contempt Fergus would never know. She turned away and set off down the path in the direction of a private chamber she often used.

'Go after her, Fergus.'

'But . . .'

'It's all right, I've been expecting this ever since you walked through the gates. It's like waiting for a spear in the back, I'd rather have it thrown and be done with it.'

'But she's your wife . . .'

'She is,' Ailell agreed. 'There is nothing like a faithful wife, my friend. And Maeve is nothing like a faithful wife. I can't change her any more than I can change the weather, so I allow her a very loose rein and let her think she's getting away with something. As long as you don't abuse the privilege, I won't complain too much about your using a bucket everyone else has drunk from.'

'I don't know if you're a fool or a very wise man,' Fergus said with some astonishment.

'Neither do I,' Ailell replied. 'But at least I've kept her, which is more than any other man has been able to do. Her winters may be bleak, Fergus – but her summers are glorious!'

He watched Fergus follow Maeve down the path. As old as me, Ailell said to himself. I hope she wears him down to a nubbin and then breaks him off.

However, Fergus made his customary appearance in the feasting hall that night, though his eyes were glazed and he moved with a pronounced lack of energy.

Bricriu waited to tease him about it until the next day. Duffach and the others who had gone into Ulster had returned to report Cuchulain on duty, ably guarding the south-eastern approaches. Relieved to be back among his friends, Duffach had settled down to a game of chess with Fergus mac Roy. The Beetle had a ponderous mind; the niceties of the game eluded him. He made ill-considered moves; he breathed heavily through his open mouth and muttered frequently to himself as he played.

Fergus found himself wistfully remembering the excellent chess contests he had once enjoyed with Conor mac Nessa.

The shadow of Bricriu Bitter-Tongue fell across the chessboard. 'I thought you were through with women, mac Roy.'

Fergus did not look up, nor did he deign to answer. But Duffach was interested. 'What's this about?'

'Our Fergus swore off females, then tumbled Maeve.'

'It's no business of yours,' Fergus growled, moving a chess piece.

Bricriu sucked on his teeth. Duffach scratched his belly and considered Fergus's move. They were using a bronze board belonging to Ailell, with gold and silver pieces on it.

Bricriu spoke again. 'Has Maeve offered to give you a chess-board like this one, Fergus?'

No reply. Bricriu smiled. 'Has Maeve given you anything at all but the friendship of her thighs, which she offers everywhere?'

Fergus drew his eyebrows down to sit on his nose.

'I was just told,' said Bricriu, 'that Maeve has put Cormac Connlongas in charge of all our men. Young and able, he is. What do you think of that, Fergus? Do you agree with her choice?'

'That's it,' said Fergus. He stood up and hit Bricriu a mighty blow on the side of the head with his fist, raising a lump. Bitter-Tongue tottered away, groaning and holding one hand to his head.

'Do you feel better now?' asked Duffach.

Sitting back down at the board, Fergus discovered that in his absence Duffach had made the winning move. 'I do not feel better,' said Fergus mac Roy.

That evening, Fergus went to Maeve again. By now he knew what she wanted of him – information about the strength and capabilities of Ulster and particularly of the Hound.

He was determined to be clever. If he gave Maeve enough information, she would be obliged to reward him in return; if he worded his descriptions wisely, she might be discouraged from ever attacking Ulster. So he let her ply him with wine and caress his body, and then, as if very reluctantly, he told her the entire story as he knew it of the birth, training and achievements of the Hound of Ulster. He also elaborated considerably for effect.

As they lay side by side in her chamber on furs reeking of stale semen, Maeve heard the story through without interruption. It confirmed her own impressions. If half what Fergus said was true – and she thought half was probably a reasonable figure – Cuchulain would be a force to reckon with no matter how many men were brought against him. He could not only fight but frighten. Preceded by such a reputation, he might terrify an army into stampeding.

Perversely, his reputation had begun to have the opposite effect on her. The more she heard about him, the more familiar and less intimidating he seemed. Once over her initial reaction to him, Maeve had been aware of a growing eagerness in herself to face the Hound again – to challenge him in serious war. He was a creature shaped to thwart her; it had become inevitable in her own mind that they clash.

But she was not about to divulge her inmost thoughts to a mere man like Fergus mac Roy. 'I'm not so impressed by your Cuchulain,' she drawled. 'I've met him, remember. Isn't he the short one with the unblemished face of a youth? He has only one body, Fergus. He can be wounded and he can die, like any other mortal.'

'If I were to name you the warriors who have already fallen at his hand . . .'

'You would bore me,' Maeve decided. 'I think you had better go and let me get some sleep, Fergus. I'm sandy in the eyes.'

Seething with dismissal and his perceived failure to awe Maeve, Fergus stalked away to his own cold bed and a sleepless night. Lying with one arm thrown across his eyes, he thought of Ulster, and of the failure of kingship.

300

He arose before dawn and began seeking out the warriors of Cruachan, regaling them with tales of Cuchulain. Perhaps Maeve refused to be impressed, but Fergus knew warriors and he knew what would frighten them. If she marched an army into Ulster, he would see that her followers were weak in the knees before they ever crossed the border, not for Conor mac Nessa's sake, but for the honour of a man who had once been king.

In Ulster, alerted by the foray of Duffach and the Connaughtmen, Cuchulain patrolled the passes and fords.

2 The group of Leinstermen led by Lorcan the Fierce came from south of Ath Cliath, looking for slaves and cattle. Harvest season had just ended; unless the winter was long and rainy, they had chosen an ideal time for their venture.

Lorcan had earned his reputation for ferocity. Having been fostered by the father of Ailell, now of Connaught, he had long since mastered the skills of war. Even Cuchulain's reputation did not discourage him when he noticed a dearth of cattle in his own herds and a decrease among his slaves.

The day was wet, the mist as thick as spittle. Laeg was driving the Grey of Macha and the Black of Sainglain, and the two men had just decided to turn around and look for an evening campsite when they heard men at a distance, singing marching songs and calling out to one another.

Cuchulain silently signalled a halt.

Stepping from the war-cart, he began to assemble his weapons. They were on a narrow roadway leading up from a ford, surrounded by a thick woodland. The raiders must come this way if they meant to proceed northward – and come they did.

The mist vomited men into Ulster.

The battle was joined at once. Cuchulain roared a challenge at the Leinstermen, and Lorcan stepped forward in answer. His arrogant glance derided the short, dark young man before him. 'This is the champion of Ulster? We'll walk over you.'

'Walk, then,' Cuchulain replied. Something in his eyes made Lorcan hesitate. 'I won't offer you single combat, Ulsterman.' With one hand behind his back, he gestured to his men to circle around Cuchulain, up the sides of the streambank, and try to take him from behind.

There were twelve of them, and one Cuchulain.

Hardhead sang, spears rained from the air. Men fell. Before Lorcan's startled eyes, the small man he had scorned changed into something he did not want to face. He raised his leather shield studded with bronze bosses and shouted a thoughtless insult to conceal his fear. 'Fatherless scum from a stagnant pond!'

Cuchulain reached out his hand and Laeg put the Gae Bulga into it.

Just a spear with a strange head and a slim shaft, but when the Hound of Ulster hurled it the weapon hummed in its flight. The few Leinstermen still alive paused to watch, their attention commanded by the death-song of the spear.

They saw Lorcan raise his shield; they saw the Gae Bulga lift in its flight, arc above the shield, and drop down behind it.

Lorcan screamed with shock and anger and tried to run but he was too late. He hurled his body sideways but it made no difference. The Gae Bulga dodged in the air with him, tearing through his body.

Cuchulain made one of his salmon-leaps and was behind Lorcan as the spear broke through the flesh of his back. The Hound seized the prongs and pulled the Gae Bulga clear.

Leinstermen were not famed for their footspeed, but on that misty day they learned to run. Within the blink of an eye, no one was left alive at the ford but the Hound of Ulster and his charioteer.

The Rage faded slowly, leaving Cuchulain's body tingling with the racing of its blood. He tossed his hair out of his eyes and turned Lorcan's body over with one foot. 'Loyal followers. They left him.' He gestured to Laeg. 'We'll bury him where he fell and raise a cairn over him; he was a brave man. But first let's claim our trophy.'

When the Leinsterman was buried, the darkness closed in. A scent of woodsmoke reached the ford, curling sweetly into Laeg's nostrils. 'There is a cottage nearby, or a dun where we might ask hospitality for the night.'

Cuchulain nodded. His blood was still racing. 'I wouldn't even mind if the family had a daughter to warm my bed,' he decided.

Later in the season, a raiding party came up from Munster, from the chieftain Curoi, and again only a few returned home to tell of their encounter with the Hound of Ulster. Poets listened and memorised the history they were receiving from witnesses; bards sang new songs in Erin's halls.

'You see,' Fergus told the Connaughtmen. 'Cuchulain is as good as I claimed.'

'Mind yourself,' Duffach warned him. 'You eat Connaught meat and applaud the deeds of an Ulsterman; sooner or later someone will say

Fergus mac Roy is easily recognised because he's the only man facing in both directions.'

Cormac Connlongas was still considered the official leader of the exiled Red Branch, a fact that rankled in Fergus's mind. Maeve and Ailell had at last given him a landholding, and he could, like other Ulstermen, have taken Connaught wives if he wished, but the leadership of the rebels seemed the only prize worth having.

He paid some fresh compliments to Maeve. She welcomed him; she was convinced he must know some secret, some weakness of the Hound's that he was keeping back.

Ailell began to feel a dark anger rising. Maeve was spending too much time with mac Roy altogether, he was beginning to appear a better man than her own husband. A day's dalliance was one thing, but Fergus had gone too far.

'Leave that Ulsterman alone,' Ailell ordered his wife as they sat together in the hall.

She almost sneered at him. 'Are your promises full of wind? Did I not ask of you a better wedding gift than any woman in Erin had ever demanded before? And didn't you promise to allow me as many rights as you had yourself? If you're taking back your promise, Ailell, the marriage is revoked this night.'

'I'm not taking back my promise,' he said sullenly, wondering why he had made such an agreement in the first place. Drunk, probably. Drunk on Maeve, who intoxicated men. 'But neither will I allow you to shame me by flaunting that man in my beard. Be content with what you have, and don't push me too far.'

She understood the warning; Maeve was sensitive to the patterns of life.

But when she was alone in her thoughts, she wondered if she would be able to stop reaching. Could she ever admit she had reached a limit? Was not such an admission the beginning of old age and death?

Wandering the precincts of Cruachan, Maeve surveyed her realm. Beyond the walls, in a huddle of wattle-and-daub huts, textile weavers and copper-alloy smiths and amber workers and brooch-makers and woodcarvers and men who shaped tools from antlers were all busily at work, providing for the needs of the ever-expanding royal stronghold.

And the mother goddess herself was at work; she, most of all.

Wind blew through grass but against buildings. Grass, being a child of the goddess, was kin to the wind, but manbuilt structures were alien,

304

product of a different and lesser creator. The forces of nature were allied against them.

Could a human hope to build anything everlasting in a world where growth was based on change?

Musing, Maeve stalked her land.

I can try, she thought. I can try.

Her elastic stride was arrogant. She was alive, she refused to be dead.

Leaf-spring bubbled in the air of Erin. Sedge warblers brought music to the bogs, curlews nested in ponds and hummocks, black bees sang their songs of production in grassy meadows.

Rushing her own season, Emer asked Flann the carver to prepare a new bedbox, carved with twisting interlace and hand-rubbed to a high sheen; a small bedbox for sheltering an infant. When the box was ready, she set it in the corner of their sleeping chamber, and the first time Cuchulain saw it, a great light came into his eyes.

'Are you. . . ?'

'Not yet. But soon, surely.'

'Indeed.' Cuchulain reached for her to make soon come sooner.

With limitless energy, he continued to patrol the eastern approaches to Ulster, sometimes alone in his chariot with only Laeg for company, sometimes at the head of a band of warriors from local clans. He urged Red Branch friends to join him whenever possible, though he himself avoided Emain Macha as much as he could. The painful memories it evoked might show in his eyes, and he wanted to be seen as invulnerable.

He was not invulnerable. There were days when he was brought back to Dun Dalgan bleeding, and his wife and physician struggled to keep him quiet long enough to heal. Each new scar was an added glory. Connaught had not yet made its move, but there were always battles to fight; heroes required them.

When he returned to his dun from some fierce skirmish, it was as if he entered a different world. The experiences he had just undergone had been shared with a brotherhood; even his opponents, as fellow-warriors, were of that brotherhood – a kinship that could not be understood by those who waited at home.

Emer would put her arms around him and say, 'You can forget all about it now, there's food waiting and fresh wood on the fire. Just sit here with me and put war behind you. Forget, forget.'

He would stare at her then as if she were a stranger, a sense of permanent alienation rising in him.

Only warriors could understand.

 He drew me to him like a magnet. No matter where I was, when Cuchulain stepped into his war-cart, a silent thunder would come rolling across Erin to summon me, and I must go to him. Those were my moments of greatest rapture. Together, we two, dominating the battlefield, spreading panic in concentric circles around us, stretched beyond our limits, both his and mine.

What else is life but a preparation for death, and the glory of the bronze-and-crimson death Cuchulain meted out to his enemies was my creation. He would be given credit for it, of course, but I did not mind, so long as the two of us were joined.

The shift of momentum that determines the outcome of battle moves on raven's wings from one side to the other. The victor will always be the man who rides with the raven.

To prepare for battle, Cuchulain parted his hair into the three sections that marked him as a champion, the crown hair coiled on the back of his head, the side hair flowing over his shoulders, the hair above his forehead glittering with gems tied into it by strands of red wool. The rest of the Red Branch now spiked their hair with lime paste in imitation of the way his arose in the battle-fury, but Cuchulain had no need of lime paste. The rest of the Red Branch painted their faces to approximate the grotesque grimace of the Rage, but Cuchulain did not need to paint his face.

He wore a fringed, five-fold mantle over his shoulders, fastened with a massive gold brooch inlaid with amber and silver. A leather warrior's apron protected his genitals, and his clothing was spattered with the dried blood of enemies, which he did not wash off.

He was the terrible Hound of Ulster. And if he was sometimes mortally afraid, no one knew.

Had Ferdiad been with him, Cuchulain might have said, 'Do you ever still feel like a child pretending to be an adult? Are you afraid the others will find out?' He could have asked Ferdiad those questions and heard honest answers. But no man would say such things to his charioteer.

So he rushed into battle, the chariot leaping across ruts and slewing sideways on wet grass, and opposing warriors screamed and charged and there was no time for self-doubt, only the sounds of metal striking metal and wood and flesh, the curse and grunt of combat, the hot hard heavy work of killing by hand, the farting and the pain, the bloodslick mud and ridiculous mistakes and occasional dazzling grace.

And at some point, Cuchulain would become what everyone expected of him; at the end of the day, there would be more trophies to send north for hanging in the rebuilt House of the Red Branch.

Moons had waxed and waned, and Connaught had not sent an army into Ulster. Cuchulain and his wife were requested to attend the king's Beltaine feast at Emain Macha to celebrate the beginning of sunseason: a command appearance of the champion.

Conall Cearnach ran to meet Cuchulain's chariot as it entered the gateway. 'I have a son, Cuchulain!'

The Hound grinned. This was the best news one man could share with another. But he could not resist asking, 'Did Lendabair endure the Pangs more bravely than you?'

'Easy enough for you to say, when you've never suffered the Pangs.' There was a brief angry glitter in Conall's deadly green eyes; then a smile surfaced. 'Cuchulain, when my son is old enough, will you take him in fosterage?'

'I will of course,' the other replied, surprised and flattered. 'But are you certain you want to send him to me?'

Conall's mouth was not shaped to form words of praise. He dug one toe in the dirt and watched it raise ridges of earth. 'Who better?' he asked gruffly.

Cuchulain understood; they were Red Branch. 'Then send your boy to me as soon as I have a son myself, Conall, and they will be raised together.' A request he had once intended to make of Ferdiad occurred to him. 'And if I should be killed before I have a son to avenge my death, will you be my avenger?'

It was Conall's turn to be flattered. 'Rely on it, Hound.'

The feast was well served and well attended. Members of clan Ulaid arrived in force to celebrate Beltaine with their leader and to admire the tributes being sent to Conor mac Nessa from the other clan-chieftains of Ulster, as was the summer custom. Wealth was pouring in through the gateways, in heavily laden carts and on the backs of sweating porters. Yet to Cuchulain's eyes, the royal stronghold appeared poorer than he remembered. Tarnished.

He told Emer, 'I think it's because the king seems dull. Have you noticed? One corner of his mouth twitches; when he thinks someone is watching, he tries to cover it with his hand. His voice is flat and spiritless, and something is dead in the back of his eyes.'

'Perhaps he's just getting old, Setanta.'

'Then I'm glad Cathbad prophesied a short life for me,' her husband replied, 'filled with glory.' He did not notice the way Emer flinched at his words.

She gladly attended the feasting with him, though whenever they were at Emain Macha, Emer could not help noticing the way other women clustered around the champion of Ulster, vying for his attention. Sometimes he would glance at her from the centre of a female tangle, and she always smiled back at him, quite unconcerned. She made a point of leaving him with as many of them as he liked for as long as he liked.

Some of the Red Branch remarked on this to Cuchulain.

'My wife knows how I feel about jealousy,' he said. 'There is none in her; her spirit is twice as big as her body.'

'You're a fortunate man,' his friends told him. After the Deirdre débâcle, jealousy was considered a dangerous trait indeed.

But when Emer was with the women at the well or in the *grianan* or at the squatting trench, from time to time she let slip a few carefully chosen words.

To Lendabair, who was Cuchulain's obvious favourite among the Red Branch wives, she complained, 'My husband snores, you know. Dreadfully. And he insists on sleeping with his head next to mine, he won't rest any other way.'

The bored and restless wife of Follaman mac Conor was told, 'The Hound has a habit of backhanding me whenever he returns from a combat.' She pointed to her dimpled cheek. 'Do you see this hole in my face? His knuckle did that.'

The pretty wife of Cethern the messenger was rewarded for her attentiveness to Cuchulain with a graphic and repulsive description of some fictitious sexual habits that Emer invented on the basis of the Hound's nickname. After hearing them, Cethern's wife did not press her bosom against Cuchulain's arm any more.

'My wife is without the blemish of jealousy,' Cuchulain boasted to all who would listen.

Conor mac Nessa's senior wife, Mugain, smiled on only one side of her face as she said, 'I envy you your happiness.'

Happiness was in short supply at Emain Macha. Misery radiated outwards from the king. The Ulaid were very aware of it, but no one wanted to speak of it openly; superstitious fear kept them from admitting to one another that their king was weakened, diminished, perhaps failing.

But the king's champion felt the lack of strength in Conor mac Nessa as he would have felt the approaching strength of an enemy. Sworn to protect both king and kingdom, Cuchulain worried. He felt increasingly obliged to take some action, but did not know what to do. What battle could a champion wage against melancholy black enough to destroy a king?

At Cruachan of the Enchantments, Maeve and Ailell were also celebrating the beginning of summer. As a gift of the season – and a subtle way of thanking her for not welcoming Fergus into her bed lately – Ailell gave his wife a present, a little hound, which she named Baiscne for its round skull. The dog was a strange creature that would never grow to normal size, but Maeve seemed to love it all the more for its flaw and cradled it to her bosom with fierce devotion.

She never caressed her own children so tenderly, Ailell recalled, watching her. Aloud, he said, 'A lashing rain is falling. Not a good omen for sunseason. We could have crops rotting in the fields and cattle standing hip-deep in bog instead of meadowland, if this keeps up.'

'Your cattle may founder in mud,' Maeve said smugly, 'but I've had mine sent to the uplands. I know how to manage cattle.' She held her little dog out at arm's length and laughed at its squirming, then drew it close to rub its nose against her own. 'Baiscne, Baiscne,' she murmured.

Over its domed head, she looked at Ailell. 'You do remember that it's your turn to serve the feast, don't you? Those cattle of yours – have you enough to roast a few oxen? I wouldn't want to be embarrassed in front of everyone with only bread to fill our guests' bellies.'

'You needn't fear that,' he answered with a flash of resentment. 'Haven't I the largest herd in Connaught?'

'Which has a growing population,' she reminded him. 'And since I have at least as many cows as you do, shall I sell you a few for the roasting?'

'You shall not. I can feed this entire province for the next four seasons without any help from a woman.'

The storm proved harbinger of a wet summer indeed, but there was a brief respite the next morning. The sun peeked from amid plumes of cloud, and rainshowers alternated with brief, bright spells. Taking advantage of one of these, Ailell ordered his cattle penned in the bawn behind the feasting hall so he could make his selections for slaughter. Not far away, Fergus and Duffach had just settled down to their latest game of chess. When they heard one of Ailell's bullocks bellowing resentfully, the former Beetle of Ulster remarked, 'That sounds very like Bricriu Bitter-Tongue.'

'Don't name a misery or it will come to you,' warned Fergus. 'I see Bricriu approaching now. The man is worse than an invasion of nettles, but ignore him and perhaps he'll go away.'

Bricriu had no intention of going away. He had pains in his back and misery to share. After complaining at length, he began circling the chessboard, commenting disparagingly on every play. Fergus grew red in the face; Duffach muttered to himself more than ever.

A scream of bovine agony lanced the air. Fergus dispatched an attendant to learn what had happened. The man ran back from the bawn to report, 'A big white-horned bull just gored one of the smaller ones. You heard the victim's death-wail.'

Bricriu cackled, 'I thought it was the lament I last heard you sing, Fergus, when Ailell put a stop to your bedding his wife. The sound of the weak bull giving way to the strong.'

This time, Fergus hit Bricriu with both fists at once, pounding the still-festering lump he had previously raised. The boil burst but did not drain. Its poison seeped back into Bricriu's head, causing increasing pain and lassitude that finally silenced his bitter tongue.

'We are better off without begrudgers,' said Fergus mac Roy.

He felt no remorse for what he had done to Bricriu. There were too many other demands on his remorse.

When the feasting concluded at Emain Macha, the Ulaid began returning to their duns and landholdings. Cuchulain lingered on. He was not comfortable amid so many reminders of the past, but he was reluctant to go back to Dun Dalgan.

Conor mac Nessa had him gravely worried.

The king was Ulster, and the light had gone out in him. His vigour dwindled visibly, day by day; his silences were too long, he even had difficulty following conversations. If rival clan-chiefs thought Conor mac Nessa was failing, they would seize the opportunity to wrest control of Ulster from the Ulaid . . . or the kings of other provinces would come to conquer the northland itself.

At a morning buttermilk-feast on the *urla*, Cuchulain found himself expressing his concerns to the king's mother.

She understood. 'Deirdre's death wasn't responsible for this. Not even the defection of so many of the Red Branch caused it. My son is a strong man, he could heal himself of those wounds in time. But the wound he may not survive is the loss of his sons. Dead by sword and spear, the posterity of Conor mac Nessa.'

'But Follaman and Cormac Connlongas are still alive!'

'Not for Conor. Cormac deserted him to run off with that wretched Fergus mac Roy. As for poor, pathetic Follaman, unfortunately Conor had his dreams invested in that eldest son of his. There is always one special one whom a man sees as himself walking into the future.' She sighed and wiped a frost of buttermilk from her upper lip with the back of her wrist.

'What's wrong with Follaman? Now that you mention him, I realise I haven't seen much of him lately.'

Nessa stood up like the old woman she had become, rising from her hips, letting her bowed back follow. 'Walk with me, Cuchulain, and we'll talk. If I sit still too long, my knees don't work properly.'

They strolled together, Cuchulain shortening his stride to hers as Nessa explained, 'Follaman is tall and broad, but he's sickly. Every season it grows worse. Always some ache or pain, or a wheeze in his chest, or a fever that refuses to cool. When you look in his eyes, you'll see no tomorrows.'

Cuchulain suddenly remembered, 'He was too tired to join us in a game of hurling the other day.'

'He's too tired even to bed his wife any more. There'll be no grandsons for Conor mac Nessa, and the knowledge is eating the king away inside. A man lives on in his descendants. Conor sleeps with his wives to try to get new sons, but nothing comes of it.'

'Why not, Nessa?'

She grabbed Cuchulain's arm and pulled his face so close to hers, he could smell her rotting teeth. In an urgent whisper, she confided, 'I happen to know that Cathbad has cursed Conor mac Nessa root and branch. He wants my son to die with no line to follow him.'

Cuchulain was appalled. 'Why would the druid do such a cruel thing to his own king?'

'Didn't you know? Cathbad's sister was mother to Naisi and his brothers. We're all of us related in some way, you can't kick a man without making another one squeal. Cathbad has avenged his sister's sons by denying my son descendants. We don't expect Follaman to see another harvest; what grandchildren will boast of the blood of Conor mac Nessa?'

Even druids felt the demands of retribution, Cuchulain thought. And they knew how to ask favours of the gods. No wonder the king was failing. But what could be done about it?

Later that same day, the tribute from the chieftain of Dal Riada was announced; the king went to the storage sheds to supervise its unloading. Follaman had taken to his bed with a fever, so Cuchulain accompanied him.

An impressive array of valuable goods awaited them. Fifty swords, fifty shields, fifty shaggy cloaks, fifty silver harness-plates, gold to the width of the king's face, ten wolfhounds, ten polished drinking horns, ten baskets of seagull eggs, and a bridle studded with carbuncles and amethyst set in silver.

'Only one jewelled bridle?' Cuchulain pawed through the assortment of goods until he found a matching second bridle and held it up for Conor to see. The king scarcely glanced at it, however.

'Wonderful workmanship on these, Foster-Father. They'll do credit to your best team,' said Cuchulain, trying to stimulate enthusiasm.

Conor shrugged. 'Put them on the Grey of Macha and the Black of Sainglain.'

Cuchulain dropped the bridles. 'I can't do that, they're your entitlements.'

'I give them to you, then. And the chariots from Fern Mag, the horses from Dun Sobairce . . . take whatever you want from the clan tributes.'

'If you don't want them, Foster-Father, they should go to Follaman, not me.'

Absentmindedly, the king ruffled the coarse hair on the head of one of the wolfhounds from Dal Riada. 'What use has Follaman now for bridles and chariots and hunting dogs? He will lead no more men into battle, nor join us in the chase.' The skin around Conor's eyes was white with pain. 'I gave my sons life; they have brought me grief, Cuchulain. Grief and sorrow.' He took the leash of the hound he was patting and pressed it into the younger man's hands. 'Here, surely you need another good dog.'

Cuchulain took an involuntary step backwards, not from the gift but from the expression of hopelessness on Conor's face. 'I already have everything I need,' he protested. Too late, he realised those were cruel words to say to the king of Ulster, who had nothing he needed.

312

Cuchulain spent the rest of the day alone, thinking, staring up at the sky or down at the earth. Night had long since fallen when he went to join Emer in their sleeping chamber in the finest of the royal guesting houses.

Attendants had prepared the champion's wife for bed. Her hair was plaited into nine long braids, looped with gold; her hands and feet had been rubbed with scented oil. Her small body was all but lost amid a profusion of cushions stuffed with sweet grasses.

Looking up with a welcoming smile for her husband, Emer saw unfamiliar lines in his forehead.

'What's the matter, Cuchulain?'

'Nothing.'

The gloomy atmosphere is upsetting him, Emer thought. He can't forget what happened here. 'We should be going home soon,' she said brightly. 'I have things to do.'

He sat down on a three-legged stool and began unwrapping the thongs that bound his soft leather boots to his legs. The thongs were stiff with mud. The season had passed when a man could go barefoot comfortably. Cuchulain worked diligently, then at last ripped the bindings free and thrust his feet into a basin of warmed water provided by the servants. 'Aaahhh.' He closed his eyes.

'Setanta?'

'Mmmm?'

'When?'

'When what?' He opened his eyes. 'When am I going to leap into that bed on top of you?' He forced a smile. 'Almost immediately.'

She was not fooled. 'I mean when do we leave for a fort with a brighter aspect?'

'Women,' Cuchulain informed his feet in the basin, 'are relentless. I don't know, Emer. When I feel as if I've accomplished all I can at Emain Macha, I suppose.'

'But there's nothing for you to do here! You are needed in the south, at the fords and passes . . .'

'I'm needed here now. I have a dual championship, remember; I am sworn to protect the king as well as Ulster.'

'Both are safe with you to defend them, no matter where you are. Now come to bed, Setanta. We won't have a harvest if we don't plough and plant.'

Cuchulain slowly straightened and stared at her as if she had imparted some rare wisdom. 'That's it, Emer. Harvest. What man can despair when his harvest exceeds his expectations?' He leaped to his

313

feet, overturning the basin of water, and began pacing the chamber, his feet squelching on the sodden rushes. Back and forth he went, something building in him with every step until the chamber was too small to contain it.

He began talking to himself, oblivious now to Emer, though she strained to hear.

'A man believes what he wants to believe,' Cuchulain was saying in a low, intense voice, stringing his thoughts together like beads. Pacing, pacing. 'As a child, I believed I sprang from a certain seed, but when I grew, I learned things are not always what they seem. The problem tormented me until I made an arbitrary decision for my own peace of mind because I had to believe *something*.'

He's talking about his paternity, Emer realised with a sense of shock. And he's saying he really doesn't know!

'If the choice I made was unwise, it was *my* choice, so I can change it,' Cuchulain went on. 'For the good of Ulster . . .'

He dropped on to the stool and picked up his discarded boots, thrusting his feet into them while his thoughts raced on, unspoken now, inside the privacy of his skull.

Sualtim. Conor mac Nessa. Lewy Long-Hand.

If I choose to believe the god has no part in me, then I do what I do alone. Without special help.

Which means the Rage comes from something inside me that is not magical but mortal. My victories – and my defeats as well, if I suffer them – are mine alone.

Unaided by a god.

Believing this, I stand as vulnerable as any other man. And if I choose to believe the Son of the Sun did not sire me, then whom shall I honour by my deeds? Whose harvest am I?

The first time Cuchulain had deliberately selected a being to refer to as Father in the privacy of his mind, Skya had been responsible. By demanding he set aside his resistance to magic and take the Gae Bulga, she had unwittingly forced him to accept the possibility of a connection between himself and Lewy Long-Hand. Or *had* it been unwitting? Had Skya known some secret of vital importance that she had tried to convey to Cuchulain by giving him the Danann spear?

His brooding had led him to that conclusion at the time.

He had taken the Gae Bulga.

But he could make a different choice. Not Sualtim, that option had been discarded long ago by acts of mutual rejection.

Drying mud flaked off the thongs as he bound them carelessly and stood up. 'Where are you going?' Emer asked, alarmed by his behaviour.'

'To the House of the King.'

'Now? They'll be in bed.'

'So much the better. There will be fewer ears trying to overhear what I have to say.' He reached for his cloak, hanging on its peg by the bed, and swirled the heavy red wool across his shoulders.

'Wait.' Emer stretched out her hand, but he was gone.

The guard at the House of the King raised his spear in challenge at the sound of footfalls approaching but lowered it as soon as he recognised Cuchulain. 'The king's in bed,' he said with a wink, 'in Mugain's sleeping chamber.'

'Send him out to me, then. I regret disturbing him, but this is important.'

'I hope so, if I have to bother him now. Here, you hold this spear and watch at the door while I'm gone.' The guard hurried away.

He returned eventually and beckoned Cuchulain to enter the hall. 'The king will join you when he's ready.'

Candles were always left burning in the House of the King at night. Though the great hall brimmed with shadows, there were pools of light every few paces revealing the stone floor, the timbered walls, the burnished gleam of metal ornament and bright enamelwork. A banked fire muttered to itself in the firepit. Wolfhounds lay piled around it like logs, sleeping. A few raised their heads as Cuchulain approached; one or two wagged feathered tails in lazy greeting.

The king came towards his visitor from the shadows, walking stiffly as if his joints ached. He wore a stern face of mountains and valleys, forested by a beard. The face of Ulster. 'What do you want? This isn't a good time to disturb me.'

For a moment, Cuchulain feared his nerve had deserted him. Plunge ahead and through, he reminded himself. 'Can anyone hear us?'

Conor glanced around. Servants were piled up like the dogs, snoring. 'Step behind this screen and drop your voice. Now, Cuchulain – what's this about?'

'Harvest,' said the younger man. He drew a deep breath. 'I thought it was important for you to realise that the king of Ulster has everything a king needs. A stout fortress, loyal warriors, the respect of his people. And at least one son of his own siring who is both strong and healthy, a son who is and will remain his loyal champion. Your harvest, Father.'

Not Foster-Father.

.The silence beat on Cuchulain's eardrums. He could not see the king's eyes; they were hidden deep in their sockets. At last he heard Conor clear his throat. 'Who told you to say this to me?'

'No one. And I will not say it again within the hearing of any other person; my words are for you alone. I will not give any man cause to accuse you of having broken a sacred prohibition. But a man must be certain of his posterity, Father.'

Saying it was easier the second time. Cuchulain let himself taste the word as it rolled across his tongue.

The silence thickened. Conor made no response at all. With senses heightened by tension, Cuchulain could hear the fleas crawling on the hounds and the insects burrowing in the thatch overhead. He began to wonder if he had made a dreadful mistake. What if the king thought he was accusing him. . . ?'

Conor mac Nessa was as immobile as one of the carved oak pillars supporting the roof. He did not even breathe.

I am a dead man, thought Cuchulain.

Then he saw the king move.

Slowly, Conor raised one hand until it came to rest on Cuchulain's shoulder. The fingers touched lightly at first, then closed with a bruising grip. A kingly, undiminished grip.

The two men faced each other, and Cuchulain could see life begin to sparkle in the king's shadowed eyesockets.

Conor mac Nessa could not trust himself to speak. His pride and his joy were communicated by touch. But when at last he removed his hand and turned away, going back to bed, he was moving with the eager, springy stride of a happy man.

A man believes what he wants to believe.

All Cuchulain's strength was barely enough to hold his elation locked inside himself until he was outside, under the stars. Then he turned in a slow circle, holding his arms wide, his face tilted toward the silent watchers in the sky.

Ulster. His lips framed the word.

Mine to defend.

Father.

Mine to protect.

Mine.

A cold wind blew across Erin, but Cuchulain did not feel it. Above him arched a vital darkness pierced by the light of a billion suns.

316

Throwing his head all the way back, the Hound of Ulster shouted unequivocally, to the stars, 'I am Red Branch!

'Red Branch for ever!'

 For ever. I find it laughable that humans, who have no concept of what 'for ever' is, invoke it so easily. They have the odd conceit of measuring time by their own life-spans, dividing it into old and new. And for some reason, they think time runs in a straight line.

Of course, I realise they cannot get far enough from their planet to viscerally comprehend the curvature of the cosmos. Early in their history, they developed the erroneous concept of straight lines, and have been misapplying the idea ever since.

I am too experienced to measure time at all. A time is a place I go into – though as in everything else, I am limited to certain eras. Some are more rewarding for me than others.

Occasionally, humans fall into a depression of the savage instinct and lose their enthusiasm for slaughtering one another wholesale. I could name you some terrible years for me . . . ah, well. Every business must expect vicissitudes.

A wise professional like myself tries to have a little something laid by for the off-season.

But I must say, the time of the Red Branch was an exciting one for me. Those warriors had delicious style.

Do I repel you? I shouldn't. I'm certain we have something in common.

Does a disaster excite you – as long as it isn't happening to you?

Can a heroic deed make your heart leap?

Do you prefer winning to losing?

Aha! I thought so.

Reject gods if you will; fortunately, their existence does not depend on you. You did not invent what you call the supernatural; that is another conceit typical of human arrogance. Latecomers, humans. Like children, they see everything only in relation to themselves. Centre of the universe and all that.

Sometimes your species makes me tired.

Cuchulain was correct, though, when he guessed there might be something of magic in every person. There is; once it burned brightly in the species, making many things possible. Now, it grows duller with each successive generation, as if passion were being slowly leached away.

317

Humans were more lively once. And for a while, the reckless, vivid warriors of the Red Branch were my favourites.

As for the Hound, shall I admit it? Love is such a big word.

But I truly loved Cuchulain.

For a while.

3 Maeve of Cruachan was restless. She twisted on the bed, unable to sleep, turning from side to side as if she lay on a wrinkle. Occasionally, she was still long enough to stare up into the smoked underside of the thatch, but soon she was tossing and turning again.

Ailell was used to his wife's moods. They had been married a long time. Many nights they lay with their heads on the same pillow, two voices mingling until they sharpened with desire or faded into sleep.

Perhaps a cheerful conversation would relax her now, he thought. He turned towards her, his affable smile revealed by the one candle left burning throughout the night in their sleeping chamber. 'Tell the truth, wife, as you lie here amid all these soft linen bedcovers. Isn't it pleasant to be married to a wealthy man?'

He had a reason for calling her attention to the linen, his most recent gift to Maeve. He had not yet been suitably thanked and bed was the ideal place for her to show her gratitude. Ailell was pleased with his ploy.

But as ever, Maeve surprised him. 'Why boast of your wealth now?' she snapped. Something other than gratitude or passion simmered beneath her surface.

'I was just, ah, thinking how much better off you are now than when you married me.'

'I was a prosperous woman before I ever met you.'

She was spoiling for a fight, then. Good enough; battle was a game he knew.

'If you were wealthy, it was the best-kept secret in Erin. When I first knew you, your only property was your woman-things and this fort, half-unwalled, with neighbouring clans plundering it at will because there was no chieftain here to teach them respect.'

Maeve sat up in bed with a movement so violent her coppery hair crackled. Her long pale moon of a face glimmered above him. Disturbed, her pet hound crouched against her, trembling.

'How dare you slander Cruachan! My father gave me this fort as a kingly gift.'

'My father was king of Leinster,' retorted Ailell. 'Don't try to impress me with your breeding, my line is as noble as yours.'

'Men prouder than you sought me in marriage. Chieftains of Ulster and Munster wanted me, firstborn sons, I might add, not latecomers like you. You're fortunate indeed that I looked at you with more than one eye.'

'Fortunate, am I?' Ailell was enjoying their skirmish. Such bed-battles could lead to further excitements. 'You set a terrible high value on yourself.'

'I always have, I know my worth.' Maeve tossed her head, stroking the trembling dog to comfort it. 'Didn't I ask for the most unusual marriage-gift ever given to a woman in Erin, because I am the most unusual of women? To win me, a man must be openhanded, I said, because I am famed for my generosity. He must also have a fine, hot spirit to match the flame of my celebrated spirit. And of course he must be without fear, because my own courage is bardsung.'

Her husband chuckled. 'I'll agree it took a brave man to marry you. But in me, you met your match – more than your match.'

She shot him a look of fire and ice. 'You think yourself better than me? In any way? Have you forgotten the most important marriage-gift I demanded? I said I would not marry unless I was allowed the rights men take for themselves, including the right to bed anyone I wanted whenever I chose. I'd never had one man without another standing waiting in his shadow, and I wasn't about to surrender my pleasures just to marry. Not when I knew any husband would continue to enjoy *his* pleasures. I demanded equality as my marriage portion, and you agreed.'

'If I agreed – and I'm not saying I did – I must have been moonmad.'

'You were amply rewarded, that's what you were,' said Maeve with a sniff. 'My gifts to you included the finest chariot ever built in Erin and gold to the width of your shoulders.'

'That seems small recompense when you consider all I've had to put up with since, and the many things I've done for you. The wealth I brought to our marriage made Cruachan what it is today.'

'Liar! You never set one stone upon another here, Ailell. Cruachan grew from my plans and my dreams, my efforts created it . . .'

'. . . out of a neglected outpost your father gave you to keep you occupied after you drove your first husband into an early grave,' her husband reminded her. 'It was only when I arrived that Cruachan began to expand.'

'Cruachan began to expand when *I* harried the Ulster borderlands. Connaughtmen were persuaded to devote their efforts to enlarging Cruachan because they feared retaliation.'

'You were taking a risk.'

'I took no risk; the warriors of Ulster were crippled by a curse. As long as we got in and got out quickly, they couldn't do us much harm.'

'You didn't know about the curse when you began all this, Maeve. You simply gambled that Conor wouldn't attack you before you could build sufficient defences.'

'Aha! So you admit I built Cruachan!'

'I admit nothing, including equality. I am your superior in every way!' Ailell found himself shouting. Maeve was as bad as a rash, she could always sting him into going too far.

'Are you indeed?' she shouted back at him. 'You have nothing better than mine, and that includes the property you boast about.' She flung herself from the bed and began yelling for her attendants. Baiscne tried to bury himself in the covers.

As the servants ran in, yawning and anxious, Maeve ordered, 'Bring my portable possessions into the hall at once. Ailell's as well. And summon counters to count them, to count everything. Each item, no matter how insignificant, is to be compared. I have to know if the scales balance.'

The unhappy servants scurried to do her bidding. Ailell groaned and heaved himself from the bed, knowing his sleep was destroyed and a bleak day would dawn. Watching as Maeve dressed in a day gown of imported *sida* that he had paid for, Ailell asked, 'Must this be done right now, woman?'

Her answering words were clipped by impatience. 'It must indeed, now is all any of us have. We could be dead tomorrow.'

The stronghold was thrown into chaos by the competition. Maeve's property was compared against Ailell's item by item – iron pots and copper bowls and bronze basins, willow baskets and wooden platters, leather buckets and pottery jugs. In housewares, the goods each had brought to the marriage or subsequently acquired were equal.

Next came the fabrics, the bales of woven flax and wool, the tunics and cloaks and belts. After these, the jewellery, massive gold lunulae to gleam from the collarbone, arm rings and finger rings and thumb rings, precious metal alloys to wear in the ears and balls of gold to hold locks of hair in place.

The hall of Cruachan soon resembled a beach upon which the entire debris of a wrecked trading fleet had been deposited. Cursing under their breath, servants scrambled over stacks of pots or ploughed through heaps of cloth – blue, yellow, red, black, green, brown, checked and striped and multicoloured.

One conclusion was drawn from the chaos. Maeve and Ailell were, so far, even.

'The livestock, then!' Ailell commanded. At first he had found the contest mildly amusing, but he lost his temper when Maeve demanded one of his smallest bits of bronze horse-ornament be weighed to see if it exceeded a similar piece of hers. 'If that woman tries to weigh my testicles and match them against her breasts, I'll denounce her for cheating,' he snarled to Fergus.

Maeve had a way of keeping life exciting; the only predictable quality she possessed was her unpredictability. Ailell thought of himself as a tolerant man who allowed her the free rein she needed for the pleasure of seeing what she would do next. But enough was enough. *He* was the chieftain; she needed to be reminded.

In Ailell, Maeve had found the one man who was willing to stand toe-to-toe with her, if adequately provoked. Both fought whole-heartedly when they fought, whipping themselves into frenzies of passion. Maeve had never found a lover to equal her husband, though she would go to her grave without admitting this to him.

In her most secret thoughts, she was tantalised by the possibility that her goading might someday drive him so far that his good nature would desert him, and he would become a wild man she could not handle. It had never yet happened, but there was always hope.

Last to be counted and compared were their herds of livestock. Everyone who had nothing else to do in the vicinity of Cruachan gathered to watch the judging of the animals. As usual, this group included Fergus, who enjoyed being on hand to observe someone else's marital strife without having a pot slung at his own head. Since he was no longer bedding Maeve, it was obvious Ailell enjoyed his company. The two had much in common. Each was born into a royal clan; each had suffered the misfortune of ageing past his prime without dying a hero's death in battle. Neither could hope, therefore, to receive the ultimate bardic accolade.

They stood hipshot, side by side, watching a herd of heifers being driven into the bawn. The stone-walled enclosure was too small to contain the entire herd. 'Every one of those is mine,' Ailell said smugly. 'My property.

'Tell me, mac Roy. You were king of Ulster before Conor mac Nessa; does the clan Ulaid boast wealth such as this?'

Fergus shrugged his heavy shoulders. 'I don't know what they have now. The last time I saw Emain Macha, it was in flames, we put the torch to everything. But if I know Conor, he's been mightily busy resupplying himself. We drove his livestock away from the fort, but he's probably recollected it and acquired more; a number of clans are tributaries to the Ulaid.'

'More clans than we control in Connaught?'

'I should think so. The rulers of Ulster have always been prosperous.'

'My wife casts envious glances at that prosperity,' Ailell remarked. 'She wants everything for Connaught because she likes to see herself as Connaught. Like a king,' he added, his eyes on the heifers in the bawn.

Some of them were trying to mount others, imitating copulation though no bull was with them.

'Cows trying to be bulls,' Ailell muttered. 'No good can come of it.'

Fergus turned his back on the bawn to lean against the stone wall, gazing out over the rolling grassland to a distant line of purple hills.

'I'll tell you something for nothing, my friend. Women cause all the trouble in the world, all the *real* trouble. I speak from personal experience. Before the one called Deirdre appeared, we were a happy lot at Emain Macha. I was no longer king, but I was content. Small worries instead of big ones, and every night I greased my knife with the Red Branch. Then Deirdre.

'Had it not been for her, we'd still be together. Me, Conor, Cuchulain, Naisi . . . the warriors of Ulster . . .' Unshed tears glistened in the yellowed whites of his eyes.

'Your heart is at Emain Macha,' said Ailell.

'Not true. You took us in, we're your men now.'

'Oh, I'm not worried about the others. But you're a torn man, Fergus mac Roy. No amount of land or cattle can make up for what you've lost, I suspect.'

Fergus turned to look deep into Ailell's eyes, seeing a grain of mistrust there amid the gleams of friendship. Quickly, he replied, 'Torn I may be, but not ungrateful! I give you my word I will never swing a sword against Connaught on behalf of Ulster. Don't worry about me. I'm too old and tired to be a worry to anyone.'

★

Fergus was mistaken. He might be tired; my own energy level falls low on occasion, though I am a goddess. But he was a born warrior, and when the bronze trumpet summoned him, his blood would leap in answer. Fergus would find himself on a battlefield again sooner than he realised. Not because Maeve craved action, but because I do.

I hunger for drama on a grand scale. The emotions war provides are my richest sustenance.

War is a transcendent experience that elicits the extremes of human behaviour. On the battlefield, some men discover courage, brotherhood, gallantry. Facing death, they find themselves to be wellsprings of humankind's noblest qualities.

In the heat of battle, other men become cowardly, treacherous, and brutal, releasing their most savage impulses in an orgy of destruction.

Two faces of war, each valid.

As true warriors understand, war is the means by which man stretches himself as far as he can go – in either direction. For this reason, human history has been shaped by warfare. And wherever battle is joined, the shadow of my wings falls across the faces of the combatants. They enter my domain, the realm of the Battle Raven who can soar to the stars or feast on the carrion of the battlefield.

The warriors are mine, in love and hate.

'How is the counting going?' asked Maeve, approaching the bawn. Since the contest began, she had loaded her arms and neck and fingers and ankles with her ornaments, displaying as much as she could at one time.

'Your wife clanks when she walks,' Fergus observed to Ailell under his breath.

'Some of that is iron. If it rains, she'll rust.'

Both men sniggered. Hearing them, Maeve felt her white cheeks mottle with red anger. She glanced into the bawn. 'Only heifers, Ailell? Have you no bulls?'

'My wife always wants to look at bulls,' Ailell said to his companion. 'If you're so anxious, Maeve, let's send for both your bulls and mine and compare them now. I may have a surprise for you.'

Runners were dispatched, herders alerted, and before the day was over, the bulls were collected for viewing. Maeve and Ailell proved to have a dozen each – but at a glance it was obvious one animal was superior to any other.

The crowd which had gathered to watch elbowed along the stone walltop, nodded to each other when the final bull was led into the enclosure with a wary herdsman on either side, guiding him with pointed cattle prods.

The animal was huge: white head, white feet, white cruel horns, and a massive body the colour of blood.

'Whose bull is he?' Maeve asked, uncertain for the first time.

Ailell smiled so broadly his ears lifted on his skull. 'I thought you were such a good cattle-manager. Don't you know your own animals? This one, as it happens, belongs to me.'

He gave her a moment to digest the information, then went on. 'He was born to a cow of yours some years ago but the poor creature was so embarrassed at finding himself in a woman's herd that he kept running away. When I mentioned it to you, you were, ah, preoccupied with someone else at the time, and you said if I was so concerned, I should take the calf myself. So I did. He grew into the bull you see. I call him Fionnbanach, the White-Horned, and he's killed any number of rivals.

'Nothing in your possession, Maeve, can remotely hope to equal him.'

Ailell was so pleased with his triumph, he failed to read his wife's face; he did not notice the clench of her jaw or the sudden black stormclouds that boiled up in her eyes. Instead, he glanced at Fergus, giving the other man a conspiratorial wink. Watch Maeve explode, the wink said.

Maeve did not explode. She was too furious for simple anger. Quivering from head to foot, she spun on her heel and stalked away.

'She'll get over it,' Ailell told Fergus. 'She wanted a fight and I gave her one. She'll never admit I've beaten her, but when she's had time to think about it, she'll come rubbing around my ankles, wanting her ears scratched – you'll see.'

Fergus watched the departing figure recede in the distance. As she breasted through space, the air seemed to shimmer around her, as if she gave off waves of heat. He cleared his throat. 'I've seen women and I've seen trouble. And that woman is going to cause a lot of trouble.'

Ailell merely laughed, and turned back to admire his bull.

Maeve sought out her herald, a man known as mac Roth. Once, he had possessed a name of his own and been her chosen praise-singer, but he had referred to himself too often when he should have spoken only of Maeve. So she decreed him nameless. Now, he was simply the son of Roth, a chastened and obedient man who ran errands for her.

'I have to have the best bull in Erin,' Maeve told him. 'Assemble a party and search the four provinces until you find him. Then buy him, borrow him, or steal him, but bring him to Cruachan to wipe the smirk off my husband's face.'

Mac Roth was a muscular man with orange hair and no chin. He wore the clothing assigned to heralds under the brehon law – a fitted linen tunic with an embroidered hem and an overmantle of only three colours. With nervous fingers, mac Roth plucked at the edge of his mantle as Maeve spoke.

'I will do your bidding surely,' he said, 'but . . . you don't want me to go into Ulster, do you?'

'And why not?'

He replied with one word. 'Cuchulain.'

Maeve smiled for the first time since seeing Fionnbanach. 'Of course,' she said so softly she might have been speaking to herself. 'Mac Roth, Ulster is the very place you must go. Find a bull for me there, one capable of killing that white-horned brute my husband thinks is so splendid.'

'But – '

'I know, I know; Cuchulain. Nothing to fear, I assure you. I've seen him myself, and there is no judge of men to equal me. But if it will make you feel safer, tell no one you come from me. Go into Ulster as a cattle-dealer from some vague location and take sufficient with you to buy a fine bull. Should you meet Cuchulain, he will let you pass; he won't want to discourage honest cattle business.

'When you find a bull answering my needs, bring him away from the Ulaid no matter what it takes, mac Roth. Let no one think I was afraid to tweak the nose of a little fellow like Cuchulain!'

Mac Roth could not say the same, but he was more afraid of Maeve. Collecting an escort whose accents were not broad enough to give away their Cruachan origins, he set out for Ulster.

An uneasy peace settled over the western stronghold. Though wet, sunseason was warm, and bees were drowsy in the meadows. On an evening when the day's sweat left his skin itching, Ailell invited Fergus mac Roy to share a bathing vat with him, and the two chatted together with ale-horns in their hands as servants dropped heated stones into the water. The vat was originally heated with fires built against its iron sides, but these were pulled away when bathers entered and hot stones used to keep the temperature warm thereafter.

After several long drinks of ale, Ailell confided that Maeve no longer shared a pillow with him.

'I thought she'd come wanting you to scratch her ears,' said Fergus.

'So did I. But now she says she'll have nothing to do with me until we are equal again.'

'Would that be so bad?'

Ailell squinted through the steam. 'Let's be frank, you've bedded her. The woman has a talent. I can appreciate the meat of many a plump haunch, but Maeve is the spice and I cannot bear to go too long without her – life begins to seem very tasteless.'

'Ah,' said Fergus, not without sympathy. 'Overpower her, then.'

'She would enjoy it too much. I can't afford to allow her any victories right now.'

Fergus slipped deeper into the water, lifting his forked beard so the hot liquid could bathe his neck. 'Slaughter your white-horned bull, then,' he suggested. 'That would balance the scales.'

'What a terrible idea! I'm not surprised your life has gone against you, mac Roy, with you having such thoughts.'

'Actually, it was the sort of solution Conor mac Nessa might have offered. He was good at thorny problems, and I learned a little by observing him.' His voice was wistful.

It was Ailell's turn to be sympathetic. 'Go back to Ulster. I mean it, I'll release you from any loyalty to Connaught. Forget about us – about Maeve – and go home where you belong.'

'I can't,' the other man said sadly, 'any more than you could slaughter Fionnbanach.'

Mac Roth returned to Cruachan, looking much the worse for wear.

Maeve had him summoned to her chamber at once. 'Your face is as long as a wet winter,' she said. 'What happened?'

'As you had predicted, Cuchulain let us pass, and in the land called Cooley, not far from his own dun, we found an animal the equal of Ailell's bull.'

'Grand news, that! But why do you look so unhappy, and where's my bull?'

'Still in Cooley, I'm afraid,' said mac Roth, taking a prudent step backwards in case Maeve struck him. She clenched her fist, but kept it in her lap. The herald continued, 'The bull is known as the Donn Cooley – the Brown Bull, as he is sometimes called – and belongs to one Daire mac Fiachna. I knew Daire at a glance as a man who'd drive a hard bargain, he has "cattle-dealer" painted all over him. A sharp step, a keen eye, a tidy way about him. But he told me he'd not sell the Brown Bull at any price, it was the pride of his clan.

'So I made him a counter offer. Lease us the bull for four seasons, I suggested, to sire sons like itself on our cows.'

'And he agreed? You brought the bull with you?' Maeve half rose, eager to rush out and see the animal at once.

Mac Roth was shaking his head. 'We didn't bring him. After the arrangement was concluded, we celebrated, my men and I, with a right-and-left-handed drinking party in Daire's guest house. And you know how it is; when a man has enough to drink, he can be foolish, sometimes he can't even hit the ground with his cloak.'

Maeve's foot was tapping impatiently. 'Go on.'

'We were drinking . . . and we were boasting . . . telling one another that it was a good thing Daire had agreed to loan the bull to us, or we would have taken it from him by force. And a servant of Daire's, who was bringing us more ale, overheard our words and ran back to his master with them.

'Daire came upon us like a flood. He said he would have killed us all if it had not been for the law of hospitality, and he threw us out of his dun, cursing us for our treacherous hearts.

'So we came back to Cruachan at the gallop, without the bull and fortunate to have our lives.'

'Without the bull. A grand animal, was it?'

'It was that. As big if not bigger than your husband's, and broader between the horns. I would say there's not an animal in Erin the equal of the Donn Cooley. A pity we had to leave him behind in Ulster, but there you are; there were only two tens of us, and nothing else to do.'

'Nothing else indeed,' agreed Maeve. But the expression of her face chilled the marrow in her herald's bones.

Dismissing him, she spent the rest of the day in thought. Determination hardened in her. The Brown Bull of Cooley must be hers, a prize all the sweeter if she could snatch it from under the nose of the Hound of Ulster.

That evening at the feasting table, she caught her husband's eyes on her and thought he was laughing at her.

Enjoy your triumph while it lasts, she said to him silently. You think I am less than yourself because I was born with a cleft instead of a dangle. Take care, Ailell – I can slice off that dangle.

One by one, Maeve interviewed the pick of the fighting men of Connaught, including the rebels of the Red Branch. Each was offered an impressive share of the plunder if he would follow her on a venture she would soon undertake. Most readily agreed; Maeve's generosity was indeed famous. Cormac Connlongas, Brocc the Badger, and Duffach the Beetle were willing to take part in a raid on Ulster in return for a sufficient share of the spoils. They considered themselves Connaughtmen now.

Mindful of the relationship that had developed between Fergus and Ailell, Maeve put off discussing her plans with Fergus until last. But there was one other Ulsterman who required special handling – the one his friends claimed was the equal of the Hound of Ulster in battle skills.

Ferdiad mac Daman, tall and blunt-faced, who never went anywhere without his body armour of overlapping plates of horn.

Since arriving in Cruachan, Ferdiad had remained strangely aloof. He attended the feasts but did not talk; he gravely accepted the gifts Maeve and Ailell offered but took no visible pleasure in them. He did not move on to his landholding, and as far as anyone knew, he never made use of his bondwomen.

Ferdiad was an enigma to Maeve, until the day she saw him glance inadvertently at her daughter Finavir of the Fair Eyebrows.

Some young women dyed their eyebrows black, in the prevailing fashion, with berry juice. But Finavir, youngest and fairest of the children of Maeve and Ailell, scorned artifice. She was so lovely she let nature be sufficient, and a number of men had begun admiring her as her childish form ripened.

Maeve summoned the girl. 'Do you know the Ulsterman Ferdiad?'

'I've seen him.' Finavir kept her eyes lowered. She was wary of her mother. Maeve demanded total obedience from her children and had little patience with their errors, as if the least failure on their part reflected unfavourably on her. But she did not want them to shine too brightly, either – not so brightly as to obscure her.

'Do you find Ferdiad attractive?'

'I suppose so.'

'I would like to be certain he is solidly in my camp. Make yourself known to him, girl. Smile at him, take him tidbits from my cooks, offer to carry his water pitcher from the well. If we should find ourselves facing the Hound of Ulster in the near future, I want to be certain of having, on my side, the man who can bring him down.'

4 On certain mornings, the fort of Dun Dalgan floated in a
sphere of sea light. Sunshine reflected from pearls of mist.
The air was suffused with soft radiance as the earth held its
breath in anticipation.

Cuchulain knew as soon as he awoke: something will happen today.

His head was clear, his body taut and eager. Leaving Emer curled in
their bed, he drew on a tunic and hastily left the chamber. Pretending to
be asleep, his wife watched him through half-closed eyes but said
nothing. He would leave like a flame blown out, and she would have to
wait until he returned, whenever he returned, in whatever condition.

You would have to marry the Hound of Ulster, she reminded herself.

Curoi's Munstermen had injured him severely, and a dozen other
major wounds had left tracks on his hide to be glimpsed as he dressed.
Emer knew them every one, every scar of every battle. She knew also
the undamaged portions of his skin that just seemed to be waiting to
have their own histories cut into them.

He faces his twentieth winter, she thought sadly, and already he's
carved up like a cow. And proud of it.

Laeg the charioteer was also proud of Cuchulain's scars. He'd been
present when the wounds were received, most of them, and passed the
weapons to his hero to fight his enemies off, and lifted the bleeding body
into the chariot and driven it home for mending. Sometimes he'd had to
draw rein and do some skilful patching himself before they reached
Dun Dalgan, just to keep the life from draining out of Cuchulain before
professional healers could work on him.

Every good charioteer knew how to staunch the flow of blood and
bind torn muscles; it was part of his training.

More than once as he worked over Cuchulain, Laeg had thought to
himself, Ferdiad could not do this for you half so well.

On the luminous leaf-fall morning when a promise of action tingled
in the air, Laeg was just wheeling the chariot out of the shed for
Cuchulain when they heard a shout from the sentry at the gate.

'Perhaps the action has come to us today,' said the Hound.

A deputation of grim-faced men arrived from the nearby peninsula of Cooley. Their leader was a well-known cattle-lord, Daire mac Fiachna, from whom Cuchulain had obtained a few beasts from time to time. But Daire did not appear to be in the mood for a bit of pleasant trading today.

'A band of impertinent strangers almost stole my seed bull,' he complained to Cuchulain.

'Cattle-raiders? They couldn't have got past me.'

'They didn't come as raiders, they were disguised as purchasers and were a little murky about their background. But they had a cart piled high with trade goods, and I thought them sincere enough.'

Cuchulain nodded. 'I remember them now. They came through here looking for a bull . . . an exceptional bull, they said.'

'And when I refused to sell them mine, they intended to steal it!' Daire burst out.

'Bring the weapons, Laeg,' Cuchulain ordered.

'Too late, that. They're gone, I ran them off. They had too small a number to make good their drunken boast.'

'Then why complain to me, if there's no work for me to do?'

'Because I fear the matter is not ended, Cuchulain. Thinking it over later, I realised they dressed and spoke like Connaughtmen. And I had overheard one mention the name of Brocc the Badger. Wasn't that one of your Red Branch who sought sanctuary at Cruachan?'

Cuchulain nodded grimly.

'My griping guts tell me more men will be coming to try to take my bull,' Daire said. 'This lot saw him, they know his quality. A larger party will be paying us a visit in time, I know it.'

Cuchulain assured him, 'Your holdings and your cattle are protected by the strong arm of clan Ulaid.'

'They had better be, or my support will go to some other clan. If he allows his tributaries to be plundered, Conor mac Nessa and his Ulaid will not occupy Emain Macha for ever!'

Cuchulain sent a runner northward to inform Conor, who understood the seriousness of the situation at once.

Maeve had no doubt grown tired of harrying the borders. Using the Brown Bull as a pretext, she could send a large party of cattle-raiders across the face of Ulster to its eastern coast, to Cooley, and plunder as she came.

Cuchulain was wise to sound an alarm.

'Tell me, Ronan,' Conor questioned the messenger from Dun Dalgan, 'does my champion expect these raiders soon?'

'He thinks it will take some time for Connaught to assemble a large enough force to feel certain of success, but said we must start preparing immediately.'

The king nodded. 'I agree. At least we're ready here.' He waved a long-fingered hand to indicate the rebuilt and strengthened fortifications of Emain Macha.

Nessa crowded close to her son. 'How can you prepare against Fergus mac Roy? That wretched traitor will come with them, you may rely on it. In his lust to harm you, he'll undoubtedly show them all the back ways and secret accesses to Ulster.'

Conor stroked his beard. 'There may be truth in what you say.' His mind raced, clear and sharp, the mind of a war-leader. A man with a future. 'Fergus knows the western country best,' he said, 'and there's been a lot of rain in the west lately. The few routes he would try are surely reduced to wetland and bogland, and if we rip up the cart roads, he could never lead the Connaughtmen through them.'

The men gathered around nodded to one another, admiring the king's wisdom. In both Leinster and Ulster, cart roads had been constructed to give access to otherwise impassable regions for the sake of trade. Split oak timbers laid over parallel birch runners were capable of supporting not only oxcarts, but war-chariots, making it possible to take such vehicles across dangerous bogs.

At the king's order, teams of men hurried from Emain Macha to tear up the cart roads, racing against time and Connaught.

In the House of the King, Nessa worried over the problem as if it were a bone. She was old and grey and gritty, but she still insisted on making her voice heard.

'Why not take the bull away from Daire and send it to Maeve and Ailell as a gift?' she suggested. 'Then they would have no reason to invade Ulster, which would mean the bull would be our only loss.'

Conor folded his arms in exasperation. 'What happens the next time someone wants something we have? Do I just give that away too, to avoid trouble? And on and on, until Ulster itself is given away?'

'Of course not. But the problem would be solved for now.'

'I've resolved too many problems on that basis,' Conor told Nessa. 'This one must be settled for all the tomorrows.'

Unconvinced, Nessa propped one elbow on the nearest table and shook her head at her son. She loved Conor, but since the Deirdre débâcle, she did not trust his judgement. It is a mother's duty to point out a child's mistakes, she told herself.

A period of tense waiting had begun that would last through the autumn. Still Connaught did not invade.

Maeve was aligning her support carefully. By a mixture of threats and promises, she persuaded Ailell to join her in her planned cattle raid. 'Once I have a bull to equal yours, matters will be settled between us, husband,' she assured him, 'and we can be as we were. But if I don't have the Brown Bull of Cooley, I'll never be able to pull the same weight in the harness as you.'

'Now, I'm expected to go with her for that animal,' Ailell told Fergus. 'She needs me, she says!'

'She needs the warriors who are loyal to you but less eager to follow a woman,' was the other man's shrewd observation.

'I have to do it. Otherwise we'll go on as we are, living two separate lives here at Cruachan and dividing the loyalties of Connaught between us. And that's no good, Fergus; it makes us too vulnerable.'

'How well I know it. I saw the Red Branch split.'

'And,' Ailell continued, 'with the new Ulstermen living here and breeding and raising families, we're going to have more mouths to feed. In a few more generations, we really will have to start reaching out. It makes sense to go into Ulster now and seize a good bull and a good herd of cows to add to our stock; we'll probably have to do a lot more of it in the future.'

Borders are always fluid; Ailell could imagine the border of Connaught shifting, expanding, as Maeve had expanded Cruachan.

Sometimes the woman made sense.

'Will you go with us into Ulster, Fergus?'

'You don't need me.'

'I'd rather have you with us where I could keep an eye on you,' Ailell said frankly, 'than left behind at my back. We have little more than one cycle of the moon until Samhain, and Maeve wants to be on the march immediately after. What do you say?'

Samhain was one of the major spokes upon which the wheel of the seasons turned. The old cycle ended with the last night of leaf-fall, the new began with the first day of winter. Death precedes life, the druids taught, so a new year must begin with winter. The juncture between the seasons of life and death was a time outside of time when spirits could most freely cross the lowered barriers between this world and the Otherworld. On such a potentially dangerous occasion clans huddled together, close to the fire.

Conor mac Nessa summoned clan Ulaid, including the majority of his Red Branch, to Emain Macha for Samhain in spite of the threat from Connaught. Fear of the encroaching Otherworld was stronger than fear of human raiders. The prudent king left the necessary guards at Ulster's primary access points, however; men who must face the terrors of Samhain alone.

Cuchulain was not to be one of them. Conor wanted his champion by his side.

The seasonal celebrations began half a moon before the feast itself, with games and contests. The opening event was the recounting by various heroes of their battle-feats during the preceding year. Bards attended this recital and memorised every word, to enter into the oral history of the clan. Everyone expected the adventures of the Hound of Ulster to be the most exciting, so he would speak last.

While they waited for the event to begin, the Red Branch warriors gathered by the Lake of Jewels to amuse themselves with a contest. Some of the women joined them, cheering as they competed with slings and stones to see who could hit the slimmest reed on the far side of the pond. The rivalry was fierce.

Emer stood watching with Mugain, the king's senior wife, and Leary's Fedelm of the Fresh Heart. Lendabair was elsewhere with Conall Cearnach, trying to persuade him to practise telling his story in more than reluctant monosyllables.

When Cuchulain's aim proved unbeatable, to no one's real surprise, the contestants put away their slings.

'He's better than ever, the Hound,' Mugain commented to Emer just as a flock of waterfowl approached the pond, circled, then settled when they felt the humans were through disturbing the water. 'Look there!' Mugain said. 'What gorgeous birds! I must have a pair of those wing-feathers to wear on my shoulders at the Samhain feast.'

'And I,' said Fedelm at once.

'And a pair for me,' chimed the other women in chorus.

As Cuchulain approached his wife, Mugain said to him, 'You're the only man swift enough to hit those birds before they can fly away again. You must get them for us.'

Emer saw how the other women turned their faces adoringly towards her husband, thinking he could do anything.

Cuchulain's mind was on the game just concluded, and the speech to come, however. 'Haven't the women of Ulster anything better to do than to put me to catching birds?'

Emer laid her hand on his arm. 'Please, my husband,' she said.

334

'Every woman here is half-blind with love for you. This would be an easy gift to give them and make them happy.'

Cuchulain smiled at her. 'An openhanded woman is finer than gold wire.' With one fond finger, he traced the curve of her cheek.

Only Mugain realised Emer had deliberately spoken so loudly that the other women could hear her and could not help being aware of the unjealous generosity of the Hound's wife.

You smug little creature, thought Mugain. Conor's fosterling has married a clever woman.

Cuchulain eased into the shallows so delicately, not a bird glanced his way. He might have been a shadow on the lake. Then, with one slam of his shield, he hit the surface of the water such a blow that many birds were stunned. A second blow sent out wider ripples of concussion, and the entire flock floated dazed and helpless, allowing him to grab them and toss them onto the bank. The laughing women scrambled for them.

When Cuchulain emerged dripping from the water, only Emer had empty hands. 'There weren't enough to go around,' she said.

'I hope you're not angry with me for that.'

'I am not. Even without fine plumage, I'm more fortunate than any other woman here. There is not one who would not share herself with you as well as with her husband. But I share myself with you alone.'

Mugain was tempted to applaud.

Grinning, Cuchulain lifted his wife at the waist and swung her into the air, whirling around and around with her until she was dizzy. 'Before we go home to Dun Dalgan, I'll capture a pair of birds for you that will make the other women gnaw their knuckles!' he promised.

He danced his wife through the air and she laughed down at him, two radiant creatures brimming with joy. For a moment, the men and women watching them felt as if they were looking at immortals, at two who would never know age or pain. Everyone smiled; they could not help it.

But Emer was glad to hear Cuchulain say the name of Dun Dalgan with longing in his voice. There, she would not have to endure the sight of other women trying to catch his eye, to touch him as he passed, to make some brief contact with the champion. He was neither tall nor golden like the king, but he was special. And any of them would gladly have taken him from her if they could.

Jealousy was the secret knife Emer turned inward, letting it hurt only herself. Conor mac Nessa's jealousy had wrought terrible destruction. No one would see Cuchulain's wife being jealous.

Though she had no birds, she went back to the fort with the other women to help them sew the plumage on their gowns. The men also began drifting toward the fort, anticipating the recital of battle-feats that would begin at sunset in the House of the King. Only Cuchulain and Laeg lingered by the lake, engrossed in a discussion of the weapons Cuchulain would need for various contests to come.

The charioteer's attention was caught by a glimpse of two more birds . . . birds? . . . flying very fast over the pond, then dropping from sight on the far side.

One was white, he thought, like a swan. The other, half-hidden by its companion, had looked black. A black swan? Was there such a creature? 'Cuchulain, did you see those?' Laeg pointed.

Cuchulain followed the direction of his finger. 'What are they? I see them on the far bank, but they're obscured by the reeds. It's a fine pair of some sort of bird, though . . . I'll get them for Emer.'

Something about the appearance of the birds, if birds they were, disturbed Laeg. No strange sighting at Samhain was to be trusted. Impulsively, he said to Cuchulain, 'Don't shoot them.'

'Do you think you can stop me?' laughed the Hound. 'I promised plumes to my wife, and there they are waiting.' He raised the sling, fired his stone, and watched in disbelief as it fell short, plopping into the water. 'My grief! I never missed such a shot before.'

He fitted a second stone to the sling, fired again, and missed again. Taking fright, the birds lifted into the sky just as he shot a third time, hurling the missile at them with angry force.

There was a confusion of feathers in the air, and the birds were gone. 'Did I hit them? Both at once?'

'I can't tell if you hit them or missed them. Where are they?'

Cuchulain waded into the lake, but there were no stunned birds floating on the water. He floundered around among the reeds looking for them. Laeg joined him to help, but without success. Cuchulain was obviously upset.

When a man fails who never fails, those who love him are made uncomfortable for him. Eventually, Laeg left, claiming the horses needed tending, but Cuchulain remained at the Lake of Jewels.

Refusing to admit defeat, he went into the water a time or two more, feeling about with his feet in the mud and debris of the bottom. No birds. And the lake was bitterly cold. Baffled and chilled, at last he gave up and lay down on the shore in an attempt to get warm, wrapping his cloak around his body and pillowing his head on a flat stone.

336

He did not mean to fall asleep. Soon he must head for the House of the King. Then, bright against the dark underside of his eyelids, a vision came to Cuchulain.

Two women approached him from the direction of the lake. One was a slender creature with the limpid loveliness of a drop of pure water. She wore a mantle of deep green and moved like a flowing stream, and she had been crying recently.

Her companion was russet-haired, tall and strongly built. An eyeful of woman, yet it was the other who drew Cuchulain's gaze.

They came to a stop beside him as he lay on the ground. 'Here is a man for you, Fand,' said the red-haired woman. 'Take this birch rod and strike him hard; I promise it will make you feel better.'

The woman in green accepted the rod and tapped it lightly against Cuchulain's legs. He started to stand up, protesting, 'What have I done to you? I would rather be friend than enemy to a woman so beautiful.'

The sadness faded from her face. Her cheeks turned pink, her eyes swept over the Hound with obvious interest. He returned the glance in full measure, lingering over the curves of her body.

'Put down that birch rod and join me in my cloak,' he invited playfully. 'I need warming.'

The red-clad woman responded by seizing the rod herself and striking Cuchulain such a blow that for a heartbeat he saw nothing but flashes of pain-coloured light. She hit again, and wherever she struck, his body turned numb. He tried to avoid her blows but could not; his knees buckled and he fell to the ground, unable to move.

She hit him again and again and again.

 Prompted by misguided impulse, I have occasionally attempted to perform a kindness. It never turns out well, and I should know better. Kindness is another of those human concepts that has no place in the natural order. Stones and hawks and comets are not kind.

But I had felt a rare spark of sympathy for Fand, wife of Manannan mac Lir, ruler of the waves. He had abandoned her, and she was as sad as if she had a human heart. Fand is the sort of sweet, unassuming creature I usually detest, actually. Cuchulain's wife, Emer, is somewhat like her, though with more spirit. Emer had once struck me with a rock, which I rather admired her for, though of course I had retaliated in my own way, in the silent darkness of her womb.

When hurt, Fand is incapable of retaliation, which is why she was suffering so. I thought it would give her relief to strike out at some masculine figure, and since Manannan was beyond her reach, I led her to my Cuchulain. Knowing him so well, I knew he could not be hurt by her puny blows. At my urging, she managed one feeble attempt, poor thing.

But it did not turn out as I expected.

I had had a secondary motive, naturally. I had decided the time had come for Cuchulain to see me in one of my other forms, something more attractive than the Battle Raven. A large black bird holds little sensual interest for the human male. And I thought it would be doubly clever to appear before him with a foil, a contrast. Beside pallid Fand, I would show to my best advantage. He would see a woman of spirit and power, an exciting creature as capable of inflicting pain as the Hound himself.

But the fool looked at her instead of me. He smiled at and desired the tepid wife of Manannan mac Lir.

So I beat him until he was paralysed and half-dead.

You see what harm is done by surrendering to a kind impulse.

5 The recitations had begun in the House of the King, but there was no sign of Cuchulain. Conor sent searchers for him, but they could not locate him until Laeg mentioned having last seen him by the Lake of the Jewels. A band of the Red Branch hurried off at once.

They found him lying motionless on the bank of the pond, with his head pillowed on a stone. His eyes were open in the light of their recently lit torches. Laeg crouched down beside him. 'What happened to you?'

'Two women . . . beat me,' Cuchulain replied through stiff lips. 'Not exactly . . . women,' he amended, panting with the effort to force out the words. 'Other.' His eyes closed. 'Otherworld . . .'

'He's been hit on the skull,' Leary Buadach declared.

Laeg felt Cuchulain's head. 'There's no bump and no blood.'

Buinne the Rough-Red glanced around nervously. The mention of the Otherworld filled his belly with ice. 'Let's carry him back to the fort and get him under a rooftree.'

'We can't,' argued Conall Cearnach. 'He's fallen asleep; there's a *ges* not to disturb him.'

The men exchanged glances and shifted their feet uncertainly. Though a cold wind had sprung up, Laeg took off his cloak and wrapped it around the body of the champion. As he reached across Cuchulain's chest, the injured man managed to whisper, 'Not asleep. Take me . . . Speckled House.'

'You should be in your own chamber. Or in the House of Pain, where Fingan and the other healers can look after you,' the men told him.

'Speckled House,' Cuchulain insisted. 'With the weapons. I defend . . . king and kingdom.'

The men of the Red Branch looked at each other, then lifted him on to their shoulders and did as he asked.

A couch was hastily made into a sickbed in the Speckled House. Emer stationed herself on one side of it, and Fingan the physician on the other. Conor mac Nessa stood at the foot while the Red Branch crowded

339

behind him, trying to peer past his wide shoulders. They were struggling to comprehend the unthinkable: the champion of Ulster paralysed and helpless.

Fingan looked up and caught the king's eye. 'I can't do anything more for him,' he admitted. 'This is no illness I recognise.'

Emer bent over Cuchulain. 'He's saying something under his breath. Something about the . . . magic people?'

'He said that before. At least he mentioned the Otherworld,' Buinne confirmed.

Reluctantly, Conor mac Nessa summoned Cathbad the druid. Reluctantly, Cathbad came. Since Naisi's death, he avoided the king's presence as much as he could, though he performed the rituals as required of him. He knew people considered his destroyed relationship with Conor as a bad omen, but it could not be helped. Anger dies hard.

Still, for the sake of Cuchulain, he would step over anger.

When Cathbad entered the Speckled House, Cuchulain at last opened his eyes. Their clear grey was dulled, and when the druid put his hand on Cuchulain's, he felt the vibration of a force that did not emanate from the man on the bed but hovered over him.

'Cuchulain suffers from a magical affliction,' Cathbad reported.

'Then cure him with magic,' commanded the king.

'Not easily done, particularly since I don't know who did it, or why.' Cathbad closed his eyes and ran his hands, palm downward but not quite touching Cuchulain, along the length of the champion's body. As he moved over the belly, the druid tensed; as his hands crossed above the groin, he nodded and opened his eyes. 'Female. This is the work of a female.'

'Some woman cursed my husband?' Emer cried. 'Name her and I'll kill her!' Her gentleness fell from her in one piece, like a shed skin.

'This is not the work of a human woman you could kill,' Cathbad told her. 'This is the most vulnerable season of the year for us, and some spirit has crossed the barrier between worlds and done this.'

In spite of a profusion of candles, the interior of the Speckled House seemed to grow darker.

Conor mac Nessa set his jaw and glared at Cathbad. 'Slaughter a white mare, create a new ritual, do what you will, but find a way to cure this man.'

Emer reached out and caught the druid's hands with her own. 'Please,' she added.

Fires burned in the centre of the standing stones, and chanting filled

340

the wind, but the next day Cuchulain still lay helpless, unable to eat or drink, growing weaker before their eyes.

Emer and Conall Cearnach had stood vigil at his bedside through the night. The Ulaid bards praised Conall as a hard man, but Emer had seen the caring in his eyes when he looked at her husband. 'Can you think of anything to do for him, Conall?'

'I'm a warrior. I've had no dealings with the gods.'

Laeg entered the Speckled House, his freckles twisted into a worried frown. 'How is he?'

'No better. Worse, if anything.'

Laeg leaned over the bed. 'I've fed and watered your team, Cuchulain. They're fine; we just need you. Get up, won't you?'

Eyeballs rolled beneath closed lids, but the Hound said nothing.

The day dragged by, and the Hound said nothing.

Members of the Red Branch came to see him, stood embarrassed looking down at him, swore at their helplessness, and went away. Conall remained faithful, never leaving the hall, even rubbing Emer's back when she felt too weary to sit up any longer. Laeg went in and out, bringing the smell of fresh air on his clothing and trying to elicit some spark from Cuchulain with chatter about the outside world, talk from the horse pens, arguments overheard.

Nothing worked.

Another night and day and Cuchulain's condition grew worse. When he breathed, his breath rasped in his throat. Conall found himself listening for the rattle that warned of imminent death.

Emer lost her temper. When Laeg appeared yet again, trying to be bright and optimistic, she whirled on him. 'I'm sick of your beard, faithless friend! You come and go as you please, you enjoy meat and ale, and my husband lies here dying! If it were you in such trouble, he would be the first to help you. But what have you done? Oh, I wish Ferdiad were here; he wouldn't let his friend down!'

Laeg gave her a long look, then fled from the Speckled House.

In the open air, he told himself he had done his best. He had encouraged Cuchulain as best he could; the Hound's illness was beyond a charioteer's skill. And beyond Ferdiad's, certainly. Emer had no reason to drag the name of Daman's son into this.

But perhaps Ferdiad would have been able to do something, a little voice suggested.

Nothing I can't do, Laeg argued.

Something . . . something . . . he walked in circles, beating his fists in alternate rhythm against his forehead.

An intuition came to him. Too vague to be even a hunch, it was all he had and he followed it.

The sickness had come upon Cuchulain at the Lake of the Jewels; a horseman with a difficult horse knows that one must often go back to the beginning and start again to cure a problem. So Laeg left the fort and made his way to the lakeside, to the very place where they had found the paralysed Cuchulain. He even found the stone where the Hound's head had been lying, a flat stone, pale grey and ordinary.

Laeg lay down on the ground in the same position Cuchulain had taken, and put his head on the stone. Whatever had happened once might happen again.

For a long time, he simply lay there, getting cold and stiff, uncomfortably aware of a pebble pressing into his back. Then he heard the sound of wings.

The exhausted Conall Cearnach had just fallen asleep, curled into a ball at Cuchulain's feet, when Laeg burst into the Speckled House. Emer had been picking listlessly at a bowl of food, which slipped unnoticed from her fingers as she saw the expression on the charioteer's face.

'I know what happened!' Laeg cried.

Conall awakened at once. He grabbed one of Laeg's arms and Emer the other, as if they would shake the information out of him, but he was only too eager to tell.

Explaining why he had returned to the lake, he said, 'I had almost fallen asleep when I heard the sound of birds nearby, and then a white seabird and a black raven lit on the grass near me. At first I thought that's what they were – but the seabird shimmered like a tear in the eye, and the raven, when I looked closely, was not a true raven. When I realised that, the earth under me seemed to fall away, as if I had dropped into the Otherworld.'

Emer drew in a sharp intake of breath. 'Go on, Laeg.'

'A voice in my head – I don't think it came from the birds, but it might have done – told me the seabird was Fand, wife of Manannan mac Lir. And when I looked at it, I believed. There were rainbows in her eyes.'

'Like jewels,' Emer murmured to herself.

'Like jewels,' Laeg agreed. 'I said something foolish then, I said,

"I'm dreaming," and the seabird replied, "The dream is ours. Don't you know that humans are our dreams?" '

'I'm not anyone's dream!' Conall protested. 'I'm real.'

Emer silenced them with an impatient gesture. 'And then?'

'And then I looked from the seabird to the raven, and I seemed to know her too. If these were magic people, she could only be – '

'Don't say it!' Emer cried suddenly, remembering with horror the day she had thrown a stone at a raven on her roof. Stupid, stupid, stupid woman, she condemned herself. Never anger the gods!

The darkness of the Otherworld breathed on the back of her neck.

'Two women,' said a hollow voice. They all looked towards Cuchulain. His eyes were open but stared upwards without seeing. 'At the lake. I wanted one . . . they struck me down.' He groaned, a sound so tortured it brought tears to Emer's eyes.

'Do you think those are the creatures he saw?' she hardly dared ask Laeg. 'Fand? And . . .'

'And the Battle Raven, the Morrigan. I do think it. He brought a curse on himself there.'

'From which one?'

Laeg shook his head. 'I don't know. I reached for the birds to try and catch them and question them' – he shuddered in retrospect at his own recklessness – 'but they flew away. Yet I did see them, Emer. I was there, and I tell you they are the ones who hurt the Hound.'

'I believe you,' she said with the faintest of smiles. 'Laeg mac Riangabra, who went to the rim of the Otherworld for us.'

Plain and bony and freckled, Laeg turned radiant.

'I believe you too,' Conall admitted. 'I know the sound of truth when I hear it. But what's to be done – summon Cathbad again?'

Emer considered. 'Gentle-Face burned his fires and chanted his chants and my husband is no better. Fingan the physician tried his remedies and they haven't worked either.' Her small chin thrust forward at a determined angle. 'It took Cuchulain's friend to untangle the riddle; Cuchulain's wife will have to do the rest.' She turned to Laeg. 'Will you take me to the Lake of the Jewels at once?'

'I will of course, but what are you going to do?'

'What I can,' Emer replied.

They made the short journey in Cuchulain's chariot, a silent ride with only the creaking of the wicker and the jingling of the horse ornaments for music.

Fand, Emer was thinking. And the Morrigan. They struck down Cuchulain.

I wanted one, he said.

Which one?

Her husband had lusted after a goddess. What woman could fight a goddess?

Her thoughts centred on the man lying drawn and shrunken in the Speckled House, wasting away as a result of his desire for someone else.

A seabird with rainbows in her eyes, Laeg had said. Surely, that would be the one Cuchulain, who loved beauty, would most admire.

Fand.

Ahead, Emer could see the shimmering water of the pond where once before she had invoked the aid of the magic people on Cuchulain's behalf, where she had called out to Manannan mac Lir, whose wife, Fand, loved jewels.

You took my jewels, Emer thought. It isn't fair that you should now decide to take my husband as well, Fand.

But what the gods had done they could undo. If anyone could save Cuchulain, it would be the magic hand that had struck him down.

If she had sufficient reason to do so.

Emer clung to the rim of the swaying chariot and tried to be longheaded.

For the champion of Ulster, there will always be women, she reasoned. It would be unnatural if he were to refuse every one that was offered to him. She should consider herself fortunate that he had not asked her – at least not yet – to accept a second wife. To help with the work, he would surely say; men always said that, didn't they? . . . Emer jerked her thoughts back to the problem at hand.

Saving Cuchulain's life must be more important than jealousy, than the passing itch of lust.

Must be. Her knuckles were white on the chariot rim.

When they reached the lake, she asked Laeg to leave her alone.

'Will you be all right?'

'What worse can befall me than a dying husband? Go, Laeg. What I must do here I must do privately.'

He obeyed because she was Cuchulain's wife, but as he drove away, he looked back at the small woman standing wrapped in her cloak beside the pond. Not for the first time, Laeg wondered at the strength of women.

344

When she could not hear chariot sounds any longer, Emer called, 'Fand, wife of Manannan, can you hear me?'

The water rippled quietly, disinterested.

She raised her voice. 'Fand! If you found Cuchulain of Ulster sweet to your eyes, hear me now!'

Wind sighed through reeds.

'He is mortally ill because of the blows he was given,' Emer cried out across the water. 'Magic has crippled him, and only magic can restore him. I am only human, I have no magic.

'But if you once looked on my husband with favour, Sea Wife, don't leave him to die. Restore his strength to him and I . . . I will . . .' This was much harder than offering her jewels. 'I will surrender him to you for whatever you want of him, if only you will save his life!'

Gold and silver and copper, carnelian and amethyst and amber, the surface of the lake blazed with colours.

Emer whirled and ran after the chariot. 'Laeg!' she was shouting. 'Laeg, wait for me! Take me back to Cuchulain!'

Emer ran into the Speckled House, where Conall kept faithful guard. 'Leave at once,' she ordered. 'We must all leave Cuchulain and bar the door.'

'Do as she says,' Laeg advised. He saw the echo of magic on the face of Cuchulain's wife, he heard the colour of the Otherworld in her voice.

So did even hard and practical Conall Cearnach.

They left Cuchulain alone and barred the door. Then they went to the House of the King to tell Conor mac Nessa.

Athairne the chief poet was among the listeners, for anything that concerned the champion of Ulster would become part of the history of the province and must be memorised and handed down, warm with living breath. Emer and Laeg took turns in the telling, and when Laeg described Fand as a seabird with rainbows in her eyes, Athairne interrupted.

'In another life, I knew her,' the poet said in a faraway voice. 'A girl like running water. And Amergin the bard . . .' His eyes brimmed with dreams and memories.

Magic is all around us, thought Laeg, glancing nervously into the shadows.

The warriors of the Red Branch were, some of them, sceptical of certain aspects of the story, and no one liked the idea of Cuchulain having been left alone in the Speckled House. But magic was a normal part of the world, even if not understood, and obviously magic had been involved in Cuchulain's wasting illness. 'What will happen now?' they wanted to know.

Emer sat in a tight knot of tension. 'I've given my husband into Fand's care,' she said, her voice strained and thin. 'Allow her until sunrise to do whatever she will.'

Conor mac Nessa nodded approval. 'Cuchulain has often told us there is no jealousy in you; now, we see the proof of it. You are a wife without blemish, Emer.'

Looking at the small, amber-haired woman, he saw the drooping eyelids and the mole beside her mouth and knew she was not beautiful as Deirdre had been beautiful. Yet suddenly he envied his Hound.

Conor mac Nessa pushed the thought away.

At dawn, a crowd gathered at the door of the Speckled House. Conall unbarred it and they entered, not knowing what to expect.

Pale and drawn but very much himself, the champion of Ulster sat on the edge of the couch and attempted a shaky grin. 'I'm better,' he said.

Emer flung herself into his arms, pressing her lips against his eyes, his cheeks, his hair. She wanted to surround him with herself and her joy, her relief. She tried to hug him all over at once . . . and then she realised the couch on which he had lain was soaked with water.

Water dripping from it, running in rivulets to the floor. Water that, in the light from the guttering candles that still burned near the bed, reflected a hundred rainbows.

Emer closed her eyes, struggling to let gratitude override any other thought.

Conor and the Red Branch were shouting and laughing and pounding one another. 'We've got him back,' Laeg cried over and over. 'We've got him back.'

The king's deep voice agreed, 'We do indeed; it only remains to get some food and drink into this man and build up his strength. As quickly as possible, I should think. Who knows when we may need him?'

With one accord, their thoughts turned toward Connaught.

At Cruachan of the Enchantments, Maeve went about her day singing. She radiated the contentment of a fully occupied woman.

Organising the cattle raid to Cooley had been a challenge, not the least of which was persuading her husband to take part. But Maeve had no doubts about the strength of the Ulster resistance; she did not want to venture into Cuchulain's territory undermanned.

Having agreed for himself, Ailell undertook to be certain Fergus

346

was also going. 'We'll give you command of your old comrades,' he offered.

'That's already gone to Cormac Connlongas.'

'Then we'll split them up and give you and Cormac three companies each, with some of the former Red Branch in each company. That should keep you both happy. Cormac is eager to face the Hound of Ulster, he tells me. Something about a twice-broken jaw?'

Fergus snorted. 'Cormac has a poor memory of the Hound if he thinks he can even that score.'

Ailell replied in a sharp voice, 'Are you afraid to face Cuchulain?'

'I am not. Didn't I train him myself? I know him better than anyone, and no man living can say I'm afraid of him.'

'Hmmph. Indeed. You were almost a father to him, some claim. Of course, it would certainly prove your realignment of loyalties beyond all question if you help capture the Brown Bull.'

Fergus looked down at his feet and counted them. Two. One left and one right.

'Well, Fergus?'

He counted the feet again. Right to left this time, but still the same number of feet. Two. Two feet. Definitely. He looked up to find Ailell staring at him. 'An answer, Fergus. I want you going with me – in the name of friendship.'

Ulster. Fergus tilted his head back and looked up at the sky.

'I suppose I will,' he said at last.

Friendship was an incentive Maeve did not trust. She had other rewards in mind. Having chosen to use Finavir as a tool, she began to see many ways to do so. At her mother's bidding, the girl was presenting her considerable charms to Ferdiad mac Daman at every opportunity, but Maeve also began to suggest, from behind her hand, to this one and that one, that Finavir could be a warrior's reward for exceptional valour. Any warrior's – he need only be willing to follow Maeve without question and do whatever she required in order to achieve the prize she was determined to win.

When Ailell learned of her offers, he was furious. 'I never felt you were a motherly woman, but I didn't expect you would try to hand out our daughter like so much bread!'

'If I'd baked the bread, I'd be entitled to give it away. Especially in a good cause. And don't look like a thunderstorm, husband – no matter who gets her, Finavir will have a hero. The man who rides off with her in his cart will have won great victories.'

'Don't you love our children?'

The look Maeve gave Ailell was one of genuine bafflement. 'Of course I do, how can you ask? You would send any of our sons into battle with the injunction to fight well and die well, and if he did both, you would be proud of him. I'm not asking Finavir to die, just to assure us of warriors we need.'

A suspicion he did not like but could not ignore assailed Ailell. 'If she, or any of our children, did die, would you weep?'

Maeve considered. 'They will all die anyway, in time,' she said slowly, 'and be returned to the earth. Should I weep for something I have always expected?' Birth and death are two faces of one goddess, she thought. But how could a man like Ailell be expected to understand?

With the advent of her first child, Maeve had anticipated loss and begun to armour herself against it. She would have Cruachan – which could not die.

On the first moonday after Samhain, the trumpet called the cattle-raiders of Connaught to assemble.

The first company was dressed in speckled cloaks. Their hair was cut square across the bottom, and each man carried a short-hafted stabbing spear. Men of the second company wore cloaks of grey and tunics embroidered with red; their weapons were pronged javelins. Cormac Connlongas, leading the third company, was surrounded by men attired in blue cloaks, their long hair drawn back and iron-bladed swords in their hands.

Fergus mac Roy was also accompanied by three companies of warriors, each distinctively dressed and armed, every one of them prepared to fight for the Donn Cooley.

Every one of them had already heard the stories Fergus could tell about the terrifying battle-feats of Cuchulain, the blood-chilling transformation of the Hound of Ulster. As they waited in the early morning light to begin their march, those memories lay behind their eyes.

In the early morning light, Cuchulain lay in bed beside his wife, still fast asleep. He had not yet fully regained his strength and slept late of a morning.

Emer had been awake for a long time.

During the night, she had snuggled close to him, and he put his arms around her. With all her young warmth, she sought to cancel out his

348

memories, to forget the water-soaked couch in the Speckled House. When his penis rose demandingly, pressing into her belly, she had felt a surge of triumph over amorphous magic. *This* was Setanta, solid and real and *hers*.

Then he murmured a name into her hair. Was the name Fand? She stiffened, instantly alert. Her nose seemed to catch a whiff of seawater, tangy and fresh. I am here with you! Emer cried out silently, locking her arms around her husband. He entered her at once, plunging hard and deep – but at the same time she received the impression of a third body in the bed with them, partially merged with his, one half-dissolved into the other.

Emer's heart leaped so wildly, it stopped the breath in her throat. Was she feeling the flesh of the Tuatha de Danann through the flesh of the Hound of Ulster, man and immortal joined, a woman of magic trying to occupy Emer's husband, to claim him with the fragrance of seafoam. . . ?'

You shall not, he is mine! Emer's whole being cried out. She clutched Cuchulain with all her strength, concentrating mind and body. In the lonely darkness, she wrestled with the memory inhabiting their bed.

A sense of excitement seized her. Child of a warrior race, she would fight for this man.

The other presence faded, then came back stronger than before. Heat pulsed from Cuchulain's body. The battle had become sexual; Emer felt the deep, sweet throbbing Cuchulain always caused in her, yet overlaid was another set of rhythms, a different range of responses tingling along her nerve endings.

Was this what *they* felt together, she asked the darkness.

She squeezed her eyes shut and pressed her face into Cuchulain's shoulder.

The climax was the exploding of suns.

Emer lay in the fading afterglow and wondered about gods and men. And who, and what, her husband was. And how much of him she would ever truly have. And who else had a claim on him.

There were so many claims made on him.

I will be faithful, she promised herself, no matter what he does. It's a pity fidelity is a woman's virtue, one men prize in their wives but not in themselves.

He was restored, that was what mattered. Over and over she reminded herself, that was what mattered.

★

And on the first moonday after Samhain, Maeve and her raiders set forth from Cruachan. Chariot-chiefs and spear carriers, slingers and men skilled with the sword, druids to interpret omens and bards to commemorate the event and satirists to insult anyone who failed in courage and physicians to care for any who were injured, herders for the cattle they hoped to steal and porters for the plunder they meant to take, plus the usual assortment of slaves and hangers-on.

An army to invade Ulster.

6 At the end of the first day's march, the cattle-raiders made their camp close to fresh water at Cúil Silinne. Scouts Maeve had sent into Ulster before departure had brought back the news of the destroyed bog roads. Fergus mac Roy had not suggested that route anyway; so far he had offered nothing helpful at all. But Maeve had immediately chosen a route along the southern reaches of Ulster towards the east coast, then northward to Cooley, passing very close to Cuchulain and Dun Dalgan: the Gap of the North which was guarded by the Hound.

Inevitable, it seemed. The destruction of the western accesses only made it more so. Coincidence is the tool the gods use to keep their workings anonymous, Maeve thought to herself.

In the first night's camp at Cúil Silinne, Maeve ordered her charioteer to make a circle of the site as the raiders came in, so she could see who was eager and who was dragfooted.

Meanwhile, Ailell had set up a tent and had his cooking things unpacked. His belly was hollow, and he was thankful to have Fergus with him, a male companion of his own rank with whom he could share the food and the battle talk. The two men traded bones and war stories beside a campfire while Maeve went on her tour of inspection, accompanied by her driver and the dog called Baiscne.

She returned with fire in her eyes.

Ailell was propped on one elbow, about to thrust a gobbet of roast venison into his mouth. When he saw his wife approaching, he gulped the food whole before she could snatch it for herself.

But Maeve was not interested in food.

She planted herself in front of her husband and confronted him with her hands on her hips. 'We would be very foolish to go one step farther,' she announced, 'with your kinsmen from Leinster in our band.'

'What's wrong with them? They came to Cruachan with me, they've followed me for years. Hard warriors all.'

'Too hard, that's what's wrong with them. They make my Connaughtmen look bad. Your lot have set up their camps and built

351

fires and filled bellies while the rest are still quarrelling over campsites. Now, your lot have harpers playing and servants polishing their weapons. If we take them to Ulster with us, they'll claim the best of the spoils as their just due.'

'Some of that will be claimed by the Red Branch men,' Fergus drawled.

'You see? Quarrelling and division at once. Your followers are making trouble the first night.'

Ailell rolled his eyes towards Fergus. Women, his expression said. 'Let them stay here, then.'

'I can't do that either. As soon as we're out of sight, they would undoubtedly run back to Cruachan and plunder it while my back is turned and the Connaughtmen are away.'

'So what do you propose to do with them?'

Fergus, who enjoyed watching other people struggling with difficult decisions, scratched his belly and helped himself to another skinful of Ailell's wine. How would Conor mac Nessa grasp this nettle, he wondered.

An idea came to him. 'Do what we did with the Red Branch,' he suggested. 'Divide some of the Leinstermen among each of the other companies. That way, we'll still have their strength at arms, but they can make no claims as a unit.'

Maeve tried to find fault with the strategy but could not. 'It was a sad day for Ulster when you vacated the kingship, Fergus mac Roy.'

'I think not. I got older faster than I got smarter.'

'We all do,' Ailell assured him.

In the morning, they resumed the eastward march, with Ailell's Leinstermen scattered throughout the band. Some of them ran out at intervals to hunt for the next night's meal, and soon the porters were staggering under a heavy load of venison, for the land swarmed with red deer.

When the raiders had feasted that night, their bellies were so gorged they could not sleep well. Duffach could not sleep at all. He sat up, crouching on his hams beside the dying campfire, rubbing his aching stomach and staring into the coals.

Others joined him, sharing the miseries of the overfed. To pass the time, they began speculating on Maeve's obsession for the Brown Bull of Cooley.

'There was a story I heard,' said a round-faced, harsh-voiced Connaughtman, 'about two pig-keepers who were friends. They may

352

have been magic people, I don't remember any more. But they may have been. Each was a proud man, and they fell to arguing over which had the finer herd of pigs. They fought over the question until their friendship was shredded, and still they fought. They fought until they killed each other and their spirits entered crows, and still they fought. Next they were worms, and fought, and when their spirits were unhoused yet again, they became – '

'Maeve and Ailell!' someone whooped.

'Not necessarily,' said the former Beetle of Ulster. 'Those two contentious spirits just might be housed in the two bulls. When we capture the Donn Cooley and turn him into a pen with Fionnbanach, we could see some mighty fighting.'

The other men laughed and stamped their feet, and the ale-skins began going the rounds again.

'I'll tell you when we'll see some real fighting,' said one of the Connaughtmen who followed Cormac Connlongas. 'When I look across my shield at the Hound of Ulster.'

Duffach reached for the ale-skin. 'Intend to kill him all by yourself, do you?'

'I could. I'm as good as he is, any day. From what I've heard, I think that Cuchulain is not a champion but a madman, and madmen are careless. Crows can drink his blood as easily as that of any other warrior, and I mean to spill it for them and take his head. Then I'll be celebrated as the one who killed him.'

Duffach raked the other with his eyes. The man was drunk, but he was tall and broad and serious. Duffach shouted towards the nearest fireglow, 'Fergus, are you awake? Come over here; we have the brave lad who's going to kill Cuchulain with us.'

Fergus soon joined them and gave the braggart a second visual examination. 'You're making a common enough mistake,' he said, 'but those who've made it before you are dead.'

'Perhaps they didn't have reason to fight as hard as I will fight.'

'And what exceptional reason is yours?'

The man hesitated, glancing at the faces watching him in the light of the dying fire. 'Maeve's offered her daughter to whoever takes Cuchulain down,' he said.

Fergus rocked slightly as if he had taken a blow, then turned and went back to his own tent. There he lay, thinking of the number of causes that fuelled this cattle raid, not the least of which had now been revealed as a determination to kill Cuchulain.

Cuchulain, who never harmed anyone unless he or those he was pledged to protect were attacked.

Cuchulain, whom Fergus most often chose to envision as the bright, bold, brawling little lad who had come to Emain Macha alone on a brilliant summer's day, armed with a hurley stick.

The rest of us grow old and crusty, Fergus thought. But not Cuchulain.

Had not Cathbad the druid once predicted a short life for him – a short life filled with fame?

His life shall not end yet if I can prevent it, Fergus resolved.

He left his tent and went in search of Ferdiad mac Daman.

Though he owned a good leather tent, Ferdiad frequently slept under the sky. The armour in which he lived made it difficult for him to be comfortable anywhere. He had hollowed out a little space for himself in the earth and filled it with moss, packed down here and fluffed up there to compensate for the bulges and hollows of his armour. He lay with his face turned to the stars.

At the sound of approaching footsteps he was at once on his feet, with a blade in his hand.

'It's just me,' Fergus reassured him. 'I got lonely for a friendly face and the accents of the Red Branch.'

Ferdiad's face could be described in several ways, but not as friendly. Since he left Ulster, he had kept it closed, denying anyone access. The thoughts behind it were his alone.

'You ate too much,' he said bluntly, 'so now you can't sleep. I never eat too much.'

'Indeed, you are practically perfect,' Fergus replied. 'I don't know how Cuchulain could tolerate you.'

His friend's name brought the faintest trace of warmth into Ferdiad's voice. 'A tolerant man, the Hound.'

'They're going to try to kill him, him specifically, you know.'

'Who is?'

'All of them.' Fergus waved his hand in a gesture meant to indicate the entire army. 'They're marching into Ulster to slaughter Cuchulain.'

'You exaggerate, Fergus. We're going after the Brown Bull of Cooley, remember? And Cuchulain will be but one of the Red Branch warriors trying to keep him from us.'

'Do you think so? What about the Pangs? By the time we reach Ulster, Conor's fighting men could be lying on their beds moaning and groaning – except for Cuchulain. He could find himself alone while all this lot hurl themselves against him. I can't sit idly by and watch that happen. It's unfair.

'In fact, I'm rather surprised you came on this expedition, Ferdiad. I never thought you would set yourself against your friend.'

'Who said I would?'

'I'm certain Maeve expects it.'

'She expects loyalty from me since she took me in, and I've given her loyalty.'

'You're so good you're boring,' Fergus commented. 'Cuchulain's good, but at least he's not boring.'

Ferdiad ignored this. 'If we do find ourselves fighting the Hound, I don't intend to be one of his attackers,' he confided. 'I'll find some other job to do for Maeve.'

'I'm glad to hear it, though that will only diminish the odds against Cuchulain by a tiny amount.' The former king of Ulster belched gently. 'There's the last of my venison leaving me. Perhaps I'll be able to get some sleep at last. But before I go, let me ask you something. You're young and strong and fast-footed. If I were to send a message to Ulster, to Cuchulain specifically, warning of this invasion – would you take it?'

There was an uncomfortable silence. At last Ferdiad said, 'I cannot, Fergus.' He sounded pained.

'Why not?'

'I told you – Maeve and Ailell granted me sanctuary, a home and a landholding, when we came here from Ulster. I can't betray them.'

'Even to see the Hound again? It used to be said of you that the two of you were closer than a man and his shadow.'

Another silence ensued. 'Honour,' said Ferdiad mac Daman.

Fergus left him then and returned to his tent. But in the night, he occasionally heard the distinctive chitinous click of horn body armour as a man wearing it paced around the campsite, unable to sleep.

Serves you right, thought Fergus.

Men who cannot rest grow quarrelsome, and before the night ended, fights had broken out in this group and that one. By dawn, many were red-eyed, and there were more bloody wounds than sphagnum moss to heal them.

'I don't think this lot can be shaped into one army,' Ailell told his wife.

Fergus had a suggestion. 'Before they waste themselves fighting each other rather than Ulstermen, why not split them into a number of groups with separate leaders and let us march apart from one another, along different tracks. We'll all come to Ulster in the end, we can agree on a meeting place.'

For a second time, the grizzled warrior won a nod of approval from Maeve. 'You've proved your value to us, Fergus. A man of your experience should be employed leading the best fighting men, so I want you to take the first group yourself.'

Fergus saluted her with an expression so bland that Ailell, who was watching, felt a powerful presentiment. You old fox, he thought. What are you about?

Waiting until the confusion of breaking camp had reached its peak, Fergus led his men out – not eastward, but along a meandering track that would considerably delay their progress into Ulster. Once they were well out of sight of the rest of the raiders, he summoned a young man he had once trained in the Boys' Troop, a fellow who still believed his former instructor to be a wellspring of authority.

'Slip away from us unobserved if you can,' Fergus ordered, 'and plunge straightway into Ulster. Get a message to Cuchulain, wherever he may be. Warn him that Connaught is sending warriors into Ulster with two goals in mind: a raid to seize the Brown Bull of Cooley and a deliberate attempt to take Cuchulain's head. I send this warning not for the sake of Conor mac Nessa' – Fergus spat out the name – 'but for the Hound of Ulster.'

Fergus waited until his messenger was safely away, then signalled resumption of the march. They had not been long underway when they heard the clatter of a war-cart overtaking them.

Maeve came along their trail at a gallop. Her red hair writhed around her furious face, and her cloak floated out behind her on the wind of her passing.

'I came to be certain your men had enough provisions to last until they could hunt or plunder,' she said. 'Good fist I made of it, coming to find out; otherwise I would never have known what an odd route you had taken.

'You aren't heading into Ulster at all, are you, mac Roy?'

Fergus tried to think of something clever to say, but his mind grated shut on rusty hinges. The attempt at misdirection was too obvious to deny; anything he might say would make matters worse.

Drawing in a deep breath, he straightened his spine to show her the full size and splendour of Fergus mac Roy, former king of Ulster, former champion of Conor mac Nessa, former instructor of the famed Boys' Troop.

Dignity was the only armour he had.

A thin rain began to fall. Maeve and Fergus watched each other through it, he with the resignation of a man who has done all he can, she with the narrowed eyes of a person trying to see into another's spirit.

'Lead your men back to join the rest of us,' she said at last, in a voice of chipped flint. 'And after this, be sure you stay where I can see you at all times.'

The march resumed. Eastward.

His strength now fully restored, Cuchulain was about to leave Emain Macha with his wife and charioteer, when an exhausted runner came staggering in from the west. 'Big cattle raid coming,' the man gasped. 'From Cruachan. To Cooley. Fergus sends . . . warning.'

Conor hastily assembled his Red Branch. 'Take bands of warriors who are loyal to you, men from clans nearest each of the approaches, and stand guard in force,' he ordered. 'Even you grey beards' – his glance swept the group – 'take weapons and men and be prepared to fight. I won't have a large raiding party of Connaughtmen crossing Ulster!'

Sualtim, formerly lord of Dun Dalgan, was among the greybeards. When the frost of winter settled into a warrior's joints, he found more time to sit by the fire, reliving his exploits verbally, than to stand leaning on his spear in some windy mountain pass. If he had done his duty and contributed strong sons to replace himself, he was allowed this diminished duty with no loss to his pride, so long as he occasionally still swung the sword. Until death, a warrior must swing the sword.

Now, every man was given an assignment, and Sualtim's post lay south of Emain Macha, though not so far as Dun Dalgan. He and Cuchulain could hardly avoid leaving the royal stronghold at the same time. Forced to occupy the same road for a while, the two jogged along together. When the silence began to seem unnatural, Sualtim remarked, 'You've left your wife back there, with the king?'

'At his suggestion.'

'Ah. Of course. She'll be safe there, with invaders going past Dun Dalgan if they mean to reach Cooley. Sensible move.'

Cuchulain looked sideways at the older man. Aren't you going to ask about my mother's safety, he wondered silently. Or have you forgotten she exists?

Laeg could feel the tension in the Hound beside him, but kept his eyes on the road and his hands on the reins. At times a charioteer must be invisible; it was the only magic required of him.

'I could have taken Emer to Dun Dalgan in full confidence of keeping her safe there,' Cuchulain said. 'The dun has been so strengthened, I have no difficulty protecting my womenfolk.'

Sualtim did not respond to this. Instead, he said, 'You'll be standing guard at the Gap of the North, I suppose?'

'I will.'

'What clans will you summon to stand with you?'

Cuchulain scowled. 'Do you think I'll need help? The Hound of Ulster?' His voice was tight in his throat. Reaching past Laeg, he lifted a weapon from the assortment carried in the chariot. 'This is the Gae Bulga,' he said, 'as good to me as a company of men, and more deadly. And those,' he gestured over the chariot rim, at the wheels, 'are sickle blades attached to my spokes. Whirling at the gallop, they can cut the legs from man or horse. Few men can even lift the sword I swing, and fewer still can face me when I'm angry.

'I assure you, Sualtim, I am quite capable of fulfilling my responsibilities to the king and to Ulster by myself alone, if need be. *I* never fail in my responsibilities.'

He hurled those last words like stones at the man who had run away, leaving a wife and small boy behind at Dun Dalgan.

Sualtim had been a warrior for a long time, he did not flinch. Indeed, he half bowed his head as if accepting a blow he knew he deserved. Then he gave Cuchulain a direct look.

'You're so young, you still think it's easy, don't you?' he said. The chariotway branched just ahead of them. With a gesture to indicate the westward direction to his charioteer, Sualtim turned aside, and as soon as he was off the *slighe* sent his horses racing away at full gallop.

Cuchulain did not turn to watch him go.

'The Gap of the North for us, is it?' Laeg asked, to be certain.

'It is, but not yet. I promised to do a favour for Leary Buadach before taking up my position. He has a kinswoman called Niamh, who is related to him by fosterage. She lives to the south of here, and her parents are very recently dead, so he's concerned about her. I agreed to collect the girl and deliver her to the safety of Dun Dalgan before the invaders arrive.'

'But what happens if Maeve gets here first, Cuchulain? If we're going to go careening around Ulster picking up all the unprotected women . . .'

'I promised a brother in the Red Branch,' said the Hound, closing the matter. 'Besides, since Fergus managed to send us a warning, I think

358

we can expect him to delay Maeve's advance as long as he can to give us time to be ready. He hasn't deserted us as totally as we thought, I hope Conor appreciates the fact. Some fathers are more responsible than others . . .' Cuchulain's voice faded away.

Laeg urged the horses to the gallop, and they hurried southward.

They had covered quite a distance when Cuchulain had an idea. 'Laeg, do you know the crossroads at Cúil Sibrille?'

'I do of course.'

'If Maeve means to get to Cooley, and hasn't been able to come through the riverlands, she will have to come by way of that crossroads. Just in case we are caught out and haven't finished delivering this Niamh to Dun Dalgan, I think I'll leave a message for her there. A little something to frighten her men and slow them down until I'm ready to face them.' He chuckled. 'Whip the team, Laeg! At the run, for Cúil Sibrille!'

Puzzled but obedient, Laeg sent the Grey and the Black at top speed. Beside him rode Cuchulain, legs braced wide, head thrown back in exultation. He was glorying in the speed and the wind whipping through his hair; the sense of going and doing that could release a man from the static pain of emotions.

He was racing Time and Fate. He might win, he might lose. But he was gloriously alive.

By the time they reached Cúil Sibrille crossroads, where two cart tracks met beside an oak forest, both men and horses were weary. They had taken only one rest, a night camp, and eaten sparingly. But at the crossroads Cuchulain was pleased to find a standing stone which he had noticed before due to a singular peculiarity it possessed.

The oak wood stretched out fingers of saplings towards the stone. Cuchulain selected one of these, tore it up by the roots, and began carving figures on it with the point of a knife.

Laeg watched as Cuchulain's blade etched abrupt lines parallel to one another in the soft wood, then slashed others at angles to make some picture in his mind come alive.

When the carving was finished, Cuchulain wiped his hands on his woollen tunic and stepped back to survey his work. Satisfied, he turned to run his fingers along the face of the pillar stone until he detected a remembered fracture.

He grinned. 'Stand back, Laeg.'

Seizing the sapling, he drove it against the stone with such force that the tree was wedged firmly into the fault line. The stone groaned in protest but did not break apart.

Laeg's mouth fell open.

Cuchulain tugged at the slender tree several times to make certain it was tightly held, then said to his charioteer, 'Find us some fresh water to drink, then let's collect that kinswoman of Leary's while we have plenty of daylight.'

Meanwhile, in spite of Maeve's suspicious scrutiny, Fergus was doing all he could to delay the progress of the cattle-raiders. He found himself with a broken chariot axle and they must wait for him, because Maeve had no intention of going on and leaving him behind to do worse mischief. His team got loose and ran away and had to be caught; some of his followers wandered off into a wood and needed to be found before the march could get underway again.

And at night, by the campfire, he told additional frightening tales of the prowess of the Hound of Ulster. Conor had made a similar attempt by sending out bards, but the effect was surely heightened when the stories were related by a gruff and grizzled warrior who claimed actually to have seen what he was telling. The firelight cast grotesque shadows on the faces of his listeners, and the dark seemed to huddle very close around them.

'When the warp-spasm comes upon him, Cuchulain turns into a monster,' Fergus assured his audience. 'A sight to scorch your eyeballs. His Rage makes his hair stand upright on his head and flame leaps from hair tip to hair tip, while a fountain of black blood bursts from the crown of his skull and pours down his shoulders, making the earth so slippery around him that men trying to close with him fall down and are helpless. His mouth gapes open; the fangs of a wolfhound glitter to rend and tear your flesh. The joints of his body twist this way and that, his erect penis goes before him like a javelin and can crush in the side of a chariot. With each hand, he can lift a full-grown ox . . . and its yoke,' Fergus added.

Late in life, he was discovering he had a gift for storytelling.

The exiles from Ulster supported his claims. Cuchulain was Ulster's hero, and his glory reflected on every man born in the province. At night by the campfires, they did not let themselves imagine facing the actual Cuchulain, but vied with one another to enrich Fergus's stories and make them even better.

In the cold light of wintry dawn, they felt differently. They glanced at each other and looked away again, their faces as grey as the light. Is Cuchulain really that terrible, each man wondered. And what will I do if he comes after me?

The march across Erin seemed to be taking a long time.

When they entered Ulster, however, Conor mac Nessa knew at once. No messenger came running to tell him; his own belly conveyed the news. One moment he was sitting on his bench in the House of the King, listening to a harper; the next moment he was doubled up in pain. His insides writhed as his belly muscles threatened to crush his organs. Breathing was impossible. He could feel his eyes bulge from their sockets. Sweat spurted along his hairline.

Sitting across the firepit from him, Nessa took one look at her son and pressed her hand to her bosom. 'Is it. . . ?'

'The Pangs,' Conor affirmed grimly.

Sent to guard the access routes into Ulster, most of the Red Branch had departed Emain Macha. Some of the older ones had remained behind to guard the king and serve as leaders for local clan-warriors. Now, Conor heard Cuscraid the Stammerer, who had been seated off to his right, begin swearing painfully with no trace of a stammer. Next, fierce Gergind whimpered like a child. Ernan of the Iron slid from his bench and curled into a ball on the floor.

'Connaught,' Conor managed to gasp to his mother as she bent over him. 'They must be bringing . . . a whole army!'

The Pangs that were attacking the fighting men of Ulster were having no effect, however, on the Red Branch rebels who now followed Maeve and Ailell. Once they had renounced the northland, the curse did not seem to apply to them. They marched upright with bristling weapons and rapacious intent, back into the land they knew.

The Ulstermen intended to stop them lay helpless, except for Cuchulain.

7 Two Connaught clan-chieftains were leading the advance, a pair who always wanted to be in the forefront where they could avoid dust in their eyes or mud spattering their clothes. They were following the main trackway leading from west to east across southern Ulster now, and the going was not difficult. The day was overcast; the brightest object to be seen was the silver trail a snail left crossing a stone.

The crossroads of Cúil Sibrille lay directly in their path.

The two chieftains ordered their charioteers to draw rein. 'Do you see that?' 'I do, but I don't believe it.'

Stepping from their carts, they advanced slowly with drawn swords. An acid odour of superstition poured from them, making the horses roll their eyes.

The two men stared at the grey pillar of a standing stone with a tree driven through its heart.

The raiders were coming up behind them with a rumble and a roar, trampling meadows and muddying streams. They had already plundered a number of isolated landholdings on their way to capture the Brown Bull.

They stopped abruptly at the crossroads of Cúil Sibrille.

The leaders gathered around the stone. Maeve, who rode in a war-cart with her dog Baiscne and an assortment of comfortable cushions, stepped down to see what was causing the delay. Brocc the Badger was just saying, 'See where some giant bird has left claw marks in the wood!'

Ailell squinted at the sapling. 'Those aren't claw marks, they're *ogham* signs.'

'You know *ogham*, don't you?' asked his wife.

Though a son of the king of Leinster, Ailell had been an indifferent pupil. 'The druid taught me, but that was, ah, a long time ago. But Fergus was a king. Here, mac Roy, read this.'

Fergus scrutinised the lines scored deep in the wood. He traced them with a blunt forefinger while the others shifted their feet and stared at the tree in the stone. He hummed in the back of his throat. Then he told

362

the crowd around him, 'This says: Do not come this way unless you have a man who can do what I have done here. And it bears the mark of the Hound of Ulster.'

A sigh rippled through the warriors as each tried to imagine himself driving a tree through a stone.

'Not a good route, this,' someone muttered.

'Are you a flock of sheep, to panic at the first sound of thunder?' Maeve yelled. 'We go this way, there is no other.'

Fergus cleared his throat. 'We could go through the forest and avoid the crossroads altogether.'

She swung around to follow the direction of his pointing finger. 'We can't get all these men through there.'

'Oh, we might have to hew down a few trees, but we have plenty of strong arms. It might take a bit longer than using the road, but do you want to risk a rebellion? None of this lot looks as if he could drive a tree through a stone, and they're taking the warning seriously, just look at their faces.'

'I am no longer pleased with any advice mac Roy offers,' Maeve said to Ailell.

'He makes sense, though,' her husband admitted. 'Which had you rather give up – the easy road or the entire cattle raid?'

'Cut down that forest!' Maeve shouted to the men.

While the trees were being felled, she paced restlessly with her hands behind her back and the dog Baiscne at her heels glancing up with eyes full of worship whenever she spoke to him. Every tree that crashed down was one less obstacle between herself and the Brown Bull.

Between herself and Cuchulain. She knew the Hound of Ulster was waiting for her somewhere along the way; she knew it in her bones as a woman knows she will meet a lover.

He will not limit my reach, she vowed.

The season was winter, the days were short. It took two of them to march the distance they would have covered in one day of sunseason. And the weather was beginning to curdle. When the cattle raiders fell into an exhausted slumber after opening a way through the oak forest, snow fell on them. In the morning, it was banked as high as the hubs of the chariot wheels, and everyone was stiff with cold. Getting underway took a long time.

But Cuchulain had made a late start himself. Finding Niamh had taken time. The girl was very young and very beautiful and very frightened, and she had hidden herself and had to be coaxed out. And comforted.

After delivering her to Dun Dalgan, Cuchulain hurried crosslands to Cúil Sibrille only to find a mire of muddied snow and slush, an *ogham* composed of footprints and chariot tracks, but no army.

'They've gone ahead of us,' Cuchulain said angrily to Laeg, who was looking unusually pale behind his freckles. 'And she's brought more than a few cattle-raiders with her – these are the tracks of an army.'

'To capture one bull?'

'She doesn't mean to stop with the bull. I tell you, Laeg, Maeve wants to humble Ulster. If she succeeds, the northland will be tributary to Connaught before any of us grow much older. Quickly, into the chariot and let's try to head her off; we may encounter some of our own warriors along the way to help.'

Laeg's face was the colour of cheese curd. 'I don't think so, Cuchulain,' he said sorrowfully. 'Can you drive? I have a problem.'

'Oh, Laeg . . . is there anything I can do for you?'

'There is,' the other said before the pain swept over him altogether. 'Tell me how you did the magic with the tree and the stone.'

'That wasn't magic. I can't do magic.'

'But I saw it!'

'I can't do magic at all,' Cuchulain said insistently, taking the reins from Laeg's fingers as the charioteer doubled up in the bottom of the war-cart.

Cuchulain knew this land by heart. He drove where no trackway could be seen until at last he was certain he was ahead of the raiders again. At the head of a stream that they must cross, he hewed down a tree to block their way, then hid Laeg and the chariot out of sight.

Soon enough two advance guards came trotting along in their war-carts, chatting with their charioteers. They were well ahead of the main body.

'Now,' said Cuchulain to the sword Hardhead as he drew it from his belt.

The sun had barely moved in the sky when Maeve and Ailell arrived to find four men's heads watching them glassy-eyed from the tops of poles thrust into the stream bed.

'We never heard a thing,' Ailell said in astonishment.

'The Hound of Ulster works very swiftly,' commented Fergus mac Roy.

'One man killed all four?'

'Without working up a sweat, I'd say.'

'But these two were famous fighters,' argued Ailell, 'and their charioteers would not have surrendered their own lives easily.'

Fergus shrugged.

'Move that log that blocks our way and let's go on,' Maeve ordered. When men did not run to do her bidding, she lost her temper. 'He only did this to frighten you! There will be no plunder for the last man to move!'

They moved.

When they reached the Plain of the Pig-Keepers, they found their way blocked again, by a much larger tree that had been chopped down and dragged across the gap opening onto the plain. Cut in its bark was an *ogham*, which Fergus read: Do not pass this oak unless a warrior in his chariot can leap it at the first attempt.

Wheel ruts approached the log on one side and went away from it on the other, toward Cooley. 'The Hound has already accomplished this feat,' said Fergus. 'Here is his mark again. He challenges us to do likewise.'

'Do it then,' Maeve snarled. 'We must have three tens of men who can do it without drawing breath.'

But they did not. One after the other, the warriors in their chariots drove up to the fallen tree, whipped and goaded their horses, then had to turn aside in failure. Several carts were smashed in the attempt, and several horses ruined.

Ailell finally put a stop to it. 'You're destroying yourselves, you idiots. If the Hound issues a challenge, we should reply in kind. Who will offer to meet him in single combat and get him out of our way?'

White eyeballs rolled in Ailell's direction. No one spoke.

'You don't know how to get things done,' Maeve told her husband. 'Send to the rear of the army, to the servants and porters and followers, and have my daughter Finavir brought up here.'

When Finavir stood with downcast eyes beside her mother, Maeve looked from one warrior to another. 'Now who will challenge Cuchulain and kill him for me?' she enquired.

A man called Fraech mac Fidaig winked at Finavir and stepped forward. 'The champion of Ulster is as good as dead,' he promised.

Leaving the group behind, he went out alone with all the weapons he could carry and began shouting at the distant hills, 'I challenge the champion to single combat!'

Maeve collected nine additional warriors and told them to go after him in case he should need assistance; she wanted to be certain Cuchulain was slain.

Ailell was appalled. 'That's not the way it's done, woman! You dishonour us. You don't understand warfare.'

Her face was set in hard lines. 'I understand winning.'

Fraech found Cuchulain bathing in a stream in spite of the cold of the day. When the champion heard someone shouting for him, he rose from the water and turned his left side toward the voice in insult.

By then the nine had caught up with Fraech mac Fidaig. 'Is that short fellow the one causing us so much trouble?' Fraech asked them with a laugh. 'I don't need help, except to carry his belongings and head back to Maeve when I go to claim her daughter. Stay here and observe how I handle him.'

He ran towards the stream. When he splashed into the water, its coldness shocked the breath from his lungs. Cuchulain, who had been in long enough to be accustomed to it, was on top of him at once.

Fraech opened his eyes to find himself staring at pebbles on the stream bed while two powerful hands choked the life from him.

When Cuchulain stepped out of the water, the nine men had fled.

They reported themselves as having barely escaped with their lives after a battle of incredible ferocity. Maeve observed there was no blood on their clothing or wounds in their flesh, and gave a disgusted snort. 'We go on,' she said. 'And we shall find better men to match against the Hound.'

But before they dragged the tree out of their way, Fergus mac Roy, for reasons of his own and with a grin on his face, leaped his team and chariot over it.

Relentlessly, the raiders from Connaught advanced through Ulster. No body of warriors came out to meet them. There was only the Hound roaming somewhere up ahead, putting obstacles in their path whenever he could, taunting and terrifying them.

The duration of Macha's Curse was nine nights. Judging from the time of the onset of Laeg's pains, Cuchulain could guess when the warriors of Ulster would begin to recover. He knew they would not all be restored to themselves at the same time, for the Pangs seemed to affect some sooner than others. But one thing appeared certain. There would be no one able to fight with him before Maeve reached Cooley and the bull.

Beside his campfire at night, Cuchulain thought of Emer. Amid the undulating hills, he missed the hollow of her back.

The only company he had was Laeg, who was so miserable he merely wanted to be left alone.

Since the days when he had served as Cullen's watchdog, Cuchulain had rarely been without a companion. His was not a way of life that allowed a man much solitude. Yet now he might have been the only person on the earth. There was no one to talk with and no one to be quiet with; only by the hills and the sky.

And an army coming to kill him.

Cuchulain hated the erosion of waiting. At the first flush of dawnlight, he stationed himself on a ridge with a long view across the grassy plain that Maeve's troops must traverse. As he faced southward, the sea between Erin and Alba was to his left hand and the undulating grasslands and woodlands of southern Ulster were to his right. Rough meadowland, broken rocky outcroppings, tumbles of gorse, and a high, wild sky surrounded him. Below him, a narrow river wound down on to the plain.

The weather was improving. A fair morning, with just enough mist lingering in the hollows to keep him from making out the details of the advancing invaders as they appeared in the distance.

I wonder if Ferdiad is among them, he thought.

In spite of the obstacles Cuchulain had thrown in her way, Maeve was satisfied that she was making progress. As they came up from a wooded lowland and swept out across a plain of winterdimmed grass, she surveyed her chariot-chiefs and spear carriers with the pleasure another woman might take in a neatly aligned row of bowls on her shelf.

'Stay closer together,' she ordered the warriors. 'And don't talk so much. When you're talking you're not watching around you, and we could be ambushed.'

The spear carrier who was walking nearest Ferdiad's chariot was a leathery man with a red hooked nose that dripped perpetually. Talking was his favourite pastime. He considered being silent worse than being ambushed. 'What does she know?' he grumbled. 'It's himself who should be giving the orders. A man who'd let his wife speak for him is no man at all.'

'Have you a wife?' Ferdiad enquired out of idle interest.

'I do have, and she knows her place. She defers to me in everything.'

'Then you don't have a wife, you have a foot-wiper.'

The spear carrier glared up at the man in the chariot. 'And what unlucky woman is sheath for your sword?'

'I'm not married.'

'There you are. You're as fit to judge me as Maeve is to lead men. Lads!' he called to the nearest marchers. 'See this fellow who knows all about women without having one wife!'

There was an explosion of derisive laughter. Ferdiad had not bothered to make himself popular among the Connaughtmen. In the feasting hall, he sat alone, his actions silently stating he did not want to be where he was. Furthermore, he was of chariot rank, exciting the natural enmity of every man who must travel on two aching feet.

'What's wrong with you, mac Daman?' someone hooted. 'Don't you like women?'

'Perhaps women don't like him,' another suggested sarcastically. 'Aren't you fully equipped, mac Daman? Is that why you hide yourself behind horny armour?'

Maeve heard the outburst of shouts and laughter. Whirling around in her chariot to see who was ignoring her orders, she almost stepped on Baiscne. The dog was no bigger than a newborn lamb, but he was cunning; he knew a small creature was safest close to a large protector. He clung to Maeve like the toes on her feet, and she constantly had to avoid trampling him.

The wind brought the insults being hurled at Ferdiad to Maeve's listening ears. Her eyes glittered. 'Every man has some weakness,' she remarked to Baiscne, leaning down to pick him up. The little dog wriggled against her chest in ecstasy. 'Mine is you,' she told him.

They were approaching a small river bordered by willow and hazel that might conceal an ambush. At Maeve's signal the raiders halted, and a party of six heroes led by Meslir of the White Knees advanced cautiously to reconnoitre the ford.

When they did not return, Ailell and Cormac took a company of swordfighters and spearmen and followed them.

They found Meslir and his companions floating face downward in the river, surrounded by crimson froth. Not a twig was stirring on the trees along the shore.

'The Hound of Ulster was here,' declared Fergus mac Roy.

Maeve and Ailell had to resort to threats and invective to get the men moving again and through the ford.

Beyond the stream, the land opened on to a broad lap between hills like thighs. From a patch of woodland, a stone came hurtling to crack open the skull of a spear carrier who was following Cormac Connlongas.

Men yelled in surprise as the spear carrier fell on his face. 'What happened?' called Maeve, urging her chariot closer. Responding to the excitement, her little dog jumped up, trying to see over the rim of her war-cart.

The next stone smashed its head and scattered its brains over the inside of the chariot.

'Murderer!' Maeve shrieked. Her voice rose to an insane wail. She flung herself from side to side, raking her face with her fingernails, tearing at her hair.

The attack of the unseen man with the slingshot was all but forgotten; Maeve commanded total attention. Ailell ordered his chariot to her side as quickly as possible, but he could do no more to help her than anyone else. He could only watch as her grief boiled over.

At last Maeve stepped from the chariot with the dog's body in her arms, feeling for the earth with her foot as if she had gone blind.

She had been raised in a society of warriors where life could be brutally short. Humans died; her young first husband had died. Long ago, she had learned to erect shields around herself by not caring too much for anyone she might lose.

But small, weak creatures could take her by surprise and crawl under those shields, as Baiscne had done. She sat cross-legged on the ground, cradling him and murmuring endearments to his ruined head. When Ailell tried to put a consoling hand on her shoulder, she shrugged him off.

'It was only a dog, Maeve.'

'Only a dog? That dog worshipped me; I was a god to him, Ailell! And Cuchulain's killed him. I'll see that Ulsterman dead in return,' she vowed through white lips, 'if it requires blood sacrifice from every warrior in Connaught.'

Maeve's vehemence startled her husband. Retreating, he told Fergus mac Roy, 'It wasn't even a very good dog. Too little to hunt anything but a bone, and crawling with fleas.'

'Lots of people have fleas,' Fergus pointed out.

Watching from concealment in the woods, Cuchulain was also taken aback by Maeve's reaction to what had been an accidental killing of her pet. His stone had been meant for a warrior on the other side of her chariot; the dog had jumped up at the worst possible time.

Search parties were already fanning out, seeking him with savage intent. An element of heightened enmity had been introduced to the conflict.

While Cuchulain dodged and hid, taking advantage of every fold and curve of the land, Maeve's men searched for him. They were afraid to go back and admit they had not found him, but at last the setting sun forced them to return to her empty-handed.

369

'We'll get him tomorrow then,' she said implacably. She was just setting the last stone in place atop a cairn she had raised with her own hands above Baiscne's grave.

Anger made her reckless. At dawn, she spread her war-carts in a broad front across land unprepared for them, hoping to catch the Hound in a net. Some chariots were damaged in the headlong rush, and their drivers had to fall out along the way to repair the vehicles as best they could.

One of the broken war-carts belonged to Orlam, a son of Maeve and Ailell. While he went to a nearby pond to refresh himself, his driver began cutting down a tree to replace the splintered cartshaft. As the charioteer worked, a youth sauntered toward him, whistling off-key. 'What are you doing here?' the fellow asked.

Glancing up, Orlam's charioteer saw a short, dark man with the face of a boy. 'Cutting this tree for a shaft,' he explained. Then, unable to resist boasting, he added, 'I'm with the great army of the west. Connaught. Best fighters in Erin. We've been smashing our war-carts chasing a wild deer called Cuchulain, but soon we'll catch up to him and take his head for Maeve of Cruachan. Then we'll take the plunder of Ulster as well. Join us and share in the loot,' he offered, smiling magnanimously at the little fellow. 'You can help me trim this wood.'

Without a word, the little fellow took the freshly hewn holly-wood into one clenched fist and stripped it clean with a jerk, peeling away bark and branches in one smooth gesture.

With his bare hand.

The charioteer felt the soles of his feet turn cold. 'Who are you?' he whispered.

'Cuchulain.'

'My grief,' muttered the horseman, ardently wishing he were somewhere else.

'Where is your master?' the Hound asked him.

'Over by the pond.'

'Come with me, then. I don't fight with charioteers.' Leading the way, Cuchulain soon found Orlam. While the Connaughtman was still reaching for his sword, the Hound removed his head with one swift slice and handed it, open-mouthed and open-eyed, to the chariot driver. 'Take this to Maeve and Ailell,' he said. 'Tell them it's in place of mine.'

Ailell sobbed when he saw Orlam's severed head, but Maeve's red-rimmed eyes were dry. 'First Baiscne and now this,' she said, as if one loss were no greater than the other.

370

She has turned to stone inside, thought Ailell. His own grief tormented him, he wondered how she could go on. The Donn Cooley could not be worth it. But when he suggested they turn back, she looked at him so wildly he swallowed his words.

'If we give up now, our dead will have died in vain!' Maeve shouted.

'Every loss we suffer will only add fuel to her fire,' her husband told Fergus. 'There's no way out of this now for any of us.'

The toll mounted. Cuchulain never appeared in front of the massed army, yet unlucky individuals encountered him whenever they strayed a few paces too far from their fellows. The bards accompanying the Connaughtmen to memorise their adventures were hard-pressed to keep count of the slain. Famous fighters fell, men who had been fostered in the households of warlords such as Erc of Leinster and Curoi of Munster. Lethan of the Stone Fort was killed, and Reun Round-Head, and all the sons of Garach were cut down as they paused to relieve themselves in a ditch.

The bards would not mention that detail in the retelling. Men slain in a war die gloriously.

Meanwhile, Cuchulain was getting very tired. In order to pick off individual warriors, he had to keep circling the main band as it advanced. Knowing this, the leaders of the companies struggled to force an army of individuals to march together as one unit.

The task proved impossible; Cuchulain caught and killed man after man who thought himself too good to stay with the pack. But his arms were so sore from swinging the sword, there were times he thought he could never lift it again. And when not on his feet fighting, he had to drive the chariot, with Laeg lying helpless in the bottom, or he could never have harried the army as it moved.

There was no time to rest. There was no time to eat. Only time to kill. His clothes were stiff with blood, and some of it was his own.

Driving the Grey of Macha and the Black of Sainglain, Cuchulain breasted a gentle rise and slowed the horses to a walk. The day was fading, a heavy bank of cloud pressed down upon the land, the wind smelled of ice. 'Laeg,' he said to the man curled up at his feet, 'are the Pangs passing yet?'

Without opening his eyes, the charioteer shook his head and groaned.

At that moment, Cuchulain wanted nothing so much in the world as one of the looks of wholehearted faith that a healthy Laeg would have given him. But Laeg no longer believed in anything but pain.

Cuchulain's heart thudded a repetitive drumbeat. Alone, it said, you are alone.

You've been waiting for me, haven't you? I knew it. I understand humans. And I knew you would look for me wherever the call of the battle trumpet sounded.

I had accompanied Maeve's raiders from Connaught, having gone there to let my anger against Cuchulain abate. I am disgusted by the shortsightedness of hard men who choose soft women. Fand, Emer, and their ilk. No real substance to them.

Let Fand heal him, it meant nothing to me. I would not begrudge her a few moments with him, I am bigger than that. I did not even mind the attention he gave to Emer, not really, though I have no doubt she was jealous of every day that he was mine. Soft women always hate me for robbing them of their men, though the part I take is something they do not want. The soft women want life to have one face only, birth and sweet music and gentle weather.

Leaving Cuchulain behind to endure the ministrations of soft women, I had winged for Cruachan, where Maeve promised to stir up a fresh cauldron of excitement. There was a bit of a soft woman inside Maeve, but there was a tiger in her, too. A pity we did not both live in a land where there were tigers – such places have warm climates. Hot summers.

As it was, Maeve set forth on her cattle raid at the start of a long, wet winter. Of course, I flew with her to lend support and encouragement – particularly encouragement.

But along the way, I lost interest in the cause of the Connaughtmen. Maeve's raiders, ricocheting from bravado to cowardice and back again as armies do, began to bore me. I longed for the solitary brilliance of the Hound of Ulster. Aware of his cleverness as he faced the invaders alone, I forgave him his recent foolishness.

Cuchulain had elected to consider himself as only human, yet like a sorcerer, he was attempting to demoralise his enemies with an illusion of omnipotence and invincibility. Had he thought to apply to me for aid, I could have shown him how to do much more. I could have taught him as I had once learned when I – when we – first came to this island where magic springs like grass from the earth.

Magic is but a label for a body of observable circumstance. To deny the reality of that which can be observed is unreasonable, which is why those who use magic effectively are those who reason more clearly than other beings. Theirs is an awareness that springs intuitively from heightened perceptions of the world as it really is. Magicians do not accept a limited reality worked out by the painful intellectual plodding of less gifted individuals.

Magic is a talent carried in the blood and the spirit, but conversely, all those abilities that humans call talent are really forms of magic. Poetry and healing and making music are simply observable expressions of the creative force that is magic.

One with a talent for magic can sense others so gifted, even if he or she never recognises the common thread uniting them. Sometimes the awareness comes strongly; sometimes it departs unexpectedly, leaving a haze in the memory. Yet each of you has encountered magic somewhere, sometime.

Do you remember?

To know a magician, look in the eyes. They are clear and aware. If you see him, he will know that you are seeing him. A magician does not hide behind his eyes; he puts everything into them to be recognised by those who know how. In every culture, the ignorant have mistaken such beings for demons – or gods.

Humans who think they can explain magic or gods have experienced neither. Yet both surround you.

Open the eyes of your spirit and see.

The moment Daire mac Fiachna had seen the warriors of his clan clutching their bellies in pain, he knew the Connaughtmen were sending a whole army to seize his bull. He hastily ordered his herders to drive the Donn Cooley and his cows into a high, hidden valley known as the Black Cauldron, a place unfamiliar to strangers from outside of Cooley. Then he waited, expecting the worst, as Maeve's raiders approached.

Dun Dalgan had stood in their path on the way to Cooley, but as they neared his stronghold, Cuchulain's attacks grew so frenzied that Ailell summoned the chariot-chiefs for a strategy council. 'If we get bogged down here fighting the Hound, we'll likely stay here until the rest of the Ulstermen recover and come howling along to surround us. Then how will you get your bull?' he asked Maeve. 'I propose we circle around Dun Dalgan, avoiding it altogether until we're on our way home again. Then, if there's time, and Cuchulain's been disposed of, we can plunder his fort.'

Maeve nodded her agreement. 'I want the bull. And I want the Hound dead.'

Neither Fergus mac Roy nor Ferdiad mac Daman commented, but Cormac and the other chariot-chiefs accepted Ailell's plan. 'If we keep him moving,' Cormac pointed out, 'Cuchulain won't even have the chance for a night's rest within his own walls.'

Word was passed to march in a wide crescent avoiding Dun Dalgan and crossing a marshland at the river Nith that offered the Hound little chance for concealment. Realising their intent, he drove his chariot at top speed on toward Cooley, hoping to intercept and hold them there.

Plundering as they went past scattered landholdings, the invaders advanced. During low tide, they crossed the sands of the bay that separated Murthemney from Cooley. As they came up from the bay, the Hound of Ulster was watching for them, sling and stones and javelins at the ready, from the height of the Stony Mountain, Slieve na Glogh.

He was disconcerted to see the dark tide of advancing men split into two rivers. To avoid missiles hurled down upon them from the heights, Maeve and Ailell had divided the army in two. One band hugged the shoreland a safe distance from the Stony Mountain, while the second, intent on plunder, made its way eastward to a long-deserted ring fort almost swallowed by briars.

Lying on a straight line that passed through an ancient grave on the shoulder of Slieve Gullion, thence to the powerful height of Emain Macha, the abandoned fort was believed to hide forgotten gold belonging to a vanished race. The bard had told the story, and Maeve's men had listened.

Half of them went in search of the gold while the rest began a systematic plunder of Cooley, demanding to know the location of the Brown Bull from every person they met.

Cuchulain was forced to come down from the mountain and pursue them. Racing, dodging, leaping into view long enough to hurl a spear or stone and then vanish again, he continued to pick off a few raiders at a time, though he saw with a sinking heart how many were getting past him. But he knew the Cooley Hills as Maeve's men did not; his homeland was only a gallop away. He did damage; men died at his hands, and the bards memorised their names and the places where they had been slain.

Cronn and Caemdele died, and Roan and Roae. The invaders ravaged Cooley and Cuchulain savaged their flanks. But he could not stop them all; many were now driving stolen cattle ahead of them or leaving piles of plunder at crossroads for their following porters to collect. They were cheerfully despoiling Conor mac Nessa's kingdom as they searched for the hidden Donn Cooley.

Cuchulain felt his anger threatening to get out of control. He had not yet turned the power of his Rage upon them; once released and its wild energy expended, he knew he would find himself spent and in need of rest until he recovered. The Rage must be hoarded for an extraordinary effort. In the meantime, he harassed the army from the west and tried to keep their plundering to a minimum, all the while adding up the score of his resentments against Maeve and her troops.

But hatred was like shadow-dappling on the hills; often the sun broke through. Several times he saw Fergus mac Roy, the unmistakable bulk of the old warrior looming into vision like a memory from a happier land. And once he caught a glimpse of a tall, sturdy man encased in some shimmering form of covering that cast off lances of light when the wintry sun touched it.

'Ferdiad,' Cuchulain said softly.

As if the other heard him, he saw Ferdiad turn towards him and lift one hand to shade his brow as he scanned the hills. Cuchulain stood unmoving. He did not try to hide, nor did he give in to his intense yearning to yell his friend's name and run down to him. He merely stood in the open for Ferdiad to see.

And by the sudden stiffening in that distant figure, he knew he was seen.

They looked at each other across soggy grassland. At that distance, only an arm as skilled as Ferdiad's could have hurled a spear with any hope of killing the Hound. But he did not reach for a spear. 'Cuchulain,' he said to himself, almost smiling, shaking his head in admiration. When he raised a hand in salute, he saw his gesture mirrored by the figure on the hill before it turned and disappeared behind a bush.

8   The questionable loyalty of Fergus mac Roy continued to disturb Maeve. Deep in enemy country, she disliked having a traitor at her back, even a possible traitor. She did not dare chain him or kill him; his old Red Branch comrades might revolt then. Besides, for his own perverse reasons, Ailell seemed to like the man.

But Maeve had always had one certain way of reinforcing alliances. Even accompanying an army, she knew how to husband her assets. When they were setting up their first night camp in Cooley, she appeared at the flap of Fergus's tent gorgeously attired in a gown of silken *srole*, fastened in only two strategic locations with gold brooches. Her hair was looped and twisted, and her fingertips were reddened with *ruam*.

'Fergus,' she said, her body swaying gently in its rustling gown, 'I would appreciate your advice and assistance. Is there somewhere private where we might talk and no one overhear? Or . . . watch what we do?' she added with a smile.

I thought I was past this, Fergus told himself dolefully, feeling an old heat rise unbidden. I really hoped I was past this.

Ailell noticed the two of them leaving camp together, melting into a nearby clump of woodland that was well-guarded enough to be safe from the Hound but also dense enough to protect those within from casual view.

Ailell pursed his lips, then beckoned to his charioteer, a slope-shouldered man called Cuillius. 'Follow that pair for me, Cuillius. At a discreet distance, of course. If mac Roy is resuming intimate relations with my wife, I want to know it.'

Fergus was a song Maeve had sung before. She knew how to move to capture his eyes; she knew how to tease him to elicit an amiable chuckle. She knew the exact spot on his body where she could place her hand to freeze him in his tracks.

She wanted something, of course, and Fergus knew it. The only question was – could he get something without giving too much in return?

Negotiation had never been one of the strengths of Fergus mac Roy.

Following her lead, his eyes on her hips, Fergus entered a stand of trees where the earth was cushioned with moss.

Twilight gave way to night.

Hidden behind a clump of trees, Cuillius observed as best he could without light. When the action between Maeve and Fergus seemed suspicious, he tiptoed closer, but they did not notice him.

Cuillius had seen a man and a woman together before – and had done his share of the hip dance – but he had never observed a performance of such studied vivacity as that of Maeve of Cruachan. He knew she was no young woman, but as he peered through the darkness at her palely glimmering body, Cuillius wondered what young woman could hope to equal her appetite.

Maeve's gown had opened all the way down the front at the first touch of Fergus's fingers. Now, she sat triumphantly astride the former king, her face thrown back, her mouth stretched in a silent laugh. Beneath her, Fergus bucked and plunged and groaned.

Cuillius felt his own body respond with a throb of hunger.

He had seen all he came for and should run back to report to Ailell, but he could not bring himself to leave. Not yet. It was a pleasure to watch that woman at work.

At last, however, he wiped the sweat from his own brow and turned away, still unnoticed by the two lying stretched on the moss. Cuillius eased out of the woods, only to stumble just as he reached the edge of the trees. Reaching down, he found Fergus's sword, which had slipped from the man's belt as he unbuckled in anticipation.

Cuillius snatched up the weapon and ran towards the glow of Ailell's campfire.

To his surprise, Ailell did not receive his report with a show of outward anger. 'She's keeping Fergus loyal to us,' was all he said. His clenched fists were held at his sides, out of his charioteer's sight.

'In his haste to demonstrate his, ah, loyalty, he seems to have lost his sword.' Cuillius extended the weapon, smirking. 'I don't think he's missed it yet.'

Ailell grinned suddenly. 'He will!'

When at last they lay spent and panting on the moss, Maeve murmured to her companion, 'There is one more little thing you could do for me, Fergus.'

'Little?'

'Simple, then. You're the only one the Hound might not kill on sight.

If you're really grateful for all we've done for you, go as my emissary to Cuchulain and find out what offers he might accept to cease his assault on my men. He can't kill enough to stop us and surely he realises it, but he is killing more than I'm willing to lose and I'm amenable to some sort of bargain.' Which might lure him out in the open where my own men can kill him, she added silently to herself. 'Prove your loyalty in this way, Fergus, and save the lives of many of your comrades as well.'

The price, Fergus decided, was not too high. An arranged truce might well be the best one could hope for in this situation. But as he and Maeve prepared to leave the grove, he suddenly discovered a vital part of his equipment was missing. The leather sheath dangled emptily from his belt, flung down along the way with other bits of clothing.

'What are you muttering about?' Maeve asked irritably.

'Go on without me,' he urged, deeply embarrassed. For a warrior to appear in public on a campaign with no sword at his side was humiliating. Eager for her own tent, and satisfied as to the results of her efforts, Maeve left him without argument, and at once Fergus began a thorough search of the area. But he found no sword anywhere. The nearest he came was a broken tree branch of about the same size. In desperation, he thrust this into his empty scabbard and returned to the camp, thankful that it was still dark, so no one would notice his loss.

But sharp eyes were watching for him. Ailell stepped out from between the tents. 'Valorous mac Roy, where is your sword?'

Fergus automatically dropped his hand, felt the rough wooden branch where a bronze hilt should be, and braced himself to endure. 'Lost in Maeve's service,' he growled. 'Haven't you noticed we're at war?'

To Fergus's relief, Ailell laughed. As always when dealing with his wife's infidelities, Ailell was torn between jealousy and a sense of inevitability, but he had come to identify with Fergus, and he admired the other man's wit in an awkward moment. 'Were you last wielding your weapon on the heights of a certain royal belly in a clump of woodland?' he asked.

Crestfallen, Fergus shook his head without answering.

Ailell clapped him on the shoulder. 'These things happen. I know about women and I know my wife. Her schemes and her itches aren't worth my making an enemy out of you.'

Fergus squinted at the other man. 'You're bigger than I would be. So I'll tell you something for nothing, Ailell. It wasn't my body Maeve wanted, that was a side issue of little importance to either of us. She wanted me to arrange a truce with Cuchulain for her.'

Ailell felt a distinct sense of relief – and of gratitude to Fergus for being honest. 'Will you do it?'

'I'll at least speak to him. It could save a lot of lives that matter to me, not the least being his own. But . . . tell me truly, Ailell. Do you think Maeve would abide by a truce?'

'Truly, I don't know. She hates Cuchulain now. But it's worth a try. The question is, can we trust you out of our sight?'

Fergus uttered a rueful chuckle. 'Your wife's made certain there isn't enough life left in me for treachery.'

At daybreak, he prepared to go in search of Cuchulain. A fosterling of Maeve and Ailell, a brash young man called Etarcomol, came up to him as he was loading his war-cart with meat and cheese and wine-skins. 'I want to go with you,' Etarcomol said. 'I have a great desire to see the champion of Ulster up close – while under your protection, of course.'

Fergus was suspicious but could hardly refuse. 'Come if you will, then, but stay out of the way. I can't promise Cuchulain will make you welcome.'

The Hound of Ulster was not difficult to locate. He had obviously been watching from a distant hill; when Fergus drove out, he recognised the solitary chariot and came down to meet him. Fergus stepped out of the chariot and advanced towards him on foot and obviously unarmed, holding out a roasted haunch of meat. 'I thought you might be hungry by now,' he said by way of greeting.

Cuchulain reached gratefully for the meat, still warm and glistening with fat. 'I see you brought me the Champion's Portion.'

The Hound's eyes, Fergus could not help noticing, glittered like grey flames in the great dark caverns of their sockets. His whole face was gaunt, cheekbones standing out in stark relief on either side of the proud and predatory nose. Whatever was gentle in the young man seemed to have been burned away, leaving only a fanatic determination to perform an impossible task.

'Indeed I did bring you the Champion's Portion,' Fergus told him with a reassuring smile. 'For the sake of the old days, I would not see you starve now. Warm to me are my memories of the time when I was your instructor as you played at hurling on the pitch at Emain Macha. You were a boy who took punishment as bravely as you gave it, and practised as full-hearted as you played. You have always been dear to me, Cuchulain.'

379

The speech pleased the Hound; for a moment, he almost heard the long-ago laughter of the Boys' Troop and the clash of the ash hurley sticks. Yet the wariness never quite left his eyes. 'Who's that with you, Fergus?' He gestured toward Etarcomol, who was leaning out of the chariot trying to get a good look at him.

'Ah, that's one of Ailell's foster-sons. He's under my protection,' Fergus added, the warning implicit in his tone. Never again did he intend to have anyone injured while under his protection.

'He's as safe from me as he cares to be,' Cuchulain replied, hunger overcoming him as he began to tear voraciously at the meat.

They sat together with their backs against a stone, and Fergus watched, pleased, while the younger man ate. Bringing the food had been his own idea, one for which he had not asked permission. When Cuchulain's jaws began to slow, he explained the situation. 'Maeve and Ailell realise the Ulstermen will begin to recover from the Pangs before many more nights pass, and when they do, they'll grind the western army to grit and gravel. They're willing to make some concessions in order to get the majority of their followers safely out of here and back to Connaught.'

'Does that mean they'll give up trying to steal the Brown Bull?'

'Do you know where he is?' Fergus countered.

Cuchulain looked at his old friend through slitted eyes. Instead of answering, he tore another strip of meat off the bone with his teeth and chewed it very slowly, very deliberately. When he finally swallowed, he said instead, 'What terms will you offer for a truce?'

'What terms will you accept?'

As he ate, Cuchulain had been thinking fast. 'Only these. I will stop attacking the army from ambush only if Maeve will send out single champions to stand against me one at a time in combat.'

'That's not a truce!'

'It is not. But neither is Maeve willing to give up without the Brown Bull. For as long as she insists on remaining in Ulster, I will only kill her men one at a time, if she accepts my challenge to single combat. But either way, I will kill them. And I cannot surrender the bull to her under any circumstances. Go back and tell her, Fergus. And tell her that, for the duration of the single combats, she is to take no plunder whatsoever out of Ulster, or the agreement is broken and I will slaughter her men by twos and tens.'

Fergus was grinning. You're as shrewd as Conor mac Nessa, he thought. The Pangs will have passed away long before you've worked

380

your way through even a portion of Maeve's warriors, fighting them one at a time. 'I'll carry your message,' he said aloud, 'but Maeve won't like it.'

'She won't like it if you stay here with me any longer, either. She'll think you're conspiring with me against her. Come, Fergus. I'll walk you back to your chariot and let Etarcomol there have a look at my face, since he's come all this way to see it.'

They shared a farewell embrace into which Fergus mac Roy tried to put the feelings he had for the younger man. His own honour forever tarnished, he briefly held in his arms a man to whom honour was everything. But Cuchulain did not make Fergus feel ashamed of himself. Rather, Fergus felt proud merely to be of the same race as the Hound of Ulster.

He stepped into his chariot, and Cuchulain headed back towards the hills. 'Aren't you going to fight him now that we've got him out here alone, in the open?' Etarcomol asked.

'I certainly am not!'

'But you were a famous champion in your day. I thought the whole idea here was to trick him into lowering his guard and then kill him, the two of us.'

Fergus was rigid with indignation. 'Who told you that?'

'No one. I just thought . . .'

'Enough,' Fergus snarled, thoroughly disgusted, wondering if Maeve had somehow suggested the scheme to Etarcomol. Taking up the reins, he drove his chariot himself back towards the camp at a brisk trot. His anger was palpable in the jolting cart.

They had gone but a short distance when Etarcomol said, 'I don't think I want to ride with a man who's afraid to fight.' He jumped from the cart.

'It's glad I am to see the last of you!' Fergus shouted after him. 'Walk all the way back, and may your feet find nothing but rocks.' He drove on in anger.

As soon as he was gone, Etarcomol looked around carefully, then set out along the path Cuchulain had taken into the hills.

Very soon, he came upon the short, dark man, sprawled in the lee of a hill, sucking the last bit of marrow from one of the bones Fergus had brought. Seen up close, the Hound of Ulster wasn't enough to frighten a duck, Etarcomol thought. He approached with one hand hovering above his sword hilt.

Cuchulain remained where he was, enjoying his food. If the

apparently lax muscles beneath his tunic had gone taut, they did not show. He had seen warriors swagger towards him before. 'Why are you staring at me?' he asked Etarcomol in a conversational tone. His voice was so low and gentle the other man could hardly hear him, so he took a step closer than he had intended . . .

. . . and got a good look at Cuchulain's eyes.

Pinpoints of light flickered in the grey irises like stars dimly glimpsed. Etarcomol mistakenly thought the champion of Ulster was mocking him.

The reputed champion of Ulster.

His temper flared. 'I'll be the first man to challenge you to single combat.'

'You don't want to do that. You're safe as you are, under the protection of Fergus mac Roy.'

'Then I throw off the protection of Fergus mac Roy!'

'You don't want to do that either,' Cuchulain advised him. In one lithe bound he was on his feet, and the hand that had held a beef bone was holding a sword. Before Etarcomol could react, Cuchulain slashed Hardhead down at an angle into the earth, then twisted his wrist and sent a huge wedge of soil flying, literally cutting the ground from beneath the other man's feet. Etarcomol tumbled backwards, landing on the point of his spine. He howled with indignation – and not a little pain.

'Now leave,' said Cuchulain, still in the same soft voice.

'I will not leave.' Etarcomol got to his feet in time to meet Hardhead again. This time the sword parted his tunic, which fell into a heap at his feet. The leather belt that held his sword, likewise cut open, fell with it.

Etarcomol dived for his weapon and came up brandishing it wildly. 'The next blow struck here will take your head or mine!'

'If you insist,' Cuchulain replied quietly. 'But it isn't my desire.'

Grasping the hilt of his sword with both hands, Cuchulain danced backwards to avoid Etarcomol's blow and then lunged forward before the other could rebalance himself. With a mighty grunt, Cuchulain brought Hardhead straight down from the top of Etarcomol's skull to his navel.

As he wiped his blade with grass, the Hound looked down at the mangled heap that had been a brash man. 'It wasn't my desire,' he said again. 'But some people don't recognise good advice when they hear it.' He carefully removed the two halves of Etarcomol's head from the ruined body, cleaned them, and wrapped them in a fragment of fabric torn from his tunic. Then he sat down to wait.

As Cuchulain had expected, before Fergus reached Maeve's armies he had begun to worry about Etarcomol and finally decided to turn back. His chariot approached at the gallop. When he saw the corpse, limbs now neatly arranged and wrapped trophy head propped on chest, he let out a cry of anger.

'You, Cuchulain, of all people! I never expected *you* to kill someone under my protection!'

Cuchulain stood up. 'I did all I could to safeguard his life for your sake. I asked him to leave, but he refused until one of us was killed. Would you rather see me lying there than him?'

Fergus looked at the body. 'Etarcomol was an arrogant man,' he said at last.

Cuchulain helped him put the remains of Ailell's fosterling, head and all, into his chariot.

The unfortunate Etarcomol, who had thus provided yet another reason for hating Cuchulain, was buried beneath a cairn of stones and the poet composed a lament for him. A lament that transformed brashness into boldness and foolishness into ferocity.

The leaders of the invasion met to discuss Cuchulain's offer. 'When he gives his word, he keeps it,' Fergus assured them. 'And this is the only arrangement he's willing to make.'

Ailell fixed a stern glance on his wife. 'Accept it, woman. It's better that he kill our men one at a time than in clumps. While the single combats go on, we can either find the Brown Bull or at least work our way back towards Connaught before the Ulstermen are on their feet again.'

'We'll stay right here until we find the Brown Bull,' said Maeve grimly. 'And until a champion brings me Cuchulain's head.'

'Since the death of Baiscne, there is no reasoning with her,' Ailell told Fergus. 'Whom can we send against the champion of Ulster?'

'There's only one man in the camp whom I'd call capable of giving him a good fight,' Fergus replied, 'and that's Ferdiad mac Daman. But he seems to have disappeared this morning.'

So he had. Searchers were unable to find the man in horn armour, and at last a bardsung hero called Nadcranntail was recruited instead. He showed a certain reluctance to face Cuchulain, but Maeve knew his weakness was women.

And she had Finavir of the Fair Eyebrows to offer.

As she had expected, Nadcranntail found the girl a sufficient inducement. The daughter of the rulers of the west would bring not only her beauteous self but considerable property and prestige to a marriage.

'Is Finavir willing to marry you?' Ailell questioned Nadcranntail as the hopeful champion was preparing his weapons. 'She's freeborn, she has the right of refusal under the law.'

Nadcranntail swelled like an inflated wine-skin. 'I know how to make women willing,' he boasted. 'Just wait until I return with the Hound's head tied by the hair to my chariot rim.'

He was a big man with a rough complexion and hands like boiled hams. Ailell liked nothing about him. 'Do you seriously intend to let him marry our daughter?' he complained to Maeve as the warrior drove out to meet Cuchulain.

'He doesn't have the Hound's head yet,' she replied. 'And while the issue is being decided, send search parties to find that bull!'

She stared after the retreating figure of Nadcranntail in his chariot, past the clutter of tents and cooking fires and war-carts and hobbled horses; past men eating or cleaning their weapons or jabbering at one another; past the pens holding choice cattle from their plunder.

But, thought Ailell as he watched her, she was not straining her eyes in hopes of glimpsing the Brown Bull of Cooley. Maeve was looking towards the hills, and Cuchulain.

A runner from the Connaught camp had advised Cuchulain of a contestant desirous of meeting him in single combat. Cuchulain made his way to the sheltered spot where he had concealed his chariot and Laeg, and began preparing himself for battle. Laeg's pains had eased temporarily, as they sometimes did, and the charioteer propped himself weakly on one elbow to watch, cursing his own inability to take part. 'Who challenges you?' he asked.

'I didn't ask. It hardly matters unless they send Ferdiad against me.'
'Would he do it?'

'Battle is his profession,' Cuchulain answered bleakly. He busied himself with his weapons.

But when he saw Nadcranntail approaching him, his heart sang with relief. The challenger was big and bold and unknown to him, and he hurled casting spears as he came. Cuchulain was so overjoyed to find himself facing a stranger that he set himself to catching the spears in his bare hands as they flew past.

Nadcranntail was taken aback. 'Who are you, to steal my spears in your two hands?'

384

Cuchulain laughed in his face. 'The champion of Ulster,' he said. 'You have come to take my head.'

'You have no beard,' the other man protested. 'Only boys are beardless; I can't take your head as a trophy, I'd be disgraced.'

The sun was shining brightly, if without heat; somewhere in the distance, a bird cawed. Cuchulain felt his weariness fall from him, and his old sense of play rose strongly in him. 'I'll offer you a trophy worth fighting for, then,' he shouted. He ran back to his camp and, with his knife, slashed hairs from the tail of the Black of Sainglain. Fashioning a crude beard of horsehair, he tied it over his ears and returned to the bemused Nadcranntail. 'Kill me now, if you can!' he challenged.

Nadcranntail lost his temper. This lad who claimed to be the Hound of Ulster was toying with him. He hurled a heavy javelin – no light casting spear this time – at Cuchulain's heart.

Nimbly, the smaller man leaped out of the way.

'Coward, you dodged my throw!'

'You are free to dodge mine,' Cuchulain answered, hurling a spear of his own.

Unfortunately, Nadcranntail was not as agile as Cuchulain. He could not duplicate the salmon-leap, and found himself mortally wounded.

A man of the Gael, he requested of Cuchulain the courtesies their people granted the dying. 'Let my charioteer take me back to bid farewell to my companions,' he said, 'and I promise my body, living or dead, will then be returned to you so you may claim your trophy.'

Cuchulain nodded his assent. The rituals of honour would be observed.

While their contest was taking place, a party of Maeve's scouts had at last found the hiding place of the Donn Cooley. Herders were sent to bring him to the camp, but the bull fully justified his reputation. He was huge and vicious and hungry-horned, and Nadcranntail was not the only Connaughtman to die that day.

When the Brown Bull was finally secured, Maeve and Ailell met to inspect the prize. He was impressive, a bovine mountain glaring out at the world from tiny red eyes while clouds of steam rose from his angry, sweating body. He pawed the earth, tearing up great chunks, and repeatedly lunged against the ropes and chains that held him.

'Now that you have him, are you satisfied?' Ailell asked his wife.

'I'm never satisfied.'

'Let me put it this way – are you willing to return to Cruachan now?'

'I am . . . but somewhere along the way I still intend to have

Cuchulain killed,' she said, keenly aware of the absence where a small dog's head should have been pressed devotedly against her.

The army turned towards Connaught, taking their plunder with them and further pillaging as they went. Cuchulain darted and danced ahead of them in a veritable frenzy of activity, taunting the Connaughtmen to pursue him in an erratic path that once again spared Dun Dalgan their attentions.

With threats and cajolery, Maeve managed to persuade one warrior after another to challenge the Hound of Ulster to single combat. And in swift succession, Cuchulain fought and killed Cur mac Dalath, Lath mac Dabro, Foirc of the Three Swift Ones, and the famous champion Srubgaile. Against this last man he used the Gae Bulga, to make four slain before the sun reached midpoint in the sky.

Srubgaile's charioteer returned to the Connaught side with the dead man's torn body. 'Cuchulain has a pronged spear that follows its victims like a famished wolf,' he related. 'No one can escape.'

'We should try to get it from him for ourselves,' Ailell remarked.

Close by Ailell stood the satirist Odran, who overheard his words. Members of the poet class of *filidh*, satirists did not rank as high as bardic historians, but they were mightily feared. Each wore an armband of very short, bristly fur, to identify his profession and refer to the bristliness of his tongue. A cruel satire was a weapon that could haunt a man beyond the grave and destroy him in the minds of his descendants. Even kings feared satirists and gave them gifts to win their favour.

Odran aspired to be chief satirist in Connaught, and he thought he saw his opportunity. As the next challenger set out to meet Cuchulain, Odran joined him. When the challenger lay dead, Odran approached the champion of Ulster. 'Give me your pronged spear,' he requested.

Cuchulain saw the fur armband but replied, 'You don't want it.'

Odran insisted. 'Give me the gift I request, or I'll destroy your reputation with a poem so cruel even children will laugh at you.'

'Then if you really want the Gae Bulga so much, you shall have it,' said Cuchulain, the thread of his patience snapping.

He hurled the Invincible Spear, and it tore Odran apart.

The man fell back dying, yet with a spark of his talent still burning in him.

'A stunning gift, this,' he managed to say before the light went out of his eyes.

The style with which Odran met his death did him honour.

Cuchulain knelt by his side until his spirit had time to leave the body, and then he took his head as if Odran had been a great warrior.

Cuchulain now knew they had the Brown Bull. He was only fighting to keep Maeve and her raiders in Ulster until the Pangs passed and the warriors of the northland could recapture the animal and defeat the Connaughtmen *en masse*. He fought in a blur, without thinking, meeting one man after another.

When Calatin, the son of Ercol, tried to trap him in a narrow fissure of rock, the Hound killed him with a single blow. On the hurling field at Emain Macha with the Boys' Troop, he had been taught to hit with deadly accuracy in very close quarters.

As he fell, Calatin hissed a warning. 'I have three unusual daughters who will avenge me, Cuchulain!' But the Hound had already turned away to go and meet his next opponent, and did not hear.

Shortly after the onset of the Pangs, Nessa had gathered the current Boys' Troop on the playing field of Emain Macha. 'You are trained as fighters but still beardless, which means you are as yet exempt from Macha's curse,' she told them. 'We have no one else to send to Cuchulain's aid. If any of you wish to stand with him against the invaders from the west, we will give you weapons.'

They were the sons of the Red Branch. Every one of them down to the smallest ran cheering to the Speckled House to claim weapons meant for grown men.

Cuchulain was their hero. Hero, model, idol. There was not one among them who was not striving to master his famous battle-feats. The opportunity to join him and fight with him was the most exciting thing yet to happen in their lives.

None of them had ever been in a real war.

From his sickbed, Conor mac Nessa heard their excited shouting. 'We can't send children to fight,' he told his mother.

'Someone has to help the Hound defend your kingdom. We went to too much effort to establish ourselves,' Nessa reminded him, 'to surrender any part of it, even a bull, without a fight. Besides, it's what they were bred for.'

Conor mac Nessa dragged himself to his feet and managed to stand, leaning against the carved doorframe of the House of the King, to bid farewell to his short-statured little army as it marched away. Freckled and scabby and sneering to hide their fear, foolish and fierce and unconsciously funny, the gang of half-grown youths swaggered past, showing off for their king.

Conor noticed, with a lump in his throat, that some of them still had dimples on the backs of their knees.

Other men's sons, going to help Cuchulain . . .

The fighting spilled out of Cooley and across Murthemney as Maeve turned toward Connaught and home. Cuchulain harried her army like a wolfpack at their heels, slowing them worse than mud, forcing man after man to stand against him and die.

Some whole companies, Maeve was furious to discover, pulled out secretly in the middle of the night and ran for home rather than submit one of their number to single combat against the Hound.

Larene the Dancer took a sword-thrust through his lung that did not kill him but doomed him to cough blood and curse Cuchulain for the rest of a shortened life. The sons of Mofemis were next to fight the champion of Ulster, one after the other, however, and they did die. One after the other. Death hung in the air, and the ravens fed.

 I found Cuchulain taking a brief rest, propped against one of his chariot wheels. Laeg lay concealed some distance away, wrapped in his cloak and his discomfort and oblivious to everything else. There was no other human to see me – or to see the face I chose to present.

Cuchulain looked up as I approached. How thin he had become! Yet he seemed to be drawing energy from his victories even as they wore the flesh from his bones. He deserved the best I could offer, the valiant Cuchulain.

From his expression, I could tell he was startled to see a beautiful woman in rich attire walking toward him. He knuckled his eyes as if I might be an apparition, but I was very real. The form I had assumed was small and slender and soft, willow-waisted, delicate and tender as spring leaves. A most boring form, actually, but one calculated to appeal to his tastes as I had observed them.

With a grunt, he scrambled to his feet to offer the appropriate greeting to a woman of obvious rank. 'Who are you?' he then enquired.

'The daughter of a southern chieftain,' I replied airily, waving my hand (soft, white, and useless) in a generally southerly direction. My voice was the cooing of a dove as I explained, 'I've heard of your courageous defence of Ulster, and I'm prepared to offer everything I have to help you.'

388

Some gift of intuition made him suspicious. He folded his arms across his chest and lowered his chin slightly. 'Why? Why not throw in with the westerners, and share in the looting of the north?'

The quivering indignation I put into my voice sounded very human. 'I'm not like that, I assure you.' Lowering my eyelids, I looked up at him through the lashes. Once I knew a lot of similar tricks. 'I am devoted to you and want only to be with you. I believe you are not . . . unkind . . . to women?'

'You've chosen a bad time,' he said bluntly. 'You've walked into the middle of a war.'

'But I tell you, I can help you.'

To my surprise – and genuine indignation this time – he laughed at me. 'A weak little woman like you can be no help to me. Or did Maeve send you? Is this one of her tricks to try to distract me? Well, it won't work, and you can trot back and tell her so. I won't waste any more time on you.'

I stood in outrage, struggling for words. How could he, in his need, refuse me? Refuse me *again*?

He had chosen me, remember – not the other way around. Now, he locked himself behind walls and thought he could do everything alone. Idiot. It's easy to forget how foolish humans can be when you don't deal with them every day. This one had more lessons yet to learn from me.

'So you reject me without even knowing what I could do for you,' I said in icy tones.

He waved a weary hand. 'Just go away and leave me alone. I'm not out here risking my life a dozen times a day for the sake of a woman's backside,' he added crudely.

Ah, yes, there are excuses for him. He was exhausted; his words revealed it. But I don't believe in excuses.

'If you won't accept my help, you'll suffer my hindrance!' I warned him. 'The next time you fight at a ford, an eel will slither between your legs and trip you. I will be that eel.'

His eyes opened very wide then, and for a moment he – almost –really saw me. 'You're no chieftain's daughter,' he said in a whisper, then, his voice growing stronger, 'but whatever you are, I can crush an eel's ribs beneath my feet!'

'You wouldn't do that to . . . me.' I tried to summon a becoming blush, but the pulsing of his anger distracted me. I realised I had made a mistake by presenting him with a mystery. Cuchulain was obviously impatient with mysteries.

He fixed his strange silver eyes on mine, and I felt the power in him. 'Get in my way and I will crush you,' he said. 'You'll carry the injury for ever unless I lift it from you with a blessing, no matter who you are. Now go and let me rest. A man will be hoping to kill me soon, and I want to be ready to give him good sport.'

Oh, he was brave. He did not understand what I was, but he could summon defiance as easily as a lad summons spit. I loved him and hated him then, but I left him. To whatever must happen next.

9 Maeve hurled man after man against him. In pelting rain, he fought with her latest champion, the two of them meeting in wintry water in the middle of a ford. They locked eyes over their shield rims just as Cuchulain felt something slither between his legs. The coils of a great eel seized him, throwing him off-balance. Its cold skin was a horror, its strength was tremendous. His opponent took advantage of the moment to bury a spear in Cuchulain's shoulder.

The sharp pain broke through the shock of the eel's attack. Cuchulain recovered enough to jerk one leg free and then slam his heel down with all his might on the eel's back; he felt bones crunch. The thing floated free of him, injured but not dead.

He had no time for it; the other man was coming at him again. This time he managed to get under his opponent's guard long enough to deliver a fatal thrust to the man's breast. Dying, the other clutched Cuchulain's shield in order to stay on his feet. Breath rattled like pebbles in his throat.

'My men . . . are watching,' the man gasped. 'Will you stand aside and let me fall . . . facing forward, as a warrior should . . . rather than backwards in defeat?'

'I will surely,' Cuchulain told him, touched by the other's gallantry. He put his arm around the dying man's shoulders to brace him until he was able to stand alone, and with the sleeve of his tunic he wiped the fine froth of bubbles from his opponent's lips.

'Now,' the man said. Cuchulain let go and he fell forward as a warrior should, attacking and not retreating.

Afterward, Cuchulain found some sphagnum moss to staunch the bleeding of his own wound, then stood leaning on his spear and watching as Maeve's men carried their slain hero away. The dead man would be given the honours he deserved.

There would be no honours for Cuchulain, no laughing feast, no hot meat, no splashing wine. He was alone.

He had killed men whom he knew to be bold men, brave men, men he would have liked to call his friends. And he would have to kill more.

Warrior. The bright bronze word seemed tarnished.

He went back to his camp, and Laeg. As always, he greeted his charioteer by asking, 'Are the Pangs fading?'

'Not yet. But the cramps haven't been as bad today, I think. And I just know if I had some warm, sweet milk, I would feel stronger.'

'Where would I get milk?' Cuchulain asked bitterly. 'Look around you. Maeve's men have been through here, there's not a cow with a teat left to pull, or a bird with a feather left for flying.'

'It would help, the milk,' said Laeg wistfully.

Even that much interest in food was a hopeful sign, and the Hound was hungry for hopeful signs. For himself, Cuchulain could not have taken a step more, he was weary past weariness. But for Laeg, he put one foot in front of the other and set off again, aware as he did so that he had somehow wrenched some back muscles in the fight at the ford – probably while he was struggling for balance with that eel wrapped around his leg.

'I seem to remember seeing a ruin of a hut off this way, with some sort of bawn attached to it,' he told Laeg. 'I'll go and see, there may be a cow even, some thin old thing Maeve's men considered beneath taking.'

'You're not too tired?'

'Of course not.' He made himself laugh. 'When was the champion of Ulster ever tired?'

He found the cottage; he found the cow. She was neglected and bad-tempered, with an udder swollen to painful proportions due to a lack of milking. No one was around.

Cuchulain was tired of the whole topic of cattle, and he had never learned to milk one. Night was coming on, he hurt all over – and the cow brandished her horns at him as if she wanted to gore him on the spot.

'Another single combat,' he groaned. In spite of himself, he managed a rueful chuckle; what if Maeve could see the champion of Ulster being intimidated by a milk cow?

The operation did not go well. She stepped on his foot and she gave only a few drops of milk, one thin squirt barely sufficient to cover the bottom of a dried-out leather pail he found hanging on the wall of the hut. When he made a second attempt, the cow kicked sideways, narrowly missing his belly with her cloven hoof. He jumped back. 'Right enough. Be brave,' he admonished himself, but the cow turned and looked at him and he stood rooted to the spot, trembling with fatigue and anger at himself. In a low voice that did not carry beyond the bawn, he called the cow every name he could think of.

The rain had ceased, but night had fallen. A thin, ragged moon peeped through dark clouds. Cuchulain was about to make a last effort with the cow, when he heard someone say behind him, 'There's an art to it you don't know.'

He turned – slowly, for his back hurt – to see an old woman hobbling toward him. A squint-eyed old woman as hunchbacked as a crow. 'I need milk for my friend, who is ill,' Cuchulain said simply.

Without replying, the crone took the pail from his hand and crouched down by the cow, resting her forehead against the beast's skinny flank. Soon the bucket was brimming with milk, so white and pure it gleamed in the darkness. The old woman stood up with an obvious effort and pressed one clawlike hand to her side, groaning.

'Are you ill also?' Cuchulain asked.

'Broken ribs. Old bones never heal. But take your milk if you insist on doing a kindness at your own expense.'

He was too tired to make sense of her words, but not too tired to forget the manners expected of a king's kinsman. 'Good health to the giver,' he told the crone gratefully, 'and the blessings of whatever god you follow.'

The timid moon suddenly dared to reveal the old woman's face; a face strangely familiar. In a curiously altered voice, she said, 'You warned me I'd carry your mark for ever, but for ever can be a very short time. You healed my ribs with your blessing, Cuchulain.' She straightened up and became fair, became young, became terrifying.

The Hound almost dropped the pail. 'I never would have done it if I'd known it was you,' he managed to say.

She laughed. 'I like that. I'll teach you to be ruthless yet.'

The moon disappeared. Night swallowed Ulster. When Cuchulain reached for the woman, his hand closed on empty air.

Only the pail and the milk were solid.

A bemused Cuchulain carried pail and milk to Laeg, but he did not tell the charioteer about his vision.

In the dark places of the night and the spirit, strange things may happen, he told himself. Or I may be going as mad as Dectera. A gift in the blood . . .

Laeg seemed a bit stronger, but he was still suffering cramps. Cuchulain had pains of his own. The accumulation of days of hard fighting meant a body lacerated by wounds, weakened by loss of blood, worn by weariness. His youth and strength were being cut away from him as he cut men away from Maeve's forces.

In the night, aching and dejected, he stood leaning on his spear in the flickering light of a dying campfire, gazing out over the plain toward his enemies. Laeg was wrapped in his cloak, asleep. A bitter wind was blowing, and one of Cuchulain's many wounds had begun seeping blood again; he could feel it under his tunic.

'I hear the voice of Neman on the wind,' he said, as if Laeg were awake and listening. Drawing his cloak more tightly around him, Cuchulain gazed sombrely at the countless small campfires of his many enemies, winking like red eyes in the distance. What was his one little spark against so many?

For days, he had fought off his loneliness and isolation, but cold and exhaustion were enemies he could not resist. Alone in the night, the champion of Ulster wanted to weep like a little boy who has just learned how terrible the world can be.

'I did not want to fail you in any way, Father,' he said softly, thinking in his heart of Conor mac Nessa. He folded himself down and lay on the earth, pulling his cloak around him, but he did not sleep. He dared not sleep. He was sole guardian of Ulster.

The Neman keened for the dead, the bitter wind her voice.

The Hound's eyes burned with sleeplessness, but still saw clearly enough to note the advance of someone striding towards him out of the night. Groaning with pain, he dragged himself over until he was between the stranger and Laeg – just in case. But as the man drew nearer, Cuchulain could sense no menace in him. Instead, he brought a sense of peace, as if the winter gale had become a warm summer breeze and the distant flickering lights were fireflies.

I'm dreaming again, thought Cuchulain.

The newcomer was fair, smooth-cheeked and fine-skinned. His eyebrows lifted into peaks, his smile was radiant. The green cloak he wore was fastened by a silver brooch of strange design and his knee-length tunic was red silk, embroidered in gold. He was splendid and kingly and had walked straight through Maeve's camp, apparently, on his way to Cuchulain – yet no alarm had been raised. It was as if no one could see him but the Hound.

He came straight on until he stood by the smouldering campfire. He seemed brighter than the flames. 'You have taken a manly stand,' he said to Cuchulain without any other greeting.

The Hound managed to sit up. His head was swimming; his shoulder throbbed. 'I haven't done very much.'

'So say you, but not your enemies. You will have help now, though.'

'Are you one of the Red Branch? I don't know your face.' Cuchulain leaned forward, trying to get a better look. 'If you've come to stand with me against the men of Connaught, you're very welcome. I can barely lift a spear any more.'

'Your wounds weigh more than you do. You need to rest and heal, that's how I will help you. And I myself will stand guard over you during that time.'

The stranger threw off his cloak as if the cold of winter meant nothing to him, and sat down cross-legged by the fire, next to Cuchulain. He smiled at the Hound as if they were old friends, and then began to sing as men sometimes sing around campfires with old friends. But his song was not one Cuchulain had ever heard before.

'Youth of Ulster, when you rise,
the mouths of your wounds will be closed.
A fair man stands watch in your place,
as the long night descends.
Rest unmolested in his care,
for succour has come to you in your lonely vigil.
You have defended cattle and fought against Fate.
There is none to match you, when chariots
travel the valleys.
A youth has done a man's work,
and made his father proud.'

Against his will, Cuchulain felt himself sinking under the weight of the melodious voice. A restful darkness opened to receive him. But before it closed over his head, he whispered, 'Who are you?'

He was already fast asleep when the other replied, 'Some call me Lewy of the Long Hand.'

During the night, the stranger brought herbs and mosses and sweet grass, and tenderly bathed and bandaged the Hound's wounds. He shook his head over a great sword slash in the young side; he frowned to see a hideous purple bruise spread from hip to groin. Between Cuchulain's ribs the flesh sank like deep cart tracks, and loss of blood had left him as pale as frost.

But Lewy of the Long Hand leaned over him, and smiled down on him, and breathed warmth on him, and in his sleep Cuchulain at last relaxed as colour began to steal back into his cheeks. The stranger fanned the fire so it kept the Hound and his charioteer warm; he tended

395

the chariot horses himself, taking them fresh water and rubbing them down with grass. When there was nothing left to be done, he stood as Cuchulain had stood, leaning on a spear and gazing out across Ulster.

In the morning a brilliant sun rose but Cuchulain slept on, oblivious. Healing.

Meanwhile, the Boys' Troop marched across the land to his aid. Marched is not the correct term, for since the defection of Fergus mac Roy, no instructor had been able to organise them sufficiently to make a disciplined unit. They ran, they leaped, they scrambled and swore and hurled stones, but they never slackened their pace. Their champion needed them.

They came from Emain Macha with their hurling sticks for weapons, and they found Maeve's armies on the Plain of Murthemney.

When a sentry came running to tell Ailell the outskirts of the army were under attack, he was at first incredulous. 'How many are there?'

'Three times fifty.'

'That many Ulstermen have recovered from the Pangs at once?'

'They are not men, but youths,' the sentry replied. 'It's that infamous Boys' Troop from Emain Macha, lads not yet old enough to take up arms.'

'And they're attacking *us*? I don't believe it.'

'Believe it,' the sentry advised. 'They've already killed several of your men.'

Maeve hurried up. She had not yet completed her morning ablutions, her eyes were puffy from sleep and the mark of her pillow was on her cheek. 'Is Cuchulain with them?' she asked at once.

'We have not yet seen him. His camp is to the east of us but a little way, yet the sun is in our eyes and we cannot tell if he is moving around up there.'

'We have to stop those boys before he joins them,' Ailell said. 'He could make a real army out of that lot.'

'They're children,' Maeve started to protest, but her husband raised his hand.

'Those children will kill your children, woman. Is that what you want?'

'Stop them,' she replied in a deadly whisper. But after a company of warriors had been dispatched with orders to kill every member of the Boys' Troop, Maeve sought the company of her daughter, Finavir. She did not enjoy being with other women, she wasted no effort on making friends of her own sex. But in this situation, a man's ears were no good to her.

'I have ordered the killing of children,' she told her daughter. 'This is a bad thing. It isn't what I set out to do.'

Cuchulain awoke in the cool of the evening. He had a bone-deep conviction that he had been sleeping for a long time. He threw aside his cloak and sat up, tardily discovering that he was neither stiff nor sore. He flexed his arms; the muscles were healed and whole. With wondering fingers, he explored his various wounds and found them closed, without infection.

Nothing hurt. He could hardly believe it.

Then he saw Laeg standing – standing – nearby. 'The Pangs?' he asked.

'Gone,' his charioteer told him.

'How long have I been asleep?'

'Quite some time, I think. I awoke this morning to find you sleeping very deeply and I left you that way.'

'Are we alone?'

'Should there be someone else?' Laeg asked, puzzled.

Cuchulain got to his feet and looked around. To the west, he saw the first flickering lights from Maeve's fires. 'I've been sleeping and left the land open to her greed!'

'Not entirely open. There have been defenders.'

'The Red Branch? They've recovered, they've joined us?'

Laeg tugged at his lower lip, then dug in one ear with a finger, forestalling the moment he must say, 'Not exactly. The Boys' Troop came from Emain Macha and attacked the invaders as you slept.'

'You're not serious.'

'I am. And a serious business it was. They killed a wonderful number of Maeve's men and wounded many, many more, but in the heel of the hunt they were all slain themselves, in a field not far from here.'

Cuchulain's full-throated roar in response was so savage, Laeg jumped backwards as if fearing for his life. 'Bring the chariot!' commanded the Hound. 'Fix the sickle blades as firmly as possible to the wheels, and fasten spears and hooks and barbs to every other surface, including the horses' harness. Run, Laeg!'

Laeg ran.

From the corner of his eye, Cuchulain glimpsed something moving beyond his campfire. When he turned his head, the stranger approached. 'You've done me no favour,' he greeted the man bitterly. 'While I slept the Boys' Troop was slaughtered. The sons of the Red Branch.'

'They would have died anyway,' the other told him. 'In your condition, you couldn't have protected them. There is no stain on your honour, Cuchulain, and now you are rested and able to fight.'

'Then stand and fight with me. Together we two can feed the blood of the child-killers to the ravens!'

'I will not stay,' the stranger said. 'The glory of this struggle is yours, not to be shared. I leave you with what I have given you, and my promise that your enemies have no power over your life as long as the heat is strong in you this night.'

The sun flared in the west as it sank. Cuchulain blinked against the dazzle, and when he looked again the stranger was gone.

But the rage remained. The Rage. Building in him, not to be denied now. 'Laeg!' he roared. 'Where's the chariot?'

From the moment Laeg awoke, still weak but free of the Pangs, he had anticipated the battle to come and been preparing for it. He had dressed in his charioteer's war-harness, as distinctive as the six-coloured cloak of a bard. A soft tunic of doeskin fitted him as snugly as his own hide. A warm, short mantle left his arms free for driving, and his head was protected by a bronze-plated cap pulled down to his red eyebrows. At Cuchulain's order, he quickly attached barbs to every conceivable surface of the chariot, even the ornamented horse-goad, until the cart bristled like a thornbush.

Holding the Rage at arm's length, Cuchulain also prepared. From his pack, he took a tunic of waxed skins sewn together with gut, and the heavy leather battle-belt that protected him from armpit to waist. He assembled his various weapons for a final check. Hardhead was ready, but so also was an assortment of shortswords and hurling spears, slings and death-balls and the terrible javelin with the bronze head and the three barbed prongs.

Laeg's eyes followed the weapon as Cuchulain himself placed it in the chariot.

'The Gae Bulga will avenge the Boys' Troop,' said the Hound of Ulster.

'Will we attack now?' Laeg asked. 'The sun has set.'

'Maeve ignores tradition, she kills children. Any agreements between the two of us are cancelled; I'll fight her as brutally as she fights, in the day, in the night, any way she wants it.' His lips drew back from his teeth as he spoke, and Laeg shuddered; Cuchulain's teeth were fangs.

The Rage was coming.

398

The Hound threw back his head and screamed his battle cry.

In Maeve's camp, they heard the sound. Men froze in their tracks. The dreadful, inhuman ululation rebounded from every hill and glen, as if all the voices of Ulster were joining in one voice.

Fergus mac Roy had just emerged from his tent to enjoy a meal when he heard that sound. His mouth went dry.

Ferdiad mac Daman reached for his sword – but he smiled.

Maeve of Cruachan took a deep breath. 'Leave your fires and your food,' she ordered. 'We have a problem.'

'You have a gift for understatement,' her husband told her.

The single chariot came racing out of the cold blue twilight. The driver made no attempt to check the two stallions, grey and black, that pulled it, but let them slam full force into a milling knot of Maeve's warriors. Blades on the chariot wheels scythed through legs and men fell, screaming. The horses trampled more beneath their feet as Laeg expertly wheeled them around and came again. Men cowering on the earth and trying to protect their heads with their hands had only one quick glimpse of the figure riding beside the charioteer, but one glimpse was enough.

A man could die of fright.

There was little left of the boy who had once been called Setanta. Cuchulain, the Hound of Ulster, had become a monster. Distorted by fury, his face was a crimson mask from which one eye bulged like a baleful demon with a life of its own. His mouth was opened impossibly wide, revealing the teeth of an insatiable carnivore, a lion eager to devour its prey. He seemed gigantic, this small, dark man; anger had swollen his muscles to grotesque proportions, and he loomed in the vision of his victims as a mountain of murder.

Worst of all was the light. The terrible light, the leaping fire that encircled his head and lifted his hair, the blaze that blinded his enemies and left them defenceless to him.

Screaming, he bore down on them. Leaning from the chariot, he did one of his famous sword-feats, killing six men with Hardhead before any could strike a retaliatory blow. Two of the six were chariot-chieftains, and their sudden deaths demoralised the men around them, who tried to run. But Cuchulain caught them.

And they died. Wherever his chariot went, men died.

Again and again he hurled the Gae Bulga, and again and again the three-pronged spear hummed through the air, caught and disembowelled its prey, and came back to Cuchulain's hand.

Terror spread out from the Hound in concentric circles.

Maeve ran from one company to another, trying to rally her men.

Cuchulain screamed again.

Apparitions of night and horror, lonely hags that prey on lonely travellers in lonely places, the very demons of the air, responded to his howl of defiance, until dark clouds boiled over the battlefield and flame leaped among them in jagged streaks. Flame flickered around the Hound. Flame burned through his bones.

Cuchulain's chariot was in constant motion, whirling at the centre of a storm of destruction. No two men could stay calm enough at the same time to mount a concerted attack on the Hound. Everyone was running, yelling, trying to tell his neighbours what he had seen, trying to save himself, trying to avoid Maeve.

The chariot sped around the encampment, killing as it went.

Spearmen famed for their accuracy sighted on Cuchulain but missed. Men leaped at him with drawn swords, but his sword met them first. Later the poets would recite: Cruaid and Calad and Ciar Nimble-Nose were killed; Ecell and Crom and Feochar and Cass and Fota and Aurith and Rochad and Mulach and Rurthech, chariot-chieftains all. Slain.

And the chariot of Cuchulain raced on to circle the camp again.

The night was a horror.

Sparks showered from the iron wheels of the Hound's war-cart, igniting fires in the winterdry grass.

Damac and Fiac and Dathi died, and the Gae Bulga killed Combirge with all his men around him.

'This is your fault, woman!' Ailell accused his wife at the height of the carnage.

'You agreed to it!' she flung back at him.

'Shame on my beard for being a fool, then,' Ailell muttered. He was more frightened than he had ever been in his life.

'What did you say?'

'I said you're getting deaf!' Ailell yelled at his wife.

For Laeg mac Riangabra, the night was magic. By the first circuit of the camp, he had known they were invincible. This is what it means to drive the war-cart of a god, he told himself. Tradition was overthrown, for what tradition could bind a god? So Laeg took the heavy horse-goad and began leaning out of the chariot to kill some men himself. The yew-wood goad with its inlaid bronze ornamentation had never been put to such good use, he thought. He preferred to use a whip for the horses anyway, the goad was just one more item to clutter the floor of the chariot. But now, it had found its true purpose.

As I have found mine, Laeg thought smugly.

He leaned out of the cart and struck another upturned face a savage blow with the goad. 'Slayer of children!' he cried.

Beside him rode Rage.

Never before had Cuchulain been so lost in crimson and gold and heat. From his crown to his groin to his heels, he burned. The pleasure was so intense as to be pain, and the pain was a goad, driving him to strike again and again. Blind and deaf, he was beyond thought. He was only action.

Someone tried to cut down the horses, and Laeg unhesitatingly seized one of the Hound's own spears and hurled it into the man before he could hurt the Grey or the Black.

Cuchulain lifted his shield and did the thunder-feat, striking it in a set rhythm with his fist until the reverberations burst the eardrums of weak-eared men. Long afterwards, survivors telling of that terrible night would remember the sound of the Hound's shield.

In distant Emain Macha, they heard thunder. Emer, who was not sleeping well, had ordered candles to be lit and was working with her distaff in the *grianan*, preparing thread for embroidery to keep her mind occupied. She lifted her head at the sound, then put down her work and went to the doorway.

As she stood looking out, southward, the king's wife Mugain, who had been keeping her company, stepped up behind her. 'What are you seeing?'

'Only the night beyond the walls, Mugain. But Cuchulain's fighting out there somewhere. I know it.'

'In the darkness? Men do not war at night, as a rule . . .' Mugain hesitated, remembering the destruction that had taken place at night at Emain Macha.

'Cuchulain's fighting right now,' Emer reiterated. 'And he's so young, Mugain. And so gentle, really. You don't know.'

'A wife always knows her husband in ways other people cannot. If you could see Conor mac Nessa through my eyes, you might not recognise him.'

'Is he gentle too?'

There was a smile in Mugain's voice as she said, 'He's of the Gael, both hard and soft. But he hides his softness, like all men. We women conceal our hardness.'

'We shouldn't have to hide parts of ourselves from each other.'

Mugain patted her shoulder. 'You're still young, my dear, or you'd know better.'

'I don't want to wear armour when I'm with Cuchulain.'

'Ah, Emer, with the passage of time, we all put on armour, if we are to survive. It gets in the way, but what can you do?'

'I'll try to go without it,' Emer told her, 'and take my wounds as they come.'

In the night, in Murthemney, the war-cart rolled on in yet a third circuit of Maeve's encampment.

One figure appeared to step from a pack of fleeing men, and for a moment Cuchulain's vision cleared enough to see him. He raised his arm to hurl the spear . . . and hesitated.

His arm went cold.

The man he faced wore a suit of horn body armour and was looking at him with a fearless expression, jaw set, eyes calm.

Ferdiad raised one hand in salute as the sickle chariot rushed by, but the spear was not thrown.

Cuchulain felt the Rage fading. When it was gone, they could kill him in his exhaustion. In guttural tones, he ordered Laeg to turn back to their camp.

'Now?' asked the disappointed charioteer. He did not want the night to end. Instinct told him this might be the highest peak of his life.

'Now,' said the Hound.

The chariot carried the monster away. Behind him he left countless men dead, head to head and foot to foot. Afterwards, the bards would commemorate the place as 'the Scene of the Sixfold Slaughter'. In the dawnlight, it would appear as a field of carnage encircled three times by the deep tracks of iron chariot wheels. The chariot had ploughed the earth; the blood of warriors had watered it. A crop was sown.

The place lay south-west of Dun Dalgan, in the district watered by the River Fane. And in a field within sight of the scene – the field where the majority of the Boys' Troop had died – stood a single pillar stone.

10 As Maeve looked out across the battlefield at the heaps of the slain, it occurred to her that the Hound's night of madness had cancelled some of her own sense of guilt for the slaughter of the Boys' Troop. The children.

She should be grateful to Cuchulain.

Cuchulain. Irresistible force, consummate killer. She had seen him. Burning, blazing, scorching . . .

She was breathing hard and her cheeks were flushed and everyone left her alone.

Fergus and Ferdiad walked the killing ground together, identifying dead acquaintances. 'It seems impossible he could have killed so many,' Fergus was saying.

'Impossible,' Ferdiad agreed, stepping over mutilated corpses and others who appeared to have died of pure fright. 'But this lot wasn't killed by old age. And the dying isn't over yet.'

'Right you are. By my reckoning, the Pangs should have faded by now. We can expect Cuchulain to start having company.'

'I'm not sure he needs it,' Ferdiad said ruefully.

'He'll be exhausted after this.'

'We're all exhausted after this. I wish I'd never come. How many dead, would you say?'

'I don't even want to guess,' replied Fergus. 'I suspect many of these men actually killed each other by accident during the panic last night. And over there are some who look scorched. Burned. Grass fires?'

Ferdiad could not shrug easily in his armour, but he raised one hand and twisted the wrist to give the same effect. 'What happens now, Fergus?' he asked.

'We have to try to get out of here, of course, and back to Connaught.'

'It isn't over yet,' Ferdiad reminded him.

'Stop saying that.' Fergus cast an inadvertent glance in the direction of Cuchulain's camp and stiffened. Sighting along his pointing arm, Ferdiad made out, in the clear morning light, the figure of one small, dark man, standing alone, facing them.

'Do you think he knows that neither you nor I killed any of the Boys' Troop, Ferdiad?'

The armoured man shook his head. 'Knowing Cuchulain, I somehow don't think that will make any difference. Now.'

Maeve was fighting for time while she tried to pull her shattered army together. 'I need a champion to challenge Cuchulain to single combat once more,' she announced.

Dead silence answered.

Maeve went to the tent of Fergus mac Roy. 'It's you or Ferdiad, and he's disappeared again.'

'I want no part of the Hound, thank you very much. I'm a fat old man, Maeve; surely you can't expect me to challenge him?'

'You can meet him in single combat, or I swear by the gods my people swear by, I'll send every man I've got against him at once, while he's still weary from the night! He couldn't do that a second time so soon, could he?'

Fergus hung his grizzled head. 'I doubt it. But . . . I'll need wine to drink first. A lot of wine. Whatever courage I can find to face Cuchulain, I can only find in the bottom of a barrel.'

Maeve gave him a bleak smile. 'It doesn't matter where it comes from, so long as you have it when you need it.'

The sun was high in the sky, shedding a light almost too bright for winter, as Fergus mac Roy approached Cuchulain's camp. He was not walking very steadily, but he was fully attired in battle dress.

Wearily, feeling depleted, Cuchulain went to meet him. 'You're a brave man, mac Roy,' he said, 'facing me without even a sword in your scabbard.'

'Oh. That. I lost it,' Fergus said rather sheepishly.

'Yet you challenge me to single combat?'

'I would do the same whether I had a sword or not. I ask you to yield to me now, Cuchulain . . . just for a little while . . . just so Maeve won't send all her men against you at once.'

Cuchulain shot his former instructor a merry look. 'I knew I could rely on you. If I yield to you . . . just for a while . . . will you give way to me another time?'

'I will indeed,' Fergus agreed thankfully.

Cuchulain packed up his camp, and he and Laeg retreated, but only as far as the swamp on the Fane River. When Fergus went back to report this small success to Maeve, some of the survivors of the previous night demanded, 'You have him running, so chase him, Fergus.'

'I have no intention of it,' Fergus replied stiffly. 'I'm an old, fat, *drunken* man, and he's far too lively for me. I don't have to face him again until all the rest of you have had a turn.'

He went into his tent and dropped the flap.

At Emain Macha, the Red Branch warriors were arising from their beds, collecting their weapons from the Speckled House, asking for their sons.

With tears in her eyes, Nessa told them, 'The Boys' Troop left here vowing they would never return until they could bring back the head of Ailell of Connaught.'

'And they've never returned,' sobbed Leary Buadach's wife. 'All those brave boys . . .'

'Every one higher than a man's waist went,' Conall Cearnach's wife said, 'to stand with Cuchulain while you lay moaning.'

In grim silence, the men of the Red Branch assembled their weapons and their war-carts and prepared to start southward.

Sitting with Conor in the House of the King, Emer ached at the thought of the lost children. The lightness of her still-empty womb seemed a blessing. 'At least an unborn son is out of the wind,' she commented.

'So is a dead one,' the king, who had dead sons, replied.

Emer had taken a stool close to his bench; now she pulled it closer. The wind of disaster that had blown across Ulster encouraged people to huddle together. The other women clustered in knots in the *grianan* or the gallery above the hall, but Emer felt comfortable being as close as she could to Cuchulain's foster-father.

Preoccupied with his thoughts, Conor absently placed a hand on Emer's hair in a gesture intended to comfort.

Suddenly, she was aware of him throughout her body. The soles of her feet and the nails of her fingers were tinglingly conscious of the physical presence of Conor mac Nessa.

Shaken, Emer excused herself as gracefully as possible and went to her chamber. She flung herself on the bed she had shared with Cuchulain, and tried to arrange her thoughts, but instead found herself speculating on whether a man who stood tall was long all over. And if so, how long? And did being a king confer some special abilities even a champion did not possess?

'Silly woman!' she scolded herself aloud. But somehow, though it was broad daylight and she had things to do, she allowed herself to close her eyes just for a moment . . . and tumbled into an unguarded dream.

When she awoke, she insisted on being given a light cart, a fast team, and an experienced driver, and was galloping south to Cuchulain even before the first of the Red Branch set forth. Along the way, she tried not to think about her dream.

The Hound allowed himself no dreams. Every breath was too charged with reality. To recuperate from the exhaustion following the Rage, he rested standing up, sleeping between heartbeats, his hands folded on the shaft of a spear and his forehead resting on his folded hands. The slightest sound alerted him. Any noise might mean an ambush from Maeve.

Maeve was planning no ambush, however. She just wanted to get back to Cruachan with no further losses. But she did not intend to go empty-handed. At her direction, a group of nervous herders was trying to take the vicious Brown Bull out of camp as unobtrusively as possible and hurry him toward Connaught before Cuchulain realised he was gone. In the meantime, the main body of raiders would stay in place and try to delay Cuchulain until the bull was safely beyond his reach.

'I have to get something out of this,' Maeve told Ailell through gritted teeth.

The arrangement about single combat had obviously been abrogated. Yet there was one challenger the champion of Ulster might yet be willing to face alone, if only for the sake of his own honour. And a battle between the two of them could buy Maeve the time she needed to get the Brown Bull safely to Cruachan and arrange a strategic retreat for her Connaughtmen.

She would not let Ferdiad avoid her any longer.

When he would not come to her summons, she sent a poet to him, the one surviving satirist with the group. Recalling the jests others had made about Ferdiad – probably the mere idle talk of rough men looking for someone to abuse, Maeve admitted to herself – she ordered the satirist to taunt him with chants mocking his manhood.

As she anticipated, Ferdiad soon came running to her, seething with indignation. 'Your man has no right to say such things to me! He called me a gelded ox!'

'He is not the first to suggest it,' Maeve said blandly. 'But I will chastise him if you like; we don't want one of our heroes upset. Of course, a *real* hero whose manhood could never be questioned has at

406

least one woman in his bed, and is willing to fight when asked.' She turned the full force of her colourless eyes on Ferdiad. Watching his face, she beckoned to her daughter Finavir to step forward. 'Since everyone knows you have no woman at all, mac Daman, perhaps you would be interested in this one?'

Ferdiad felt an invisible snare jerked tight around his mid-section. Only a fool would refuse such a blatant offering – particularly when the woman being offered was a daughter of the rulers of Cruachan. And if he did refuse, there would be no controlling the tongues of the satirists. They could make the name of Ferdiad mac Daman a symbol of shame throughout the land, such was their power.

He let his eyes linger on Finavir. He had noticed her before; worse fates could befall a man.

Reading his thoughts in his eyes, Maeve smiled. 'Of course, you must prove yourself worthy of my daughter, Ferdiad, and do something to win her devotion. We have seen no examples of your vaunted prowess yet. It is as unproved as your manhood.' The warmth that had been in her voice was gone now. Ferdiad had never seen colder eyes, even across a shield.

'Be my champion and challenge the Hound of Ulster to single combat,' Maeve said. 'And should you decline this request, I assure you the satirists will shout not only your lack of manhood but your absolute cowardice from every high hill in Erin.'

Ferdiad stared at the woman. He had no doubt she meant her threat. And it was a potent threat indeed: dishonour and humiliation.

'Your offer is overwhelming,' he told Maeve. 'Even so . . . the Hound of Ulster has been more than a brother to me. I don't want to fight him.'

'Are you afraid of him?' Maeve spat. At her words, Ferdiad unconsciously balled his fists – and she noticed. 'You *are* afraid!' Her eyes narrowed with cunning. 'So what he says about you is true.'

She caught Ferdiad off guard. 'What does Cuchulain say about me?'

'Only that he is glad you never went to challenge him, because killing you would have been too easy. Some of the charioteers who have taken our real heroes out to meet him reported that he scorned you as a coward, but I didn't believe it myself until this moment. Where is that satirist?' She looked around as if she could not wait to tell the poet the shameful truth of Ferdiad mac Daman.

Blood beat like hammers in Ferdiad's temples.

He had heard satirists cut the legs off decent men. Having left Ulster and his clan and . . . admit it, and Cuchulain . . . behind, he had nothing left but his reputation as a man and a warrior. And Maeve meant to strip that from him.

Could Cuchulain have thought it was cowardice that kept Ferdiad from challenging him?

He did not know.

He could not bear to have the Hound think he was afraid.

Maeve was watching him. Finavir was watching him. Ailell, who had joined the group, was watching him.

Ferdiad hunted in his throat until he found his voice, then said, 'Send word to the champion of Ulster. He has one more single combat to fight – if he dares. At the ford of the River Dee.'

He stalked away to prepare himself.

'Maeve,' Ailell asked his wife, 'who told you Cuchulain accused Ferdiad of cowardice?'

'No one. I simply used the man's own pride as a weapon against him, a tool to force him to do what I need done.'

Ailell gave his wife a look of mingled admiration and disgust. Then he went to find Fergus. 'Ferdiad has agreed to challenge Cuchulain to one final single combat,' he explained, 'and I want you to carry the message.'

'Why is she doing this now? And why me?'

'To give us time to get the bull away and prepare our own retreat. Our forces are in bits after the Hound's attack on us, we have to get injured men on their feet and able to march. And I'm the one asking you to carry the challenge, because I know you as a friend to both men.'

'The warriors of Ulster may be here soon.'

'All the more reason to hurry, then. If a single combat is taking place when they arrive, they won't intervene but will wait until it's decided, and by the time the contest is over, our wounded men and the Donn Cooley can be halfway to Connaught. Lives can be saved on both sides, Fergus.'

Why me? Fergus thought again, silently this time, but with bitterness. Nevertheless, he set out for Cuchulain's camp, feeling there was nothing else to be done.

He found Cuchulain and Laeg sitting side by side on a fallen tree, cleaning weapons. 'Ferdiad mac Daman challenges the champion of Ulster to single combat,' Fergus announced formally.

Cuchulain put down the sword he was cleaning. 'I don't want to.'

'You're not afraid of him.' It was a statement, not a question.

Cuchulain's reply was also a statement. 'I love him. That's why I don't want to hurt him.'

'Do you think you could . . . kill him?' Fergus wanted to know. 'Aside from his skill, he has that special armour.'

'I know about his skill and his armour. What I don't know is how he could have been persuaded to challenge me now.'

Fergus helped himself to a seat on the log. Laeg obligingly moved over to make room. 'They're saying in camp that Maeve offered him her daughter Finavir,' Fergus said. 'Nothing new, really, she's offered the girl to every man who's challenged you in exchange for your head. Of course, no one's collected so far.'

Cuchulain looked astonished. 'Ferdiad is willing to fight me for a woman?'

'Apparently so. He's preparing himself now. He intends to meet you at dawn, at the ford.'

Cuchulain stood up, turning his back on the other two. For a long time, he simply stood immobile, looking out over Murthemney. Then he said, 'Fergus, carry my agreement to Ferdiad mac Daman. And it's a good thing you came as messenger. If any other man had brought me such news, all Maeve's armies would not have been enough to save his life.'

He sat down and began sharpening his sword blade. He did not speak to Fergus again. Laeg, however, met the older man's eyes and shook his head sadly. 'They are well matched,' said the charioteer, worried.

'They are,' Fergus agreed with a heavy heart. Feeling old and cold, he wrapped his shaggy mantle more tightly about him and returned to the camp of the Connaughtmen, where he lost himself in drink and was incoherent before sunset.

Shortly before sunset, however, Laeg ventured out to look at several snares he had set for game – and saw the glow of a fire where none should be. Stealthily advancing, a drawn sword in his hand, he made an unexpected discovery.

And returned to Cuchulain in high good humour.

The Hound's mood was sour. He barely grunted at Laeg.

'Cuchulain, I think you should know – '

The Hound lifted a hand. 'Quiet. Do you hear something?'

'That's what I'm trying to tell you.' Laeg's excitement was bursting out of him like juice from over-ripe berries. 'Cuchulain, what are you doing tonight?'

'Cleaning myself and resting, what else should I be doing before combat?'

'Indeed. Well, think on this. When Ferdiad comes to the ford in the dawnlight, his body will no doubt be freshly bathed by the fair Finavir. You should receive the same attention as your opponent, don't you agree?'

'I don't need you to wash me.'

'Nor am I offering. But Emer will.'

'Emer!' Cuchulain grabbed Laeg's arm in a grip so crushing that the next day the charioteer had to drive the team one-handed.

'The sounds you hear are coming from her camp just over that hill, in the Meadow of the Two Oxen. She came in a racing chariot to be with you, and assures me the warriors of the Red Branch are following as soon as they are able.'

Laeg could not tell if Cuchulain heard his last words or not. The Hound had vanished into the night, running up the hill towards the meadow.

Alone by the campfire, Laeg hummed to himself as he made a meal of snared rabbits and cheese. Then he rubbed grease into Cuchulain's various leathers to soften them; he held up spears and swords and squinted at their surfaces in the firelight, giving them a few more strokes on the sharpening stone to be certain they were deadly.

Laeg had never liked Ferdiad mac Daman very much.

11 Emer was waiting when Cuchulain came rushing to her out of the night. Without a word, she enfolded him in her arms. They clung together, feeling life in each other.

She had meat and barley wine waiting and fed him well. 'I'm glad you're here,' he said simply. 'But how did you know?'

When she laughed, her nose crinkled. 'Oh, Setanta!'

After he had eaten the meat and rubbed the grease from it into his muscles to keep them supple, he reached for her again. The cart driver and the spear carrier who had accompanied her took themselves off to stand guard. Stretching out by the campfire, the Hound pressed Emer's head into the hollow of his shoulder. He would not enter her body before the battle. He had a greater need of her: the comfort and absolution women have always given their warriors.

In a few terse words, he described the situation.

'I can't believe a man you've called your dearest friend means to fight you to the death,' Emer said.

'We're often forced to believe things we don't want to.'

She pressed closer, her tawny hair brushing his cheek. 'How dangerous is he to you?'

'Ferdiad?' Cuchulain gave a hollow laugh. 'Very. We've tested ourselves together many times, and if any man can kill me, he can. In strength and skill, we're well matched, unless . . .'

'Unless?'

'Nothing. We're well matched. And we know each other's style and weaknesses, know every shift of weight and slash of sword. Fighting Ferdiad will be like fighting myself.'

'Then must you do it?'

'My honour is pledged as champion. I have to accept a challenge. And one of us will have to die,' he added prophetically, knowing neither of them would stop short of death.

He closed his eyes then, and Emer wrapped her arms tightly around him. She lay with him moonlong, and when he wept in his sleep, she knew.

By sunrise, Maeve's camp was feverish with excitement. Even the injured were reluctant to take advantage of the time that had been bought for them by setting out at once for Connaught. Everyone wanted to watch the fight between Cuchulain and Ferdiad.

Maeve was waiting for her elected champion when he emerged from his tent. Detecting a hesitation in his step, she asked sharply, 'Has your nerve failed you?'

Ferdiad's chin came up. He rewarded her question with a hostile glare. 'Not even on the rim of the world would my nerve fail me,' he said.

Maeve caught a glimpse of Finavir out of the corner of her eye, the first time she had seen the girl that morning. Aware that the satirist was standing close enough to overhear what was said, she asked her daughter, 'Have you seen mac Daman without his armour on yet?'

The warriors were crowding around, listening and leering. They were not schooled in mercy.

Finavir looked at Ferdiad and then looked away, saying nothing.

The satirist laughed. 'Go to your battle and prove yourself,' he said, 'or by this time tomorrow no man in Erin will share his drinking horn with you and no woman will ever welcome you to her bed.'

Above the edge of overlapping plates of horn, the back of Ferdiad's neck turned red. He signalled for his charioteer.

Meanwhile, Emer was pleading with Cuchulain to let her accompany him to the river. He refused. 'You would only distract me. Besides, Ferdiad may not even come.' But just then they heard the tattoo of approaching hoofbeats on the other side of the Dee. Cuchulain stepped into his chariot, and Laeg drove him away.

Ferdiad reached the ford first. Wheels grating on gravel, Laeg drove in a flamboyant, spinning circle to present the left side of insult to him, then pulled the horses back on their haunches so violently they reared.

The two champions left their chariots to face each other across the water.

'So you did come,' Cuchulain said softly to the familiar, rough-hewn face.

'And you. I bid you welcome.'

'Once, I would have been glad of your welcome, Ferdiad. Now, you're just an invader plundering our land.'

'I'm a warrior for Connaught, come to prove my strength!' Ferdiad shouted so the distant line of watching westerners could hear him.

Still soft-voiced, Cuchulain replied, 'I can stand against anything you hurl against me, as we once stood together against Ayfa. Do you remember?'

Ferdiad blinked. 'Best we forget such boyhood attachments. They have no place here; we have the work of men to do.'

Stung, Cuchulain said, 'If that's what you want. If you can forget we shared one bed and one sleep, so can I. The friends who fought together and hunted together and talked until dawn together are gone from my mind. Prepare to defend yourself, invader!' cried the Hound of Ulster.

Throwing out his arms, he inflated his lungs until the seams of his leather battle-tunic creaked. His look of youth fell from him. In its place, the coarse, derisive, taunting war chant of a champion boomed out across the water. In the Boys' Troop, both he and Ferdiad had been taught the insults calculated to infuriate an enemy and make him careless, and now they hurled them at each other across the ford.

Each knew the phrases to most wound the other. Reluctantly at first, then with mounting vehemence, they used them. Men who know each other's secrets make terrible enemies.

Listening to their shouts as they carried on the wind, the druids who had accompanied Maeve from Connaught nodded their heads at one another. 'No end for this but blood and death,' they agreed.

On the banks of the ford, the taunting rose to a crescendo, then stopped. Red-faced and breathless, whipped to a frenzy of anger, the two warriors glared at each other. 'Your chariot reached the ford first,' Cuchulain called. 'You choose the first weapons.'

'We will open with the battle-feats Skya taught us,' Ferdiad decided.

A momentary warmth flickered in Cuchulain's eyes.

They took up round sharp-rimmed shields and sheafs of light spears and began throwing at one another, but each man watched the direction of the other's glance and read his arm. The spears sped over the water to lodge in the rims of the shields, then were hastily jerked out and flung back, buzzing like so many bees as they darted from one side to the other. But no dart got through. Cuchulain and Ferdiad danced on their opposite banks, spinning their shields, catching the points on the rims, and in time they began laughing as one fine toss after another was made and parried.

'They are playing *games*,' Maeve muttered darkly.

'They are warming their muscles and testing each other,' Ailell assured her. 'The serious fighting will come later. You are seeing a true test of champions, woman; settle down and enjoy it.'

Maeve had a pile of crimson cushions brought and propped against her chariot, and she leaned on those as she watched. She was a good gallop from the ford, but the day was bright and she saw clearly; she was unwilling to miss a detail. If any man inadvertently stepped into her line of vision, she swore at him in a way to shame the cruellest satirist.

From time to time, her hand slipped down, seeking a silky head to pat, but Baiscne was not there.

By the time the sun stood high, it was obvious the exchange of light spears was proving nothing, merely blunting the points of the weapons.

'It's still your choice as long as the light lasts,' Cuchulain reminded Ferdiad.

'Heavy javelins, then.'

Cuchulain tossed his light shield and spears to Laeg and took up a heavier shield of tough leather, and a sturdy javelin bound with flax. Similarly armed, Ferdiad met him again and they fought, but neither could gain an advantage, though more than once their weapons drew blood.

The day was short, night owned the winter. When the light began to fade and neither man had overcome the other, Ferdiad called, 'Let's break this off and resume tomorrow.'

'Good enough,' Cuchulain agreed. He tossed his weapons to Laeg, and he and Ferdiad looked at each other once again across the stream.

Then, without saying anything, they waded out and met in the middle.

The spectators could not tell who moved first, for the twilight was falling very rapidly and obscuring their vision. But it was obvious the two men stood still for a long time, face to face – then suddenly threw their arms around each other's necks.

'Are they giving up?' Maeve screamed in outrage.

'Not a bit of it,' said Ailell. 'They'll fight tomorrow, but the sun is setting now. This is a battle of champions, it has its own rules.'

'I know the rules of war,' his wife said.

'Do you?' Ailell turned his shoulder to her and began talking animatedly to Fergus mac Roy instead.

Cuchulain and Ferdiad came splashing out of the ford together, waving to their charioteers to join them. They oversaw the grazing of their horses in one field; they put their foodstores together and divided them equally, so neither would receive more nourishment than the other for the next day's work. They examined each other's wounds and Cuchulain ordered Laeg to give Ferdiad's charioteer some of his own healing potions.

414

Then each man retired to his night camp on his own side of the ford, but they lay on one earth, looking up into the same wilderness of stars.

At dawn, they met again.

'Today, you choose the weapons,' Ferdiad said.

'Stabbing spears,' Cuchulain replied. 'And chariots.'

'See there!' Ailell told his wife. 'They're getting into it now.'

'See there,' his wife responded, 'on the far shore beyond Cuchulain. Men. The first of the Red Branch are arriving.'

'They won't interfere with the contest. Nothing will happen while those two are fighting.'

'But a lot will happen after,' said Fergus mac Roy.

To fight with chariots meant leaving the ford and meeting on dry land. Laeg and Ferdiad's driver went together to select a level place free from stones, which took some time to find. Without exchanging words, Cuchulain and Ferdiad stood side by side and waited until all was in readiness.

'Take the sickle blades off my wheels,' the Hound ordered Laeg. 'Ferdiad's cart has none.'

'Leave them on,' the other man said. 'I can defeat you just as easily.'

'I won't fight you that way.'

'Very well, take off the blades, but hurry up.'

Cuchulain let his eyes meet Ferdiad's then. 'Are you so anxious to die?'

'I'm not afraid of it.'

'I've never known you to be afraid of dying – only of living,' Cuchulain said softly, as if the two of them were alone in some peaceful place, exchanging the confidences of friends. 'Skya understood you very well when she gave you armour to wear.'

'You've seen me without it.'

'I have.' Cuchulain's jaw tightened. 'But when you are dead, I'll leave it on you. No one will see you vulnerable again.'

Ferdiad should have replied with a spirited denial of any possibility of defeat, but instead he only searched Cuchulain's face with his eyes, then turned away and went to his chariot.

The second day of battle was savage. The chariots wheeled and spun and raced at one another, taxing each driver to the utmost. Men from both Connaught and Ulster crowded around the field, cheering their champions, forgetting their differences in the excitement.

But Maeve could not help noticing that the ranks of spectators kept growing as more and more Ulstermen arrived. Still, her armies outnumbered them substantially. Recovering from the debilitating effects of the Curse of Macha took some men a long time; male bodies are not designed to endure birthing pangs.

Leaning far out as the chariots passed each other, Ferdiad and Cuchulain stabbed again and again, forcing their way past one another's guard, drawing more blood. When the horses were heavily lathered and almost out of control, they drew rein by mutual consent to allow them to rest, then began again.

At last Cuchulain called, 'Our horses are almost ruined and our charioteers are sagging as they stand. Shall we break it off until tomorrow?'

'We shall,' Ferdiad agreed gladly.

They met again and embraced, signalling a halt to hostilities. Both men were grimy with sweat and dirt and smeared with blood. Their clothing was soaked. In their eyes, each saw a mirror of the other.

'You look awful,' Ferdiad said with a shaky laugh.

'We're well matched, I've always said so.'

'You have supporters arriving, will they bring you fresh food?'

'I hope so.'

'I'm well supplied. I'll send you some of my meat and wine.'

'We'll share the meal,' agreed Cuchulain.

They sat together at the edge of the chariot field while their drivers tended the horses. Their wounds were by now too severe for charioteers to deal with, so healers from both sides were summoned to apply poultices and chant incantations. A runner from Maeve's camp brought a jug containing mead mixed with eggs and bull's blood to give strength to their champion, and Ferdiad called for two cups so he could share it with Cuchulain.

When he stood up at last to seek his bed, on his own side of the ford, he moved very stiffly in his armour.

'You should take off those horn plates and let us care for your wounds properly,' advised the physician Maeve had sent.

Ferdiad glanced at the Hound of Ulster. 'My armour never comes off again,' he said.

'That's a promise,' came the answer, softly spoken.

The two men slept the troubled sleep of exhaustion that night while two armies watched from opposite sides, their campfires glaring like angry eyes.

The third day of single combat dawned bleak and cold. In an iron-grey sky, no bird flew, no wind stirred. Brittle dead grass crunched to

416

the stepping foot as men dragged themselves from their beds, huddled around campfires chafing their hands together, blew on their fingers to warm them before shuffling off to relieve themselves.

On the east side of the ford, Cuchulain opened his eyes and missed the glow of the sun. On the west, Ferdiad opened his eyes and stared up at the lowering clouds.

They met again.

'I think you look worse than I do today,' Cuchulain greeted his opponent. The expression on Ferdiad's face was painful to him: dull-eyed and filled with shadows.

The Hound had faced many men in battle and many times observed the subtle change when the inward spirit made its decision to give up fighting. Often the warrior himself was not consciously aware, but the choice had been made, and sooner or later there would be a fatal mistake.

Not Ferdiad, Cuchulain thought. Not Ferdiad!

The battle had to end and there could be only one ending, but Cuchulain denied it.

He taunted Ferdiad more viciously than ever, trying to put the will to win back into him. But when he saw the shoulders brace and savagery leap into the eyes, he regretted the cruellest of his words. Should he die, he did not want them to be the last thing Ferdiad had heard him say. 'Is there any reason for the two of us to want to kill each other?' he called out.

'You fight for the honour of Ulster,' the other man replied. 'Are you offering to set that aside?'

After the briefest of pauses, Cuchulain said, 'Name the day's weapons.'

'Swords,' said Ferdiad mac Daman.

Though the Ulstermen were trying to keep her away from the scene of battle, Emer winced with each clang of the great iron swords as they clashed, plainly audible. 'Let me go to him!'

'Stay back,' she was told by men who understood. 'You'd only get him killed.'

On one arm, each warrior carried his sturdiest full-length shield, in his other hand his favourite sword. The black shield of Cuchulain protected him as best it could while Hardhead did the work of ten swords, but Ferdiad's skill held up throughout the day. The two men fought until flesh and bone could fight no longer, and each had hacked great wounds in the other.

417

Yet the combat remained unresolved.

At the end of the sword-day, they did not meet and embrace. The matter had gone too far and too long; the ending pressed heavily on both of them.

They showed each other their backs and sought the solace of their separate camps. Their horses did not share a grazing that night, nor their charioteers a cooking fire.

Ferdiad found the night a thousand winters long. Some time before dawn, he admitted to himself that this must be the final day. He arose wearily and began preparing. Rubbing his eyes, his half-awake charioteer hurried to help him.

On his head, Ferdiad placed a crested battle helmet brave with red enamel and richly coloured carbuncles. He fastened a leather battle-apron over his body armour, then had his driver place a large flat stone atop that, covering much of his chest and belly, and strap the thing in place with leather thongs. 'I would not be surprised if I had to face the Gae Bulga today,' Ferdiad explained. 'I make ready as best I can.'

He reached the ford first, and by the time Cuchulain arrived, he was running through a dazzling repertoire of battle-feats, giving the impression of being very fresh and formidable.

'Look at him, Laeg,' the Hound said admiringly. 'Should my strength fail me today, you must taunt and insult me to keep me fighting. I'll rely on you.'

Then he called out to Ferdiad, 'I am here, but I want you to know this before we begin. I am aware that a woman sent you here by offering another woman as a prize. But not for any woman born would I have undertaken to kill you.'

Ferdiad faltered in his display. One of the spears he was juggling fell unnoticed as he turned towards the Hound. 'Know this,' he said slowly. 'It's not for the sake of any woman born that I undertake to kill you.'

'Then why?' Cuchulain asked in surprise. 'You have been my team-mate, my forest friend – why agree to this deadly combat?'

With something like a sob in his throat, Ferdiad answered, 'Because I'll be forever dishonoured if I refuse. You don't understand . . . Maeve has threatened me with the undying satire of the poets. Men will jeer at my name for a hundred generations unless I prove myself against you today.'

'Only honour compels you to do this?' Cuchulain said, as if in disbelief.

'Surely you can accept that. Honour is everything to you,' Ferdiad

418

replied in a dull voice. His eyes were blank. 'The choice of weapons is yours today, Ulster.'

There is no way out for either of us, Cuchulain thought bitterly. Sencha the brehon had once taught him, convinced him: Honour is the treasure no one can take from you; honour is the shield no one can penetrate unless you let him.

Now, honour had brought the two of them to an icy river on a bitterly cold day to try to kill each other for something neither could touch or taste or hold in his hands.

Honour has somehow failed us, Cuchulain thought, wishing he had time to puzzle it through. But there was no time left. 'Bring any weapon you like,' he told Ferdiad, turning away before the other man could see the conflicting emotions in his face.

Baring their feet for the water, they met at the midpoint of the ford, and they came to kill. Cuchulain leaped at Ferdiad first, but the other man met him with a blow to the belly that sent him spinning away.

'He brushes you aside as a woman brushes off a clinging child!' Laeg at once taunted from the riverbank.

Cuchulain scrambled on to the high point of the bank above the ford and hurled himself off in the salmon-leap, feet extended to knock Ferdiad's shield away. But just as his feet touched its surface, the other man struck the shield such a blow from the inside that the Hound was thrown backward into the water.

Laeg yelled, 'He crushes you as a millstone crushes malt! He swallows you in one gulp as an eagle swallows a fish!'

Shaking off bright droplets, Cuchulain flung himself at his opponent a third time, only to be repulsed again. Laeg felt his heart skip. He knew Ferdiad must be fresher; Cuchulain had fought so many times before. Furthermore, the charioteer was beginning to be afraid the Hound could never force himself to strike a fatal blow against his friend. In desperation, Laeg screamed, 'If you fail Ulster as her champion today, the bards will forget your very name!'

At that moment, like an eerie echo, a second voice joined his. The raucous screech of a huge raven tore the air, an inhuman cry sounding strangely like human words: 'Arise, Root of Valour!' A caw of mocking laughter followed, sarcastic, derisive.

The change began before Laeg's eyes. Cuchulain and Ferdiad had been more evenly matched than he ever suspected, but after the transformation he saw taking place, the contest would no longer be even. Laeg gave an explosive sigh of relief.

Answering an irresistible summons, the Rage invaded Cuchulain's blood and bones.

He made a futile effort to fight it off for Ferdiad's sake, but then the taunting inhuman laughter rolled over him, refusing mercy, and the anger leaped in him and the great red glory sizzled through him with the drumbeat and the heat and the lust . . . and when the voices ceased, he did not know. He heard only the roar in his ears.

To the farthest side of Maeve's encampment, they could hear the terrible roar of the Hound of Ulster.

Maeve's eyes dilated.

Beside her, Ailell said sombrely, 'Look in the sky. The first of the ravens has come to feed.'

The thing that Ferdiad found himself battling was immense, red-mottled, out of control. Hideous and gorgeous, war exemplified. He had seen Cuchulain's battle-fury before, but never fully appreciated the paralysing terror his victims felt; now he knew.

Perversely, he welcomed the moment. He might die, but before he did, he would know his full measure against the Hound.

With an incredible effort of will, Ferdiad shook off the pall of fear and attacked instead of running away. His own battle yell mingled with the savage baying of the apparition he fought, and the water foamed white around them.

Knee to knee and belly to belly they struggled. Their shields were pressed together so forcefully that they split; their sword blades grated against each other with a scream of their own.

In spite of himself, Laeg put his hands over his ears.

The teams that had brought the two chariots to the river panicked at the sounds coming from the stream and reared in terror, rolling their eyes.

There was one breathless moment when the battle might have gone either way, Ferdiad's inspired manhood finding its highest expression against the champion of Ulster. But in the madness of their two reddened faces straining together, breath gushing from the nostrils of one into the nostrils of the other, the creature who had been Cuchulain looked into Ferdiad's eyes and remembered.

Campfires and high stars and smoky nights. A friend to whom you could divulge the deepest feelings of your spirit. Love met and matched . . .

In that heartbeat, Ferdiad got his sword past the Hound's shield and plunged it into his chest.

420

Hot blood poured out, taking the magical heat with it.

Sparks swam in Cuchulain's eyes.

'RED BRANCH!' Laeg screamed at him from the riverbank.

Staggering backwards, Cuchulain dropped Hardhead into the swirling and bloodied water. He half turned and called in a failing voice to his charioteer, 'Bring the spear.'

Laeg whirled and ran to the chariot. He was back at once, slipping and sliding down the muddy bank, holding the Gae Bulga high above his head.

Cuchulain dropped on one knee, his strength rushing from him. As Laeg hurried towards him, the charioteer slipped and fell forward. The water tore the Invincible Spear from his fingers and carried it downstream.

Only the three in the water and the raven above in the sky saw what happened next.

12 Both men had been fighting barefoot, using their toes to grip the stones in the stream bed and keep their balance in the water. Half-submerged now, Cuchulain was supporting his upper body on propped arms to keep his head from going under. As the Gae Bulga came towards him, he managed to lift one foot out of the water and somehow grasp the shaft between his toes. Then he threw it.

The aim of his foot did not have to be accurate, nor the thrust behind it strong. This was the Gae Bulga.

Ferdiad flung himself backwards, but there was no escape.

The spear sang to itself as it flew.

The bronze head with its barbed prongs struck and shattered the stone he had attached to protect his vital parts. With no diminution of force, it passed through his leather battle-apron and tore open the plates of horn no weapon had pierced before.

Ferdiad felt as if his entire body were suddenly filled with barbs.

The head of the spear broke through his back, and he tumbled sideways against the exposed roots of an old tree reaching down into the river. The pain was so excruciating, his body only allowed him to feel one jolt, then rejected sensation completely. Ferdiad did not faint, but a fatal numbness told him he was a dead man.

Upstream, Cuchulain was dragging himself to his feet. Laeg hurried to support him, draping one of the Hound's arms across his own shoulders. His warrior had taken a fearful wound in the chest, but to Laeg's experienced eye it looked survivable.

'I believe I am killed,' a faint voice moaned.

Cuchulain pulled free of Laeg and splashed over to Ferdiad. As he bent down, the other man opened his eyes and said in the accusing tones of a small boy, 'You didn't fight fair.'

Cuchulain crouched in the water beside Ferdiad to stroke his face, chafe his hands, smooth his wet hair out of his eyes, whisper, 'I didn't mean the insults I shouted at you. Can you hear me? You know they were just part of the ritual, Ferdiad. Ferdiad?' Getting no response, he

422

gathered the larger man, spear and all, into his arms, and carried him out of the river. On to the Ulster side.

There, Cuchulain – he was Cuchulain now, the monster had vanished into the darkness within him – sat down cross-legged to cradle his friend's head and shoulders in his arms. In an excess of tenderness, he kissed Ferdiad's bloodless forehead again and again, though he was close to fainting from his own blood loss.

When Ferdiad next opened his eyes, Cuchulain asked, 'Shall I draw the spear?' The sight of its shaft rising from his friend's breast appalled him.

'Don't. I'll die if you try it.'

'You'll die anyway,' Cuchulain replied, with a sob in his throat. 'I used the Gae Bulga.'

'The Gae Bulga, is it? Ah, then. But you were good at the foot-throwing feat today. I saw you. Remember when we used to practise it together? At Skya's I was good too . . .'

'Don't try to talk, save your strength.'

'For what? Have we a race to run, Cuchulain? Or is there an enemy we should be facing together?' He coughed weakly. 'We men of the Red Branch . . .' His eyes flared wide. 'Ah, Cuchulain, I was Red Branch too. And it is hard to die by your hand . . .' His head lolled lifeless in his friend's lap.

From the west side of the ford, Ailell watched one figure emerge from the riverbed carrying another. 'They're going to the east side,' he reported. 'The victory is to Ulster, then.'

Maeve made a strangled noise and turned away. She did not watch as the Hound carried his dead friend away from the Dee and laid him on the grass while Laeg circled ineffectually around him. She did not see Laeg at last withdraw, to go and stand talking with Leary Buadach of the Red Branch in order to give Cuchulain a little time alone with Ferdiad's body.

The details of the aftermath did not interest her. Over and over, she repeated, as if she could not make out the meaning of the words, 'Cuchulain won. Cuchulain won.'

'Of course he won,' Ailell snapped. 'I expected it, didn't you? I think even poor Ferdiad expected it. He left here loaded down with every conceivable weapon, but he didn't look very hopeful, did he? He knew what the Hound of Ulster is, and so do we all.'

'Do we?' Maeve asked. She turned around and shaded her eyes with her hand, looking across the river now towards the small, dark form of one man sitting on the grass, cradling another in his arms. 'What would you say Cuchulain is, Ailell?'

Her voice cracked saying Cuchulain's name. Ailell gave her a measuring glance. Was she losing control? She had never been beaten; some people could not stand losing. 'Let's not waste time discussing the Hound, Maeve. Do you see that line of men across the river? They're Red Branch warriors, and we killed their sons in the Boys' Troop. If they don't know it already, they're sure to find out soon, and unless I'm very much mistaken, they won't consider the death of Ferdiad sufficient to avenge their sons. We'd better break camp now and run for our lives.'

She gave him a distracted look. 'This isn't the way I planned it.'

'War never goes the way anyone plans it, woman! Tie up your strings and let's get out of here. I'm fond enough of my head to want to keep it a while longer.'

'Red Branch,' Maeve said. 'The Red Branch doesn't hurt women; they're famous for it. Isn't that true? Didn't I hear it somewhere? Conor mac Nessa . . .'

'Oh, come *on*!' cried the exasperated Ailell, grabbing his wife's arm and pulling her along behind him like a pony on a rope.

From the far side of the ford, the men of the Red Branch had watched the single combat. When it ended, they respected Cuchulain's grief; there was not a man among them who had not knelt beside a dying friend. But a few brief words with Laeg had told them the fate of the Boys' Troop, and they could not stand idle. Skirting the place where Ferdiad lay, they formed into companies and prepared to attack the Connaughtmen – a band Cuchulain had already depleted considerably.

After speaking with the men of the Red Branch, Laeg went back to Cuchulain. He found Ferdiad's charioteer there, standing awkwardly to one side. 'I have to take mac Daman's body back,' the man said.

'I wouldn't try it yet,' Laeg advised him. 'Wait until the champion of Ulster has finished mourning him, or I might have to deliver your dead body to Maeve along with Ferdiad's.'

Heedless of his own injuries, Cuchulain held his friend's body in his arms and wept for him. Every word of praise admirers had showered on Cuchulain he now gave to Ferdiad, commending his valour, his manly beauty, his singularity. Ravaged by battle cries, his voice rasped in his throat, but he continued until it was only a whisper of grief.

Laeg stepped forward then, and Cuchulain looked up at him. With gestures, he indicated that the charioteer was to cut the dead man open and remove the Gae Bulga.

Laeg shrank back. 'Don't ask it of me.'

'I must,' Cuchulain struggled to say. 'It's something I can't do myself. Cut out the spear but leave his armour on him; I promised.'

Cuchulain turned his face away while Laeg freed the deadly spear. Then he gathered the ruined body in his arms again. 'I am broken and bloody,' he whispered to it, 'and Ferdiad's chariot stands empty.'

He was not a bard, yet by the ford of the Dee a lament came to him and demanded to be chanted. There was no other to lament the son of Daman, no other who knew him so well or loved him so truly. Magic welled up in the champion of Ulster and formed itself into words, and the listening charioteers wept as they heard them.

In a voice so broken and torn that the blood welled in his throat, Cuchulain paid his tribute to his friend.

> *'All was play, all was sport,*
> *Till Ferdiad came to the ford.*
> *We had the same teachers, we shared the same breath.*
> *One our life, one our spirit, one our courage in arms.*
>
> *All was play, all was sport,*
> *Till Ferdiad came to the ford.*
> *Ferdiad, furious, fiery lion, huge as a mountain to me*
> *Yesterday. Today, he is only a shadow.*
>
> *All was play, all was sport,*
> *Till Ferdiad came to the ford.*
> *Now the games are over, the laughter changed to weeping.*
> *He should have lived for ever. Now, I am doomed to live.'*

The ragged voice fell silent. Cuchulain passed a hand across his eyes, gasped, and fell over on to the earth.

Laeg ran for help.

Emer came at once, bringing a healer with her. After the briefest of examinations, the physician told the champion's wife, 'He has suffered enough wounds to kill any mortal man three times over. I can staunch the flow of blood, perhaps, but beyond that I can do little. If Cuchulain lives, it will be because he forces himself to live.'

He signalled for bearers tc come and carry the Hound's unconscious body a safe distance behind the Ulster line. Emer walked beside the litter every step of the way, holding one of her husband's hands in hers and murmuring to him, 'Live for me, Setanta. Live for me.'

In the Connaught camp, Maeve seemed dazed. Ailell ran frantically from one group of men to another, trying to get leaders to lead and marchers to march. 'All the fighting that's gone before will seem as nothing compared to what's coming now,' he warned them. 'We've stepped into a hornet's nest up to our knees. Cuchulain held us here too long; we stood around watching like gape-mouthed idiots until our enemies outnumbered us. Move fast now, or there'll be more widows than grass in Connaught!'

'Not much grass in Connaught anyway,' commented Fergus, who would have felt depressed no matter what the outcome of the combat. 'Stones are the principal crop.'

'I'll stone you, mac Roy!' warned Ailell. 'Get in your chariot. Or had you rather wait here, and see how the Ulstermen treat traitors?'

'I don't need a demonstration,' Fergus assured him, beckoning to his charioteer.

The invaders set off westward as swiftly as possible, with the Ulstermen at their heels. Led by the Red Branch, the northern forces were swelled by the addition of men who had never claimed warrior rank before and were hungry for the chance. Conor mac Nessa's favourite messenger, Cethern, acquired a war-cart and driver and went in the forefront of the charge, yelling in a fair imitation of Cuchulain's battle cry.

No man could resist pursuing a fleeing enemy.

But Cethern was not a trained warrior. When he caught up with the Connaughtmen, the first one he attacked dodged his clumsy sword-swing and plunged a spear through him.

Cethern's driver carried him back to the camp where Cuchulain was being treated. In spite of his injuries, the Hound had struggled back to consciousness, though it was not a place he enjoyed being. He kept envisioning Ferdiad dying in his arms. To distract himself, he watched one of the healers working over Cethern's wounds.

The messenger was not used to pain; it made him wild. When the healer told him, 'I'm afraid you won't survive this,' Cethern shouted hysterically, 'Then neither will you!' Seizing the sword that lay by his pallet, he slammed it into the healer's head and cracked his skull.

With a groan, Cuchulain raised himself on one elbow. 'That's it,' he told Cethern. 'Now you'll never get anyone to care for you.'

'I don't like bad news,' Cethern muttered, twisting in his pain.

Cuchulain looked toward Laeg and Emer, who sat beside him. 'Laeg, is the king with us?'

'Following soon. He wanted to gather additional warriors. But many of his people came with us.'

'Fingan the physician?'

'Indeed, it is he who cares for you.'

'Summon him for Cethern as well, then. But be careful to warn him that the patient is very particular about the nature of the messages he receives.'

Exhausted, Cuchulain sank back and closed his eyes, but Emer was smiling. His small spark of humour gave her hope.

When Fingan entered the leather tent that had been hastily erected to shelter the injured men, Cuchulain sensed his presence and growled at Cethern, without bothering to open his eyes, 'Remember I'm the king's champion. If you do an injury to his physician, you'll have to fight me.'

'Oh.' Cethern lay back quietly then and let Fingan examine his wound. Then he asked the physician, in somewhat chastened tones, 'How do you see my future?'

'Don't expect calves from your cows,' Fingan advised him. 'However, if you are bathed in a mash made from the marrow of beef bones you may recover enough to live a few more seasons – provided you give up fighting, which is not your true work, and sit quietly out of the wind.'

After Fingan had gone, Cethern whispered to Cuchulain, 'As soon as I'm healed, I'm going to fight again.'

The champion of Ulster opened his eyes and gave him a long, sad look, then turned his face away.

Meanwhile, Conor mac Nessa swept down from the north, gathering every kinsman and ally and clan-chief who owed him tribute. When his warriors reached southern Ulster, he directed them to divide into two great wings, so they could trap the Connaughtmen between them.

The region they entered had been ravaged by plunderers. The raiders had not only taken cattle and burned homesteads; they had seized able-bodied young men and fertile women, yoked them together, and dragged them off to be slaves. While Cuchulain mounted his lonely defence, Maeve's men had scattered like chaff on the wind, seizing everything they could.

As the king's chariot rolled past, old women ran out of burned, roof-fallen houses to try to seize his hands and kiss them. 'My son . . . my daughter . . .' they pleaded. 'Return them to me!'

In one of the chariots accompanying Conor rode the ancient grandsire of Leary Buadach, a snaggletoothed old man with three wispy strands of hair left on his head. Ilech was his name, and the chariot he rode in was as old and decrepit as himself. The team that pulled it consisted of two small dun-coloured horses with sunken backs and sunken eyes.

When Ilech joined the gathering army of the north, some of the younger men hooted with laughter. But Conor mac Nessa, who no longer felt young himself, silenced them. 'Close your mouths,' he commanded, 'for age lies waiting in all our bones.'

When they caught up with the first contingent of Connaughtmen, Ilech halted his team and stepped from the chariot. As if he had all the time there was, he patiently removed his clothing one piece at a time, and folded it on the splintery floor of his war-cart. Then he collected enough rocks to fill the chariot until there was barely room in it for him. Urging his horses on, he drove to the scene of battle.

So strange was his appearance that men stopped fighting to gape at him, and there were any number of caustic comments about his withered private parts, hanging for all to see. In their amusement, the Connaughtmen crowded close, chortling at the useless old man. 'Look at his skinny tool and his empty balls!' someone chortled – just as Ilech picked up the topmost stone in his cart and hurled it with deadly aim.

He injured a number of those crowding around to laugh at him before they could knock each other aside and get away.

Of all the Red Branch warriors who had stayed with Conor mac Nessa after Fergus fled to Connaught, not one held himself exempt from the battle against Maeve and Ailell. None doubted they would face former comrades. But the story of Cuchulain's combat with Ferdiad challenged them to set fraternal feelings aside.

'Be as ruthless as the Hound,' they urged one another.

Meanwhile, the Hound of Ulster lay on a pallet made of cloaks folded over moss, feeling his wounds throb. 'You're healing,' Fingan told him. 'You shouldn't be, but you are. You'll be on your feet again and able to join the king by the time he has the invaders surrounded.'

'Wonderful news,' said Cuchulain. He sounded supremely un-interested.

Realising the desperation of their situation, Ailell dispatched a messenger to Curoi of Munster, reminding the southern chieftain of various alliances and kinships established through fosterage between his own clan and clans in Connaught.

428

Curoi gathered a band of warriors together and started to Ailell's aid, but he made no great haste. Judging from the attitude of the wild-eyed messenger, the war was already lost. Curoi was a prudent man. He preferred to be on the winning side. Losers, in his experience, kept little loot.

On his way north, he found himself trying to negotiate men and chariots across hills so strewn with stones that one cart after another was broken. 'I didn't come all this way to be a carpenter,' Curoi announced to his followers – and turned back, though he insisted his bards record his effort in their memories, in case Ailell should charge him later with a failure of kinship.

Meanwhile, as the deer scents the hounds, Ailell smelled the Ulstermen closing around him. He had taken Maeve into his chariot with him because he did not like the way she looked or sounded; Cuchulain's victory at the ford had brought on a dangerous lethargy. As they jounced along together behind a pair of trotting horses, he turned to her to enquire, 'Where's mac Roth?'

Her skin was pasty; her crisp hair hung in lank strands. 'Why do you want my herald?' she asked dully.

'He has sharp eyes and some experience of the Ulstermen. I want him to slip over that ridge there and be our lookout; tell me how near our enemies are.'

'Perhaps mac Roth is dead,' Maeve said. 'Perhaps the Hound killed him. He kills everything.'

The nearest spear carrier spoke up. 'I know where mac Roth is; I'll bring him to you.'

Fergus drove up and halted his chariot beside Ailell's to wait for the news as mac Roth was sent to reconnoitre.

With the Ulstermen in pursuit, the invaders had been driven farther south than the route they had originally followed into Ulster. They had left far behind them the steep ascents through heather and over runs of rock. Breasting a low ridge, mac Roth could look north to the sparkling waters of one lake and south to another. Gently undulating land fell away into valleys and hollows cloaked with fog. As islands rise from a lake, hilltops emerged from the fog to be bathed in prismatic colour as the wintry sun glanced off the banks of moisture.

Mac Roth took one long look, then ran back to report to Ailell, 'I saw only a dense fog swirling through the low places, lit by flashes of bright colour.'

Fergus snorted. 'The fog you saw was the breath of the Ulstermen, and the flashes of brightness were glints from their spearpoints.'

'I can't understand why I haven't killed you long before now,' Ailell remarked to the former king of Ulster.

'Anyone can kill an old fat man,' Fergus said. 'I'd advise you to send your runner back for another look, though; you need a more complete report than he's given you.'

'I don't care how many Ulstermen are out there, we're a match for them,' Ailell insisted. But he waved mac Roth off for a second look.

This time, the herald returned with the dark freckles standing out clearly on a face gone white. 'There's a mighty force assembling on a hill, and they've put up a high seat for their leader by piling up sods and covering them with a cloak. The man who has taken his place there is extremely tall, with a beard of mingled gold and silver and hair lying in ripples down his back. He wears a pleated tunic dyed purple, and a shield is leaning against his knee, with the golden figures of animals on it.'

'His beard is forked?' Fergus inquired. 'And his sword gold-hilted?'

'Indeed.'

'Conor mac Nessa,' said Fergus mac Roy.

'Other companies approach him from other directions,' the herald went on, describing the leaders of each. Fergus solemnly named them one by one: great names of Ulster heroes. Leary the Battle-Winner, Cuscraid the Stammerer, Buinne the Rough-Red, Owen Hard-Hand. And many others, every one a name to strike fear into brave men. Some were tall and hard and golden, others were swarthy and fiery-faced; some looked kind and others harsh. But they were all trained warriors with trophy heads to their credit.

And they were fresh, while the invaders were exhausted.

There seemed no end to the heroes mac Roth was listing.

'I didn't know Conor mac Nessa could command so many warriors,' Maeve said, as the recitation continued.

Her husband gave her a sour look. 'Didn't you bother to find that out before you began this?'

'War looks easy from the outside,' Fergus commented to no one in particular. 'You just gather some big husky men and go and bash someone harder than they can bash you.'

'Now I know why I don't kill you,' Ailell told him admiringly. 'Because you say things like that.'

Mac Roth's knees bent, and he leaned against Ailell's chariot. 'I'm tired from talking and the tale not yet told.'

430

'Then say the rest before you collapse. Tell us what you haven't seen,' Maeve said, entering the conversation.

Mac Roth brightened minimally. 'I haven't seen Conall Cearnach, whom I would recognise. And I haven't seen the Hound of Ulster. But there were more companies coming up when I turned and came back to you. Everywhere I looked, I saw men and horses instead of fields and hills.'

'In Conor mac Nessa, you have seen a man with a great following,' Fergus told him.

'You had to say that, didn't you?'

'Don't look so sour, Ailell. I only spoke the truth.'

'Then I had better go to Conor myself and arrange for some sort of truce until we can prepare ourselves.'

'By then, Conall and Cuchulain may have joined their friends,' Fergus replied cheerfully.

Instructing her attendants to keep a close watch on Maeve – and keep her safely in the centre of the armies – Ailell set out for Conor's encampment. He had dressed himself in his royal best, but was all too aware of many days' grime buried in the folds of his skin. To ensure he would not be attacked mistakenly on the way, he took only a small honour guard with him, demonstrating kingly courage.

The Ulster sentries passed him through their lines without comment.

Conor mac Nessa did not do Ailell the honour of standing as he approached. 'You're Maeve's husband,' was all he said.

'I am a son of the king of Leinster, as well you know!' the other man retorted, standing tall.

Then Conor stood. He was taller. 'You take the responsibility on yourself for this invasion?'

'I am not a man to hide behind a woman.'

Conor gave him a smile as cold as winter sun. 'Whether or not you are a man at all remains to be seen. Are you here to challenge me personally to single combat?'

The suggestion was so unexpected, and so unwelcome, Ailell started to answer several times before he could find the right words. Then he said, 'We are too important to risk in battle, and your champion lies wounded; I would not want to take advantage.'

Conor mac Nessa laughed out loud. 'You invade my kingdom in the winter, then claim you don't want to take advantage?' The men around him made comments Ailell did not care to hear. The king of Ulster added, 'Why are you here, then?'

'I've come to offer you a truce until the next sunrise. My men, frankly, need to rest and regroup, and I'm sure you'll want to scout the countryside, since you're in unfamiliar territory.'

'But I'm not. That hill rising to the north, for example, is Uisnach. An ancient stronghold, which I have many reasons for knowing. The spices that will season my meat tonight were purchased at last season's Beltaine fair there. Sea-traders bring them great distances to trade for well-made Ulster tools. You are in my lap, Ailell, and I can slap you as flat as an insect on my thigh.'

'Warriors insult one another, kings fight with their dignity,' was Ailell's answer. 'I offer you a truce until sunrise, mac Nessa. Or are you so uncertain of your strength, even though you have me surrounded, that you must fight now, before your men lose their courage?'

Conor stroked his forked beard. 'Truce until sunrise,' he agreed.

Meanwhile, Cuchulain was driving his wife and his physician frantic. 'I defied Maeve's armies at the Gap of the North, I deserve to be with Conor to see them defeated!'

'The victory will be yours entirely,' his wife assured him, 'because you held them off until the king could arrive. Haven't you seen enough of killing for a while, Setanta?'

He turned the full force of his brilliant grey eyes upon her. 'I have. But I'm not allowed to look away.'

'Oh, bind him afresh and let him go,' Emer told Fingan. 'He will make himself more ill just lying here fretting.'

On either side of the open area between the two armies, warriors seethed like new ale. The most experienced men slept; the others fought the next day's battle over and over in their minds, until their weapons were dulled.

Only the sentries, keeping their lonely watch, owned the night. Across the empty space, they looked towards one another and occasionally called out, offering a drink of ale or a crust of bread, or asking about relatives they might have in common with some man on the other side.

The night at the far edge of winter was crisp and cold, and the same wilderness of stars looked down on them all.

Walking through the camps, bards chanted to the men as they lay on the earth, reminding them of the courage of their grandsires and urging them to brave deeds. Throughout the night, the trained cadence of their voices rose and fell. It comforted those who were awake and sank through the ears of those who slept, deep into their brains.

Within their tent, Maeve and Ailell sat open-eyed. Every so often, she would stand up and look out, as if the night might have magically passed away. 'By now my new bull must have reached Cruachan,' she kept saying.

'I'm tired of hearing about your new bull. Do you know how many of our best men are dead because of him? How can we face Conor mac Nessa with the remnant that's left us? Cuchulain has destroyed the cream of the battle leaders; our remaining war host will be just a body without a head, running in every direction.'

'Cuchulain's dead,' she said. 'Surely he died of the wounds Ferdiad gave him.'

'I doubt it. He was still strong enough to carry Ferdiad out of the river, and that was a big, heavy man.'

'Cuchulain's dead,' Maeve repeated.

 Of course he wasn't dead.

Maeve's concept of death was, naturally enough, at variance with mine, as she was operating within a human frame of reference. For all she consciously knew, death was a darkness and an ending. Many people believe that. Some fear it, others welcome it.

Then there are those who envision life after dying. The Gael like to imagine a wonderful island off to the west somewhere, which they called Tir-na-n-Og, a paradise where no one ever died and heroes could fight magnificently, be slain, and rise again to enjoy another battle.

If such a place existed, I would find it boring. The whole point of killing someone is to put an end to them, at least to a certain extent. The immortal spirit cannot die, but the mortal body certainly can and should. And not just to feed me on blood, either.

I envy humans their temporary death and darkness and the loss of memory it brings. They awaken fresh and new, somewhere else, past pain forgotten. The most cruel of fates is remembering; you would not want to hear a fraction of the terrible things I remember.

But then, I have lived a very long time without the refreshment of dying.

In the coming confrontation, many men would die. As Cuchulain in his chariot hurried to the scene, gritting his teeth against unhealed injuries, I flew with him for a while, invisible in the darkness.

433

I enjoy being one of the few birds who flies at night. Ordinary ravens don't, you know. Aside from owls and bats, the dark skies were mine.

But I grew impatient with our slow pace and went ahead to savour the event awaiting us. From a long distance away, I could hear the bards chanting. It's hard to resist joining a chorus. When your voice is only a harsh cawing, the effort to sing is an embarrassment, but I had other voices available to me.

13 On the night wind, Neman sang her song for the soon-to-be-slain, and men waiting for battle listened.

Some wrapped their cloaks around them and crept away to hide in hedgerows and hollows, or drown in bogs, or wander half-mad through dense forests, or even make their way safely home, to sit as old men by their hearthfires regaling their grandchildren with tales of their heroism in the Great Battle.

Others stayed to fight.

In his own leather tent, Fergus was preparing for the next day in his own way. The sound of someone trying to be unheard arrested his hand just as the wine-skin was nearing his lips. More silently than one would expect from a man of his bulk, the old warrior slipped to the entrance of the tent and stood listening as two younger men, whispering to each other to be quiet, tried to creep past him.

'Where are you going?' he boomed out suddenly.

A powerful hand clamped each by the back of the neck and dragged them together into the tent of Fergus mac Roy.

Both looked thoroughly miserable. They stared at him, each other, and then their feet.

'Home,' one admitted finally. A long-faced lad with lank yellow hair and body to match, he did not appear to be good fighting material anyway.

But the other was broad and bull-necked, with a sturdy trunk set atop heavy thighs. His knees and his toes turned out in a graceless way, yet he had a resolute face and Fergus knew him for an able spearman.

'You, Nelleth – I didn't expect you to be a deserter. Where's your courage?'

The sturdy man looked up. 'It's the brave ones who leave, Fergus. The cowards stay and fight, because they're afraid of what others will think if they don't. You can go with us if you like, but we're not staying. Those men are coming to *kill* us!'

'Get out of here then,' Fergus snarled. 'You'd be no good tomorrow anyway.'

'I knew he wouldn't tell on us,' the yellow-haired man muttered as the two hurried from the tent. 'He understands.'

At dawnlight, the first contingent of fighters made their way to the agreed-upon battlefield on a nearby plain. The lowest in rank went first. This was to be a formal war.

Ailell met Fergus emerging from his tent. The former king's eyes were red from drink or sleeplessness or thinking. 'We expect great things of you today, Fergus,' Ailell told him.

'Gladly would I do them if I had my good sword,' the other answered. 'I would send heads flying like hailstones, I would pile severed limbs higher than the highest cairn, if I had my faithful weapon. But it is lost,' he added, trying to look doleful.

Ailell threw back his head and bellowed with laughter. 'You're in great good fortune, old friend! The glory of battle will not be denied you for want of a suitable weapon, because I happen to know where yours is!' With a snap of his fingers, he sent an attendant running to bring the weapon in question.

Fergus gave him an accusing look. 'You had this all along.'

'I did,' Ailell replied, unembarrassed. 'My lad stole it while you lay atop my wife. Now, I expect you to wield it in my name.'

Fergus held out his hand and felt the familiar hilt slide into his palm. 'Take it,' Ailell advised him, 'and even your score with Conor mac Nessa.'

'I . . .'

'Think of all the things he did to you. You stood as his foster-father and raised him as a prince, son of a king, yet he tricked you into betraying your honour, and he murdered young men under your protection. Friends of yours. Think of the sons of Uisnach who lie in their graves because of him, Fergus mac Roy. And go and fight the king of Ulster.'

Ailell strode away, leaving Fergus turning the sword over and over in his hand.

Dark birds flew screaming through the sky. The druids who accompanied Maeve and Ailell interpreted their cries as, 'Woe to Ulster, Hail men of Connaught!'

The druids with Conor mac Nessa heard, 'Hail Ulster, Woe to the men of Connaught!'

A lone chariot approached the battlefield and drew rein. The Hound of

Ulster sagged against the chariot rim. His wounds had begun to bleed again.

Cuchulain had pushed himself so far past mortal endurance that at last even he must admit it. Dying in battle did not frighten him, but he did not want to collapse in front of everyone before striking or being struck. 'I'll rest here,' he told Laeg. 'For a while, until my strength returns. Go to the high ground and watch the progress of the battle and report back to me.'

Laeg dutifully trotted back and forth, describing the scene as thousands of men swirled darkly over the plains. In the chaos, it was impossible to make out many details, but when the chariot-chiefs arrived with a cry of war trumpets, he was able to pick out the various ones by the colours of their cloaks and the style of their drivers.

'And the king himself is fighting,' he ran back to tell Cuchulain. 'I saw him go down among the highest-ranked with his sword in his hand.'

Cuchulain groaned. 'I should be standing between him and his enemies.' He tried to walk, but his bones turned to water and he fell. Laeg ran to him and made a pillow for his head from his cloak. 'Just lie there and rest; just lie there. You'll be better soon, then you can go. Or must I tie you to the chariot wheel to keep you here?' he asked, only half in jest.

With no champion to protect him, Conor mac Nessa was a formidable figure. The tallest of the kings on the battlefield that day, he had armed himself with the white heat of anger, and it glowed from his every pore. He had seen the first lot of rescued Ulstermen and women whom Connaught had meant to take as slaves, had seen them with the rope halters still around their necks and the terror unquenched in their faces.

The battle was truly begun. Singing and chanting, leaping high into the air to display their energy, clashing their weapons against their shields, the warriors advanced on each other. Animals in the distant woodland fled from the cacophony of warring.

The initial charge would be one of blind passion, two walls of men hurling themselves against each other in an attempt at an early rout through intimidation. A forest of spears whistled through the air. The war-carts surged forward, the hero in each looking for a man of equal rank to oppose him. Amid the indiscriminate slaughter of hundreds, intense single combats took place, chieftain against chieftain, charioteers leaning back against the reins to use their entire strength to force the excited horses to wheel and hold close.

A chariot brilliant with dyed plumes spiralled in on another and Fergus mac Roy found himself facing Conor mac Nessa.

Conor lifted the great shield Ocean and looked at his former foster-father over its rim.

The tattoo of approaching hooves brought Cuchulain, staggering, to his feet. The worst of his weakness had passed. He shook his head to clear it and saw Conall Cearnach's chariot racing toward him.

Conall's charioteer, a man called En, drew rein, and Conall jumped from the cart. 'Why aren't you fighting?' he asked Cuchulain.

'I will be soon enough, midday at the latest,' the other predicted. 'Have you any meat with you, or strong mead?'

'I do, and you're welcome to it. As soon as I recovered from the Pangs, I had to check on my own clanhold, but I've come as swiftly as I could. I'm not too late, am I?'

'You're not indeed,' Laeg said as he came running to join them. 'The battle's just getting good. You haven't missed very much beyond the opening exchange of insults.'

'I'd rather fight than talk,' said Conall Cearnach, 'so I've come at the right time.'

'I'll be along behind you,' the Hound assured him. 'Tell us, Laeg – how are the Ulstermen doing?'

'Brilliantly. They're tightly massed right now. En and I could drive our carts over them from one side to the other without a chariot wheel or a horse's hoof breaking through to the ground beneath. They'll plough Maeve into the earth.'

Though screams and thuds and oaths and whinnies and spear hums and sword clangs surrounded them, Conor and Fergus met in what seemed the silent heart of battle. The frenzied activity on every side had nothing to do with them as their eyes locked over their shield rims.

This has been a long time coming, Fergus thought. 'Who am I seeing?' he called aloud in challenge.

'A better man than you, mac Roy,' came the answer in the deep, familiar voice. 'A man who will defeat you today. A man who never turned his back on the clan Ulaid. Is that the blood of my people I see reddening your sword?'

'You see the blood of my enemies on my blade.'

'We were all sons born of the same mother – Ulster.'

'Ah, but you turned yourself into my enemy, Conor mac Nessa. And

438

you know just when and how you did. This is for Naisi!' Letting the old grievance give strength to his arm, Fergus raised his sword for a mighty downward blow that Conor barely deflected with his shield. The great shield called Ocean boomed out its warning. The king was under attack.

Conor's own sword flashed its reponse. He tilted Ocean so its sharp rim would cut his enemy's arm if Fergus came too close, while simultaneously he tried to drive under the other man's guard. The charioteers struggled to hold the horses still, but both teams were frantic with excitement, backing, sidling, moving the carts apart.

By mutual consent, the warriors jumped from their chariots to continue their combat on the unmoving earth.

Neither was young, though Conor was a generation newer than Fergus. Both men had trained in the hardest of schools. Their swords raised and fell and lifted again, and they swore cruel casual oaths with each gasp of breath.

All that had once been between them was cut and slashed with their swords.

Then Fergus cast his shield aside and gripped the hilt of his weapon with both hands, in order to bring down a blow capable of cleaving the other man in half.

At that moment, two arms wrapped around him from behind; two hands closed on his wrists.

'Don't,' said Cormac Connlongas.

Looking over Fergus's shoulder, Conor saw his own exiled son preventing the blow that might have killed him.

Fergus quivered throughout the length of his body. From the time Ailell had pressed his sword back into his hand, he had been working himself up into a fighting fury. His honour, that much-abused thing, would not let him refuse the battle, and once committed to kill, he had been committed to attack Conor mac Nessa. Go for the head – the first instruction a young warrior receives. He was an old professional and had trained scores of young men in the art he knew; it had come back to him easily enough. There was no love left in him for Nessa's son. Betrayal is the death of love.

But when the killing blow was stopped, he knew he could not mount another. 'Who do I strike, then?' he asked Cormac hoarsely.

'Anyone and anything,' the young man told him. 'Pour out your anger on those three hills over there, if you like; strike the tops off them, if you want. But remember you were born and will die Red Branch, and do not kill your king.'

He opened his arms, Fergus swayed, righted himself. Then, with a howl wilder than all those around him, he turned and plunged into the press of fighting men.

Before Conor could say anything to Cormac Connlongas, his son had also lost himself in the crowd.

Even from a distance, Cuchulain recognised the booming warning of the shield called Ocean. 'Conor's in danger!' he cried. Laeg made a halfhearted effort to bid him take more rest, but Cuchulain brushed him aside, leaped into his chariot, and seized the reins himself. Leaving his charioteer in his dust, he drove off toward the battlefield.

Laeg began to run after him, knees and elbows pumping.

In the heat of battle, many warriors had flung off their tunics and were fighting naked in the old style. They felt no winter winds, nor even the pain of minor wounds. Pressed together, hacking and stabbing, fearing and exulting, they were senseless and mindless as Cuchulain's chariot dashed up to the outskirts of the fighting.

Another war-cart came towards him with a grizzled hulk of a man in it, his iron helmet lost somewhere, his eyes red-rimmed. He automatically raised his sword in challenge.

'Fergus mac Roy,' Cuchulain called. 'I yielded to you. It is your turn to yield to me.'

Squinting, Fergus looked into the dazzle of midday sun and finally recognised the Hound's face. 'Yield?' he asked, as if he did not understand the word.

'Yield to me, and all your followers with you!' Cuchulain roared back at him. 'You promised!'

'I promised.' A warmth like gratitude spread across the other man's face. 'I *did* promise!'

A runner sought Ailell and found him among his Leinster kinsmen, trying to urge them to rally against the superior numbers of the Ulstermen. 'Fergus mac Roy has left the battlefield and taken half the exiles with him,' the runner panted.

Without blinking, Ailell replied, 'Should that surprise me?'

Almost at once, a second runner reached him. 'The Hound of Ulster has joined the fighting.'

'Of course,' Ailell said. 'And the sun will set in the west tonight. Some things are inevitable. Take word to my chieftains to prepare the best retreat they can.'

Earlier in the day, Ailell had prudently advised his wife to move to the heel of the army, out of harm's way. He had expected the usual argument, but she had gone rather meekly – for Maeve. 'Perhaps someone there will know if the Brown Bull has safely reached the borders of Connaught,' was all she said.

She stood quietly while her chariot carried her westward. Behind her, the sounds of battle; somewhere ahead, the sanctuary of Cruachan.

Some vital spark had been extinguished in her, and she knew it. She remembered, almost as a casual observer, the restless energy of the woman who had made Cruachan a mighty stronghold and come east on a tide of soaring ambition. Where had the energy gone?

She looked down at the cupped and rutted earth of the cart track her driver was following. Audacity had brought her a long way, but of all she hoped to win, what would she be taking home with her?

Not the humbling and subjugation of Ulster. That was being decided in the battle going on behind her, but the issue was hardly in doubt – Conor mac Nessa would win.

Cuchulain's heroism had guaranteed it.

Cuchulain.

She would have the Donn Cooley, of course. Several had already told her the Brown Bull and his herders had passed this way days before, and were therefore in Connaught by now. Ostensibly, she had accomplished her goal. And no matter how the battle turned out, some of Ulster's plunder would be carried to Connaught too, if only concealed beneath the tunics of defeated warriors.

Warriors. Cuchulain.

The poets would be singing of his accomplishments during the cattle raid of Cooley for a thousand years, Maeve knew. He would never be dead; he was already immortal.

She had sought immortality by defeating him. Now, in a creaking chariot jolting over muddy earth, she admitted to herself that she had wanted more. She had dreamed of bringing him back to Cruachan with her, his wild beauty chained to her war-cart, his flaming spirit forced to admit the supremacy of hers, his glory dimmed by hers . . .

Glory. 'So war is about glory after all, Fergus,' she said aloud.

Her charioteer was not named Fergus. He cast her a curious glance, then turned his attention back to the horses. The woman had been mumbling to herself all day; he was frightened of her.

Trying to relieve a persistent ache in her back, Maeve arched her spine and lifted her chin toward the sun. Its heatless light fell on a face hollowed with fatigue. The sun.

Cuchulain.

Why did her mind keep turning back to him?

Because he had scorned and refused her?

Because he had refused to be beaten, to be dead, but continued to live in her brain, his features burned into it as if with a heated iron rod. Warrior, killer, enemy of life and growth . . .

Maeve leaned forward and beat her brow against the heels of her hands. Alarmed, her charioteer looked around for help, but they were alone for the moment, suspended between the last cluster of warriors who still considered giving battle and the first group of women and porters who were already setting their faces to the west and gathering up their belongings.

'Let me at least be remembered as long as Cuchulain is remembered!' Maeve cried aloud. She felt something tear inside her and gasped. It could not be . . . she was past the age when a woman bled . . .

The hot gush poured down her legs. She could smell it, saltsweet. Womanblood. 'Stop the chariot,' she commanded, 'and call for help. I need a shelter of shields around me.'

Meanwhile, Cuchulain in his chariot cut his way through the warriors from the west. Some he killed and some he shoved aside, and many scrambled over each other to get out of his way. Spearmen and foot warriors were not ashamed to run from him, but the chariot-chiefs snarled at him and fought back. One by one, his sword took them down, and when a man kept himself beyond its reach, he sent the Gae Bulga to seek and kill him.

Soon even the surviving chieftains were fleeing the Hound of Ulster. They thought they saw him in every man who stood upright in a war-cart. Confusion gave way to pandemonium, and the momentum of battle was with Ulster.

The Hound drove in a wide circle like a shepherd gathering his flock, sending some of the Connaughtmen back in blind panic into the spears of their allies. Whenever he saw a white and frightened face turn towards him, he roared and raised a recently taken head, shaking it by the hair. Following his example, the other Red Branch warriors began to circle the invaders also, forcing them against one another, so many were trampled and killed by accident.

Cuchulain's widest swing brought him at an angle to a cart track lying westward of the battlefield. There, he saw a crowd of men huddling together, making a wall with their shields. He reined in his team and approached at a walk. The tired horses tossed their heads gratefully and exhaled great clouds of vapour on to the frosty air of late afternoon.

'Stand back!' someone called to Cuchulain, shaking a spear at him.

He almost smiled. 'Who orders it?'

'Who refuses me?'

'The Hound of Ulster.'

He heard a smothered exclamation behind the shield-wall.

Stepping from his cart, Cuchulain shouldered his way between the shields. No man dared try to stop him. Within their circle, he found Maeve of Cruachan crouching on the earth, her blood pouring on to it. She turned a pinched, drained face towards him and bared her teeth like an animal.

The horrifying image of Macha on the racecourse swept through Cuchulain's brain. He took an involuntary step backwards.

Of all the confrontations Maeve had once imagined with the Hound of Ulster, this was the least foreseen. The flooding reassertion of her womanhood left her helpless. The eyes she turned towards the warrior were glazed, like those of a druid offering sacrifice. Yet in their depths, an insatiable hunger lurked.

She extended her hand to Cuchulain. 'Spare me . . .'

The same thing happens again and again, Cuchulain thought, wondering. Yet the pattern can be broken. Now. Here.

'I would be justified in killing you, Maeve, but I give you mercy instead. I don't hurt women.' Thrusting his drawn sword back into its sheath, he left the circle of shields and the woman who crouched there, longing for immortality.

Her famished eyes watched him go.

Then one of her spear carriers foolishly said to her, 'Lucky for you you're only a woman.'

The field of battle presented a charnel aspect. Once, Cuchulain would have been in the forefront of the victors claiming their trophies, but some of the men he had killed had been Red Branch exiles.

The Hound took no trophies. Instead, he gathered a company to harry Maeve's troops as they fled westward, pursuing them as far as Ath Luan before turning back to rejoin Conor mac Nessa.

The Great Battle was over. The ravens were feeding. All that remained was for the counters to add up the dead and the poets to celebrate the heroes.

As the army of Ulster tended its wounded and raised cairns over the fallen, the sun smiled an early heat. By the time the warriors began to return to their homes, the women were preparing the feast of Imbolc, the celebration of the lactation of the ewes.

Upon reaching Emain Macha, the king ordered a magnificent bronze war trumpet to be hurled into the lake, to mark another war.

14

'The worst thing,' complained Daire mac Fiachna of Cooley, 'was Maeve's getting away with my bull after all.'

Seated in the House of the King for the Imbolc feast, the cattle-lord was not in a celebratory mood.

'The worst thing,' contradicted Leary Buadach, 'is the quality of this wine. Conor, are you certain this is the best we could import from the Middle Sea, or whatever that place is called? It's undrinkable, I could strain sheep urine through my shoes and get a better taste. I think the sea-traders have robbed you this time; a man could die of thirst in your house.'

'The Brown Bull is more important than the sourness of the wine,' Daire said.

'To you. But if the sea-traders have begun to think they can dump their inferior merchandise on us . . . well, you wouldn't understand, Daire. You're only a cattle-lord.'

'And what shield would you hide behind, if not my good leather?'

'I don't hide from anything!' Leary was on his feet, red-faced, eyes bulging.

The king's imperious voice commanded, 'Enough, both of you!'

'He insulted me,' they yapped in unison.

Conor mac Nessa shook his head. 'Leary, sometimes I think it's a pity you weren't born twins – then you could be twice as belligerent. And twice as stupid,' he added in a lower tone. 'As for you, Daire, while I appreciate your grievance – '

'No one appreciates the problems of a cattle-lord,' the man from Cooley said dolefully. He committed the grave offence of interrupting his king, and Cathbad the druid scowled, but Conor let it pass. He was determined to see no tree of contention grow from a tiny seed if he could help it.

'We take the risks,' Daire was saying, 'raising livestock and worrying about the weather and being raided by everybody old enough to take up weapons for the fun of it – and what happens? You all trot off and have a lovely war and bring back grand stories and cartloads of trophies, but you don't bring my bull. Overlooked in your sport, was he?'

'Maeve's men had taken him out of Ulster before we were aware he was gone,' Conall explained. 'But we defeated them so soundly Ulster's honour is untarnished, and there'll be no question of tribute.'

'What about my bull?' the frustrated cattle-lord cried.

His bull was causing problems on its own. The herders charged with taking him to Cruachan had had a dreadful time with the beast. Some swore they would give up cattle and develop an interest in sheep. Or geese. Or whittling. As savage and unpredictable as he was magnificent, the Donn Cooley was a force of nature.

As he approached Cruachan, the animal sensed a climax to his journeying. He could smell the herds of Maeve and Ailell, the heifers waiting for him with their tails flung over their backs. Fertile females. Breeding season. And the scent of another bull!

The Brown Bull lost what little tolerance he had for the small two-legged creatures who kept pulling and poking at him like so many irritating gnats. More important matters of sovereignty demanded his attention. Planting his huge cloven hooves, he lowered his massive head and bellowed a royal challenge.

A bellow of equal force answered him.

Enraged to hear the voice of a rival, Fionnbanach crashed through the tightly woven branches of his pen and lumbered across the grassland to meet the Donn Cooley.

By another road, Fergus mac Roy and his band of Ulster exiles were returning to Connaught because they had nowhere else to go. When they heard the roaring of the two bulls, they ran towards the sound in time to encounter the forefront of Maeve's army rushing up, also drawn by the cries of lust and fury emanating from the two great beasts.

Ulster exiles and Connaughtmen rejoined to watch the titanic struggle about to take place on the Plain of Cruachan. The bravest of the warriors was not foolhardy enough to attempt to prevent the battle.

Brown Bull and White-Horn galloped towards each other, the thunder of their passage shaking the earth. They came together with the crash of mountains colliding.

But after the first blind charge, something went wrong. The Donn Cooley reared like a horse in an attempt to paw open the top of his enemy's skull. Fionnbanach, his equal in cleverness, threw himself sideways to avoid the blow. The Brown Bull's hoof slammed harmlessly on to one of the gleaming white horns and was impaled on it, holding the antagonists locked in an awkward embrace from which neither could break free.

Bulls bellowed, dust roiled.

Of all those present, Fergus mac Roy had the least enthusiasm left for living. 'It would be a great pity to bring this wretched overgrown calf so far,' he said, 'to have his reputation lost now.' Dismounting from his chariot, Fergus edged up to the bulls and jabbed the Donn Cooley viciously in the flank with his spear. 'Tear yourself free and show us if you were worth the trouble! Good men are dead because of you.'

When the angry bull tried to lunge sideways in order to gore Fergus, the impaled hoof was torn free. Fionnbanach snorted. At once the Donn Cooley turned back to his rival and lowered his head in challenge. Nothing else mattered. They had no god but killing, and were eager to offer sacrifice.

The battle they then waged had an atavistic grandeur beyond any human warfare.

Great chunks were torn from the earth by their feet; the distant hills rang with their cries. They circled and charged and drew back and attacked again, and again, and again, while the men of Connaught marvelled at their stamina. But at the end of the day, the Donn Cooley finally succeeded in driving both horns deep into Fionnbanach's side. With a tremendous grunt, the Brown Bull lifted his enemy clear off the ground, taking his weight on his own huge shoulders. Fionnbanach's death cry shivered the air.

Brandishing his opponent on his horns, the Donn Cooley broke into an uncertain trot, the pendulous flap of flesh at his throat swinging. A few men attempted to herd him towards Cruachan, but when he whirled on them, they hesitated, transfixed in horror at the sight of the dead bull impaled upon the living one. The beast went one way and then another, and men shouted directions to each other while trying to stay clear of him themselves.

The scurrying humans added to the Donn Cooley's confusion. Why was he in this strange place? He was tired and wounded and lost. The wind had shifted; he no longer smelled cows. A lake glimmered. He splashed into its shallows and lowered his head for a drink in spite of the terrible weight pressing down upon him. The water tasted wrong, but the coldness cleared his dim brain enough for a simple thought to take hold.

Home. Water that tasted right. Grass that tasted right. Not like this. Upland slopes and wind that smelled of the sea. High meadows and paths winding through gorse; paths his feet knew. His cows. His. *Home*.

This was not his place. The two-legs could not keep him here. He had just proven his supremacy over a more formidable opponent than any mere two-legs.

Surging out of the lake, the Brown Bull turned decisively towards the east and began to pick up speed.

'Stop him!' shrieked Maeve.

Fergus mac Roy found himself squarely in the beast's path. He did not know which way to run; he was not even certain he wanted to run. He watched almost stolidly as death bore down on him. Then the Brown Bull swung just wide enough to avoid him. Having done his killing, the animal only wanted to go home.

For one heartbeat, the eyes of the two warriors met, and a long look passed between them. In the bull's tiny, red-rimmed eyes, Fergus saw the reflection of his own deepest longing.

Brandishing his sword, he yelled in a voice of unmistakable kingly command, 'Let him go!'

The other men were only too glad to obey.

Maeve could only watch in frustration as the immense Brown Bull, his dead enemy still on his horns and rivers of blood streaming down his shoulders, set off for Ulster.

Parts of Fionnbanach would subsequently be found strewn all along his route.

For the rest of the short drive to Cruachan, Ailell avoided looking at his wife's livid face. He was aware of the perfect irony of the bullfight, but did not expect Maeve to accept it as final. She would rest and recover like the earth in winter, and then . . .

He pulled his chariot away from hers and fell in beside Fergus mac Roy. They had come a long way together, they might as well share what remained of the adventure.

'My mouth has a bad taste in it,' he admitted to Fergus. 'And not just because the Brown Bull got away from us.'

The other man nodded sympathetically. 'I think our mouths are filled with the dust raised by a misleading woman.'

'I couldn't have said it better myself,' Ailell replied. 'As soon as we get back to the fort, why don't you join me somewhere private and we'll share a cask of wine, just the two of us. Without women. To settle the dust.'

'I cannot refuse you,' said Fergus mac Roy. 'There is a *ges* on me.'

448

By the time the Brown Bull was sighted in Ulster, people were beginning to relax in their clanholds, assured they need fear nothing further from Connaught for a while.

Pleading his wounds, Cuchulain did not go to Emain Macha with the king to celebrate Imbolc. Instead, he took Emer home to Dun Dalgan.

As his chariot rolled through the countryside, grateful Ulster folk ran out of their homes to throw the first greetings of the season into his path. The Hound acknowledged their tributes with a gravely courteous nod, but he did not shout his victories or flourish trophies.

His silver eyes brooded behind their screen of lashes.

For much of the journey, he was thinking about time. Youth assumes immortality; he had thought the future a boundless golden meadow, an endless summer day. But Ferdiad's death had shown him time had limits. There was so much of it and no more; no infinite future in which everything would come right again.

His time with Ferdiad had ended. The exchanges of friendship were concluded; no additional tokens of affection could be given.

Not fair! he wanted to cry to some god, somewhere.

Why didn't I anticipate death, when I have seen so much of it? Why didn't I say to him all the things I now wish I'd said . . .

Everyone will die, he realised with a sick thrill in his belly.

Emer will die. Emer will die!

What haven't I said to her? What haven't I done for her? Why didn't I realise how fragile she is?

With a kind of desperation, he began counting the people whose deaths would be painful to him. His wife, his king. His mother. Laeg. Fergus mac Roy (admit it, definitely Fergus). Conall Cearnach, Leary Buadach (him too), and so many of the Red Branch. His brothers, the family he had chosen for himself.

Hearing a faint groan, Emer put her hand on Cuchulain's arm. He was thinking of Ferdiad, of course. Since the battle at the ford, she knew Ferdiad had been almost constantly in her husband's thoughts.

The small hand on his arm recalled Cuchulain to an awareness of his wife. His tiny, mortal wife. He felt a flood of guilty solicitude for having ignored her. 'You shouldn't be standing for so long,' he said with an intensity that surprised Emer. 'There's a cushion in here – somewhere – here, sit on this and let your feet hang out the back.'

He began to try to move her around as if she were an old and helpless woman.

449

'I don't need to sit down, Setanta,' she protested. 'Riding in a chariot is much less uncomfortable when you stand up, because then your knees and ankles absorb the jolting. When I try to sit down in a cart, every bone I have is shaken loose.'

'But we mustn't let you get too tired. You're a woman, after all, you should be treated gently.'

'I wouldn't mind being treated gently,' commented Laeg in an amused drawl. 'Why not give Emer a try at handling the reins, and I'll sit on the cushion for a while and hang my feet out the back?'

'Are you tired?' Cuchulain asked at once. He turned such a penetrating gaze on his charioteer that Laeg was taken aback.

'I'm fine, Cuchulain. Really! I was only joking, you don't need to look so worried.'

'But if you're tired, or you don't feel well, we can camp right here. There's no need to strain yourself.'

'What's wrong with him?' Laeg whispered to Emer out of the corner of his mouth.

She had no answer.

By the time they reached Dun Dalgan, both she and the charioteer were feeling smothered by an insistent blanket of solicitude. The Hound could not do enough for either of them. And when he reached the fort, he ran to his mother's chamber and embraced her as if they had been exceptionally devoted. He hugged her, he pressed her to his bosom, he devoured her with his eyes – though, as usual, she hardly seemed aware of him at all.

Soon it was obvious Cuchulain had undergone a profound change; not the usual transformation associated with the Hound of Ulster.

Unknown to anyone, he was thinking about dying. He thought about death as constantly as he had thought about sex while growing into manhood. Secretly, because there was no one left to whom he could confide these thoughts.

Ferdiad was dead.

And I am going to die, Cuchulain told himself. Me, personally. Die. The light will fade from my eyes. They will put me in a hole in the earth, and the dirt will crumble into my nostrils. A black, airless hole. I won't be able to breathe, just lie in the dark. Rotting.

He had believed himself fearless; now, he realised he had simply chosen to disbelieve in the possibility of his own death. But Ferdiad had made him a believer again. He, Cuchulain, would also die, there would be no repeal of natural law just because he was special and unique and precious to himself.

He would die.

I am mortal, he thought. Mortal, nothing else. Like Ferdiad, or Emer, or Conor mac Nessa.

There will be only the darkness for all of us; we are going into the unrelieved dark.

The darkness lay waiting for him like a sickness in his bones. Waiting for him and for everyone he loved.

He had been as self-centred as any other bold young man who is praised and idolised. Never deliberately inconsiderate, he had been thoughtless and others accepted it, for youth is thoughtless.

Now, he went to the opposite extreme. He treated others as if he expected them to be snatched away from him at any moment. He dogged Emer's footsteps, watching fascinated while she trimmed wicks and mended tunics. When it began to get on her nerves, she snapped at him, but he smiled blandly and continued.

'Being cherished is lovely,' Emer complained to the silent Dectera, 'but the novelty has worn thin. Besides, he acts as if I'm breakable. When we're in bed, well, it just isn't the same.'

To a mindless woman, Emer could confess just how tepid Cuchulain's passion had become since he returned from the cattle raid. At first, she had blamed it on his wounds, which were severe and would take time to heal. But as he regained his strength, he continued to be tentative in his sexual approaches to her, as if she were something so fragile he hardly dared touch her at all.

She missed his excessive, incredible, magical heat.

But Cuchulain's view of Emer had been as altered as his view of time. She was so precious he tiptoed around her. He could no longer imagine tearing her clothes from her as he had once done; what if he inadvertently caused her an injury, and she sickened, and. . . ?

He hardly dared touch her at all.

As sunseason advanced, the days lengthened, until twilight became only faintly less luminous than sunlight, and the evenings were sweet with the scent of meadowland and grainland. People stayed under the sky until the stars appeared, and even the season's soft, warm rains did not make them seek shelter.

Yet by the time Emer and her husband lay in bed together at last, she was not tired, nor ready for sleep. She would prop herself up on one elbow and look down hopefully at Cuchulain with all the invitation she could muster in her eyes. He would stretch out one gentle finger and trace the curve of her cheek, or stroke the hollow of her throat with such delicious tenderness that her flesh burned wherever he touched. The gentle caress continued to the point of madness and beyond, and she wanted to scream out at him, 'Grab me!' But she never did.

When he entered her, it was no longer with the exultant power of an eagle spreading wide wings over his mate. Now Cuchulain only touched his wife as softly as the brush of a moth's wings, and if she allowed herself the smallest gasp of pleasure, he stopped at once and asked her if she was all right.

I may become as mindless as Dectera, Emer warned herself.

She was a healthy young woman raised in the household of a hosteler and cattle-lord. To anyone but her husband, she had no reticence about describing her dilemma. Yet no one else seemed able to understand.

'Are you trying to say he's impotent?' the physician asked.

'He's not at all, it's just that he's very . . . gentle.'

The man frowned. 'Surprising. Well, I suggest, if you want him to give you fiery sons, you start feeding him ground bulls' testicles mixed with strong red wine.'

'It's not sons I'm worried about.'

'Then you should be, that should be your first consideration, woman! We want a litter of young warriors to follow the Hound of Ulster! Now go home and get started on it.'

So she went to a crone famed for the efficacy of her herbals, and was told, 'The best remedy for a flaccid rod is to rub it three times a day with a potion I'll make for you. This never fails. I bury a live crane in a wide-necked bottle in a bog for three cycles of the moon, until a sufficient quantity of fluid collects in the bottom of the bottle to be mixed with germander and cress into the potion. The weakest rod stands up straight with this remedy.'

'He's not flaccid,' Emer protested.

'Then why have you come to me? You have no complaint, girl. I wish I were your age and my old husband had a good stiff rod.'

People began to say to one another behind their hands that the Hound's wife was growing as moody as Cuchulain himself, staring off into space with such a melancholy expression on her face.

Maybe the old herbalist is right, Emer tried to tell herself. I have everything, and I'm not satisfied.

But that didn't help. The evenings were too long and warm and glowing, and as Cuchulain healed, his hard, muscular body filled her

452

thoughts to the exclusion of anything else. Until he touched her, and it was not like the touch she remembered and wanted.

Finally, she did cry out, 'Grab me!' and he drew back, appalled. 'I might hurt you.'

'I'm not afraid,' Emer assured him laughingly, thinking he must be teasing her in the old lighthearted way.

'But *I* am.' Cuchulain rolled over and turned his back to her, leaving his wife sleepless and perplexed.

The wheel of the seasons turned, and turned.

The days grew long, then began to shorten again. Small, dark blue bilberries, first of the wild fruits, were ripening and grain nodded heavy-headed on the stalk, awaiting harvest and the festival of Lughnasa.

Lughnasa. A song for the sun, primal source of light and heat, indispensable mate of the earth, who ripened the fruit of her dark womb.

Samhain, Imbolc, and Beltaine could be celebrated under roofs, but for Lughnasa great assemblies convened in high places under open sky, to be nearer the god. Their song of thanksgiving would be dedicated to Lugh, Son of the Sun, most brilliant figure of all the vanished, unvanquished Tuatha de Danann.

Throughout Erin, the preliminary ceremonies of the season began with ritual meals served to strengthen the harvesters for their task. The privilege and duty of cutting the first corn was the prerogative of the king, or the ranking chieftain or patriarch of a region. Accompanied by his wife, who would formally identify the site of her earliest sowing, the man cut the corn with a silver sickle while witnesses chanted in hushed and reverent voices.

Cuchulain was chosen by popular acclaim to make the first cutting of corn for Murthemney. Emer paced proudly beside him into the field she had sown beyond the walls of Dun Dalgan. When she pointed out the grain to be taken and the silver sickle made its flashing curve through the air, she felt the closing of a vast, invisible circle. Ploughing and sowing, weeding and chasing away marauding birds, praying for sun or rain as needed, they had spent long days in partnership with soil and sky. Now, the partnership was culminating in a heap of golden grain to carry them through the winter until planting season began again. With their own chapped hands and aching backs, they had wrested their survival from the land; the cyclical magic was completed.

In that numinous moment, personal problems seemed too trivial for thought. Emer gave a small sigh of contentment, and Cuchulain grinned in understanding. 'This is the best time,' he said softly.

'The best time,' she echoed. Catching his fingers, she entwined them with her own, and they walked back to the fort together, swinging their linked hands between them.

The harvesters moved into the field quickly to finish cutting the grain, for Lughnasa was often, perversely, a time of rain. But as Murthemney prepared for the three days of festival, the skies continued to burn blue with a beaming sun.

Sun Day. The Gael gathered on their hilltops. On a height overlooking the plain of Murthemney, they began arriving long before dawn, the adults chafing their hands against the chill and reminiscing about the festivals of other years, while the children ran and shouted and chased one another as children do. The high, solemn event of sunrise would quiet them soon enough.

As Cuchulain came up the hill, the druids began chanting. You will die too, he warned them in his head. All your chanting is powerless to hold back the dark. He shuddered. Beneath his short woollen mantle he wore only a knee-length tunic of fine *sida*, with a heavy gold torc around his neck. Chill dawn wind was pressing the tunic against his body, revealing every contour.

Beside him, Emer could not keep her eyes from her husband. But like the other celebrants, he was now gazing towards the east.

The light came from the east. A sudden leap of light as clear as a tear swelled to fill the sky until even the memory of night was forgotten. Lugh hurled his golden spears into a rosy dome and his golden chariot followed. A thousand throats responded with a moan of awe.

Sun Day.

Emer watched Cuchulain's profile against the glowing sky. As the sun rose, he began to smile.

Lughnasa. He tilted his head back, imagining himself sinking into the cauldron of the sun. Lost in light, swimming in sunshine. The morbidity that had obsessed him began to melt away. Thoughts of death and darkness could not survive that radiant, living blaze.

Lughnasa.

Help me, thought Cuchulain. I am afraid of the dark.

Warmth washed over him, burning through wool and silk to sink deep into his bones. The light did not destroy the darkness, but simply relegated it to its natural and necessary role in the cycle of existence, something that would come, and end, like the night.

454

While the triumphant sun climbed higher, Cuchulain felt as if he momentarily grasped the ungraspable meaning of life. He opened his arms and cried out, but no one noticed. A thousand other people were similarly entranced in worship.

Above green and misty Erin, the sun rose in splendour.

Lughnasa.

Harvesting continued while the three-day feast was served. The men working in the fields had eaten their fill before the reaping began; now, it was Cuchulain's turn to savour the cakes made of his first cutting. In the rebuilt feasting hall of Dun Dalgan, fresh rushes had been laid on the floor and small children played happily on them while their elders ate and drank and celebrated, all care temporarily set aside.

Days after the feast ended, healers and herbalists would still be soothing overextended bellies.

On the final night of festival, Cuchulain found himself uninterested in food or ale, yet still hungry. Ravenous. A heat was in him, the sun burned in his veins. The hand he laid on Emer's shoulder in her bed was not gentle, but fiercely demanding.

She met him with a passion as fierce as his own. He felt her teeth in his shoulder and the pain was pleasure. As he had surrendered to the sun, Cuchulain surrendered to joy. Death happened, but so must life, and he was refilled with life.

'Setanta!' Emer gasped in delight.

He rose in splendour above her; she could see his eyes gleam in the dusky chamber. Then he plunged down between her thighs and filled her with his heat.

For a moment, he lay still, throbbing inside her. When he began to move, she moved with him. Theirs was a single rhythm of taking and giving; taking everything they wanted, giving everything they had. Without restraint.

Feeling Emer's glad reception, Cuchulain fleetingly wondered why he had let anxiety make him timid. He would not make the same mistake again, he resolved. Reach out, *live*.

He drove deeper into her and felt the familiar slow spasms of ecstasy begin at the base of his spine.

'Now,' she whispered. 'Now, Setanta!'

Now and now and *now*.

For a time, they lay resting in each other's arms, content to stroke and murmur. Then she cuddled closer and he fitted himself more firmly against her, and suddenly the rhythm seized them again, irresistible and demanding. The bed was soaked with their sweat, but they did not know how to stop.

At last Emer said with a shaky laugh, 'You're going to kill me.'

'I am not. We're immortal.' Then, in a tight voice, 'Fight me.'

The last thing she wanted was to resist, but Emer made herself struggle until his manhood rose yet again in triumph. When she fell asleep, the first rays of morning were seeping through the cracks in the chamber walls.

Cuchulain was still awake, watching the light.

15 Emer was not with child. Cuchulain tried to conceal his disappointment to avoid hurting her, but at Lughnasa he had felt so certain he could impregnate the world, he could scarcely believe her belly was not swelling. Yet life was surely in him, demanding to be passed on.

Cuchulain found himself beginning to look with speculative interest at other women.

The king sent Conall Cearnach to join with him in a mild skirmish between two clans of southern Ulster, and when the two of them came back to Dun Dalgan after settling the matter, Emer knew Cuchulain had been with another woman. Conall's wife, the elegant Lendabair, had accompanied her husband, and she confirmed Emer's suspicions with a shrug. 'It is the way of warriors,' she said. 'Particularly the heroes of the Red Branch; everyone offers them women. Does it bother you?'

'Not if he returns to me,' Emer replied truthfully.

And he always did.

Yet as time passed, the matter of the child they did not have lay between them like a small blue sorrow.

There was always work for Ulster's champion, and many times the Hound was summoned to defend this dun or that from its neighbours. He went willingly, with his old zest, and while away from Emer he availed himself of whatever local hospitality had to offer, living a life hot and physical. He appeared neither to brood nor grieve, but kept his own counsel and was invincible, season after season, year after year.

The only difference between this life and the one he had lived before Ferdiad's death was the fact that he never used the Gae Bulga again. He would not even take it out for demonstrations, but kept the Invincible Spear wrapped in oiled leather in the bottom of his war-cart, seemingly forgotten beneath all the other weapons.

Nor did he allow the Rage to transform him.

Each time they faced an enemy, Laeg waited eagerly, only to be disappointed. He began to suspect he had dreamed Cuchulain's powers. 'Aren't you ever going to use the Gae Bulga?' he finally asked.

'I win without it.'

'You do indeed, but . . .'

'I win without it,' Cuchulain repeated, closing the subject.

Not until next sunseason, after a particularly arduous struggle against a marauding band of Leinstermen, did Laeg ask, 'Why didn't you . . . change? In your battle-fury, you could have smashed that lot in half the time. I think they were actually disappointed they didn't get to see the monstrous Hound of Ulster.'

'I think *you* were disappointed,' Cuchulain told him.

He would not discuss his feelings about magic with his charioteer. He had never discussed them with anyone but Ferdiad. Thinking of Ferdiad, he said to himself, Now, I wear armour too, but mine is invisible. I have grown a layer of calluses over my spirit.

He had become hard, and he was proud of the fact. There was no need for the Gae Bulga or the Rage; he was cunning and experienced, he could meet other heroes on their terms and defeat them as a man. A man of the Red Branch.

He thought he wanted nothing more.

Five winters after the cattle raid of Cooley, he and Emer made their seasonal journey to Emain Macha for Samhain. Conor mac Nessa greeted his champion warmly. 'I've been doing some building,' he said, gesturing to indicate additions made to the House of the King. 'The druids conduct many of their rituals there now, so I've made some alterations to please them.'

'Have you won Cathbad back to you?' Cuchulain asked.

Conor laughed. 'You see through my little scheme. So did he, actually; I doubt he'll ever forgive me.' His deep voice sobered. 'And I doubt I'll ever see a son of my sons ruling Ulster. Unless you produce one, my Hound.'

'I'm doing my best, Father,' Cuchulain told him in tones too low for anyone to overhear.

Conor grinned and punched him on the arm. 'So I hear, so I hear! There's even a rumour about you and the wife of Curoi of Munster.'

'I think she started that one herself, I hardly know the woman.'

'But she knows enough about the Hound of Ulster to want everyone to believe she's found favour with you.'

Cuchulain's eyes twinkled. 'Then I won't insult her by denying it. That would be ungenerous, and I'm always generous to women.'

The incident seemed insignificant at the time.

458

He went on an inspection tour of the royal fort. A number of round timber buildings had recently been constructed to provide additional storage facilities, and the House of the Red Branch had even been enlarged to allow all the king's warriors to be quartered there at the same time.

A number, however, insisted on sleeping in lesser halls. Memories of the destruction of the earlier building were still too vivid.

Beyond the palisade, Cuchulain saw new duns and homesteads indicative of a growing population. The signs of prosperity that peace allows were everywhere.

'There's too much fat on us,' he commented to Conor. 'When Maeve is ready, she'll be back with another army, and this time she may bring invaders all the way to Emain Macha.'

'Much good will it do her, I've made Emain Macha impregnable. Look around you. Higher earthen banks, more walls of stone and timber, more naked iron and gleaming bronze. What attack could breach this stronghold now?'

The autumn sunshine was so dazzling, Cuchulain was forced to blink. In the moment between the fall and rise of his eyelids, he saw, or thought he saw, a different Emain Macha, eerily silent, great earthworks topped by nothing but grass, huge halls swallowed by time, timbered palisades rotted away, milling throngs vanished. Wind and ravens were the only tenants.

Then he blinked again, and the familiar scene was restored. With relief, he watched a porter in a coarse, undyed tunic trot past, balancing an immense load of faggots on his head to feed the royal hearthfire.

'Let's go and prop our feet up,' suggested the king of Ulster.

Several days later, Cuchulain happened across a group of gawky boys sitting in a semicircle under some trees, listening gape-mouthed to a storyteller.

They were the new Boys' Troop. Watching them fondly, he wondered if he had ever been as awkward and incomplete as these lads appeared.

They were obviously fascinated by the bard's recital. Cuchulain envied them their carefree absorption in myth, so much more enduring than forts. The trained voice was recounting deeds of shimmering implausibility, yet they captured the young audience in a net, filling them with dreams and aspirations of their own.

Cuchulain was about to turn away when something in the myth struck a familiar chord.

He stayed rooted where he was, eyes gradually widening.

The bard was so engrossed in word-weaving, he was unaware of the dark man in the shadow of the trees, staring at him as he told of the boyhood deeds of Cullen's Hound.

 More cold and drizzly winters passed, and more damp summers. Dismal island this, from my point of view. Which is the only one I accept.

Numerous single combats took place, but no serious major warfare. Herding and hunting and farming, the Gael were neglecting to kill one another in appreciable numbers.

The Erin of those days was too rich in resources, and therein lay the problem. Freed from the threat of hunger, its inhabitants were in danger of being corrupted by such peaceable pastimes as music and poetry.

Erin had a potential for paradise almost unique on a planet where most humans were scrambling to feed and clothe themselves.

I could not allow paradise.

Furthermore, I was bitterly disappointed in Cuchulain. He was not living up to his potential – after all I had done for him! The gifts lavished upon him were not being used.

And much as I might have wished otherwise, the responsibility for him and his actions was mine as a result of his early commitment to me.

In spite of that commitment, he had repeatedly rejected me, however, which I could not forget. I do not want you to think me vindictive, but I am alive. I do have feelings.

He had also rejected the god within himself, which was even more serious.

So it happened, inevitably, that destiny must close around him like a vice. Having given himself to the Battle Raven, he could not expect to be allowed a reflective voyage into placid old age, losing his hope and finding his sorrow in the futility of existence.

Making the necessary arrangements – and you have no idea how much work is entailed in my profession – I would have pitied Cuchulain if I could, but fortunately pity is not one of the burdens I must bear.

I found it necessary to make a number of trips across Erin, goading and encouraging, and many people heard the sound of my dark wings in the night sky. Women bolted their doors and kept their children inside when I passed.

Though I like children, actually.

460

I had loved the child Cuchulain had been. I hoped he would prove to be one of those rare humans who would embrace his fate with nobility when the time came.

I would know soon enough.

This man and that man challenged Cuchulain as the years passed, and this man and that man died. Their sons and kinfolk nursed their grievances and waited their time.

A grudge never falls on stony soil.

Like the rest of Ulster, Murthemney was prospering. The distribution of landholdings became a pressing concern, and at last Conor mac Nessa, accompanied by Sencha the brehon and various members of the Red Branch, journeyed south from Emain Macha to hold a court at Dun Dalgan. The fort itself was not large enough to contain all of the king's retinue plus the patriarchs gathering from the region, together with their families – each clamouring for their own interests – so it was decided to call an assembly at Baile's Strand, not far from the fort.

Tents were set up, trestle tables arranged, a fair and a market day sprang into being. Crowds gathered. To amuse the king, a chariot race was arranged on the white sand at the edge of the sea. Conor mac Nessa lounged on a high seat covered with black wolfskin, his eyes narrowed against the glare off the water as he watched the racers.

Suddenly, he sat up straight. 'What is that I see coming?'

Following his pointing finger, the others saw a boat breasting in through the surf. A small boat, leather hides stretched on a wooden frame, it contained only enough men to row and to manage the single square leather sail – and one boy. A boy who carried the shield of a warrior and wore a fine crested helmet covering his hair.

The bottom of the boat grated on the beach. Men ran forward to help pull it higher, beyond the tide. The boy stood to one side watching them like a prince instead of a labourer.

He had a haughty face, what could be seen of it beneath his helmet. His age was hard to guess, for he was lanky and yet muscular, caught somewhere between childhood and manhood. But the weapons he carried were a man's weapons.

Cethern's son, who had become the king's herald, asked the stranger's name, but received only a cold stare in reply. When he asked a second time, the boy told him, 'I give my name to no one. It is my own property, and I keep it to myself.'

'Strange boy, this,' Conor muttered behind his beard. 'Who would let a young lad come over the sea unattended except by boatmen? They might have robbed him.'

Overhearing, the boy replied, 'They would not dare rob me. I could kill them all before the first laid hands on me.'

'You are very confident for a little fellow,' laughed Leary the Battle-Winner.

'I am,' came the answer. Reaching down, the boy selected a pebble from among the many littering the beach. He fitted it to a sling carried in his belt, and in one smooth gesture turned and shot a gull out of the distant sky.

'Well done!' applauded the king. 'I would have that boy's name; I want to know what manner of people bred him.'

The youth stood with his legs apart and his shoulders back, meeting Conor's blue eyes with the fierce, proud stare of a hawk. 'I tell no one my name.'

Everyone was watching. Having his people see a mere boy defy him did not sit well with Conor mac Nessa. 'Will one of you take this boy into that field and teach him some respect?' he asked of the nearest members of the Red Branch.

Conall Cearnach stepped forward. He wasted no effort on words, but hurled himself at the boy.

And a moment later, found himself lying on the sand with the lad standing over him.

Conall shook his head to clear it, then grabbed for one of the boy's legs to jerk it out from under him. But the lad skipped nimbly aside and delivered a powerful kick to Conall's skull in passing.

The warrior rose, his broad jaw set, a look of blind fury in his deadly green eyes. He attacked the boy as he would have attacked a man, and the two grappled furiously while a crowd gathered around them, cheering Conall on.

But in the end, their cheers were wasted, and Conall hit the ground again. This time, he lay there, breathing hard, listening to the ringing in his ears.

Conor stepped off his high seat. 'You have overthrown the mightiest warrior here today,' he said to the boy. 'Now, you must tell us your name so our bards can praise you.'

'I will not,' the boy answered.

Conor was perplexed. He glanced around until his eyes met those of Cethern's son. 'Cuchulain isn't here yet, so I want you to go at once to

462

Dun Dalgan and tell him I need him immediately. This lad's refusal is an insult to the king of Ulster.'

At Dun Dalgan, Cuchulain had been occupied for days with preparations for the king's visit, often working late into the night beside his clansmen and servants. When Conor adjourned to Baile's Strand, his champion took advantage of a little peace and quiet to steal a nap before going to join them. He was asleep in his sleeping chamber when Cethern's son – who had never been informed of *gessa* on the Hound of Ulster – burst in upon him.

'There's a lad on the beach who challenged Conall Cearnach and threw him down! The king wants you to come at once, Cuchulain!'

Snatched from sleep, Cuchulain sat up and knuckled his eyes. His head felt fuzzy on the inside. As his brain cleared, he was astonished that anyone had the temerity to awaken him. 'Where's my wife?' he asked, wondering why Emer hadn't intercepted the herald.

'Off somewhere with the other women of the Red Branch, doing woman-things. You have your own job to do as the king's champion, though, and I bid you to hurry.'

'Go find and my charioteer, then. And tell him to be certain my weapons are in the war-cart.' Dismissing the herald, Cuchulain prepared for combat.

The broken *ges* gnawed at the back of his mind, making him uneasy.

As he and Laeg neared the beach, they could see people gathered in knots. The strange youth stood apart from them, cheeks flushed, head high in defiance. When Conor saw Cuchulain approaching, he went to meet the chariot. 'I won't be threatened by an unknown boy who comes out of the sea. Make him give you his name, my Hound.'

The crowd formed a circle around Cuchulain and the stranger.

When asked his name by the champion, the youth replied, 'I am sworn not to tell it.'

'I'll have to kill you if you don't; you're insulting the king. There is no desire in me to kill a mere boy, so set your oath aside and live.'

The boy cast a wary glance at the increasingly hostile crowd, its ranks now swelled by a group of women who had come to see what was happening. But he stood his ground. 'I cannot set an oath aside.'

'An honourable answer, but an unfortunate one for you,' Cuchulain told him. 'I must challenge you to combat then. You are still a boy, however, so you are free to refuse.'

'I cannot refuse a challenge. I cannot give way to any man.'

Cuchulain glanced towards Conor, but the king's expression was implacable. Such stubborn defiance could not be ignored, even coming from a stripling boy.

'Show me your best feats, then,' said Cuchulain to the stranger.

'I will do more than show you battle-feats. I will kill you.' With these words, the boy ran back to the boat and took out an assortment of weapons. He tossed his spears and caught them behind his back; he balanced his shield on a rock and ran around its rim without setting a foot on the ground; he balanced the point of his sword on the bridge of his nose with his eyes closed.

'Whoever that boy is, hard men bred him,' said Conor mac Nessa. 'I don't want him to be able to go back to such people and report how prosperous Ulster is.'

From his chariot, Cuchulain selected a light casting spear. He threw it at the boy, who caught the point easily on the rim of his shield and threw the spear back at Cuchulain in one smooth motion, narrowly missing putting a new parting in the champion's hair.

'My grief!' Cuchulain returned to his chariot and selected a heavier weapon. With Hardhead in his hand, he told the athletic young stranger, 'I must have your name now, or I'll kill you where you stand.' His words were hard, but his voice was low and quiet; the boy liked the sound of it. He liked his adversary's grey eyes too; eyes that did not stab into his but instead seemed to invite him to enter their luminous depths.

'There is no man living to whom I would rather give my name,' the youngster said. 'But I cannot. So we will have to prove ourselves against each other.' From his assortment of weapons, he selected a sword as broad and heavy as Hardhead, though it had no ivory on the hilt. The watching warriors were surprised at the ease with which the slender youth handled the heavy blade. Then he adjusted a shield on his arm, balanced his weight on the balls of his feet, and screamed his battle cry.

Cuchulain came to meet him.

He could not allow himself to think of his opponent as a boy, a child. He was the champion, and this warrior, whatever his age, was his enemy. The tough shell he had built around his spirit stood him in good stead now, for when he drew back his arm for the first blow, it did not hesitate, though seen close up the lad's face was heart-wrenchingly young.

But not too young: the determination to kill or be killed was already hot in his eyes.

Cuchulain met the first blow and took it on his shield, surprised at the strength behind it. He immediately responded with a mighty swordthrust of his own, which the boy successfully avoided, only to pivot and come back with a downward slice that would have been fatal if it had broken through Cuchulain's defences.

'They are well matched,' Conall Cearnach said in disbelief.

The fight was now in deadly earnest. The difference in age was forgotten by combatants and spectators alike. Since he had fought Ferdiad in the ford, Cuchulain had never found himself so hard-pressed. The boy was desperately quick, and he had the stamina of youth. For the first time, Cuchulain realised his own reflexes were a hair's breadth less swift than they once had been, and his famed agility did not come quite as easily as it always had before.

How quickly the wheel of the seasons had turned.

They fought. From one end of the strand to the other, they fought. Neither wasted breath on insults; they struggled in panting silence, and the watching crowd was equally silent, afraid to make any noise that might fatally distract their champion.

'You don't have to let him defeat you, Cuchulain,' Laeg whispered under his breath, knowing the Hound could not hear him. 'You don't have to lose.' He clenched his fists and tried to force his thoughts into Cuchulain's mind.

Someone went for Emer, and she came like a running deer, her eyes huge. But she did not cry out, merely watched. Silently.

The struggle could not last for ever. Perhaps he had fought one too many battles, or perhaps, as he and the boy were pressed knee to knee, something in the lad's face caught Cuchulain by surprise, and he was less careful than he should have been. But the youth succeeded in knocking Hardhead from his hand, and the great sword went arcing out over the sand to fall into the hissing surf at the edge of the sea.

'A weapon!' Cuchulain cried out desperately to Laeg.

In another heartbeat the charioteer had a weapon in his hand and in another heartbeat he was tossing it to Cuchulain.

When the boy saw his opponent being thrown a javelin, he dropped his sword and seized a javelin of his own. Then he stepped back to give himself space in which to make the throw.

No sooner had Cuchulain lost Hardhead than he realised he might actually be beaten. Yet he was the champion; a defeat for him was a defeat for Ulster and the king. With an inward wrenching, he loosed the grip he had held on himself for so long and let the Rage burst free. Then his fingers closed around the shaft of the weapon Laeg tossed to him; and with hardly a pause in its flight, he sent the Gae Bulga on its way.

465

Seeing the flame of hero-light blaze around the man's head, the boy suddenly knew whom he fought. He hurled his javelin to one side, deliberately missing Cuchulain.

But the Gae Bulga never missed. Humming, it tore its cruel way through the boy's body and pinned him to the sand.

The sand turned crimson.

Cuchulain ran to the lad and knelt beside him. The boy tried to raise one hand; a heavy gold ring glinted on his finger. 'You are as good as she said you were,' he managed to whisper.

'She?' Cuchulain was staring at the ring.

'My mother. Ayfa. You wanted my name – she named me Cunla in honour of my father, who is called . . .'

'Cuchulain,' moaned the Hound of Ulster.

This second agony was so much worse than the one he had experienced with Ferdiad beside the ford that Cuchulain thought he must surely die while his son still breathed. But he did not die. Lifting the bleeding boy into his arms and cradling him against his heart, he turned a terrible face towards the watching warriors.

Men gasped at the sight of that face.

Still half-transformed into the monstrous Hound, but equally transfigured by human grief, Cuchulain appeared to be neither god nor man.

'This is my son,' he said in a choked voice to Conor mac Nessa. 'If you look at his hand, you will see a ring on his finger that you once gave me. My curse is on the woman who placed it there, for she has killed him.'

'Father?' a faint voice murmured. At the sound of that incredibly precious, unfamiliar name, Cuchulain bent his head over the dying boy. 'Are these the men of the Red Branch around us?'

'They are.'

'Will you call each of them by name for me, then? If I had lived, I would have been proud to join their company of heroes.'

'You are of their company,' Cunla's father told him, fighting back tears he had never thought to shed.

As Cuchulain held the broken body – so slight now, so fragile! – the Red Branch warriors came forward and he identified them one by one, letting Cunla's dim eyes try to fix each famous face in memory.

Somewhere between Cuscraid the Stammerer and Ernan of the Iron, Cuchulain felt the body in his arms grow heavier, and knew its bright spirit had fled.

Yet he continued to call the roll of the Red Branch, and each knelt in turn to look on the face of the champion's son.

When the last warrior stepped aside, Emer took his place.

She was crying unashamedly. She held out her arms and took half her husband's burden into them. Together they cradled the dead boy, bending tenderly over him until their two heads touched above his.

Cunla of the Reddened Spear was buried beside the strand, and the warriors of the Red Branch raised a pillar stone over him with their own hands.

Afterward, when Baile's Strand was empty of all save sea and sky and the lonely monolith standing like a sentinel, Cuchulain returned to the beach with the Gae Bulga in his hands. At arm's length, like a sacrificial offering, he carried the Invincible Spear that had slain Ferdiad and Cunla.

The shaft felt like an extension of his arms. His will and the will of the spear had, together, performed impossible feats. Made him champion.

Destroyed the irreplaceable.

He slumped on to the beach and turned the shaft over and over between his fingers, staring at the weapon as if he had never seen it before. The cruel bronze head gleamed in the sealight. 'Do you think Macha Fleet-Foot was grateful for her gift of speed on the racecourse at Emain Macha, Ferdiad?' he asked softly.

His grip on the spear's shaft tightened. The expression on his face did not change, did not distort, did not lose its humanity and give way to the grimace of the Hound. Yet the shaft creaked in protest as his fingers tightened, tightened, tightened. Exerted an impossible pressure that did not relent until, with a loud crack, the ash wood split throughout its length like a tree struck by lightning.

Cuchulain turned his attention to the head of the Gae Bulga. Still wearing an abstracted, almost dreamy expression, he twisted the solid bronze until the metal responded with a scream of almost human agony. Indifferent to the sharpened prongs, he crushed the spearhead in upon itself until only an unrecognisable mass of crumpled metal remained.

With a mighty effort, Cuchulain hurled the ruined spear far out to sea. He had already turned his back when it struck the surface and disappeared beneath the waves.

16 For seven winters after the disastrous cattle raid of Cooley, Maeve kept peace with Ulster. She appeared to be content with Cruachan of the Enchantments; she boasted of it as before, and proudly showed visitors the numerous duns and outbuildings spreading across the plains, like spokes to its hub. Cruachan was the centre of a powerful kingdom, and Maeve was the centre of Cruachan.

Ailell wisely avoided provoking her, and only the bravest of men would mention bulls or cattle-breeding in her presence.

'We have grown old, Fergus,' Ailell told the former king of Ulster. 'Too old for any more martial adventures. Pleasant it is to sit with fingers laced across a round belly and contemplate past achievements, knowing you need not get up in the cold before dawn to undertake new ones.'

'You and I may feel that way,' Fergus agreed, 'but do you really believe Maeve is reconciled to it?'

'Just keep your head down and hope,' Ailell advised.

But in their season, the travelling bards came to Connaught and told of the other kingdoms of Erin: of Munster and Leinster and Ulster. And of the Hound.

'They are still singing of him,' Maeve muttered to herself as she sat on her bench in the hall of Cruachan. 'Ailell, did you know that everywhere but here an epic saga is told of our cattle raid, a saga in which Cuchulain is the hero and I appear a fool, outmanoeuvred by a beardless man?'

'I doubt if anyone calls you a fool, Maeve, nor have I heard this epic you describe.'

'Only because no one dares repeat it here. But the bards refer to it sideways, the way you look at serving women.'

Her husband raised his eyebrows to his hairline. 'What serving women?'

Maeve ignored him and went to listen to the latest bard.

This one had a story of more than passing interest. 'The Hound of

468

Ulster,' he related, 'has made a bad enemy in Munster. Blanad, wife of Curoi the king, has long been interested in Cuchulain, and in an effort to attract his attention, she sent him a message claiming her husband was cruelly mistreating her. She begged him to rescue her from Curoi's fort during a period when she promised her husband would be away.

'Cuchulain could not bear to hear of any woman being abused, so he took a band of Red Branch warriors with him and followed the road to Munster.

'Curoi, however, was a wise man who knew his wife's nature, and though he told her he was going to be away, he came back to his fort secretly to spy on her, just in time to intercept Cuchulain and his men. He accused the Hound of trying to steal his woman, and a dreadful battle ensued. Eventually, Curoi received a wound that was to kill him, and Blanad – in real fear at last – fled north with the Ulstermen.

'Cuchulain intended to deliver her into safekeeping at Emain Macha, but before they could reach the northern fortress, the woman was slain. One of her husband's musicians had accompanied her, pretending he was devoted to her but actually planning to take revenge for Curoi. During an unguarded moment, he killed both himself and the faithless wife. Now, the eldest son of Curoi mourns his father and nurses a bitter hatred for the Hound of Ulster.'

'The name of this son of Curoi?' Maeve asked eagerly.

'Lugaid. Lugaid mac Ros; Curoi was his foster-father, but they were as close as two teeth in a mouth. This same Lugaid had once hoped to marry Emer, the woman Cuchulain took as wife.'

'He must indeed hate the Hound of Ulster,' Maeve said, with obvious satisfaction. 'A man like Cuchulain makes many enemies. Every trophy head in his collection has a living relative somewhere.'

When she repeated the story to Ailell, he was mildly surprised. 'I wouldn't have expected Cuchulain to steal another man's wife.'

'He claimed he wasn't trying to steal her, but to rescue her. He had told his companions they would take Blanad to Emain Macha and put her under Conor's protection, but I dare say Lugaid doesn't believe it.'

'The rest of the story is true, though?'

'I heard it from a poet's mouth.'

'Poets are sometimes criticised for having their facts wrong, let me remind you.'

'Poets are not concerned with facts, but with truth, Ailell. They may confuse facts, but they make no mistakes about truth.'

Walking the footworn pathways winding through Cruachan, Maeve wondered what truth the poets would tell of this stronghold. Would it be remembered for being the home of Maeve, who was defeated by the Hound of Ulster? Or would it not be remembered at all, a place of no consequence?

The constructions of man are only as famous as the men connected with them, Maeve told herself.

Or the women.

The fort of the woman who defeated the invincible Cuchulain would be famous for ever.

Her restless feet slowed long enough to allow her to run the palm of her hand along the sun-warmed top of a stone wall, slowly and with love.

Mac Roth the herald was sent throughout the kingdoms and clanholds of Erin to learn the names and grudges of those who might have the most reason to hate Cuchulain and the most strength to bring against him.

Ailell found Fergus in the ale hall, snoring gently with one cheek pressed against the rough wood of a tabletop. A puddle of ale spilled from his overturned horn was slowly soaking into the wood.

'Wake up, Fergus, you can't sleep on the table. If you must sleep here, get under the table with the rest of them.'

Fergus opened one crimson eye. 'What difference does it make?'

Exasperated, Ailell grabbed his friend by the shoulders and tried to wrestle him to his feet, but the man was a dead weight. He staggered, he fell, and Ailell found himself somehow pinned beneath the mountain that was Fergus mac Roy. 'You're crushing me,' he protested in muffled tones.

Fergus heaved to one side and reopened the same eye. This time, it observed dirty rushes and part of some woollen garment dyed bluish-grey. Sloes produce that colour, he mused dreamily. Someone's been dyeing their wool with sloes. My mother liked that shade.

Ailell scrambled to his feet, swearing. Catching Fergus under the armpits, he hauled him into a semi-sitting position and propped him against a bench. 'Can you hear me?'

'I cannot. Unless you're offering me another drink.'

'Forget drink. There's going to be a new war against Ulster.'

'In that case, Ailell, I'll need two drinks.'

'Don't you understand? Maeve's gathering another army and counting on the Pangs to protect her again. There are the usual promises of plunder, of course, and we took enough out of Conor's

470

kingdom last time to encourage men to go with us once more. But my wife's real purpose is revenge.'

Fergus considered this statement, then opened both eyes. 'Revenge?'

'For the humiliation she suffered during the cattle raid.'

'Your wife once told me she thought a war of revenge accomplished nothing.'

'She changed her mind, Fergus, as soon as she found herself aggrieved.'

'Isn't that the way of it?' Fergus asked his huge, chapped hands as they lay like dead animals in his lap. 'Isn't that always the way of it?' Then, to Ailell: 'Who's she taking with her?'

'Every man in Erin with a grudge against Cuchulain, it seems. Erc of Leinster, Lugaid from Munster . . .'

'You needn't name them all for me,' said Fergus wearily. 'It might take the day. Are you going?'

Ailell eased himself on to the bench next to Fergus. 'I thought I was past battle after that great foolishness of the cattle raid. Still, Maeve is my wife. And I think I've been missing the chariots and the trumpets and the shouting.'

'A sight I'd rather miss, I've seen enough of it already.'

'She doesn't intend to take you anyway, Fergus. She says you would be more hindrance than help.'

'And so I would,' Fergus agreed. 'Never would I make it easy for someone to attack Cuchulain.'

'Shorten your face, old friend. We may do him no damage at all; we couldn't kill him last time, remember.'

With these heartening words, Ailell left the ale hall. As soon as he had gone, Fergus set about draining every cask in the place.

Another Lughnasa had been celebrated in Murthemney, and a fine harvest of grain was stacked in the haggard at Dun Dalgan. Cuchulain's wife joined the other women at the threshing floor near the kiln house, because these were oats of her planting and she was responsible for them. She would use some of them to bake the flat oaten cakes Cuchulain preferred above any other form of bread.

Emer held a flail, as did the woman facing her, for the threshers worked in pairs. As the grain was threshed, it would be swept into a pit in the corner of the threshing floor, leaving the straw to be dealt with separately. The women had hardly begun their task when they heard running feet and shouting.

'Word from the west, word from the west! Ulster is attacked!'

Dropping her flail, Emer hurried to the hall.

Cuchulain was there ahead of her, listening with stormy eyes as a messenger reported, 'Ulstermen to the west are already beginning to suffer from the Pangs.'

'Invasion,' Cuchulain said. 'Maeve, then.' He had no doubt.

There would be little time to prepare. 'Send our bondwomen and their children into the secluded glens of the mountains,' he told Emer. 'My mother too; make certain she is safe. I would not be surprised if Maeve put the torch to Dun Dalgan this time.'

'But won't you be here to protect it?'

'I have to be at Emain Macha to protect the king. Maeve took the Brown Bull once; this time, she is surely after something else.'

'Maeve is a hideous, horrible, unwomanly woman, and I hate her!' Emer said vehemently.

The ghost of a smile played across Cuchulain's mouth. 'I wouldn't describe Maeve as unwomanly. She's just a different sort of woman.'

'Beautiful, is she?'

He shrugged. 'I'd call her the scrapings of the pot compared to you or Lendabair. Or Niamh, that kinswoman of Leary's,' he added with a gleam in his eye that Emer pretended not to notice.

When Dun Dalgan was as secure as he could make it, he set out to protect his king and Emain Macha, taking Emer with him.

Meanwhile, invaders were bruising Ulster with iron wheels and trampling feet.

For Ailell, the adventure was somewhat dulled by a sense of repetition and a general lack of exuberance on the part of the participants. This was not the merry band of cattle-raiders who had set out from Cruachan seven years before. These were grim men whose primary purpose, like that of Maeve, was the annihilation of Cuchulain.

Only when the champion of Ulster was dead would they despoil his province.

 Maeve, I had realised, was no longer quite sane. Her fixation on killing Cuchulain, which had driven her to relinquish her former view on the futility of seeking revenge, was an example of her mental imbalance.

Not that I have anything against revenge, you understand. I am its ultimate and only true beneficiary.

But the human mind is a model of the cosmos, with its polarity

472

between what one might call the male and the female principles. The male, like the sun, pours out creative energy. The female, like the earth, absorbs and transforms that energy. Destruction occurs when the polarity is upset, for its balanced tensions provide the cohesion that holds the universe together.

For some peculiar reason, for several thousand of their years humans have endeavoured to confer supremacy on the male force, while relegating the female to a secondary position. Dangerous, of course, as Maeve intuitively knew. But in trying to re-establish equality, she had mistaken her opposite for her enemy.

The spectacular Cuchulain embodied all that was male and threatening for Maeve, so she had become obsessed with the idea of destroying him. Moreover, in refusing to kill her because she was a woman, he had unwittingly insulted her by implying she was less than his equal.

Now, she must kill him to prove him wrong.

For the first time in eons, I found myself dreading a human death. There is some blood that even the Morrigan does not wish spilled!

On the eve of departure, Maeve and Ailell had served a sumptuous feast to the chariot-chieftains who had come to join their armies, men from every part of Erin except Ulster. Fat and prosperous Ulster.

While the chieftains were enjoying their meat and ale, Maeve had the chief bard of Connaught recite the names of their kinsmen whom Cuchulain had slain. The list was long, and by the time it was completed, the hall was filled with sullen, angry muttering.

Maeve then beckoned to someone concealed behind a screen. A trio of hideously deformed women crept forward, their humped backs and gnarled limbs casting weird shadows on the walls in the light of pine-knot torches. At the sight of them, the brave chieftains of Leinster and Munster shuddered in revulsion.

'My foster-father, Ercol, had a son called Calatin,' Maeve explained to her allies, 'who was killed by the Hound of Ulster seven years ago. These are Calatin's daughters. Their father had always believed they had been given unique gifts to balance their deformities, and had requested that, should he ever be killed, his daughters be fostered by Ercol's druid.

'The druid was a man of extraordinary ability, who could walk into the mind of another person as easily as you or I walk into a sleeping chamber. He recognised what Calatin had suspected in the three

473

twisted girls, so he took them out into the loneliest, stoniest places of Connaught and began to dance patterns in their minds.

'Day after day, season after season, the druid whirled through the minds of Calatin's daughters until they could form the patterns as well as he could. Better, for there were three of them together. They could make rain fall, reshape smoke, give the trees voices . . . and perform darker deeds as well.

'Eventually, the druid died, exhausted from his efforts, but he had accomplished what Calatin wanted – made of the dead man's daughters a weapon for vengeance.

'We are going to take them to Ulster with us,' Maeve said, 'and no matter how powerful he is, or how well he withstands sword and spear, Cuchulain will not escape the claws of Calatin's daughters.'

Even Ailell looked appalled. The three sisters writhed in the firelight like unclean growths sprung from the floor of the hall.

Seated near the door, Fergus mac Roy was also chilled by the sight and purpose of the creatures. When he thought no one was watching him, he slipped outside and went in search of a runner, someone he could trust – or bribe – to carry a warning to Ulster. 'Tell Conor mac Nessa to keep Cuchulain out of Maeve's reach no matter what happens,' was the message he dispatched.

When he returned to the hall, Fergus was met by Maeve's icy stare and realised she had guessed his mission. From the side of her mouth, she whispered an instruction to the daughters of Calatin. One hairless, birthmarked creature raised a bony arm and made peculiar gestures in the air, then pointed her longest finger at Fergus mac Roy and laughed.

A tingle began in his toes. The hall faded around him; the sound of voices became a meaningless buzz in his ears. He felt worn out, helpless. Tottering from the hall, he stumbled to the nearest sleeping chamber and fell across the bed. He looked around vaguely, but did not recognise the chamber except to know it was not his, but he could not hope to reach his. He could no longer stand up at all. He lay with his mind wandering amid random memories.

Until Maeve's return from Ulster – whenever, in whatever condition – Fergus mac Roy was condemned to the weakness and senility of a man who had survived a hundred winters or more. Tended and mocked by servants who cleaned up his bowel movements and wiped the drool from his lips, he would not know when the men of Erin marched away to invade the northland. Nor would he see Calatin's daughters riding in honour among them, in a special four-wheeled wooden cart prepared

474

for their comfort, with curtained sides and an embroidered canopy suspended from poles ornamented with bronze.

Fergus's message did get through, however, and a white-lipped Conor mac Nessa, already suffering from the Pangs, received the unwelcome news that the foremost purpose of the invasion was the destruction of Cuchulain.

'Has my champion arrived in Emain Macha yet?' he asked a servant.

'He has, he's unyoking his chariot now. His charioteer is in the same condition as yourself,' the servant replied, thankful for once to be born to a lowly station.

Conor turned towards his mother. 'Nessa, you and the women will have to use your cleverness to keep Cuchulain away from Maeve until we recover our strength and can defend him ourselves.'

Nessa's eyes were faded by age, but sharp with undiminished intelligence. They sought out Cathbad, who, like the rest of the *filidh*, did not suffer from the curse afflicting the warriors. 'I need your help,' she told the druid.

He seemed to draw back into the hood of his cloak. 'For the king?'

'For Cuchulain.'

'Then I'll help you, of course,' Cathbad assured her.

Reaching Dun Dalgan unchallenged, Maeve and her armies learned that their quarry was no longer there, but north at the royal stronghold. Maeve did not bother to put a torch to Cuchulain's fort. Nor, she announced, would she tire her men further by marching them to Emain Macha.

'We'll set up camp on the plain of Murthemney,' she said, 'and bring Cuchulain to us here, alone and unaided, without a man at his side or the walls of Emain Macha to shield him.'

Since this was Maeve's war, Ailell had let her direct it herself, so far, but now he was puzzled. 'How do you propose to do that? If he is with the king, why should he come out? Will you tempt him again with challenges of single combat?'

'And allow him more victories to swell his fame? Under no circumstances, husband. You forget – I have a weapon capable of reaching Cuchulain wherever he is. Even if he has been warned and made every prudent preparation, I can get to him.

'I have the daughters of Calatin.'

Cuchulain was standing guard at the main gate of Emain Macha when the first sounds rang through his skull. He had been resting in the warrior's posture, leaning on a spear driven at an angle into the earth, with one knee bent and that foot resting upon the rigid knee of the leg that supported him. His folded cloak atop the spear's shaft formed a cushion for his armpit, and he was relaxed but wary – until he heard the distant but unmistakable clash of arms and the roar of warriors.

In the indrawing of a breath, he had assumed fighting posture. Yet the female sentries who had taken over duties in the gatetower called down to assure him, 'We see nothing!'

'Open the gates and let me go out to see for myself.'

Emer ran forward, followed by Cathbad of the Gentle Face, to intercept Cuchulain. 'Stay inside where it's safe,' she urged. Cathbad added, 'I sense a trick. Some unclean magic stinks in the air like belly gas.'

'But I hear a war chant,' Cuchulain insisted. 'The invaders are coming. I can't cower in here, I'm the champion! Can't you hear the trumpets calling me to battle?'

'I don't hear anything but the wind and the cawing of birds,' Emer assured him.

The sentries in the tower heard nothing either, though Cuchulain asked them repeatedly. Peering out across the land of the Ulaid, they saw rolling hills and glimmering ponds and clustered woodlands, but no armies.

In the clustered woodlands out of sight of their searching eyes, however, the daughters of Calatin were at work. They had left the comfort of their canopied cart and made the journey from Murthemney to Emain Macha in swift chariots, and now they crouched among the trees, contorting their bodies and weaving their fingers into patterns to speed the creations of their minds into Cuchulain's skull.

His ears rang with the shouts and jeers of an advancing army.

Pushing Emer aside, Cuchulain began unbarring the gates.

Cathbad tore at his hands. 'Leave it, Hound!'

'I cannot!'

'It's an ambush, I tell you.'

'I'm the champion, I have to go,' Cuchulain insisted.

Emer interposed her slender body between her husband and the gate, and took his face between her hands. 'Ah, Setanta, when did I try to keep you from battle? But just this once, I ask you to stay with me; we women have charge of your safety now.'

He made an effort to listen to her words, but they kept getting lost in the percussion of hooves, the clang of spears being struck

476

against shields, the taunting insults of warriors shouting challenges to him.

'There is one place he might be safer, Emer,' Cathbad suggested. 'Glen na Bodhar, the Deaf Valley. High hills shield it on all sides, and few sounds enter from outside; whatever Cuchulain's hearing now might not reach him there.'

'Come with me to Glen na Bodhar then, Cuchulain,' Emer immediately pleaded. The other Red Branch wives, joining with her, added their voices, but still Cuchulain stared longingly at the gates and the conflict he imagined beyond. When Emer tugged at his arm, he shook her off.

She caught the eye of Conall Cearnach's wife. 'Lendabair, help me. A wife is too familiar to a man, he makes no special effort to please her. You ask him. He just might do it for you.'

Lendabair stepped forward, pleased with Emer's public admission that she might have some influence over the champion that his own wife did not. Cuchulain had admired her elegant form more than once, and she had never hesitated to respond with her warmest smile.

Standing so close to him that her breath stirred the hair on his temples, Lendabair murmured, 'I'm so frightened, Cuchulain. If there is an army out there, my husband lies helpless to protect me. Please take me away from here to some safe place before any fighting begins, will you? Take us all to the Deaf Valley, the women will be safe there no matter what happens in Emain Macha.'

With an effort, Cuchulain concentrated on her words enough to make sense of them. Women. Protect. He must protect the women. He let her lead him away from the gate, and the farther he got from the south side of the fort, the more the sounds of invasion faded from his ears. He managed to hitch his team to his chariot, and then, accompanied by the women, left the fort through the small water-gate on the north side.

The women encircled his war-cart so closely that he could not have turned back without running some of them down.

Once they entered Glen na Bodhar with its encircling hills, he seemed calmer. The sounds of war had faded away, and he was willing to believe they had been a trick of the mind, as Cathbad had said. The women took turns distracting him with songs and games. One played a harp while another held Cuchulain's head and shoulders in her lap, stroking his dark hair. Emer encouraged everything, so long as he was willing to remain with them.

Soon Calatin's daughters sensed Cuchulain's absence from within the walls of Emain Macha. They shrieked and jabbered and pranced until a wind arose, swirling a pile of dead leaves upward. The leaves did not blow in one direction only but scattered, north and south, east and west, searching.

In Glen na Bodhar, Cuchulain began to chafe at the loving restraint of the women. 'If I shelter here any longer, the bards will tell that I was afraid,' he tried to explain to them.

Fedelm of the Fresh Heart said, 'What the bards may tell future generations isn't nearly as important as keeping you alive.'

'It is to me,' Cuchulain argued. He was becoming increasingly agitated. He turned his back on the women and went in search of his chariot horses, which he had unyoked and turned loose to graze in the valley. Emer ran after him and hung on his arms, digging her heels into the mossy earth. 'Dearest of all men in the world, please stay just a little longer!'

He turned a frighteningly blank face towards her; he was like a man who had had too much to drink and was unaware what he was doing. A wife was just an impediment; he pushed her away impatiently.

Looking around desperately for help, Emer saw Niamh nearby. Leary Buadach's lovely kinswoman Niamh, a woman of rippling hair and high-arched foot. Emer summoned her with a glance. 'Put your arms around Cuchulain quickly,' she said in a low, urgent voice, 'and put your mouth on his mouth. If you value his life, hold him here.'

'I cannot!' Niamh protested. 'And you watching!'

'Then take him into that glade where the bushes will hide you, but take him, woman! He can't think clearly now, you must make him aware of you to the exclusion of everything else, or we will all lose him.'

Understanding, Niamh placed herself in Cuchulain's path with a smile of heated invitation. She entwined her arms around his neck, and with the gentle weight of her supple body she pressed him, step by step, into the glade. The dazed man tried to resist her, but the swirlings in his head made clear thinking impossible. The bushes closed behind them.

'Do you think he understands what is happening?' Fedelm asked Emer.

'Part of him does.'

'I couldn't send Leary into the arms of another woman so freely, even to save his life.'

Emer smiled sadly at Fedelm. 'Then you don't love him enough. Or you love your pride more.'

478

I have grown and learned, she thought, remembering Fand.

The leaves blowing on the wind passed over sheltered Glen na Bodhar. Below them could be seen the Grey of Macha and the Black of Sainglain, peacefully grazing near a feather-ornamented chariot.

Calatin's daughters had found Cuchulain.

In the glade with Niamh, Cuchulain heard the battle cacophony building again in his ears, and struggled against his confusion. As Emer had told Fedelm, he was partially aware of the true nature of the situation. He resented the influences clouding his mind. There were brief moments when he knew very well that the sounds of an army were not real, but illusion.

Magic, he thought angrily, when he could think. His fear and mistrust of magic came back to him. A man should rely only on the tangible, he told himself, on his strength and skill and tough, clear mind. Being forced into a passive role, twisted and turned by forces beyond his control, infuriated Cuchulain. If only he could break free . . .

Then magic washed over him again in waves, blinding him to everything but the imperative of battle. Fading only when held at bay by the strength of a woman's arms.

In Murthemney, Maeve waited on piled cushions at the mouth of her tent, patiently looking northward toward the peak of Slieve Fuad, which marked the way to Emain Macha.

A dark purple storm-line was gathering over Conor mac Nessa's stronghold.

Niamh emerged from the glade to report that Cuchulain had fallen into a fitful sleep. At once Nessa put her to work helping the other women prepare shelters, lashing branches together and covering them with cloaks.

The clouds sank lower, becoming dense fog that settled into the hollows as if it meant to stay for ever. Muffled sounds took on an eerie quality that made the women apprehensive. 'Perhaps we should take Cuchulain back to Emain Macha,' Lendabair suggested. 'I don't like this.'

'I don't like it either,' Emer said, 'but I don't dare take him out in the open yet. And who knows what may be happening at the fort?'

While the man slumbered on, occasionally crying out some incomprehensible syllables, the women finished the shelters and spread out to collect drinking water and firewood.

Every tree limb and twig she found was saturated with damp, so

Niamh wandered farther and farther away from the others, searching for wood dry enough to burn. She thought she heard Emer calling to her and headed in the direction of the voice, but after a few steps fog surrounded her, obliterating the landscape on every side. When she tried to call out, the fog filled her throat so she could not speak. She turned back, hoping to retrace her steps, but the way was unfamiliar, and she could hardly see anything.

With a twinge of terror, Niamh realised she was lost.

Lendabair had found a clear stream and was just lowering a cup into it, when she heard the call. She straightened up and answered, noticing that the voice was moving away from her and sounded as if troubled. One of the other women was obviously in difficulties, so Lendabair hurried to help.

The fog closed around her.

Emer was in a thicket relieving herself when she thought she heard Cuchulain shout. She ran towards the sound of his voice as soon as she could, but upon leaving the thicket, she got turned around in the fog. Her husband's voice rang out again, the cry of a man in mortal peril. Half-crying, stumbling over roots, beating at the air with her hands, Emer fought to reach Cuchulain through an impenetrable blanket of choking mist.

17

Cuchulain lay dreaming. He thought he slept on piled furs in his bedchamber at Dun Dalgan with Emer nestled beside him, a linen coverlet tucked under her chin.

But her imagined presence was no comfort to him. He was gravid with grief. Since the death of Cunla, there was no escape from sorrow, even in sleep. A leaden mood seeped into his brightest dreams, tarnishing them.

An image of Ferdiad flickered across his closed eyelids. Cuchulain reached out eagerly, but the face faded as swiftly as it had appeared, leaving him in his darkness. Like other verities Cuchulain had once trusted, friendship had betrayed him into pain.

His sleeping mind pondered this with the clarity of thought that sometimes illumines dreams. Is it possible, he asked himself, that I misremember the flavour of our friendship? We fought each other to the death – does that not show I was mistaken about the love between us?

He tried to recall specific words and deeds that would prove him wrong, but his memory was slippery. The more he clutched, the more he lost. Ferdiad began to seem like a phantom he had created to satisfy his own need.

Need? Need of what?

Need for another like yourself, came the answer. Need not to be trapped in solitude between the dark-before-birth and the dark-after-death.

Need not to be alone.

I'm not alone, Cuchulain averred. I fight in single combat, but all Ulster supports me. Men imitate me, women pursue me. I am the Hound.

You are alone, replied the voice that sounded like his own voice. You are alone for ever, that is what it means to be human. Ashes and death and dying, and the most a man can hope for is to be put into a dry grave.

Where did I hear those words before?

Then Cuchulain remembered . . . and the memory became a dream from the past, relived again.

Looking down from a height, he saw the child Setanta standing with his mother in a windswept field as some member of the Dun Dalgan guard was being buried, a man who died of the bloody cough. Beside Dectera were two other members of the guard, ruddy Gaelic warriors with innocent mouths and hard faces. One was saying, 'Good enough he's going into a dry grave. A terrible disgrace it is when they put a man into a wet grave. I'd never go into one, myself.'

The second man rolled an eye at the overcast but rainless sky, then looked back to the burial. 'It's a big mystery,' he said. 'A big jump.'

'Ah, it is,' agreed the first. 'But if you don't take this jump, you're not in for the next one.'

The sleeping Cuchulain reached for Emer to ask her about this puzzling remark, for Emer was good with riddles.

But his groping hand found only empty space.

Cuchulain was shocked out of sleep.

He found himself sitting bolt upright and alone on a makeshift bed of moss and branches. A wet, cold fog clung to his lips.

'Emer?' he called.

An answer echoed through the fog. Someone he thought to be Niamh came toward him, weeping. 'Arise, Hound of Ulster,' she said. 'Dun Dalgan is burned, and all Murthemney laid waste.'

Before Cuchulain's numbed brain could fully digest her words, a second form emerged from the mist, one wearing the face and figure of Lendabair. 'Go quickly, great warrior, and avenge your dead,' this image urged, 'for Maeve's men have come here as you slept and taken your wife away to toss on the points of their spears. Her broken body goes ahead of you to Murthemney.'

With a terrible cry, the Hound lurched to his feet. 'My grief, it is hard to trust in women! You held me here long enough for disaster to overtake us; I will never forgive you.'

They reached towards him with wraithlike arms. He spun around and ran in the direction where he thought his chariot waited.

The fog parted to form a clear path that led straight to his war-cart. He could not pause to wonder at this, however, for the din of battle had begun again, ringing through his brain until there was no room for thought, only for action. Thoughtless action seemed the answer to everything.

Mocking laughter hung on the fog, but Cuchulain did not notice.

Beyond the chariot, his horses stood quietly cropping grass. As he approached, the Grey of Macha lifted its head and looked at him. From the back of the cart, Cuchulain took a bridle and shook it at the horse to bid him come, but the stallion backed away instead. Frowning, Cuchulain took the other bridle and tried to catch the Black of Sainglain, with similar results. The horses would not let him come near them. The nervous Black even broke into a lather.

They trotted from him and he ran after them, feeling his heart hammering. Emer dead. Dun Dalgan burned. Himself alone in this fog-cursed valley.

At length he succeeded in driving the Grey into a pocket formed by a stand of trees. Trapped, the horse halted, but each time Cuchulain approached, the stallion turned his left side towards his master. 'You've never behaved like this before,' Cuchulain reproached the horse. 'What have I done that you insult me now?'

The noble neck arched, the great head lowered as if in contrition. The Grey stood his ground then and let Cuchulain come up to him, but when he went to put on the bridle, he saw tears form in the stallion's eyes and start to roll down his grey face. Crimson tears, the colour of blood.

They dripped steadily on to the earth at Cuchulain's feet.

He made himself finish harnessing the horse, and then was able to catch the Black as well. But when he led the pair back to his chariot to yoke them to it, he found his war-cart broken.

 I had broken the chariot. A spasm of that very human emotion called love had overcome me, quite to my surprise, making me forget my duty. With claws and beak, the Morrigan attacked Cuchulain's chariot, thinking to damage it so badly he would not be able to go to Murthemney until the spell cast by Calatin's daughters faded. Their magic was powerful but transitory; one clear, bright sunrise and Lugh would be able to burn the enchantment away.

Such a gesture was a mere aberration on my part, of course, and as futile as it was foolish. Old Fergus mac Roy had taught his pupils well – any of them could effect quick battlefield repairs; and with roots and thongs and strips torn from his clothing, Cuchulain bound his war-cart together again. Clumsy repairs made in haste, but still sufficient.

Watching from the trees, I scolded myself for having tried to interfere. I knew the part assigned me more clearly than any human ever recognises his. Those who seek the immortality I know must be all

483

of a piece, without self-doubt or second thoughts. To be candid, I had not expected my feelings for Cuchulain to affect me so strongly. Having given in to them once, I was afraid I might do so again.

I must not; I must not! His was the free will; he had made the choice.

But I would go with him. I could not help it.

The path that had opened through the fog to allow Cuchulain to find his chariot now formed a clear lane ahead of him, showing him the way out of the valley. Still he hesitated. His thoughts roiled. Something had entered his head, his Celtic head where all life really took place, and was deliberately confusing him . . . women? Were there women who would be unprotected and in danger if he left. . . ?

He looked back to discover that the fog had formed an opaque barrier behind him, closing up to make a wall of convincing solidity. An unreasoning fear of that fog gripped him. He could not clearly remember if there were women beyond it, somewhere . . .

He would go on then, he decided, to Murthemney. To Murthemney, where Dun Dalgan burned . . . and Emer lay dead. With a sob, he urged the horses forward.

When he had gone, the fog gradually lifted. The women found one another; Emer and Niamh and Lendabair came together beside the bed of crushed mosses that still bore the imprint of Cuchulain's body.

They realised they had been misled, deliberately lured away from him by voices in the fog. Now he was gone, and they began a desperate search to find him, but eventually were forced to admit he was no longer in Glen na Bodhar. The track of his chariot wheels told its story.

'He could be anywhere by now,' said Niamh. 'The Grey and the Black are the swiftest horses in Erin.'

Emer sat down suddenly, heedless of the damp ground. She put her hands over her face and said between her fingers to the other women as they crowded around her, 'He's gone to be killed. I can't bear this any longer. I wish he would die and be done with it; every battle he fights puts another spear through my body.'

Fedelm bent over her. 'A great shame it is, you saying such things and you a warrior's wife.'

'I'm a woman,' Emer said bitterly. 'I have feelings too. Everything has always been done for him, his way. When is it my turn?'

Cuchulain stopped briefly at Emain Macha before setting out for Murthemney. If possible, he wanted to take his charioteer with him, so he could meet Maeve in true champion's fashion.

As he neared the fort, the light was fading. From the byres came the voices of women, singing to the cows to get them to let down their milk. Servitors called out to him, but he did not answer their questions; he could not tell anyone what had happened in Glen na Bodhar, because he did not know himself. For the same reason, he did not report to the incapacitated king, who would surely try to stop him.

He found Laeg twisted into a knot on his bed in the House of Red Branch. 'It's the worst day so far,' the charioteer gritted through clenched teeth. 'Perhaps I'll be better . . . tomorrow.' He gasped as a cramp seized him; his spine bent like a bow.

'I'll go on without you,' Cuchulain decided. 'Bring another chariot and follow me when you can.'

'Follow you where?'

'To Murthemney, to fight Maeve.'

Laeg struggled to get up. 'You can't, you mustn't. Wait for us . . .'

'I can't wait. Dun Dalgan's been put to the torch and they've taken Emer to kill her.' He turned on his heel and ran from the hall.

'Who told you that?' Laeg called after him weakly. 'We haven't heard any such thing.' But Cuchulain had gone.

He drove southward at a mad gallop. Somewhere along the way, he heard the brittle sound of wings above his head.

In Maeve's camp, the warriors prepared their weapons. 'It's almost Samhain,' remarked Erc of Leinster, a big man with a drooping red moustache, to Lugaid of Munster. 'If Maeve succeeds in luring Cuchulain to us, it should take no more than a gentle push to send him over the lowered barriers between life and death.'

Lugaid replied, 'I wouldn't want to make anything that easy for him. Walking dung heap,' he added under his breath. 'Champion of Ulster, indeed.'

Erc propped one bare foot on his knee and contemplatively scratched its callused sole. He preferred to fight barefoot even in the dead of winter. 'Tell me, Lugaid. Do you think Cuchulain really can be killed?'

'Anyone can be killed. I hardly believed my foster-father could die, but he did, thanks to Cuchulain, though Curoi was a man so full of magic, his bones sang as we buried him.'

Erc put down his foot. 'Sang songs, you mean?'

'They did. The women who were keening over Curoi's burial were badly startled; their mouths snapped shut like a trout's snapping on a fly. But the music of the bones was seductive, and soon they began to sing with it. A song about a red deer, it was – he had always loved the hunt.'

A man of the Gael, Erc was interested but not overly surprised. 'You might as well sing grief as cry it,' was his comment.

Cuchulain drove through the night. Infected with his passion, his horses seemed tireless. Occasionally, he remembered them long enough to allow them a brief walk, but soon he was yelling at them to resume the gallop. Inside his head, Dun Dalgan burned, and Emer . . . and the voice of the battle trumpet called, and the war cries taunted . . .

From time to time, the Grey of Macha flicked an ear backwards to listen to his master's ragged breathing, or rolled an eye to catch a glimpse of the white, set face. The horse's eyes glowed with sorrow.

Dawn took Cuchulain by surprise. Night had seemed a permanent condition befitting his mood. Ambushed by light, hills and valleys began to reveal themselves, intruding on the mental scene of death and flame.

Cuchulain shook his head and rubbed his eyes.

Laeg will be annoyed with me for driving these horses at a gallop at night, he found himself thinking.

It was the first reasonable thought he had had in a long time.

A thin edge of gold outlined the eastern horizon. Cuchulain drew in a deep lungful of cold air and realised he was hearing nothing more than the creak of the chariot and the thud of horses' hooves. His head ached with the echoes of battle noises, but he could no longer hear them. They belonged to some fevered dream. And in that dream, someone who looked like Niamh – almost – and like Lendabair – almost – had told him impossible tales.

Impossible.

He yanked on the reins. The stallions lowered their haunches, skidding to a halt.

Cuchulain stood frowning in his chariot, wondering how much of his memory he dared trust. He thought he recalled reaching Emain Macha, and then some time later he was almost certain Cathbad had been warning him of a trick, a ruse . . .

Cuchulain stepped from the chariot and squatted on the track, examining the cupped and rutted mud. There was no sign of a large army having recently passed this way. Maeve's forces were still to the south, then. Had he been lured from Emain Macha to leave the stronghold defenceless? But why, if she was southward?

The light was increasing. He recognised familiar landmarks and knew he had come most of the distance to Murthemney in his wild drive. Should he go back? Something was wrong, his bones warned him, but his enemy was still in front of him somewhere, and lifelong training held him to the attack.

He remounted his chariot and drove on again.

The sun rose higher, burning his mind clean. He leaned forward, as if his own shift of weight could push his horses to greater speed.

Soon he would know the truth about Emer, Dun Dalgan, all of it: truth, not shadows and dreams.

He realised that the raven that had followed him throughout the night had deserted him. Glancing around for her, he speculated on the strangeness of a raven flying at night and wondered why it had not puzzled him earlier.

Clouds of steam rose from the sweat-matted coats of his horses, who had already grown their long hair for the winter. Turning them from the *slighe*, he found a stream where they might drink, and knelt beside it with cupped hands to slake his own thirst while his team sucked eagerly at the cold water. When his belly was filled to gurgling, Cuchulain splashed water on his face and stood up, looking around.

Then he saw the woman at the bend of the stream below him.

He started towards her to ask if she knew anything of an invading army. But as he approached her, the woman raised her head and looked at him, and his feet stopped moving of their own accord.

Her face was white, her hair was russet, and the garments she washed in the stream were his own. Blood ran from them, staining the water.

Badb. Prophetess of doom. One of the aspects of the goddess of war.

The vision of Badb washing blood from Cuchulain's tunic told him all he needed to know. A trap had indeed been set for him, and cruelly baited. But as the supreme champion, he could not refuse the challenge. Honour demanded a reckless, immediate response of unhesitating courage.

Good enough, Maeve, he thought. I am coming as swiftly as possible. I am not frightened merely because a dark goddess shows me her face, and blood runs red in a stream.

He ran to his horses. In a few heartbeats, the chariot was heading south again at a headlong gallop.

Cuchulain's eyes continually scanned the horizon for signs of Maeve's army, but he saw none. Then Murthemney lay open and undisturbed before him. When he saw Dun Dalgan unburned, he gave a great shout of relief.

After a swift examination to assure himself his fort was unharmed,

Cuchulain turned aside and made his way to the glen where he had sent the womenfolk for safekeeping.

His stallions picked their way along a narrow track half hidden by nettles. Woodland appeared to bar the way, but with a sure hand Cuchulain guided his team among the trees until they reached the head of a narrow valley surrounded by yew and holly. At the heart of the glen was the encampment of the women.

They had built simple shelters with practised skill, weaving wicker walls roofed with branches in the manner of the seasonal huts cattle-herders made for themselves as they moved the animals from pasture in the booleying time.

Because there was no rain, the women were taking their midmeal outside as Cuchulain drove up. Seated on a split-log bench, Dectera was obediently opening her mouth as an attendant fed her bread and bacon. The women forgot their food and rushed forward to welcome Cuchulain, however – even Dectera came forward, though her eyes were as empty as ever, with no sign of recognition in them. In one hand, she carried a forgotten cup of wine.

As the women crowded around him, Cuchulain stepped from his chariot and gave a formal greeting to his mother. 'I'm relieved to see all is well with her,' he told her nearest attendant.

The woman shrugged. 'Every day is the same.'

'Keep her hidden safely until the foreigners have left Murthemney,' Cuchulain instructed. 'I'm going now to challenge Maeve's army.'

At his word, some obscure impulse prompted Dectera to lift her cup and hold it out to him like an offering. Touched at the gesture, Cuchulain reached for it.

Then he looked down at the contents of the bowl of polished agate. He saw and smelled blood.

With an inarticulate cry, he dashed the cup from Dectera's hand. The liquid spattered on her gown and his legs.

'My grief!' Cuchulain cried. 'A man is truly alone when his own mother offers him blood to drink.'

The crowd of women recoiled.

Just then, a single benevolent ray of sunlight stroked Dectera's hair. She lifted her chin. She appeared to stand taller. Her eyes met Cuchulain's. 'Stay here in safety with us,' she said in a clear voice.

Her women gaped in astonishment. No less surprised, her son caught her hands with his own. There were tears in her eyes. She was back, he realised – all the way back from whatever far land she had so long

488

inhabited. Worn and reluctant but aware, Dectera was gazing at Cuchulain with growing intensity.

'I can't stay,' he told her as gently as he could. 'I've been challenged to fight and I must go, my name depends on it.'

She made a small sound of distress. To comfort her, he offered the one truth he had never doubted. 'A great name outlasts life, Mother. And I will have a great name.'

She nodded; he was certain she somehow understood. Pulling one age-spotted hand from his grasp, she stroked his cheek. 'Then go,' she said, 'and be your father's true son.'

Her words robbed him of speech. All the things he might have said to her dried in this throat. He caught her in a hard embrace for as long as he could bear it, smelling her hair and the unfamiliar, old-woman scent of her; then he walked blindly to his chariot. Only at the head of the valley was he able to look back and see her standing there, still watching him, one hand lifted in farewell.

Driving crossland, he eventually glimpsed an alien dark line against fading fields. Maeve's army was lying in wait for him south-west of Dun Dalgan.

Cuchulain needed no druid to remind him it was the eve of Samhain. As the battle was his to initiate, he would not begin until the sacred night had passed. Morning would be soon enough to answer the demands of honour, and he would have had time to prepare himself and organise his thoughts as a warrior should.

Taking care that no one from Maeve's camp should see him, he located a small hollow screened by hazel trees where he could camp for the remainder of the day and the night to come. With the dawn of the new year, a most auspicious time, he would challenge Ulster's invaders.

For the end of autumn, the afternoon was warm. Deep golden light slanted across Murthemney Plain as the sun began to set, and a dark bank of purple cloud moved in from the north. Against its face appeared a brilliant rainbow in six distinct colours, like a bard's cloak. Cuchulain sat propped against a tree with his legs extended and his ankles crossed, allowing himself the luxury of contemplating beauty.

A beauty intensified by the knowledge that tomorrow would be a battle morning.

Quiet, he told himself. Quiet and calm. Be a clear pool in which the trout lie at the bottom, waiting.

As the sun sank lower, he ate a sparse meal of dried meat and oaten cakes. He gathered bits of wood for a small Samhain fire, just enough to honour the spirits without alerting Maeve's sentries to his location. Then he methodically prepared his weapons and battle-dress for the next day. The Grey and the Black were thoroughly rubbed down with handfuls of sweet grass before being hobbled and released to graze nearby.

In the hushed moment of the sun's death, Cuchulain heard a lone druid voice rise from Maeve's encampment, beginning the solemn chant that called upon those who had crossed the barrier to return to the world of the living for one night and share the feast.

Out of long habit, Cuchulain had set aside part of his own meal for the Samhain feast. This he now arranged in tiny piles for his dead, whispering their names. Ferdiad's was hard to say; Cunla's was impossible. He bowed his head over his bent knees, listening to the hammering of his heart, and then flintstruck the spark for his own Samhain fire as the living fire of the sun disappeared from the sky.

Around the hidden hollow where the champion of Ulster was encamped spread the lap of Erin. High sky, yielding earth, unyielding stone. Nothing else was of permanent importance, even battles of life and death. The land's possession of itself was total.

Brooding by his campfire, Cuchulain sensed this. Should he die tomorrow, it would not change the essential Ulster, the earth beneath his feet.

So why dare the darkness, he asked himself, aware of how much he enjoyed life, how sweet he found the smell of wood-smoke, how delicious the murmuring music of blood in his veins.

Because a great name outlasts life, came the answer. Obliteration is more terrible than death, and immortality can be won through deeds.

Cuchulain wrapped himself in his cloak and stretched out beside his tiny campfire to gaze at the flames.

After a while, he realised a face was gazing back at him from them. A blunt, rough-hewn face. You could still turn back and live, suggested Ferdiad mac Daman, who had not wanted to die.

A second flame flickered to reveal another, younger face, one composed of equal parts of Cuchulain and Ayfa the warrior-woman. Maeve does not yet know you are here, Father, said Cunla. And the warriors of Ulster are recovering from their Pangs. If you return north and wait for them, soon a great army will be able to fight beside you.

Cuchulain's eyes stung. The living are not alone on Samhain.

Their concern moved him deeply, but he gave the only answer he could make. 'I can't go back,' he explained to the fire. 'Not while there

490

is the slightest chance the Hound of Ulster could win tomorrow. I don't want reinforcements. I want to face the invaders alone.' As he spoke the last words, his voice rang in his chest like a deep bronze bell.

The spirits watching from the flames understood. You have made yourself the champion, they agreed. This is your battle.

Cuchulain settled back to wait, and they stood the long watch with him.

But he could not sleep. His head, he was distressed to discover, was not as calm as it needed to be. An awareness of some preparation he had not completed gnawed like a mouse in his mind. Weapons, chariot, battle-dress – what was not in order?

Yourself, drawled the husky voice of Ferdiad mac Daman from the Samhain fire. *You* are not complete.

Cuchulain sat up abruptly, glaring. 'I am! I'm the champion!'

Champion, sighed Cunla. Tell me, Father – if you die tomorrow, can that one word possibly contain all you knew and felt and were?

The question startled him. His lips framed a hasty answer, but then Cuchulain stopped. And thought.

If he were honest, he had to admit that Emer had helped him uncover aspects of his nature he had not guessed before her: qualities of tenderness and nurturing that were essential to the man he had become. The term *champion* did not indicate them. Nor did it express what he had learned about being a friend with Ferdiad and the men of the Red Branch, about being a son to Conor mac Nessa, about the agonised weight of fatherhood he had discovered with Cunla. All this was part of him.

Yet something was still missing. His bones told him. Some vital element was lacking, a fragment without which he was incomplete on the eve of the greatest trial of his life.

If only he could find it in time, anything might yet be possible. Even victory.

Cuchulain sat staring at the dead fire, chilled by the realisation that being champion was not enough.

 From beyond the farthest rim of the firelight, I had watched, seeing into Cuchulain's spirit as he struggled with his final preparations. Pagan and barbarian and even myth, future generations would call him, yet he brooded over the same thoughts that have always set humans apart from other beings. Nothing I could do would make this easier for him. He had come to

491

the ultimate choice dictated by the terrible, enviable gift of free will. Lacking that gift, I could only watch.

He would not be deciding between life and death, for they are the same after all, two faces of one condition. He also had two faces. At the height of his Rage, the Hound of Ulster embodied the glamour of violence. But he also had another side, and soon he would have to choose between desolate reality and the true landscape of his heart.

Even I could not foresee the outcome.

18 The women of the Red Branch had been distraught over Cuchulain's disappearance. No one doubted he had gone to meet his death. Emer and the others had returned to Emain Macha as swiftly as they could, once they were certain Cuchulain had left Glen na Bodhar. But by the time they got there, Laeg could only tell them, 'The Hound's driven on to Murthemney to face Maeve. He thinks something's happened to you, Emer; he thinks the invaders have you. I couldn't persuade him to wait, but I'm going to follow him at once, as soon as I can make my legs stop trembling.'

'I'm going to follow him now,' Emer said. 'It's almost Samhain, the most dangerous time. What chariot can I take? I have to be with him!'

With an effort beyond any he had thought himself capable of, Laeg finished throwing off the effects of Macha's Curse. He caught Emer's thin wrist in one hand and held on grimly while forcing himself to straighten his torso, then his legs. The cramps faded. His head was spinning, but his determination was rock-solid. 'I'll drive you,' he told Emer.

Meanwhile, the other women were spreading the news through Emain Macha. The king and the warriors of the Red Branch responded with the same rush of desperation that had strengthened Laeg. To have their champion stolen from them by trickery and guile was insupportable. No hero worthy of the name was willing to lie quietly recovering for three or four more days while Cuchulain was deliberately slaughtered.

Conor mac Nassa announced, 'We'll march tomorrow.'

'I'm ready today,' claimed Conall Cearnach, brandishing his sword. When the weapon wavered in his grasp, the king frowned.

'Tomorrow, Conall,' he ordered.

Emer refused to wait. She was determined to go at once, and as Conor pointed out to Nessa, 'If anything happens to her, Cuchulain will take my head. I want you and the other women to restrain her any way you can. Tie her up and hold her in the *grianan* if you must.'

Nessa nodded. 'If anything happens to Cuchulain, you should marry

493

that one, you know. She'd make a better wife for you than all the rest of them laid lengthwise.'

Conor, who had had the same thought and pushed it angrily away, pretended to be shocked.

On his own, Laeg took a chariot from the royal shed and started for Murthemney without waiting for the rest of the Red Branch. He drove faster than ever in his life, not caring if he killed the horses. He must be with the Hound to face Maeve.

Cathbad of the Gentle Face made a rare appearance in the House of the King as the warriors were assembling. Fixing a cold eye on Conor, the old druid intoned, 'Mark well the pattern you see here. The pattern of Deirdre and Cuchulain.'

The men exchanged startled glances. Some, their ears still ringing with weakness, thought they were not hearing correctly. But Cathbad was obligated to share his druid vision. 'Only death could free Deirdre from the curse of her beauty,' he said. 'And only death can free the Hound of Ulster from the curse of his honour.'

With a swirl of his hooded cloak, Cathbad left the hall and went north to the circle of standing stones to commune with the spirits, for it was the eve of Samhain.

On the following morning, Cuchulain awoke before sunrise, surprised to find he had slept after all. He awoke completely and at once, moving from night to day in one breath. Birds were twittering sleepily in the branches nearby. A thin rime of frost crunched under his feet when he stood and stretched, yawning.

His fire was cold and dead.

He went to check on the horses. The Grey of Macha lifted his head and started to nicker a greeting, excited by the approach of a friend. The growing light revealed another chariot advancing cautiously, the horses white with caked lather and mortally exhausted. Laeg, pale but on his feet, greeted Cuchulain as he stepped from the war-cart.

'I followed your wheel tracks. The Red Branch is about a day behind me, and Emer is secure at Emain Macha, as I tried to tell you before.'

Emer was alive . . . and safe . . . and Laeg was here . . . Cuchulain tried to speak around the lump in his throat, could not, and contented himself with pounding his charioteer on the shoulder.

'You'll do the fighting, but at least I can do the driving for you,' Laeg said. 'And cheer you on to victory.'

'Are you so certain of our victory?' Cuchulain could not help asking.

'Indeed I am. I can almost see it already, you challenging Maeve's

494

champions to single combat as you did before, killing them one by one until Conor and the Ulstermen arrive to bludgeon the whole mass into the earth. The king might chase Maeve back to Connaught and burn Cruachan around her ears. She'll need more than magic to protect her this time.'

'Magic?' Cuchulain lifted one dark eyebrow.

Laeg repeated the women's account of events in Glen na Bodhar. 'It was an enchantment,' he concluded, 'a trick, as Cathbad said.'

Cuchulain nodded. 'Reject magic in all its forms, Laeg. It's an ugly, dangerous thing.'

The charioteer gazed at the Hound, seeing the visionary silver eyes, the form so readily changed from humanity to monstrosity and back again. 'But *you're* magical, Cuchulain!'

'Don't ever say that to me.' The grey eyes stabbed Laeg with blades of ice. 'I'm no more magical than you are.'

Chastised, Laeg busied himself with Cuchulain's team.

Meanwhile, the three daughters of Calatin returned to Maeve's camp. Exhausted, they wanted bowls of milk to drink and lumps of fat to chew, but Maeve insisted on questioning them before feeding them. She had made too many mistakes in her campaign into Ulster seeking the Brown Bull; she meant to give no man cause to criticise her strategies this time.

'We finally lured Cuchulain away from Emain Macha,' the weird sisters reported. 'Even as we speak, he is encamped nearby.'

Maeve's eyes lit with triumph. 'Has he any allies with him?'

'His charioteer is joining him, but otherwise he is still alone.'

'What of his weapons?' Ailell wanted to know.

'The terrible Gae Bulga is no more, but the champion of Ulster carries many other weapons, swords and slings and spears. The first three javelins he hurls in battle against you will kill three kings,' the women added in prophetic tones. They could say no more. White-eyed, they collapsed in odiferous heaps, their mouths gaping for food.

Maeve gestured to her attendants to feed them, then turned to Ailell. 'I don't want my noble allies killed. How are we going to get those javelins away from Cuchulain before he does damage with them?'

Ailell rubbed his ribcage and squinted his eyes, remembering. 'Seven years ago, a poet who was with us demanded a gift of Cuchulain and received a spear. The hard way. It might work again. No one refuses a request from a member of the *filidh*.'

'We'd better find men who don't know what happened seven years ago,' said Maeve.

For the sake of his noble kinsman Erc of Leinster, Ailell set about interviewing the poets who had accompanied the armies, and finally located two satirists and an apprentice bard who had not been on the cattle raid seven years before, nor yet learned the story of Odran the satirist.

As he gave them their instructions, Ailell felt no regrets about sending them to their possible deaths. His primary concern was to protect the men of kingly family who had allied with Connaught; if the three poets had not yet memorised enough history to know the danger they were in, it was their own misfortune, he thought.

There were good reasons for learning every possible detail of the past.

Midmorning of the first day of winter, Cuchulain's chariot advanced towards the lines. Gorgeous with plumes of red and black, it boasted gleaming, deadly sharp sickle blades attached to its spokes, catching and reflecting the light of the sun with every turn of the wheels. A forest of spears stood upright in the war-cart beside Laeg and Cuchulain. At the charioteer's command, the Grey of Macha and the Black of Sainglain arched their heavy stallion-crested necks and plunged against the restraining harness, as if they could not wait to get at the enemy and rend them with teeth and hooves.

Erc of Leinster was the first chariot-chieftain to observe the Ulster champion's approach. Baring his teeth in a mirthless grin, he ordered his own charioteer forward to meet Cuchulain.

'Do you come to challenge me to single combat?' Cuchulain shouted as the space narrowed between them.

Erc shook a spear in the air. 'No single combat this time. You are Ulster; we are joined together to bring you down. Ask whatever gods you pray to, to accept your blood when it flows.'

'Ask on your own behalf,' Cuchulain yelled back at him, 'if your blood is not too sluggish to flow at all, Leinsterman!' At his signal, Laeg wheeled the horses in a wide circle, turning the left side of insult toward the invading armies. From the corner of his eye, he watched them, trying to guess how many there were. A vast roiling mass of men, like salmon in spawn.

Cuchulain lifted a huge oval shield of tight-drawn leather studded with bronze bosses and drummed it with his knuckle and elbow until thunder rolled across Murthemney Plain, promising doom to his enemies.

496

Erc had rejoined the main body of the army and watched impassively as Cuchulain advanced on them. When the chariot was near enough, a figure in a poet's cloak pushed through the ranks of men and ran out to Cuchulain.

'You have fine javelins in your chariot, and I am afraid to be without a weapon; this is my first war,' the young satirist said. 'Give me one of your spears before the fighting begins.'

Cuchulain glanced down at him. 'You're one of the *filidh*, you're not in any danger.'

The satirist had his instructions. Shaking his head stubbornly, he reiterated, 'Give me one of your spears or I will put a blemish on your name throughout Erin.'

The warrior's face darkened. 'Take your spear, then,' he cried, tossing one of his javelins toward the poet with such force it passed the man altogether and went through the body of a foot-warrior standing slightly behind him.

Lugaid of Munster ran forward and jerked the spear out of the dying man, who was one of his, while the man's heels were still drumming the earth. In one smooth gesture, he hurled the weapon toward Cuchulain's chariot.

So sudden was his action that Cuchulain, surprised, had no time to shift his shield. The javelin thudded into Laeg's breastbone.

'Hold!' roared the champion of Ulster in a voice so commanding Maeve's armies obeyed.

He sank to one knee in his chariot, bending over his driver as Laeg collapsed. There could be no doubt the wound was fatal. The spear had gone through bone and angled into a lung. Frothy red bubbles escaped with every breath Laeg drew.

Sensing disaster, the Grey and the Black stood still, rolling their eyes and snorting warnings at anyone who tried to come too near.

The charioteer rolled his eyes downward, trying to assess his wound. 'I can't possibly die now,' he said in a weak but matter-of-fact voice. 'You need me.' Then he felt the tide rising in his lungs. 'But if you must be your own driver, Cuchulain . . . remember, the Black pulls to the left when he's excited . . .'

Laeg's last words had wings; his spirit rode them out of his body.

How swiftly he had gone, Cuchulain thought. Dead, yet his face was still as freckled as a boy's. He lifted Laeg's body and carried it from the chariot. The surrounding warriors watched, still transfixed by the power in the Hound's command. No matter how much they might want

Cuchulain's blood, they understood ritual, and the death of a hero's charioteer was an event to be respected.

Cuchulain carried his friend away from the faceless mass of the invaders and laid him on the earth beneath the arching branches of a silver birch, beside a tranquil pool. With one hand braced against the white trunk of the tree, he murmured his farewells to Laeg mac Riangabra.

Alone, said a voice within him. Now you are totally alone.

He went back to his chariot and gathered up the reins. This time, he did not gallop recklessly but circled the horses in a cadenced trot, giving himself an opportunity to look for gaps in the wall of shields now raised against him. He drove in a second, larger circle, challenging, attempting to impress, but simultaneously assessing his enemies.

He could not let himself think about Laeg any more, at least not until this was over. Laeg had become the past. He must think only of the present, if he hoped to see the future.

The men who had come with Maeve and Ailell were variously attired in princely cloak and ragged woollen tunic. Some had leather bound to their legs; more were barefoot in the old style. Many of them, Cuchulain noted with sardonic amusement, now dressed their hair with lime paste to make it bristle like that of the Hound of Ulster in his battle-fury.

And they all had murder in their eyes.

Refreshed by a brief rest, the daughters of Calatin had come to see the battle. They stood beside Maeve's chariot, next to that of Ailell, within a secure ring of armed guards. As Ailell watched Cuchulain advance, he could not help thinking there was something both glorious and ugly about forcing one man to face an army alone.

It would not be possible to live with Maeve if she lost this one. On the other hand, Ailell admitted to himself, he really did not want to see Cuchulain die. He slipped unobtrusively from his chariot and walked back through the ranks, unwilling to watch what would happen next.

A second poet, also wearing the fur armband of a satirist, stepped forward to meet Cuchulain. 'I ask a spear of you,' the man called.

Cuchulain frowned down at him. 'I've given one gift today, I am under no obligation to give another, even to a poet.'

'Then I ask the gift of Ulster,' the satire-maker replied. 'If Ulster doesn't give it to me, I will condemn the province as a land of unhospitable chieftains and cowards who lie in their beds whining instead of coming out to fight. I will say all Conor mac Nessa's famed Red Branch have become old women.'

'I won't have Ulster reproached for my deeds today,' Cuchulain said. Since Laeg had fallen, he felt as if he were encased in ice. He did not care if he killed one of the *filidh*; he did not care what he did. Reaching for a spear, he hurled it at the satirist and tore out the man's throat, then immediately raced away in another wide circle, shouting insults at the armies of Erin.

Erc of Leinster ran forward to take the weapon from the dead poet's neck. He called to the daughters of Calatin, 'Who did you predict would die by Cuchulain's second spear?'

'A king surely,' they answered.

'You said that for the first spear,' he reminded them, 'yet Lugaid only killed a charioteer with it.'

The three weird women shouted in unison, 'Lugaid killed the *king* of the charioteers! You hold a weapon of equal destiny.'

'We'll see about that,' Erc muttered, hurling the spear after Cuchulain with a mighty throw that all but tore the sinews from his shoulder. But a chariot being pulled at the gallop over broken ground offered an uncertain target. The javelin did not strike the Ulster champion. Instead, it arced downward to strike the Grey of Macha, who screamed.

The stallion dropped to his knees. Cuchulain vaulted over the chariot rim and swiftly cut him from the traces. Blood was pouring from the horse's nostrils. 'Go and save yourself from this slaughter,' Cuchulain said into a curving grey ear.

The stallion managed to get to his feet and stagger away. With only the Black of Sainglain left to pull his chariot, Cuchulain drove on, the cart slewing sideways.

'You have killed the king of the horses!' Calatin's daughters were shouting to Erc of Leinster.

A third figure emerged from the army to intercept Cuchulain. 'I claim the gift of a spear to protect myself,' said a young man who wore no satirist's armband but was dressed in a six-coloured cloak, his premier entitlement as an apprentice bard. Having seen what had happened to the two men who had made similar requests before him, he looked decidedly apprehensive. But Ailell had given him an order, and he was a man of Cruachan.

'I've given gifts already in my name and the name of Ulster,' said Cuchulain. He was fighting to control the Black of Sainglain. Tension in the atmosphere and his unprecedented lack of a teammate had maddened the horse. 'Leave me alone and live,' Cuchulain advised the bard.

'Give me the gift I must have, or the bards of Erin will remember Cuchulain as a man incapable of fathering!'

The warrior's face went white. 'Lie,' he said, between clenched teeth. He could not let himself think of the truth; remembering Cunla at such a perilous moment could unman him. To silence the would-be historian's voice, he threw a javelin straight at the man's heart.

Lugaid of Munster removed it from the twitching corpse. 'The third spear,' he said to those clustering around him. 'The king of charioteers, the king of horses, and now. . . ?'

They turned to watch Cuchulain coming at them again, screaming defiantly from a lurching one-horsed chariot on the far edge of control.

The king of champions.

The invading army answered his challenge with a roar. Seeing him impossibly outnumbered and alone in a crippled war-cart, each man dreamed of being the one to kill the Hound of Ulster.

He recognised the sound of bloodlust. If he were to survive, he must release the Rage, and release it now. He could sense his battle-fury slumbering inside him, latent but living. An explosion of sufficient violence might yet stampede his enemies.

But since Cunla's death, he had suppressed the Rage so totally, he could no longer summon it at will. It burned beyond his reach like an ulcer in his belly.

Scenting the kill, the men of Erin advanced.

High in the sky, a huge raven screamed a warning.

Cuchulain knew that cry. Glancing up, he saw her. War and death were her gifts; he need only scream his own hatred in unison with her to have the Rage break free. Another ecstasy of transformation, another rapturous surrender of self into glorious, murderous madness and the earth of Ulster would run red with blood again. No one within the Hound's amplified reach would be spared . . . sweet lust of savagery . . .

NO! NO MORE!

With an incredible effort of will, Cuchulain turned his face from the raven and closed his eyes.

At once the dark future was filled with unfathomable light.

And Lugaid hurled the spear.

His aim was perfect. Cuchulain felt as if a fist had struck him. There

500

was no pain, merely jolting shock. When he caught at the rim of the chariot to steady himself, the reins slipped through his fingers and the Black stepped on one, breaking it as he lunged forward. The startled horse lashed out with a hind leg and crushed the front of the wicker chariot. In a panic now, he continued to kick, fighting for his freedom. His wild plunges overturned the war-cart, and Cuchulain was thrown out amid a welter of splintered wood and waving plumes.

One iron wheel was still spinning as the Black pulled loose and galloped away, dragging bits of harness.

With a sense of surprise, Cuchulain looked down to see the shaft of one of his own javelins emerging from his body. If Laeg was with him, the charioteer would know just how to work the head free, slowly and carefully, so he might recover.

But Laeg was dead. And the men of Erin were gathering around him shouting, congratulating each other, eager to see him dead also. Several tweaked the spear shaft until he felt the buried head tear his insides past healing.

Lugaid looked down at him. 'I have killed you, champion of Ulster,' he said. With a vicious twist, he pulled the spear free and brandished its bloody point over his head.

Somehow Cuchulain forced the ghost of a smile. 'I've felt better,' he admitted. His soft voice was almost inaudible; his throat threatened to close up. 'There's a thirst on me,' he told Lugaid. 'May I have a last drink at the pool where I left my friend?'

Lugaid glanced around, gathering in his companions with his eyes so all would witness his magnanimous gesture. 'You may of course, provided you promise to return to me so I can claim my trophy.' The amount of blood pouring from the man's body assured him Cuchulain could not escape.

'If I'm too weak to come back here, I give you leave to come for me.' As the men of Erin watched, Cuchulain dragged himself up on one knee, then gripped the wreckage of his chariot and levered himself to his feet. Maeve joined the circle around him, but he did not spare her a single glance.

'No man can walk with his bowels torn open like that,' she said with certainty – then stared in disbelief as Cuchulain clasped his belly together with his hands and made his way across the grassy plain to the pond where Laeg's body lay.

He was performing one final ritual in which no one else had a part. Understanding this, the warriors followed him with their eyes only.

With great difficulty, he knelt among the reeds at the edge of the dark, clear water, and drank. His blood ran from him into the pond. An otter of the sort his people called water-dogs crept out of the reeds to lap at the crimson liquid, then dived beneath the surface when Cuchulain tried to splash his face.

He knew none of the invaders would wash him after he was dead.

His feet were turning cold. He made himself stand, though it seemed to take for ever. He was avid to look upon Murthemney one last time.

There was something tantalisingly familiar about the area where he found himself. He shook his head to clear his eyes of a growing mistiness, and saw that west of the pond was a field he knew, and in that field stood a pillar stone.

A grey pillar stone standing alone in a field south-west of Dun Dalgan, like a giant's finger pointed at the sky.

Step by agonised step, Cuchulain made his way to the stone. He did not have the strength to return to his enemies; they must come for him here. Removing his short mantle, he wrapped it beneath his armpits and then around the stone, binding himself upright. He drew Hardhead from his belt. The sword's weight dragged his arm downward, but his stiffening fingers closed in a grip only death could release. When they came for him, Cuchulain would meet his enemies on his feet, as a champion should.

 There was nothing left for me to do but be with him. He had made the choice that was his to make, but I was bound to him until the end. So I settled above his head on the stone where he had first seen me, to wait with him.

Will you understand if I say I was very proud of Cuchulain? Though he had rejected me, I loved him more than I have loved anyone before or since. I could see the spirit within the flesh.

Cuchulain gathered himself. Against his back, the surface of the stone was rough and cold. There was not enough warmth left in his skin to warm the rock, yet there was heat in his centre blazing like a forge fire, melting separate metals into a unified whole.

In his ultimate moment of heroism, he was, as man is, most truly himself. Yet he also felt a growing awareness of immortality. Years of questioning were resolving into a realisation: only the spark of divinity that animates a human being is capable of lifting him to the heights for which he most hungers.

502

Dying, Cuchulain accepted the god within himself, and was glad.

His wounds meant nothing, he had suffered so many wounds. Even grief was dissolving in a flood of opalescent light he sensed beyond his closed eyes. Radiance was beaming upon him from somewhere nearby, and in that radiance his father waited.

Maeve's men crept towards him. Cuchulain heard their tense whispers and the rattle of spears as they formed a circle, warily keeping their distance. The sight of the slumped figure beneath the glaring raven was more frightening to them than the healthy Cuchulain had been. A glow illumined the champion's features, the manly and mature face still as beardless as a boy's. The bravest of his enemies could not bring himself to step within reach of the Hound's sword while the hero-glow lingered.

The raven raised her wings in menace, warning them.

Cuchulain was almost ready. His enemies were only a circle of shadows surrounding him, and he was no longer afraid of shadows. The salmon-leap would carry him safely past them to his father.

'I have been the best I could be,' Cuchulain whispered to him.

He heard the answer. He felt the love.

With the careful, calculated grace of a champion at his peak, Cuchulain gathered himself. And when the time was right, he made the most splendid of all his leaps.

Into the light.

Having obeyed the heroic imperative in every particular, Cuchulain was gone. He had earned in full measure the Champion's Portion. The path he trod was narrow, torn between opposing obligations, and sometimes there had been no right choice to make – only the least wrong one.

Let no man envy him. Nor forget him, for he deserves his immortality.

You may ask what happened to the Red Branch afterwards. The story is simply told. I was an observer, though my heart wasn't in it. But the warriors always summon me.

Conall Cearnach had long ago promised to exact vengeance from anyone who killed Cuchulain, for what was suffered must be answered in kind. He was the first of the Ulstermen to arrive on the scene – though not the first to strike a blow for the slain champion.

The Grey of Macha claimed that honour. The wounded stallion returned when the hero-light had scarcely faded from his master's face. He attacked the men around the pillar stone so savagely they fled from him yelling. With teeth and hooves, he did great damage to them before collapsing from loss of blood. In the excitement, I found myself alighting on the shoulder of Erc of Leinster and pecking at his eyes before I quite realised what I was doing.

Abashed, I flew to a nearby tree. When all the light was gone from Cuchulain's face, Lugaid of Munster summoned enough courage to claim his trophy. He almost tiptoed to the stone, though, ready to run if the champion so much as flickered an eyelash.

He stood as far away as he could, seized the head by the hair, and severed the neck. Simultaneously Cuchulain's sword hand leaped in a final spasm and Hardhead cut off Lugaid's sword hand.

He fell with an awful cry at the foot of the pillar stone. My pillar stone.

His Munstermen took Cuchulain's hand for satisfaction, and bound up their chieftain's stump to keep him from bleeding to death. Maeve's followers, apprehensive about the wrath of the Ulstermen, were anxious to leave the place and fled south, carrying the injured Lugaid with them.

They had not yet reached the valley of the River Liffey when Conall Cearnach caught up with them, the Red Branch at his back.

Conall was almost as wild in his grief as the Hound had once been in his Rage. When it was over, he returned north with the heads of Lugaid and Erc and many more besides. And the head and sword hand of Cuchulain of Murthemney, wrapped in silk.

504

Emer opened the wrappings herself. She would let no one else touch them. It was, indeed, his head. Strangely enough, death had not filmed the silver eyes, but had filled them with the shine of stars.

Conor mac Nessa ordered a burial prepared appropriate for the fosterling of a king.

On the night wind, the voice of Neman wept.

When Cuchulain's body and head were laid in the earth, Emer flung herself into the grave and demanded that the two of them be covered over together.

'We cannot!' protested the king, shocked.

She looked up at him with a tranquil face, from which the green flecks in her eyes shone like spring leaves. 'Many were the women, wed and unwed, who envied me until this day,' she said. 'Now, my gentle companion no longer will leave my side to go to another woman.' She paused, thinking of the one rival for whom she had never conquered her jealousy. Then her lips curved in triumph. 'Nor can he leave me to be with the Red Branch.'

She unwrapped the silk once more and set her warm mouth against her husband's cold lips. Then, as easily as if she were shrugging off an unwanted gown, Emer's spirit slipped free from her body.

In the end, Cuchulain no longer belonged to me at all. He was finally hers, that small, soft woman's.

For all his strength, Conor mac Nessa could not endure watching a second double burial. He went a distance away and wept like a child; even his mother did not dare disturb him.

He was a king and a man, and it is not easy to be either.

War followed – inevitable, of course. War and war and war, and in time each of the heroes of the Red Branch met his death in his own way.

Ulster has known little peace since, so I should be content.

But more often than I wish, I think of Cuchulain.

Ireland,
Two Thousand Years Ago . . .

While there is no historical verification for the existence of Cuchulain, Conor mac Nessa is recognised as having been a king in ancient Ulster, northernmost kingdom of Ireland. The Annals of Tigernach date his reign around 30 BC. The region he controlled was almost impenetrable then, shielded by river and bog, mountain and forest. One valiant warrior could have staged a solitary defence of the few eastern fords and passes giving access to the interior, and in this way Cuchulain's deeds may have become legend.

Pre-Christian Erin was divided into four provinces, each ruled by a king. Munster lay south of Ulster, with Connaught in the west and Leinster in the east. A fifth, royal Meath, would eventually emerge as the seat of a high king who would claim tribute from the provincial kings, who in turn dominated the chieftains of the various clans in their territories.

Ireland, which would never be invaded by Caesar's legions and would therefore escape Roman influence, was a small island brimming with natural resources. Heavily forested with primordial hardwoods, it possessed rich grasslands in its central plain, an abundance of game, and much gold in its rivers and streams. There is evidence that the early Irish conducted some trade with the Mediterranean cultures; they lived comfortable, even luxurious, lives for their time.

The society was based on that of their Celtic ancestors, the foundation folk of Western Europe. The Celts were never a nation but an assortment of tribes speaking variants of one mother tongue and sharing similar customs. Successive waves of settlers from the European mainland moved into the British Isles in the millennia preceding the Christian era. Last to invade and conquer Ireland were the Gael, a Celtic tribe arriving around 500 BC, according to most authorities.

506

In insular Ireland, the Celtic culture would thereafter remain virtually unchanged for over a thousand years.

Kings did not inherit their titles. They were elected according to the archaic Brehon Law that is, second only to the Code of Hammurabi, the oldest known codified law system. Warriors constituted the nobility, for this was a heroic warrior culture like that of Homer's Mycenae. A king such as Fergus mac Roy was chosen from among contenders who must belong to the senior line, or branch, of the dominant warrior family, or clan. Thus, Fergus came from the Red Branch of the clan Ulaid.

In order to win kingship, every aspirant had to undertake a series of gruelling physical and intellectual contests administered by brehon judges. By this method, the most worthy man was identified. A king not only served as warlord and distributor of plunder and trade goods, but also as the living embodiment of the strength, wisdom, and virility of his people. A blemish could disqualify a man.

Social classes were strictly ordered. Immediately below the warrior nobility were the non-noble but freeborn cattle-lords. Of comparable rank with the nobility, however, was the professional class, or *filidh*. Bardic poets, brehon judges, physicians, and druids were members of the *filidh*. Peculiar to Gaelic society, a chief poet ranked second in status only to his king.

Roman historians of Caesar's time described the druids of Gaul as priests. From native sources we deduce that Ireland's druids could more accurately be called professors of the natural sciences. The majority of Irish gods were nature gods; the druids attempted through their rituals to manipulate the environment. They observed the arrangement of stars, the attributes of water, the properties of trees. They studied the stomachs of cattle and the urinary patterns of humans.

Irish druids were the learned men of their people, charged with instructing the sons of kings. They were also seers and prophets, wizards who invoked the mysterious Otherworld that was so much a part of the Gaelic consciousness. According to a surviving fragment of bardic poetry, only druids could interpret portents from the realm where 'spirits meet spirits and jostle in the dark'.

Unlike Continental druids, those of Ireland do not appear to have practised human sacrifice. They did incorporate into their rituals the stone circles and pillars and tombs left by an earlier race. They also used stones as well as wood for *ogham*, which was a technique whereby a series of lines and slashes could be used to represent simple messages.

507

Celtic peoples were not literate, they mistrusted the written word; the *ogham* of the druids was the closest they would come to writing. Examples of *ogham* stones may still be seen in Ireland today.

So far-reaching were the abilities of the druids that some scholars use the term instead of *filidh* to apply to the entire professional class – with the exception of poets.

Because in early Ireland the basic economic unit was the cow, cattle-lords who maintained large herds were of great importance in the tribe. So were skilled craftsmen who provided the necessities such as weapons, and the necessary luxuries such as ornaments and jewellery. A famous smith like Cullen of Ulster possessed sufficient prestige to invite his king to his feasting table.

Farther down in rank were the freeborn who owned no property but farmed the communal lands of the clan or worked in various menial capacities. Below them were the bondsmen and the slaves, who did the hardest labour, but even these had certain protections under the Brehon Law. The maltreatment of a slave could dishonour a king.

The custom of fosterage, or exchanging children between warrior families to strengthen alliances, was common. Kings were supported by tributes exacted from the other clans in their kingdoms. Each provincial king maintained a personal army, like Conor mac Nessa's Red Branch, in addition to being able to call upon the warriors of clans tributary to him. Every clan had its own warriors, because warfare between clans as well as between provinces was the means whereby the Gael kept their fighting skills polished. On an island that would see no additional invaders until the coming of the Vikings in AD 795, heroes could only remain heroes by proving themselves against one another.

So ancient Erin was a land of tribal kingdoms living by agriculture, raiding, and fighting each other for cattle and slaves and landholdings. The custom of having champions contend in single combat could save many lives in an underpopulated land, unless too much animosity developed on both sides. Then, warfare was brutal.

Among the Continental Celts, women had sometimes held chieftainly rank and had often fought beside their men, as Caesar recorded. A more patriarchal system developed among the Gael of Ireland, though women still owned property in their own right, and the standing of a freeborn woman was the same as that of a freeborn man.

Maeve was not called queen of Connaught in her own time, for Ireland had no regnant queens by then, merely female consorts to the ruling kings. Maeve did defy tradition by acting as a warlord, however, in the old style.

Beyond Ireland, some Celtic women continued to be involved in martial pursuits. The Britons would soon have their fierce Boudicca, and during the Red Branch era, Skya ran her school for heroes on the island that would someday bear her name: modern Skye, off the coast of Alba, which is called Scotland today.

The king was so valuable to his followers as a symbol that a personal champion was chosen to represent him in battle, though he retained the option of wielding weapons. A king who was actually unable to fight would have lost his kingship at once. Like his people, he was controlled by the rigid demands of honour, the built-in discipline of the brehon system.

To be the king's champion was the highest honour a warrior could receive, until Cuchulain became famous for being the recognised champion of an entire province. While Conor mac Nessa ruled from Emain Macha, near the modern-day city of Armagh, Cuchulain reputedly guarded the borders of Ulster.

Strongholds of the nobility such as Emain Macha and Cruachan were not towns; in this totally rural culture, there were no real towns. Most commercial trading took place at 'fairs' held at crossroads throughout the land. The king's dun was a residence and garrison housing no more than his family, guards, and necessary attendants. But the forts were also used for the lavish entertaining that was expected of a king, to hold supporters and intimidate possible rivals with a show of power. Dominant clans could be challenged and overturned; every leader must be wary.

Constant competition for supremacy was a fixed feature of Gaelic life.

Modern scholars have verified many details from this period that may appear anachronistic to the layman. The ancient Irish passion for bathing and the custom of offering heated water to guests for washing is but one example. The exquisite details of Gaelic craftsmanship defy reproduction by modern techniques, and hint at a highly developed artistic appreciation. They were a contradictory blend of refinement and savagery, the old Gael.

The poems they composed and handed down through their bards sing with deep reverence for nature, celebrating with gentle wonder the grace of a red deer or the tracery of bare branches against a winter sky. Yet such sensibilities did not prevent warriors from taking trophy heads on the battlefield with the same zest modern hunters show in collecting deer and elk. The epics of Ireland introduce us to a race of passionate, earthy dreamers, who loved their friends and slaughtered their enemies with equal enthusiasm.

For readers who would like to know more about these vivid, extraordinary people, a selected bibliography is included that lists both basic source material and general historical and archaeological information.

On Raven's Wing was written by drawing upon the vast body of bardic tales still in existence in various forms and translations. Most of them are fragmented and episodic; often it was necessary to assign an arbitrary chronology where none existed. But Cuchulain, the Irish Achilles, runs like a bright thread through all these stories, including a number that are not repeated here but deserve to be read in their own right.

On Raven's Wing represents a search for a skeleton of possible truth beneath the glamour of myth, yet in dealing with ancient Ireland one can never totally divorce fact from magic, for they were the two faces of one reality for the Gael.

As Cuchulain says within these pages, 'A man believes what he wants to believe.'

Selected Bibliography

Colum, Padraic. *Treasury of Irish Folklore*. New York: Crown Publishers, 1967.

Dillon, Myles. *Early Irish Literature*. Chicago: University of Chicago Press, 1948.

Dunn, Joseph, trans. *Táin Bó Cúalnge (Cattle Raid of Cooley)*. London: David Nutt, 1914.

Gantz, Jeffrey, trans. *Early Irish Myths and Sagas*. London: Penguin Books, 1981.

Gregory, Lady Isabella Augusta. *Cuchulain of Muirthemne*. London: John Murray, 1902.

Heroic Tales from the Ulster Cycle. Dublin: O'Brien Press, 1962.

Hoagland, Kathleen, ed. *1000 Years of Irish Poetry*. New York: Devin-Adair, 1981.

Joyce, P. W. *Social History of Ancient Ireland*. London: Benjamin Blom, 1913.

Kinsella, Thomas. *The Tain*. Dublin: Dolmen Press, 1969.

MacNeill, Eoin. *Celtic Ireland*. Dublin: Academy Press, 1981.

MacNeill, Maire. *Festival of Lughnasa*. London: Oxford University Press, 1962.

Moelmuiri Mac Ceileachair. *Leabhar Na H-Uidhri (The Book of the Dun Cow)*, compiled circa ad 1100. Dublin: Irish Academy, 1870.

Muir, Richard. *Reading the Celtic Landscape*. London: Michael Joseph Ltd., 1985.

O'Curry, Eugene. *Manners and Customs of the Ancient Irish*. London: Williams & Norgate, 1873.

O'Rahily, Cecile, ed. *Táin Bó Cúalnge* (from *The Book of Leinster*). Dublin: Dublin Institute for Advanced Studies, 1984.

O'Siochain, P. A. *Ireland: A Journey into Lost Time*. New York: Devin-Adair, 1963.

Senchus Mor (The Ancient Laws of Ireland). Dublin: Courtesy of Trinity College Library.

Tymoczko, Maria, trans. *Two Death Tales from the Ulster Cycle*. Dublin: Dolmen Press, 1981.